Lord
of
Darkness

Lord
of
Darkness

BY

ROBERT
SILVERBERG

ARBOR HOUSE
New York

To Sue

CONTENTS

He that is shipped with the Devil must sail with the Devil.
　　　　　　　　　　　—ENGLISH PROVERB

God is English!
　　　　　　—JOHN AYLMER
　　　　　　　　An Harborowe for Faithfull and Trew
　　　　　　　　Subjects, 1558

BOOK
ONE:

Voyager

ONE

ALMIGHTY GOD, I thank Thee for my deliverance from the dark land of Africa. Yet am I grateful for all that Thou hast shown me in that land, even for the pain Thou hast inflicted upon me for my deeper instruction. And I thank Thee also for sparing me from the wrath of the Portugals who enslaved me, and from the other foes, black of skin and blacker of soul, with whom I contended. And I give thanks too that Thou let me taste the delight of strange loves in a strange place, so that in these my latter years I may look back with pleasure upon pleasures few Englishmen have known. But most of all I thank Thee for showing me the face of evil and bringing me away whole, and joyous, and unshaken in my love of Thee.

I am Andrew Battell of Leigh in Essex, which is no inconsiderable place. My father was the master mariner Thomas James Battell, who served splendidly with such as the great Drake and Hawkins, and my mother was Mary Martha Battell, whom I never knew, for she died in giving me into this world. That was in the autumn of the year 1558, the very month when Her Protestant Majesty Elizabeth ascended our throne. I was reared by my father's second wife Cecily, of Southend, who taught me to read and write, and these other things: that I was to love God and Queen Elizabeth before all else, that I was to live honorably and treat all men as I would have myself be treated, and that we are sent into this world to suffer, as Christ Jesus Himself suffered, because it is through suffering that we learn. I think I have kept faith with my stepmother's teachings, especially in the matter of suffering, for I have had such an education of pain, in good sooth, that I could teach on the subject to the doctors of Oxford or Cambridge. And yet I am not regretful of my wounds.

I was meant by my father to be a clerk. My brothers Thomas and Henry and John followed my father to the sea, as did my brother Edward, who was drowned off Antwerp, only fourteen years old, the week before my birth. That news, I think, broke my mother's heart and weakened her so that the birthing of me killed her. My father, doubly grieved, resolved to send no more sons a-sailing, and so I was filled with knowledge out of books, even some Latin and some Greek, in the plan that I should go up to London and take a post in Her Majesty's government.

But the salt air was ever in my nostrils. My earliest memory has me in my stepmother's arms at the place where the Thames flows into the sea, and shaking my fist at a gull that swooped wildly to and fro above me. Leigh is such a town, you know, as will manufacture mariners rather than clerks. Since early days we have had a famous guild of pilots here, taking charge of the inward-bound traffic, while the men of Deptford Strond in Kent provide pilots to the outward bound. It was the Kentish guild and ours that King Henry VIII of blessed memory incorporated together as the Fraternity of the Most Glorious and Indivisible Trinity and of St. Clement, which we call the Trinity House, and it is the brethren of Trinity House that keep all England's ships from going on the reefs. My father Thomas held a license of that guild, which took him a dozen years in the winning; and his son Thomas, now dead like all my clan, was a pilot, too. And a time came when even I found myself dealing with quadrants and astrolabes and portolans in strange waters, though such piloting as I knew was in my blood and breathed into my lungs, and not taught to me in any school. It was God who made me a pilot, and the Portugals, but not Trinity House.

Another early thing that I remember was a visitor my father had, a great-shouldered rough-skinned man with hard blue eyes and a shaggy red beard and a stark smell of codfish about him, though not an unpleasant one. He snatched me up—I was then, oh, seven or eight years old, I suppose—and threw me high and caught me, and cried, "Here's another mariner for us, eh, Thomas?"

"Ah, I think not," said my father to him.

And this man—he was Francis Willoughby, cousin to Sir Hugh that was lost in Lapland seeking the northeast passage to China—shook his head and said to my father, "Nay, Thomas, we must all go forth. For this is our nation's time, we English, going out to be scattered upon the earth like seeds. Or thrown like coins, one might better say: a handful of coins flung from a giant's hand. And O! Thomas! We are bright glittering coins, we are, of the least base of metals!"

I do recall those words most vividly, and seeing in my mind the giant walking to and fro upon the continents and over the seas, and hurling Englishmen with a mighty arm. And thinking then, too, how frightening it must be to be hurled in such a way, but how wondrous to come to earth in some far land, where the sunlight is of another color and the trees do grow with their roots in the air, and their crowns below!

My father nodded his agreement, and said, "Aye, each race has its special destiny, and the sea now is ours, as empire-making was for Rome, and conquest was for the Normans. And I think our people will indeed go far into the world, and embrace it most exuberantly, and bring this little isle of ours into a clasp with every distant land. And the Queen's mariners will know a good many strange places, and peradventure some strange fates, too. But not my Andy, I think. I think I will have him stay closer by me, to be a comfort for my older age. I may hold one son back, may I not? May I not, Francis?"

And I thought it most unfair, that if all we English were to be flung by the giant, and exuberantly embrace distant lands, that I alone should be kept from the sport. And I told myself in private, while my father and Francis Willoughby jested and laughed and drank their ale, that I, too, would have my turn at those strange places and strange fates. That I remember. But I also remember that when Francis Willoughby had taken his leave, and the warmth of the moment had cooled, I allowed those dreams to fade in me for a time.

I was, as I say, destined to be a clerk. But as I studied, I watched the coming and going of the ships and listened to the talk of my father and brothers, and a different desire arose in me. My brother Henry it was in particular, the first privateer of our family, that led me to the sea. Henry was the second son, bold and impatient. He fought greatly with my father, they tell me. (All this happened when I was small, for that I was so much younger than my brothers.) "You may happily ply between Leigh and Antwerp, between Antwerp and Leigh, if you like," declared this brazen Harry, "but I long for a broader sea." He went out from home and was not seen for a time, and then one day he was back, taller than my father now and his skin almost black from the tropical sun and a cutlass-scar across his cheek, and he jingled a purse of gold angels and threw it on the table in my father's house and said, "Here, this pays for the lodging I have had at your hands!"

He had been to sea with John Hawkins of Plymouth, to raid the Portugals in West Africa of blacks, and sell them in the New World to the Spaniards as plantation slaves. And he came back rich: more than that, he came back a man, who had gone away little more than a boy. John Hawkins went again to Africa the next year with five ships, and Henry was with him again, and also John my brother, and when they returned, sun-blackened and swaggering, they had pouches of pearls and other treasures. I was still a child then. My brother Henry walked with me along the shore and told me of fishes that flew and of trees that dripped blood, and then he gave me a pearl that looked like a blue tear, hung from a beaded chain, and put it about my throat. "With this pearl you may buy yourself a princess one day," said my brother Henry.

Again Henry and John went to sea out of Plymouth and took slaves from Guinea and carried them to Hispaniola, but this time the Spaniards were sly and the English captain, John Lovell, was a dullard, and they came home with neither gold nor pearls, but only the tint of the hot sun on their skins to show for their pains. "All the same," said Henry to my father, "the voyage was not entirely a loss, for there was a man aboard our ship who has the grace of a king, and he has plans and schemes for doing wonders, and I will follow him wherever he sails." That man was the purser aboard Lovell's vessel, and his name was Francis Drake. I lay awake upstairs listening as Henry and John told my father of this man, of how he bore himself and how he laughed and how he swore and how he meant to grow rich at King Philip's expense, and I imagined myself going off to sea with my brothers when they signed on with Francis Drake.

That was mere fantasy, for I was not yet ten. But Drake and John Hawkins sailed, and my two brothers sailed with them on Drake's *Judith*, and now my third brother Thomas, the eldest, went also with them. How my father raved and raged! For Thomas was licensed by Trinity House after his years of study, and was guiding those who traded at Channel ports, when this fit of piracy came over him. "Who will be our pilots at home," my father demanded, "if all the mariners rush to the Indies?" Yet it was like crying into the wind to ask such things. Thomas had seen the pearls. Thomas had seen the angels of gold and the gleaming doubloons. And methinks he envied our brothers their scars and their swarthy skins.

Everyone knows the fate of that voyage, where Hawkins and Drake were forced by storms to take shelter at San Juan de Ulloa on the Mexican coast, and there by Spanish treachery were foully betrayed, so that they barely escaped alive and many of their men were slain. One of those who perished was my brother Thomas. You might think that my father would draw dark vindication from such news, as people do when their warnings are ignored, but my father was not of that sort. He mourned his firstborn son properly, and then he sought out Francis Drake and said, "I have given three sons to your venture, and one of them the Spaniards slew, and now I ask if you have need of a skilled pilot who is not young when next you go to raid their coasts."

What, you say? Was my father maddened by grief? Nay, he was only transformed. The mere hunger for treasure had not been enough to draw him from his duties in the Channel and the North Sea. But the cowardly and lying way the Spaniards had fallen upon unsuspecting Englishmen, with the loss of so much precious life, had altered his direction. He wanted nothing now but to help Drake take from Spain whatever he could, in partial repayment for the life of his son. "There are more ways of serving God and the Queen," my father told me, "than by piloting ships into the mouth of the Thames."

So in 1570 he was with Drake on the *Swan* to harry the Spanish Main, and again in 1571, and a year later he was one of those from Drake's *Pasha* that seized the royal treasury at Nombre de Dios on the Isthmus of Panama. The torments of that voyage, the fevers and disasters, were God's own test indeed, but my father must have prospered beneath such burdens, for when he returned after a year and a half he looked miraculously younger, more a brother than a father to Henry and John, and all three lean and hard and dark as Moors. I went to Plymouth to meet their returning ship. I was then nearly fifteen and grown suddenly tall myself, and I think the disease of piracy was already bubbling in my veins. I embraced my father and my brothers and then they thrust me toward a robust man of short stature with a fair beard and dainty garments, whom I took to be some lord or gallant, and gallant indeed he was. "You see, Francis," my father said, "I have kept one son in reserve." And Drake cuffed me lightly on the arm and ran his hand the wrong way up my newly sprouting soft beard and said, "God's blood, boy, you have the gleam in your eye! I know it well. I tell you this, that you will journey farther than all your brothers," and so I have, into a realm of darkness so terrible and so strange as never a man of Essex imagined.

For the next few years there was little privateering. Her Majesty had no stomach for war with Spain, and patched up a peace with King Philip, and not even Drake dared to tamper with it. My father returned to his piloting, my brother Henry went off with Frobisher to seek the Northwest Passage, and I know not what became of my brother John, though I think he may have gone to Ireland, where he died in some wild feud ten years after. And I? I had my first taste of the water. At sixteen I was hired aboard the *George Cross*, a 400-ton carrack in the merchant trade, that hauled casks of claret from Bordeaux. She was a slow and clumsy old tub, three-masted, square-rigged on fore and main with lateen mizens, not much like your pirate brigantine or your caravel of exploration: a coarse heavy thing. But when you are at sea for the first time you find any vessel a wonder, most especially when land is out of sight and the hard waves wash at the hull. Knowing that my father had from my birth intended that I live a safe life ashore, I felt some fear when I came to him for permission to sign on. He looked at me long and said, "Henry has put the Devil in you, eh? Or was it Drake?"

"Sir?"

"When we landed at Plymouth, and we saw how you had grown, Henry said to me, Master Andrew is too sturdy now for a lubber's life. He must have said something of the same to you. And then Drake, with his prophesying of your travels—he overheated your soul, did he not?"

"Aye, father. It was like that."

"Tell me the sea is calling you. Tell me that it is a pull you are unable to resist."

I shifted from one leg to another, uneasily, not knowing if I were being mocked.

I said, "It is not entirely like that."

"But?"

"But I would go."

"Then go," he said amiably. "You'll be in no jeopardy in the Channel, and you may learn a bit. Will you be scrubbing decks, d'ye think?"

"I have some learning, father. I will be tallying records, and making bills of lading."

He shook his head. "I would rather have you scrubbing decks, and I myself had the learning put into you, too. That was an error. You were meant for the sea, boy. But I suppose no harm is done, if you have a sailor's body, and a clerk's wit. Better that than the other way round, at any rate."

And with that somewhat sidewise blessing he let me sign on.

I look back across forty years at that boy and I confess I like what I see. Green, yes, and foolish and silly, but why not, at such an age? Quiet, and diligent, and tolerant of hardship, such little hardship as I had known. I had stubbornness and devotion and the will to work, and I had some intelligence, and I had steadfastness. From my father I had inherited something else, too, the wit to know when it is time to change one's course. There are those who sail blindly ahead and there are those who tack and veer when they must tack and veer, and I am of that latter sort, and I think it has been the saving of my life many a time.

For eleven months I served on the *George Cross*. I knew some seamanship before I went aboard, from what I had heard at home and seen in the Thameside docks; that is, I knew not to piss to windward, and which side was larboard and which starboard, and what was the quarterdeck and what the forecastle, and not a whole much more. I had little hope of learning a great deal waddling about between Dover and Calais, but as it happened the old carrack went wider than that, to Boulogne and Le Havre and once to Cherbourg, so I saw something of storms and concluded a few conclusions about winds and sails. That would be useful to me, though I knew not then why. There was aboard the ship a certain Portugal as the carpenter, one Manoel da Silva, very quick with his hands and with his tongue, who long ago had married an English wife and given up Papistry. He had a fondness for me and often came to the cabin where I struggled with invoices and accounts, and in his visits he spoke half in English and half in Portuguese, so that by and by I picked up the language from him: *um, dois, tres, quatro*, and so forth. I learned that I had a skill with language. And that would be useful to me one day also.

In those months I grew a liking for good red wine, I discovered the way of walking a deck without sprawling, I had my first real fight and gave better than I got, and, long overdue, I left my aching virginity in the belly of a dark-haired French whore. Thereafter I worried about the pox for days, without need. I found I could sleep well on hard planks and I came not to mind the drench of salt spray. My body hardened and my legs lengthened, and I told myself I was now a man, and the sound of that had a good ring in my ears. Betimes I imagined myself a thousand leagues from home, on my way to the Japans or Hispaniola or Terra Australis on a voyage that no one would ever forget. Well, and I was only plying a tub between England and France, ferrying wine.

Nor did I even then think to make the sea my trade. For all my eagerness to straddle the globe and see strange lands and marvels and fill my purse with Spanish gold, my true and deepest notion was to set by some pounds and one day buy me the freehold of a farm, and marry and prosper, and live comfortably in hard work and the bosom of a family, reading books for pleasure and attending the plays betimes in London, like a gentleman. At the end of my year's voyage I found I had set by not as much as I had expected—two shillings less than two pounds. But even that seemed a fair fortune for a lad of seventeen, and more than I could have earned ashore, for in those days a skilled work-man—a thatcher, say—could hope for no more than seven and sixpence a week, out of which must come rent and clothing and food and all, and a young clerk hardly that much. So I went to sea again after two months at home.

This time it was a farther voyage, to Flanders and Norway, and the year after that all the way to Russia aboard a vessel of the Muscovy Company, and a cold time I had of it then. But these journeys were making a complete sailor of me, for each time I did less clerking and more seamanship, and I was finding my way around the maps and charts, the compasses and leads, not because it was asked of me but because my curiosity led me to know at first hand what sort of trade my father and his son Thomas the pilot had plied. So the years of my early manhood went.

In those years the Spaniards began once more to break the truce between their lands and ours, and the Queen sent Drake out to punish them with the loss of gold and silver. This was in 1577, and it was destined to become a voyage around the world, though that was not Drake's first plan. My brother Henry was with him aboard his flagship, the *Pelican*, that Drake would rename *The Golden Hind* in mid-passage.

My father, too, applied for command of another ship, the pinnace *Christopher*, but he was refused with thanks, on account of his age. I also would have gone, but my father would not let it, saying, "Thomas is dead and John is fled to Ireland and Henry sails with Drake, and I want one son for England." I could have thwarted him in that, but I had no heart for it. He was suddenly old, and he did not so much forbid me as implore me, and how could I say him nay?

So Henry Battell went with Drake through Magellan's Strait and up to Valparaiso and on to loot the gold of Peru, and to unknown northern lands of horrid fog and cold, and out into the South Sea to the Spice Islands and Java and Africa, and home again in just short of three years, leaving his left arm behind, that had become inflamed by a poison dart on some tropic isle. In the meanwhile Andrew Battell sailed four times to Antwerp and thrice to Sweden and once to Genoa. Which I suppose is no small travelling, but hardly a patch on going to the Spice Islands or Java, and often I thought ruefully of Drake's prediction of how far I should journey. Who could possibly go farther than Henry, who had encompassed the globe? But there is voyage outward and there is voyage inward, as I would learn, and my twenty years inward to the heart of African deviltry took me farther indeed than Drake himself could have gone, as I will relate.

Yet I thought my sailing days were over by the time Drake and his men had come home. I was two-and-twenty, and by thrift and sweat I had earned my freehold, and I had my land and I had my wife. Her name was Rose Ullward of Plymouth, and she was small and dark, with sparkling eyes. I blush when I tell you that that is almost all I remember of her, save that she was a barmaid at the licensed house that her father kept by the docks. We lived as man and wife a year and some months. Together we went to Deptford that spring day in 1581 when Queen Bess made Francis Drake a knight; because my brother was a man of *The Golden Hind*, we were allowed on board, and I stood so close to the Queen that I could see the pockmarks on her cheek. She was a fine royal woman, quite tall and handsome, and I was almost weeping for being so near her. A great crowd attended on that day, so that the bridge laid from shore to the ship collapsed, and two hundred people were thrown into the Thames, though none was injured or drowned. I jumped in to save several, and Henry also, thrashing about valiantly with his one arm. Sir Francis embraced me as I shivered on deck afterward, and said, "I know you, fellow," which amazed me, for he had met me only once and that many years before. But the men of my family have all had a single face, and he must have seen Henry on my features. It was a happy moment.

Soon my Rose's belly was swelling, which gave me joy but also fear, for I remembered how my mother had died with me in childbed. Such misplaced worry! In brooding about imagined perils we often fail to see the real foe stealing upon us. Three months before her time Rose took the smallpox, and perished swiftly of it, and my unborn child of course with her. In that same dark season my father died, of an apoplexy, in his sixty-third year.

I have never known such bleakness. For the only time in my life all heart left me, all faith, all strength. I wandered as if in a dream, wifeless and fatherless and childless. In my foolish sorrow I turned to the taverns, and neglected my farm and drank up my savings and drank also the six pounds I inherited of my father, which is no small quantity of drinking, and in time everything was gone and the bailiffs came to tell me I had lost my land. Then did I sign on in Leigh as a clerk in the customs-house. I was barely four-and-twenty and thought of my life as almost ended, though in truth it had hardly begun.

At the lowest ebb the tide turns. In the year 1586, after an interminable dreary time of this waking slumber, I came to my senses and looked about me and saw that the world was still beautiful, and I began to recover into life. I fell in love, I pledged myself to marry again, I began once again to amass the money to buy me a freehold; in short, the interruption of defeat and black dejection was put at an end for me. And out of these renewed hopes and ambitions I came by easy stages to take up my long-abandoned career at sea, for how else could I come quickly by the wealth I needed? And by one step and another I set myself all unknowingly on the path that would carry me far from home for so many years, to Africa, to the torments the Portugals laid upon me, to the royal courts of Kongo and the Angola, to the jungles of coccodrillos and elephantos and the broad plains spangled with zevveras and gazelles; I began my long journey to the side of that diabolical Jaqqa cannibal, Imbe Calandola, the incarnation of the Lord of Darkness, whose lieutenant I became and whose monstrous wisdom rings to this day in my soul like terrible discordant music.

TWO

HOW DID it happen? Why, I fell in love.

Her name was Anne Katherine Sawyer. She was but fifteen. Her hair was golden, not mere yellow like mine but the golden gold of the gold of Ophir, and her skin was fair and her lips were sweet. She was the daughter of the registrar of customs. I had seen her about the place as a pretty child, and then one day I woke and saw she was a child no more, and I felt the blood coursing again in my veins, that had been slow and sluggish since the day my wife Rose closed her eyes. I strolled with Anne Katherine along the docks, I spoke with her of Antwerp and Muscovy, I told her of my brother, who had sailed with Drake, and my father, who had seized Spanish treasure at Nombre de Dios, and I touched her shoulder one day and her elbow the next and her hand after that, like a boy afraid of frightening his girl with overmuch forwardness.

A bit of a coquette is what she was, and as things grew more urgent she held me lightly apart from her body when first I attempted her. But desire burns in woman as it does in man—let no fool tell you otherwise—and in time she yielded her maiden treasure to me, which was not a shameful thing, for I knew I would have her to be my wife. I gave her, for a token, the pearl on a beaded chain that I had had long ago from my brother. All the next day I was dizzied with the memory of my hands to her silken thighs and my lips to her round pale breasts, and the sound she made—soft, soft—when I went at last into her. And I dreamed of doing such things, night after night, all the nights of our life together.

But first there was money to put by all over again and land to buy, perhaps even the same that I had earlier lost in my folly. And also it was unseemly to marry her so young, sixteen or seventeen being more fitting. I looked about for service on some merchantman, but there was little to be found, as times were hard then in England. Nor was there even piracy to turn to. God's death! That was a terrible time for me, and no one to blame but myself.

What brought me up out of despond was the mighty audacity and vacuity of King Philip, that sent the Armada of Spain against England in the summer of 1588. When our great captains gathered to meet that troublesome attempt—Drake and Hawkins and Frobisher and the rest—every seaman in the land was there to do the work, and there among them was I. If I had had my way I would have been on board Drake's flagship *Revenge*, next to my brother Henry, but I was too obscure for that, and had my berth on a lesser though not contemptible vessel, the privateer *Margaret and John*, of two hundred tons and a pretty turn of speed.

I need not retell here how we English, with the help of the winds and storms, scattered and routed the silly Dons and sent them fleeing up around Scotland to smash themselves on the Irish shores: you know all that. For me the weeks of battle were an especial joy, both for giving my strength for Queen and country and for getting the whiff of the sea into my nostrils once more. You should know that until that summer I had secretly thought myself but half a man, since I had sailed only in clerkish ways while my father and brothers were by way of being heroes, and since in my life at home I had lost my land and made myself a figure of shame. But all that was mended now. I had sailed heavy seas; I had fought our enemies without fear; I had enrolled myself among the heroes of the realm.

There was aboard the *Margaret and John* a man of Leigh, one Abraham Cocke, who had much to do with the shaping of my life thereafter. This Cocke was a sour sort, with a ragged brown beard and one eye asquint, who had known my brother Thomas in boyhood and later had taken up the trade of piracy. Ill luck it brought him, for he went raiding along the coast of the Brazils in the ship of Drake's cousin John, and a little short of the Rio de la Plata was captured by the Portugals, who kept him prisoner several years. From this captivity he was delivered at last by the Earl of Cumberland, who while marauding on that same Brazilian coast fell in with a Portuguese vessel aboard which this Cocke was serving, and rescued him back to England. That was in 1587. Cocke's sufferings taught him nothing but greater greed for Spanish gold, and he hungered to return to the lands where he had come to such grief. He told me this on a summer day of dead calm and heavy sluggish air as we followed the Armada from Portland Bill to Calais Roads.

"This war will be the shattering of Spain," said Cocke to me. "King Philip has pissed away much treasure on the building of these doomed galleons of his, and he will need to milk the Indies for gold aplenty to renew his coffers. When this work is done, I will put myself between King Philip and his gold. Will you join me in that, Battell?"

"Aye," I said, and in that single short word I spoke away twenty years of my life.

Cocke told me that every year great store of treasure is transported overland out of Peru to the port of Buenos Aires on the Rio de la Plata, and from there it is shipped along the coast to Bahia in Brazil, where four or five caravels wait to carry it to Spain. It was Cocke's intent to intercept the treasure-ships between Buenos Aires and Bahia, not by brutal force but by making a lightning swoop with two small vessels of great swiftness. I saw this plan as being much to my favor. If God gave us strength, I could earn as much in that one piracy as in ten years of scribbling invoices aboard merchantmen, and I could have my land and my Anne Katherine, and finally set about the making of sons and the reading of books. And then farewell to maritime life, for I was somehow come to be thirty years of age now, and longed for the shore and my warm bed and Anne Katherine beside me in it.

When the business of the Armada was finished and the Spaniards were ruined, I spoke of my intent to Anne Katherine. I feared she might object to my going privateering, as women sometimes take exception to such doings, but not she. With a smile as broad as the sun she said, "By all means, go and harvest gold. For the Spaniards only steal it from the poor Indians, and have but the Devil's claim on the stuff themselves. Why should we not have some of the use of it, too, who are peaceful folk whom God loves?"

Henry, too, gave me his blessing. I think I was an embarrassment to him—the unlucky younger brother—and he hoped this voyage would settle me in life at last. He himself was becoming a great man then, having fallen in with Walter Ralegh, and planning with him an expedition in search of the great treasure of El Dorado in Guiana. Which some years later it seems he undertook, and my brother left his bones along the banks of the Orinoco for his troubles, but I know little of that.

Cocke raised his money and bought two pinnaces of fifty tons each, the *May-Morning* and the *Dolphin*. We sailed from the River Thames the twentieth of April, 1589, I having spent all the night before in the arms of my Anne Katherine, and the fragrance of her sweet breasts still in my nostrils as we stood forth into a greasy fog. "When will you be back?" she asked me at the hour before dawn, and I said, "Before Christmas, with pouches of golden doubloons, and we will marry by Twelfth Night." Though that she had had not a moment's sleep her eyes were bright and her face was fresh and clear, and I saw the love and God's grace in her good smile. She was of eighteen years then, already growing a little old for marriage, and I bitterly begrudged the year's delay. But without gold I could not be marrying, if we were to live properly ever after.

In all my wanderings ahead, the image of Anne Katherine burned brighter in my memory than do the faces of the saints among the Popish. But many a strange thing befell me before I saw that face again, and when I came at last to the seeing of that face it was a passing strange thing in itself, a seeming miracle. Of that tale in its proper moment, though.

On the sixth and twentieth of April we put into Plymouth, where we took in some provision for the voyage. The seventh of May we put to sea, and with foul weather were beaten back again into Plymouth, where we remained some days, and then proceeded on our voyage. As England fell from sight behind us I saw the great curving green sphere of the open sea and cried out for joy, for I was on my way into the world at long last, that vast round thing so full of wonders and splendors and marvels.

Running along the coast of Spain and Barbary we put into the road of Santa Cruz de Tenerife, one of the islands called Canary. Here I breathed the soft air of the lands of eternal springtime, with so many perfumes upon it that it made me wild. Jesu! Such beauty and such strangeness! I had a friend aboard ship, Thomas Torner of Essex, who had been the Tenerife way before, and Torner said to me, "This is the isle of the Raining Tree, which is enveloped by a cloud every day at noon. The tree's great branches absorb much moisture, which travels quickly downward to gush in great streams from its roots into certain cisterns placed nearby. And the whole water supply of the island is had from this one tree."

My eyes went wide and my heart thundered. For I had come on this voyage to gain gold, aye, but also to see marvels. The Raining Tree of Tenerife! Well, so be it. God wot, I saw no such tree there, though I found another of which I had heard much. This was the famous Dragon's-Blood Tree, that dripped scarlet blood. Thus I described it to Torner, as it had been described to me. But he only laughed and said, "Andy, Andy, it is no such thing! Come and see!"

He pointed to me the Dragon's-Blood Tree, and there were many of them indeed on the isle. A fine peculiar tree it was, too, fat-boughed and swollen, with leaves like long daggers, and when you pulled the leaves off, there was a bit of a red stain left behind. I wonder how many of the other travelers' tales have been inflamed and magnified in that fashion, from Marco Polo's day to ours. Yet I swear to you by the wounds of God that I tell you nothing but the truth in this my narrative, and if anything I make what I experienced seem more sober than in truth it was.

We were carrying with us the kind of little vessel called a light horseman, or rowing-boat, which we had in two pieces. On the quiet shore of Tenerife we assembled this craft and thenceforth carried it alongside us, for in-shore venturing. When that was accomplished we put to sea.

Not far south of the Canaries is the usual place for turning westward for the Atlantic crossing. We did not do that. Instead we clung to the coast of Guinea and rounded the great hump of Africa, as if Captain Cocke planned to take us to some destination other than Brazil. I know not why that was, whether it was sheer incompetence on his part, or honest error, or hope of encountering some treasure-ship of the Portugals in those waters.

It was a bad time for us. We were becalmed, because we were too near the coast. For days we were driving to and fro without puff or wind. In this time most of our men fell sick of the scurvy by reason of the extreme heat of the sun, and the vapors of the night. From that misery I was spared, owing to my faith in God or more likely the strength of my frame, but it was hardly easy for me, standing double and triple watches, and going about among the sufferers to give them ease. We baked under the great yellow eye of fire above us. My skin was darkening as my brothers' skin had, and I knew I would cut a swaggering figure with it in Essex now, but this was not Essex, and I felt as though I were turning to leather, fit only to bind books in. We ate little but salted meat and dried peas in those days.

When we were within three or four degrees of the equinoctial line we fell in with the Cape de las Palmas, a happy place far down the side of Africa where it has its grand curving to the eastward. The people of this cape made much of us, saying that they would trade with us; but it was but to betray us, for they are very treacherous, and were like to have taken our boat, and hurt some of our men.

From this cape we lay south-west off; but the current and calms deceived us, so that we were driven down to the isle of São Tomé, believing that we had been farther out to the sea than we were. I knew we were astray badly, and at night I often lay awake in the heat thinking of my Anne Katherine's fair white breasts with their little delicate pink tips that grew so hard under my hands. I was getting no closer to Anne Katherine in this journey past the African shore, and getting no closer either to the Spanish gold that was to be my marriage-money. So I felt sadness and sometimes a choking rage. And when I thought of her breasts growing hard I grew hard myself, elsewhere, and rolled myself on my belly and eased myself with my hand, as sailors must do.

Yet for the heat and my sorrowful loneliness and the scurvy and the wearisome salt cod and all the rest, still would I not have traded places with a landsman for anything. For this was the great adventure of my life that I was embarked upon.

Being in distress for wood and water, we went in between São Tomé and a smaller island called Las Rolas, a mile off the southern tip. With our light horseman we went on shore at this small and high and densely wooded island, thinking to fill our casks with sweet water. Here we found a village of blacks, for the Portugals of São Tomé are accustomed to sending their sick or weak slaves to this island to let them recover their strength. We took from them a great store of oranges, and also the fruit known as plantain, which is long and yellow, and starchy in the mouth. Beynonas is what the Portugals call this fruit. But of water we got none, since there are no springs on this island and all their supply comes from the rainfall, which is not often. They drink also the wine of the palm-trees in place of fresh water. We sampled that, but for all its virtue it was no substitute for water. Having refreshed ourselves with the fruit of this island, we burned the village. And running on the east side of São Tomé we came before the town there, which is a slave-depot for the Portugals. But we dared not go close to it, for the castle was well fortified with heavy guns, and they fired at us until we were far beyond range.

Then we lay east and by south toward the mainland, and after a time swung about back toward the island of São Tomé, for our casks held only rusty dregs now and our need of water was pressing. On the west side of the island we came to a little river which runs out of the mountains, and we went on shore with our light horseman, with six or seven butts to fill with water.

But the Portugals were waiting for us with one hundred men lying in ambush. When we reached shore they came upon us, and killed one of our men and hurt another. The dead man was a boy of Southgate whose name I forget, with exceeding pale fine hair, almost like flax. A Portuguese ball caught him high on the forehead and I remember the brightness of the blood staining that fair hair, though his name is gone from me. He could have been no more than seventeen, and in that moment all the beauties of the world were lost to him forever. It was the first time I had ever seen sudden death, though not, God wot, the last. We fled to our boat and got aboard, and afterward we stole ashore at another place and took the water we wanted.

Now at last commenced our westward journey.

We lay west-south-west into the sea: and being some fifty leagues off, we fell into a shoal of dolphins, which did greatly relieve us, for they did follow our ship all the way till we fell in with the land on the other side. There was joy in seeing these great fishes sporting and leaping in the sun, and seeming almost to laugh, or perhaps to smile, at their own agility. But the crossing had many hardships for us. During the long passage on the vast gulf, where nothing but sea beneath us and air above us was to be seen, we often met with adverse winds, unwelcome storms, and even less welcome calms, and being as it were in the bosom of the burning zone, we felt the effects of sultry heat, not without the frights of flashing lightnings, and terrifyings of frequent claps of thunder. These were the horse latitudes we were in, or the doldrums. No breezes blew and the ships were often stilled and idle. One awful day we were given the other side of the Devil's hand, when terrible gales abruptly struck us, and we dipped so far to our sides that the yardarms touched the waves. On the masts danced a weird blue glow, blinding in its brilliance, that gave me terror. But a sailor calmed me, saying, "It is Saint Elmo's fire, that speaks of divine protection." He dropped to his knees and prayed. As did I, and the sea grew calm, and we went onward at a good pace.

The heat was great and the deck was like an oven, and the tar melted in the seams. We slept poorly. We had little to do, and that was a trial. And yet there was no anguish in this crossing for me. I felt gratitude that I was strong and healthy and able to do my sailing, into a realm of dolphins and blue fire and even the pale and glistening flying fishes of which my brother had told me when I was a boy, and which I now saw with mine own eyes as they soared above the breast of the sea.

In thirty days we sighted land. The dark line before us was Brazil. I looked toward that place and a kind of dizziness came over me, and such ecstasy as I think the poets must feel. For in the eye of my mind I saw the lands west of Brazil sweeping on and on toward the sunset, over to Peru, and I knew from my brother Henry's tales that the great South Sea lay beyond, and on the far side of that sea such places as Cathay and India and the Japans, and then Africa. In brief, I had a vision of the whole world as a single ball, league upon league of miracles, God's own fullness of marvel. And I had another vision of England's sturdy men sailing on those seas to all corners of the globe, and planting the flag and making themselves homes and increasing our wealth and pride. How wondrous to be alive at this time, in so great an adventure!

And then I remembered that I was only a penniless man of Essex who wanted nothing more than a wife and a farm, and that I had come to this strange place to take from the Spaniards and the Portugals the gold they in turn had taken from the Indians. And I laughed at my own swollen grandeurs and set about mending a sail, which was my task for that day.

We ran along the coast of Brazil until we came to Ilha Grande, southward of the Line. This is a fine lofty island most green and lavish with trees. We put in on the mainland side and haled our ships on shore, and washed them and shoveled out the ballast so we might scrub the bilges, a foul job but a needful one. We refreshed ourselves and took in fresh water. No inhabitants did we see in this part of the island, but it is very fruitful. When we had been there some twelve days there came in a little pinnace heading south, to water and to get some refreshments. We surprised it in our harbor and took it prisoner, and brought from it a Portugal merchant, who seemed in fear for his life.

Abraham Cocke sent for me and said, "You speak the Portuguese tongue. Ask him when the treasure-ships come."

Now such Portuguese as I knew had years of rust upon it, and this Portugal was in such terror he all but beshit his pants and he chattered in the teeth when he tried to speak. So our conversation was like that of blind men discussing whether the sky be red or green. But the words returned to me, enough to comfort him that he would not be slain by us, if only he dealt honestly with us. Even then he only shivered and prayed and named all the saints a hundred times each.

"He is out of his wits in fright," I told Cocke.

The captain nodded his head. "It is because he knows what would happen if matters were the other way round, and one Englishman were taken by a ship of Portugals. Tell him we gave up burning Papists long ago, and want only information from him, not his soul."

I spoke as I could and finally the man grew calm and said two treasure-ships would leave Buenos Aires within two months to sail to Bahia, near this Ilha Grande. He also said without being asked that on the other side of this island lived a degradado, a banished man, with a plantation full of fruits that would nourish us. Since our bread and our victuals were almost all spent, we allowed the Portugal to lead us there. And indeed we found the plantation and its owner, and took from him great stores of plantains, and a few hogs and hens and other things.

Captain Cocke now divided our party, putting some of the men of the *Dolphin* aboard our *May-Morning*, and leaving the *Dolphin* behind at Ilha Grande while the rest of us went south to meet the treasure-ships at the Rio de la Plata. That seemed foolish generalship to me at the time, as had so many other of Cocke's doings. We had few enough men as it was, and to split our number was hard to understand. I have had more than twenty years to reflect on that, and still I have no answer to the mystery, and I know I never shall. What became of the *Dolphin* and her men I also do not know, though I think they stayed only a few days more at Ilha Grande and went home to England. At any rate we filled our hold with the degradado's plantains and departed from his island. Cocke spoke long and loudly of the gold that soon would replace the plantains belowdecks. When you looked at his face—which was not easy, since that his eyes went in different ways and would not meet yours—you saw in it a glow of avarice, as if he were staring at mountains of doubloons. So it was; yet there is a good old English saying, "A crowing cock lays no eggs," and thus it was with this our good Cocke. For in my life I saw as many cock's eggs as I did doubloons out of that voyage.

THREE

A LONG bleak time we had of it going down that fertile coast.

The third night, or the fourth, there was such a strong south-easterly wind and squalls that it threw us awry, and we sought a sheltered spot to anchor in. But where we came to shore there were a dozen Indians waiting. They were dark brown and naked, and had no covering for their private parts, and they carried bows and arrows in their hands.

They all came with determination toward our boat. Nicholas Parker, the second mate, made a sign to them to put down their bows, and they held them down. But he could not speak to them or make himself understood in any other way because of the waves which were breaking on the shore. He merely threw them some baubles and a little cap, which pleased them, and one of them threw him a hat of large feathers with a small crown of red and gray feathers, like a parrot's. I think they perceived that we were not Portugals and therefore would not harm them.

These Indians had holes in their lower lips and a bone in them as broad as the knuckles of a hand and as thick as a cotton spindle and sharp at one end like a bodkin. Some were covered in a motley way with stripes of paint of a bluish black. We made gestures to them and they to us, and then four or five girls appeared out of the woods. They were very young and most pretty, especially to men who had not touched soft skin in many months. They had abundant long hair down their backs, and their private parts (of which they made no privacy) were tightly knit and almost without hair, and so comely that many women in our country would be ashamed, if they saw such perfection, that theirs were not equally perfect. "I will buy one or two maidens from them," said Nicholas Parker, laughing broadly, and we encouraged him in this, for these girls were well made and rounded. "What price will they have? Something shiny, I think," he said.

But then the Devil took a hand in the dealings. A sailor from Portsmouth, a huge clumsy lout or ox, chose to stumble forward to put his hands on one of the Indian maids. That was bad enough; but as he lumbered toward her a vine in the sand caught his boot and he fell headlong. His musket began to fly from his hand. He seized it as he dropped, but such was his position that it appeared to the timid Indians that he was getting ready to fire. They fled in an instant and favored us with a shower of arrows from afar, which did no harm but put an end to our parley, and we purchased no tender maidens that day or any other. After that we did not find Indians, or for that matter any good harbors, nor did we see hide nor hair of the Spanish treasure-ships out of Buenos Aires, though we tacked back and forth in the sea-road searching for them. Abraham Cocke began to look coldly upon me, as if he thought I had let the Portugal merchant beguile me with lies, or had misunderstood his language. And so we were six-and-thirty dreary days of it until we came to the Isle of Lobos Marinos, which is in the mouth of the Rio de la Plata.

This island is half a mile long, and has no fresh water, but abounds with seals and a larger animal, a sort of sea-horse. There were so many of these creatures that our light horseman could not push through them to the shore unless we beat at them with our oars: and the island is covered with them. Upon these seals we lived some thirty days, lying up and down in the river, and were in great distress of victuals apart from that meat. Then we determined to run up to Buenos Aires, and with our light horseman to capture one of the pinnaces that waited at that town. But, being so high up the river as the town, we were struck by a mighty storm at south-west, which drove us back again, and we were fain to take refuge at the Isla Verde—that is, the green island—which is in the mouth of the river on the north side.

Lack of victuals discomforted us mightily, and we were not able long to remain there. So downcast were we that we gave over the purpose of the voyage altogether, and made a melancholy retreat back to the northward to reconsider our intentions. Now we came to the Isle of São Sebastião, lying just under the Tropic of Capricorn. There we went on shore to catch fish, and some of us, I among them, went up into the woods to gather fruit, for we were all in a manner famished. And on this island my life as a free man ended.

I think it befell on Twelfth Night, this calamity. There is cold irony in that, for I had promised my betrothed Anne Katherine we would be wed that night, in all my innocence, not knowing that Abraham Cocke would foolishly sail halfway down the side of Africa before making toward Brazil, or that we would waste weeks here and there and here and there without finding the treasure-ships. In the tropics all is upside-down, and Twelfth Night falls in the dead of summer, and it was a day of most fearsome heat, that made me fond for snow. I stood high on the hillside plucking a soft sweet purple fruit from a tree with leaves bright as mirrors, and O! I heard cries and screams, and looked downhill to see a band of naked Indians rushing upon our people from hiding. These were no childlike folk with gifts of feathers. All had bows and arrows and some carried knives that they must have had from the Portugals, and they attacked so fast there was no time to put match to powder, but only to flee. Flee! Aye, so it was. Within a moment there were corpses on the beach and Englishmen clambering into the boat or merely swimming desperately out to the *May-Morning*.

Well, that is fair enough, to take flight when surprised and sore beset. I thought I knew what would happen next, that is, that Cocke would turn the guns of the ship against the Indians, and terrify them to surrender, and then send the light horseman back to the island to collect our dead and to recover those of us who had been picking fruit in the

hills. But that is not what happened. The light horseman reached the
ship and the men scrambled aboard; and before my stupefied gaze the
May-Morning hoisted anchor and rigged her sails and made briskly for
the open sea. I could not believe it. I dared not cry out, knowing it
would only bring the Indians upon me, and anyhow my voice would
have been blown apart in the wind. But something in my soul cried out,
and loudly, so that I thought my forehead would burst from the roar
and thunder of it. Treachery! Cowardice! Had Cocke forgotten me, or
was he so pissing his pants with terror that he would make no attempt
to regain me, or was it simply that he did not care? I was abandoned,
that was the sum and total of it.

Jesu! How I wanted to rend and tear things asunder in my fury!

But I am, God wot, a man of balance and even temperament, and
my first fine rage passed quickly, and I examined my situation. Was I
a castaway? Well, then, I was a castaway, and not the first since the
beginning of time in such a pickle. Perhaps there were others nearby of
the same lot. I squatted down beside a plant that was all barbs and
prickles, so I would not be seen by the Indians who still infested the
beach, and considered the case.

Primus, Cocke might not yet have fully abandoned me. Perchance he
would take a census of his men when safe out from shore, and in counting
the missing would recall he had left a few to gather fruit, and would
come back for me. Perchance. And perchance the Queen would marry
the Pope, but I did not intend to wager high stakes on it.

Secundus, so long as I lived I was not yet dead, even though abandoned. I must try to survive, and find other English, and build some
sort of boat to take me across to the mainland. For we were only five
leagues from Santos, where the Portugals had a town of fair size.

Tertius, if I had allies perhaps I might capture a pinnace in Santos,
and sail away from Portuguese territory. For the Portugals were my
enemy, ever since King Philip of Spain had conquered their land nine
years past and made himself king over it, too. God's eyes! How hard
all this would be, and how needless! Between one moment and the next
our lives can be wholly transformed, while our backs are turned.

Out of fear of Indians I spent the night on the hillside. I made a
gloomy dinner of purple fruits and slept in snatches, standing watch
and watch with myself, so to speak, now awake and now taking some
winks. In the morning all seemed quiet and the Indians were nowhere
about, nor, I do say, was the *May-Morning*, not even a dot of white
against the far horizon.

I went cautiously down the slope to the beach, tearing my trousers

often on the demonic fanged plants. Six of our men lay dead with arrows
in them, men whose names I knew and whose friendship I had valued.
Their bodies were twisted and wretched of their last agonies, which told
me that the arrows must have been tipped with poison, as is the custom
here. I resolved to bury the dead men in the afternoon, but it was one
of those bold resolutions easier to make than to keep, for I had nothing
to dig with but my hands and some seashells, and a grave must be six
feet deep. I put the task aside for another time.

I went around a little headland to the far side, where the shore was
rocky. Here I saw things stirring by the seaside, as the tide went out,
and I crept on my hands and feet like a child, and when I drew near I
beheld many crabs lying in holes in the rocks. I pulled off one of my
stockings and filled it with crabs, and I carried it to a hollow fig-tree
where I found an old fire smouldering from some lightning-stroke. Casting the crabs on the coals, I cooked them and made my dinner out of
them, and so the day passed.

So I lived three or four days alone. Again I tried to bury the dead,
but the earth ashore was hard and full of rock, and at the beach the sand
slipped and fell about as I dug it, so that I could not make graves. I
would have tied rocks to the men and buried them in the sea, but I had
no cords for tying, and it seemed un-Christian merely to push them into
the water, where they would float and bloat in the surf and be eaten by
vermin. So I did nothing, except feel shame that I left them unburied.
The stink of them became noisome and the sight of them was a reproach,
so I moved on around the edge of the island and passed by a fair river
that ran into the sea.

Here I thought to make my abode because of the fresh water. But I
had not been there scarce the space of half a quarter of an hour, but I
saw a great thing come out of the water, with great scales on the back,
with great ugly claws and a long tail. I knew it not, though later I would
learn that it is the animal known as the coccodrillo, or in some parts
called the allagardo.

This monster put me into a fright close to perishing. It came toward
me and I would not flee, nay, could not, but strangely went and met
it, as though drawn by sorcery. When I came near it I stood still, amazed
to see so monstrous a thing before me. It was like a diabolus, a mage,
something from Hell come to fetch me, and I yielded utterly to its malign
power. Hereupon this beast seemed to smile, and opened his mouth,
and thrust out a long tongue like a harpoon. I commended myself to
God, and thought there to be torn in pieces, but the creature turned
again and went into the river. And I burst out into laughter, not that I

saw any jest, but only the deep jest that is the frailty of our flesh, the ease with which at any moment our bodies may be parted from our souls.

The next day I walked farther around the island, fearing to tarry in that place, and I found a great whale lying on the shore like a ship with the keel upwards, all covered with a kind of short moss from the long lying there. As I examined this marvel a familiar voice cried out, "Andy, for the love of Jesus!" It was Thomas Torner, who had made his camp on the whale's far flank.

An immensity of joy rose in me at the sight of him, for he gave me hope that I might escape this place, which would not be easy for two but was well nigh impossible for one. We embraced like brothers.

"I feared I was left alone," I told him.

"Nay, there are several of us," said Torner, and led me around the whale's heavy flukes. "Look ye," he said, and I beheld three others of our company, Richard Jennings and Richard Fuller and one other whose name the years have washed from my memory. These men had been in divers separate places at the moment of the Indian attack and each had fled a different way into the forest, and one by one had come together here. "God's wounds," cried Richard Jennings, a great burly man half as high as an oak tree, "Do you know, Battell, that we were betrayed and abandoned by Cocke the cockless, and will live the rest of our lives among these crabs and other insects?"

"Aye," I replied, "I know of our betrayal, for I saw the ship depart. But as to the second part I say you nay, friend. I think we will see England again."

"Do you now? Will dolphins carry us there?"

"God will provide. And if He do not, we must provide for ourselves, or indeed these crabs will be our neighbors forever. Are there others of us here?"

"Just we four," said Torner, "and you are the fifth. I think there are no others in the part of the island behind us. Were there more in your direction?"

"Only six dead men, rotting and unburied on the beach. But five of us are enough to build a boat and take it to the mainland," I said, and explained my plan of capturing a Portuguese pinnace in Santos and using it to cross the ocean by small hops and skips and jumps. They listened intently and without scoffing. Fuller was a carpenter's mate, which gave us a great advantage in this project. We spoke of searching for a fallen tree, and hollowing it for our hull, and such things, and as we talked I understood that I had silently been elected the leader of these men. It surprised me greatly, for I had only a deckhand's skills and had never held authority of any sort, indeed had in some ways been cramped and diminished by being the youngest of so many brothers. But that counted for nothing here. I was thirty years of age, and strong of body, and such failings or smallnesses of spirit that might have afflicted me in youth were unknown to my companions and had no bearing. I think also it was my determination to reach England again that gleamed like a beacon out of my soul, and gave them courage, and had them turn to me; for until I came upon them, these four had been concerned only with finding food and shelter, and had given no thought to a plan of recovery.

We lunched on the meat of the whale, which was still unspoiled though not much to my liking, and talked long and earnestly of our strategies, and afterward we commenced a search for wood with which to build our craft. Whether we would have fulfilled this project is a question I can never answer, but I tell you that the planning of it gave us hope, without which life would have been cruel indeed for us. An ocean separated me from my Anne Katherine. A tropic sun burned my skin. Buzzing things hovered in clouds, and bit and stung. Nightmare creatures dwelled in the rivers and could march upon us in any moment. Yet I did not despair, for what use has despair? And my strength became the strength of the others. I talked of schemes that even I knew were sheer madness, and made them sound plausible. The one I most clearly remember was a notion of journeying up the whole coast of this southern America, and from isle to isle in the West Indies, and northward aye to Virginia, where Walter Ralegh had founded a colony on Roanoke Island. In my mind that distance was not so great, although in fact it is nigh as far as sailing to Africa, and we would be in enemy waters all the way. But the idea, rash or not, sustained us for a few days. And in the end the rashness of it mattered not at all, since we never had a chance to put it in practice, owing to the return of the Indians to the island.

They came upon us as stealthy as cats. A canoe laden with them landed on the west side of our island, and they made their way through the woods and emerged out of the mists of dawn, surrounding us in a ring with drawn bows. Their bows were long and black and their arrows long also, with heads of sharpened cane, and they would have skewered us wonderfully had we given any resistance. But to resist was folly. These Indians were naked, and some were painted in quarters with their paints, others by halves, and others all over, like a tapestry. They all had their lips pierced; some had bones in them, though many had not. All were shaven to above the ears; likewise their eyelids and eyelashes were shaven. All their foreheads were painted with black paint from temple to temple, so that it seemed they were wearing a ribbon round them two inches wide. Their chieftain spoke to us in jabber, or so it seemed, "Umma thumma hoola hay," and words like that, which he repeated five or seven times.

Torner said to me, "You have the knack of languages, Andy. Tell him we mean no harm, that we are enemies of the Portugals, and hope to be friends of his folk."

"Shall I say it in umma and thumma?" I asked.

The chief spoke again. I tried to imitate it, though learning a language at the point of an arrow is wondrously ticklish. We might have spoken nonsense back and forth at each other all morning, until they lost patience and slew us, but then the chief said a few words in unmistakable Portuguese, and the words were, "You come with us."

To my comrades I said, "These are tame Indians, that belong to the Portugals, I think. We will not be slain, but I think will be made slaves."

"Better to be slain," muttered Richard Jennings.

"Nay," I said, "dead men never escape, but lie dead forever. Slavery is less permanent. And these Indians do but save us the trouble of getting ourselves to Santos."

So the Indians took us over to the mainland in their canoe, a boat that they had made of a whole tree. When we came to the shore of that place we saw a town of some hundreds of people, very silent, and out of the silence we heard the ringing of a bell. "It must be Sunday," said Torner, and we all spat, for we knew by that bell that the Portugals were at their Mass, and at that same instant the friar was holding up the bread of sacrament before the people for them to worship it. So it was, for the Indians marched us right to the church, and would have thrust us clear inside. But a Portugal in leather breeches came out and forbade it, saying, "You may not enter. You are not Christians."

I translated that for the others and high color came to Richard Fuller's face and he cried, "I would not enter that building even to shit in it!" and such. The Portugal, I think, understood some English, or else he knew the essence of Fuller's words from his tone, for his eyes grew very cold and he took from his neck a heavy crucifix of silver, and put it in front of Richard Fuller's mouth and commanded him to kiss it. I knew what Fuller was apt to do, and I began to say, "Have care," but it was too late, for Fuller had already gathered in his mouth a gob of spittle and let it fly over the image of Jesus and the Portugal's hand. Whereupon the Portugal took his silver idol and struck it across Richard Fuller's mouth to split his lips and break his teeth and send blood into his beard, and then thrust its end into Richard Fuller's gut so hard that the man retched and puked; and then he waved his hand and the Indians took Fuller away toward some trees behind the town. We never saw him again. I could not then believe that one European would have another one slain in this strange land for mere disrespect for a Popish idol, except perhaps a Spaniard might, but I thought higher of the Portugals. So I believed they only had Fuller kept in solitary confinement to punish him for impiety. But since those days I have seen much of the world and its cruelties, and I now know that blood is shed for even more trivial reasons, sometimes for no reasons at all, by Portugals and Spaniards and French and Dutch and everyone else, and even an Englishman is capable of murdering a man for a fancied or real slight to his religion, though perhaps he would hold court on him first. Did not King Henry have a man's head struck off for eating meat on Fridays, and others for denying certain tenets of the Creed, and did not Queen Mary burn good Protestants like roasting-oxen for speaking out against the Pope? I think this is not the way of Jesus, but it is the way of princes and men, and not uncommon.

The rest of us they made captive in the cellar of a storehouse for a few days, chaining our wrists and ankles with manacles, and letting us eat by giving us bowls of the mashed root called manioc, that we had to lick with our tongues like dogs. The governor of that place came to us and spoke with me, asking why we were intruding in the territory of the Portugals, were we spies or only pirates, to which I made reply that we were settlers going to the Virginia colony, blown far off course and shipwrecked in the Brazils. "So you will be," he said, "shipwrecked a long while in the Brazils."

I think he wanted no part of us, for very shortly a sloop arrived at Santos and took us off to a larger town that the Portugals had built to the north, in the mouth of the river called the Rio de Janeiro. On this journey we passed the Ilha Grande, where Cocke had left the *Dolphin*, and saw no trace of it. In the Rio de Janeiro we remained four months. Here there were two things of importance, a Jesuit college and a great sugar-mill on an isle called the Island of the Governor. Jennings and the other man were sent to be servants at the College of Jesus, I suppose swabbing the floors so the friars would not soil their robes when they knelt, and Torner and I were turned out to the sugar-mill. I know not which pair of us fared worse, those that slaved for the Popish scholars or those that broke their backs to feed that mill: I dare say Torner and I suffered greater pain of the body, and the other two a larger pain of the soul. But we had no chance to compare notes, because after we were separated I never encountered the other two afterward, and for all I know they are still there, maybe Jesuits themselves by this time, old and bowed and fluent in Latin and skilled at singing the Mass, God pity them.

For me it was an education of a different kind. They had me on a bark going day and night up and down for sugar canes and wood for the mill. I had neither meat nor clothes, but as many blows as a galley-slave would receive, and Torner as well. We talked daily of escape, but there was little chance of that, the mill being on an island and the surrounding waters said to be full of man-eating fishes. We were desperate enough before long to risk testing if that were true, except that the case seemed hopeless, there being nowhere safe to flee. The Portugals had enslaved certain tribes of Indians and made them do their bidding, but a little way beyond the town the Indians were wild, and they too were man-eaters. Cannibal fishes by sea and cannibal men by land: prudence argued that we stay awhile where we were, since we were only being beaten, which is less barbarous a fate than being eaten.

I know not whether the warm and gentle waters of that estuary indeed do hold man-eating fishes, but of the cannibal Indians I have no doubt. In the second month of my captivity I and Torner and a dozen Portugal soldiers were despatched inland a short way, to collect timber of a certain rare kind, and we were set upon by a tribe called the Taymayas or Tamoyas, who are the most heated enemies the Portugals have in these parts. They tethered us and carried us away deeper into the forest, and a Portugal named Antonio Fernandes said to me, "Make your peace with your God, for these people mean to eat us at their festival." We were kept in their village, near a river full of allagardos and huge serpents, and other strange beasts. I recall one as big as a bear, and like a bear in the body, but with a nose of a yard long, and a fair great tail all black and gray. This beast puts his tongue through ant-hills, and when the ants are all upon his tongue, he swallows them up. Torner said, "And can you find such joy in monsters, when you are about to die?"

I made answer: "I live all my life as though I am about to die, and find such joy meanwhile as I can. And you and I are too stringy and tough from our labor to make good meals. They will dine on the Portugals first."

In sooth I could not credit that men could have a taste for the flesh of other men. The more fool I, for this world is full of cannibals that happily devour all they can hold, as I have come to know better now than any Englishman who ever lived. But I was right in one thing, that these Taymayas would eat the Portugals first. Their devilish feast began that night. The Indians came to us and selected the most plump of the Portugals, who cried out, "Jesu Maria!" and other such things, and called upon the saints. He could just as well have called upon the trees, or the allagardos in the river. They drew him forward by his rope and a lusty young man came behind him and struck him two terrible blows with a club, cracking open his skull and killing him. Then they took the tooth of some beast and unseamed his skin, and held him by the head and the feet over their fire, rubbing him with their hands, until the outer skin came off.

I watched this thinking I was in a dream, and thinking also that at this same moment my Anne Katherine was quietly reading a book, and the great Queen Elizabeth might be sitting with her courtiers, and actors are on the stage of the Globe, speaking the lines of a play, that is, there is a civilized world somewhere that knows nothing of these matters, and here is Andrew Battell of Leigh in Essex sitting in a wild jungle watching a plump young Portugal being trussed for dinner. Truly this was no dream, and never did I feel further from the world into which I had been born than in this first episode of great horror, which by God I wish had been my last.

They took from him his head and gave it to their chief, and then the entrails to the women, after which they jointed him joint by joint, first hands, then elbows, and so all the body. After which, they sent to every house a piece; then they fell a-dancing, and all the women brought forth a great store of wine. And later they boiled every joint in a great pot of water, and made a broth of it. I witnessed all these things in such shock and disgust that I thought I would die of it. For the space of three days the Indians did nothing but dance and drink, day and night. After that they killed another Portugal in the same manner as the first. But they did not get to enjoy his bounty, because a rescue party of Portugal troops burst upon the village just then with muskets blazing, and set us free.

Free, aye, but for me it was only the freedom to escape the dinner-pot, for they had me swiftly back at the mill slaving like a weary mule. Torner beside me said, "I almost regret being saved, for that was a quick death, and this is a living hell that may engulf us for fifty years." And then he smiled and said, "Nay, Andrew, spare me your talk of preferring life to death at any cost. I know you too well by now, your stubbornness, your perseverance, your faith that all will end happily."

"Would you truly rather have died, then?" I asked.

"Nay, I think not," he said, and we went back to our toil.

But though I never yielded to despair, yet did I feel it nibbling at my soul, for the weeks were passing and I longed for England and Anne Katherine and the cool gray skies and the clear sweet streams that were not all deadly with coccodrillos and the like. Why, it must be spring in England now, I thought, April or May of the year 1590, the land greening and the flowers bursting, and I am here in a land that knows no winter, a slave, and unto what purpose? A year of my life had passed away from England: how I lamented that!

A year of my life! Yet my captivity was only beginning.

In our fourth month at the Rio de Janeiro a Jesuit friar came to Torner and me, one who spoke some English, and said, "Will you embrace our faith, and come to our Mass?"

I did not strike him, as another man might. I did not spit. I did not cry out that the Catholic faith is treason to England and I was no traitor. I am not excitable in that way. Though I felt all these things, I said only, "I would not. We have our own English faith, and we prefer it, for it is the only consolation we have just now."

The friar sighed. He was not a cruel sort. "We could keep you here at our College, if you took up our way. But otherwise you are to be sent from here, for they want no heretics at the mill."

"Where are we to be sent?" asked Thomas Torner.

"São Paulo de Loanda," replied the Jesuit.

"Jesu!" cried Torner. "To *Africa?*"

FOUR

TO AFRICA, indeed, to that dark and steamy land from whose vast bosom gushes a milk of mysteries and horror.

The Portugals had seized a foothold there long ago, sailing south and south and south until they rounded the continent's tip, that was the Cape of Bona Speranza, and went on to India. Thus they had built a vast empire the spread of which makes the mind grow dizzy in contemplation of it. This was at a time when we English foolishly had no interest in going far to sea, but were content to sail only to Flanders or Portugal or France, or sometimes to Iceland or Newfoundland for the fishing. Up and down both coasts of Africa the Portugals had founded cities and fortresses for their trade, which was in all the wondrous goods of the land, gold and spices and the ivory of elephantos, but most especially slaves: and it was to one such outpost, nine degrees south of the equinoctial line in the land called Angola, that Torner and I now were shipped.

It was a long and worrisome voyage, for the winds were contrary and the gales blew in our teeth much of the time. We rode a broad and heavy carrack, some three hundred fifty tons or maybe larger, with an ingenious great lot of sail, spread on masts patterned after the Dutch scheme. That is, there were topmasts with caps and fids, carrying topsails of great size and topgallants above them, which I had never seen before at close inspection. But for all that, the vessel was hard pressed to beat her way eastward, and we wallowed miserably in rough and sinister seas.

Cold furies and hot rages ran through my spirit. I could not bear being a prisoner. I wanted England, and Essex, and Anne Katherine, and my patch of land; and I could not have them; and often I thought of throwing myself into the sea, if only I had the chance. But that was only hollow bravado, I knew. For all my pain I would not have surrendered myself to death, not then or ever.

Torner was my bulwark. This sole remaining companion was ten years my elder, a staunch weatherbeaten man who had sailed in many seas. Ofttime he lost heart himself, but at a different time from me, so that we cheered one another alternately. "See, now, we'll be home before you can say Jack Sprat!" he cried. "As we strike forth into the Atlantic some good English brigand will swoop upon this old scow and take it prisoner, and ship us aboard!"

That did not befall. But it was pleasant to dream upon it.

The first three days Torner and I were kept in chains, as though the Portugals feared we would seize the ship if left to our own. The metal was rusty and rough and chafed us most cruelly, so that our wrists bled and blazed with pain. We lay on deck like cords of timber, bound and stacked, and the seamen walked around us and paid us no mind, or sometimes glared and spat, or made the horns at us with their fingers, or did the cross with their hands as if to ward off the malign influence of demons.

I hated that hatred of theirs. What had I done to them? Refused to praise God in the Romish way? Sworn my allegiance to an English Queen instead of to their crazed King Philip, whom they despised themselves? That was the only true difference between us, that I was an Englishman and they Portugals, and yet they looked upon me as if I were a Turk, or some ravening fiend out of the nether hells. Why? Why? God's truth, I had no hate for them, only for their religion. I do plead guilty to a certain dislike for their oily Portugal looks, but that only because such folk were unfamiliar to me and I preferred the good clean open-hearted look of Englishmen.

The sea-spray stung my eyes and in the rolling of the ship I was often bruised and once some great bird with a white breast and blazing red devil eyes flew slowly across the deck and dropped its dung on my forehead. Which gave the Portugal sailors much to laugh upon, and they did pound the decks with the flats of their palms in amusement at my expense.

But when the first heavy weather struck, there was need for all hands to work the rigging, even us. We were set free, rubbing our cramped tethered limbs to ease some blood back into them, and sent aloft to tug at the cords. And so we toiled beside those who had mocked us so sharply. It would have been no huge task to nudge one or two of them with an elbow and send them tumbling to their dooms as we scrambled about the topmasts; but that was madness, gaining me nothing but a watery death myself, or worse, and I forgot the scheme. And in a day or two the hatred of these men for us subsided: now we were fellow hands, was all. Though we ate apart and dined on slops, we were not again chained, and no one seemed to care that we were supposed to be prisoners. Aye, and where could we have escaped in mid-sea, save into the mouths of the sharks?

Our shipmates were a sullen and a surly lot. They fought often with one another and spoke in foul curses, and made mock of their officers behind their backs. Sometimes to their faces as well, and one morning in mid-ocean I heard loud shouts between a black-bearded crookbacked seaman and the second mate, which grew more angry until suddenly the seaman struck the second mate to the deck with a blow that shattered his nose and sent blood spurting an amazing distance. When that happened everything stood still upon the ship: the men in the rigging froze, and those working the pumps stood like statues, and those tightening the lanyards and tackles let go the ropes. The man who had struck the blow looked at his own hand as though he had never seen it before. For one does not strike officers at sea and live.

The man was seized and within an hour he was tried and his fate was set, and it was to be the lash. Every hand not needed to work the ship was called into assembly, and the seaman was tied to a mast, and a gigantic Portugal with arms as thick as anyone else's legs was the wielder of the whip.

Now I am not one of your Londoners who goes out to every execution and stands with the crowd from earliest dawn, waiting to get a good view. I see no entertainment to be had from attending a beheading, with all that gore and welter and the dead head held high afterward, or going to a burning, and seeing good human flesh char to a crisp while hideous cries break the air. And though I know the favorite of the crowds is the drawing and the quartering, where they hang some poor soul until he is half dead, and cut him down and cut from him his privy parts and take from him his entrails and burn them in his view, and only then to behead him and divide his body in sections, it was never my pleasure to witness such a festivity. It is not that I am overly womanish and finicky and easily sickened by harsh sights, but only that I am a man of Essex, never raised to enjoy the city amusements: let the wicked be properly punished, say I, but I will take my sport elsewhere. But this flogging I did watch—I had no choice, for all hands attended, and I could not help but look on. The crookbacked sailor was one I notably disliked: he was one of those who had most jeered us when we were in chains, and I had felt his spittle and worse, and once when Torner and I were given a little wine to drink he had knocked my bowl from my hand, in seeming accident. So I scarce regretted that they were doing him to death. Yet flogging is a terrible way to die.

They ripped from him his shirt, laying bare his ill-matched shoulders and his little hump, and the lashes commenced falling. You know that the whip used at sea is no small horse-flicking thing, but a great horrific leather monster, and as it rose and fell and rose and fell it cut the villain's flesh apart like a saber. Sweat oiled the body of the enormous whipper until he glistened like a buttered statue. I heard the whistling of the whip in the air and the crack against flesh and muscle, and on the fifteenth lash the man seemed to lose consciousness, and on the twentieth he stopped moaning, and still the whip descended, with scarce a pause for the whipper's breath. It cut the man to tatters. There was no need to go all the way to one hundred, for bone was showing by the fiftieth or earlier, and the deck was stained; but to the end they went, and then the ship's priest gave Popish blessings to what certainly was a dead man, and they sacked him and put him over the side. For days afterwards I saw when I closed my eyes that whip coursing through the air. And I saw also the anatomy lesson that they had made out of the sailor's back, that discourse on flesh and muscle and bone. To Torner I said, "If they ever ask me to choose my death, remind me to select the headman's axe."

"Aye. Who would not? But only a fool strikes an officer, and a flogging is a good education for a fool."

"And for all the other fools who saw it done," I said.

After that there was less bickering on board, and ready obedience to the orders of the mates. The stains remained in the boards for many a day. Well, and the English fleet must do its floggings just as grimly; but I am in no hurry to observe the niceties of the method a second time.

Of all the Portugals only one spoke sociably to us the whole voyage. This was a certain Barbosa, a peaceful man with a pleasant way, who was some sort of tax-collector for King Philip, and traveled an endless weary route between Brazil and Africa. He was older than the others, with a fine taste in clothing and an elegant broad-brimmed hat that he wore cavalier-fashion, shoved down over one eye. He spoke good English, and often at dusk he came to us as we stood by the rail, and talked of the land toward which we were going.

The Portugals, he said, had but a tiny purchase there. They had gulled several of the African kings into taking them in, and even into swallowing the holy bread and wine of the Romish rite and christening themselves with Portuguese names, so that this blackamoor monarch was now Don Affonso and that one Don Alvaro, and the Duke of This and That, the Marquess of That and This. But for all that there were mere little islands of Portuguese civilization on the African coast surrounded by great dark pools of monstrous night, and warfare was constant between the Portugals and their unwilling hosts, and also with a cannibal tribe called the Jaqqas that roved like demons in the back country. Barbosa was of two minds of all this. "It is a deadly land, full of vile malarias and secret venoms. And yet it has beauty and riches, and we will make of it, if God give it to us, another Mexico, another Peru."

"King Philip has enough of those already," I said.

"Aye, but this will not be King Philip's! He does not meddle in the lands overseas that were Portugal's before the two kingdoms were joined," said Barbosa, "and King Philip will not rule Portugal forever." And he looked about, perhaps wondering if he had been overheard, though why any other of these Portugals should mind that Barbosa was treasonous toward the Spanish king is hard for me to comprehend.

A day came when Africa darkened the horizon, weeks later. And as our vessel glided on a glassy sea into the harbor at São Paulo de Loanda in the land of Angola, the boatswain came to us with our chains and indicated with tosses of his head that we should submit to them once more.

This Sãŏ Paulo de Loanda lies on a great bay, called the Bay of Goats, that provides a tolerable haven for shipping. The closing of this harbor is made by a certain island known as Loanda, which means in the language of the place "bald," or "shaven," because it is a very low place without any hills. Indeed, it scarce raises itself above the sea. This island was formed of the sand and dirt of the sea and of a rivermouth a little south of the town, the River Kwanza, whose waves meeting together, and the filthy matter sinking down there to the bottom in the continuance of time it grew to be an island. It may be about twenty miles long, and one mile broad at the most, and in some places only a bow-shot's width from side to side.

As we passed by this island Barbosa said to Torner and me, "On that isle the black King of the Kongo has his money-mine, and pulls forth each year great store of wealth."

"Gold, you mean?" said Torner.

This Barbosa laughed. "Nay, good friend. Shells of the sea is what these simple folk prize the most!"

He laughed as if to scorn it, a great curling hard-eyed laugh of contempt, and told us how women go on the beaches and at depths of two fathoms and more they scoop up sand in their baskets, and afterwards take little curved shells, smooth and bright, from the waste matter. These are the money of the land. "Gold and silver and other metals are not money here," declared Barbosa. "In sooth, with these shells you can buy gold and silver, or anything else! But these are only silly savages, do you see?"

We laughed with him, Torner and I, for we saw it as comic, and passing strange, that pretty-colored shells should be valued even above gold.

But at that time I was still new to the far corners of the world, and I looked at everything with the blinkered eyes of ignorance and narrow compassion. Time has given me a shade more of wisdom, and I think now that there is no one righteous path in anything, but that each path is righteous in its own way, and so why should pretty shells not be beloved to these people even as pretty yellow or white metals are to us? All are scarce goods to find, that must be scavenged from the earth with toil, and all have beauty, and none has much use except as an article of commerce. Yet I could not have argued such matters with Barbosa at that time. Nor, by the bye, do I share with him now the thought that the people of this land are mere silly savages; but all this wisdom was very costly in the learning.

Angola shimmered in the clear torrid daylight like a land of dreams, none of them happy ones.

Torner had drawn me a rough map. Angola sits along the south-western coast of Africa, about midway between the great bulge of Guinea to the north and the Cape of Bona Speranza to the south. Running above Angola on the coast is the kingdom of the Kongo, joining to it as Spain joins to Portugal, and above that is another kingdom known as Loango, and there are sundry other smaller kingdoms inland from these three in those parts.

Strange names. Rumbling mouthfuls of sound. Mpemba, Mbamba, Mbata, Nsundi, Mpangu, Soyo. The province of the Ambundu. The territories of Wembo, Wando, Nkusu, Matari. The regions of the wild men, the flesh-eating Jaqqas, Calicansamba, Cashil, Cashindcabar. Devil-names. Names of harsh music, full of drums and shrill skirling outcry.

Some of these names Torner told to me, as we peered on the map he had scrawled. Some of them I heard later after, whispered to me in the forest by frightened men. I bear scars to remind me of those names now. Drops of my blood lie in the dark moist soil of those places, and from my blood great ollicondi trees have sprouted in these years past, and cedars and palms, and trees without any names at all. I have seen with my eyes the province of Tondo and the great city of Dongo and the river called Gonza, and more, so much more that my brain fills and overflows with the bursting memories of it all. Kingdoms: Angola, Kongo, Loango. Dreamlands.

Nay, though, not dreamlands to their own people, but right and proper dominions, such as are Portugal and France and Sweden in our world, or England herself. The King of the Kongo is the supreme monarch, whose title is Manikongo, and both Angola and Loango are deemed subject to him. But the powers of that king have greatly been diminished of late, and in any event the Portugals have made a jest of all the solemnities of these kingdoms by imposing their own government and their own worship and their own customs as far as possible upon the black folk.

Captive though I was, dismally far from home with no hope of returning, yet did I behold this new place with eyes of wonder. And the sky-high green-crowned trees ashore were things of miracle to me, and the heat of the air, and the smells, the sounds, the dazzle of the light.

Our weighty vessel made its way as deep into the harbor as it dared, and cast its anchor. And then small boats with oars and sails came to fetch us. These were made of palm-tree wood, joined together and framed after the manner of our boats. As we were conveyed to the mainland we saw the channel full of these boats, taking fish, for these are rich waters, heavy with sardines and anchovies, and also sole and sturgeon and an abundance of wholesome crabs.

We drew up to the shore. And saw a grim platoon of somber-faced Portugals waiting for us, dark-haired, dark-eyed, swarthy-skinned little men, sweltering in their full armor under the terrible sun. As though we were a company of great Judases, Torner and I, that durst not be let escape.

They glared most foully at us. Their hard cold staring eyes were stones that they would have hurled at us to pierce our skins. I felt the pressure of their hatred, that dull heavy hostile weight, as I had those first few days of our ocean crossing. And I gave them glare for glare, scowl for scowl. Am I your enemy? *Porque?* Because my country is your country's enemy? Because my Queen is the Pope's enemy? Because we will not sit and mumble at our devotions, and call upon the saints and other false gods? Because we loathe the Latin singsong, and have our own lawful book of prayer? Well, then, so be it, Portugals, I am your enemy! But only because you choose to be mine.

They jeered. They shouted things in their thick-mouthed lingo, not knowing that I understood the half of their foulness. They cursed the

Queen as an excommunicated whore and the daughter of a whore and witch. They said the same of my mother and Torner's. I kept my peace, though it was hard. Jesu, it was hard! I would have cried things at them of the Pope and the stinking luxuries he wallows in, and the monks who fill themselves on altar wine and couple in the cloisters like devils, and such stuff, but worse. Yet I kept my peace.

I said only at last, in my best Portugee, as they marched me onto the dry black earth of their city, "The Devil will chew your souls, ye Papist swine," and left them gasping in amazement that I knew their tongue.

The town, for the supposed capital of a supposed great empire in the making, was small and shabby. This part of Angola yieldeth no stone, and very little wood, and the buildings I saw were largely made of bulrushes and fronds of palm, covered with earth. There were of course certain structures much more grand, the governor's palace and the houses of government, and the great-steepled red-walled church, and the high-palisaded fort.

Torner and I were prodded like sheep, or more roughly than that, through the midst of this place, down dusty mazes of scurfy streets. Everything was hot and dry, the rainy season having given way to the long time of no rain that is the only way to tell winter from summer in these latitudes, the winters being parched. As we proceeded, some Africans came out to stare, first a few, and then great crowds, like floating swarms of bulging white eyes in a cloud of blackness.

"Why do they look so fiercely at us?" I said to Torner. "Is it such a miracle, then, that two Englishmen should be paraded here?"

"It is your hair, Andy, your yellow hair!" he answered me.

Beyond doubt it was, and soon the boldest of the blacks crept forward to touch it lightly, as if to find out whether it was made from spun gold, I suppose. White skins were no longer strange show for these folk; but fair hair, I trow, must be a vast novelty, the Portugals all universally being a dark-thatched people. So they stared at me and I at them. What a splendid complex world, where some are pink in our fashion, and some are red and some yellow-skinned, and some are ebon! These Angolans were pure black, both the men and the women, some of them somewhat inclining to the color of the wild olive. Their hair was curled tight and black, though I saw in a few a slight red tint. Their lips were not as thick as those of such other blacks as I had seen in other lands, and their cheekbones were precious sharp. The stature of the men was of an indifferent bigness, very like that of the Portugals. The women looked strong, with deep and heavy breasts, which they exposed without shame.

What would become of me in this place was utter mystery to me. I

knew not why the Portugals had troubled to ship me here nor what use
they would find for me, and nothing was certain save that I would be
a long time in seeing England again.

They thrust us forward to the fortress. The sun was fire in my eyes,
blinding them, and then I fell blinking and muddled into a dungeon
both damp and chill, carved out of the earth. Torner and I lay side by
side in a great dusky mildewed chamber, with a barrier of sharp stakes
between us. Our ankles were bound with light chains, so that we could
not run without stumbling, but our hands were left free. The Portugal
soldiers hovered around us, stinking of garlic and oil, poking their faces
close upon ours, prodding us here and there to see if we had bones and
ribs, and finding that we did, and prodding us again. Like superstitious
heathen they made the sign of the cross often at us, and waved their
beads and other toys about, and spoke to one another in a Portuguese
so barbarous, so crusted with nonsense, that I could make little of it,
except that they were instructing each other that we were to be kept
without comfort.

And then they left us. "God bless Queen Elizabeth!" I called after
them. *"Dieu et mon Droit! England, England, England!"* and more such
things.

There we remained in darkness and misery for three or four days,
receiving meals from time to time but otherwise ignored. Insects paid
us visits, spiders with fur, and small chittering things, and lizards of the
night. The stink of piss and shit was all we breathed. Barbosa had said,
as we parted from him in the plaza of the town, that we would soon
know our fates, but I wondered if these ill-gendered Portugals had simply
forgotten us. Finally, though, came a clanking of gates and a rattling of
distant locks, and Barbosa appeared, holding a guttering taper. Two of
our jailers were with him, but they lay back some paces.

The good man was kind enough to bring for us a bowl of the wine
of the country, which is made from palm-juice: for such courtesy may
his saints give him peace, may his Madonna hold him in the bosom of
her repose. The wine was milky and powerfully sweet, and had a tingle
to it.

"Are you being fed?" Barbosa asked.

"Not often, and not well, but we are not being starved," I said. "They
give us a sort of porridge, mainly. Are we to be left in this hole forever?"

"There is a problem," said Barbosa. "The old governor is dead, and
all is confusion here, and warfare with the blacks is threatening. The
King of Matamba and the King of Kongo and the King of Angola have
made league against us, and the Jaqqas lurk on the other side, hungry

for evil meat. There will be war. At such a time the officials here can give little thought to you."

"Then let us go, if we are too much trouble!" Torner cried. "Set us free to make our own ways toward home!"

Barbosa shook his head sadly. "You would not live a week, my friend. This is no country for such adventures. You must stay in São Paulo."

"Why are we kept?"

"They will find uses for you," said Barbosa.

"What?" shouted Torner. "Never!" said I, in the same instant.

"Uses," said Barbosa. "We are so few, and the blacks are so many. The administrators have decided to employ captive English here, of which you are the first."

"It is folly," I said. "We will never serve. And if they send enough of us to this place, we will rise and swarm upon your pitiful troops, and take this empire for Queen Bess."

"I pray you, no such talk," said the Portugal mildly, "or the hotbloods here will have your heads."

"Does it matter?"

"It might, to you, when the moment comes."

Torner said, "What counsel can you give us?"

"Patience, endurance, silence. Offer no defiance, and hope for better days. The death of the governor puts everything into paralysis here, for he was such a man as holds the center of all authority, and when he is gone there is only empty air, a vacuum through which whirlwinds swirl."

This governor who had lately died, he told us, was one Paulo Dias de Novais. The garrison had elected its captain-major, Luiz Serrão, to his place. "Serrão in his time was a fine soldier. But he is old and weary," said Barbosa, "and he is forced to fight a war little to his liking. I think he will make no disposition of you twain until his other problems are behind him. And that day may never arrive."

"So we will rot here without limit?" I demanded.

"Jesus and Mary give you comfort," the good Portugal said gently. "Better for you that you had never left England, but here you are, and I will remember you in my devotions, for I think it will be long before you see daylight again."

In that, however, the kind Barbosa was mistaken.

Hardly a day later we were called out of our dungeon and summoned to the governor's palace for an audience with this Serrão. He was old and heavy, and he sat in a slouching way, breathing thickly, for that he was fleshy and ill, with unhealthy grayish skin and beads of sweat bright all over him. For a long while he stared at us as if we were some strange beasts of foul stench, and I looked back at him with rage and detestation, for that this man was our single foe here, the one with power of life and death over us, and stood between us and home, and I knew he would not set us loose.

At last he said, "The letters tell me you are dangerous brigands, that sought to overwhelm the government of the Brazils. Is this so?"

"Brigands, yes," I answered. "But all we sought was some of the gold of the Indies, out of the treasure-ships of the Rio de la Plata." There seemed no purpose in holding to the pretense that we were innocent Virginia settlers, when we were plainly condemned here.

"You speak our language well, though your accent is poor."

"It is the language that is poor. I speak it as well as it deserves."

"Oh? Are you so full of fire, then? That you rail at the man who owns your life?"

"I rail at you because you own my life, sir."

"I did not ask for you," said Serrão. "To me you are a burden, a thorn in my side."

"We did not ask for you, either."

Serrão peered into my eyes. "Shall I feed you to the coccodrillos, and be rid of your nation? You are a buzzing in my ears. Saint Michael spare me from receiving more of you."

"And Saint George spare us from dwelling long among you."

"Be silent!"

At that sudden outroar from the sluggish and ailing Serrão, Torner looked toward me and said, "For Jesu sake, Andy, don't enrage the old man!"

Serrão said, "The other English, he understands nothing of our speech?"

"Very little," said I. "Afterwards will I convey the meanings to him."

"Is he as full of wrath as you?"

"More," I said. "His tongue trembles with disgust of all your kind, but he can say it only in English."

Serrão nodded, as though hardly caring that we were such firebrand rogues, and fell silent again. He toyed with some carving at his belt, and picked at his nails with his dagger: a fat old soldier, who must once have been valiant and quick, though there was little sign of that now. Very likely he was sore vexed with Paulo Dias for dying at such a time. He looked up after a while and said, "What am I to do with you."

"Put us aboard the next ship for Lisbon, and we will find our way from there to England."

The old man laughed. "Yes, and give you a thousandweight of ivory to recompense you for your time in our hands, also. Are you good sailors, brigand?"

"Excellent good."

"What skills do you have?"

"I am a pilot," I said coolly, "and my companion is a gunner."

These lies did I tell to make us seem more important, for had I said we were mere deckhands I feared the Portugals would value us little, and perhaps slit our throats to have no more trouble of caring for us. In this I think I was right. Serrão said in a mumble, "A pilot. Good. Very good. Our pinnace that plies between here and Masanganu is short-handed of crew, and we will let you serve aboard it."

"That we will not do," I replied.

"Are you defiant?"

"Indeed."

He made a scowl, as though I had struck him with my fist in the rolls of fat at his belly, and had let some air out of him. I kept my eyes glittering cold. Yet strangely I found my loathing of him difficult to maintain: he was old, he was ailing, he was weary, he was mortal, and by an accident of fate he sat in judgment over me, which perhaps he liked no more than I did. I took this to be weakness and softheadedness in me, and attempted to banish such a way of thinking, and glowered down upon him as I might upon some sly and cozening Italian Cardinal who lay nightly with his own sister.

Serrão said, "Why do you refuse?"

"I am Queen Bess' to command, but not yours, and surely not King Philip's."

"Talk not to me of King Philip. He is no king of mine, except by distant decree, of which I know nothing. I ask you to go on our pinnace, that has need of crew."

"Crew it yourself, old man."

He seemed to be holding himself in check. In a slow steady way he said, "What are my choices? I could slay you out of hand, and say you were determined heretics that preached falsely to the blacks. But no, I am not hot for that path. I could send you to your dungeon, and let you stink and moulder down there until your bones shine through your skin. Is that to your liking? But then I must feed you once in a time, and otherwise give care to you. Or else you could serve under our command."

"That we will not, if we must rot for it, or feed your coccodrillos with our flesh."

Serrão lapsed back against his chair and drummed with his fingertips on its arm, which was made of some scaly serpent-skin, and said, "You are stubborn and you are stupidly stubborn. So be it: back to your cell."

The guards began to tumble us from the room.

Torner looked to me and said, "What is it?"

"We are offered berths on some ships of theirs. I have told him nay, we will not serve."

"Brave fellow!"

Brave indeed, but perhaps not without folly. For as we hied ourselves back through the soul-frying sticky heat toward the depths and bowels of the fortress, I felt an alteration of my position coming over me. I thought to myself that I was being noble but nobly foolish in my patriotism. They could well leave us in the dungeon a year or five or forever. We might conceivably die down there of the damp, or of a spider's bite, or of some inner flux, in two more weeks. How would that serve the Queen? How would that serve our own needs and dreams? Was it not better to obey these Portugals, and come up into the sunlight, and do their bidding until perhaps they pardoned us? I would find it hard to enter their service, but it might be either that or perish, and to perish out of stubborn patriotism may be a fine thing, but not half so fine as seeing England again.

To Torner I said, "I have changed my mind."

"What?"

"In the dungeons we stand no chance. Aboard their pinnace we may find the beginning of the way home. What say you, Thomas?"

"Will you serve them?"

"Aye, I will. I think it is wiser."

"Then so will I, Andy."

I halted and said to the Portugals who were prodding and pushing me in the kidneys with their truncheons, "Wait, I would see the governor again."

"Another day," one guard replied.

"No!" I cried, thinking it might be months. "Go to him, tell him we reconsider, or it be on your head!"

The Portugals conferred; and then they relented, and took us back to Serrão, who looked that much older and more weary for the ten minutes that had gone by.

"I yield," I said. "We will serve."

"You are shrewd to do so. So be it." And he waved us out.

Once more we were conducted to our dungeon, and now I explained to Torner all that had passed between Serrão and me in our earlier conversation. He shrugged when I said our choices had been to serve or to die miserably in our chains, and laughed at my promoting him to gunner and me to pilot; but he blanched when I named Masanganu as the place where we were to be shipped.

"You know it?" I asked.

"Barbosa told me of it once, when we were at sea," said Torner. "It is a fort somewhere in the hot interior of this land, which guards against the wild tribes beyond. The Portugals all dread it, he said, and no man will go thither if he can prevent it, for it is a place where men die like chickens of fevers and plagues." Torner looked to me and I saw more anger than fear in his eyes. "That fat old villain has found the easiest way to rid himself of us. Masanganu! A place where men die like chickens, Barbosa called it. Where men die like chickens."

FIVE

THIS PINNACE of the governor's was a modest vessel even as pinnaces go, with a spar awry on its foremast, and its mainsail baggy in the Arab fashion, so that it tended to bury the bow. I was glad we were not called upon to take it to ocean water, for I suspected such a craft would yaw unpredictably with a following sea or with slight changes of wind. But all we had to do was sail it somewhat up the River Kwanza, a distance of one hundred thirty miles.

This river has his mouth a short way below São Paulo de Loanda on the coast. The pinnace that waited there had a small crew indeed, barely enough men to cast free the anchor and set the sails: small wonder they were pressing Englishmen into their service. These Portugals were sadly overextended in Angola, but a few hundred of them to fill all the garrisons, and enemies congregating on every frontier. Aboard the pinnace the master and pilot were one man, a fleshy-faced Portugal named Henrique, and the others were but common yeomen who did as they were told, nothing more.

Nine days we were going up the river of Kwanza, in which time one Portugal yeoman died and another fell mortally ill. The country here is so hot that it pierceth their hearts. We moved slowly in terrible silence broken by terrible sounds: by day the wild screams of birds, by night the ghastly music of the leopards and lions and jackals and hyenas. "We have but one blessing," said Henrique to me, for he was courteous and showed us no disdain, "that we are making our voyage in the dry season. For in the wet, black flying insects come at us thick as clouds, and we breathe them and eat them and blink them in our eyes."

Coccodrillos lurked on muddy banks, smiling their coccodrillo smile that I remembered so well from Brazil. When we drew near them, they silently slid off into the dark water. In riverside lagoons water-birds by thousands waded about, feeding on hapless small creatures. There were black-and-white storks of sinister aspect, which to me seemed harbingers of death; and also another great bird with a bill strangely shaped like unto a great spoon. And along the shore was reedy green papyrus with tops like fans, far taller than a man. While beyond that the jungle lay, palms and vines and such intertwined into an impenetrable wall. Sometimes we saw the river-horse or hippopotamus, only its huge nose above the water, and its broad glistening back. And sometimes the coccodrillos were so thick on the banks that their heavy musk made us want to puke.

The strangest sight of all that we beheld was neither coccodrillo nor river-horse, though, but a man of human kind. This was perhaps halfway up the winding course of the river, just beyond a great lake called Soba Njimbe's Lake. Here, on a flat place of land by the edge of the thick jungle, stood alone by himself a black of enormous height and huge depth of color, pure jet in hue, with a purplish undercast to him. He was altogether naked but for a girdle of beadwork that did not at all conceal his privy parts, which were frightful in size. He wore on one hip a kind of dagger and on the other a longer weapon, and leaned on a heavy target or shield of much size, and stared off into the distance, taking no more notice of our passing craft than if we were beetles on a drifting strand of straw.

There was about this one man a strangeness and a presence most commanding, and such a sense of silent menace, that made him a sort of Lucifer or Mephistopheles, and I knew at first instant he was nothing ordinary. Beside me one of the Portugals made a little grunting sound and he dropped to the planks and began such a crossing of himself, such a torrent of Ave Marias and Pater Nosters, that I saw I was not the only one to have such a feeling.

To Henrique I said, "What is that person?"

"Some prince of the Jaqqas," replied the pilot. "We see them of times along this road, making pilgrimages that are outside our knowledge."

"Jaqqas? The man-eaters?"

"The very same," said Henrique. "Followers of the Lord of Darkness, devils out of the pit!"

One of the other Portugals had fetched an arquebus, and was aiming the thing now at the creature on the riverbank. Henrique hissed and pushed the snout of the weapon aside, saying, "Nay, fool, would you have us all in the stew-pot by nightfall?"

In another moment the river took a hard curve, and the Jaqqa was gone from our sight. But the image of him was burned into my mind and lingered long.

Henrique said, "They are a plague. They come and go like ghosts in the wilderness, or like locusts, rather, devouring everything in their path, destroying, showing no quarter. And yet we know not if they are our enemies or our friends, for sometimes they serve our purposes, and sometimes they fall upon our encampments like the hounds of Hell." He shuddered. "These Angolese people, and the Kongo folk, are but human beings with dusky skins and woolly hair, and we understand them, and when we look into their eyes we see souls looking back, and when we touch their flesh we feel the flesh of mankind upon them. But the Jaqqas—!"

He left the words unsaid.

Onward we went through the killing heat, which wrapped around us like a heavy cloth. On the sixth day we stopped at a village called Muchima, where the Portuguese had founded a presidio, or fort, in order that we might get medicines for our man who had fallen ill, the other having already died. Only three Portugals lived at this presidio, which indeed was more of a hut of boughs than any sort of fort. But all about them was a village of blacks, fifty or eighty souls, of a friendly sort, innocent and gentle, that lived mainly by fishing. We passed a night there.

For company that night all of the Portugals, even Henrique, took girls of the tribe as bed-partners, except for the one who was too ill for such sport, and one other who I think had taken an oath not to touch woman that season, in return for some favor granted him by his beloved Virgin Mary. Torner also was offered a woman, and most gladly accepted, and I, too, but I refused. My refusal was the occasion of some merriment among the Portugals, since I was so robust of body and rich of health that they could not understand it. "Are you a sworn monk?" Henrique asked me. "Or is it that you prefer the love of your own sex, in which case I think we must slay you and feed you to the coccodrillos, lest you corrupt our voyage."

"Neither the one nor the other," I made answer. "But I feel no urge toward woman in this foul heat."

In truth that was no truth. My loins ached, and in my dreams I saw only breasts and thighs and buttocks and fleecy loins. But the fleece that covered those loins was the golden wool of my Anne Katherine. God wot I am no saint, and had taken no vows of fidelity neither, and yet I could not at that time put myself into the body of some stranger woman merely for the easing of my lusts, not when the palm of my hand could serve the same purpose with lesser sin. Especially when the stranger woman was of black skin and oiled with some rancid stuff, and had strange scars carven on her cheeks by way of decoration, and perhaps a bone thrust through her nose. To use such a woman would be almost like using cattle, that is, not a fitting partner for an Englishman. So I thought—God forgive me!—in my haughtiness, me only a year and some months gone out from Essex at that time.

Therefore I slept by myself that night, which I was greatly weary of doing, a year and some months being a long while to sleep by one's self. In the morning when we resumed our journey Torner came to me, as we poled our way through a place of shallows and rocks, and said, "They gave me for my pleasure a girl of thirteen years. Her breasts were new, and stood out straight from her chest like this, and felt like globes of a firm spongy stuff. Among these folk it is a sin for a married woman to lie with other than her husband, even as it is with us, but their girls they pass freely around."

"And had you delight, Thomas?"

His eyes gleamed like beacons. "Aye, Andy! Aye! Not that she was greatly skilled at it, and she had an odd way of wanting to receive me, crouching on her knees. But I turned her over and spread her fairly, and oh! Andy, it was so good a feeling, after this long a while."

"Although she had no skill?"

"What matters is that? I was not marrying her," said Torner, "only relieving my need. She lay there with her eyes open and her legs apart, and did little, so that I yearned for a good London wench that knows her arse from a table. But yet, Andy—but yet—!"

"What of her teeth, filed to points? Did that not unnerve you?" I asked.

"God's death, but it would if she had gone crawling on my body with her face! I'd have shriveled to a thumb's-length, with those devil-teeth gaping around my yard! But that is not the style of loving here, I think me. And merely the looking at the teeth caused me no distress, for after the first glimpse I kept my eyes elsewhere, and later I kept them closed." Torner laughed and pummeled my arm. "And you? Too proud to tup a black wench?"

"Too much mindful of my Essex maid," I said softly.

"Ah. Essex is far away, and will you remain chaste until you get there again?"

"How can I know that?"

"But for now you do, is that it?"

I nodded. "For now. I've kept chaste this long, at no small cost; maybe the habit of it is settling in on me."

"Nay. I've heard you groan in desire many a night, Andy."

Color came to my face. "Have you, now? Go to!"

"It's truth! Why, in that dungeon last week you lay moaning and sobbing in your sleep, and then you snorted, and then you were still. Don't you think I know those sounds, lad?"

"Perhaps you do."

His hard blue eyes were close to my own, and his smile was a wicked one as he said, "D'ye think Anne Katherine lies chaste while you rove the seas?"

I struck him.

I hit him with the flat of my hand, against the cheekbone, a hard push rather than a blow, but hard enough to buckle his knees and send him reeling. Three or four Portugals came upon us, not wanting a brawl among us English, but Torner rose, shaking his head to let the bees loose from his ear, and grinning, and saying, "You slap with good force, lad."

"You spoke out of turn."

"Aye, and I'm sorry for it. It was a shameful thing I said."

"She is no maid. I had her myself more than once, but I was the first, Thomas. I know that for certain, and I think I am yet the only one."

"I pray that you be right. I wish you all joy of her love."

"And the years will pass and I will not return," I said, "and a time will come when she thinks me dead, and then she will go on to another man. But I think that time is not yet. I choose to think it, Thomas. She is but nineteen, or perhaps twenty by now, and I think she will give me another year."

"You are betrothed?"

"Aye. I had a wife once that died of the pox, and now I fear I have lost a second before we were wed, and while we both still live. Are you married?"

"I am," said Torner. "With three boys from her."

"And does she stay faithful to you while you voyage?"

"I make no inquiries of that, good Andy. My trade keeps me apart from her long months at a time, and now may keep me from her forever. Am I to stay pure for such lengthy spans? And if I am not, should she? But I make no inquiries on that." He laughed broadly. "How old do you be, Andy?"

"I was born in the month of Queen Bess' accession."

"So you are thirty, I think. A man of middle years, and yet you seem very young, in some ways."

"Aye," I said. "I had a late start, and I lost a few years through grief and confusion in my early manhood, when no wisdom entered my head. But fear not, Thomas: I am no fool. Filed-teeth wenches with breasts that stand straight out do not arouse me this week, that is all." And we laughed and embraced, with pummeling of backs, and went on with our deckside chores.

But a heavy melancholy settled over me. I saw Anne Katherine shimmering in the air before me, and she was weeping and garbed in widow's weeds. And I thought me, How strange, that I am here in this land of filed teeth and scarred cheeks and coccodrillos and Lucifer standing naked on a riverbank, and England so far away, lost to me belike forever. It is the price of empire, as Francis Willoughby long ago said, that some of our people be scattered like seed into strange ground: but why was it me that was so scattered? Torner might well be right, to console himself with whatever consolation lay at hand, for our lives that we knew in England were gone from us, and we were something other in this place, stripped of vows and identity, as naked to our pasts as that Jaqqa by the river is naked to the air.

And then I thought, Nay, I am Andrew Battell of Leigh in Essex, and I will remain Andrew Battell to the last, a man of Essex, and, God grant it, I will see Essex again, and Anne Katherine, and my family's own house.

And now I think, knowing the things that that young man on the river-pinnace could not know, knowing all that I have done and had done to me in these twenty years and more gone by since then, Am I still Andrew Battell of Leigh in Essex, or am I transformed, am I magicked into a changeling? And I answer, Yea, I still am Andy Battell, but a larger and more strange Andy Battell than ever was planned for me when my father engendered me. And though I have done such deeds as an Englishman would hail as monstrosities, yet am I still God's own man, and mine own, for aye. Do you comprehend that? I comprehend that. And, God willing, so will you, by the time I come to the end of my tale.

A bleak river-fog descended, making our voyage perilous, and in that heavy grayness my melancholy lifted. I found myself too much occupied with my duties to care that I was an exile and a prisoner, and in stray moments I even found myself wondering what it would have been like to lie with some blackamoor girl. We skirted the muddy shores. Out of the mists came fearful mooings and bellowings, of such creatures I knew not what, but that they were not the sheep and cattle of England. The mist raised a bit, and we saw that a second river was pouring into the Kwanza. This was the Lukala, flowing from the north-east, and just beyond this meeting of the waters lay the presidio of Masanganu.

Henrique trembled as he pointed toward the small stone fort. "This is a terrible place," he said. "It is the unfirmest country under the sun.

You shall see men in the morning very lusty, and within two hours dead. Others, that if they but wet their legs, presently they swell bigger than their middles; others break in the sides with a draught of water. I dread this place."

"Are we to be here long?" I asked.

"Some weeks."

"That could have been worse."

He looked full upon me. "O, if you did know the intolerable heat of the country, you would think yourself better a thousand times dead, than to live here a week. Here you shall see poor soldiers lie in troops, gaping like camels for a puff of wind. Husband your strength, Englishman: you will need it."

"Why then is there a fort in such a place?"

"To keep check on the blackamoors, that they do not invade us from without. If anyone is to descend on São Paulo de Loanda, they must needs come this way, or else along the river that lies to the north, the Mbengu, which is not so easy for transit. And there is another reason. There is beyond here a place called Kambambe, as far inward as Muchima lies behind us, and in Kambambe, they say, great mines of silver exist."

"Indeed?"

Henrique guffawed. "See, the pirate is excited at once by talk of treasure! Know you, English, that we have not yet managed the discovery of the mines of Kambambe. But we know the silver is there. We think that it is the outermost of the mines of King Solomon, in fact."

"Aye?"

"Aye. Some there be that will say that Solomon's gold, which he had for the Temple of Jerusalem, was brought by sea out of these countries. And as we make our way to the heart of this land, O English, we will have ourselves Ophir and its treasures, to match the treasures of Peru and Mexico that the Spaniards have had."

I listened attentively to all Henrique's talk of the mines of King Solomon, and made note to bring such news to the ear of Queen Elizabeth if ever I returned home. I would have liked to place upon her hearth another Peru, another Mexico.

Poor Henrique saw no golden treasure. Under the ghastly weight of the hotness of Masanganu, which hung upon us like a falling sky, he took a flux and lay shivering with ague in the little house where the Portugals keep their sick there, and every week the surgeon came to him and did a letting of blood, but it gave him no surcease. I visited him and saw him growing into a skeleton day by day, the flesh burning away in his sweat. He had begun by being a plump and hearty man, and now he was a death's-head and bones, an awful sight, death in life. At the end of two months there was nothing left of him, and he succumbed.

Then an officer at the Masanganu garrison whose name was Vicente de Menezes came to me and said, "You are described in the journals as a pilot, English."

I was taken aback an instant; and then I recalled the lie I had lied to Luiz Serrão.

"Aye," I said.

"Well, then," said this Vicente de Menezes, who was gaunt and green-complexioned and seemed to have the hand of death on him as well, "the pinnace must now be returned to São Paulo de Loanda, with despatches and certain goods, and Henrique is dead. You are commanded to carry her down the river in his place."

I did not debate the point. No pilot was I, but I had some smattering of the art, and none of the Portugals about here looked to be even faintly skilled. And I think at that point I might have done many things to get myself alive out of Masanganu's furnace heat, even unto kissing the image of the Madonna, or mumbling Romish jargon—aye, even that, I think. Merely to take command of a Portugee pinnace was a small thing in the saving of my life. So I moved another inch toward my transformation: it might now be construed that I had become an officer in the service of King Philip. God's blood, the twists and turns life inflicts on us!

And the twists and turns of the river: those at least I remembered, for I am gifted that way. What enters my mind sticks there with a fearful grip. We loaded our cargo, and took our leave, with a crew half the size of the one that had set out upriver, for Henrique and two of his men were in their graves now, and one other was too ill to depart. Those under my command showed no disdain toward me for my Englishness. Why should they, who only wanted to flee this hellish place? They would take orders from the Antichrist if he stood on the quarterdeck.

So we embarked. When we came to Muchima, a day and a half downstream, we saw smoke rising above the palm-trees long before the village appeared, and then came the village. A destroying angel had visited it; or a pack of demons, more likely. A hurricane of murderers had swept through here. The place was sacked and wholly ruined, with corpses everywhere, and steaming mounds of torn-out entrails, and other charnel horrors. It was a hideous sight. The palm-trees that give the wine had been cut down at the root, and the plantations had been dug and rendered waste, and all the fish-nets torn, and the bodies of the people were most hellishly mutilated and sliced apart. So much blood soaked the black earth that it was as crimson underfoot as though we walked on gaudy carpets, or the robes of Cardinals. The Portuguese presidio, too, was sacked and one of the Portugals lay dead and weltering in it, and the other two were gone.

"The Jaqqas, it was," said one of my men.

Thus I came to understand that the lone black prince we had seen standing on the bank was a forerunner, perhaps a Jaqqa scout and perhaps a notifier of impending doom. The devilish scourge had come to this town and taken all life, even the cattle and dogs. We sought for the bodies of the missing two Portugals, but did not find them. "They are eaten," a yeoman said, and the others all nodded their agreement.

Torner amazed me by showing tears. For the Portugals? Nay, for the girl he had had, the file-toothed wench on whose unenthusiastic body he had vented his cravings. From one smoking hut to another he wandered, looking for her remains among the frightful carnage. I came to him and took him by the arm and said gently, "What, are you so concerned for her?"

"She was warm and soft in my arms. I would at least give her a proper burying."

A Portugal came up to us to inquire when we would be going on. I explained quickly that first we sought this certain girl's body, and he shook his head.

"Nay," he said. "The Jaqqas kill everyone, but not the boys and girls of thirteen or fourteen years. Those they take captive, and raise as their own. All the rest they slay, and many they eat, but not those."

This I repeated to Torner. We returned to the pinnace. Such total destruction stunned and froze me. What, was such evil upon the earth in our Christian day? These happy folk snuffed out, and for what? For what? Their very palm-trees cut down, that gave sweet wine? I thought on it, and it was like staring into a wizard's glass, and seeing such a realm of deviltry and monstrosity that I was thrown into sore fright, as if Pandemonium had broken through upon the earth and would conquer it all, one spot at a time. I felt a sickness of the soul. And in time another kind of sickness; for the next day the first throbbings of fever announced themselves in me, and as we hurried downriver, my head pounded and my skin ran with sweat and my bowels gave way, and I saw things all in pairs, so that I was hard put to steer my craft safely free of the banks of coccodrillos, and by the time I came upon São Paulo de Loanda I was filthy sick. I thought my last hour was galloping toward me.

SIX

PHANTOMS VISITED me in my fevered sleep.

First came a horde of lanky Jaqqas, led by one who was a veritable Jack-o'-legs, nine feet tall and black as night. I lay tossing and moaning on some foul straw pallet and out of the darkness of the jungle appeared these diaboli, with their eyes blazing like circlets of white flame. About me they marched, round and round and round. One of them played on a flute fashioned of bone, and one wore over his head and shoulders a coccodrillo mask, all snout and teeth and smile, and one beat on a drum that was made of human skin, still showing birthmarks and other such blemishes. And they sang to me in their Jaqqa tongue, but I understood their song, which was a song of death, a song of fury.

> *The burning is the joy*
> *The torment is the pleasure*
> *The killing is the fine delight*
> *The eating is the crown of*
> *all.*

And so forth, long skeins of doggerel imbued with a hellish vigor and enthusiasm.

Before my dreaming eyes these black fiends fell upon the village, and I knew it to be the village of Muchima, where I saw them arrange in a secret circle and burst inwardly on the hapless fisher-folk, and strike them with their spears, and slit their gullets with knives of bone or polished wood, until the dead lay in heaps. Whether I closed my eyes or kept them open I saw the same sight, a slaughter most dread, followed by a feast much like the one I had viewed in Brazil, of human meat. There was one difference, that instead of devouring their victims one by one, these Jaqqas took an immense cauldron the size of a barque or caravel, and filled it with water that at once bubbled and sparkled, and thrust the villagers into it by the dozen, so that they floated and drifted while they boiled, and the meat came loose from the bones. And when it was cooked the greatest of the Jaqqas, the giant one with a body like a god's and a dangling long member like a black serpent, took to me a thigh and an arm and said, "Here, English. Take and eat! Take and eat! In this flesh will you be healed!" And I had no choice but to eat, but lo! the meat was tender and graceful, and power poured into my ailing body, until I rose from my bed and danced among the Jaqqas through the smoking ruins of the harmless village.

Such was my phantasm. There was no truth in it but only that of a disordered mind. But there was prophecy in it, I would discover. There was vision and oracle. A day would come when I would witness at close range the Jaqqas at their play, and though what took place was very little like that of my fever-dream, yet there were certain monstrous similarities indeed.

The Jaqqas sang and danced and feasted and were gone. And I lay sweating and vomiting, thinking, I must not yet be dead, because I feel pain in every joint, and death is said to bring relief from such dismay.

After the Jaqqas, there came into my room Her Protestant Majesty Queen Elizabeth.

She was garbed all in resplendent white, with sparkling gems set into her robe, and a trim of white ermine that had been brought her from the dukedoms of Muscovy. The crown was on her head, with spikes of gold that rose as high as long fingers, and atop each spike was a little ruby or emerald carved most cunningly in the shape of a man's head, just like the pickled heads of the traitors that stand on pikes along London Bridge. She carried the scepter and the orb as well, but these she put down, and she leaned over my bed so that her lustrous red hair dangled in my face and I felt her cool sweet breath and saw the luminous wonder of her smile.

"Poor Andy," she murmured. "How you suffer for me!"

And took my hand in hers, and stroked it to draw the heat from my flesh, and said softly, "I remember how it was, when I had the pox and was like to die of it, and everything was alpha and omega for me all at once. It's like that for you, is it not? But I recovered and you will recover of it, too, and grow strong, and when you return to me I will name you Duke, eh, Andy? The Duke of Angola. The Earl of Masanganu. And give you land and castles and ten thousand pound a year, for you are my only son, in whom I am well pleased."

And much more drivel of the same sort, telling me tales of the court, the doings of the Earl of Leicester and Lord Burghley and Sir Walter Ralegh and all that crew, and then she spoke of her dread sister Spanish Mary, Mary Tudor, who died in the year of my birth, and who would have had us all Papists if she had lived. The Queen whispered to me of Bloody Mary's chilly couplings with her husband, the very same Philip who has become King of Spain and Portugal, and told me such mocking gross things as I blush to reveal in this telling, for that they came not out of any true gossip but only out of the stews of my own mind, however fevered. She told me also similar tales of the Pope and his catamites, and then she said, "And if you die on this bed, Andy, take not the unction from the Portugal priest, but go with my own dispensation, that frees you of all blame, for I am God's vicar in England," and such stuff. And wiped my forehead with a damp cloth, and gave me sweet thick syrup to drink, and rested my head against her breasts, which were wondrous soft, contrary to the vile stories that are told of her. But I was fevered. For as the Queen cradled and caressed me she was transformed in my melting brain to my sweet Anne Katherine, whose breasts I knew well, and soft indeed they were. In the deep valley between them I had my repose, and she ran her fingers over my matted and tangled hair and sang of love and peace.

"Good Anne Katherine," I said. "Take me to you!"

Her body was bare, all pink and gold, and from it came the fragrance of grass in springtime and violets in bloom, or lilacs, and she opened her arms to me and gathered me to her. And my body rose to her, my manhood stiffened and I felt the warm wet place between her thighs where I was to go, and as I entered her something happened that was passing strange, for she darkened and grew smaller and became my other wife Rose Ullward, that had died of the pox. The change took only a moment from the fair woman to the dark, the tall to the small, and I cupped her breasts, which were wondrous round and full for so tiny a woman, and put my face into the hollow beside her cheek along her shoulder, and ran my lips along her skin, but the skin seemed cold to me. And well it might be, for the Rose I embraced was the Rose who lies to this day in the churchyard at Plymouth, all bone and staring eyeless sockets, which gave me great horror.

I screamed long and severely from that vision. And there came someone to comfort me, who patted my brow and spooned a medicine between my lips. I dared not open my eyes, fearing another skeleton, but a familiar voice said, "Have no dread, Andy, you are mending well." It was my father. I looked to him and there he was as in life, dressed finely with tight dark hose and fine velvet breeches and a brown leather jerkin, and a doublet all chased with patterns of gold, and the cloak of a great gentleman, and leather purse at his waist, saying, "You were ever my pet, my favorite, the child of my late years, and I will guard you now, I will defend you against all harm, for I am your father and your mother both, and your pilot as well in this sea of storms." I clasped his hand and he turned to smoke and was gone, which seemed to me to say, There is no true pilot except for yourself, and you must sail your own course in this world, where no other soul can truly aid you. But perhaps I am wrong to take such phantasms so earnestly.

I know not how long I tossed in these dreams. It may have been days or weeks or months.

There were many more. My mind was wholly cut loose from its moorings and I could not distinguish between dream and wake, day and night. Sir Francis Drake came to me and vowed to teach me all his craft of the sea, I know, and then there was a priest who offered me Romish comfort, with wafers and wine, which I think I may have accepted, and I do recall Thomas Torner's young Muchima bedmate, with her firm breasts, jutting in that manner of newly sprouted ones, and her little teeth filed to sharp wedges. She ran her mouth over me, kissing me and nibbling me, the way a barber might cup for the ague, raising little welts here and there, which I did not find objectionable. I found nothing at all objectionable, after a time, in anything. Let the Jaqqas dance in the room, let my Anne Katherine become my Rose become a skeleton, let Papist incense burn, it was all the same to me, for I was dying and the things of this world were all one, they had no heavy significance: baubles of air. I had sup with Bloody Queen Mary one hour and her father Great Henry the next. I had good Jesus and all His disciples, and Peter and James and Thomas did a juggling-show for me that made me laugh and clap. I danced with coccodrillos in a fine galliard. I dined at the court of the High Khan of Cathay and with the Grand Duke of Muscovy, and I walked down the long marble gallery of the lords of Byzantium, and I drank the golden wine of Prester John. I coupled with dolphins and serpents and the daughter of Pharaoh. I wandered into ages yet to come and into time gone by. I floated from one miracle to another, in a daze, in a rapture, and I had no wish for it ever to end.

But end it did. The world became more real about me day by day, until I emerged into the true truth of my surroundings. And then I would rather have returned to my dreams and my fevers.

I saw myself in a room with earthen floor and an earthen roof, an underground chamber, pierced at top by a circular skyhole that admitted a wan beam of light. My furniture was only a miserable pile of straw and a bucket of slops beside it, and there was a palisade of stout poles barring my door, with a chain across it, so that I was not sure whether I was in a hospital or a dungeon, or some of both. Which latter I soon discovered to be the case.

I was weak as a puppy. I could not rise. I touched my face with a quivering hand and felt my cheek all stony and hollow, like a skull's, and rough uncouth beard sprouting everywhere. My eyes were blear, but I could see well enough my naked body before me, fleshless, the hip-bones rising to view like scimitars, my skin loose and slack and yellowish, my manhood shriveled and shrunken like that of a man of ninety years, limp and sad against my thigh. So I was not dead, but I was far from being alive.

The gate was let back and a woman entered my cell. I could see her but dimly, but she was slender and seemingly young, with a bodice and robe of some dark velvety stuff, and a kind of surplice over her shoulders woven like a net out of fine fibers, and a veil on her face. I took her to be a nun, though I was puzzled to see gold chains around her neck, and that she had a cap of black velvet trimmed with jewels. This did not seem nun's garb to me.

"Are you awake, then?" she asked in Portuguese.

"Aye."

"And in your right mind?"

"I cannot be so sure of that. What place is this?"

"The hospice of Santa Maria Madalena, in São Paulo de Loanda, where you have lain ill these months past."

"Months? What month is this?"

"It is the month of the Feast of São Antonio."

"By God, I know not your saints! What month of the calendar?"

"June."

That smote me hard. First, that I had dozed away half a year here, out of my mind; and second, that now two years had slipped by since my leaving England. My life was fleeing and I was becalmed, helpless, lost.

The woman had brought me food. It was a bowl of some mashed stuff, floating in a light sauce. She crouched beside me and offered me some with a wooden spoon, saying, "You must regain your flesh. You have eaten very little. Will you try it?"

"What is it?"

"It is a thing called manioc, that we take from the ground and roast, a whole root, and grind into flour. It will make you strong again."

I remembered this manioc from Brazil: a plant of the Indians, that I suppose the Portugals had brought with them to Angola. I had eaten it often, with no great fondness, but now I took it, and the broth in which it lay. The first spoonful filled me with such appetite that I signalled at once for another, but that was rashness: by the time the second one hit bottom, my stomach was sorely griped from the first. I waved the bowl away. She waited patiently. The spasm passed and I was hungry again, and took more, less greedily, a kitten-sip of the stuff. Then a little more. Then a pause, and then yet more. And I felt the griping begin again, and smiled my thanks, and said politely, "*Obrigado*, sister," which to the Portugals is thanks.

"I am Dona Teresa da Costa."

"Is it you that has cared for me all these months?"

"I and some others. They would have let you die, at first, but that seemed too harsh, and we came to give you medicines, and a little soup when you would take it."

"I am most grateful," I told her again. "What is your order, sister?"

She laughed a little tinkling laugh. "Ah, nay, I am no nun! No nun at all!"

"And yet you serve in the hospice?"

"It was for my pleasure," she said. "You looked right splendid when they took you from the pinnace all unconscious, with your golden hair adangle, and your fair English skin, and all. I had never seen such hair and such skin, and I would not have had you die. Can you eat more?"

"I think not."

"Something to drink?"

"Some water, only."

"I will fetch it."

She was gone a long time. Before she returned I felt the fever climbing in me again, and knew that I was far from healed, perhaps still in risk of my life. I began to shake, and as she came to me I turned on my side and delivered myself of all that she had fed me, in such racking pukes that I thought my guts would spew out my mouth and snarl by my side. Then, as quickly as that had happened, I was calm again, sweaty, trembling, but the heat was gone from my forehead. I begged her mercy for having inflicted such foulness on her, but she only laughed, and said, "There has been worse, much worse, in your illness."

As she wiped the spew from my face I looked closely at her. She was no more than eighteen, I saw, and of surpassing beauty. Her eyes were set far apart and narrow in that wondrous Portugal way the women sometimes have, and her skin was deep-hued, an olive tone, and her hair, jet black, was thick and lustrous, tumbling in heavy loops and coils. Her lips were full, her cheeks were high and sharp, her carriage was regal.

"I will try more manioc," I said, and this time I kept it down.

She bade me sleep, but I told her I had slept for months, and wished now to learn something of what had gone on in the world outside my cell. There was another Englishman in São Paulo de Loanda, I said: where was he, could he not be sent to visit me, or was he under imprisonment?

"I know not," she said.

"His name is Thomas Torner, and he was with me on the pinnace when we came from Masanganu."

"Yes, that I know. It was he who carried you on shore when you fell ill. But he is not in São Paulo de Loanda now."

"Gone back to Masanganu?"

"I think he is fled," she said. "Or perhaps perished. I know nothing of this Englishman."

Which saddened me and sorrowed me greatly. What escape could he possibly have managed? I asked her to make inquiries, and she did, to no effect. Later I learned that Torner had disappeared not long after our return from Masanganu, slipping away in a manner most mysterious. But a party of Arab slave-traders had been along the coast just then, selling captive Moors from the desert lands to the far north, and it was suspected by the Portugals that Torner had somehow insinuated himself among them, bribing them or begging such mercy as the sons of the Prophet are willing to offer. What became of him beyond that I know not, whether he was sold in slavery himself, or made his way through the kindness of the Arabs to some civilized land, but I have had assurance that he did in time reach England safely.

With Torner gone I felt monstrously alone in this strange dark land. He had been a boon companion, a man of my own kind with whom I felt comfortable, and a wise head against which to toss ideas; and now I was by myself among a wild stew of Portugals and Jaqqas and Kongos and all the dozen other kind of blackamoors, with no one to guide me but my own wit. That was a heavy burden, though I think I bore it well enough as things befell.

My talking with Dona Teresa left me weary and she went from me, which was to my regret, because her presence gave me vigor. She seemed then to me a saint of charity and kindness. I slept and woke and slept and woke, and others brought me food, and then on the third day she returned. I was stronger, strong enough to reach a hand toward her as she entered, and to try to sit up a bit.

When I had eaten I said, "I think I will soon be able to leave this bed, and walk a little. And then I want to go out into the sunlight and quit this hole."

"Ah, you may not."

"In truth? Why not?"

"Because you are imprisoned."

"Nay," I said. "I dealt on that matter with Governor Serrão. He invited me into Portuguese service, and I agreed, and I served as pilot on the governor's pinnace when I brought it down from Masanganu. Why imprison me now?"

"No one knows. The decree was set down, and you are not to be freed. Outside this room a guard stands at all time, to restrain you from leaving."

I had to laugh at that, me too weak to put my legs to the floor.

Then I leaned toward her and said, "Dona Teresa, are you my friend?"

"That I am," she said. And in that moment I for the first time doubted her, because I saw a glint in her eye, a strangeness, a kind of Satanic mischief, even, and I wondered how much a saint she might truly be. Where came those thoughts I hardly know: I think it was her great beauty that frightened me, and a certain foreignness, the full extent of which I did not then understand, that made me wary of trusting a Portugal no matter how kindly. But even as I was having these misgivings of her she said warmly enough, "What service can I do?"

"Go to Governor Serrão," I urged, "and remind him that he and I came to a treaty, and that I said I would serve faithfully and—"

"Governor Serrão is dead."

"Ah, then! When?"

"Many months past. There was a war against King Ngola and his allies, which went badly for us, and soon afterward Serrão fell ill and died. The troops elected the captain-major once more, Luiz Ferreira Pereira, to take his place. It is Governor Pereira who ordered you imprisoned."

"Why?"

She shook her head. "That is not known. Perhaps he simply did not want to think about you, since he had so much else on his mind. There was an order posted, that the Englishman is to be kept apart, as prisoner. Which made no difference to you, since you raved and dreamed, and everyone thought you would die anyway, though you did not. When you have your strength again you will be transferred to the prison at the presidio."

"Nay, nay, nay! Will you go to this Governor Pereira for me, and tell him how Serrão dealt with me, and that I am more useful to him in his service than in his jail?"

"But Pereira is gone to São Salvador."

I was blank at that name. "Where?"

"It is in the land of Kongo. He left three months ago, and I think he will not return. They said he had urgent business to do there, but I think he is only in fear of the Jaqqas, who are said to be gathering strength to invade this territory."

"So there's no governor here at all?"

"None."

"Who rules?"

"No one. All is without center or motion here. They say a new governor is on his way from Portugal, but we are not sure. We wait. We live. Time goes by."

Once more I felt helplessness overcome me. These Portugals! The fat old governor dead, the new one fled, the next one not yet come, and what of me, what of me? Was I to rot forever, while they went about their ninnyhammer foolery? Well, and well, there was no use fretting myself over that now. So long as I had not the strength to walk as far as my own pisspot three feet away, it mattered little whether I was in the hospice or in the dungeon. And perhaps by the time I was strong enough to rise, the new governor would be here.

My strength did indeed come quickly back to me, in the weeks that followed. I was served occasionally by Dona Teresa, but more often by black nuns of the hospice, and always it disappointed me when one of them came into the cell and not she.

But she was there often enough, and slowly I learned things from her about herself. She was in fact just eighteen: I was right in that. And she was no Portugal, or rather, only by parts. I found that out by asking her how long it had been since she had come out from the mother country, and whether she had been born in Lisbon, which made her laugh. "Ah, nay, Andres"—so she called me, Andres—"there are no women of Portugal in this place."

"What are you, then, a witch-child? A changeling blackamoor?"

I was closer to the truth than I knew. She told me that she had been born in the Kongo, in that same city of São Salvador where Governor Pereira had now sequestered himself. The Portugals had arrived in that neighboring kingdom to the north nearly a hundred years before, had settled there and had extended themselves into the blood and veins of that land in a peaceful invasion, filling the Kongo folk with Portuguese ideas and ways, and filling the Kongo women with something else, which you can imagine. Taking the black women for their wives, they brought forth a race of mixed blood, and then later Portugals married into those, and so on and so on until a strange interbreeding became the rule, producing such wonders as Dona Teresa. To my eye she looked a pure Portugal. But some of the blood in her veins was Kongo blood.

Knowing that of her, I understood my early moment of fear. She had done nothing but serve me, dutifully and without cavil, in my illness. Yet I misdoubted her for being a Portugal, and now I misdoubted her worse, since I had no idea where her real loyalties might lie, except to herself, and to the mixed blood that coursed within her. The jungle had its savage imprint upon her somewhere.

She had not been in Angola long—I think she had arrived only some months before my coming. What she chose not to tell me was that she was the mistress of a certain great fidalgo or grandee of the Portugals in the Kongo, one Don João de Mendoça, and upon the death of Governor Serrão this Mendoça had removed himself to Angola, thinking to make himself powerful there.

When she had told me these things of herself, I asked her also to tell me of events in the Angolan land during my time of delirium.

That was much, and none of it good. Shortly before Christmas Governor Serrão had completed his preparations for the war he had so little stomach to fight, and moved against the enemy. His army came to just one hundred twenty and eight Portuguese musketeers—with three horses—and some fifteen thousand native allies, armed with bows. That sounded to me like a mighty force indeed, but Dona Teresa shook her head, saying, "The black folk here are gentle, and frighten easily. And when they are faced with the armies of King Ngola their loyalty to Portugal quickly melts."

This King Ngola was the ruler of the place, for whom the Portugals gave the land its name. Serrão took his army across the River Lukala and advanced east to a place far inland, where Ngola was waiting for him with a huge force of his own and the troops of the King of Matamba and a detachment sent by the King of Kongo and also, said Dona Teresa, certain forces of the Jaqqas known as the Jaqqa Chinda.

"Do the Jaqqas then make alliances with other peoples?" I asked.

"When it suits them," she replied. "Just as the wind makes alliances with seamen, when it fills their sails and sends them where they wish, and other times comes upon them in gales and snaps their masts. We never know, until we find out."

Fat old Governor Serrão was so shitstricken by fright that he desired to retreat before this preponderous enemy army, but his officers impelled him to attack. One of those who urged the battle on him was the same Captain-Major Pereira now in hiding in the neighboring land. On the last Monday of the year the Portugals met their foe and were most terribly defeated, and fell back many leagues toward Masanganu. In this withdrawal, it is said, Governor Serrão fought valiantly against his pursuers and ably protected the rear guard of the Portugals. For some time the army lay besieged at Masanganu, until reinforcements came up from São Paulo de Loanda and relieved them. Soon after this disastrous campaign Serrão took to his bed and yielded up the ghost, and was succeeded by Pereira.

"And now?" I asked. "With Pereira fled, will the city be invaded?"

"We wait," she said. "We pray. We watch for omens."

I thought secretly it would be no great disaster for me if King Ngola or the Jaqqa Chinda or any other of these heathens came in here and put São Paulo de Loanda to destruction. With luck I would show them I was no enemy to them, and my yellow hair might be the flag of my freedom. And if the ocean ran red with Portugals' blood, what was that to me? I held no love for them; I had not yearned to be here; what had I had from them, in these two years, but chains and dungeons and mush to eat, when I would fain have been in England?

Yet I kept these thoughts to myself.

There was no invasion that month, or the months thereafter. My strength grew under the care of Dona Teresa and the black nuns of the hospice. I took my first few tottering steps; I held down solid food, and even some wine; I washed and dressed myself; I left my cell, under guard, and walked weakly in a courtyard of the hospice. Once I came to a place where a mirror was, and I saw my face and knew how close I had come to death: for I was haggard and weathered, with deep seams in my cheeks and a raccoon's rings around my eyes, and my color was bilious and my look was rheumy—and this after months and months of recovery! I have always known that my Protector watcheth over me, for in our harsh world it is a triumph simply to live beyond childhood, but I think I must have more lives than most cats, and that I surrendered one or maybe two with that plaguey ailment that I got in fever-cursed Masanganu.

Now the return of my health brought me little joy, though. For as soon as I was seen to be walking and putting meat to my bones, a fine-feathered captain of the Portugals came to me and said, "You are transferred to the prison. Make yourself ready and come with me."

I protested, but in vain. I demanded to speak to the governor, but of course there was no governor. I urged that I was already enrolled in the service of the colony, as a pilot on the governor's pinnace. Was that madness, to beg to toil for the Portugals, and be shipped, if I won my suit, back to Masanganu, that had all but slain me? I think not. For it is hateful to moulder in a dungeon, and pride must be put aside when freedom, or a semblance of freedom, can be had.

This captain, who was a decent man as Portugals go, felt sympathy for me. But Governor Pereira had ordered that I be imprisoned, and a prisoner I must be, since there was no governor here to countermand Pereira's foolish order, and no one else dared take it upon himself to find another disposition for me.

So I was hauled roughly back to the presidio on the heights of São Miguel overlooking the town. And when I angrily pulled my arm free from one of the Portugals who was conveying me thither, another struck me from behind with his cudgel such a blow in the kidneys and I fell gasping and vomiting, and thought I would give up my spirit there in the dust.

They returned me to the same beshitten subterraneous dungeon where Torner and I had been penned on our first arrival in São Paulo de Loanda. And the gate closed. And there I sat in the dimness and the stench. And there I was forgotten once more. My jailers brought me food twice a day, and water, and once a week they asked if I wanted to have a priest hear my confession, which I declined. Of other human contact I had none, for more weeks than I care to sum.

I thought I would go mad.

I wondered if it were better to have died.

It was one of my deepest testings. I had no Torner to amuse me with rough seaman's talk and gossip of home; Dona Teresa did not visit me; the kind Barbosa, who had brought me wine on my first stay in this stinking keep, was no longer in Angola, or else had given up concern for me. I petitioned my jailers constantly for an audience with some authority of the colony, and they answered me with jeers, or spittle, or sometimes with their fists, which split my cheek and cracked a rib another time.

"Will you have a priest?" they asked again and again.

"Nay," I said, "he will not free me, will he?"

SEVEN

IN THESE dark months of bitter solitude I found only one entertainment, which was to hold conversation with imagined companions out of my lost happy life.

Anne Katherine I often addressed, saying, "This gold of the Indies I bring to you, to hang between your breasts and dangle from your ears and shine on your wrists."

To which she replied, "And will you go to sea again, Andrew, now that you have won this treasure?"

"Nay, never. All that hauling of ropes and lines, all that furling and unfurling, the tarring and mending, the sun and the black thirst swelling my tongue—nay, nay!"

"But it was your great adventure, love."

"Indeed so, and I would not have missed it. But the harbor is reached, and now it is time to sow and reap, and dine on cheese and wine, and see increase, and give thanks and sleep in a good soft bed, and one day to die in bed, too, full of years. Come here to me, sweet."

And her breasts in my hands, and her lips on my lips, and our tongue-tips touching and our breaths mingling, and our bellies meeting—yea! Our seed rushing one to the other, and her sighs soft in my ear—

I spoke with my father. "Tell me the secrets of your craft," I begged him, "so that I can be of use to these Portugals, and lever myself into freedom."

"And would you aid them, then?"

"It is not so bad a thing. Do I serve God better working at a trade at sea, or lying in my own piddle in this black hole? Tell me of piloting, I pray."

"You must first learn the tools," he said. "Your task it is to know the water, the capes and shoals, but also your position in the universe, and for that you must have tools. Here: this is your cross-staff. See, hold the end to the eye, and move the cross-piece thus, until it corresponds exactly to the distance from the horizon of the star you observe, and that will tell you your altitude from the horizon. Do you see? At dawn and at dusk this is your guide. And this, here: this is your astrolabe, that you hang from this ring, and move the disk so. And here: study this book, the treatise of the Jew Pedro Nunes, on the uses of the compass, and such fine matters."

"There is so much to know, father!"

"Aye. Twelve years, to make a proper pilot. Caping from one landfall to the next, taking the soundings of lead and line, telling the hours, making your memory into a rutter for all the world, mastering the currents and tides, keeping your charts safe and adding to them for those who follow after you—so much, so much! And you will be a pilot for the Portugals?"

"Nuno da Silva piloted for Drake, father. And Simon Fernandes, the Portugal, was it not he on Walter Ralegh's *Falcon* in '78 in that doomed venture of Sir Humphrey Gilbert?"

"Aye, boy."

"Why, then, an Englishman can pilot for the Portugals, or for the Dutchmen, or for the Egyptians, if need be. What matters is serving God through properly doing your task. D'ye see that, father? D'ye see that?"

And Rose Ullward I summoned out of the shades, my dark little first wife, whose father had the tavern in Plymouth. She peered at me, squinting in the darkness, and said, "You be Andrew that was my man, be you not?"

"That I be."

"I knew you so little. Our time was so short. Be I remembered well by you?"

"In faith, not very. But I loved you, that I know."

"Now you love another."

"Because you were taken from me by death. God's breath and eyes, woman, will you be jealous from the grave?"

"I am not jealous. I was betrayed by fortune. When you return from captivity, will you return to her or to me, then?"

"How can I return to you?" I asked.

"We will meet on the farther shore. You and I, and the good Jesus, and Great Harry the old King, and everyone else who ever lived and bled. Will we not? You said you loved me, Andrew."

"And that I did. And you are the only wife I ever had. But when you went from me, I found another."

"Aye. The way of the world. I wish you joy of her. But think of me, from time to time?"

"That I pledge," I said, and sent her back into the realm of shades, for this imagined conversation was leading me into turbulent waters.

After her I summoned my brothers Henry and Thomas and John, and even Edward, who drowned before I was born, and talked long and earnestly with them about their lives and hopes and their skills, their fears, their purposes. I had Sir Francis Drake to lunch and John Hawkins and Sir Walter Ralegh, who was overbearing and shrewd and frighted me some. I spent a few hours discussing matters of state with Her Majesty. I had King Philip to my cell, that dour and bleak old monk of a king, and quizzed him on his creed and made him admit the Papist way was false and a mockery to the Gospels. I roved farther afield, and had the Great Khan and Prester John and the Sultan of the Turks. I got me poets, Kit Marlowe and Tom Kyd and others of the sort, and bade them read me plays, which I made up out of my own head, the play of Queen Mary and the tragedy of Samson and the play of the King of Mexico and the Spaniard conqueror. Oh, and they were such plays as would not have disgraced the Globe in London, I trow, but I can tell you not a line of them today.

In such fanciful ways my months ebbed by. Also did I pace my dungeon and count its paces, and get such other exercise as I could, and breathed as deep as I was able to make myself, despite the stench of the place, to keep my lungs in trim. And I think after my early despair I came to a kind of tranquility, like a friar in the desert: no longer bewailing the discomforts and disappointment of my life, but only taking one day at a time, as God's decree upon me. I am in my way a fair philosopher, I suppose: I seek not to rail against the unalterable, nor to spend my energies moving the immovable.

One day at last I had a visitor other than my jailers. Dona Teresa it was, like a ray of golden sunlight lancing through the thick mud walls of my prison.

Her dark beauty glimmered and glistened in the shadows. Her eyes had a wondrous gleam and her lips, so full and broad, were shining, moist, heavy with the promise of delights. And I had mistaken this woman for a nun, once, in my sickness!

"I thought you had abandoned me," I said.

"Poor Andres. I could not get leave to visit you, until a certain friend returned to the city from duty in the north, and by his authority granted me access. Do you suffer?"

"Nay, it is a glorious palace, and the feasts are beyond compare. It is only that I miss the hunt sometimes, and other little pleasures not available to me here, the morris-dancing and the games of bowls on the village green."

"These words are mysteries to me."

"What season is it?"

"The rains are upon us."

"But not the armies of King Ngola?"

"Nay, there is peace. A new governor is coming to us, Don Francisco d'Almeida."

My heart quickened. "Will you petition him for my freedom?"

"That I will," she said. "And I will speak with another great man of the colony, Don João de Mendoça, who is known to me. I will bring you out of this place, Andres."

"I pray it be soon."

"What will you give me, if I have you set free?"

I could not fathom that. "Give you? What have I to give? You see me in rags, and less than rags. Where is my hidden store of gold, Dona Teresa? Do you know a secret that is secret even from me?"

"I know where your gold is," she said.

"Then tell me."

She came to my side and put her hands to my hair, coarse and tangled and foul, but still yellow, still the fair English hair so scarce in these lands.

"This is gold," she said. She touched my beard. "And here is more of it. Holy Maria, but you are filthy!"

"There is little bathing here, Dona Teresa."

"I will remedy that," she said, and stroked my hair again. And looked long and strange at me.

I had not seen such forwardness from her in my hospital days. For certainly there was flowing between us now such currents as I know pass between man and woman, and my long solitude had not deceived me in that: a woman does not toy with a man's hair, and fondle his beard, to no purpose. In the hospital I lay withered and naked before her, fouled by my own body's foulnesses, and she seemed no more than a helpful woman of the city, doing a service to a hapless ailing man. But this was something quite other, now, this sly flirting, this playing at the game of coquetry and subtle desire.

As she stood close beside me she reached into her garments and took forth some small object, that she rubbed most lovingly against each of her breasts in turn, and then pressed to her belly and downward to the joining of her legs. After which she took this thing and put it in my hand, and folded my fingers over it, and, smiling secretly, stared most hotly into my eyes.

"Keep this by you," she said, "and all will be well."

I opened my hand and looked upon it. It was a wooden carving, cunningly done of some very black wood, that showed a woman with a swollen middle as though with child, and heavy breasts, and a deep slit carved in the place of her sex, and there was hair fastened to the head: five or six strands of dark coarse hair much like Dona Teresa's own. When I touched this little idol with my thumb it felt warm to me, with the warmth of her own body impressed into it; and it troubled me, for it smelled of witchcraft.

"What is this thing?" I asked.

"A talisman," said she, "to protect you from harm while you are in this place, and ever after."

"A devilish little amulet, you mean?"

"An amulet," said she, "but not devilish."

"I think any amulet is the Devil's manufacture."

"A crucifix, too? Is that not an amulet?"

"Aye," said I. "I do abhor all that sort of stuff, even the ones claimed by the Papists to be Christian."

"Well, and abhor not this one," Dona Teresa said. "For it will guard you, Andres." She folded my fingers over it again, and, whispering close, said, "Take it. Keep it close by you. Do this for me, will you, in return for the services I have done you, and will in the future do you. Will you, Andres?"

"I will," said I reluctantly. "But only because it is your gift, and I think fondly of it, that it came from you. For I tell you, I do abhor any amulet of the Devil."

"I say again, it is not of the Devil."

"It is no Christian thing, though."

"Nay, that it is not." She put her fingers to her lips. "We are Christian here, but we know some of the old ways, too, those that are of merit.

This is one. Keep it by you, Andres, close against your body, and all will go well for you." Then did she put her hand over mine, that held the talisman, and she said, "One thing more, though. Keep it from the sight of the Portugals, for they do not understand these matters. And if they should find it, I pray you do not say you had it of me. For I am thought of by them as full Portuguese in my ways, and I would not have them knowing I do follow a few of the old teachings. Eh, Andres? Will you pledge me that, Andres?"

She frightened me. I felt it was a Devil-trap she was leading me into. Perhaps it was because I had lately written in my mind that play of Samson who was snared by the Dalila who destroyed him, that woman of another tribe, in enemy employ. And here she was, yet, toying with my very hair, as Dalila had with Samson's. Aye, I feared Dona Teresa. I feared her for her beauty, which was overwhelming, beyond that of any woman I had known, and I feared her also because she was part Portugal and part African, which is to say, Papist on one side and demon-worshipper on the other, but not an atom in her that was English. At that time of my callowness I looked upon women who were not English as something terrifyingly other, for all that I had chosen a French one to lie with first, as a boy. To me Dona Teresa was a bubbling pot of mysteries and magics, a stew-cauldron of unknown perils. And then, too, I suspected that she might be spying for her Portugal masters, which made me naturally cautious of revealing my heart to her.

And so I was wary with her and did not reach to embrace her, which I think she was inviting me next to do. But I did accept the little idol from her.

She felt my coolness and retreated after a bit, and said, hiding her annoyance well though not completely. "It was not easy for me to gain permission to visit you."

"Will you come again?"

"Do you want it?"

"Why have you come?"

"When you were ill, I nursed you. I feel an ownership of part of your life, from that. Now you suffer again, in a different way, and my soul goes out to you."

"You are most kind, Dona Teresa."

"They say I can come every second day. I will do so."

She looked to me as if waiting for me to refuse that. But I did not. Uncertain of her though I might be, I was not so foolish as to spurn the first companionship I had had in many months. Thus I told her I welcomed her return, and indeed it was no lie. I spent the day that followed counting away the hours. She had broken entirely the rhythm of my solitude, and I could not employ the little diversions now, the conversations and fantasies, that had whiled the time. Despite myself Dona Teresa had unsettled my philosophical equilibrium and reawakened me to life.

When she returned she brought two things with her, that she carried one at a time into the cell. The first was a flask of wine: not the sweet palm-wine of the blackamoors, that Barbosa once had given me, but true claret of Portugal, whose taste I had all but forgotten.

"This was not easy, either," she said. "It is rare stuff."

"You do me great kindness. Come, let us draw the cork!"

"Not so fast, not nearly so fast." She put the wine aside and went beyond the palisade, and came back a moment later bearing a broad basin and a great rough yellow sponge. "Put off your clothing," she said to me.

"Dona Teresa—"

"Do you think your odor is fragrant?"

"Nay, they issue no perfume to captives here. But this shames me, to put off my clothes before you this way."

"In the hospice you lay with no clothes at all, and you had no shame of it then."

"I was far from my right mind."

"But the shape of your body comes not as news to me. And if we are to sip wine together, you must be more clean. Come, sir, do as I say!" She snapped her fingers at me as though she were a queen.

On that day she had chosen to wear a light bodice, cut very low, that all but revealed her breasts. They gleamed out from their captivity like fine polished carvings of precious wood, round and smooth and dusky-bright, reminding me of the breasts of her little idol. I felt myself swept along on a tide too powerful to resist.

But yet I was determined. Still did I intend to remain faithful to my Anne Katherine, whatever temptations this Dalila dangled at me: and if the words sound overly innocent to you, as they do to me, yet I will not deny them, for that was my intention, poorly conceived but deeply felt. I knew I might remain the rest of my life in Africa, and then my fidelity would be a fool's medal, but thus far, thus far at least, I meant to cling to it, having held it so long already.

So I intended, at any rate.

Yet to clean my body was not a bad idea. I have always felt a fondness for bathing. I suppose if I were a grandee of the court, I would be content with powders and unguents and perfumes, and never once put my skin into water; for that is how they do it, so I hear. But simpler folk of the outlying towns have cleaner ways, and especially those that go to sea, for one often stands naked in a driving rain and the touch of water against the skin is neither unfamiliar nor painful, but rather becomes to be enjoyed. Here in my dungeon I was much bothered by the crawliness of the filth that was accumulating upon my sweltering body. So for all my uneasiness with Dona Teresa I did drop my clothes, and made as though to take the washbasin from her.

"I will do it," she said.

There was no refusing. She wet her sponge—a harsh thing, not long from the sea, that scratched like briars—and scrubbed it down my back, and then my shoulders, and she spun me around and sponged my chest, not gently, so that my skin began to tingle and a rosy hue came into it. "How foul they have let you be!" she said. "Look, the water runs in dark streams from your hide!" I thought she had done with me when my upper body was cleansed, but no, she was most devilish thorough, and took her sponge over my belly, more kindly this time, and down my thighs, and along my legs both front and back.

In doing this service, which she performed as calmly as though she were swabbing a statue, she traveled most intimately close to my private parts, though she took care not actually to touch them. Yet she might just as well have caressed my privities fondly with her hands, for the effect was the same on me, that had not lain with a woman in two years and some. Her eyesight alone, casting its beam on my flesh as she knelt to rub my haunches, would have been enough to inflame me with lust. I strived to keep my body in check. I felt the sap rising in my loins, I felt my member quickening with life, and it was most shameful to me to know that it was getting stiff. I did not dare look down. But I could tell without looking that my mast was up, and royally so. And my heart thundered, and my throat went dry, and I recited the catechisms and other such dreary things to keep myself from throwing myself upon her, for how could I let myself do that?

How, indeed? When I meant to be faithful to a fair young woman in England, how give myself to a dark wench out of the jungle of Africa?

You smile. You say, Go to, only a monk would have retained his fidelity, or a eunuch, under such provocation. A man and a woman alone in a locked cell, and the man naked and the woman nearly bare-breasted, and so long a chastity for him, and the temptation so overpowering—surely the man would yield, and quickly and gladly, in that circumstance. I smile, too, at the recollection. But I was there, not you, and I swear by the bloody palms of Jesus that I kept myself chaste that day.

But not, I needs must add, in any way that was creditable to me. For as this bathing of me continued, my mind went hazy as with sunstroke and my vision clouded and my perceptions became narrowed down solely to that aching rod sprouting from my loins. And I sucked breath deep into my lungs and knew I could no longer withstand the gift of what seemingly was so freely being offered. I was on the verge of reaching for her, to take her to my pallet and push up her robe and slide myself deep into her harbor, with all thoughts of England and Anne Katherine and chastity blasted from my mind. Then suddenly she rose and stepped back and said, coolly, with a brusqueness, "There. Now at last you are properly clean. Clothe yourself, and let us enjoy our wine."

It was like a mug of cold vinegar hurled in my eyes. I stood there stunned, my soul all full of desire and she already halfway across the cell and tugging on the cork of the claret. It was all I could do, I trow, to keep myself from stumbling toward her and throwing myself upon her, for I was not much different at that moment from a catapult that has been fully wound up: that is, once the mechanism is set in motion, how can the catapult help but discharge its load? The only thing that held me back and let me master myself once again was the awareness that I might have misread her entirely. Perhaps there was no flirtatiousness in her manner and no provocation intended by the freedom she had taken with my body. Perhaps she had no shred of desire for me at all, but saw me merely as a foul-smelling prisoner who needed cleansing. And perhaps it was all a test, to see if I could be trusted, and six guards lay in wait outside the cell to fall upon me at her first outcry of rape.

That was a cooling thought indeed. Fear overcame yearning. For I was among Portugals that might cheat at any game, even this, and mayhap they looked only for a pretext to hang me. To assault a woman of their nation would be sufficient charge, and she could well be part of a plot to open me to such a charge. At once my member droped and I turned away, and found my shabby clothes.

Dona Teresa, pretending unawareness of all my states of changing mind—I know that she was pretending—smiled most graciously and offered me a goblet of wine.

We drank together like lord and lady. We kept piously far apart, and talked of trivial things. I was bewildered and utterly disarrayed by the games she had played on me; my jaws ached of tensing them, my eyes throbbed, there was a band of fire across my forehead. The wine eased me, but only somewhat. I think I grew drunken, a little, and I stared more at her bosom than at her face, which she noticed, but she gave me no further provocations, and I kept my distance. In time she said she must leave, and she collected the empty bottle and the goblets and tucked them in a straw bag, and came toward me and smiled and flashed me such a look of direct and blatant invitation as like to have melted my kneecaps. But before I could comprehend it and conclude what response

I should make, she kissed me lightly on the cheek, a sister's kiss, a butterfly grazing, and sweetly wished me well and took her leave.

That visit much muddled my mind. In the days that followed I relived it a thousand times in memory, wondering if it had been her intent to make me so asweat with desire, or if I had wrongly imagined her motives. That I had meant to remain chaste was sure; that her sponging had magicked all chastity out of me was equally sure; but had I been toyed with? Or was it only that I was overripe for loving and was coming to see my fidelity as mere romantic folly? I knew not my own mind. I was overmatched with this Dona Teresa, I suspected: she was too cunning a player of the game of man and woman, and I far too simple.

When she visited me next, a few days later, she came swathed in black garments trussed as secure as a nun's, and neither kissed me nor gave me looks of the eyes, but was proper and chaste with me. On the next visit from that she was more playful, and wore flimsy clothes again; on the next, she stayed only a few minutes, and was coy and remote. I never seemed to see the same Teresa twice running. And on the next she came in garments so light she might as well have been naked, a rain-soaked shift through which I saw everything, her dusky breasts and dark nipples, and the socket of her navel, and the three-pointed mat of dark curls below. It was too much. I knew for sure, the moment she slipped off the cloak to show me the wonders of her body barely hidden by that faint fabric, that she was playing a devil's game with me.

"I have brought more wine," she said.

"Will you bathe me, then, as you did that other time you came with claret?"

She laughed prettily. "Are you uncleanly again?"

"Nay, I am clean enough. But the sponging made a good preamble to the wine."

I was altogether in her spell. My eyes traveled her body as though it were the map of the highway to paradise.

Coolly she said, "I have not brought the basin with me, nor the sponge. And if you need no bath, why take the trouble to have it, sir?"

"Because it gave me pleasure."

She pretended to chide me. "Sir, you are a prisoner! You are not entitled to pleasures!"

"The wine?"

"Oh, that. It is for your health alone."

"Bathe me with that, then."

"You forget your place," she said, sounding stern, but her eyes were sparkling and her smile was bold.

I went toward her. I was the aggressor, no denying it: but she had so maneuvered and chivvied and manipulated me that I was altogether her toy, and if I seemed to be the forward one, it was only an illusion, for I was moving along a path that had been wholly preordained by her scheming. My hands went to her shoulders. I pulled her close against me. She stiffened and pretended to be shocked, but it was mere pretense. That much was apparent. "Sir," she cried. "Sir, what is this?"

I made no answer. I brushed at her shift, trying to sweep it from her, but in my need and my anguish I was clumsy, with fingers of wood, and even while she squirmed and feigned resistance she managed to reach about and touch some catch, so that the thing opened and fell away like fog in the morning sun. At the sight of her breasts I came close to releasing her and backing off, for her nipples were brown and the wide circles that surrounded them were brown. It was the African in her blood revealing itself. The women of Portugal and Spain, I know, have darker skins than those of England, but the ones I had lain with in my days aboard the merchant vessels had the breasts and nipples of an Englishwoman, more or less, a deeper hue of pigment but not brown like this, and in the baring of her breasts Teresa displayed the strangeness within her soul.

Not that I saw anything dreadful about African women, though they were not then particularly to my taste; but it was the *mixture* that put me off, the mingling of the blood of two worlds. Dona Teresa was a creature beyond my knowledge of women. I felt ensnared by the Devil, a slave to dark forces.

But I was enslaved also by another force that hammered and beat within my own veins. And so I covered those alien nipples with my quivering hands and gripped the dark satiny globes and pressed my mouth to hers, while she pulled away my clothing. And we sank down together to the damp earthen floor and her thighs parted and she received me, for she was more than ready and there was no need for the prelude of stroking and opening that many women prefer.

And O! and O! and O! all thought went from my mind!

Her back was arched and her legs wrapped themselves about my body and her fingers dug into my back, and down below I felt the hot sweet moist hidden mouth of her consuming me like the hungry mouth of a starfish, and there came a rising tide within me that altogether swept me away, nor did I fight against that. Buried deep in that lovely nether mouth, in that warm comforting harbor, I yielded up my ghost in a cannonade of lunatic explosions that entirely unmanned me, and left me dead and gasping on the floor by her side.

She laughed, a light and tinkling laughter, and ran her hand through the golden fur of my chest.

"So eager, Englishman, so hurried! But I forgive you. It has been a very long time, has it not?"

"A thousand years."

"The next time will not be so far away."

"Nay. Hardly another three moments, I trow."

She cradled me against her breasts. My fingers roved her skin. In the aftermath of lovemaking it had the look of finely burnished bronze, and her hair below was crisp and closely coiled, another secret sign of the Africa in her veins. In the touching of her I felt my manhood return almost at once to life.

I rolled free and embraced her again.

"This time more slowly, for your impatience will not be as great, eh, Englishman?"

"Aye," I answered. And gave the devil her due.

EIGHT

SO WITH those first thrustings of flesh into flesh, commenced what I must now recognize to be one of the greatest adventures of passion that I have known, possibly the most grand of all, that transformed and wholly altered my life. I did not suspect such a thing at the time. I had no sense of anything of significance having its beginning, but merely that I was a lonely sufferer far from home who had tumbled into the snares of the Fiend. Dona Teresa, having cozened and dangled me until I was little more than a cunny-thumbed fool, had pried my much-vaunted chastity from me and in so doing had demonstrated—probably not for the first time—the power of her wiles over a helpless man. If I had been a Papist, I think I would have feared for my immortal soul, and gone bleating to the confessional the moment she left my cell.

But I am no Papist, and though I am a God-fearing man I am not a Church-fearing man, if you take my meaning. I do not think souls can be lost by the thrusting of a few inches of firm flesh into some hot little slit, even if it be not the right and proper slit that one has sworn to use exclusively. Though I felt myself to have been pushed and prodded by her into doing something that was only partly of my desire, yet that in itself did not make her the Devil's agent, did it? She had played with me, and had had something from me that doubtless she had sought for good reason, and had given something to me that met my need.

I felt no shame and no guilt neither, I must declare. For chastity is like an inflamed boil, which, once pricked, heals and subsides quickly, and does not recur, and when the inflammation is gone is lost to memory. I knew that I loved Anne Katherine no less for having coupled with this stranger-woman on the floor of an African dungeon. And I knew also that my hope of seeing England and Anne Katherine again was slight, so slight that it was little more than monkish madness to attempt to preserve myself chaste until my homecoming. Not even Ulysses had done that, dallying as he did with Circe and Nausicaa and I forget how many others on his long journey toward Ithaca.

(But of course his Penelope *had* remained chaste. Aye, but that's another matter, is it not?)

After that first passionate hour Dona Teresa left me, and did not come to me again for two days. Which left me hungry for her company, and kept me busy in my mind replaying our sport. Each time I heard gates clanging, my sweat burst out and my loins came to life, but it was only some guard, bringing me gruel or porridge or other dreary mess. But in time she did come, and again, and again many times.

"How is it," I asked, "that you can be so free now in this prison? You come and go as if you are the captain of guards."

"Ah," she answered, "that am I not, but the captain of guards is my friend. It was he granted me the right to come to you."

Startling hot jealousy blazed in my flesh, for I thought I knew what she meant by "friend."

"That dandy, you mean, with the fancy purple breeches?"

"That one, yes. You know him, then?"

"I met him once. It was he who took me from the hospice to the dungeon."

"He is Fernão da Souza. He is young and ambitious, and he means to be a mighty man in Africa one day."

"As do they all, these Portugals, eh? Your friend Mendoça, who you say will grant you my pardon, he also hopes to be great in this land."

"Indeed. And Souza thinks by pleasing me to please Mendoça, who is more powerful. So he lets me use him, by coming here and visiting with you as often as I like. In return for which he uses me, by having me say good things of him to Mendoça." Mischief flickered like heat-lightning across her features. "D'ye see, Andres, how simple it is for me?"

"If one has such beauty as yours, anything is simple."

"Beauty is not the secret. Cleverness is. I understand what I want, and therefore I seek it and get it."

"And what is it you want from me, then?"

"Would I tell you outright, Andres, d'ye think?"

"Aye," I said. "For you know me to be a bluff and open man, and deviousness is not the medicine to use on me. But I answer plainly and openly to a straight request."

"So you do."

"Then what part am I to play in the epic of your life, Dona Teresa?"

"Why, you will take me to Europe."

"What?" I said, amazed.

"It is my great dream. I am an African woman, you know, who has seen only Kongo and Angola, and all the rest of the world is only a fable to me. Do I seem European to you, Andres?"

"Aye, very much."

"I am not. Yet I study being European. I speak like a European and I wear Portuguese clothes and I carry myself in a Christian way. I hate this place. I am tired of heat and rain and drought and rivers full of beasts that devour. I drink fine wine and cover myself with powders and perfumes and imagine that I am a woman of the court, but all the while I know this is mere savagery, with Jaqqas in the jungle that would eat me if they could, and great elephantos smashing down the trees, and such. I want to hear music. I want to attend the plays. I would have my portrait painted, and enjoy flirting with dukes."

"So, then, lady, I am to convey you to Lisbon? To Madrid?"

"Why not London?"

"Shall I spread my cloak and fly by it, with you clutching on? Ah, I cannot fly! And I have not even the cloak!"

"You will leave Africa one day, Andres."

"It is my every prayer."

"And you will take me. Yes? You will bring me before the Queen Elizabeth, and say, Here is a woman of the court of Kongo, who desires now to be your lady-in-waiting."

I smiled and said, "You much mistake me, Teresa, if you think the Queen and I are playfellows. But this much I promise you: aid me to escape, and I will seek to bring you out with me when I flee this land."

Ah, such lies we tell, when smooth thighs and hard-tipped breasts are close at hand!

Was it a lie? I think that at that moment it was God's own truth, and I saw the two of us in the eye of my mind escaping Africa together, settling out in some sturdy little craft along the coast and upwards to the Canary Isles and the threshold of Europe. But how could I do such a thing? Escaping of my own would be taxing enough; taking a woman would more than treble my risks and difficulties. And then, even if I did—to march into England with a woman of this sort on my arm? Easier to carry in a brace of elephantos, or a little herd of fleet zevveras. Introduce her to the Queen? Aye, and introduce her to Anne Katherine, too, and then have the three of us married by the Archbishop of Canterbury, shall I? But those were all second and third thoughts of a later hour. Just then I took my promise half-seriously, in the way we take cheering fantasies. That I would escape Africa one day seemed altogether possible, for it was my great goal. That I would take Dona Teresa with me was at least worth allowing in hypothesis.

Meanwhile I was a prisoner, and she had found a way to visit with me, and we now were constant lovers, with a rich and powerful lodestone force pulling our bodies together in a vehement and most ecstatic way. It seemed more than natural, that ceaseless yearning of the flesh.

And indeed it was, for she said one day, "Do you still have by you the little talisman I gave you?"

"I do. I keep it on a cord, around my waist, sometimes, to remind me of you, and when I sleep it is against me, or beneath my head."

"And you had such scorn for it, when I gave it!"

"Well, but it is from you, and so I have grown fond of it."

"I did lie to you concerning it," said she, with a wanton grin.

"In what way?"

"That it was an amulet of protection. It is not that."

"What is it, then?"

She laughed playfully. "An amulet of love," said she. "To bind you to me, to make you crave me. For I did crave you, but you never looked upon me with desire, so that I thought I must have recourse to some greater power. Was that not wicked of me?"

"Ah," said I, amused and uneasy both at once: for this was witchcraft, and I feared witchcraft. Yet did I tell myself that it was not the amulet that inspired this lust, but simply her beauty; although I felt some doubt of that in the depth of my soul, and some fear, that in keeping it close I was exposing myself to deviltry.

She brought me wine. She brought me little cakes. She bathed me with her sponge when prison filth grew too deep on me. She opened her body to me joyously and freely, and we developed vast skills at the sport of love, so that prison was less of a torment to me than prison is generally thought to be. Yet was I still a prisoner.

"The new governor will be here in a few weeks' time," she told me. "Then shall I intercede with him, by means of Don João de Mendoça, and have you set free from this hole."

"And shall I still see you, when I am free?"

"We shall have to go about it secretly. But we shall go about it, I pledge you that!"

"And if your fine Portugal friends discover us, what shall become of me? Back to the dungeon? Or worse?"

"They shall not discover us."

"Aye, you are practiced in these crafts, I know. If you were a man, I think you would be governor of this place before you were thirty."

"If I were a man," she said. "But I shall be the governor's governor instead, and have the rewards without the burdens. Is that not better? Considering that I am not a man, and am by that disqualified from holding office. Why is that, d'ye think, that women may not hold office?"

"In England they may," I pointed out.

"In England, aye! But these Portugals think otherwise. They think a woman good for only two things, both of them done in bed, and the second one being childbearing."

"The other is not done in bed, Dona Teresa."

"Not by you and me in this bedless cell, perhaps. But customarily—"

"Nay, I mean cookery," I said, "for is that not the other thing women do, when they are not with child?"

She laughed heartily at that, and gave me a broad nudge.

Then, more serious, she said, "What offices may women hold in England?"

"Forsooth, Dona Teresa, the very highest! Surely you know we have a Queen, and had another Queen before her!"

That did not awe her. "So I am aware," she said. "Your Elizabeth, and your Mary that was half a Spaniard. But queening is only an accident of birth. If there is no son, then the daughter must have the throne, or the power will be lost to the royal family, is that not so? Even the Spaniards, to whom a woman is nothing, have had queens, I think."

"Aye, Isabella of Castile, for one, and mayhap others."

"But what other offices in England do women hold? Do they sit in your courts and go to your councils?"

I thought a moment. "Nay, it is impossible."

"Impossible, or only unthinkable?"

"There are no women in our Parliament. We choose none for our Judiciary."

"And as your priests? Any women?"

"Nay, not that, either."

"But you have a Queen. She is supreme, and has heads stricken off as it pleases her, and looses the forces of war. Below her, nothing. Eh, Andres?"

"It is so. Save for the Queen, our women are subject to their fathers and husbands in all things."

"So it is the same for all you Europeans. A clever woman must rule by ruling her rulers, unless she be a queen. Do you regard me as clever, Andres?"

"You are the most clever woman that ever I knew, though it may be that our Elizabeth is more than your match. But perhaps no one else."

"Then I shall gain what I crave," she said, "which is majesty and might, or at the very least some strength of place. Fie, a woman has more privilege among the blackamoors of Kongo than they grant her in Europe. The blacks have had queens, too. And their women may own property. Yours *are* property."

"You speak of the Kongo folk as 'they' and 'blackamoors.' You speak of the Portugals as 'these Portugals.' Do you stand outside both peoples, then, and look upon them all as strangers?"

Her face grew downcast. "In some degree I do."

"Outside both, a member of neither? Is that not painful to you, to have no true nation, Teresa?"

"That was not of my choosing."

"Who were your parents?"

"My father was a Portugal in the court of Don Alvaro, the Manikongo, that is, the black king. He was an adviser on military matters, and served the Manikongo bravely when the Jaqqas invaded his kingdom and drove the king into sanctuary on the Hippopotamus Island. He was Don Rodrigo da Costa, a very great man. He is dead now, of a fever taken while in battle."

"And your mother?"

"Dona Beatriz, whose father was Duarte Mendes, the viceroy at São Tomé. They say that she was beautiful, that she resembled me much, but was darker, having more African blood than I. I never knew her. She died when I was a babe."

"That grieves me. I also lost my mother early."

"The Jaqqas took her, and I suppose used her in their feasts." For a moment her eyes showed pain, and anger. Then she looked to me and said, "If she had lived, she would have been a great woman. I will be great in her stead. I will find the place where power is in this land, and I will seize possession of it. Unless"— and she smiled wantonly—"unless you bring me forth from here when you escape, and take me to England. In England I would also be famous and great. Tell me of England, Andres."

"What would you know?"

"Is it cold there?"

"Nay, not very. The land is green. The rain falls all the year long, and the grass is thick."

"I hear of a thing called snow."

"There is not much of that," I said.

"Tell me what it is."

"Snow is rain, that freezes in the winter and falls from the sky, and covers the countryside like a white blanket, but not often for very long."

"Freezes? That word is unknown to me."

I groped and fumbled for explanations. "On the highest mountains of Africa the air is cold, is it not?"

"Yes."

"And are those mountains not covered at their crests by a whiteness?"

"So I have heard. But I have not seen it."

"The whiteness is water, that has been turned hard by the coldness, and made into snow, and also into ice, which is snow pressed tight. But why talk so much of snow? England has little snow. It is a mild cool land with sweet air, and fine fleecy clouds, and sometimes the sky is gray with dampness and fog, but we have come to love even that."

"You scorn the Pope there."

"Aye, that we do!" I stared at her. "You know of the Pope? What is the Pope to you?"

"The Pope is the King of Christendom," said Dona Teresa. "The Pope is the right hand of God, and King Philip and all his subjects are subject to him."

"You are a Christian, then?"

"My father was Don Rodrigo da Costa, and I am no savage, Andres," said she with much show of dignity. "Why do the English mock and defy the Pope?"

"Why, because it is madness to be governed by a religious authority that is seated a thousand miles beyond seas and mountains, and that judges questions of English law by the standards of Italy and Spain and sometimes France, but never by those of England. The Pope conspires to dethrone our Queen. The Pope would deliver us into the power of our enemies of Spain. The Pope has strived always to tell us what we might do, and sometimes he has succeeded; but at last Great Harry overthrew him—"

"Great Harry?"

"King Henry that was the eighth of his name, the father of Queen Elizabeth."

"Overthrew the Pope? Nay, how was that possible? The Pope still reigns in Rome."

"In Rome, aye. But we have broken free. And spared ourselves from greedy monks who bleed the people of their wealth, and spared ourselves from ignorant mummery and mumpsimus nonsense, that chanted at us in an ancient language and smothered us in the reek of incense and the crying out to idols."

"Why, then, you are not Christians!"

"Christians we are," I said, "but we are English, and that makes a difference in all things."

"Aye," she said. "English have yellow hair and hate the Pope. Those are the chiefest differences. You must tell me more of England another time. And of yourself: you must tell me of your boyhood, and of your schooling and how you came to go to sea, and if there be anyone you love in England, and how you fell prisoner into the hands of the Portugals, and many other such things. But we will talk of those things later."

"Later, aye."

"And now let us talk no more," she said.

To which I concurred, for she moved against me and drew her satin-smooth skin across my chest, and once more she magicked me in that brazen way of hers, engulfing, devouring, that starfish mouth drawing me in. She had no shame: that was the essence of her. Dona Teresa lay at the center of her world and all other things pivoted about her, and that which she desired was that which she took, be it jewels or fine clothes or the bodies of men. Yet there was an ease and an openness about this which made it not at all unseemly: it was as if she were a man, merely following her star, as we do. Why is it that ambition in a man is a virtue, and in a woman is shrewish discordance? Why is it that lustiness in a man is a mark of strength, and in a woman a stigma of wickedness? Aye, there are fallen women aplenty, but never a fallen man, except only those who have had high positions and let themselves foolishly tumble from it.

I learned much about the world from Dona Teresa da Costa in our feverish couplings on the floor of that murky stinking prison cell. I learned that a woman could be much like a man in certain aspects of character without giving up anything of her womanhood, if she be clever enough. I learned that an entire sex has been left to waste in idleness and chatter, for that we suppress them to our own advantage. I learned that in the darkest heart of Africa could blossom grace and intelligence and vigor that would give honor to any kingdom.

All these things I might have learned, I wager, from close study of my own Queen. For surely Bess is a prince among princes, a woman with all man's attributes and those of woman, too, and she gives the lie to those who say that the sex is simple and weak. But it has not been my privilege, nor shall it ever be, to strut like a Leicester or Ralegh in the halls of Her Majesty: but Dona Teresa has afforded me close instruction indeed, her eyes glistening near to mine, her tongue-tip tickling the tip of mine, her hardened paps burning like fiery coals against my breast, and, moreover, her dark and mercurial mind open to my inspection, so that I could see her intentions and projects as clearly as, I think, anyone ever did. I would not compare her to my fair pink-and-gold Anne Katherine, for they were as unlike as one planet is to another, as orange Mars to dazzling Venus; but yet I sometimes found myself putting Dona Teresa's forwardness against Anne Katherine's timidity and shy uncertain way, and Dona Teresa's snorting fury of lust against Anne Katherine's tender and sweet embrace, and in such comparisons I felt ashamed and guilty of making them, for the olive-hued woman of Africa emerged far the more brilliant in the matching. Which is why, I hazard, we should not stray from our own beds to those of strange women, lest we discover things we are better not knowing.

Under Dona Teresa's ministrations my captivity was not, then, the most painful of captivities to endure. There were bruises and discomforts aplenty, for sometimes the jailers grew angry with me, or I with them, and they beat me for my insubordinations. Thus I came to lose a forward tooth. Dona Teresa observed that, and asked at once for the name of the man who had injured me, so that she could have him punished for it. "Nay," I said, "I stumbled and struck my face by accident," I said, for I feared that the guards might take vengeance on me if I informed, and might even slay me. Other than such little things, though, mine was a comfortable life, with a woman of great qualities to be my consort on many a day, and excellent wine sometimes to drink, and little treats from the finest banquets of the city. Yet for all that I was not born to dwell in an earthen cavern, and I yearned for the sunlight and for freedom.

How many months had it been? I had lost all count. A season of rain and a dry season, and rain again and drought—was that not the full cycle of the year twice over? Was there yet an England? Was Elizabeth still its Queen, or had the Spaniards come again with a new and less feckless Armada? Anne Katherine, what of her? How fared my brother Henry, and his patron Ralegh, and the great Sir Francis Drake, and did the Thames still run past London to the sea? Lost, lost, all lost to me. Dona Teresa's supple thighs and bobbling breasts were comfort but not comfort enough, as I raged and paced and suffered in my dungeon, and counselled myself to a philosophic calm, and raged yet again.

At last she came to me and said, "The new governor is here, Don Francisco d'Almeida. He has come with four hundred and fifty foot-soldiers and fifty African horse, all picked men, and he is full of bold plans. He has a project for an expedition clear across Africa, and a chain of forts to protect the road from here to the sea that lies on the other coast."

"Very bold indeed," I said. "And have you spoken with him, and will he let me from this hole?"

"I have spoken somewhat with him."

"And?"

"He is a vain and idle man."

My spirit, which had briefly soared, plummeted like Lucifer, who tumbled all the day long from heaven. "That is, he will not set me free?"

"He is occupied with his projects. Chiefly he is in struggle with the Jesuit fathers here. They claim rights in his government, and refuse obedience to the civil powers."

"It is ever thus with the Pope's men. And it is ever thus with these dim-souled governors here. Am I to moulder down here forever, Teresa?"

"Peace, peace. Having failed to win the ear of Governor d'Almeida, I have turned to Don João de Mendoça."

I had long ago lost faith in the powers of this Mendoça. It seemed plain that he himself was unable to gain headway in Angola, in that he had dwelled here at a time of no governor without being able to take command, and had been set aside to some degree by this silly new governor out of Portugal, Don Francisco. But now Dona Teresa had arranged an interview for me with Mendoça, just as I had come to think no action ever would be taken on my behalf. "He will see you tomorrow," she said, "and he intends to enroll you into his service."

"Can he do such a thing?"

"He can do as he pleases. Now that Governor d'Almeida is here, and stands revealed as a fool, it is Don João's time to make his reach for power. Be of cheer."

"So shall I be."

She caught my wrist by her hand and drew me close, ear to her mouth. In a low voice she said, "One thing, only. Give no clue to him that anything has passed between you and me save geographical instruction, or it may go hard for both of us."

"Geographical instruction?"

"Aye. I have come to you all these months to be taught the globe, and the oceans, and the countries of Europe. Nothing more. Nothing more."

"Don João de Mendoça is a jealous man?"

"He is a man of pride."

Which confirmed what I had already guessed, that she was this Mendoça's mistress, that she was using with him that which lay between her thighs as one of the instruments of her ascent. Well, and well, I had not thought her to be a virgin, nor to lie alone on those many nights that she was not with me.

It did not matter. I was of cheer. With her hand on Mendoça's privates she might yet be able to squeeze me out my freedom.

NINE

IN THE morning there came to me that fancy-breeched captain of the guards, Fernão da Souza, another whom I suspected that Teresa had conquered. As was his custom he was most nobly dressed, all lace and spotless gloves and scented boots, and satin sleeves and pearl-trimmed cuffs of great flare and breadth: a young man, tall for a Portugal, fair-complected, with just enough of a look of shrewdness and ambition in his eyes to take the curse off his foppishness. "You are summoned," he told me, "to come before Don João de Mendoça, who out of the greatness of his heart has granted you the opportunity to make yourself of use. Clean yourself and put on these garments."

No foul-smelling ragabones for Don João! I sponged myself and clad myself in decent simple clothes, and went forth from my cell and out, blinking and astonished, into the huge blaze of daylight. And into the plaza of the town, and beyond the church to one of a small group of houses done in the Portuguese style—that is, fashioned out of boards, and with a second story, instead of being a thing of light framework and mud and thatch. This was the palace of Don João de Mendoça, whom I found already at his midday meal when I was brought in.

Mendoça was a man of much presence and authority, who in any sort of society would rise to a position of distinction. What he was doing in this remote colony, instead of dwelling at Lisbon and dealing in high affairs of state, I surely could not imagine, though later I found out what should have been evident enough to me: with a Spaniard on the throne of Portugal, Don João saw little hope of advancement in his homeland, nor, as a younger son, had he inherited great lands and wealth. So like so many other men of spirit he had gone to the tropic lands of empire, where all things begin anew for those with zeal and ability.

He was a man past middle years, forty or somewhat beyond that, which left me wondering how he could cope with the demanding passions of his paramour Dona Teresa. In stature Mendoça was low, but yet his shoulders were of great breadth and his chest was deep, so that when sitting he seemed a person of power and majesty. It was the same with

Sir Francis Drake, who was not tall, but dominated by easy force at a counciltable. Don João's flesh was full but firm, his skin was swarthy in the Portuguese way, his eyes were large and very glistening. He was dressed finely, yet not in the overdone dandified way of Captain da Souza: his was more restrained a costume, in tones of black and gray, with black velvet slippers. The feast that was spread before him was a royal one, I thought, although served on simple pewter dishes rather than fine plate. In many bowls and tankards and platters were the foods of the country, fruits and vegetables that I did not recognize, and meats of several kinds, all in deep and thick sauces, and reeking of the spices that the Portugals so love, their garlics and saffrons and capsicums and the like. Two kinds of wine were on the table, and beakers of beer or ale also. Don João had a platter to his mouth and was sipping of a heavy golden sauce, and with great deliberation he finished his sip, and hacked him a piece of what I took to be mutton or veal, and speared it prettily with his knife and chewed at it most delicately. Then he took a vast deep draught of his pale wine, and wiped his lips, and looked up toward me, and I saw in him a man well satisfied with his meal.

"Dona Teresa tells me you speak passable Portuguese," he said without other word of greeting.

"Aye, that I do."

"Where did you come by that skill?"

"By stages, sir, since I was a boy in England and my brother taught me some."

"Your accent is too broad, though you have the words and the sense quite aptly. You speak our words in the flat English way, without music. Speak you more in the throat and in the nose, do you take my meaning? Put some thunder in your vowels. Put some savory spice in them. I think it is your English food, that is so empty of taste, that causes you English to speak your words in such a flavorless way. How do you say your name?"

"Andrew Battell, sir."

"Sit you down, Andrew Battell. Will you eat?"

"If it please you."

"Eat. There's enough here for a regiment." He pushed vessels of meat and gruel toward me, and a goblet and some wine, and other things. I was perplexed by such plenty, having lived so long on foul prison fare leavened only by those tasties that Dona Teresa had smuggled to me. As I hesitated he stabbed a slab of meat and put it before me, and I took of it, for fear of offending against his hospitality. It was meat that looked to be mutton, at a glance of it, but to my tongue it was not in the least muttonous, more in the direction of veal, though not far in that direction, and it was covered with a sauce of hot pepper and onions that was like live coals in my mouth upon first touch, though I quickly grew familiar with it. Don João watched me with curiosity as I ate the strange meat and then a second piece.

"You like it, then."

"Indeed I do. What sort of meat is this, sir?"

"A vast delicacy. You know not how fortunate you are."

"And its name?"

"It is called in these lands *ambize angulo*, that is to say, a hog-fish, because it is as fat as a pork."

"It has neither the savor nor taste of a fish."

"Nay," said Don João, "for it is no more a fish than you or I, though it lives in he rivers. It is the animal that in the New World the Indians call the manatee, that has two hands, and a tail like a shield. It never goes out from the fresh water, but feeds on the grass that grows on the banks, and has a mouth like the muzzle of an ox."

"A creature passing strange."

"Indeed. There are of these fishes some that weigh five hundred pounds apiece. The fishermen take them in their little boats, by marking the places where they feed, and then with their hooks and forks striking and wounding them. They draw them forth dead of the water, and in the kingdom of the Kongo all such creatures that are caught must be taken straightaway to the black king, for whosoever does not incurs the penalty of death. Here we suffer under no such restriction, and we eat it often. Will you have more?"

"In some while, perhaps. This richness of food surfeits me, after so lengthy a captivity."

"I see. But it improves your Portuguese. Do you comprehend that this sauce has sharpened your inflection, and made you eloquent?"

"Not the sauce, I think, but only listening to your words," I said.

"Are you a flatterer, then?"

"Nay, I mean no flattery. It is only that I have a good ear, and in following your way of speech, I improve my own."

"Ah. Well said. You are clever, and learn things quickly."

To this I made no reply.

Don João went on, "This meat is of the thigh of elephanto, and this is a porridge, that takes the place of bread in this land. And this is a bean they call *nkasa*, that they stew. The oil is the oil of the palm-tree, this being no land for olives. And the wines are the good wines of the Canaries. We have not enough salt here, but otherwise we dine well. Why are you a prisoner, Englishman?"

"For that I was captured."

"Yes. Yes, I know that. In Brazil, was it?"

"Aye, sir."

"But prisoners are useless weights. If we did not kill you, we should have put you to some function."

"That has been done. Governor Serrão used me in a voyage to the presidio of Masanganu, some two years past. But when I returned I fell ill, and upon my recovery I was jailed, I know not why, and I have languished ever since in one of the dungeons beneath the citadel."

"You are a pilot?"

"That I am."

"And willing to serve?"

"It is not my prime choice, but I prefer it to captivity."

"And your prime choice?"

"To return to my England. I have a betrothed in England, and my only dream is to go back to her and make her my wife, and spend the rest of my life on land."

"Yet you were a pirate in Brazil."

"A privateer, sir, seeking to win some gold with which to buy my land."

"To steal some gold, you mean?"

"It would not have been the gold of Portugal, Don João, but rather that of Peru, already stolen once by the Spaniards, and not theirs by God's main design."

"Ah," he said, and said no more a long while, but mopped his bowls and searched in them for more bits of meat. In time he said, "I like you, Battell."

"Thank you, Don João."

"I do. You have a rough English honesty about you that pleases me. You do not fawn, you do not lick. When I thought you might be flattering me you said, Nay, I am only copying your way of speech, where one of the captains here might have given me a lengthy song about my elegance of style. I will let you go home, I think."

I had not expected that. It stunned me so that my tongue was nailed to the roof of my mouth and my jaws hung slack like those of a witless gaffer.

"If you will do some service here first, that is," he continued.

"Name it, sir!"

"We are shorthanded of mariners here. There is trade to do along this coast, to the kingdom of the Kongo and beyond it northward into Loango, where they have riches that they will exchange for baubles—the teeth and the tails of elephantos, and the oil of palms, and the cloth also that they make of palms, and much more, which we can have for beads and looking-glasses and rough cloth. Of ordinary seamen there are enough, but scarce anyone to command them, and do the navigation, and keep our pinnaces off the reefs. I would have you do some piloting for us, a few voyages, six months' worth of service, perhaps, or a year, and if you acquit yourself honorably we will put you aboard a ship for Europe, and God go with you."

My face grew red and I stammered with joy, for this answered all my prayers.

"Don João!" I said. "Don João!"

"Will you serve, then?"

"Aye. And gladly, if I buy my liberty with it."

"Done, then. Take ye another piece of the hog-fish."

He shoved the platter at me, and in my delight I cut me a great huge dripping slice, and crammed it down all at once, so that I like to have choked on it but for the gulps of Don João's precious wine of Lanzarote that I took with easy abandon. He watched me without objection. Already I felt myself halfway back in England, Africa dropping away from me like a sloughed skin, and the morsel of manatee meat in my mouth, strange flavor and fiery of spicing, seemed to me the last strangeness I would have to swallow. O! but I was wrong in that, and strangeness aplenty was waiting for me down the channel of time, and the meat of the gentle sluggish mud-grubbing manatee was hardly the worst of it. But just then I was bound for home, at least in the fancies of my mind, and I thought to myself that this Don João de Mendoça was unlike all other Portugals and Spaniards, a man of sympathy and compassion and true grandeur. I could almost have kissed his boot, but that I have never been the boot-kissing sort to anyone, and might find it hard to make such obeisance even to Her Majesty.

He said, "Dona Teresa speaks highly of you. I think her judgment is the proper one."

"She is a perceptive woman."

"Indeed. A rare woman indeed. I have known her many years, Battell. Her father died young and heroically, in the Kongo, and I have been her guardian."

And something rather other than a guardian, I told myself, but did not say it. A rough English honesty I might truly have, but rough English honesty does not extend to rash looseness of tongue except among fools.

Yet I saw Teresa in my mind's eye, naked in my cell and oiled with sweat, crouching above me and lowering herself to encompass my pestle within her mortar, and then setting up such a grinding as would turn marble to powder; and I knew that if that image were to leap from my mind to Mendoça's I would find myself no sea-pilot at all, but a galley-slave or something worse. And I saw also Mendoça, naked and sleek and plump, with his knees between Teresa's thighs and his hands clasping both her breasts, and *that* image kindled a fire of turmoil in my own breast that was so dismaying that I compelled myself hastily to think of manatees instead, and elephantos, and the shining fishes of the tropic seas. While my head so swam with these pictures, Don João continued to talk, prating of Dona Teresa's virtues, her wisdom and command of the arts of music and poetry and her shrewdness, which he said was the equal of any man's, and her beauty, telling me of her keen luminous eyes and supple limbs and cunning lips as though he were describing some woman of a far-off land. Well, and he had good reason to be delighted in her, and to praise his own good fortune by praising her this way to me. I understood his zeal only too clearly.

It was time now for an end to my audience with him. We had arrived at our compact: I would do some piloting, and then he would turn me loose. It seemed strange to me that the Portugals, who had found all these lands and the far side of Africa as well in the days of Prince Henry the Navigator, these Portugals who had gone off into the misty beyond and discovered even India, would be so reduced as to press an English pilot into their service, in the very seas where Bartholomeu Dias and Vasco da Gama and their other great mariners had won such repute. But evidently the Portugals had fallen upon low times, if they had to have the Spaniard Philip for their king, and why not, then, the English Andrew as their pilot, me who had had only the lightest of training for that task? I thanked Don João de Mendoça once more for his generosity of spirit and also for this meal of rare delicacies.

He clapped his hands and two slaves appeared to clear the table—blacks of some other region of Africa, with flat noses and lips like fillets of beef. One had the ill fortune to stumble and splash some drops of an oily yellow sauce on Don João's garment, staining it, and with a single smooth unthinking motion Don João scooped up a pewter boat holding another sauce, a fiery hot one, and dashed it across the slave's face and into his eyes, so that the poor brute cried out and covered his face with his hands and dropped to the floor, rolling over and over and sobbing. Don João spurned him with his foot, pushing him aside, and the slave, crawling on his knees, scuttled from the room, for all I know blinded, or at the least in mighty pain. So it is with these Portugals. Don João was in truth a man of sympathy and compassion and all of that, civilized and humane, maybe the best of all his kind, but even he, for a few spots on his sleeve, would deal out a terrible agony to a fellow creature. It was a useful lesson to me, not that I really needed it, in the complexity of human nature, that I should see Don João as a superior being of great merit, and that he should in reality be quite far from perfection. But perhaps that is a lesson in the simplicity of human nature, namely, my own, that I should have expected total goodness in a Portugal. The unhappy slave might at least be grateful that he did not serve a Spaniard; for then his master might have had him flayed, or worse, for those small flecks of grease.

TEN

AND THEN did I take up the honorable and exalted trade of ocean-going pilot, the finest of all maritime professions, which my father had mastered in his twelve years of Trinity House, and which my late brother Thomas also had attained. It humbled me to be following in their path without having undergone their long and strenuous licentiate period, and it struck me as hugely ironical that I would do my piloting for Portugals instead of for the Queen.

But I had no fear of doing it badly and disgracing all the Battells of time past and time to come. Don João had said it himself, that I am clever and learn things quickly. I mean no immodesty, but it is true. And also I was then no novice at sea, having made a voyage from England to Brazil, and one from Brazil to Africa, along with many lesser ones in the seas of Europe, even as far as Muscovy, and I had not made those voyages with my eyes closed. Finally I had already had one taste of piloting, when I sailed Governor Serrão's pinnace down the Kwanza from Masanganu to São Paulo de Loanda, and though that is not the same as going out into the Atlantic, still, it calls for some skill.

What is it, this craft of piloting, that I value so high?

It is nothing less than the heart of navigation: the art of guiding vessels from one place to another when land or navigational marks are in sight.

I do not mean to scorn the science of navigating in the open sea, which is the province of the ship's master, unless master and pilot be combined in one individual. That is called grand navigation, and it is no trifling aspect of seamanship. A Magellan or a Columbus or, supremely, a Drake who points his bow into unknown seas is scarce to be mocked.

And yet, I must say, what is grand navigation once one is out in the great waters, except the doing of the same task day after day, that is, keeping the wind to one's back and the deck above the waves, and seeing to it that you sail toward sunset if westering is your aim, and the other way if you would go the other way? Whereas the pilot—ah, the pilot must cope with a thousand thousand perils, and have every science at his command to prevent disaster, and his task is full of intricacies in every moment.

Mind you, the pilot does not have land constantly in sight. The prudent seaman does not often choose to keep close inshore—there are too many dangers and mysteries there—but rather prefers to take himself to deeper waters, beyond what we call the kenning, which is the distance at which the coast is visible from the masthead. But it is the pilot's duty to sight capes and headlands often enough to be sure of his vessel's position. Where the territory is well known, he has his rutter or portolano to tell him of the points he must watch for: his book of charts, compiled by generations of his predecessors, marking each promontory, each island, each snag or speck that is a landmark to him. And where he sails an unknown coast he must use his wits to learn the landmarks, and use his instruments when no landmarks are ready at hand for him.

So we feel our way, with compass and lead, with cross-staff and quadrant, with astrolabe and plumb-bob. We strive never to veer dangerously close ashore, nor to let ourselves be driven perilously far to sea. We must know the winds and the stars and the messages of the clouds.

There is more. A time comes in the voyage when landfall must be made; and then there are new pothers, for the pilot must deal in shoals and reefs, in tides, in sudden bores and currents. The moon rules the tides and the pilot must then live by the moon in her phases, or risk running his ship aground and running himself to the land of simpletons. So it was a sizable assignment that Don João was offering me, made doubly difficult in that I had never seen these African waters before—unskilled pilot bluffing his way in unfamiliar seas!—and triply difficult for having as my companions a crew of Portugals who had no reason to love or respect me or to share with me such knowledge of the route as they might themselves have.

The pinnace I was given was the *Infanta Beatriz*, a larger vessel than the one I had had on the river, perhaps seventy or eighty tons. Perhaps it was more of a caravel than a pinnace, in fact, for it had three masts, including one little one at the stern-castle, and her sails were lateens, that would let her run before the wind and also go near it, that is, sail with a side wind. But in addition there was some mongrel arrangement for square-rigging her on the fore-mast, if need be.

They let me go aboard her to make examination and grow familiar with her. For to a mariner a new ship is much like a new woman, that needs a little getting used to. All women have the same parts, in more or less the same places; but yet they differ in size and shape and in their workings, and even an expert saddleman takes a few moments to learn the way of her. With a ship even more so. The hull is below and the masts overhead, but there are many varieties of placement within that arrangement, and one must seek out and know ahead of time the details of sails and spars and spirits, shrouds and tacklings, braces and stays, ratlines and cables, and all of that. So I wandered about, discovering the *Infanta Beatriz*. She was tight and sturdy, a handy ship, promising ease of sailing. There was a cabin for me in the poop, though small, and for my guidance I had some instruments and also various books of tables, old and much water-stained but still useful: an ephemerides, an almanac, a table of tides, and a rutter-book. Not one of these gave the complete information of the coast, yet each held a part, and by employing them all and the protection of God besides I thought I would be able to find my way up the coast the first time. After that I should be able to manage it less hesitantly.

The crew was a smallish one. The master, who was my superior officer and had command of all and responsibility for the cargo, was one Pedro Faleiro, who seemed to me weak-willed and short-tempered, but not evil. Of others we had a carpenter and a caulker and a cooper, a gunner, a boatswain, a quartermaster, and a company of ordinary seamen, all roguish and lame-spirited, that struck me very different from English sailors in all respects. Yet they seemed to know one rope from another, which was all I would ask of them. I think I would not have cared to cross the ocean with such men, but a journey of fifty or one hundred leagues up the coast and back was a different matter.

Though I was English and not a Papist, they were outwardly friendly to me, and Faleiro and some others invited me to take the Mass with them on the eve of sailing. "Nay," I said, "it is not my custom," and their faces clouded, but only for an instant, and they let me be. So off they went to their Romish mysteries, their swallowing of wafers and guzzling of wine, that is, their eating of the body of Jesus and the drinking of His blood, as they themselves will admit to believing they are doing.

I would not have minded some word or two of God's blessing myself before putting to sea. But there happen not to be any chapels of the Anglican rite in this part of Africa, and I saw no value to me in the Latin ceremony, which is not a conduit for the divine power but rather an impediment to it. Instead I went off apart by myself and looked toward the sky, and said within my soul, "Lord, I am Andrew Battell Thy servant, and I have fallen into a strange fate, which no doubt Thou had good reason for sending upon me. I will do Thy bidding in all things and I look to Thee to preserve me and to keep my body from peril and my soul from corruption. Amen."

I remember that prayer well, because I had many other occasions afterward to use it, as my African years lengthened and the dangers that menaced me grew ever more horrific. And I think it is a useful prayer. I do believe that if one turns directly to the Lord and speaks openly and plainly to Him, that it is a thousand thousand times more effective than any telling of beads and lighting of candles and muttering of Pater Nosters and Ave Marias and kneelings and grovelings before some priest in fine brilliant robes and majestic pomp.

When I had done praying I returned to my dark cell in the presidio; for, though I was no longer under guard, they had not given me any prettier quarters. A place in the town would be ready for me when I returned from my voyage, they said. (There was no need to guard me now. They knew I would not flee. Where could I go? How? I could not swim to England.)

Soon after, Dona Teresa came to me. She wore a dark cloak and a veil across her lovely face.

"You see I keep my word," she said.

"I am most grateful."

"Don João spoke of you warmly, and with great praise. He says you are a man of skill and strength and shrewdness, and that in your blunt way you have a kind of diplomacy, and that you are altogether commendable."

"Aye, that I am."

"And you are possessed of great modesty, too."

"Aye, Dona Teresa! I am famous for it, and rightly so."

"You have other gifts, too, for which you could be famous also, but Don João knows nothing of those."

"Nay," I said. "I told him, as we sat over our wine and our hog-fish stew, how many times I had enjoyed your body, and how admirably I had tupped you, and what sounds of extreme pleasure I was able to bring from your lips. And he gave me congratulation, saying that he had sweated like a Dutchman over you without achieving your ecstasy, and he wondered if I had any secret of it that I could impart to him. So thereupon I said—"

"Andres!"

"—that it was simple, that one need only put one's mouth close to your left ear—"

"*Andres!*"

"—and speak to you in English, saying certain inflammatory words such as 'cheese' and 'butter' and 'tankard', and upon hearing those words you went into such frenzy that it took all of a man's vigor to ride you without being thrown, and—"

"I pray you, stop this!" she cried, holding in her laughter but letting some giggles escape.

"—and straightaway you would reach your summit of pleasure, from merely the sound of some English. So Don João thanked me and commanded me to instruct him in my language, which I have done, and when he seeks your body next you will, I think, hear him speak some of the fine old words of English at intimate moments, whispering to you, 'cobweb' and 'cutlery' and such like. And I advise you, Dona Teresa, to respond with much movement of your hips and thrusting of your middle and gasping and moaning deep in your throat, or else it will give me the lie, and I will lose standing and prestige with your Don João."

"You are a very foolish man," she said fondly.

"I am set free after long months of prisonhood, and I think it has softened my brain with excitement."

"Will you speak to me in English?"

"An' it please you, I would speak to you in Polack, or in the language of the Turk."

"Speak in English."

"I am thy faithful servant and highest admirer," I said in English, with a bow and a grand flourish.

"Nay," she said, "not yet, not yet! Whisper these things in my ear, as you said, when we are intimates!"

"Ah. Surely."

She unwound the veil and laid bare her elegant face, which more and more seemed to me to have some hidden blackamoor beauty in its features—that fullness of the lips, that breadth and height of the cheek-bones. And then with a similar gesture she doffed her cloak, pivoting and whirling while unshipping the small catch that clasped it at her throat, and I saw that beneath the cloak was nothing at all except the supple nakedness of Teresa, her breasts swaying and tolling like bell-clappers in bells, her thighs glowing darkly in the dark shine of my cell. And at that sight so suddenly revealed I felt an access of joy that all but had me shouting out an hurrah. She came to me and I stroked and rubbed her with my eager hands and felt her beginning to writhe beneath my touch, most especially when I put my fingers to that plump tight-haired mound at her belly's base. She made hissing sounds and spoke to me in words I did not know, but which I think must have been of the Kongo tongue that was native to her mother's grandmother, and as I went into her her eyes rolled as those of one transported. The keenness and wildness of her passions were almost frightening. We went at it with right regal fury, and I could not help but give play to my wit, which hearkened back to our foolery with words, and at one moment of delight I put my lips beside her ear and murmured such English words as "stonemason" and "turnip-greens" and "scavenger," the first that came to my mind.

Which made her shriek with crazy laughter and pound my back with her hand in a fair savage way, and down below I felt her squeeze me tight, in that style of having a little fist concealed in there that some very passionate women have, and she cried, "Ah, Andres, how I do love you, Andres!"

And with the using of that word "love" a chill passed over me in all my overheatedness. For I thought of Anne Katherine. I had taken care not to do that for quite some long time, but now she came rushing into my guilty soul. I told myself that these are deep waters indeed that I sail, if Teresa and I have taken up with the light sports of word-play, that are the mark of lovers, and that has carried us onward to talk of loving. For mere coupling like rutty cats in a foreign land is one thing, which may be forgivable when lust overtakes one's chastity, but love is quite another, and perilous.

Then I told myself what I should have thought at the first: that oftentimes people speak of love when their bodies are entwined, and it is a human thing, a failing of the moment. One always loves the person who is giving one's body extreme pleasure—at least at the instant such pleasure is being administered—but that is not the same thing as the love that bonds man and woman across the decades. Or so I told myself.

And put the question from my mind, and had my pleasure in good hard hot pulsing spurts, and fell gasping over Dona Teresa. And we lay quiet a long while, until she rose and recloaked herself and went from my cell, wishing me a bon voyage.

ELEVEN

THE NEXT day we sailed. I thought my piloting would be put to the test at the very first, in the finding of our way out of the harbor of São Paulo de Loanda, through all the shoals and shallows. But there was no need. The crewmen knew the road across the Bay of Goats, and did it without my instruction, following the buoys and marks and taking us past the tip of the isle of Loanda and into the open sea.

Yet I marked well what they did; for another time I might have to find the way of my own.

There was some challenge soon after, as we beat our way northward. Not far north of São Paulo de Loanda a river reaches the sea that has several names, the Mbengu or the Nzenza, which the Portugals choose to call the Mondego. Under whatever name it roils the waters with its outflow, and had to be gone around with care, which we did, and then it was straight sailing.

Shortly I discovered that my apprehensions of difficulty in my new trade were for nothing. It was a fair sea and we had no great journey to make, only fifty leagues to the mighty river of Kongo, that the Portugals call Zaire. That is their way of speaking a native word, *nzari*, which has the meaning simply of "the great river," and a great river it is, one of the greatest, I trow, in all the world. To reach it we sailed with land-winds pushing us, creeping still all along the coast, and every day we cast anchor in some safe place either behind a point or in a good haven. There were a few small tasks of decision to make as we journeyed, but on the whole I think a child could have done the piloting, and it gave me no high opinion of the Portugals of Angola to think they had waited this voyage until they had a captive Englishman to read their charts for them. Oh, I did some gaping and some squinting, and I came out with my astrolabe and looked most solemn, and measured stars with my cross-staff very gravely, and from time to time fed my compass needle with my lodestone to renew its magnetism. And took some soundings, and did my timekeeping, and had things done with tacks and sheets and bowlines, and all of that. I wanted the Portugals to prize me highly.

The place of our going was an island in the mouth of the River Zaire, which in my orders from Don João de Mendoça was called the Ilha das Calabaças, that is, Calabash Island. When I looked to my charts, meaning to find the outermost of the isles of the estuary, that island was marked, Ilheo dos Cavallos Marinhos, which means Hippopotamus Island. I asked Pedro Faleiro about this, saying, "I will find any island I am asked to find, but you had better keep your names more orderly."

Faleiro smiled. "They are the same place, Calabashes or Hippopotamuses. We have a town there, where we do our trading."

I had heard that name before, Hippopotamus Island, but I had to roam some way into my memory before I found it. Dona Teresa had spoken of it, I recalled. Her father, she said, had fought bravely and died there at a time when the Jaqqas had erupted into the kingdom of the Kongo. I asked Faleiro if he could tell me anything of that, and he said, "It was long ago, before my coming here. But they still relate tales of it, to remind us of the fury of the devil Jaqqas."

And a tale of horror and ferocity he unfolded, that made me think of the worst stories of history that I had heard, the diabolical Mongol hordes that had overrun Europe in ancient times, or the vengeful Turks, or the Huns of long ago, that had blackened whole provinces. But this seemed worse, for it took in not only the destruction of settled peoples, but the eating of human flesh, which I think those other monsters did not practice.

The Jaqqa cannibals, Faleiro told me, had come into the Kongo out of the forests along the south-west flank of the kingdom and had gone rampaging northward to the royal capital, São Salvador, which lies inland, well away from the great river. This befell, so far as Faleiro could reckon, in the year of 1568. I was a boy of ten in that year, dreaming in Leigh of going someday to sea. And in that very moment of my childhood by the placid banks of the Thames hundreds of thousands of fugitives had desperately been crossing the land of Kongo with the hope of escaping the murderous appetites of the Jaqqas.

Into São Salvador the Jaqqas came, said Faleiro, like a tide of fire. It was a great city then, far more resplendent than it had been ever after, and infinitely greater than São Paulo de Loanda. They set it ablaze, and murdered in terrible ways anyone they could catch, and piled up the dead and ate their fill of them until they were glutted and belching with the meat of mankind. Meanwhile the survivors set up a huge migration: the people of São Salvador, not only the Manikongo or king and all his court, but also some hundreds of Portugals that dwelled there, fled into the countryside, causing such confusions there as the Jaqqas might almost have worked themselves, and setting in movement vast hordes of innocent folk that went running through the forest until they came to the banks of the Kongo. There they found some islands on which they might take refuge, most particularly this Hippopotamus Island or Calabash Island that we were now approaching.

They came in there in such numbers and in such awful closeness that plague broke out among them, and famine, and thousands died every day and had to be thrown into the river. And yet the Jaqqas rampaged behind them, forcing more and more and more of the gentle Kongo folk into the zone of the river. Some were literally pushed into the river itself, by the crowding and the pressure of those that came behind them. Those became feasts for the coccodrillos.

Then happened something else that Faleiro spoke of with a kind of pride, which filled me all the more with horror. For the Portugals thereupon took advantage of all this fright and tragedy, by coming down in caravels from their slave-peddling island of São Tomé in the north—the same that I had seen when sailing with Abraham Cocke—and rowing in longboats out to the islands to make slaves out of the sufferers.

Faleiro thought his was a right shrewd deed. "They brought food, d'ye see? And the father sold his son, and the brother his brother, because they were starving, and a great profit we made of it. And carried the slaves off to São Tomé and thence to the New World, to their great benefit, for I think they would all have died if they had remained on the Hippopotamus Island."

Hearing this, I thanked God I was made an Englishman and not a Portugal. For although we ourselves have trafficked in slaves to good profit, at least we buy our merchandise honorably from the dealers both Moorish and Negro in such commodities, and do not shamefully come to desperate starving folk and offer them bread in return for their children. And in thinking this I wondered for the first time, but not for the last, which were the greater devils: the Jaqqas who had worked all this destruction, but who were like wild forces of nature without souls or consciences, or the Portugals who seized advantage from it, and were supposedly Christians who had pledged themselves to the way of Jesus.

Among those who were caught up in that charnel madhouse at the river's mouth was the mother of Dona Teresa da Costa, and Dona Teresa's father also. And I believe Dona Teresa herself was born in that time of chaos, living in a world gone mad with the bonfires of the Jaqqas blazing on the horizon and so many people dying each day.

Well, and well, no horror lasts eternally except the one that the preachers promise to sinners, and I think those Portugal slavers will feel the heat of that at Judgment Day. But it was other Portugals who honorably ended the torment by the river. Don Alvaro the black king sent a message to his ally King Sebastião of Portugal—they had a king of their own in those years, before the Spaniards swallowed Portugal—the King Sebastião sent word to his men at São Tomé to cease stealing slaves and to begin the rescue of the unhappy sufferers. And so the Portugals at São Tomé put together an army of six hundred men and went down to Hippopotamus Island and gathered the remains of the Manikongo's forces, and waged war against the Jaqqas.

It took two years of bloody campaigning, but in the end the Portugals drove the Jaqqas out and restored the Manikongo Don Alvaro to his throne at São Salvador, and built a wall for him around his city to secure it. And the Manikongo then vowed himself a vassal of Portugal, and paid a tribute for some years in *njimbos*, that is, the cowrie-shells that are the currency of the land, for he had neither gold nor silver to pay. But those Jaqqa wars were the end of the Kongo as a real kingdom, for afterward it was greatly weakened by famine and plague, and the strife of its chieftains and provincial lords, and the hellish enterprise of the slave-buyers. And the Portugals, seeing their puppet kingdom collapse in the Kongo, began to remove themselves toward their southern colony of Angola and make that their base for activities in western Africa.

It was in the driving back of the Jaqqas that Dona Teresa's father Don Rodrigo showed his valor, until he took a fever and died. And it was in the defense of Hippopotamus Island that Dona Teresa's mother was stolen and, in all likelihood, consumed by the cannibal warriors. So the place that lay before us was closely linked in my mind to her, that woman whose lips and breasts and thighs, so sultry and siren-like, were fresh in my memory. And now we made our course toward that island.

Entering the mouth of the Zaire was no child's task, and there I earned my keep as a pilot. You should know that the Zaire is a river that swallows all rivers, a tremendous torrent that by comparison makes our Thames seem like a stream. I would match it against the great Nilus of Egypt and the giant many-mouthed river in America that they call the Amazonas, for size, and I could not say which one has pre-eminence. While moving northward toward it I was compelled to stand well out to sea, sometimes as much as fifteen miles, for that the waters offshore are very shallow and the surf is evilly fierce. Keeping steady watch through my glass, I saw a long wall of high red clay cliffs, and then came to that which I knew from my charts to expect, but which must have astounded the first Portuguese explorers into silent amazement: the frightful onrush of the river into the ocean.

It comes down out of the land with a dark hue, which is the mud that it carries from Africa's heart. And it drives this color forty, fifty, even eighty miles into the ocean, so that the waves breaking near shore are a strange and surprising yellow-brown color, and the ocean itself is deep red, a muddy bloody hue. And all this is fresh water, though it lies in the ocean: we could drink it, if so we wished. This river torrent emerges from the land between two broad spits like the claws of a mighty crab, that make what seems to be a natural harbor, a dozen miles or greater across, inviting mariners to enter. Here the red clay cliffs give way, and there are level beaches of sparkling sand, and behind that a forest of ollicondi trees, that must be the most swollen colossal trees in all the world, and then the blue wall of distant mountains somewhere eastward of all that.

So inviting a harbor, yes. But O! the entering of it! The terrible entering of it!

For the river comes forth with a violent roar and crash and beats itself upon the bosom of the sea like an awful flail, and our small pinnace was a mere cockleshell against such might. With the aid of the sea breezes I made my way slowly and cautiously into the Zaire's vast mouth, thinking I was putting myself into the maw of a dragon. And though it was fair going at first, the river narrowed and narrowed and narrowed yet more, until it was scarce a mile across, with walls seven or eight hundred feet on its banks. The narrower the river the more furious its flow, in that there was that much less space here for all that volume of water to pass, so it must pass the more vigorously. We ran against a seaward current of ten knots that boiled and seethed, with whirlpools looming suddenly with loathsome sucking noises right beneath our keel. Now the Portugal sailors looked to me. I saw terror in Pedro Faleiro's face, and knew why I was there.

"Tell us, pilot! Which way? Where the channel?"

There are times when it is best not to think in any solemn slow way, but to act according to your sense of the moment. At such times, if fortune goes with you, you become an arm of the sea, an adjunct of the winds, and everything flows through you without meeting resistance, and you know without knowing what must be done. So it was with me. I had studied the rutter and I knew something of the best way into the estuary, but I looked at no charts now. I put myself in a commanding place and gave signals to the men working the ropes and lines and to the one at the helm who gripped the whipstaff, and tacked her and swung her and leaned her into the wind, and felt the currents running below me like the blood through my veins, and called for readings on the fathoms as my leadmen sounded them. And ten thousand mile of river thrust against me out of Africa's unknown core and I would not let it say me nay, but beat my way on and on and on, until at last the worst of it was behind me and we were in the estuary, moving through quiet channels where we were shielded from the worst of the onrushing force by the river islands that lay just ahead.

Ah, I thought. That is what sailing is! I had never known its like before.

And as we glided into the mouth of the Zaire, making our track between swamps and mud-flats and other such shallows, looking toward the saw-edged grass that rose three times the height of a man, and toward the hordes of coccodrillos whose eyes gleamed like emeralds out of their long nightmare heads from the sandspits, and listening to the flame-colored parrot-birds standing in the palm-trees, and seeing a hippopotamus arise from the water, more like a vast round-nosed pig than like the river-horse that its name would have us see, and opening its gaping red mouth as though to belch us back to Brazil—as I saw all these things, I felt a hand come to rest lightly on my shoulder, and did not look around, for I knew I should not see the owner of the hand, and the hand tightened in a fond grip and my father the master mariner Thomas James Battell of Leigh in Essex said to me in a voice that only I could hear, "Well done, my son, well done indeed." And my eyes became moist, out of pride that I was my father's son and worthy of the name.

Before us lay Hippopotamus Island, or the Island of Calabashes, or call it what you will.

Having Faleiro's story of warfare and destruction fresh in my mind, I was surprised at the peace of the place. I suppose I expected to find bloody bodies scattered in mounds at the shore, or vast scenes of devastation. But that was idle of me, for all those monstrous events were twenty years in the past, and matters had long since calmed here. There was a little harbor, and a native town, and a Portuguese settlement of no great size, and after the turbulence of the river I found this place most placid, most welcoming.

This was my entry to the kingdom of Kongo, which once was the greatest realm of all this part of Africa, perhaps surpassing even the fabulous land of Prester John in far Ethiopia, but now is much fallen from high estate, owing to the bloodthirstiness of the Jaqqas and the different evil practiced by the Portugals upon these people. It was a light and open land, golden yellow in the grassy places—for there had not been rain in a long while—with fine dust drifting easily. But as is true everywhere in Africa, behind the open plains and easy sunny places there always lies a jungle, and the jungle is ever dark, dark.

This first taste of Kongo was pleasing to me. I saw myself at the gateway to a land which, although black, was in its way civilized. In Angola I had seen little except São Paulo de Loanda, which is wholly a Portuguese settlement created by them from the ground upward, and such blacks as dwelled there had come from elsewhere to be pressed into the service of the white masters. And on my journey to Masanganu I had seen but a few small villages, from which I had learned little of the nature of the people. But now I was in a true black nation, which was a novelty to me.

The people of the Kongo call themselves the Bakongo and they speak a language called Kikongo, in which I became fluent as time went along. They live by farming and other settled arts, understand the crafts of metalworking and textiles, and are by way of being Christians, though I will testify that their Christianity is but a shallow overlay, a sort of coat of glossy sacred varnish that covers the deep and strange paganism beneath. The giving of that love-idol to me by Dona Teresa is a fair example of that. In their capital city of São Salvador, which I was not to visit for some good long while, they do wear Portuguese dress, much of it quite fine, and give themselves Portuguese names and put on many other such pretensions of civility. But here on this island it was not quite that way. The place was small, but most exceeding hot and moist, and nothing about it showed much mark of great advancement. The native town was fashioned of light structures of branches and earth covered with thatch, much as I had seen at São Paulo de Loanda, and the streets were a muddled maze, so that, small as the town was, a stranger would instantly become lost in it. The people did not wear any European finery, but only a simple piece of red or green palm-cloth wrapped like a kilt about them from waist to feet, leaving the breast bare. Some of this fabric was quite finely worked, with pleasing decoration, but nothing like that which I would see later in the cities; most of it was rough stuff, for these were mere common people.

The Portuguese town was very tiny and not pleasing to me. It had eight or ten Portugals living there, gloomy-looking men in the main, whose appearance was ill-kempt and bedraggled. They had with them some black concubines, practically naked, and there were bastard babes running about, and dirty, fly-bedeviled dogs of uncertain breed. "Fie," I said to Faleiro, "are these men convicts, that they look so worn?"

"They are the garrison, and do guard this place against invaders."

I laughed at that. "An invasion of mosquitos? An invasion of mice?"

"What if the Dutchmen were to come here, or you English, and try to pry the Kongo from our influence?"

"And would these sad old men drive them away, then?"

"They fly the flag. It is important to fly the flag. Other Europeans respect a flag. So long as they are here as representatives of our land, there will be no foreign invasion."

"And if the Jaqqas come?"

"Ah," said Faleiro, with a little shudder. "The Jaqqas are another matter."

I understood the unhappiness here. These were forgotten men in a forgotten place. The Portugals now concentrated their energies in winning Angola, and had their other main base well up the coast at São Tomé to do their slave-trading; but the Kongo, once so great in their schemes, was hardly more than anything to them now, and there was no future for those who maintained the ghost of an empire here for Portugal. Yet it had to be done, and these were those who did it, and also those remaining at São Salvador. I readily comprehended now why so ambitious and capable a man as Don João de Mendoça, after having devoted himself to the Kongo for so long, had removed himself to Angola in the pursuit of his ambitions. But these poor souls could not do as he had done.

Well, and that was hard for them, but no concern of mine. No one had compelled them to go to Africa, as I had been compelled. They stared at me sourly, knowing from my yellow hair that I was something out of the ordinary, and when they heard that I was English some of them made the sign of the fig at me in scorn, since that England and their homeland were enemies now, but I gave it back to them, and the sign of the folded arm as well, and would have no mockery from them. Faleiro spoke with them and they let me be after that. I disliked their mangy town and went back to the native one, where the people did look upon me as if I had come down from a different world. But they were friendly, and in their timid dainty way begged to touch my hair and beard.

We performed our trading business quickly and in enormous profit. This island was a depot for the merchants of the hinder lands, who brought such treasures as the teeth of elephantos to trade with us. These teeth are of great size, being only the two forward ones, that are called tusks, and ivory is carved from them. Another sort of thing that the Portugals purchase here is the golden wheat of the kingdom, that is called *masa mamputo* by the natives. This is not true wheat at all, nor is it native to Africa, but it is the stuff called maize or Indian corn, that comes from the Americas and was introduced here by the Portugals. The last commodity we had at the Hippopotamus Island was the oil of the palm, that they produce out of the pulpy fruits of the slender and graceful palm-trees that grow everywhere about. This is extracted from the fruit as oil is extracted from olives, and is most excellent in cooking: I came to prefer my food cooked in it and now find the oils of Europe greasy and strange to my taste. Its color and consistency are that of butter, though it is more greenish; it has the same use of olive oil and butter; it may be burned; it may be used to anoint the body. We acquired great store of it here.

And what did we give in return for this abundance of tusks, and that golden wheat, and the oil? Why, long glass beads and round blue beads and trifling little seed beads, and looking-glasses of the most vile manufacture, and red coarse cloth, and Irish rugs, which were very rich commodities to the Bakongo folk. We received for one yard of cloth three elephanto teeth, that weighed one hundred twenty pounds. I was ashamed to do such dealings, but when I saw that the natives were joyed to have our scurvy merchandise I let my objections drop away from me, for who am I to say which is more valuable, an elephanto tusk or a yard of cloth?

So quickly we laded our pinnace and got ourselves back onto the bosom of the great river. Which swept us like a cork out to sea, and I caught hold of the wind and turned us south, and coasted us skillfully back to Angola. And stood like a king in triumph on the deck of the *Infanta Beatriz,* bare to the waist and sunburned dark, with my hair long behind me in the breeze that came out of the hot lowlands, as we made our way into harbor at São Paulo de Loanda. For it had been a successful voyage and I had done well, and had won my own respect in the business of piloting. And one's own respect is the hardest of all to win, if one be an honest man.

Don João de Mendoça clapped me lustily on the back and praised me or my work and fed me on buffalo and other strange meats, and gave me his good wines, and said, "Well accomplished! And next week off you go again, even farther, to the land of Loango for a greater cargo."

Indeed I was ready to go. And go and go again, as often as they did care to ship me, for a year or so. I would keep my bargain, and then they would keep me theirs, and send me off to England as a free man.

Aye! To bargain with a Portugal! Ere I saw England, how many voyages there would be, and what monstrosities of event, and what pains, what deaths, what torments! But I predicted nothing of that to myself then. I supped with Don João, and I spoke a trifle boastfully of my getting into the estuary of the Zaire, and then I went to my new little house in the city to plan for my next voyage. There did Dona Teresa come to me soon after, and there did we have a joyous reunion of our bodies and our spirits, and afterward, when I lay alone and drowsy, an amazing thought did enter my mind. For I realized that even though I had been taken captive and sent into slavery to these Portugals, and had endured much that was not to my liking, I had emerged into a happy life. I was a happy man, by God, and could not deny it! Only one thing was lacking to me, and that was my return to my native land; but even that seemed less urgent, now that I was out of dungeon and had won a place among the Portugals here and had a skill that I practiced well. That amazed me: to find myself happy. Yet it was the truth, at that moment. And in a week, the voyage to Loango; and in a year, perhaps, the voyage home to England. All journeyed well for me.

Aye! Would that it had been so!

BOOK TWO:

Pilot

ONE

NORTHWARD AYE I went, in quick course, on my second trading voyage in behalf of Don João. Loango was my destination, which is a kingdom that has its beginning fifteen leagues to the north of the River Zaire.

Do you wonder at the ease with which I became an officer of the Portuguese maritime? That I should have no qualms and pangs of conscience, that I should take so swiftly to piloting of their vessel and earning them their tons of richly valued elephanto teeth? Nay, but I did not see myself as any traitor to Her Majesty by so doing. My choice was to serve, or to lie and rot in dungeon. If I proudly chose the second of those, and if perchance some venomous creature did creep upon me in my cell and bite its poison into me, would I then ever again see England or serve the Queen? But by undertaking these voyages along the coast I could preserve my life, I could increase my health, I would gain in knowledge of piloting that might some day be of use to Her Majesty— and I stood at least a chance of regaining my liberty. Or so I told myself, over and over a great many times, whenever this debate erupted within my soul, until a time came when it erupted no longer and I did my duties without self-inquest.

This land of Loango was an easy voyage from Angola, with no terrible river-mouths to enter as on the last one. Upon the appointed day I did go down to the port at São Paulo de Loanda and I found the same ship as before ready for me, the *Infanta Beatriz*, and much the same crew. This was comforting. Already on board were Faleiro the master and other men I had come to know, whose names I remember well after these many years, and they were Andrade and Pires and Cabral and Oliveira, who did clap me on the back and give me good grinning smiles and freely offer me the harsh thin wine that they keep in leather sacks. These men had seen me do brave service piloting them into the maw of the Zaire, and now all prejudices owing to my being English were forgot among them. They called me "Andres" or more often "Piloto," that is the Portugal way of saying pilot, and I got from them no further stares or hard glowering looks. The only time I held myself apart from them was when they were at their devotions, for I would not take the Mass or sing their Latin songs, or venerate the crucifix and image of the Madonna and other holy idols that they had brought on board. Instead at such times I went off quietly and knelt and talked to God in good plain English words, unburdening my soul and sometimes saying what words I could recall of the offices of matins or evensong. The sailors took no offense at this, for they no more expected me to transform into a Papist than they would expect a blackamoor to begin turning white of skin.

So we sailed up the coast with good breezes past the awful Zaire and to a point called Cabo do Palmar, where Loango commences. Here there are many palm-trees, giving the place its name. Five leagues beyond it is the port of Kabinda, which many ships use to water and refresh themselves. The terrain is one of woods and thickets. And seven leagues northwards of that place is the River Kakongo, a very pleasant place and fruitful. This is a strong river whose waters discolor the sea for seven miles, though that is nothing to what the Zaire achieves. At its mouth is the town of Chiloango: here is great stock of elephanto teeth, and a boat of ten tons may go up the river.

I tell you these places because I was the first Englishman to behold them. At four leagues from Kakongo is the river of Luiza Loango. Its depth where it meets the sea is only two feet, owing to a sand-bar, but once your vessel is within, it finds a fair waterway for over an hundred miles. Ten miles upriver is the town of Kaia, one of the four great seats or lordships of the kingdom of Loango. I did not go there on this voyage. And two leagues northward along the coast is a sandy bay, where a ship may ride within a musket-shot of the shore in four or five fathoms. Here is the port of Loango, the capital city of this kingdom.

"Come, Piloto," said Pedro Faleiro as we cast down our anchor and made ready to go ashore. "You will accompany us to the city, which I think you will find different from such places as you may already have seen."

"Tell him about the king and the bell," said our boatswain, Manoel de Andrade.

Faleiro laughed. "Aye! The king and the bell! Listen well, Andres, for it could cost you your life to be careless in this."

And he said that it was forbidden in this land to behold the king taking food or drink, on pain of death. When the king drinks, the bearer who carries the royal cup of palm-wine also holds a bell in his hand, and when he gives the cup to the king, he turns his face away and rings the bell. And then all that be there fall down upon their faces, and do not rise until the king has drunk. "Which is very dangerous for any stranger that knows not the fashions," said Faleiro, "for if anyone sees the king drink he is straightaway killed, whosoever he may be."

"Whosoever?" I asked.

"Aye. There was a boy of twelve years, which was the king's son.

This boy chanced to come into the chamber when his father was in drinking, and beheld him. Presently the king commanded the boy should be dressed in fine apparel, and given food and drink. This was done; and afterward the king commanded that he should be cut in quarters and carried about the city, with proclamation that he saw the king drink."

"It is not so!" I cried.

"You would give me the lie?" said Faleiro, looking angered.

"Nay, nay, good Pedro," I said, touching his arm. "I mean only that my mind will not accept such horror."

"Accept it, and accept it well. For if we are so lucky as to be granted audience with this king, listen ye sharp for the bell. We are not exempt from the rule."

"Would they cut one of us in quarters, then?"

"We are few and they are many. I know not whether they would attack us, and if they did, we have our muskets and they have none. But we ought not put it to the test."

"And so we must grovel on our faces when the king is in his cups?" I asked.

"Turning away the face is sufficient, for us," answered Faleiro.

Andrade said, "It is the same when the king eats, but there it carries less risk, for the king has an eating-house that he enters alone, and the door is shut behind him, and he knocks before he comes out. Yet even so, sometimes a fool will stumble into this house and spy unwitting on the king, and for this he always perishes."

I felt a shivering, despite all the heat of the day. "This sounds devilish to me, or mad."

"It is their belief," said Manoel de Andrade, "that the king will shortly die, if ever he is seen at his food or drink. And so he protects himself. For if he slays the one who sees, then his own life is spared, they do think."

"Ah!" I cried. "Now I understand, and in sooth it makes goodly sense!"

But I was speaking with deep irony—which my Portugal companions did not notice, I suppose, for they gave me odd looks, as though to say the English must be as mad as the Loangans. I did not trouble to explain myself. Indeed it did make a sort of sense, that *if* one believes a certain thing, then it follows naturally that one must take proper action to ward off its evil. The trick is in believing. To the Papist the actual and real blood of Christ is in the chalice from which they sip, and I think the King of Loango would have difficulties believing the truth of that. By God, *I* do!

Hearing such tales as these, I was in a taut and most sensitive mood as we went toward Loango. We entered the city on foot, leaving a small band of men to guard the ship. And entering that place was for me like entering a land of dreams, a place where phantoms did walk abroad in open daylight. The strangeness of those first moments there was something I could taste in my mouth, as if I had taken some piece of metal against my tongue, and I can remember that taste of strangeness to this day.

Yet the strangest thing about that strangeness is how swift it passes. I have entered many places as alien from my native land as Loango, and each time I have felt as though I am passing into another world, where light and sound and all else have different qualities. But yet I adapt and assimilate most speedily. Is that some special aspect of my own character, I wonder, or is it universal? The former, I think. There are those who never adapt to anything unfamiliar, and go through life speaking only their native tongue and eating only their native foods, and if they are exposed to other foods or climes they sicken quickly and die. Yet I do adapt. I never came to like the heat of these African lands, which is severe: the heavy wet air hangs about you like a woolen cloak that may not be shed. But since there is no escape from the heat, it becomes unremarkable. One lives with the heat the way one lives with the ache of an old wound, and takes no notice of it. And wherever I found myself, I incorporated into myself whatever I could not shrug away. I spoke the language of those about me, be it Portugal or Kongo or Jaqqa. I ate— God save me!—the things they ate. I breathed their air. Thus it was that Loango, which I entered as if I were entering the domain of Belial or Moloch, lost its strangeness early for me, and came before long to seem most comfortable, and pleasing, as though it were some cozy town along the Thames. And in after years, when I needed refuge, I took my refuge there and found it much to my liking. I think this is a curious quality of my soul, but I make no apology for it. For if I had not had it, I trow, I would have gone to feed the worms many years ago.

The main town of Loango is three miles from the waterside, and stands on a great plain. The streets are wide and long, and always clean swept. The place is thick with people, more than can be numbered, though you might not know it because the plantain-trees and palms and other vegetation are so profuse that they hide the dwellings that are built among them. On the west side of town are ten great houses that belong to the Maloango, as the king is known, and outside the door of his main house is a broad open space where he sits, when he has any feastings or matters of wars to deal with. I found it not easy to imagine Queen Elizabeth squatting outside her front gate to debate with the Privy Council. But, then, I found it equally hard to imagine the Privy Council pressing their faces into the dust whenever the Queen's cupbearer came to her beck.

From this open place goes a great wide street that runs the length of several musket-shots, and at the other end of it there is a great market every day, that begins at twelve o'clock. Here they deal in victuals, hens, fish, wine, oil, and grain, and in the excellent cloth they make from palm-leaf threads, fashioning it into velvets, satins, taffetas, damasks, sarsenets, and such like. Here also they deal in copper bracelets and in a wood that makes a very fine scarlet dye. But though Loango has an abundance of elephantos, the teeth of them are never sold in the marketplace, but always by private treaty.

The people of Loango are pagans. They wear fine garments of palm-cloth or woven grass that drape them from waist to feet, like a sort of kilt, of fine workmanship. They go circumcised after the manner of the Hebrews, as is true of all the peoples hereabout except the Christian folk of the kingdom of Kongo, who keep their members intact as Europeans do. The King of Loango is an ally with the King of Kongo, and in earlier days, when the King of Kongo was very powerful, the King of Loango was his vassal.

It was the middle part of the afternoon when we came into the city. Few people were about, under the horrid glare of the sun, but as word passed that the Portugals had come, the numbers of those in the streets increased. And once again the presence of a blond Englishman doubled and redoubled their curiousness: they whispered, they pointed, they crept forward almost unto touching range. With my hair and skin gleaming in the brilliance of the sunlight I felt that I was become Apollo of the Greeks, and I did smile and stretch forth my arms to the multitude and pretend to be giving them solemn blessing, until Pedro Faleiro tapped my ribs and said sourly, "Spare us this comedy, Piloto."

Through these gathering throngs we made our way to the royal compound so that we might present our compliments and credentials. The Loangans parted before us with that awe and deference that the colored folk of the world show so readily to Europeans, and by which the Spaniards and Portugals have been able to conquer so much territory with such small expenditure of lives. Is it that they take us indeed for gods, I wonder, or do our white skins persuade them that we come from the spirit-world and must be obeyed? Certain it is that if the Mexicans and the Peru folk and all the other conquered nations had risen up, and had been willing to sacrifice fifty of their lives for each of the invaders, they would have hurled King Philip's troops to perdition and preserved their empires unto their own keeping. But they did not do it.

As we came upon the royal buildings Faleiro showed me one group to the south side, all encircled with a palisado of poles, and said, "This is the harem."

"I know not that word," I replied.

"It is Moorish, and means, the place where the king's wives are kept. No man may enter that zone and live."

It was so many buildings that it looked to be a village of itself. I felt amazed. "God's own passion," I cried, "how many wives does the man have?"

"One hundred fifty and more," said Faleiro.

"Jesu!"

"That is a trifle. The old king that was here before him had twice that number. And four hundred children by them. Or was it four thousand, eh, Andrade?"

"Four hundred, I think," said the boatswain.

I shook my head. "Quite enough. One hundred fifty wives! Jesu, if he visit one a night, it would take him half the year to tup them all!"

Faleiro gave me a leering look. "And would such a regimen be to your liking, Piloto?"

"Nay," said I most truthfully. "Better one wife, and clasp her dear body a hundred fifty times a year, than a hundred fifty and embrace them once apiece."

And that set me thinking of home, and house, and wife, and awakened the sadness and homesickness that lay always not far beneath the surface of my soul. And also did all this talk of women and tupping arouse in me dark hot thoughts of Dona Teresa, that I did miss most intensely from my life. Ah, then, was it the loss of Anne Katherine I mourned, or my absence from the witching Portugal woman? I did not know. I did not know at all, and that threw me into a new despond. For I would not then admit that Anne Katherine and all our plans had entered into the realm of vapors and mist for me, and that it was the silken thighs and hard-tipped breasts of Dona Teresa that I craved. But yet had I brought Dona Teresa's little witching-statue with me, and kept it close beside me at all the time, and rubbed it now and again, as if I were rubbing her own flesh; and the touch of it made my ballocks heavy with desire and fiery recollections. This much dismayed me, for it was witchery, and witchery I do dread greatly: but though I had thought often of hurling that little idol into the sea for the sake of Jesus, yet had I not done it, and could not, for Dona Teresa's sake. And all these thoughts did roar through my head just then, that stirred me into confusion.

The rough Portugals did not have the wit to see that I was brooding, but jostled me and joked with me about what it would be like to be a king, and own such an abundance of wives. But I felt no gaiety and my mind was on other matters that they could not comprehend.

And then they told me that if any man be seen trespassing in the royal harem, if he be taken in a woman's arms or merely speaking with her, they both are brought into the marketplace and their heads are cut off, and their bodies quartered, and for all that day they lie thus sundered in the street. Faleiro had seen just such an execution, and Andrade also at another time.

A man of our company named Mendes Oliveira, that had the best command among us of the language of this realm, spoke with some grandee who came out to meet us, and arranged for us to attend the king at his court-meeting. This happened every day between one in the afternoon and midnight, and was about to occur now; so we were quickly conducted to the main palace. Which was no true palace, but only a large arching-roofed building of wickerwork and straw and mud, hung with carpets and crimson tapestries to make it look more grand. It was full of noblemen, sitting upon white carpets upon the ground. That they were noblemen was clear certain, for they were most nobly dressed, in the garments of palm-cloth most splendidly worked, of the brightest yellow and scarlet and blue, and they also had hanging in front, apron-style, pretty and delicate skins, such as the skins of panthers, civets, sables, martens, and the like, with their heads left intact. For even greater show they had flung about their bare shoulders a kind of round surplice called in their language *nkuto*, the which fell below the knee and was woven like a fine net, out of palm fibers: the links were bordered with fringed tufts, making a very graceful effect.

There was a long time when no one spoke. Then the king entered and went to the upper end of the house, where a sort of throne was set for him. Unlike his nobles he was dressed in extreme simplicity, in a short loin-cloth of the purest white, and another band of white cloth about his head. The blackness of his skin and the whiteness of these stark garments gave him an overwhelming kingly radiance, a brilliance, that far outshined the gaudiness of the others.

He was a strong-built man, going somewhat to fat. When he took his seat all the others clapped their hands and saluted him, crying, "*Nzambi! Ampungu!*" Which I learned afterward means, "O Most High God." For this king of Loango is thought by his people to be God Himself, and I suppose if he were to meet the Pope, he would expect the Pope to kneel to him, the Maloango being of a higher rank.

The king accepted this homage pleasantly until he had had enough. Then he looked toward us and uttered a greeting, or so we thought, that went, "*Byani ampembe mpolo, muneya ke zinga!*"

"He is bidding us welcome," murmured Oliveira, who replied loudly in Portuguese, "In the name of His Most Catholic Majesty Philip the Second of Portugal and Spain, we thank thee, O King of Loango, and may the blessing of God and His Son descend upon thee and all thy kingdom." Or words to that effect, said most resonantly, which he then repeated in the native tongue.

It was not for many years that I came to understand the real import of the Maloango's greeting, when I did hear it again, with time having given me a fluency in his language. For the words *Byani ampembe mpolo, muneya ke zinga* have actually the meaning there, "My companion, the white face, has risen from underground and will not live long." A strange greeting indeed! But not at all meant as a threat, though Oliveira, had he comprehended its sense, might well have construed it so. Its meaning rises from the belief of the blackamoors that the white man is a ghost that ascends from the bottom of the ocean with his ship, and so long as he keeps to shipboard he will live forever, but once he comes ashore, he is doomed to an early death. This, I suppose, because so many Portugals have succumbed to fevers and fluxes in this land. And that perhaps explains why they give us such deference, since we have the holiness of imminent decease overshadowing us like dark gleamings.

These formalities and others like them ran on for some hours. Oliveira interpreted for us, but I think not very well, for he frowned and strained to hear, and muttered to himself as if not understanding, and when he translated for us, I think he was inventing the half of what he told us, for it made precious little sense to me. I listened with care, of course knowing nothing of what I was hearing, but I did succeed in learning some five or six words simply from having them repeated in certain contexts that left me no doubt. It seemed not a difficult language, once your ear be attuned to it, and privately I considered that I might win more safety and privilege among the Portugals if I came to know the native tongues better than they did, they apparently having little aptitude for such things.

After long and wearying parley, coming to no purpose that I could discern, the king did call for drink. There was on either side of him an official to serve this purpose; the one on the right it was who handed him the cup, and the other on the left gave warning to the assemblage, by means of two iron rods about the bigness of a finger, and pointed at the end, which he did strike one against the other. Straightaway the whole gathering dived for the ground, as Faleiro had said they would do, and hid their faces in the sand so long as the irons continued making their noise. It was an astounding spectacle to behold those grandees in their fine robes, every one groveling down on his nose while the monarch took his wine. We did not, but all of us spun around and looked another way, and I closed my eyes besides, lest some reflected bit of the king's image glance into them while he drank and cost me my life.

When all of that was done, the nobles rose up again, and according to custom did signify that they wish him health, with clapping their hands, that being a sign of respect, as with us in Europe the putting off the hat. Wine now was distributed generally to the house, and a meal was served also, of fried fish with a sauce of honey, and a thick porridge made of the ground-nut, which is a pea, somewhat bigger than ours, the pods of which grow in the roots, underneath the ground. This last stuff was improved by the juice of a hot pepper, the *pili-pili*, that was like eating fire. It produced in the mouth an intense burning sensation and made the sweat stand out all over my skin. I thought I would perish of tasting it, and even the Portugals, who eat a lustier diet than we English do, were hard put to swallow much of the stuff. But I did eat my fill and gradually accustomed myself to it, and in time, over the months and years ahead, I would come so much to dote on the *pili-pili* that food without it came to seem devoid of taste, as it still does for me.

There was some obstacle toward our buying the elephanto teeth we had come here to purchase. I know not what it was, for the Portugals would not confide with me on so delicate a matter, and I was not privy to the urgent conferences between Faleiro and the officials of the Maloango's court. Perhaps it was a religious problem—the season not being right for commerce—or perchance the Loangans were seeking to increase the price of their goods; but I was not told, and I did not ask. These matters did, however, create a delay of many weeks in our leaving Loango.

We lived in small rude houses built especially for us, and were fed on the native foods. We talked often of going hunting for game, but we did not do it, on account of the great heat, which I think made us all lazy. Likewise we did not touch women. Faleiro told me that women were available to us—not citizens of the city, who were jealous of their virtue just as Christian women would be, but slaves, who were abundant here. But I had no hunger for them, and I think none of my companions either, except possibly one or two of the lustiest, and those not often.

Mostly did we spend our days resting, playing games with dice or knives, and drinking the heavy sweet palm-wine, and talking of our homelands. These Portugals were generally coarse folk, and I never once heard them speak of anything but gaming or wenching or drinking or fighting or gathering treasure. Not a word came from them concerning poetry or plays, that any Englishman who was more than a common churl would have been brim-full with discussing. One day when I told them of the richness and joy of our theater, and of Master Marlowe's

play of Tamburlaine that I had seen, and the wonderful play of Hi-
eronimo and the Spanish prince that was done by Thomas Kyd, they
looked upon me as if I were speaking in Greek, and paid me no heed.
And one of them that was named Tristão Caldeira de Rodrigues, that
seemed to have a special dislike for me, did scowl and hawk up a great
wad of spittle almost at my feet and say in his idle lolling way, "These
English sailors would have us think they are all poets and scholars, to
shame us. But I think they do but feign their poetry, and give themselves
high airs, for that the English have long been only a race of peasants
and clod-grubbers, and are shamed by it now, and do lately pretend to
a finer breeding."

"Ah, and are you so finely bred, then?" I demanded hotly, with a
rage beginning to pound in the vault of my head, for it was only by
heavy effort that I could rein in my temper.

"You have heard my name," said he disdainfully.

"It means nothing to me."

"I am not at all surprised," replied this Caldeira de Rodrigues, and
turned himself from me as though I had been dissolved into air.

I might have called him out for a brawl, but that I still had some
mastery over myself, knowing that whether or no I be pilot for these
men, I still was in a subservient place. And yet it was a close thing, my
fury being so strong at his mockery: only the touch of a hand on my
arm—Cabral's, I think—kept me at the last from leaping at him.

I learned from others, a little after, that this snotnosed scornful jay
was the son of one of Portugal's great dukes, and close kin to the old
royal family that had fallen from power: and so he was far superior in
birth to almost anyone else of Angola, except perhaps for Don João de
Mendoça, that was also of high origin. Caldeira de Rodrigues and his
elder brother Gaspar, they said, were exiled from Lisbon for their ruin-
ous high living and stark criminous pastimes, which went too far even
for men of their great standing, and were sent to Angola to sweat themselves into some semblance of virtue. He was a man of eighteen, very
slender, pretty almost in a womanish way, though there was an ugly
and hard glint in his eye, and a dagger at his hip that I knew he would
be quick to use. His face was marred by a purple blemish of the cheek
that took back some of the prettiness, and his beard grew only in places,
with foolish barren patches between. All in all I liked him little, and
was sorry to have him among my shipmates.

During this time of delay I sometimes did wander about the district,
either by myself or with one or two of the more amiable Portugals, and
rarely without some blackamoor guards also following us to see that we
did not cross into holy ground. That thing we nearly did, one time,

when we walked back toward the harbor and spied one of their idols, a little black image that is known as Kikoko. Kikoko is a *mokisso*, that is, a witch-spirit, that lives in a little house along the main highway, and everyone who goes by him claps hands, or makes a gift, as an offering.

I knew these *mokissos* had great power over the blacks, and I thought that power might extend even to us: for who knows how long the reach of the Devil's arms may be? All that I heard led me to tread cautiously in the witch-world. In Loango, they said, this *mokisso* will sometimes take possession of a person in the night, and he babbles frantically for the space of three hours. Whatever the frantic person speaks, that is deemed the will of Kikoko, and all the tribe obeys it, and they make a great feast and dancing at the house of the one who speaks.

Though I had much respect for this evil being, yet did I want, out of curiosity, to look upon Kikoko in his little house. But the blacks stood before him and made a frightful gesture at me with their spears, and I weighed anchor swiftly and went elsewhere.

There was one diversion concerning these idols. A new one had been carved and was arriving by sea from a town to the north, when it slipped from the hands of its bearers and fell into the water. Though they sought mightily for it, they could not uncover it below, which was deemed a great calamity. The king of the land sent for us, and told us what had befallen, and asked if we had some way of bringing up the statue. Very few of the Portugals were able to swim at all, but I had that skill, so I stripped off my garments and went down, and thought I had sight of the *mokisso*, but the water was too deep and my breath not sufficient, so that I came to the surface empty-handed.

"I will try again," said I.

"Nay," said Faleiro, "do not drown yourself on behalf of these pagans, Piloto, for we do have greater need of you." And I did not dive a second time.

On another occasion Cabral and Andrade showed me the burial grounds of the kings of Loango. This was at a place called Loangiri, two leagues without the town. Here the teeth of elephantos were thrust into the ground all about, to make a great shining white palisado, and the whole burying-place was ten roods in compass, that is, a fine estate for anyone. Cabral said, "These elephanto teeth alone, if we could but have them, would be worth half a kingdom. But also, beneath those mounds, they have buried with their kings all manner of treasure, pearls and jewels and such, of a value too high to count."

I stared at him wide-eyed, this Cabral having seemed to me to be a man of honor, as honor is reckoned among the Portugals.

"But surely you will not covet the things of a cemetery!"

With a shrug he said, "But this is not consecrated ground. They are but pagans, and if they choose to waste their precious things by burying them, why, it is our duty to God to unbury them, and carry them off for some use."

"Your duty to God," said I in wonder, "to rob the dead?"

"They are but pagans," Cabral repeated.

And he and Andrade spoke of a time to come, when Christianity would be spread into this land of Loango, and the priests intended to persuade the king at that time to have his ancestors reburied in a Christian graveyard. "And at that time," said Andrade, "we will take all these heathen treasures from the ground, to our own great profit and the saving of the peoples' souls."

"Aye," I said, but not aloud, "save their souls by stealing out of graves. Look to your own souls, Portugals!"

But we did not trespass that day upon the royal burying-place. We only stared in awe at that great wall of lofty elephanto teeth that ringed the place, and I smiled to see the greed that glistened in the faces of my friends Andrade and Cabral, and after a time we returned to the town.

Two

By slow and easy stages Faleiro began to prevail in his negotiations, and it seemed sure that the Loango folk would trade with us at long last. I was heartily glad of that, for this idleness wearied me, and I was eager to feel the sea-breezes against my face. I confess with no little shame that I longed also to return to the arms of Dona Teresa in São Paulo de Loanda: for although I had managed to be virtuous enough for several years of chastity after leaving England, I had had my slumbering lusts reawakened by her, and it was not easy now to return them to their disciplined repose. So betimes at night I imagined her satin-smooth breasts in my hands and her thighs wrapped tight about my hips, and I played such fantasies with her in my mind as previously I had been wont to do with Anne Katherine. Anne Katherine herself, I fear, was becoming only a shadow in my memory by this season, for it was four years now and some months since my leaving England, and all my prior life was growing pale and unreal to me, like something I had once read about in a book. The bright sunlight of Africa did eclipse for me the poor pale gleam of England. Africa was become my only reality now.

So I dreamed of Dona Teresa's tawny nakedness and I gobbled the fiery stews and porridges of Loango and I roamed the town to study its ways, learning a bit of its language and discovering of its customs. I found another *mokisso*-house near the port, where an old woman dwelled named Nganga Gomberi, which means the priestess of the spirit Gomberi, and the blacks told me that once a year a feast is made there, and Nganga Gomberi speaks from underneath the ground, giving oracles. I asked to be let to see this old witch, hoping she would cast a horoscope that would waft me back to England, but they would not show her to me.

I saw an even stranger thing, that is, a white Negro, as white as any white man, but with curling hair and thick lips and a flat nose. This was in the marketplace, when I heard a great stir and a murmuring, and there he came, with the crowd giving way on all sides. Oliveira was with me, and he said, "Hsh! Keep care! That is a holy man!"

"God's blood, what is it?"

"It is called a *ndundu*, which is born white and stays that color all its life. They are always brought up to be witches, and serve the king in witchcraft. He has four of them, they say, and no man dares meddle with them."

Indeed, this *ndundu* was passing through the market sampling this food and that, taking a bite and a bite and tossing away, and all this while he was allowed to go as he pleased. He came within five yards of me and turned to stare, for I with my blond hair was as strange to him as he was to me. Our eyes met, and his were red, *red* where mine were blue, the red eyes of a demon from Hell, that I have never seen otherwise.

Toward me he did make certain holy gestures, that were like the writhing of a madman, with much waving of the arms and crooking of his fingers. And in a hissing voice he cried out, an evil croak, saying, "*Jaqqa-ndundu! Ndundu-Jaqqa!*" The meaning of that is "white Jaqqa," which even then I understood, though I could not fathom the sense of the appellation. And he did say other things, just as mystical, which left me sore bewildered. We looked at one another a long while, and then I looked away, unable to meet that diabolical gaze any more; and I felt a chill even in so much smothering heat, as though the gates of the Inferno had opened before me and released a blast of the icy wind of Satan. White Jaqqa! What madness was that? Ah, and I would learn; but how did he know?

While we were thus becalmed at Loango there were three special prodigies, that is, things that were out of the ordinary even for the people of Loango.

The first of these was a miracle of the king, to make rain fall. It was the rainy season then, but all had been dry for some weeks and the people were suffering, for the crops could not thrive. So according to the custom and usage of the land they came to the king and begged him to bring the rain, and he did decree a great rain-making festival, which we all attended. On that day all the lords and armies of the surrounding districts came to Loango and held a tournament and display before the king, brandishing their spears, dancing and leaping about, and showing their skill with the bow and arrow. The best of these was an archer who would have put Robin Hood and all his men to shame, and did such wonders of splitting one arrow with another, and bringing down birds on the wing, that I did not think were possible except in storytellers' tales. When he had done his feats he came forward and spoke with the king, who embraced him and gave him food and drink with his own hand.

Then the king took his place upon a carpet spread on the ground, some fifteen fathoms long and broad, made of the fine fabric *nsaka*, which is a stuff resembling velvet, and sat upon a high throne the height of a man, covered entirely in leopard-skin. He commanded his *ndambas* to strike up, these instruments being pieces of palm-tree stems, five feet long and split down one side: notches are carved on the edges of the split, and they rub these notches with a stick to make a weird and unearthly sound, like the rasping of gigantic crickets. Also they have an ivory trumpet made of elephanto tusk, called the *mpunga*, hollowed and scraped light. With these *mpungas* and *ndambas* they created a truly hellish noise. After they had sported and shown the king pleasure in this way, he rose and stood upon his throne, and beckoned to the great archer, and received from him his bow and arrows. I thought the king himself would shoot them, but no: he bestowed them on a high priest, or rain-witch, who stood by his side all daubed with paint and feathers. Also beside the king were the four albino monsters, *albino* being the word the Portugals use for these white blackamoors; and with them were various other witches and mages of the tribe, even the old Nganga Gomberi woman. There was a great awesome sounding of the drums and trumpets, that made me want to cover my ears with my hands, and set the Portugals to work crossing themselves furiously and muttering their Latin, and the high rain-witch aimed his bow toward the sky and fired his arrow with all his might, so that it went up in a great arc and vanished far off.

And then, you will say, nothing happened, and the dearth of rain did continue for another four months, and all the land was turned to desert. So I would myself have expected, from such pagan folly as this. But I must tell you that upon my mother's soul I speak the truth when I report that within a few minutes a small white cloud did appear in the southeast, and then a darker cloud, and then the sky was thick with them, good black clouds of rain, and before an hour had passed we were having such a deluge as would have sent Noah to cover, for rivulets were running through the streets and dust was transformed instantly to gobs of mud. How does one explain it? One does not explain it. One ascribes it to the dark power of witchcraft. Or else one says that it was, after all, the rainy season, and rain must come sooner or later even in a dry year, and very likely the king had waited until signs of rain could be seen afar, and had chosen that day to hold his great rain-making festival. And was it witchcraft truly? I cannot rightly say. For it is the case that the king did not fire the arrow himself, but gave it to his priest. I think if the king was sure he could make rain, he would have drawn the bow with his own hand; but by giving the task to the priest, he protected himself against the chance that it would have no result. Priests can always be punished if they fail to bring rain; princes, in my experience, are not much interested in taking the responsibility for public failures.

That was the first of the three prodigies.

The second was but three days afterward, when light rains still hovered about the place. I was in the market exchanging a few of the cowrie shells that go for money here for a piece of the palm-cloth brocade, all done finely in green and red and yellow, from which I meant to make a mantle to shield me from the worst of the sun. Of a sudden I heard a shrill music from afar, a sound not unlike the bagpipery of the wild Scots, that punctured my ear in a painful way. At this piercing and frightful sound all activity ceased in the marketplace. Next I did hear men chanting, as men will do when they pull some heavy load or bear some great burden, a deep slow steady grunting song, I think made not of words but of mere sounds. All this came from the west, from the ocean side of the city.

Then there entered into view what seemed to be a coccodrillo of mighty dimension that floated in the air. But of course that was not the case: this coccodrillo, which was as large as any beast I hope to see, easily eight yards in length and perhaps more, was being borne on the shoulders of some eight or ten men. They struggled under its vast weight, chanting their stern rhythm to keep themselves moving forward, *oom oom OOM oom oom, oom oom OOM oom oom*, staggering and straining, their eyes all but popping out of their shining black faces, while about them danced and capered three or four musicians playing on their pipes and flutes. This uncouth procession came forward into the very center of the market; the black who was the commander of the carriers gave a cry, and thereupon all did kneel to their knees and roll aside, allowing the great coccodrillo to fall to the ground.

Its eyes were open but they had a gloss on them, and the horrid toothy mouth gaped but did neither close nor open further, for the animal was dead. Indeed such a smell came from it that my guts heaved and fairly leaped into my throat: for not only was there in the air the musky reek of all coccodrillos, that is loathsome enough, but also there was from this one the stink of corruption, of deathly decay. I stepped back some paces; but the townsfolk did press forward, crowding around, and setting up such an excited clamor that my thin newly won knowledge of their language was defeated, for I could not make out a single word, so frenzied was their outcry.

This display went on a long while, to my mystification. Was it some custom of the community to bring their slain coccodrillos to the marketplace and crow over their downfall? How, indeed, had this one been slain? I saw no mark on its body, though there was a kind of swelling about its middle, a bloat, that made me think it might have been poisoned. I could learn nothing. But at last came some of the grandees of the city out from the direction of the royal compound, led by a tall and bulky person in elegant scarlet robes, who had the look of a grand minister about him. This individual drew from his garment a long iron blade, which he thrust forthwith into the side of the coccodrillo in the place where the bloat was.

O! and the gushing forth of vile fluids! O, the stink, the foulness! In great calmness this high minister did slash at the monster's thick hide, cutting it with no small effort, and thereby liberating such a flow of evil bile as to make me gag and choke. Yet did I not turn away, for I have this certain quality that I scarce do understand, of looking with fascination upon certain repellent and frightful things, of being drawn to them by a kind of magical attraction. So I watched; and this functionary of the court, when he was done slashing open the belly of that leviathan, did thrust his arm into the hole, and grope around within, reaching even unto his shoulder, and suddenly, grimacing and grunting, he pulled forth something that I could not at first recognize, and which I then perceived to be a human arm, partly digested and much melted from its true shape. At this sight a heavy cry went up from the onlooking populace. Still did the official tug; and the arm was attached to a body, and the body to a chain, and the chain led to a second body, and a third, and this revelation of horror and death went on and on, passing all belief.

In time there were eight half-eaten bodies lying in a ghastly sequence on the ground, and the coccodrillo, thus emptied of its prey, had a flattened and shrunken look. The court official, satisfied that no more victims lay within, arose and removed all his garments, for he was entirely beslimed with gore and muck, and boys came to him and cleansed him with buckets of water; and, taking on new garb, he strode off toward the palace to tell the tale of this event. Whilst the populace, crowding around, set up a lengthy commentary on all this in low murmuring tones.

I saw a merchant who I knew to have some Portuguese, and I touched his arm and said, partly in that language and part in his own, "Pray tell me what has befallen here."

And he explained that this coccodrillo was so huge and greedy that he had devoured an *alibamba*, that is, a chained company of slaves, that had been at work along the shore of the nearby river some days back. As the unfortunate captives did their toil, one had slipped and fallen to the muddy bank where the creature lurked; and, springing upon him with that terrible speed which coccodrillos demonstrate when their appetites are aroused, it had eaten the man whole. But by the suction of its maw it had pulled the next in the chain toward him, and the next, and the next, gobbling each in his turn, there being no escape, each terrified slave watching as his predecessor was devoured. Until at last the entire *alibamba* of men was well within the coccodrillo, and I know not how many yards of chain besides.

It was the indigestible iron that paid him his wages, though, and murdered the murderer. For even a coccodrillo, even a giant among giants such as this, has his limits; and it lay sluggish and torpid for days, striving to encompass its formidable meal, and it might in time have absorbed them all, taking some months at the task; but the chain was beyond its capacity. So it weakened and bloated, and boys of the town were assigned to watch him day and night in his final throes, and when his death was upon him these bearers hoisted him to their shoulders and carried him to the public square. The official that had cut him open was the regulator of slaves, who needs must keep a tally, and note down the death of any human property. The which he had done, and the episode was closed. I looked on as other slaves now appeared and cleaned away the eight awful corpses as if they were so much trash—taking them, I think, to the town's bone-heap and scrap-yard. But the chain that had held the *alibamba* of slaves and drawn them to their dreadful deaths was most carefully rinsed of all slime, and carried off to be used anew. For some days thereafter it was the talk of the town, that the coccodrillo had had such a capacity for meat, and that it had died of its own gluttony; but not a word of remorse did I hear for the slaves that had perished. Perhaps my understanding of the language was not then perfected enough to register such subtleties. In any case I was haunted by the sight in my troublesome dreams three nights running, and in my waking hours I yearned ever more passionately for England and her good sweet Thames, that holds no such devilish monsters. And where, even if such things were apt ever to happen, the victims would be pitied some, and wept over, and put into a Christian grave for their last repose.

And that was the second of the Loangan prodigies.

But the third, which followed a week after that, had the deepest impact of the three, though it was the simplest event. How, you ask? Why, because although the eating of slaves by a coccodrillo in so great a number was an amazement and a marvel, it meant no threat to those who were yet undevoured. And the drought, grave matter though it might be, was more of a hardship than a catastrophe. But this third thing did portend a universal downfall, though in itself it was so slight. For it was merely the finding of a lone black man dead in the forest of ollicondi trees that lay between the city and the royal burial-ground at Loangiri.

A lone black man! Yea, but rather more than that.

Once again the event came to my awareness through the sounds of pipes and flutes, but this time, instead of playing in wild skirling sounds, it was more like a dark dirge, so slow and mournful that it all but wrung tears from my eyes. It had in it all the sadness that ever was, all the loss and grief and misery that Almighty God ever had sent amongst us to test our faith in Him. Then came a single drummer, beating a dead-march on a drum whose head was covered with the skin of that lovely black and white horse of the plains that they call here a zevvera. This too was so poignant a sound that it pierced the very soul. I was with Faleiro and Cabral when this music was heard, and we turned to one another in shared alarm, and Faleiro said, "I like this not. What calamity do they announce?"

"It could only be the death of the king," I hazarded, "for what else here would merit such melancholy stuff?"

"God forbid it," cried Faleiro, making the sign of the cross half a dozen times swiftly. "For if it is so, we are lost. When the Maloango dies the world stands still, and everything is given over to weeping. There is no hunting, the market is closed, the forge and the anvil grow silent, it is forbidden to go out at night."

"Aye," said Cabral, "and one may not laugh or cry out or even sneeze or cough, and there is no cooking of meals, and they do not go to the wells. Let us pray the king still lives. In the funeral week if a dog barks it is slain, if a ram bleats it dies."

But these fears of the two Portugals were not long in troubling us: for the nobility began to issue from the royal palace, and among them came the king himself, borne by slaves atop his high throne. Which reassured us and at the same time increased our concern, since that we knew that the Maloango made no public appearances except when some grave occurrence had befallen his kingdom.

We stood still as stones while the pipers and the drummer went past, and then came the center and cause of this eerie procession. Out of the forest road walked very slowly four warriors of the realm who carried a broad shield of elephanto-hide stretched over a wooden frame; and on that shield lay a naked man, dead, his limbs dangling all asprawl. They brought him before the king and laid him down, shield and all, and backed away, and the musicians were silent, and the entire city was silent.

Then there did burst from the throat of the Maloango such a wailing and outcry as could rend the soul to hear it. You would think that he grieved for his own most dearest son, like David crying for Absalom. Yet was not this the king that had ordered a child of his issue quartered for coming untimely upon him as he drank wine? Now he wept, he moaned, he shredded his headdress and hurled it to the ground. Not even Mary beweeping the Savior could have set up such a vast lamentation.

"What is it?" I asked Faleiro. "Why does he shriek so?"

"This is a prince of the Jaqqas that lies dead here," replied Faleiro in a hoarse whisper.

I moved as close as I dared, for a better look. Indeed the dead man seemed to be of some tribe other than the Loangan. He was of large stature, slender, with great elongated arms and legs and a high slim neck, yet also he had nobly developed muscles, that lay like cords of metal beneath his sleek midnight-hued skin. He wore nothing but a double rope of white beads about his narrow hips, and on his bare shining chest there was painted, strangely, the sign of the cross in some thick white paint, that gave him the look of a Knight Templar which had gone out to take the Holy Land from the infidel. His cheeks were covered with ridged scars, six down this side, six down that. In the grimace of his dead mouth I saw two of his upper teeth gone and two lower, which seemed done by way of ornament, since his other teeth were strong and good.

From his length and majesty I thought this might be that same Jaqqa prince I had seen standing alone in the clearing along the River Kwanza, that time just before the massacre of the village of Muchima. But no, this was a different man, although somewhat similar of body. For I remembered that that other prince, naked and leaning insolently on his shield, had possessed a male member of phenomenal length, like unto a black serpent hanging halfway down his thigh, and this man was

constructed in a more ordinary way, though yet scarce worthy of anyone's contempt. Even in death a kind of frightsome radiance was about
him, a mysterious invisible glow, something like the halo that a devil
might have if devils had halos of the sort that saints are widely said to
have.

I saw on him the marks of his death. For his chest was somewhat
crushed and twisted, and one side of his body was bruised, as though
he had been injured by some great beast of the forest. It was Faleiro's
idea that this Jaqqa had been surprised by an elephanto, which had
seized him in his long nose and squeezed him and perhaps hurled him
against a tree to his perdition, and I think that was the case.

The King of Loango now left off his wailing and began a speech, of
which I could understand perhaps every sixth word, and in which the
words "Jaqqa" and "Imbe Calandola" were repeated over and yet over.
Faleiro struggled to hear, as did Cabral, but I could tell that they scarce
understood anything. And though I could follow the words, I knew so
little of Loangan customs that I could not easily arrange them into sense.
But by conferring among us three, we puzzled out the truth of the king's
speech.

Which was that one Jaqqa generally meant many; that in all likelihood
this Jaqqa was a scout, come to investigate the desirability of making
war against Loango; and that the death of this man, though it was not
the doing of any Loangan, might well bring destruction upon the entire
city.

Faleiro spat and kicked against the ground. "We must leave this place
at once!" he said, in a fury.

"Without our cargo?" I asked.

"If needs be. I will not stay here when the Jaqqas come."

"We are charged to return to Angola laded with elephanto teeth," I
said, "and all the other goods that come from this place. How now, can
we flee after waiting so long, and bring back nothing?"

"Piloto, this is no concern of yours!"

"It would be an embarrassment to show such cowardice."

Faleiro's eyes went bright with rage at that last heavy word, and he
reached toward his sword. I being unarmed except for a small knife, I
felt that my last moment might be upon me. And deservedly so, for I
had spoken foolishly. What was it to me, if these Portugals prospered
or did not prosper? I was but their prisoner, their indentured servant:
if they chose to go back to Don João and say that fright of the Jaqqas
had driven them off empty-handed, what shame would attach to me?
Yet it galled me to have wasted so much time here without making trade,

even if I was to have no share in the profits of the voyage. But Pinto Cabral came between us and made peace before Faleiro could strike, and I fell back, coming to my right mind and saying in a low voice, "I beg pardon. These are not my decisions to make."

"Yea, Piloto. Stay here if you like, and let the Jaqqas stew you alive. But we will leave."

While this dispute had unfolded, the Maloango had continued to instruct his subjects. I returned my attention to him and found that he was laying schemes for defense, ordering the city to prepare for an incursion of the cannibals, and sending scouts off into the forest to search out the enemy force. And soon everyone was running about in frantic hurry, while we withdrew to plan our retreat from that place.

Yet after this first hour of excitement things grew more calm. Drums sounded in the forest, near and farther away, that were the sounds of Loangan scouts talking to one another, sending back word by a sort of code, and what they seemed to be saying, so I did learn, was that no Jaqqas were near at hand: the dead man had been an isolated wanderer. That eased the crisis somewhat. The next day there was a ceremony of great pomp in which the Jaqqa was buried, at a special burial-place deep within the forest. I think the Maloango, by showing this respect to the Jaqqa's corpse, hoped thereby to ward off the anger of his fellows.

There was one especial surprise for us. When the king became aware that Faleiro had ordered our departure, he sent word that he wished at last to conclude some trade with us. And after all this long delay, we did indeed engage in active bargaining, buying from them with our rugs and our beads and our looking-glasses the elephanto tusks that we had come there to obtain. This exchange, too, may have had some mystical significance, the king thinking to please his gods by obtaining our shiny merchandise from us and putting it on their altars: at least, I can find no reason otherwise for this sudden willingness to have commerce, after that we had been kept waiting so long. We filled our hold with ivory and with palm-cloth, and also with something else of high value, that is, elephanto tails. These were of no worth to the Portugals, God wot, but were much prized by the blacks of Angola, who wove the hair of them into necklaces and girdles; I learned from Faleiro that fifty of the coarse hairs of the tail were valued at a thousand reis of Portugal money, which is the same as six English shillings. So we were obtaining these tails from this land rich in elephantos in order to trade them elsewhere for slaves, and thus the circle of merchandising doth go in these territories.

Within two days we were fully laded and ready to go. In that time we slept very little, remaining vigilant always against the Jaqqa attack, for we thought the man-eaters might come like ghosts from any direction, without warning.

The same thought was in the minds of the blacks, and they were constantly on guard, their faces so drawn and fearful that I thought sure they would soon begin to die of their own timidity. These Loango folk were more terrified than if an army of giant coccodrillos were heading toward them.

At this time one of our number took advantage most shamefully of the disarray of the Loangans. I had my first clue of this when I saw two of the lower Portugal sailors trading among themselves, and haggling over a fine knife of African manufacture, with great green jewels set in its hilt. I happened upon them and took the thing from them to admire it, and turned it over in my hand, and said, "Where did you come by this? I saw nothing like it in the marketplace!"

"Ah, it is an old one," said they, "which a poor ancient woman was selling, to pay some high expense of hers."

That sounded believable enough; but soon after I saw the same thing, a bargaining between two of the most common men upon a disk of splendid ivory carved most strangely. And I asked some questions, and then some more, and what I learned was this: that the sly and shameless Tristão Caldeira de Rodrigues, under cloak of night and at a time when the Loango people were too concerned with Jaqqas to expend men properly on guarding their holy places, had crept out to the sacred cemetery-place at Loangiri and had despoiled one of the finest of the graves, carrying away a sack of treasure for his private enrichment, and selling off a few pieces to the others to cover certain gambling debts of his.

I suppose it was my place to bring the matter to Faleiro, or to ask counsel of Mendes Oliveira or Pinto Cabral, and not to take it into my own hands. But already had I my choler aroused by this worthless young man, and fate brought him across my path just then before I saw any of the others. And so I taxed him with his crime, and asked if the tale I had heard were true.

He gave me a saucy glare, as though to say, "How dare you reproach me, English clod-grubber, English ruffian!" And shrugged, and would have walked away.

But I took him by the wrist and said, "Answer me, is it so?"

"And if it is, what is that to you?"

"It has great import to me."

"Ah," he said, "you are co-religionist with these blacks, and take it as a sacrilege. Eh? But let me tell you, Englishman, if you touch me on the arm again, or anywhere else, I will put the point of my dagger into your privates, if you have any."

"You talk boldly, boy. Let us see how bold you are, when the demon-*mokisso* of these blacks reaches out, and hurls you into the sea for your impiety."

"What, and do you believe that?" he said, seeming genuinely astounded.

"That I do."

"Nay," he said. "You are a fool, Englishman! There are no demons here! There are no gods! There are only treasures for the taking, and ignorant naked savages who must surrender them to those who are their betters."

I regarded him with much coolness and said, "They tell me you are the son of a duke, and I am only the son of a mariner, so I should not lesson you in matters of courtesy. But I tell you this, that we English peasants, dirty and ignorant though we be, have sufficient respect for the dead, whether they be white or black or green of skin, to let them sleep unperturbed, without going among them to filch away their treasures. That is one matter, and not a trifling one, but it is merely a matter of courtesy, which may not be of importance to you, for you are a duke's son and above all such little fine punctilios."

"Indeed," said he, "I will hear no instruction from you on points of breeding."

"Nor should you. But hear at least this: these people have gods and demons, even as we, and surely those dark beings do guard their holy places. And we are about to undertake our voyage southward in troublesome seas. I tell you, sirrah, that your greed here may well bring a curse upon our voyage, and cost us all our lives: and I will not be pilot on a doomed voyage."

At that he looked somewhat sobered, though his glare was chilly as ever, and the purple birthmark on his cheek did blaze in bright token of his fury at my interfering with him.

I said further, "I will go straightaway to Master Faleiro, and tell him I will not sail, and I will tell him why."

"Will you, now?"

"And if he has also plundered, and cares nothing for what you have done, then so be it: I will remain here, and have my chances with the Jaqqa hordes, and let you all sail pilotless out into whatever fate awaits you."

Caldeira de Rodrigues now did shift his weight from foot to foot, and look most discomforted, and say, "A curse, you think? On an old yard where ancient bones do moulder? Come, Piloto, this is foolishness!"

"Not to me, and I know something of the sea, and I will not go venturing on a ship that bears a man that is marked for the vengeance of the spirits."

"And you will tell this to Faleiro?"

"That I most assuredly will."

He was silent a long while. Then he said, with the gleam of the seducer upon his eye, "I will share with you, half and half, if you will be silent."

"Ah, and allow me to share the curse as well?"

"But who can be sure that there will be a curse?" he cried.

"And who can be sure that there will not?" said I.

Again he considered. And it seemed to me that I had struck deep to his shabby soul, and frighted him: for callous he might be, and airy and mocking, and guided only by his own greeds, but no man can wholly ignore the power of the unseen world, save at his deadly peril. Thus I think a dispute went on within Tristão Caldeira de Rodrigues, in which he did balance his great avarice against his love of life, and bethought himself of the perils of the sea, and, I believe, considered for the first time that there might truly be witch-fires protecting the treasures of the Loango-people's dead ones. I saw all this moving about on the face of that worthless youth, his anger at me for interfering with his theft warring with his own fear of perishing by shipwreck. And I believe also another thing did hold high urgency in his mind, that he was intent on keeping Faleiro from knowledge of his crime, either because he thought he might lose his stolen goods to the master, or that the terms of his exile in Angola were such that he dared not be taken in the act of performing such looting, out of fear of heavy punishment.

At any rate, he did much calculation in very few moments; and then he said, giving me the thoughtful eye, "If I return to the cemetery that which I have taken, will you swear to say nothing to Faleiro?"

"That I will, most heartily."

"And may I believe such an oath?"

"Do you take me for a villain? I have not the fortune to be a duke's son; therefore must I make do with mine honor alone."

"You are a troublesome meddler, Piloto, and a fool."

"But not a rogue, sirrah."

"Keep a civil tongue, or I'll have it out with my blade!"

His threat gave me no unease.

"We were speaking of your returning what you had stolen," quietly I said.

"Aye. And I will put back everything, since you leave me no choice.

But I will exact some kind of payment from you for this. And I will not conceal from you that I despise you sorely for forcing this returning upon me."

"Despise me all you like, good friend," said I, for I saw that he was a coward, and this was all bluster and bravado, and that he was compelled to yield to me. "But at least no curses will be brought down upon my ship for your sake, while I am at sea."

He drew himself up tall, which was not very tall, and put his nose near mine, and said, "I give not the smallest part of a cruzeiro for your fear of curses. I think that is woman-folly, to fret over the vengeance of blackamoor-ape spirits. And so far as the matter of respect for the dead is concerned, why, I have no respect for these monkeys living, so why should I respect the dead ones? But there is this to reflect upon, that your fear of witchcraft is so great you cannot be dissuaded from running to Faleiro with your tale, and if you do that, it will go badly for me. So I could kill you where you stand, or I must return what I have rightfully acquired by my courage and skill. I should kill you, in good sooth. But I think I will not do it. I will take back the treasure."

"I will accompany you," I said.

He glared fire at me then. "Is not my word sufficient?"

"It is a dangerous thing, slipping into that holy place. I will go with you, and stand watch for you, while you restore what you have taken."

I thought then he would indeed make an attempt on me; and I saw his fingers quivering, as though to go to his dagger. I was ready for him. I think he knew that. So although his hatred for me did smoulder and reach almost to the flashing point, yet did he subdue his wrath, which was most wise of him. Together we went to his quarters, where he had secreted in an oaken chest an astonishing array of marvels, all manner of precious gems and little splendid carvings of ivory and the like. Most sullenly did he gather these things, and in my company he took them back to the graveyard, and would have dumped them without ceremony on the open ground, but that I urged him most menacingly to put them below the earth. Which he did; and I think even then he toyed with the idea of murdering me in this lonely place ringed by vast elephanto teeth, but that he was too craven to make the venture. Give him five or six bravos, and surely he would have had them hold me while he slit my gut. But he would not face me alone, and wise of him, aye.

So I had earned his double enmity, both that I was a mere crude Englishman, and that I had compelled him to give up his purloined treasure. I cared nothing for that. One does not go to sea with a man who has called down upon himself the wrath of the invisible world. Those sailors who took the prophet Jonas onto their ship in ancient

times, when Jonas had been disobedient unto the Lord, found themselves
in the midst of a tempest, that did not subside until they cast forth Jonas
into the sea; and so, too, in this instance was I certain that Caldeira de
Rodrigues' plunder of the dead would cause us all to suffer. Therefore
had I risked the loathing of that shoddy and shameless young man, for
it affrighted me far less than the anger of the unknown deities of this
place.

As we took our leave of Loango the city was hectic with concern, and
barely saw us go. The four albino *ndundus* of the king were mounted in
a high station to chant prayers, and various witch-women went about
making sacrifices to the powerful *mokissos* of the nation, and so on, just
as the cathedrals of Europe must keep busy when an onslaught of the
Turks is predicted. Everywhere it was incense and bonfires and drums
and pipes and chanting, with somber-faced Loangan soldiers striding up
and down drilling with their weapons, and so on and on, everyone active
in the preparations for defense against the imagined attack of the onrushing anthropophagi.

Thus we left Loango with our rich cargo of goods and sailed back
toward São Paulo de Loanda. Which had been a very fine voyage for
me, and exceeding instructive in the ways of that foreign land.

THREE

WE STARTED us southward in high good spirits, for our hold was full
and the profit would be great, and there was not one of us but yearned
to be in the capital city again. But though I had gone myself to the
graveyard with Tristão Caldeira de Rodrigues to make him undo his
impiety, yet did it soon become clear that we still had a reckoning of
the most heavy sort to pay for his crime, and that our sturdy little ship
was indeed now accursed.

The wind was good, if strong sometimes beyond our needs, and the
sky was fair as we made our way down the coast. But we were still some
distance north of the mouth of the Zaire when we had an omen of an
ill-fated journey, for at the noon hour one day we came across a fish,
and no one knew what fish it might be. It was like a whale of no great
bigness, somber-looking and evil-countenanced, that frightened away all
the other fish that traveled with the ship. It stayed with us all day, and
the next it was still there, and it left us not at all, but stayed in front of
the vessel throwing up great spurts of water, and peering at us from its
small baleful eyes.

Then a dry sour wind did come from the south, very hard, like water rushing down a gulley, or like a river of air coursing fierce through the air. This wind made us all most impatient with one another, as though it excited a morbid action in our veins. And then there were flashes of lightning above us, but no rain, only a greater and greater dryness.

The Portugals were all much alarmed by that, as was I, for we had only rarely seen lightning without rain, and always it was a boding of nothing fortunate. The air was now so hot and parched that one felt as if one could strike blue sparks by the snapping of the fingers, and that if one were to turn too quickly into the wind, one's clothes would burst into flame.

Faleiro came to me and said, "We must be prepared to strike sail quickly, for this wind could become evil."

"Aye," I said. "If it shifts to westerly, I would fear it, and I pray it does not."

We were vigilant; and still the wind came out of the south, hotter and harder, standing us stock-still in our track. We were well out to sea now, with the coast only a thin faint line. There was much praying aboard the *Infanta Beatriz*, the men dropping to their knees at every slight change in the intensity of the air, and crossing themselves and doing their game with their beads. I also was no stranger to prayer at that time, and I saw even the vile Tristão Caldeira de Rodrigues at his devotions. I looked to him as if to say, "You see? The demons of Loango are searching for the one who did profane the dead!" But he would not meet my gaze at all, and shifted guiltily away. I think he feared I would denounce him to Faleiro, and have him thrown overboard as a Jonas in our midst. In truth the idea did cross my mind. And also it crossed my mind that Rodrigues might forestall such a move on my part by slaying me; so I did not sleep all that night, and kept my weapon close beside me in case he came creeping like an assassin.

Another thing that I considered, but only briefly, was that *I* might be the root and cause of this terrible wind. For was I not carrying a little witchcraft statue that Dona Teresa had made for me, and did I not, from habit, rub it from time to time, which was a kind of veneration? I thought that might have incurred upon me the anger of God, that I should be praying to a heathen deity, and invoking a lust-charm. Once again, as I stood by the rail of the ship, I contemplated throwing my little Teresa-*mokisso* into the water, to spare us from the menace of the sea. But I could not do it. The thing was precious for having come from her hand, and summoned to my mind all the passionate hours we had spent entwined in one another's arms. To cast it overboard was to cast

Dona Teresa overboard: I could not. She held me in her unbreakable grasp.

And had I not already made voyages with this idol by my side, and were we wrecked then? If I were to be punished for idolatry, surely it would long since have happened. So I kept the carving by me, and prayed that I was not thereby taking upon myself the guilt for the death of others.

And the wind rose and rose and rose, and the air grew yet more dry and hot, and then befell what we had all feared, for it shifted and blew out of the west, and drove us willy-nilly across a wild and lurching sea toward the unknown coast. In this violent veering our sails bellied out like the cheeks of Boreas, so that we thought the fabric might not hold, and began to lower them. But before we could, the strong wind ripped the mainsail off its yard. When we saw that we had lost our sail, we all ran to take in the foresail, before it be stripped also. Now the waves which bore down from the west and those which mounted up in the east so swamped us that each time she rocked we thought the ship was going to the bottom; but yet we preferred to risk the waves striking the ship athwart to being left without any sails.

God's blood! How we toiled!

We had not quite finished lowering the foresail when the sea did strike the *Infanta Beatriz* athwart. At the same instant three waves broke over her, so huge that the lurches she gave burst the rigging and the mast beams on the larboard side.

"Cut down the mast!" Faleiro cried.

His words were all but lost in the wind, but no matter: we each of knew what had to be done. We found our axes and set to work felling the mainmast, when it broke away above the rings of the fiddle-blocks, as if we had felled it with one stroke, and the wind threw it into the sea to starboard, as if it were something very light, together with the top and the shrouds. Then we cut the rigging and the shrouds on the other side, and everything fell into the sea.

Being now without our mast or our yards, we made a small mast out of the stump which was left us of the old one, by nailing a piece of a spar to it, and made a yard for a mainsail out of another spar, and so on. But all this was so patched up and weak that a very slight wind would have been enough to carry it all away.

All this happened so swiftly, and amidst scenes of such chaos, that I had scarce any time to reflect on the sad mutilation of our lovely little pinnace, nor on the perils that were mounting about us. But we had some respite after a time, the wind relenting a little; and while we worked, we exclaimed on the turns of fate, that had had us so rich with cargo at one moment, and wondering at the next if we would survive at all. But that is the true life of the sea.

They came round with rum for us as we worked. The man who gave me mine was Caldeira de Rodrigues, and I leaned close and looked him eye to eye and said, "What now, duke's son? Is there not some force striving to repay you for your crime?"

"Keep your voice low."

"Ah, you still worry about your skin! Well, and I think we may all be swimming, before long. Finish your rounds, and go you and ask Jesus for forgiveness."

He gave me a cold look and said, "When this is done, I will have your life from you, Englishman."

"Ah, indeed, I brought the storm to cause you inconvenience, is that it? Go to, scoundrel: anger me enough and I'll send you over the side, and then, I think, the storm will abate! But look at the injury we have suffered for you!"

He moved away, fearing I meant my words, which to some degree I did. But worse injury was coming. For now we were helpless in the sea, though we had cobbled together masts and sails of a sort; and we were being driven onward, and night was coming, and who knew what shoals might rise from the sea to harry us? I went to my charts, but they gave me little news. We were still many leagues out to sea, but these were tropic waters, often shallow where one least expected it, and the charts were sketchy, and there was no pilot alive who knew all these waters, least of all me, so hastily impressed into my office.

Darkness fell. The wind seemed more quiet, and the sea a little still. We talked of the repairs we would make in the morning, and the resumption of our voyage. Some men went to their berths. I remained on watch, with Faleiro the master, and Pinto Cabral. Then the wind rose again, and the sea began to foam, and in the very pit of the night we heard suddenly the terrible sound of the waves breaking on nearby rocks. Then, for our sins and by God's equable and hidden judgment, the *Infanta Beatriz* that we had no way of controlling did run upon a shoal.

"We are lost!" cried Cabral, and I thought he might well be right.

When the ship struck, it gave three great frightful knocks, and at once the bottom of the vessel was cast up above the water because of the extreme roughness of those submerged rocks. I heard the sound of shattering timbers, an awful grinding and splitting sound, and felt the spume and spray pour over me.

The most evil aspect of this wreck was that it befell by night, in such darkness that we could scarce see one another. Men came rushing from the depths of the pinnace, crying out in fear and confusion, for they faced death in the roaring seas with no knowing where safety might lie. The breaking up of the ship, the cracking of the wood which was all being ground to splinters, the falling of masts and spars, made so hideous a clatter and noise that it fair to burst our brains.

Then came another flaring of that rainless lightning, which gave me a moment's vision of our surroundings. We were flung up upon rocks that jutted partly from the sea at this tide, though by the sliming and seaweed of them I could see that within some hours they would be wholly submerged. By a second flash of God's bolt I managed to jump to the nearest of these rocks, and cling to it; and by a third I looked back and saw that though the ship was altogether destroyed, the longboat of her still was intact.

We were thirty or forty men, though, and the longboat would hold perhaps a dozen, and we were some leagues yet from the shore. I turned to gather men to salvage wood for rafts, and stumbled over a figure who lay upon the rocks, groaning: a mariner who had been flung free of the ship in the wreck, doubtless. As I groped for him in the darkness, to which now my eyes were growing a little used, a wave splashed us both, and he began to drift away, and in another moment would have been lost in the night. Though my own life was at risk by so doing, I slipped into the water and, swimming with the greatest difficulty in my heavy boots, did make after him, and catch him by a leg, and draw him in my arms toward the shoal. The lightning came again, and told me that this was Pinto Cabral I had saved, which pleased me, Cabral being a good man. It might just as readily have been Caldeira de Rodrigues for whom I had risked my life, and I was not so fine a Christian that I would have cared to do such a thing.

"The ship is in danger," Cabral did murmur, coming awake now that he breathed air instead of water.

"The ship is entirely destroyed," said I. "But the boat survives. Come, put your arm over my shoulder." And, slipping and sliding upon the sharp rough slimy rocks, we found our way back upon the broken decks. I saw some men striving to lower the boat, and others crowding about it, fighting to get on. There was no sight of Faleiro, which left me in command, as pilot. At once I rushed to the ones who struggled, and cried, "Are you mad? If you all enter the boat, it will go down, and all of you with it! Hold back, let us consider. We are safe here, for the moment."

Yet did they continue to fight like mad wolves to enter the boat. I seized them one by one, and hurled them back, calling upon them to regain their wisdom, and I took some hard blows as I fought to help them keep their lives. But then Faleiro appeared, with a great bloody bruise on his forehead, and stood beside me, and together we were able to bring order.

Though the wind still howled and the sea raged like a ravenous beast, we kept command and took stock of our situation. It seemed that some eight or nine men were dead: some killed in the breakup of the ship, which lay impaled and sundered upon the shoal in the saddest way, and others thrown free like Cabral, and swept off into the night before they could be aided. The others clung to the sides of the boat and we waited for morning. The waves broke very fierce over the reef and fell off at once with great violence to the south-east, in which direction the sea appeared to be running.

In the last hours of darkness there were many tears, and signs of contrition and repentance for sins. I heard them at their litanies and rituals, and asking for God's mercy, which I also did in my own English words. Some waved crucifixes on high, or pictures of the Virgin, and in great weeping asked her to save their souls, for they thought their lives were doomed. But by first light we saw there was some hope. We found the ship's ropes, and out of the planking of the deck commenced the construction of some small rafts, a task that took us less time than I thought it would. Now the storm was gone away, and the day was hot and fair. What was most sad was that the ship was burst open, and some of the vast elephanto teeth were strewn upon the shoal like match-sticks, and our fine fabrics and other good articles of trade; and the rest of the cargo was in the water, beyond all salvaging. Yet were we still alive, most of us, and for that we gave thanks.

When the rafts were built, Faleiro looked to me and said, "Well, Piloto, and can you lead us to shore?"

"I will do my best," said I. "Come, let us take the tide while it is running high, and leave this place at once."

It was agreed that I was to ride in the longboat, since that I was the pilot and must not be lost. Faleiro would command one raft, and Pinto Cabral another, and the third, that was the largest, would be led by a man named Duarte Figueira, who had shown great coolness and strength in the wreck.

The others drew lots, for who was to have the safety of the longboat. Nine were chosen, and they did rejoice greatly, with a kind of crazy jubilation. Also did we stock the boat with such things as we could rescue from the ship, weapons and ropes and tools, but not much. Of food-stores we had scarce any. The tide was now at its fullest, and the shoal was altogether submerged, which freed the rafts and boats, and let us get away: and a good thing, too, for at that moment a great wave came up, and split the ruined *Infanta Beatriz* in sunder, so that the two halves of her fell off and were swiftly carried down, leaving only some part of her hull that was impaled on the rocks.

At the last moment there occurred something that would return to trouble me sorely in after times. For the wave did sweep Cabral's raft close alongside our longboat, and suddenly Tristão Caldeira de Rodrigues, that had a place on the raft, did stand up, looking like a madman with that purple mark of his ablaze on his face, and cried out that he did not intend to die in an uncovered raft that was at the mercy of the sea.

I saw him making ready to jump into the longboat, which was overfull as it was.

"Nay, you may not!" I shouted. "You will swamp us!"

But he was already in mid-leap. We could not have him with us, for we would all be lost. Though Caldeira de Rodrigues was a man of slight build, he carried a sack in his arms, doubtless containing things that in his greed he had saved from the ship, and from the look of his effort it was of great weight. His lunatic leaping would up-end us for sure.

So I did not hesitate. It was no mark of my dislike of him, that which I did: I would have done the same had it been Cabral, or Faleiro, or anyone else, for we could not afford the loss of the longboat. I seized the handle of my oar, and as he sprang through the air I rammed him hard in the belly with it, and thrust him back toward the raft.

He hung in mid-air for a moment like one suspended by a rope, which was a fate I think he richly deserved. His eyes were round with amaze, his mouth was gaping, his birthmark flashed like a beacon-light. Then he fell and dropped beneath the waves, still clutching that sack of his. The longboat, at the same time, tipped far to the side and shipped some water, but righted itself in a moment. I looked down, and thought I saw a glimpse of Caldeira de Rodrigues, and waited for him to bob to the surface. But he did not. Mayhap my blow had knocked the wind from him and stunned him, yet even so he should have floated up in a little time. I think, though, that he held his sack in such a deathly grip that he would not release it, and the weight of it drew him downward and drowned him.

"You will suffer for that if ever we see São Paulo de Loanda again," said a man at my elbow. "His brother is certain to have vengeance."

With a shrug I made reply, "I will face that problem when the time for it comes. If he had reached the longboat, we would all be in the water now with him."

"Aye," said another. "There is truth in that."

We waited a moment or three more, but there was no sign of him. I believe I do know what was in that fatal sack: for I suspect that when he agreed to return his stolen booty to the graveyard, he did keep some of it back without my knowing, and carried it upon the *Infanta Beatriz*, and had it safe in his arms during the wreck, and it was that stuff, so precious, that carried him down to his death. Well, and a proper death it was, if so be the case: for I think it was the curse on the grave-robber that brought the storm onto us, and caused the loss of our ship and all its treasure, and took the lives of some innocent men.

FOUR

AND SUCH was the piteous end of our joyous and prosperous voyage to Loango. Now, under a cloudless and merciless sky that gave us no surcease from the terrible hammer of the tropic sun, we made our way landward in our distress. But some worse horrors even were yet awaiting us.

By God's great mercy, the wind was out of the west, and not an evil one, and we rowed our boat and poled our rafts in brisk order. Soon the shore was clear in view. From the look of it, and my memory of the coast as we went northward, we were perhaps midway between Loango and the mouth of the Zaire, and how we ever would get back to São Paulo de Loanda I did not know. But I gave that question little heed: sufficient unto the day was the evil thereof.

Though we managed to remain in close formation most of the journey, the raft commanded by Duarte Figueira veered somewhat to the north-ward as we neared the land, and, try as he might, he could not make headway back nigh to us. At the time that seemed of little consequence, for we thought we could reunite on the shore: but in fact that separation of his raft from us led to a sore and tragic calamity in a little while.

The current now ran swiftly north-easterly, and our rowing and poling were no longer of avail. We were simply swept up and carried toward the shore, and had no say in our going, and merely prayed that we would not be cast up on some fanged rocks. Nor did that befall us, for when we were close we saw that the shore here was flat and sandy, with a good many little spits and islands and peninsulas of low stature, the product of some inner river, much like the isle of Loanda in the harbor of São Paulo de Loanda. So we glided to an easy landing, the longboat and Faleiro's raft and Cabral's at one such spit, and Figueira's at another, with perhaps three hundred yards of open water separating him from us. We unloaded our pitiful little goods, and cried out to them, "Come over! Let us all be together!" But when they attempted to pole their raft to our place, they could not achieve it: the water was too shallow, and the pole became mired as it were in a quicksand. And when they tried to come about to us from the landward end, it was the same thing. The landward side of their spit was all muck, and they could not pass.

So there we were in two parties, come to land on a pair of sandy spits that jutted out like the two prongs of the letter V from the true shore, with shallow open water between them, and impassable swamp at the inner end. Well, and we could rest awhile, I thought, and then return to our rowing, and move on along the coast to some more hospitable place.

Meanwhile we foraged on our little spit for anything that might be useful to us, for we had salvaged not much in the way of edible stuffs from the wreck. Some flagons of wine, a bit of cheese, some quince jelly, some waterlogged bread: that was about the whole of it, and it would not last two days.

"What do you find?" I asked Cabral and Faleiro, when we came together from our foraging.

Their faces were dark. "Small serpents," said Cabral. "A kind of rat. Some crabs."

"And a few sprigs of bush," said Faleiro, "with no fruit upon them."

"Well, then we will be eating snakeskins and toasted bones before long," Cabral said, making a smile on it, though we all knew it was no jest but the truth.

"And after that," said I, "we will be eating one another."

"Ah, and are you a Jaqqa, to say such a thing?" Faleiro demanded sourly.

"God forbid," said I. "Let us take our lives, before it come to that!"

Yet sometimes in jest the most frightful things are foretold.

We made a melancholy cold meal, and wandered our little kingdom, and waited for night, and slept poorly, and waited for morning. And morning, when it came, revealed a monstrous thing. For although it had not been possible for us to reach the land by crossing the quicksand, certain folk had been able to come the other way, at least on the adjoining point where Figueira and his seven or eight companions were. I was looking idly out to sea, and dreaming of a vessel that would come to rescue us, when Cabral grasped my arm most fierce and cried, "Look! Across the way!"

"Jesu preserve us," I said.

For a demonic band of dark naked figures now surrounded our companions on the other spit. Like revelers out of Hell had come some dozens of long-legged graceful men, who pranced and capered in a weird dance, throwing out their arms and legs with evident glee, and circling round and round.

"Mother of God!" said Faleiro, in a voice like that of one who is being garroted. "They are Jaqqas!"

And so they were, and now a true nightmare unfolded before our eyes, nor could we wake from it, but must witness every grisly ghastly moment.

How the man-eaters had come out onto the point, God alone can say. Perhaps they knew some path through the quicksanded pitfalls, or else they had come swimming up from the other side, or in boats: I never knew, I cannot tell you now. But they were there, and as our hapless shipmates knelt and prayed most fervently, the cannibals fell upon them, one by one slitting their throats.

We could do nothing. Our only weapons were knives and swords, that were of no use at such a distance.

"Blood of the saints!" roared one grizzled old Portugal of our band. "We must save them!" And he went struggling out into the water, brandishing a blade in each hand; but he got no more than a dozen yards, and found himself mired up to the knees, and it was all he could do to return to shore. At which the Jaqqas looked up from their slaughter, and gestured mockingly to us, and laughed, and called out as though to say, "Wait ye your turn there, and we will come and have you next!"

And so we watched. And cursed, and raved, and shook our fists, and were utterly helpless.

Our friends were entirely slain. Figueira himself was the last, a tall and noble-looking man of silvered hair, who called upon Heaven to avenge him, and then the long knives went into him. And after the killing came worse, the butchery and the cooking. God's truth, it was a terrible sight, much more grievous than that other cannibal feast I had witnessed long ago in Brazil, for these were men I knew by name, that had only just survived a dread ordeal by sea, and did not merit such a fate as the next thing. From scraps of wood and old dried seaweeds and the like the Jaqqas did build a fire, and cut our men into several parts, some three or five of them, and roasted them before our eyes, and sat crosslegged in a merry way, gnawing at haunches. God's death! I was thankful only that some hundreds of yards of open water separated us from them, not so much that it gave us safety, but that we did not see that dread feasting at any closer range. For it was vile enough, at that distance.

It went on and on, the roasting and the eating. And I think that the worst of it all was that in our starved state, the aroma of that roasting meat did arouse in us a hunger despite our horror, so that our mouths ran with rivers of spittle and our stomachs griped and yearned. And what monstrousness was this, to stir with such famine at the smell of man's cooking flesh? But so starved were we that we could not tell ourselves it was unholy to yearn for some of that meat: it could have been mere pork, for all that our ignorant noses were able to tell.

I know not how many hours the ghastly feast proceeded. But at length it was over; and the Jaqqas rose, and slung over their shoulders the bodies of those men whom they had not consumed, and in their ghostly way did steal away, over a little rise in the sandy spit, and vanished on the other side.

"They will come to us next," said Faleiro in gloom.

"I think they are sated for now," I said.

"Ever looking on the brighter side, eh, Piloto?" said he. And it was true, in good sooth: for what value is it to take ever the darkest outlook? We placed guards, and for all the rest of the time we dwelled in that place we looked out day and night for the coming of the Jaqqas. But they did not come, either because they could not reach our shore as readily as they had the other, or because they had satisfied their needs here and now were journeying to some far destination to perform the next of their foul celebrations.

Yet it was hard enough, living there, to walk about with the memory so bright in us of what we had witnessed. A thousand times I wished I had looked away, and closed my eyes, while that feast was happening. But I could not; none of us could; we had witnessed every terrible instant of it, and it blazed now, and for long afterward, in my soul.

After a few days, though, it began to seem to us that our fallen companions were the fortunate ones. For there was next to nothing to eat in that place, and if we had not had the good luck to locate a spring of fresh water we would have died a death even more frightsome than theirs. As it was, we were hard put to live, and Cabral's jest was amply fulfilled, for we were reduced to such things as gnawing on bones, and chewing scraps of snakeskin, and sucking roots. I thought often of the hardships I had known since leaving England, and nothing seemed worse than this, though perhaps I was mistaken in that: but the hardship of the moment often seems far greater than those endured in other days. I lay staring out to sea, much, and dreamed of home, and sometimes of Anne Katherine and sometimes of Dona Teresa, whose amulet I took from my pocket and studied long. But the sight of it, its breasts and cleft of sex and smooth shining buttocks, did stir distressing desires in me that I could not fulfill, and I regretted bringing it forth. And also did I continue to wonder whether I should be carrying such a talisman at all, it being forbidden by my church and by God Himself to place faith in idols.

Well, and that evil time ended, as all evil times of my life have late or soon come to their end. A vessel out of São Tomé, going south on business to São Paulo de Loanda, passed that way and saw the timbers of the *Infanta Beatriz* upon the shoal; and, thinking there might be survivors, approached the shore, where the hand of God directed it to us. So were we rescued, and given food and clothing, and a place to sleep, and bit by bit we began to recover from our ordeal. And as we neared São Paulo de Loanda I felt almost myself again. But within my mind now forever were certain images and pictures I would gladly have scraped out. I saw, and still see, Tristão Caldeira de Rodrigues hanging suspended in mid-air after I had struck him with my oar; and I saw the dark teeth of the shoal by lightning-flare, with our tight little pinnace wrecked upon it; and I saw, most bitter and painful of all, the demon Jaqqas dancing about our crewfellows, and slaying them, and falling to most heartily on their flesh. Ah, what a world it is, I thought, that has such wolves in human guise loose upon it!

So I was of somewhat a brooding mood by the end of that voyage, which had begun so well. But it is not my nature to dwell morosely on darker things, and I was glad enough to be alive, when I came stepping ashore at São Paulo de Loanda.

I found that much had altered in that city during my absence.

The new governor, Don Francisco d'Almeida, had begun to put his mark upon the place. The slopes of the hill leading up to the high fortress were bustling with fresh constructions. Thousands of blacks did toil under the terrible blaze of the torrid sun, building a palace for the governor far more majestic than the old one, and homes also for the governor's brother, Don Jeronymo d'Almeida, and for the various other great fidalgos who had accompanied this governor out from Portugal. All these were very grand structures of lime and stone hauled from great distances and covered with tiles of Lisbon, very dignified and awesome, much enhancing the look of the city; for the whiteness of the lime and the merry blue and yellow of the tiles did dance most playfully upon the eye in the bright sunlight. Down below there were many other dwellings a-building, and barracks for the hundreds of new soldiers that Don Francisco had brought with him to Angola. This work had been accomplished at no little cost of native lives. For although all seasons are hot in that place, the rainy season often is more hot and evil than the dry one, and d'Almeida had compelled his people to work regardless of any heat, so that many of them fell in their tracks and died, for all that they were accustomed to such a clime. This I learned from Don

João de Mendoça, who by now had taken me as a sort of confidant. "They bury a dozen blacks a day," he said, with a scowl, "and still d'Almeida shows no restraint. He wants his palace done by winter."

"Is the man mad?"

"Nay, Andres, not mad, only stupid. Very, very, very stupid." Don João looked at me long and deep. "That is no way to treat one's work-men." I remembered that Don João was the man who had in an angry moment dashed a bowl of spiced sauce into the eyes of a careless slave. But then he added, "It is wasteful to work all those men to death, for some of them have skills that will be not easy to replace," and I under-stood that Don João's objections were objections of economy, not of morality. He laughed and said, "Still, one day Don Francisco will be gone from here, and his palace will remain for the using of his successors. I suppose that's something good to come out of this."

Don João did not need to tell me that he had great hopes of dwelling in that palace himself. Anyone with eyes would know of the rivalry between him and d'Almeida: Don João the stronger and shrewder man, Don Francisco the holder of the royal commission. That the governorship should have gone to Don João upon its last vacancy, no one in Angola did doubt; but Don Francisco was higher born, and he had the better connections in the mother country. It was cunning of Don João to make no show of resentment at having been passed over for the governorship, yet must it have been bitter for him, since suddenly Angola was full of new men, the satraps of Don Francisco, and these must also stand between him and true power in the colony. This Don João concealed from me, for he was not one to protest openly his dissatisfactions.

When we were done with these matters, the talk turned to my sor-rowful voyage. Here he had lost grievously, since he was a major owner of the cargo that had gone down with the pinnace; but again he made light of that matter.

"There will be other voyages," said he. "And I trust you will play a great part in them, for I have heard much from Faleiro of your valor and skill."

"The skill is what I inherit from my father," I answered. "As for the valor, it was only what was needful to save my life."

"And the life of others, so I am told. All the men do speak highly of you."

"Glad am I to have earned their respect."

"Their respect, and more. For on your next sailing, you shall have a share in the proceeds. It is not right, to send a man off at risk of his life to be pilot for us, and not let him claim his just part of the return."

This surprised me greatly, that the Portugals would divide a share for me. But I gave him only warm thanks, and not a hint of any ungracious thought.

He said, "Tell me of the events of your voyage, Andres, before the wreck."

The which I did, in much detail, dwelling hard on the strange things that had occurred while I was in the land of Loango. Of the rainmaking and the great coccodrillo he took but light notice; it was the tale of the dead Jaqqa that most aroused him. He had me describe it in every detail. When I mentioned the white cross that was painted on the cannibal prince's chest, he slapped the table, and roared out loud, crying, "By the Mass! They are jolly devils, those Jaqqas!"

I saw nothing jolly about them: to me they were devils, and hyaenas, or wolves in human form. But peradventure Don João had never seen them feeding on his shipmates.

I said, "What meaning has the cross to them? Surely they be not Christians."

"Why, no, surely not. And it has no meaning for them, I suppose, but they find it a pretty thing. Or else they mean to mock us. Or perhaps they are become Jesuits, and that is their new sign of office. No one understands why the Jaqqas do the things they do. I think they are not human. But none of these blackamoors have any much sense of real Christianity, no matter what they babble in the church of a Sunday. Do you know, Andres, that when I was in Kongo I often saw good Christian Negroes putting the holy cross to pagan use? In one place there was a pile of horns of wild animals surrounded by branches, a sort of altar, and a cross was mounted above it. It is an ancient superstition of theirs that they can witch their animals when hunting them, with piles of horns, and it must have seemed to them that the cross would be an even more powerful *mokisso*, so they added it to the pile. I thought it clever of them."

"And I, too, Don João. Why not use all the superstitions one can find, when one is hungry?"

He raised his eyebrows at me and I thought he would be angry, but then he eased somewhat.

"The cross is to you a superstition, then?"

Uncomfortably I said, "We are taught in England that Jesus died on the cross for our sins, even as it is taught by the Roman way. But we believe that it is Jesus who is holy, and not the wood on which He died. We have cast aside our old images and idols."

"Have you now," said Don João. "And does it not frighten you, to live without their protection?"

"It was but false protection, sir. For when we destroyed our holy relics, our images of the saints, and the like, there was no plague come upon England, nor any vengeance of our enemies, but rather we have prospered and grown far wealthier than we were in the old days, and when King Philip sent his Armada, we were not harmed, but—"

"Yea," said Don João darkly. "I wonder why it is, that the Lord encourages such heresies as England's. But be that as it may: we are far from such quarrels here. I showed the hunter's cross to a priest, who grew all indignant, and broke it and burned it to pieces, saying it was blasphemy to use it so, and perhaps it was. Well, let the priests burn the Jaqqas as blasphemers, too, if they can catch any. Have you seen these Jaqqas, Andres? Other than the dead one at Loango?"

I looked upon him in amaze, and cried, "Have they not told you, that they devoured some of our men, after we had been cast up on shore?"

"Nay, not a word!"

I found myself atremble from the recollection. "It was the most fright-some thing I ever saw. They appeared like phantoms, in a place ringed round by quicksand, and fell upon the stranded men, and slew them, and—" With a shudder I said, "I saw it all. But need I paint it for you now?"

"I was told only that many men were lost in the wreck."

"That was how half the dead man perished, to the appetites of Jaqqas, after they had escaped the wrath of the sea."

And I looked away, that he might not see how pale I was, nor how shaken by the dread memory.

He seemed unaware of my emotion, for he went on talking in the lightest way, saying, "They are bold fellows. Perfect savages, with not a trace of humanity in them. I saw some, once, that we hired to do a battle on our behalf—for they will hire themselves out, you know, when the mood takes them. They were like a band of devils, so that I kept looking to their shoulders, to see if the black wings did sprout there. Yet were they well behaved and quiet. I hear they keep a market in their territory somewhere inland where man's flesh is sold for meat, like sheep and oxen, by the weight. By the Mass, I wonder what method they use for its cookery, whether they stew it, or roast it, or bake in an oven!" He patted his ample stomach. "God forfend it, Andres, but sometimes— sometimes—I am curious about its flavor. I confess that thing to you that I would not tell even my confessor, and I know not why, except that I think you are a man to my humor. Would you eat man's flesh?"

"I have seen it done, Don João, when I was a captive of wild Indians in Brazil. I was not tempted." I would tell him nothing of the effect that the smell of the roasting meat had upon me, when I was so hungered on that sand-spit.

"And if your life depended on it?"

"I think it would not," said I staunchly. "I could live well enough on roots and leaves and berries, and the small beasts of the wilderness."

"Nay, I mean, if you were told, Eat this meat or we will slay you, and the meat were man's flesh?"

"A strange question, Don João."

"I do put it to you."

With a shrug I said, "Why, then, I think I would eat of it, if I must! May God spare me from that choice, though."

"You *are* to my humor!" he cried. "Wiser to eat than to be eaten, ever! Come, Andres, have some wine with me. And then to your own amusements." He poured me a brimming goblet of sack and said, handing it to me, "Will the Jaqqas attack Loango?"

"I cannot say. The Loango people fear it greatly."

"You have heard the tales of that time when the man-eaters struck at São Salvador in the Kongo, have you not?"

"The time when the king of that land was fain to flee to the Hippopotamus Isle?"

"Aye. In '69, it was. They will come here some day, Andres. They will come everywhere, in time. They are God's own scourge, loosed upon the world." He said this mildly, as though he might be talking about the coming of a breeze from the west, or a light shower of rain. "I think they mean to eat their way from nation to nation, until they have devoured all the world. They have a king, Imbe Calandola by name, whose appetite is said to be limitless. Why is it, do you think, that such destroyers are spawned among us again and again? The Turks, the Mongols, the Huns of old, the Assyrians of whom the Bible tells us—now the Jaqqas, and their grand devil Imbe Calandola, are the latest of that sort. They speak for something that exists within us all, do you not think? Eh, Andres? That love of destruction, that joy of doing wrong? God's own scourge! There is a beauty in such evil. Eh, Andres? Eh? Here: have more wine." He sat back, laughing to himself, scratching his belly. He was very far gone in his cups, I did perceive. His speech was thickened, his meanings monstrous. I did not know what to reply in the face of such amazing words. We were silent a time, and then he declared, "I will find me a few tame Jaqqas, Andres. And I will feed them on some useless Portugals to make things more quiet in this city. I will let them take a meal of Jesuits first, I think. And then the whoreson fool d'Almeida and his poxy friends. Hah! And my own cook shall brew the sauces for them, that is a master of his art." He laughed, and drank, and laughed, and drank. I watched, wondering. Before long, I did feel certain, he would fall asleep of his own drunkenness. But instead Don

João did quite the opposite, sitting up in his chair and pushing his wine-glass aside, and saying to me in altogether a sober voice, no longer slurred nor strange, "There is much trouble here between Don Francisco and the Jesuits, and it will grow worse. I tell you, the man is stupid. He does not know how to handle those priests, and soon there will be open warfare between him and them."

"Will priests take up arms, then?"

"Nay, I mean no actual war. But some kind of struggle is sure, and it will disrupt our lives. You know, the Jesuits came to Angola in the days of Paulo Dias, and they have always had a hand in governing here. Dias was strong and wise, and he kept control over them by consulting them in all matters of state, and letting them believe that they were high in his councils. Serrão, when he was governor, and Pereira after him, had so deep a barrel of other problems that they paid the Jesuits no heed, which let the priests collect new powers unto themselves. This, d'Almeida has tried to curb, and he is doing it the wrongest way, as he does everything. He threatens the Jesuits, and he should be seducing them."

"In what way," did I ask, "do the priests seek power?"

"Why, by claiming that the blacks are their spiritual flock, and they must be the sole shepherds of them. Already they make intrigue to construct themselves the only intermediaries between the governor and the native chiefs, so that in a short time the chiefs would do the bidding of the Jesuits, and not the governor."

"But that would mean that the Jesuits would command this country!"

"That is my meaning in precise, Andres. They would relegate to the governor the power to make war and defend our frontiers, and keep all else of substance to themselves. And soon we would need no secular authority here at all, for the holy fathers would have builded themselves into the great power of the land. Well, and d'Almeida does not like that, and for that I applaud him: but now he schemes to forbid the Jesuits to meet with the chiefs at all. That is not the way. They must gradually be taken out of power, so gradually that they do not themselves understand what is happening to them."

"Is such a thing possible, to cozen a Jesuit?" I asked. "We are taught in England that there is no one subtler nor more crafty than a member of that sly confraternity."

"Yea. They are diabolical, Andres. They are veritable Jaqqas of the Church. Still, they *can* be controlled. Paulo Dias knew how to do it. I know how to do it."

"And how do matters lie now?"

"We have had a meeting of the governing council. D'Almeida announced that the Jesuits have been using their spiritual influence most shiftily to induce the friendly chiefs to withhold obedience from the civil powers, and he did call for authority to deal with that. Which was granted him, by a vote of his brother and his cousins and other such leaders, I voting contrary. Now will he proclaim, this day, that any Jesuit seen entering the camp of a chief or holding conference with one is to be hanged."

"What, hang a priest?" I exclaimed.

"It will not come to that. The priests are too strong for him. They will break him, Andres. Which would not be so bad except that we are surrounded by enemies in this land, and we have wasted years since the death of Dias, gaining no advantage for ourselves. Leadership is what we need here, not poltroonish squabblings of this kind."

"Aye," I said, knowing what leader he did have in mind.

"But if d'Almeida falls, there will be months or even years of fresh turmoil before order is restored. We can ill afford that. Let me explain to you, Andres, how I do believe we must conduct ourselves, if we are to achieve our purposes here."

And so he expounded, at some great length. But I had lost interest in the details of all these intrigues. The moment he had spoken of the wasting of years, I was most forcibly and poignantly brought to reflect upon my own waste of years as a captive here, and I fell to brooding, paying him no heed. He did drone on and on about the iniquities of Don Francisco, and the remedies he proposed for them, and I listened little, so that he took me by surprise when suddenly he said, "And what is this, Andres, have you committed murder?"

"Sir?" said I, startled.

"There is to be an inquest upon you, I am told. You are charged with the wanton slaying of Tristão Caldeira de Rodrigues, that was a man of high birth."

"He was a scoundrel, and a thief!"

"Well, and if he was? His blood was royal, or close to it. Come, Andres, what is this crime? You may be open with me. I knew the man a little: there was no merit to him. Yet if you have indeed slain him—"

"I took his life," said I wearily, "but it was to save the lives of many other men. It was not murder. When that we were wrecked, he essayed to force his way into a longboat that was already too crowded, and I drove him back, and he fell to the water and drowned."

"Ah," said Don João, pouring more wine.

"Drowned, furthermore, because he would not let go his hold of the treasure-sack he clutched in his hand, that was full with the precious goods he had stolen from the grave-site of the kings of Loango, and weighed him down, so that he went under. It was the stealing of these things, moreover, that I think did lead to the downfall of us all: for angry demon-gods did send hot dry winds upon us, and rip away our sails and drive us onto a secret shoal, all in the midst of a fair and pleasant day."

"Ah. Ah," said he. "Ahah."

And for a long while he sat with his eyes closed, and held his wine-cup close against his chest, and I thought he had fallen to sleep, so sluggish and slow was he from all his drinking. But then he looked about at me and said, "Was it truly as you say?"

"Upon mine honor."

"Then it is true," he said. "Be there witnesses?"

"Ample, unless their fear of the dead man's brother brings them to lie against me."

Don João nodded. "The brother. Aye. It is the brother who brings this charge: Gaspar Caldeira de Rodrigues. Another worthless man, a pestilent rogue. He will cause you much difficulty, for he is bent on vengeance."

"And will I be prisoned again for this? I tell you, sir, if I am, I would rather die first: and take this Gaspar with me, when I do go."

"Prison? It could be, if the inquest finds against you."

"Then I will slay him!"

"Soft, soft, Andres. There is the inquest, first. Over which I think I shall preside." He stretched out his hand toward me and smiled and said, "We must arrive at the truth. But I think I know it already: for I do know you, and I somewhat know Gaspar. And I would not readily part with my Piloto." He yawned most broad, and belched, and rubbed his swelling belly. "Go, now, Andres. I grow torpid now, and would rest. We will talk on these matters another time. Go: and beware. This Gaspar makes an evil enemy, and he may not wait for the inquest to have his vengeance."

I left him and returned to the small house that they had given me, a pleasant one on the seaward side of town, where good winds often blew. Mine eyes I did keep sharp, lest Brother Gaspar and his comrades spring out at me with drawn swords, but it did not happen. I was in a troubled mood, over this inquest, yet I was not greatly surprised, knowing the influence Gaspar Caldeira de Rodrigues wielded here. Yet the truth would be my defense, and I had the support, so I fervently hoped, of Don João de Mendoça, and though truth alone might not be sufficient, the strength of that most powerful fidalgo might perhaps see me through.

As I made my way to my dwelling I saw some proclamation being read in the great square, with soldiers standing to attention, and much ceremony. I neared it and discovered that it pertained to intercourse between the Jesuits and the native chiefs. But I was tired, and did not care to hear more just then on that subject. Turning homeward, I lay down and slept a time, and then came a soft rapping at my door, in the night.

I parted the curtain and saw Dona Teresa in the darkness.

"You come so late?" I asked, for it was not like her.

"Don João is elsewhere."

"Nay, I saw him only at midday."

"That was at midday. Tonight he is in conference with the governor and the council, and it will last for hours. Oh, Andres, Andres, will you not ask me in? I feared so much for you! When they said your ship was lost, how I grieved, how I mourned! And how I prayed!"

"To Jesus and Mary, or to your *mokisso?*"

"Mock me not," she said sharply, half wounded, and half angered. "Let me in!" And she thrust herself through the door and into my arms.

In the short while since my return we had not been alone together even once, though I had passed her one time on the plaza, and at a distance we had exchanged a cautious glance and a secret smile. Now she slid against me and greeted me with a tigerish hungry kiss. She wore only the lightest of wraps, moist from a gentle rain that was falling. She raked her fingers fiercely down my bare skin, and drew her breasts across my chest. There was heat coming from her. I cupped her round teats and found her nipples swollen and firm, and she made a little hissing noise as I did tenderly squeeze them.

"Andres!" she cried. "Oh, I prayed! I longed for you so!"

"As did I for you."

"Truly?" said she, and her eyes held an inquest most severe. "Did you think on me at all?"

"Constantly." I brought forth her little statue, that I had stroked so often, and held it high. "A thousand times did I touch this witchy thing, and tell myself it was your breasts I touched, and not a piece of wood!"

"Ah. I feared for you, all the time you were in Loango. It is a dangerous place."

"It seemed not like that to me."

"They are not Christians there. They hold to strange ways."

"And you, the maker of idols, you are Christian?"

"Yes!" she cried, in deep wrath. "Never say I am other!"

"But the idol—"

"A precaution," she said. "I am Christian, but I discard nothing valuable."

We stood only inches apart, both so crazed with desire that we could not move, but went on chattering. She told me fifty times how she had died deaths for me, and prayed to every god of Africa as well as all the saints and the Madonna that I would not be harmed in Loango or perish on the sea, and I told her how I had tossed and twisted in desire for her. And yet we did not move. Until at last she let her light wrap fall to the ground, and she urged me impatiently toward my rumpled bed, and I followed in haste.

The rain became less gentle, and drummed the thatch of my dwelling with much vigor. In my nostrils was the scent of Dona Teresa's body, harsh, acrid, the lust-scent that all animals do have, and at that moment she seemed no more than an animal, sleek, quick, a thing of the jungle. She lay down and planted the soles of her feet upon the bed, and flexed her back so that her buttocks were in the air and her body arched. By the dim light of my single candle I saw her taut and spread for me, a dark foreign creature with every muscle quivering, the strength of her thighs showing in the contours of them, and the jet-black hairy diadem between them pulling me like a lodestone. I went to her and fell on her and into her in almost a single motion, and she relaxed the torsion of her frame and eased us both down to the surface of the bed, and there we lay motionless a moment, content merely to have our bodies joined again after so long a sundering. Her eyes gleamed with a wantoning.

Now that we were united some urgency went from her, and slyly she said, holding her hands to my hips to keep me from movement, "Had you many black maidens whilst you were north?"

"Nay, not a one."

"Ah, perfectly chaste, Andres!"

"I was not allured by what I did see."

"Swear it by God's Mother!"

"I will swear by God Himself, I entered no woman's body."

"You lie," said she coolly and pleasantly, beginning now to pump her hips in a slow, steady, maddening way. "You had a dozen of them, little ebony wenches with sweet hard breasts, and you never thought once of me. I can still smell the smell of them upon you. I can see the marks of their little bites on your shoulders."

"Then you see with witch-eyes, for there are no marks."

"What are these?" she asked, and touched me in a place where I had scraped my arm on barnacles when scrambling upon the rocks of the shoal that had wrecked us.

"I fought with a coccodrillo last week," I told her, "and it nipped me once or twice before I split his jaws in twain."

"Ah," she said. "I am relieved of all my fears. Better you hug a coccodrillo than a wench of Loango, eh?" And she laughed, and I laughed with her, though this pretended jealousy of hers seemed something more than mere pretense to me, beneath its outward playfulness, and that was discomfortable to me. But she moved her body in a changing rhythm now, ever swifter, and I ceased thinking of anything at all save the conjunction of our flesh. I drove deep to the center of her and the little quivering motions of her ecstasy did begin within her and a new scent arose from her, a sea-scent, musky and tangy, as the discharge of her pleasure commenced. Though it had been many weeks since I had known such discharge myself, I held myself in check, waiting her out until the highest moment of her ascent, and then, releasing all control, shouting out into the low strange bestial growl of her delight, I did give myself up to the completion of our loving, which went through me like the force of a hammer's blows. And I fell athwart her, panting, sweaty, laughing giddily, and we held one another, and rolled from side to side, and lightly slapped each other and kissed and pinched. The world seemed calm and full on her course now. For when man and woman love, and pass together through the fulfillment of that loving by the flesh, they enter out of the world of turbulence into a new and silent realm of tranquility that might almost be of a higher sphere of existence, so I do think. Would that we could remain there forever, as the angels do in their crystalline abode! But then, I suppose, we would never know the joy of the ascent, if we dwelled always above the clouds.

After a time we slipped our bodies apart and Teresa, rising from the bed, stepped naked outside the house to douse herself in the rain. She returned clean and glistening and said, "I must leave now. When Don João sends for me tonight, I must be in my own bed as his messenger comes."

"This conference you spoke of—"

"It is about the Jesuits," she said. "You heard this afternoon's proclamation?"

"Very little of it. Don João told me there is strife between the governor and the Jesuits."

"Indeed. D'Almeida has decreed that any Jesuit who meets with a *soba* must die."

"So was I told."

"There is more. When the decree was read, and nailed to the door of the priests' residence, the Jesuit Prefect Affonso Gomes did tear it off, and burn it. And sent word that he would excommunicate the governor, if he persevered at this." She frowned and said, "Is that painful, to be excommunicated?"

"It means only to be cut off from the sacraments of the Church," I said.

"Yes, that I do know. Forbidden to take the Mass, and no confession, no absolution, none of the rites of birth or marriage or death. But is that all? I have heard of this excommunication, but I have never seen the thing done. Is it done with whips?"

"It is done with words alone," I said.

"Ah," said she, and peradventure she was a trifle disappointed. "Then there is no peril in it?"

"But there is," said I. "It is not only that one is deprived of the whole rigmarole of piety that the Catholic faith does adhere to. But all Christians must scorn the excommunicated one, and turn away, and give him no aid, even if he lie bleeding and broken in a ditch. Did you not know that?"

"I have been taught these things, but when I was a girl. We have had no excommunication here, Andres. Why, even if there be no whips, still it sounds like a very grave thing!"

"So I do suppose. But much depends on the effectuality of the powers of the excommunicator. When our King Henry denied the authority of the Pope, in the matter of putting aside his first wife Catherine, the King was indeed excommunicated, but we in England paid no heed to that. And again another Pope did excommunicate our good Elizabeth, when I was a boy, for issuing us a prayer-book and giving us Protestant bishops. But once more it was like the mere blowing of the wind to us, and had neither meaning nor substance."

This bewildered Dona Teresa, who after all was a Catholic if she was any sort of Christian, and knew nothing of our heretical ways, excepting that we had contempt for the Pope. I suppose she could not rightly be called a pagan, for she had been reared truly in her Church and had received its sacraments and all of that, but yet I knew, from her faith in idols and witchcraft, that it was only skin-deep to her, as it is to all these converted folk of tropic lands. She knew which was the Virgin Mary and which the Savior, and other grand things of the creed, but I suspect that the nice points of doctrine were cloudy and murky to her, and had no real essence, other than that her mother and father had told her to hold God in awe. Perhaps I do her an injustice: perhaps the priests of the Kongo had made a true and deep Catholic of her. I know not. Could she hold that faith and the pagan one of her black grandmothers with equal force? I think she was capable of that: nay, I do know it! I think she had as much doubt of my faith as I did have of hers, and admitted me to be a Christian only because she did not know what else I might be deemed. For I appeared to believe in God and His Son in a right Christian manner, yet the Pope, that was her grand *mokisso*, was only the blowing of the wind to me.

At my door she said, "They tell me there is a quarrel between you and Gaspar Caldeira de Rodrigues."

"So it appears."

"And is it true, that you slew his younger brother?"

"I caused his death, that I admit." And I told her how it had befallen. "But I accept no blame for it. Do you know this Gaspar?"

"A little," said she.

"Is he as cowardly as his dead brother?"

"Of that I know nothing. He is a clever man, and ambitious. Walk carefully until this matter is resolved, for I think he would harm you."

"Then pray for my welfare, as though I were in peril on the sea."

Her eyes glistened. "I will do more than pray. I will use all the unseen forces at my command, against his malevolence."

"Ah, then you admit to witching!"

She put her finger to my lips. "Not a word of that! But I will guard you." Then most shamelessly did she caress my manhood with her wanton hand, so that I would have drawn her back to the bed, but she would not let it. "Until next time, my love!" And she was gone.

I thought for some while of all these troubled matters, the inquest, and Don João's struggle with the new governor, and the doings of the Jesuits. But then it all fell from my mind, this squabbling among tricksome and quarrelsome Portugals, this Papist tug-of-war for power over the pitiful blacks whom they had so cozened and gulled and enslaved and exploited. I dropped into a sound sleep, and was gone from the world well into the morning. And when I awoke I did know at once, from the uncommon silence of the city, that something notable had occurred.

I dressed and took my breakfast, which was brought me by one of the slaves assigned me by Don João—I, a miserable prisoner, did have three slaves as servants!—and went forth into the center of things and looked about. The grand plaza was all but empty. A platoon of soldiers marched back and forth before the compound of the Jesuits, on which some new proclamation had been nailed. High above, at the presidio, other soldiers drilled. All work had ceased on the new constructions along the slopes, and very few natives could be seen anywhere. I thought to go to Don João's palace to discover the turn of events, but I was halted by the captain of the guards, Fernão da Souza, who emerged suddenly from the commissary and said, "You would do well to stay to your house today, Englishman."

"What has happened?"

"The governor has confined the Jesuits to their quarters, and says he will put to death any of the priests that comes into view. Father Affonso is said to be preparing a writ of excommunication against the governor, and shortly may appear to proclaim it in the plaza."

"Madness!" said I.

"Which, the governor's decree, or the prefect's?"

"Both. What will be done when the priest steps forth. Is he to be shot down on his own doorstep?"

Captain da Souza—credit him with that much—did look dismayed greatly. "No one knows, my friend. We do not shoot priests. We do not disobey our governor. But we cannot hold faith with both factions at once."

"If you were a common soldier," I said, "and you were told to shoot down a priest, would you obey?"

"I think not," he said after some pause.

"Well, then, Governor d'Almeida is lost."

"So do we believe. But there may be deep dispute before that becomes clear to him, and I think there will be fighting, for the governor, when that he came from Portugal, brought troops who may be more loyal to him than to any Jesuits. We shall see. I advise you to keep yourself out of the path of the shot, eh?"

Which was not advice that I needed to hear twice over. I withdrew to my own place, and passed the time there, and during that day nothing of consequence happened, nor the next, nor the one after that. The Jesuits held to their compound, the governor to his palace, and soldiers were the chief occupants of the plaza. When I grew weary with the game of watching and waiting, I went down to the harbor, and fished and waded, and talked with the port officials, who were expecting the arrival of a ship from Brazil and held little concern for the matters going on in town. I fancied myself boarding that ship and seizing her captain and forcing him to sail me to England, but it was only the idle folly of a hot moist afternoon.

Then it came to be Sunday, and I wondered if the church would remain sealed, with no Mass offered. But on this day events began to occur. I peered into the plaza and saw troops here and there and there, all in some anxiety and suspense. Don João de Mendoça rode by, passing from the governor's palace to his own, and though he saw me he did not speak, nor did he gesture. Then the governor himself emerged, in a group of his kinsmen. I had not yet ever spoken with this Don Francisco, though of course I had seen him many times from afar: he struck me just from the look of him as a coward and a weakling, with a soft face and heavy-lidded sleepy eyes, and a long thin beard that did not hide the outlines of his chin. He dressed in the most amazing fantastical way, a costume that might have seemed too pompous for an emperor, too gaudy for even Prester John, with yards of gold braid and a glittering helmet inlaid with rows of precious stones. This morning he strutted about, gesticulating grandly and showing the greatest animation as he inspected his troops, examined their weapons, spoke words of encouragement. Some dispute within his own advisers seemed to be in progress also, and from time to time men did come to him, and there were angry words shouted back and forth.

Dona Teresa appeared. She greeted me with high formality, and I the same to her, neither of us showing any hint of an intimacy. And she said, "They are going to do the excommunication this day. The Jesuits will come forth at noon."

"And will Don Francisco defy them, d'ye think?"

"Would you? Defy the power of God? Aye, I guess you would, in that you are heretical."

"I would not defy God, nay. But what proof have I that these Jesuits hold divine authority, other than they say they do?"

"Why, they are anointed priests!" she cried.

"They are but men. When they leave their proper province of sacred matters to meddle in affairs of state, they must set aside such cloak of holiness as they claim to wear. If I were Don Francisco and I meant to govern here, I would not let the Jesuits usurp my authority."

"Now they will put the curse of God on him, though, and all will be lost for him."

"Do you think King Henry of England feared the curse of God when he cast forth the Roman faith from our land in a similar struggle? Or did his daughter Elizabeth, when she did the same?"

"They were very rash. Unless they did so for reasons of state."

"Indeed!" I said. "They were wise princes, and knew what was needful to defend their people against foreign tyrants. And so they feared not the curse, for God alone knows who He means to curse, and not any priest. And the dispute was not truly a question of forms of worship, that involved things of the spirit, but rather it was of matters temporal."

"How so, do you say?"

"The Pope was making league against us with the Holy Empire, to hurt our trade, when Henry was King. This did Henry thwart by making Protestant alliances, and ridding our land of spies and traitors. And in my own time were we greatly threatened by Spain, and King Philip sought to rule over us, and wreck our England the way he has drained his Spain and now Portugal, too. We were full of conspirators in priestly robes, scheming to kill our Queen and give the land over to him. God's death, woman, do you believe that these quarrels we have with the Papists are truly over niceties of prayer-saying? That we care so deeply whether we speak our service in English or in Latin? It is politics, Dona Teresa, it is politics, it is national interest that governs the way we church ourselves!"

She nodded. "So I do begin to understand."

"And thus is it here. Don Francisco must fight, if he would remain governor. If he do not prevent the priests from denouncing him, then will his government here be broken."

"That is what Don João believes is to befall. The power of God is too great for Don Francisco."

"And is the power of a musket-shot not too great for the Jesuit prefect?" I asked.

"Don Francisco will not attempt to harm the priests," said Dona Teresa calmly. "They are God's messengers, and God would destroy him if he lifted his hand against them, and he knows that. Politics is not everything. There are false faiths and true faith, and when the true faith speaks, only a fool would offer defiance. So do I believe, Andres." She smiled and took her leave of me, and moved on across the plaza to her dwelling-place.

To which I made no response but a shrug. I had heard before from believers in true faiths, and I knew better than to dispute with them. That disputation is folly. They will have no argument; their minds are set. If the number of our breaths is fixed at birth, it is wanton to waste any precious two of them on such debate as that.

As I stood alone at the edge of the plaza, though, meseemed me I had spoken some too strong on the political side of our break with the Church of Rome, and had not given enough weight to matters of faith. Not that I would ever hold that our faith is the *true* faith, and all others be wicked heresies. I merely feel that ours to be the better faith, the more effective one in yielding up the bounty of godly life. For I do believe the Papists long ago became deeply corrupt, and turned away from the way of Jesus, with their incense and their bright brocaded robes and their jeweled thrones and palaces for their Cardinals and Popes, and that we in our Protestant revolution have swept aside all such foulnesses, clearing a straight path between ourselves and God. I never knew Popery at home, born as I was with Queen Mary already in her grave, but my father did, and he spoke often of how under the old religion people were kept ignorant and helpless, not knowing how to read, not permitted even to know the Bible save as the priests would teach it, which was not always as it was written. That was a religion that did not let us speak outright with God, but forced us to go through intermediaries. That is not good: it discourages thinking. Why is it that we English are so bold and venturesome, and the Papist peoples in the main so sheeplike, so willing to obey even the falsest and most evil of leaders? I think it is because we have chosen a better way, that gives us a deeper comfort of the soul. And I know we were right to free ourselves from whatever ties of faith there were that put our England at the mercies of our enemies. Our change in religion does serve our national interests well; it also well serves our souls. It is no accident that all the seagoing men of England are staunch Protestants, and do so fervently hate Papistry: it is because we are patriots, and also because we have spirits that are clear and free, unfettered by superstition, that we have gone out to rove so widely in the world.

It was nigh upon noon now. The day was dry and windless and the huge sun gave us a killing heat. At the stroke of the midday hour the gates of the Jesuit compound were thrown open and into the plaza did come four priests in the fullest uniform of their profession, not simple monkish robes but the complete vestments and sacerdotal ornament, so that they did shine like beacons on the brilliant sunlight.

At their head was the prefect of their Jesuit order in Angola, Father Affonso Gomes. He was a tall and wide-shouldered man with the look and bearing of a warrior: very dark of complexion, with fierce blazing angry eyes and great mustachios jutting outward and a hard tight face with cheekbones like knifeblades. There was nothing of the sweet mild Jesus about this man. He had the face of a great Inquisitor, one who would not only be joyed in the roasting of heretics but who would turn them gladly on the spit with his own hand. The other three priests were far milder and gentler of demeanor, with that scholarly and inward look that Jesuits often have; but even they were at this moment solemn and bleak-faced, like soldiers on the eve of battle.

They were accompanied by some dozen or more of their followers and associates, that is, acolytes, altar-boys, incense-bearers, and other such supernumeraries. These bore with them a sort of portable altar, in the form of a broad bench or table of massive design, that they carried to the center of the plaza and proceeded to cover with robings and draperies of samite and red velvet and such, and to place heavy silver candlesticks upon it, and vessels of incense, and all the related trappings and appurtenances of ceremony, as if they were going to perform a coronation before our eyes, or a royal marriage. They brought from within their church also their holy images, of the Savior and Mary, and two great crucifixes of silver inlaid with gold and pearls, each of which was sufficient in value to have paid a whole English county's duties and imposts for half a year. I watched in wonder as all this holy treasure was arrayed and configured with marvelous enormous patience and care in the midst of all the town under that great heat. The plaza, which had been nigh empty, now began to fill. Every Portugal in Angola appeared to be there, Don Francisco and his party gathered in this side, and Don João with Dona Teresa there, and soldiery, and merchants and slave-dealers and tavern-keepers, and some thousands of the native population both slave and free, all standing like sheep in the fields, still and silent.

I understood now why Don Francisco was helpless against these Jesuits. How could he dare order his troops to open fire, as he had threatened, and slay the fathers before all the town? This Father Affonso was so fearsome that he did seem capable of brushing aside the musket-shot with some sweeps of his hands, as we might dismiss a buzzing mosquito. And in all this Romish pomp even I felt a tremor of awe, and could well imagine the terror such show would inspire in one who shared the faith. This was no mere business of politics and a struggle for power, though that was at the root of it: the very armies of God seemed drawn up at Father Affonso's back, and this say I, to whom Jesuits have always seemed more villains than men of holiness. If a heretic Englishman could be so moved, what then would a Portugal feel, or a credulous black?

Then Don Affonso began to speak, and as he did so my awe gave way to scorn and angry contempt, for I knew myself to be among foolish barbarians.

His voice was deep and rolling, and his words were in Latin, slow and somber, so well laced with special words of churchly use that I could scarce understand any of it. But I think it was not meant to be understood, only to terrify. On and on came the grand torrent of sonorous incantations—for incantations is what they were, a solemn magicking most repellent—and as he spoke he sometimes turned and took a silver bell from a silver tray, and lifted it high and tinkled it, and put it down and seized two mighty candlesticks and raised them aloft, and so forth, a whole pompous theater of rite and pageantry. I heard the name of Don Francisco d'Almeida mentioned several times, and when I looked toward the governor I saw him pale and twitching, with sweat glistening on his white forehead, that just now was several degrees whiter than its normal swarthy shade.

There was furthermore a great show of turning to the other priests and taking from them certain books and chalices and I know not what other items of Papist equipment, and passing these things one to the other in some preordained sequence. I marveled at how intricate this ceremony was, and how well rehearsed. Again the two candlesticks were held high and lowered, again the bell was tinkled, again the Latin words boomed forth, all this accompanied by any number of signings of the cross, and now and then a frightful stretching forth of the arms as though lightnings were about to shoot from the Jesuit's fingertips.

Then—and he spoke in the Portugal tongue now, so that everyone could understand, even the blacks—Father Affonso declared:

"Whereas thou, Don Francisco d'Almeida, hast been by sufficient proof convicted of contumacy and blasphemy, and defiance of Holy Mother Church, and after due admonition and prayer remainest obstinate without any evidence or sign of true repentance, therefore in the name of the Lord Jesus Christ and of His Father and of the Holy Spirit, and before all this congregation, do I pronounce and declare thee, Don Francisco d'Almeida, excommunicated, shut out from the communion of the faithful, debar thee from all churchly and temporal privilege, and deliver thee unto Satan for the destruction of thy flesh, that thy spirit may be saved in the day of the Lord Jesus."

And with those terrible words he dashed the lighted candles to the ground and extinguished them, and did ring his bell, and brandished the holy Bible and slammed it shut, and seized a chalice and bore it high and marched off toward the Jesuit compound, followed by his three colleagues and all his company of underlings, who carried the altar and its rich gear along with them.

There was shrieking and uproar among the blacks. There was consternation among the Portugals. I caught sight of Don Francisco, looking apoplectic and his face all a mottled red, whirling around and striding toward his palace, with his brother Don Jeronymo and other close associates all very grave following at his heels. I saw Don João de Mendoça standing placid, his arms folded and an odd little smile on his face. I saw Dona Teresa with her eyes wide and her mouth parted, as though just now she had beheld Satanas Mephistopheles flying across the face of the sun. I saw Captain Fernão da Souza in hot discussion with some other of the soldiery, all of them looking stunned and amazed. And so it went about the plaza: everyone had expected the excommunication, and yet most were as sundered from their senses as if they had been taken entirely by surprise, and did not know what now to think or do.

And I? I, who had felt that tingle of awe at the setting up of that portentous altar under the sun's blazing eye?

I felt sick with grief at the foolishness of mankind. This did seem altogether insane to me, this waving about of bell and book and candle, this chanting of frightsome words, this throwing of spiritual thunderbolts in the name of God's tender Son. It was as magical to me, and as heathen, as those doings in Loango with albino witches and houses of *mokissos* and the blowing of trumpets to bring rain. Why, the very coccodrillos that lie roaring and blowing on the river-banks would never be so shallow as give credence to such stuff; only mortal men, hokusing themselves soberly with noisy formulas and sacred gibberish, could swallow it down. Did Father Affonso believe he had truly separated Don Francisco from the mercy of God? Did Don Francisco believe it? Or was it all for outer show, to frighten the foolish and strip away from him the power of the governor by making the ordinary folk feared to approach him, lest they, too, be sent to Hell? I do not know. But this one thing is sure, that the blacks of this country have fallen between two sharp mouths, if they are to be governed either by corrupt and venal authorities civil or by these ferocious priests, and which government is kinder for them, no man can say. And a second thing also, that I was unable to see little differences between this high Christian ceremony I had witnessed and all the various heathen rites done with masks and wild dancing and painted skins. It is all equal madness. It is all folly. Bells, books, and candles have no power. There are true unseen forces, but not nearly so many as we believe, nor would they rule us so sternly if we did not admit them to our souls. We would not be assailed half so often by devils, had we not taken the trouble to invent so many of them.

FIVE

As I made my way homeward from the excommunication, I found my path blocked by a slender and agile-looking man in tight blue velvet breeches and a flaring scarlet jerkin, who looked at me most evilly, while rubbing his hand up and down the shaft of his sword as though stroking his lustful male member.

I knew him at once to be Gaspar Caldeira de Rodrigues. He had his brother's shifty whoreson eyes and weak scornful smile, and the same sort of poxy beard that grew in patches on his face. But he was taller, and more robust, and somewhat less cowardly and slippery of bearing. Behind him stood four more of his sort, ugly and dour, and I moved instantly into a readiness to defend myself, fearing an attack and determining to send at least half of them to Hell before they despatched me.

He said in a cold way, "Hold your place, murderer. I would speak with you."

"I am no murderer," said I. "But I am able to slay, as you will find out if you test me."

"My brother did you no harm."

"Let the court be the judge of that, Don Gaspar."

"I have spoken with those who witnessed your killing of him. The court will hang you, if you live long enough to be hanged."

"Ah, and will you add murder to the crime of suborning witnesses, then?"

"I would not soil my blade on you," he said. "But my brother had other friends, of less noble birth than I, who may not be so finicking nice."

"Yes, your brother was indeed noble. Nobly did he plunder graves, and nobly did he attempt to enter into a longboat that had no room for him, and nobly did he clutch stolen treasure to his breast even if it drowned him. Are you equally noble, Don Gaspar?"

His wrath blazed high. He strutted toward me, and stroked his sword all the more flagrantly.

"Noble enough not to slive you apart in the street, which is what you deserve, Lutheran dog! I will let the court have its rightful turn with you. But I tell you this, Englishman: if you come free away from the inquest, through some chicane of your master Don João, then you shall have me to answer to!"

"And your friends as well, I suppose? Or will you challenge me man to man?"

For reply, he spat at my feet, and made a snorting in his nostrils, and whirled, and most pompously marched away.

My first impulse was to laugh: for he was so comic, so puffed with pride, with his strutting and his caressing his sword and his threats, and his "Lutheran dog" and other such ponderous menacing expressions, that it was tempting to take him for a clown. Yet I knew that to be error. It is just such men—inflated like pig-bladders, puffed with pride of their own breeding and merit—that are most dangerous, for they are weak, and do cover their weakness with such action as they deem to look bold in the eyes of other men. One who is truly strong can shrug, and laugh, and walk away from strife that is beneath his honor; but the weakling who must feign strength has no such wisdom, and it is he who strikes the coward's blow in the dark, he who pursues his enemy with mean vindictive whining persistence until, by deceit or malign conspiracy, he attains the triumph he must have. Another man, learning how his brother had perished, would grieve for the loss of his kinsman but hold no malice against the slayer. But I had in sooth won me a perilous enemy here. One oftimes must fear the hornet more than the lion.

Yet if I guarded myself, I might not for a time need to face warfare with him. Like his brother, he was vain and idle and craven, and also

I think was in so precarious a state of exile that he could afford no more crimes on his hands. He hoped the inquest would condemn me and save him the trouble. But afterward, if I emerged with my acquittal, it would be a different matter, and I could expect much trouble from him.

I put him for the moment from my mind.

The inquest now was delayed. For, as Don João de Mendoça had predicted, the authority of Governor d'Almeida was wholly shattered by the excommunication. It was not at all the same thing as a King Henry or a Queen Elizabeth having been condemned by a distant Pope, while yet remaining secure and powerful in England. São Paulo de Loanda was then a small city; everyone in it professed to be a loyal Catholic, save for those blacks who were secret pagans and the one English Protestant unwillingly in residence; it was impossible for d'Almeida to carry out his civil functions while he remained outside the communion of his faith. Anyone who dealt with him or did his bidding risked the same dread excommunication: therefore was he isolate. If he emerged into the city he would seem an unapproachable figure, like some leper, or a carrier of plague: therefore he remained immured in his palace. And a governor who may not go forth, and who cannot lawfully be served, is no governor at all.

For several weeks the city was nigh a city of the dead. No business was conducted and the streets were empty. Neither the Jesuits nor the governor were seen at all. There were meetings of the powerful men of the place, one faction led by Don Jeronymo d'Almeida and the other by Don João, but what took place at these conferences, I know not. My only news came from Dona Teresa, but even she was little apprised of what was happening, except that a negotiation was in progress to determine who should be the new governor of Angola, Don Francisco's rule being entirely ended.

I went quietly about my business, taking care not to involve myself in the fractions, and keeping a wary eye out for Gaspar Caldeira de Rodrigues and his friends. Now and again I crossed their paths, and there was sour glaring aplenty, but they took no action against me.

The ship from Brazil arrived in the midst of this, bearing some few new colonists and also none other than the gentle Barbosa, who had returned to oversee the taxation of the colony. By chance I was at the docks as he came ashore, and he looked at me with such amazement as though he beheld a ghost.

"What, Battell, here still, and alive?"

"Aye. Would a small thing like a shipwreck injure my health, d'ye think?"

"Shipwreck? What shipwreck? It was the bloody flux I thought would carry you off. They said you would not live."

"Ah, but I did, and much has happened since that time!"

We embraced each other warmly. It was two years since last I had seen him, this now being the April of '93. He seemed leaner and more than two years older, but he was as elegantly dressed as ever, in sea-green breeches and a fine light cloak of lavender hue, and a high-crowned narrow-brimmed hat.

He drew back and inspected me and said, "You look healthy enough. What is this, now, have you been to sea?"

"Aye. When I came forth from my illness I went to prison awhile, and was forgotten there, and then was drawn up from oblivion and hired by Don João to pilot his pinnace along the coast, in the ivory trade. The which pinnace was lost in my most recent voyage, coming home from Loango, but as you see I stayed afloat, and I think will be sailing again before long."

"This is not the fate I thought was marked out for you," said he. "You have your freedom, then?"

"Freedom of sorts," I answered. "I have a house and servants, and they tell me that on my next voyage I am to be given a share of the profits, which be kind of them, though not a tenth so kind as simply letting me go home to England. That thing will they not do, although they have made airy promise of it, if only I undertake a few more voyages for them first. But I think there will be neither voyages nor profits this season, owing to the civil war that we soon will have."

That startled Barbosa. "Civil war?"

"Aye," I said, and told him of the troubles between Don Francisco and the Jesuits, and now this maneuvering between Don João and Don Jeronymo. All this he heard with much show of dismay and distress, for Barbosa was a decent man, and strife among Portugals gave him much pain. At the end of my recital he shook his head most sadly, and walked about in a small circle.

Then he said, "They are fools to do these things. With so many enemies gathering outside the city, they cannot allow themselves the luxury of contending for power within. I will speak with Don João."

"Telling him what, may I ask?"

"To give over, and wait his time. The faction of d'Almeida holds the royal commission, for the moment. Don João is the best ruler for this place, but only if he come to power by legitimate means." Barbosa seemed journeying in thought a moment. Then he smiled and took his arm and said, "How strange it is, and how fine, that you who came here as a scorned prisoner should live, and even thrive, and have servants! I am greatly joyed to see your good fortune. Will you dine with me tomorrow night?"

"Most gladly," said I. "I would take high pleasure in your company, and I hope you will share with me such news as you bring from the world without. For I am mightily curious about events." And I did laugh. "How strange it is, yes, Senhor Barbosa, that I endure here, and prosper, and now am even invited to dine with an official of the Portuguese court! It was not what I imagined when first I set sail for America. There are times, senhor, when this adventure seems but a dream to me."

"From which you would readily awaken, I venture, and find yourself in your bed in England."

"Aye, perhaps. But instead when I wake I feel the heat and moisture close against my skin, and see the strange heavy trees of scarlet blossoms beyond my window, and hear the beasts of Africa bellowing in their jungle. And I know it is no dream."

"Say, then, it is a dream within a dream. You are in England still."

"That is a pretty fancy, Senhor Barbosa," I said, smiling with it. "Would that it were so!"

Barbosa's goods now had been unladed from the ship, and slaves were come to fetch him into town, carrying him in a sort of litter made of cords, much like a hammock. Throughout Angola and the Kongo it is the custom for great personages to be borne in such hammocks when they go about, especially in the rainy season, when the paths are muddy underfoot. Barbosa asked me to accompany him; but there was no other litter to hand, and we did not care to wait while the blacks returned to town to fetch a second one, and Barbosa would not have me walk alongside whilst he was borne. Then the head slave proposed that I be carried in the arms of two or three of the strongest blacks, but that seemed absurd to me and most objectionable. So in the end we dismissed the carriers and walked to the town upon our own legs, which I suppose was not the proper deportment for a man of Barbosa's rank.

While we were still some distance out, a young Portugal of the militia appeared, running, who halted when he saw Barbosa. He was in full armor and did stream with his sweat. Looking somewhat surprised to discover us going by foot, he saluted and said, much troubled by hard breathing, "I seek the fiscal registrar Lourenço Barbosa, newly arrived from Brazil."

"I am he," said Barbosa.

"I am instructed to tell you that Governor Don Francisco d'Almeida has resigned his post this morning, and that you are to report with the most extreme swiftness to his brother Don Jeronymo, who at the urgent request of the council has taken up the reins of government."

"Ah," said Barbosa, and he and I did exchange glances. "Is all peaceful in the city, then?"

"All is peaceful," the soldier said.

"And how fares it with Don João de Mendoça?" I asked.

The soldier looked toward me as though I were some serpent with legs. "I have no instruction to speak with you, Englishman."

For that disdain I would readily have slain him, were I not unarmed and he encased in leather and steel. But Barbosa diverted my sudden rage by mildly saying, "His question also has interest for me. I pray you speak."

"Don João has been detained for his own safety, since there are those of the d'Almeida faction that have made threats against him. But he is unharmed and in no peril."

"Ask now about the Jesuit fathers," I requested of Barbosa.

But the soldier now deigned to reply to me direct. "The Jesuits are within their compound. Don Jeronymo will meet with them tomorrow to discuss a reconciliation of the civil and spiritual powers of the city."

"Then all is well," Barbosa said. "Come: let us proceed to the new governor and pay our respects."

"Have you no bearers?" asked the soldier.

"They have been dismissed. I have spent these many weeks past aboard a small vessel; my legs need stretching." With this Barbosa smiled most graciously, and we continued onward, escorted now by the soldier and by half a dozen other Portugals who, I discovered, had been waiting a short distance along the road.

The city was peaceful indeed. Soldiers stood posted at each corner of the plaza and outside every of the municipal buildings, and in front of the Jesuit compound as well, and before the palace of Don João. No one other was in sight, nor was there any sign of any strife. Whatever upheaval had taken place in São Paulo de Loanda that morning had been swift; and, I learned shortly thereafter, it had as well been entirely bloodless, which was an amazement to me.

The situation was much as the soldier had described. Disgraced and most utter disheartened, Don Francisco had resigned his governorship that morning, or had had it taken from him. He was now in seclusion and did make ready to leave Africa for Brazil upon that ship that had newly arrived. There had been a brief but somewhat stormy meeting of the council, at which the names of Don Jeronymo and Don João had been proposed for the office, and it was made clear by the supporters of Don Jeronymo that they held a stronger position. Don João had caused his name to be withdrawn, but not before there had been angry words and even a brandishing of knives between a cousin of Don Jeronymo, Balthasar d'Almeida, and a certain João de Velloria. This Velloria, a Spaniard, had been a soldier in Angola for many years and was deemed one of the most valiant warriors there, having distinguished himself greatly in battle against the natives. He was, as well, a devoted ally of the Jesuits. For that reason he abhorred the entire clan of d'Almeida and had thrown his support to the side of Don João de Mendoça, to no avail; and in the words that followed, either he or Balthasar, it is not known, did curse each other's mothers, and the like. Don João, urging Velloria and Balthasar most strongly to put their weapons by, had stopped the quarrel and, for the sake of tranquility in the city, did offer his allegiance to Don Jeronymo. Now Don João was confined to his own residence under guard, João de Velloria was under more grievous arrest in the fortress, and Don Jeronymo d'Almeida held control of the city.

My own condition, I saw, was precarious. From the harsh tone of that soldier's voice to me when I was walking with Barbosa, it plainly seemed that I was listed as an adherent to the side of Don João, and therefore I must be far out of favor. Which proved to be the case. When I reached my little cottage I found all my servants gone, and two dour Portugals posted as guards on my doorstep.

"Do you keep my house safe from lions for me?" I asked in a pleasant way.

Not so pleasantly they made reply, "Get ye inside, and remain within, English!"

I did as they bade me. This was no occasion for heroism. Officially I was yet a prisoner of war in this place, for all that I had been allowed to live in the semblance of freedom for a long while. My privileges had grown out of the happenstance that Governor Serrão had taken me into Portuguese service by first using me as a pilot, and Don João had renewed then those privileges by sending me on my two trading voyages northward; but Serrão was long dead, Don João now was fallen, and quite likely I was fallen with him. I counted it fortune that I was merely under house arrest. It might well be, I thought, that by nightfall I would be back in chains, in the familiar old dungeon on the hill. Don Jeronymo had no great reason, after all, to take to his bosom an Englishman, most especially one that was affiliated in loyalty to his enemy Don João.

That I did not go to the dungeon was entirely the working of the good tax-collector Barbosa. All that afternoon and night I did remain in my house, visited by no one and without food or drink; and in the morning I was summoned forth, in tones less rough than before, and conducted to the hall of government. In the room of the tax-roll keeper I found Barbosa, looking weary and unaccustomedly shabby in yesterday's clothes, as though he had not slept at all. He beckoned me sit and said, "Have you been mistreated?"

"Other than some starvation and thirst, I would not say so."

"They have not fed you?"

"Not even prisoner slops. I've been penned in my own home, or what I call my home, in this land."

Barbosa gave signal to a slave that he should bring a meal for me.

"It has been a busy night," he said. "I am supposed to be a financial officer and not some keeper of the peace. But I think I have drawn all these contending sides together. Do you hold any hatred for Don Jeronymo d'Almeida?"

"I know the man not at all. I have had no dealings with any of the d'Almeidas."

"Nay, you are Don João's man. Well, and that must be at an end. You must swear yourself loyal to Don Jeronymo, or I cannot protect you further."

Somewhat overzealously I did reply, "I will swear loyalty to anyone, so long as it will keep me out of that dungeon!" And I said, "Was it you, then, that had me set free this time?"

"It was."

"Again I must thank you. I have from you a great overplus of kindly treatment, Senhor Barbosa."

He shrugged my thanks aside. The slave entered with a tray of food and a beaker of palm-wine for me, and whilst I ate Barbosa said, "This colony can afford none of these disputes over the holding of power. During the quarrel of Don Francisco with the Jesuits, the *sobas* of the province of Kisama, which lies to the south and the east of us, have broken themselves free of their allegiances, and we must pacify them anew. Don Jeronymo knows this. At this moment he is closeted with the Jesuit Father Affonso, repairing that breach. When he has Father Affonso's blessing, he will gain the allegiance of Velloria and the other soldiers who are respectful of the Jesuits, and everything will be healed, so that we can send armies into the field."

"And what role have you designed in this for me?" I asked.

"Why, you are the pilot of our navy! Don Jeronymo means for you to sail to the island of São Tomé, and obtain fresh soldiers to aid him in his warfares."

"Then I am to be trusted, even though I am known friendly to Don João?"

Barbosa said, "Don João is to be leaving Angola shortly. He has agreed to undertake a mission to the court at Lisbon, to seek more troops for this colony, and weapons and horses."

That news was most disagreeable to me. I had not thought Don João could be dislodged from this place. It was still my hope that he would come into the government, and show favor to me, and permit me to take my departure for England. His going from Angola could only be a calamity for me, especially in that the inquest over the death of Tristão Caldeira de Rodrigues still awaited me.

I said, "Don João allows himself so easily to have Don Jeronymo rid himself of him? I am surprised."

"There is no room in São Paulo de Loanda now for Don Jeronymo and Don João both. Yet Don Jeronymo dares not raise his hand against Don João, who has many friends. Therefore he finds a pretext for Don João to take himself to Portugal, and Don João finds an honorable way to leave a place where he has lost all his power, and both men are spared further conflict."

"And when Don João returns? Will there not be strife all over again, then?"

"Ah, that will not be for many months, or even longer. Much can happen in that time, and it is idle to speculate upon it so soon." Barbosa put his thumbs to his eyes and stroked them, and delicately yawned. "It is agreed, then, that you will serve the new governor most faithfully?"

"It matters not to me who is governor," I said. "Only that I do remain alive and out of the dungeon, until such time as I can find my passage to my own country."

"You are a wise man, Andrew Battell."

"Be I, now?"

"You live not by pride but by good sense. You see your true goal far in the distance, and you make your way toward it shrewdly and without confusion. That I do admire."

"No sailor ever reached home by sailing into the jaws of a storm," said I. "I try to keep my sheets aligned so that I will move ever forward, or at least not find myself capsized. Shall we dine tonight as we first discussed, Senhor Barbosa?"

"Another night, I beg you, good Andrew," said Barbosa with great sweetness. "Tonight I must confer again with Don Jeronymo. Am I forgiven this default?"

"Indeed you are," I replied. "Let us meet another night, when you be less sorely pressed by these urgent matters."

SIX

WITHIN A few days all was restored to calmness in the city of São Paulo de Loanda. Don Jeronymo did make his peace with the Jesuits; the excommunication of Don Francisco was raised, and that unhappy fidalgo took ship for Brazil, glad, I trow, to see the last of Angola. João de Velloria was released from prison and given again the rank of captain-general, that he had had formerly. Don João de Mendoça also was relieved of all restraints, although he did choose to remain in seclusion. And I, too, was freed from my house arrest. A lieutenant of Don Jeronymo's bore me a message from the governor, saying that I was to make ready for a voyage to São Tomé, and would receive my more specific instructions from Don Jeronymo in a short while.

The matter of the inquest now demanded a disposal. But this, which I had feared so greatly, proved in the event to be a hollow formality. Such great affairs had taken place in the city that the slaying of an unruly mariner, even if he be a duke's son, had become a trifle, forgotten by everyone but the aggrieved Don Gaspar. And though I had no longer the hand of Don João raised above me for a shield, yet were my services required by the new governor Don Jeronymo, and so I could not be expended in such vengeful doings.

Thus a court was summoned, before a judicial officer of the faction of Don Jeronymo, Don Pantaleão de Mendes, much wrinkled and glum of face. The thing was done in an hour. Don Gaspar rose and denounced me for slaying his brother, saying I had coveted certain valuable goods of his, and reminding Don Pantaleão of the dead man's high ancestry. I spoke my piece. Then Pinto Cabral did rise, and Pedro Faleiro, and Mendes Oliveira, all my companions of the voyage, and say how it was that the late Caldeira de Rodrigues had attempted to force his way into the longboat, and had been kept from it by my quickness and valor, to which they all swore by solemn oath. And that was all.

"Death by misadventure," Don Pantaleão decreed, and assessed the costs of the inquest against the plaintiff, and the case was closed. But as we left the room, Don Gaspar did pluck my sleeve, and hiss and scowl, and vow his vengeance.

"I am not done with you," said he.

"I beg you," said I, "fry other fish, and let me be." And put him from my mind.

The upheaval being ended, I had me my dinner with Senhor Barbosa.

There was a fine house at his disposal while he was in São Paulo de Loanda, and we were served by a multitude of slaves, some in good liveries, for Barbosa was ever a man who cherished fine dress. We ate splendidly of many meats, partridge and pheasant both, and the wild boar called here *mgalo,* and little oysters of a great succulence, and the strange fruits of the land, such as the mandonyns and beynonas and ozeghes. All this was cooked most elegantly in the European style, with fine sauces, and accompanied by a plenitude of excellent wines of Portugal and the Canaries. I did stuff myself shamelessly like one who has been long in desert lands, though Senhor Barbosa was himself content but to taste a trifle here and a trifle there, the merest of morsels.

I heard from him, at this grand feast, of some doings in the world: such that Drake was still harassing the shipping of King Philip. "He has gone into the port of Coruña in Spain, and destroyed a new Armada that was under construction," said Barbosa. "After which, he took up with Don Antonio, that is the pretender to the throne of Portugal, and landed with him at Lisbon, intending to establish him as king."

"Brave Sir Francis! But to what result?"

"Ah," said Barbosa, "very little, for we Portugals seem not eager to die to have back our former dynasty, and the expedition did fail. Now Drake lies under disgrace in England, the Queen being angry at him for having provoked King Philip so, and for not having succeeded at what he began. He is off raiding the Azores and the Spanish coast, and fears to return home."

"He is much mistreated. And what else is the news?"

There had been, he said, another great voyage by Thomas Candish, who had sailed around the world commencing in Anno 1586. I knew somewhat of this Candish, who was of the Suffolk gentry, and was trustworthily said to be one of the cruelest and least loving captains ever to take ship. Barbosa told me that he had sailed from Plymouth with five vessels some two years past, and had raided Brazil, attacking the town of Santos by surprise when its people were at Mass, and taking everyone prisoner within the church. "Yet this invading was a failure," said Barbosa, "owing to the negligence of Candish's deputy in charge of the attack, one Captain Cocke—"

"Cocke?" I burst in, feeling an angry hammering of my heart at the hearing of the name. "A small sour-faced man, is he, with one eye askew?"

"That I know not, for I never saw the man. During this time I was at Rio de Janeiro."

"Tell me what negligences he did work."

"Whilst he was in possession of Santos," Barbosa said, "he paid no heed to the Indians of the town, who did carry out from it everything in it, all kinds of necessaries and provisions, leaving the place bare. So that the English found themselves shortly in extreme want of victual, worse furnished than when they had come into the town, and after five weeks were forced to quit the place."

"It sounds much like the Cocke I knew, that abandoned me on a desert isle four years back, and sundered me thereby from all the life I led."

"Ah, so that is why the color rises to your face at his name, and anger enters your eye!"

"I wish scarce any man ill, except this one Cocke. Who I see still thrives, and marauds in American waters, and does carry himself as foolish and foul as ever."

"Perhaps no longer," replied Barbosa. "For under the command of Candish this entire fleet proceeded south to Magellan's strait, but it was now past the season for navigating that region, owing to the delay at Santos, and the English ships were scattered by extreme storms. We heard no more of them thereafter. So perhaps your foe Captain Cocke lies at the bottom of the Southern Sea."

"I would sooner have had God blow him to Africa," I said, "and waft him into this harbor of Angola, and give him into my hands." And I curved my fingers most fearsomely, thinking what joy it would be to have them around the throat of Abraham Cocke. Which strong feelings gave me great surprise, for I am not usually of so vengeful a humor: but it must have been Barbosa's generous pouring of the wines that had set me into such a fever of hatred.

Of worldly events, the making of wars and the changing of princes, Barbosa could impart little that was recent, owing that he had been in remote colonial regions these past two years. But there was some news for telling. He had heard that there had happened a vast coming and going of Popes, no less than four of them in that time, one reigning a mere twelve days. But that mattered little to me.

There was strife, too, in Spain, where the people of Aragon had rebelled against King Philip, but had been put down by Castilian troops. Whatever distressed Spaniards did give me keen pleasure, but I did not say that to Barbosa. In England the Queen still reigned most gloriously, though her treasury was hard pressed for funds, on account of the expenses of maintaining armies in the Netherlands and in Brittany to keep the ambitions of Spain in check. There were, he said, a good many burnings and hangings for reasons of religion in England still, and those who died were not only Catholics who did intrigue against the Queen, but even some Protestants who had gone too far in the Puritan direction, and called for the abolition of the bishops. To speak against the Church of England from either direction now was deemed sedition, if Barbosa told me true; and I think he did, for these holy slaughters were, I believe, as repugnant to him as to me.

At length all the news was told, and I could eat no more and drink no more, and Barbosa summoned slaves to take me in a hammock back to my cottage. As I rose to depart he caught me lightly by the arm and said, smiling, "It cheers me that you have fared so well in this land. When first I saw you and the other Englishman lying chained on the deck, as we set out from Brazil to this place, I grieved for you, for your lot seemed dark, and I did not think you had the look of a rogue. I hoped you would withstand your pains, and I said a prayer for you; but I did not think you would achieve what you have achieved in your captivity."

"It has been God's blessing, and mine own very good fortune."

"And so may it continue. But beware: there are true villains all about you here."

"The Jaqqa man-eaters, d'ye mean? Or Don Gaspar?"

He laughed. "The Jaqqas! They are but bad dreams, nightmare-monsters that will do you no harm if only you stay out of their jungles. Nay, I mean closer to hand. I know not how much substance there is to Don Gaspar's threats. But there are many here who would sell you for their own advantage. This is no city of saintly men, nor saintly women, neither. Watch your steps." And so saying, he released me and let me be borne away into the night.

His parting words did trouble and alarm me as I crossed the city under a sliver of a moon. A veil of warm air draped me heavily; great green moths and dark hairy bats and the strange birds of the night fluttered close past my head; I heard a distant thick sound that might have been the trumpeting of an elephanto, or the bray of some ugly hyaena, I knew not which. I reached my cottage weary and much jangled, with my mind full of Barbosa's talk of enemies, and of assassins and lost ships and hangings and the deaths of Popes and kings. What had been a delightful evening had somehow ended in quite another way. But though I lay down troubled, the wine soon mastered me and I fell into a heavy sleep, and when I woke I was cheerful once more, with gratitude toward God for having spared me nigh unto thirty-five years, and humbly did I entreat Him to grant me thirty-five more, and show me all the lands and wonders of His great empire.

It was many days before the new governor summoned me. In that time a ship arrived from Portugal, bearing letters and parcels and casks of wine, and other pleasant things, and also some priests and a few soldiers and a supply of muskets and shot. When its cargo of ivory and hides and copper and such had been put aboard, it would return to Lisbon, and Don João de Mendoça would sail with it.

As well as one other person, whose leaving gave me great grief.

This other voyager was Dona Teresa da Costa. I had not thought that she would accompany Don João, since that it might seem improper for him to appear in Portugal with a woman of mixed blood who was his mistress. But Don João had other thoughts on that.

I learned this from Dona Teresa herself. Her visits to my cottage had been fewer and farther between in these days of uneasy politicking in the city, with spies everywhere on the governor's behalf. But on the eve of the sailing of the Portugal ship, almost, she came to me at midday, and as we made ready to lie together she said, with a strange and mischievous look to her, "Let us take our pleasure slow and cunningly today, Andres, for I think it will be a long while before we embrace again."

"And why is that?"

Her lips trembled and her eyes sparkled, and she could barely get her words out, until finally she said in a wild blurting way, "I shall be in Portugal! I travel with Don João!"

That news unmanned me, and I could not conceal my misery. I rolled free of her and gaped at her.

"What, will you leave Angola?"

"It has ever been my dream to see Europe. I begged most piteously, and Don João granted it. I will behold true cities, and great cathedrals, and the high fidalgos of the court in their fine robes." At these prospects was she all aglow. "Perhaps we will visit Rome, or Paris! Have you been to these places? Are they greatly distant from Portugal? Why, Andres, why do you look so downcast at this my great joy?"

"Because I shall never see you again."

"Nay, I will be back! Six months, seven—the time will go by like a moment!"

"Not for me," I said. "I would not gladly spend even six days without you. And I think you will never return."

"That is untrue."

I shook my head. "Don João has fallen from power here, but he is so great a man that Don Jeronymo cannot allow him to remain. You do not realize it, but this journey is intended to take Don João forever from Angola. He will be permitted to come back never. And if you go with him, you will be exiled all your life."

"None of what you say is true," said Dona Teresa coolly.

"They have kept the truth from you. And what will become of you, in Portugal? You will be a curiosity, a nine-days' wonder, and then be forgotten. And the first winter will kill you, for even the mild winters of Portugal are like nothing you have ever known. I pray you do not go, Teresa!"

"You are ignorant of our purposes," said she, all self-possession and confidence.

"Which are?"

"Do you not think we know why Don Jeronymo wishes Don João to make this journey to Portugal? That is, not to obtain reinforcements for the armies here, but only to be rid of him: yea, we understand that. But can you not see what value there is to Don João to be in Portugal, and how he can turn it to his own uses?"

"I see it not," I said.

"Why, Don Jeronymo has no royal commission to govern, but was merely elected by the council in his brother's place, after the folly of Don Francisco had put an end to his rule. When we are in Lisbon, Don João will apply to certain powerful allies he has there, and gain for himself the royal warrant to hold authority, so that when we return he will at last be governor. And Don Jeronymo will be the one to fall."

I had not thought of that.

"It is an excellent plan, Teresa."

"So we think. He who is closest to the throne is the one who emerges with the highest rank. That was Don João's mistake, when he did remain here before, after Governor Pereira fled, and let Don Francisco come from Portugal bearing the royal seal. Don João does not make a mistake twice. So we will be back, I assure you, and it will not go well for Don Jeronymo when we are." Her eyes flashed with the familiar wickedness. "Come, now, take me in your arms, Andres!"

"I cannot," said I.

"And why is that?"

I indicated my lap, and the limpness of my member.

"All this talk of your going has discouraged him," I told her.

"Pah! A moment's work!"

And she bent over me, so that her breasts did hang like heavy moons above my thighs, and drew them swaying from side to side, laughing, and I felt her hot breath on my belly and the tips of her teats on my yard. And it rose at once, as always it did in Dona Teresa's proximity. And when it did she mounted me, sitting astride, lowering herself to my spear until I was altogether engulfed in her, and crying out jubilantly. I cried out also, and seized her smooth buttocks in both my hands and rode her up and down on my shaft, until the sweat poured in rivers from both of us, and the natural oils of her body did flow and mingle with mine, and the gaspings of pleasure began in her. She was splendid to behold, with her head thrown back, her dark hair streaming long, her back arched, her breasts aimed high. In each our turn we took our pleasure, and rested, and began again, and more slowly brought each other again to ecstasy, lying now on our sides in the close warmth of the day, staring eye to eye. How precious she was to me then, in her alien beauty, her tawny dark-eyed glory! I could not bear the thought of her making so long a voyage away from me. I would burn for her all the while.

I could not tell you how many times we did the act of love that long afternoon, but it was a creditable number, I assure you, and I was not the first to weary, though I was nigh on being twice her age. We lay back at last.

She said, then, "Oh, and one thing more. When we are in Lisbon, Don João and I are to be wed, by a Cardinal of the Roman faith, in full pomp and majesty. But nay, be not so dejected! The governor's wife will not be too proud, I pledge you, to keep an Englishman as her lover, when she returns to São Paulo de Loanda. Am I not faring finely, Andres? Am I not faring finely?"

SEVEN

HER SHIP embarked for Portugal. Governor d'Almeida made a great public show of going to the harbor and bidding Don João and Dona Teresa farewell, displaying more anguish over Don João's departure than he had shown when his own brother Don Francisco had crept off into shameful exile. I saw that such mariners of the colony as Pedro Faleiro and Manoel Andrade, that had sailed with me on my two voyages along the coast before, were on board the very same ship, as overseers of cargo. Seeing Faleiro thus depart was a puzzle to me, for if he was not here, who was to be the master of the pinnace that soon would sail for São Tomé?

I had the answer swiftly to that. For soon after the sailing of the Portugal ship I was sent for by Don Jeronymo the governor, to interview with me on the subject of the São Tomé enterprise.

This Don Jeronymo was the younger brother of Don Francisco d'Almeida and could not have been more than five-and-twenty years of age. Nevertheless he appeared a far more consequential person than his brother, being tall and imperious, with a princely bearing about him. It seemed to me that Don João would have a formidable task in displacing this man from the governship, royal commission or no.

He stood throughout our entire meeting, and though I am a man of more than middle height he well overtopped me, so that I felt somewhat ill at ease. Briefly he questioned me on my willingness to serve his government: to which I replied truthfully enough, that my continued welfare depended on my loyalty to my masters here, and therefore I was entirely at his service. He stared at me long and hard, as if trying to read my soul and see if I meant to betray him in some fashion for the advantage of Don João; and his eyes were as fierce and penetrating as those of the Jesuit Father Affonso, who had pronounced the excommunication. But the intent of treachery was not in me, and so how could Don Jeronymo find it there?

He said, "Are you able to read, Piloto?"

"Aye."

"Read this, then."

And he did hand me a document, all beautifully lettered on a piece of white parchment. I had some trouble with it, both because it was written in so fine a hand and because my knowledge of the language of the Portugals was only a speaking knowledge, not a reading one; but I made my way through it well enough and looked up all amazed, saying, "Am I to be captain of the pinnace, sir?"

"This is your credential to present to the governor. You are pilot and master. We have too few men to spare: you will be short of crewmen, and you will have to play two roles yourself. Have you commanded before?"

"Never."

"Only piloted?"

"Aye," I said, not volunteering to tell him that even my piloting experience was limited but to two voyages on this coast and one up the river to Masanganu.

"Many pilots have become masters after," said Don Jeronymo. "They tell me you are very capable. I count on you to carry yourself well."

I was honored by this; but also it gave me thought that I might be doing treason against England, to be taking command of a Portuguese vessel, which was a new and higher degree of service for me. It was one thing to serve as pilot, and another indeed to be the master of a ship, Portugal being formally at war with my own land. Yet I told myself it could make no difference what cap I wore aboard my vessel, so long as I committed no hostile acts against England. And I had no further time to think upon these things, because Don Jeronymo was drawing forth other documents that I was to present to the governor at São Tomé, one that set forth the problems of the Angola colony and requesting a force of some hundreds of soldiers to aid in pacifying the restless *sobas* of the outer provinces, and another that pledged that the São Tomé men would be permitted to harvest here as many slaves as they felt was proper, in payment for their assistance. When I had read these things Don Jeronymo's secretary came, and sealed them all with thick brown wax, and so it was settled, that I should have charge of the voyage.

They had built a new pinnace, or rather had rebuilt one, taking an old wreck that was sitting off the isle of Loanda and putting her seaworthy. She was the *Dona Leonor*, not quite so tight and pretty as the *Infanta Beatriz*, but not vastly different in general, and she would do. But my crew was shorthanded indeed, owing to the losses by shipwreck and Jaqqa ferocity, and I had barely half the complement there had been on the Loango journey. Some of the men were known to me, such as Mendes Oliveira and Pinto Cabral and Alvaro Pires, but most were newcomers to Angola, having arrived off the recent ships from Brazil and Lisbon. If they were startled to find themselves having an Englishman as their captain, they said nothing about it; but perhaps they took it easily, thinking it was no more strange than anything else they had encountered thus far in Africa. I made my preparations swiftly and we took ourselves out to sea on the fifteenth day of June in Anno 1593.

This isle of São Tomé lies in the Gulf of Guinea some two hundred leagues northwest of the mouth of the River Zaire. Four years previous I had paid a brief call there, when I had been shipping with Abraham Cocke aboard the *May-Morning*, and the current or else the ignorance of Captain Cocke, or his greed, had carried us very far south of our course. Now, coming upon São Tomé from the other side, we had a hard time of it, for dry northerly winds were blowing in our teeth all the while, and we beat our way up the coast with no little expenditure of effort.

To avoid the outflow of the Zaire I took the pinnace a fair way out to sea, and that went well, but I was almost discomfited very badly in going back toward land, when I intended to halt for water and provisions at Loango. The great merit of being both master and pilot is that you are accountable to no one save God and your conscience; during our difficult passages I kept my own counsel, made a brave face of it, consulted much with my rutters and charts, and did such a shortening and lengthening of sail, such a shifting about of ropes and lines, that no one dared say me nay. We had one very bad moment when the wind veered violently from north to west in devilish gusts, a wind so strong it seemed to have a color, a light purple hue, and I was painfully reminded of the wind that had heralded my late calamity. It kicked up a high roughness of the sea as we wallowed about. Three great green waves broke over the ship and the lurches she gave burst the rigging and the shrouds on the larboard side, and one of my men was swept away and lost. But then it grew quiet, and we made repairs and continued onward to the coast, where soft waves beat mildly against the white line of the sands. At Loango we discovered the town safe: the Jaqqa encroachment that they had feared so greatly had not fallen upon them, and all was prosperous, for which they gave high credit to the *mokissos* that guarded them against all demons.

Beyond Loango the waters were new to me, but my charts provided me good guidance and it was only a matter of battling the contrary winds, which a sailor finds as much a part of daily routine as is pissing or putting on boots. In all these slow weeks, though, the hardest time for me came when the wind was gentle and we were making good passage. For at that hour I was standing on the bridge with Mendes Oliveira my lieutenant, both of us idle and looking toward the west, where the dark blue bowl of the sea seemed to curve away into emptiness for a thousand thousand leagues. I turned to Oliveira, a man of forty years with a weatherbeaten ugly face and a long narrow white beard, and said lightly, "This sailing goes slow. I think Don João will be in Portugal before we get ourselves into São Tomé."

"Nay," answered Oliveira. "That will be not."

I pointed north-west, vaguely toward Portugal, and said, "His ship departed in May. If it be not in Lisbon by now, it cannot be far from there."

"That much I grant you, Piloto. But though the ship may be near Lisbon, Don João is not."

"I cannot comprehend you."

Oliveira leaned close. "Shall I tell you a secret, that I had from Pedro Faleiro before he embarked on that same ship?"

"Speak it."

"Don João is already dead. The order was given by Don Jeronymo, to certain agents of his aboard the ship, that on the seventh day out to sea they were to seize Don João and hurl him over the side, and report him lost by mischance."

"*What?*"

"Aye, I swear it! Faleiro was drinking with the men who were hired to do it, and Andrade also, and in the tavern the two did boast that they had been paid in gold to do Don João to death, and also his mulatto concubine Dona Teresa, who—"

"Nay!" I cried, in a voice so great that it made the masts quiver. "Nay, it cannot be!"

And indeed I believed in that moment it was impossible, that Don João was too wise and well connected to fall victim to such a plot, and that my dark and dark-souled Dona Teresa, so luminous of intelligence and guided moreover by her *mokisso*-witching, would surely be proof against all such villainy. In the deepest pit of my soul did I deny their deaths: but then, as the tide will flow inexorably back upon rocks that have been laid high and bare, so too did fear and doubt come to sweep onto that denial and flood it with uncertainty, and after uncertainty came terror, all in the next instant. For even the mighty and the well guarded can be undone by a determined enemy, or else kings would never fall to assassins; and after my first refusal to accept their deaths came the sudden reversal of that, the agony of doubt, the dread that it was so, that my ally Don João was gone forever and that Dona Teresa, whose witchcraft had insinuated so deep into my heart and loins, would never again return to me.

Oliveira, not knowing why I was so moved and not yet realizing that I was already half berserk, said in his same quiet way, "Aye, the two of them would be given to the sharks, so it was arranged, and thus Don João never would trouble Don Jeronymo again. A pity, I did think, for Don João was a shrewd man and also a just one, and might well have—"

"Jesu!" I bellowed, and hurled myself against Oliveira as though he were Dona Teresa's own murderer. My hands went to his throat and dug deep, so that his eyes began to start from his face and his cheeks turned purple, and I shook him and shook him and shook him, making his head loll on his shoulders like the head of a child's straw-stuffed poppet, and he made thick gargling sounds and slapped without effect against me, feeble as a babe. As I throttled him I continued to roar and cry aloud, and nearly the whole ship's company came running to see what was the matter, forming a ring round us but no one at first daring to intervene in this dispute between master and second-in-command. Then Pinto Cabral, who was a wise and thoughtful man, laid a hand to my shoulder and said a few words in a gentle way, believing me mad, and in that moment I regained my senses enough to release Oliveira and hurl him from me. He went sprawling across the bridge and fetched up in a corner, trembling and gagging and stroking his throat. I too trembled, and more than trembled: I shook, I convulsed as though in a fit.

Never before had I experienced any such earthquake of the soul. I crouched against the planks, pounding my knuckles into them while tears hot as burning acid did roll into my beard and drip between my knees. To the eye of my mind came a hideous vision of ruffians seizing Dona Teresa in the night, all soft and bleary of her slumbers, and taking Don João, who slept beside her, and carrying them to the rail of the ship and hurling them swiftly and silently into the dark, perhaps slitting their throats first so that they could not call out for aid, and then Dona

Teresa entering into the maw of the sea, Dona Teresa vanishing forever from sight, Dona Teresa food for the sharks—she who had spoken of being married by a Cardinal in Lisbon, she who had yearned for Rome and Paris, she who had dangled her lovely breasts across my thighs to wake my manhood, a day or two before she had sailed, she now wholly rapt into that dark and cold and enormous watery shroud—no, no, no, it was beyond thinking! I was wholly broken by it.

I know not how long I did crouch there, shaken and dazed and numbed, whether it was ten seconds or ten minutes, but at last I conquered my grief to some degree and arose, and in a low growling voice did order the seamen back to their duties, gesturing at them with my elbows and not meeting their eyes.

I went to Oliveira, who still rubbed his throat, where marks of my hands were beginning to show. He looked at me in terror, thinking perhaps that I meant to finish the job. I knelt by him and said, "Are you badly harmed?"

"Piloto, you all but slew me!"

"It was a sudden madness that came over me. I am much abashed. Can you rise?"

"Aye."

"Come, then."

I helped him up. His eyes were still wide and his face very red, and he was shivering as though we had passed into Arctic seas. Even now he was uncertain of me, and stood poised to run from me if my present softness were only a prelude to another attack.

Most of the crew still watched. I whirled to them and cried, "Away from here! Back to your tasks!" To Cabral I said, "You are in command for this hour." And I said to Oliveira, "Come to my cabin with me. I will make amends to you with some good brandy-wine, and we will talk."

"You frightened me greatly, Piloto."

"It was a madness," I said again. "It will not return. Come with me."

In the narrow space of my cabin I uncorked the dark smoky brandy-wine and poured a strong dose for him and another for me, my hand still shaking so badly that I all but spilled it in the pouring, and his the same, so that he all but spilled it in the drinking. In silence we had our liquor, and at length I said, "The tale you told me gave me a deep disruption of the soul, and for the moment drove me wild with grief. I greatly regret this attack on you: I hope you will forgive me."

He ran his finger about his sweaty collar. "I will survive, Piloto."

"You understand how it is, when a man hears terrible news, how sometimes he strikes out at the closest at hand, even if it be someone entirely innocent?"

"Such things happen," said Oliveira.

We drank us a second drink.

Then he looked at me and said, "May I speak with frankness, Piloto?"

"Indeed. Say anything."

"We are not close friends, are we, but only men who have sailed together twice or thrice. And you are English, and I a Portugal, so there is little in common between us. But yet I would not want to see you come to harm, for I think you are a skillful pilot, and a man of good heart, and moreover—"

"To the point; if you will."

"I approach the point, Piloto. It is quite plain to me that you were powerfully stricken with grief at the news I gave you, and your great emotion speaks much for your loyalty to Don João, who was your especial protector, I am aware. But nevertheless—"

"You misunderstand."

"By your leave, let me to finish. I urge you to master your grief and put aside all feeling for Don João; for to mourn him too openly is unwise. It marks you as the enemy of Don Jeronymo, and I know in truth that there are those on board this ship who have been told by Don Jeronymo to watch you closely, lest you prove in some way a traitor to him. Any show of despair over Don João, or continued loyalty to him now, is perilous and rash."

"I thank you for that warning. But my despair was not for Don João."

"Not for Don João?" he said, blinking.

"If you can relive in your mind that moment when I sprang upon you, you will know that you had just told me Dona Teresa also had been marked out for death. Do you recall that? I am slow sometimes to calculate consequences, and I had not realized at the first, hearing from you of the plot against Don João, that it did extend to her as well."

"Ah."

"And thus when you told it to me—why, something snapped in me, d'ye see?"

"So it is true, then," said Oliveira.

"What is?"

"That you were the lover of Dona Teresa." And so saying, he cowered back, expecting me to leap upon him again. But all I did was laugh, in my surprise.

"You knew of that?"

He looked me slyly and, I think, a trifle enviously. "It was rumored in town. She visited you often, both when you were in the fortress and after your release, and we thought perhaps it was not merely to discuss the weather, or to play at dice. We talked much of your good fortune, to come here as a slave and then to find yourself at once in the arms of Dona Teresa."

"Do you think Don João heard those tales, too?"

"I know not what Don João heard and what he did not, for we were not close companions, after all."

I closed my eyes and gripped my brandy-wine flask tightly, and took a gulp of it, down deep in a single swallow. It calmed me some, but behind the burning of the brandy in my gut there was another sore fire of anguish, over Dona Teresa and over Don João, too, though that in a different way. It amazed me that I should grieve so keenly for a Portugal and for a halfbreed woman, I who was English and betrothed to fair golden-haired Anne Katherine of fading memory, but so it was, and I saw the depth of the change in me, how fully I had been thrust into this African world. And I saw, too, how frightful a place it was and how many perils loomed on all sides, reefs and bergs and floes, with these plots and counter-plots all unsuspected by me, and even myself the subject of rumor, secret surveillance, and, for all I knew, fatal conspiracy. I thought long on all of this, while Mendes Oliveira stared at me, too frightened of me to speak or to withdraw. At length I corked the bottle and arose and said, "We will talk no more of these things, eh? But I thank you for all you have said, and I beg you once again to pardon me for my madness against you. And I will be grateful for any other guidance you can give me, if I be in further danger. Agreed?"

"Agreed, Piloto."

And he backed out of the cabin, glad, I suppose, to be gone from there.

EIGHT

VERY OFTEN in the remainder of that voyage to São Tomé did I think of Dona Teresa, and often, too, of Don João de Mendoça, and the knowledge of their fates lay upon my bosom like a cold stone lodged between my ribs, and would not ease. Never did I lose hope of their survival, but my conviction that they were lost was stronger. As the days went by, though, that dull heavy pain of the knowledge of loss moved to a lesser zone of my awareness: it did not diminish, it did not pass, but it no longer was in the forefront of my mind. I think that is a natural process of healing. I had experienced it before, in deaths much closer to my soul, those of my father and brother and early wife Rose. We never forget the dead or cease to lament our losing of them, but the sharp edge of the pain is quickly blunted, and we learn to live with the absence that has entered our lives.

Moreover the work was fearsome hard, this beating against those ill and most contrary winds, and I had no time to give over to sorrow. Some nights I slept not at all, and others only in winks and snatches, for that a dry harsh wind from the north threatened always to turn us about, and set us catercorner to our true direction. I could not abide the risk of losing another ship. And these Portugals of mine were surprising foolish sailors, who knew everything about the sea save how to out-think it, and it was needful that I instruct them at all times what they were next to do. I told myself often that if these men were the sort of mariners who had served in the ships of Prince Henry the Navigator and the other great Portugals of ancient high repute, why, they would have scuttled themselves out of folly ere they had sailed as far as Cadiz. But that was a hundred and fifty years gone, that time when the Portugals discovered the depths of Africa and first rounded the Bona Speranza, and I suppose a hundred and fifty years is duration enough for a race to decay and grow simple, though God grant it happen not to England.

But by one way and another I did bring the pinnace safe into São Tomé, a place of dark repute, for which I bear no love.

This island is the capital of the slaving industry that the Portugals do operate in Africa. It is a small place, oval in shape or almost round, about fifteen leagues in length from north to south, and twelve in breadth from east to west. It stands out from the mainland one hundred eighty miles, right opposite the river called Gabon. The chief port-town of São Tomé lies in the northerly part of the island, directly under the equinoctial line.

The Portugals have owned this place over a hundred years. The climate of it is very unwholesome, and an abundance of men died here in making the early settlement. But when those Jews who would not accept baptism were expelled from Portugal in the year of 1493, thousands of them were exiled to this São Tomé and forced to marry with black women fetched with Angola, producing, in the process and fullness of time, a brood of mulattos that is the present population of the island. Half-Jew and half-blackamoor in ancestry, they yet are Christians now and boast of being true Portugals; but their constitution is by nature much fitter to bear with the malignity of that air than that of Europeans. There are a number of Portugals here, too, making a race so mixed as to be beyond any easy understanding.

I took the *Dona Leonor* into the harbor of the town, which lies betwixt two rivers in a low flat ground. It is a town of some four hundred houses, most of them two stories high, and all of them flat-roofed, built of a sort of hard ponderous white timber. A rampart of stone protects it on the sea-side, and on a high point above it rises the well-fortified castle of the place, which I remembered well, since its guns did fire most heavily upon us when the ships of Abraham Cocke passed by here in Anno 1589.

We had come in an unkind season; but all seasons are unkind here. There are two rainy and two dry seasons at São Tomé, the rains beginning at each equinox, when the sun, standing straight overhead, draws so much water from the sea that when it drops down again as rain it is like Noah's deluge. The vapors rising from the black marshes under the violent heat create thick stinking fogs that make the air malignant, and compel the natives to lie at home at such times. But the deep clouds do at least shield the place from the worst furies of the sun, which in the dry seasons is intolerable, as it was when we arrived: the soil we found so burning hot that it was scarce possible to walk upon it without cork-soles to the shoes.

This is a most fertile place. The soil is generally fat, mixed with yellow and white earth, which by the dew of the night and the extreme rain of the wet seasons is rendered very proper to produce many sorts of plants and fruits, and, in swampy grounds, prodigious lofty trees in a short time. They plant ginger here, and manioc that grows as big as a man's leg, and four sorts of potatoes, and much else. A principal crop is sugar: there are in this island above seventy houses or presses for making of sugar, and every press has many cottages about it as though it were a village, and there may at each be some three hundred persons that are appointed for that kind of work. All together these places make about fifteen hundred tons of brown sugar. The canes grow exceeding tall, but for all that do not give so much juice as they would in Brazil, perhaps because there is too much rain for proper ripening. Another thing they grow is cotton, and also wheat and grapes and such.

But the mainmost crop of São Tomé, that they harvest with great zeal, is sprung from the seed of Adam.

This is a place where they deal in the souls of men and women and children, which is a most frightful trade, and keenly cruel. Slavery is an old thing in Africa, far antedating the coming of the whites, and as it is practiced among the Africans it is no more reprehensible, I trow, than many another habit of the world. But the Portugals have refined it, here at São Tomé, into something most monstrous.

Slaves are a simple commodity to the folk of Angola and the Kongo and Loango. They are taken in wars between tribes, or are sold by their own tribesfolk to settle debts or to guarantee loans or in payment of blood money, or are placed in servitude as a punishment for theft, murder, or adultery. Once in slavery, the slave has no rank in the land, but is a mere piece of property, transmitted by inheritance or disposed of as his owner wishes. Yet other than in lack of freedom the condition of the slaves is hardly different from that of the free men. They must by law be treated properly, fed and housed, cared for in all ways. They are permitted to marry, even to marry those of free rank, and if they are diligent they can save enough to purchase their freedom, though only a few are known to do so.

All this have I seen with mine own eyes. I would not be a slave to anyone, at any time; yet will I attest that these slaves who are slaves in Africa to other black folk do not have a severely harsh life, and are more like the serfs and peasants of our older times in Europe. But how different a matter the Portugals have made of this custom of slaving!

I think they do not understand that the slaves are human beings. They regard them as mere articles of commerce, like the stacked tusks of elephantos or so many bags of pepper: something to be brought swiftly to market and sold for the best price. Strong slaves are valued, weak or sickly ones are discarded like lame horses. The demand for this mer-chandise is immense, for there are great plantations to be worked in the New World, and the Indians of Brazil and the Indies are poor laborers, who die or run away rather than serve their masters. But the Negro folk are good workers, and are sent by thousands upon thousands over there. The slavers of São Tomé rove all the coast, and go far inland, rounding up their human chattels and herding them toward the island. Where there are established slave-markets, the Portugals buy, exchanging liquor and gunpowder and such things for men and women. But also do they take by force, going into the jungle and stealing harmless folk away from their lives. And I have told you already how, when the Jaqqas did raid the Kongo and cause famine there, the Portugals of São Tomé went down to the isles at the mouth of the Zaire and bought children away from their own starving parents, for a few grains of food. But that is not the worst of it. For then—naked, badly fed, chained together— these people once they are enslaved are conveyed in great discomfort to the island, and laded upon evil vessels, and sent off to America with no regard for their welfare or comfort.

While I waited for my audience with the governor of São Tomé, I had me a good observing of the workings of this slave trade, and it sickened me mightily. Each day new hordes of slaves did come in from the mainland, and were stood in a certain shed to be branded, as we do

brand sheep with a hot iron. I saw a branding one day, with slaves
standing all in a row one by another, and singing a song of their nation,
something like *mundele que sumbela he kari ha belelelle*, for all the world as
if they were about to enjoy some happy festival. And one by one they
were taken off by Portugals who put the hot metal to their flesh, stamping
them on the buttock or the thigh, the men and women both. Most did
not even cry out at this, though some fell from the pain. I watched this
many minutes in horror, hearing the sizzle of the iron against flesh and
smelling the smell of the burning, and finally I asked a Portugal, "Why
do they show no fear? Why do they not cringe away from the iron? Are
they so childish ignorant that they cannot know it will hurt?"

And he laughed and said, "Nay, they know it hurts. But we tell them
that they that have not the mark will not be deemed persons of any
account in Brazil, and so they are eager for the branding."

Ah, the poor beguiled blackamoors!

And then they must wait for the next slave-ship that will depart. So
they lie on the bare ground every night in the open air, without any
covering, which makes them grow poor and faint. Some from the inland
that are not used to the terrible climate of São Tomé fall ill, and they
are allowed to die without medicine, which seems to me a very poor
husbandry of one's crop; but the Portugals say it is just as well that those
die here, for if such inferior workers were shipped and sold and then
they died, it would give the slave-sellers a bad reputation, and this culls
the weaklings before they come to market. I suppose that there is some
degree of sense in that, though I think there would be greater merit in
preserving and strengthening the slaves, and curing and feeding them,
than in allowing some by negligence to perish. That is, if one ignores
all matter of human consideration and approaches this thing purely in
business ways.

The time of waiting may be only a week or two, or maybe many
months, if the seas are stormy. But then the ships come for them. The
Portugals have constructed great dreadful slave-vessels, and it is pitiful
to see how they crowd those poor wretches, six hundred and fifty or
seven hundred in a ship. The men were standing in the hold, fastened
to one another with stakes, for fear they should at last rise up and kill
the Portugals. The women were between the decks, and those that were
with child in the great cabin, and the children in the steerage pressed
together like herrings in a barrel, which in that hot climate occasions an
intolerable heat and stench. The voyage is generally performed in thirty
or thirty-five days, the trade-wind carrying them; but sometimes they
are becalmed, and then it is longer, often much longer, and I think then
the suffering must be horrible. Before any ship departs, the Portugals

cause the slaves they load to be baptized, it being forbidden under pain of excommunication to carry any to Brazil that are not christened. This, too, I witnessed, the forcible making of a great many new Roman Catholics, who by whips and hunger would be taught to love the mother of God and all the saints. On the ship I saw, all the men were given the name of João, and all the women the name of Maria, and the priest did exhort them all every one to confide in the mercy of God, who never forsakes those who sincerely rely on him, adding, that God sends afflictions to punish us for our sins. Well, I cry amen, for I also believe that God does not forsake those who love Him, though I hold that He sends us afflictions not as punishments but as a discipline, to make us stronger. But I do wonder how much those blacks understood of all that. They were no longer singing *mundele que sumbela* and the rest of that cheerful sound, but now were putting up cries that made a dismal harmony indeed.

This trade does profit the Portugals extremely much. Yet I trust they will pay it all back with full interest thereon, at the final Judgment, when they must look into the faces of their Maker and perhaps all their saints besides. And yes, I know that we English have carried our share of slaves, even such great men as Drake and Hawkins partaking in the trade. But those slaves were all bought fairly, I trow, not stolen by us from their homes and families, and they were not treated near so cruel in shipment. I do not like slavery and if I had the running of the world I think I would not encourage it; but I recognize it to be a part of life, like illness and mortality, and I cannot truly say I oppose it, only that it should be done with some regard for the welfare of the enslaved, and not in the way of the Portugals.

There was a certain delay in seeing the governor of the island, in that he had gone to the mainland of Guinea on some matter of importance. So we were obliged to take up residence until his return. This was alarming to us, São Tomé being so unhealthful a place, almost as terrible as Masanganu, that had nearly been the slaying of me from fever. That same fever is common on the island, and I am told it usually carries off newcomers from Europe in less than eight days of sickness. The first symptoms are a cold shivering, attended with an intolerable heat or inflammation in the body for two hours, so as to throw the patient into a violent delirium, which at the fifth or seventh fit, or the fourteenth at most, makes an end of most persons seized with it. I feared this daily, but Cabral told me I would not take it, for I had had it before, as had all the men of my crew. This Cabral, who was a short and supple man with one leg a trifle longer than the other, had been in Africa many years and was wise in its way, and I did rely on him greatly for matters of such advice. "If one takes the Masanganu fever," said he, "and one survives it, one is thereafter proof against it, if he live a temperate life. But only the fortunate few survive it. You are robust of constitution, Piloto, and I think the gods do favor you."

"Aye, they must," said I, "or they would not have given me the benefit of so much exile from my home, and other little gifts of that kind."

"We are all far from our homes," said Cabral. "But I think you have known some joy mixed in with your harms, in your wanderings abroad."

"That I have, good friend. I will not lament."

The island also suffers of smallpox, Cabral did warn me, and also a colic that is attributed by some to the excessive use of women, and by others to the morning dew; and there flourishes there a bloody flux of great deadliness. But the thing I most dreaded, in that suspended and discomfortable time of waiting, was one malady called *bichos no cu*, which is a sort of dysentery very common there. The nature of it is to melt or dissolve men's fat inwardly, and to void it by stool, so that one dwindles and goes. The symptom is an extraordinary melancholy, attended with a violent headache, weariness, and sore eyes. As soon as these things manifest themselves, said Cabral—for, seeing that I was hungry for knowledge of the lands I entered, he did regale me with all manner of tales—they take the fourth part of a lemon peel, and thrust it up the patient's fundament, in the nature of a suppository, which is very painful to him. If the disease is not inveterate, this certainly cures him; but if this remedy proves ineffectual, and the disease so malignant that there comes away a sort of gray matter, they infuse tobacco-leaves in salt and vinegar for two hours, and pound it in a mortar, and administer a clyster of it to the patient; but because the smart of it is violent, they have two men to hold him. "Even two," said he, "may not be sufficient: I saw once a man break free of three, and rush to the water to cool himself, where he was straightaway devoured by a coccodrillo."

"Which eased his pain of the fundament, at the least."

"Aye," said he. "But it is a drastic remedy, Piloto."

Cabral having filled me with such harrowing news, I feared this disease much, but neither that nor any other malady befell me in São Tomé. No man of my crew fell ill, either, except one that took the venereal pox, but it was cured with mercury, not without giving him great pain.

One thing that I did acquire, though, while waiting in the island, was a female slave.

This happened greatly to my astonishment, for slave-owning is foreign to my nature. In truth I did as you know have three slaves in São Paulo de Loanda, but they had been bestowed upon me without my seeking, and I regarded them only as servants, not as property. I have never thought it fitting for an Englishman to own the life of a fellow human being. Yet did I make purchase of one in São Tomé. But it was for good and proper reason, I do believe, and I did not hesitate or scruple to do it.

It befell in this way. There was a sort of pen for slaves, called by the Portugals a *corral*, in the main plaza of the town hard by one of the churches. One morning I was going past this corral, which was well laden with slaves, when a voice from within it called out to me, "*Senhor, em nome de Deus,*" which means in Portuguese, "Sir, in the name of God!" I had not expected a prisoner of that slave-corral to cry out in Portuguese, nor to talk of God. Therefore I halted and did scan that close-packed mass of black naked flesh, until I saw who had spoken to me. She was a girl of no more than sixteen years, altogether bare with not even a scrap to hide her loins, which some of the women had. She was tall and well fashioned, with good clean limbs and high breasts that stood out straight forward, as the breasts of African girls do until they have had a child. Her skin was smooth and unblemished save for certain tribal scars that the Negroes do inflict upon themselves, and for the tattoo of slavery freshly applied, that blazed like a scarlet stigma upon the inside of her thigh just below the crotch. She was not so much black in color as a warm brown, with almost a tincture of red underlying it, quite unlike the hue of the people I had seen along the coast, and her eyes were bright and clear, with a distinct look of intelligence in them. Beckoning to me, she continued to talk in the Portuguese tongue, saying, "Jesu, Maria, the Holy Ghost, saints and apostles," and the like, and came so close to the fencing of the corral that she could thrust her arms through. "Sir," she said, "save me, for I am a Christian."

At that a guard did appear within the corral, a foul squat one-eyed Portugal with a whip in one hand and a cutlass in the other, and he shouted at her and cracked the whip in the air, so that she turned and cringed before him. With a rough gesture he ordered her away from me, which wrung from her a look of such sorrow as did cleave me to the heart.

"Wait," I said. "I would speak with her!"

"And who be you?"

"Emissary from His Grace Don Jeronymo d'Almeida, Governor of Angola," said I with a flash of lightning in my eye to cow him. That sort is cowed easily enough. "I am inspecting these slaves, and I pray you give me no interference."

He glowered sullenly at me, and in a low surly voice said, "What business does Angola have with our slaves?"

"I need not discuss such matters with you, friend. Get me this girl from out of your pen, so that I may talk properly with her, or it will go hard with you."

"Will it, now?"

"By the Mass, I'll have your other eye cut from you!" I roared, and had difficulty keeping myself from laughter at hearing myself swearing a Roman oath.

My sword was out and my face was red with fury, but I was still outside the corral and he and the girl within, and he could have chosen to leave me there, looking a fool. But it seemed that he had tested my resolve as far as he dared, for he signalled me around to the side of the corral where the gate was, and unlatched it, and sent the black girl through it to me, saying in no very gracious way, "You must not keep her outside for long."

"Long enough to learn what I wish to know," I said, and drew her a little aside, away from the gate. She was staring at me in wonder and awe, as though I were some deliverer come down from Heaven. And, looking upon her as she smiled so shyly, I found myself thinking it would be a pity to send her back into that cage of slaves from which I had plucked her. I think it was in that moment that the wild idea of buying her began to form itself in my mind.

To the girl I said, "How did you come to be in there?"

But she was not fluent enough in Portuguese to understand me readily. I realized then that she knew only a scattering of words, and had been rehearsing those most carefully, in the event that anyone drew close enough to the corral to pay heed to her. So I said my question again, more slowly, and doing a little dumb-show and miming with my hands to help convey the meaning. This time she comprehended, after some moments. She said a few words by way of reply, and I nodded and encouraged her, and she spoke again, more clearly, her confidence at the language increasing as she saw that I was inclined to be gentle and patient with her. And by slow and painful exchanges we did manage a fair degree of communication.

She said, squatting down to scratch a map of sorts in the soft earth, that she came from an inland province of the Angolan territory, a place called Kazama in the land of Matamba, that was tributary to the King of Angola. Jesuit missionaries had passed that way and built a small church and converted the people to the Roman faith, or more or less, and she had been baptized by them under the name of Isabel. She told me also her native name, but for once my ear for strange sounds did fail me, for the name was so awkward on my tongue, such a twisting sneezing clicking thing, that I was unable to say it after her, though she told me three times. I could not even put it down rightly on paper. So I called her Isabel, though I found it not easy to do, Isabel being so European a name and she being such a creature of the dark African interior; afterward I usually called her "Matamba Isabel," and then just "Matamba," which she accepted as her name even though in truth it was the land from which she came, and not a person's name at all, as if she had wanted to call me "England." But all of that came later.

She had fallen into slavery by double mischance. Two years before— so I think she said—a marauding band of Jaqqas had stolen her from her village, and would have made her one of their own kind—it being the Jaqqa custom to adopt into their tribe the boys and girls of thirteen to fourteen years of the villages they plundered, as I had already learned at the time of the massacre at Muchima. But she had slipped away from the cannibals in the darkness of the jungle and, wandering most boldly by herself, had drifted westward into some part of Angola where the folk of a settled village found her. These, to pay for certain goods that they desired, had sold her to an itinerant slave-trader. He in turn had brought her to the coast and conveyed her to the Portugals; who had branded her and had penned her here in São Tomé until such time as she could be crammed aboard one of those stinking abominable unhealthful slave-ships to be sent into servitude and early death in America.

"God's blood!" I cried. "They shall not have you!"

I suppose it was wrongful of me to single out one girl from all these others and say that she should not be enslaved. Were the others not human as well? Did they not also have hopes, fears, pains, ambitions, and all that human cargo? Was not each of them the center of his own universe, a proud and noble creature of God? Why say, *this* one should be spared, *this* one is not deserving of such bondage, but *those* must remain.

Yet this one did seem superior to the others, and of such qualities that it was an evil thing to enslave her. I know there is an error of thinking in that. Slavery is not a condition to be imposed only upon the inferior. If it must be imposed at all, it should be handed round impartially to anyone, and if God has decreed that blacks be shipped in chains to America, why, then we should not pick out certain blacks that catch our favor and say, You are exempt, you are too fine for such service. And yet the injustice of turning this girl into a sort of pack-animal did cry out to me with a hundred tongues. She held herself so high, she seemed obviously to have such unusual qualities of mind and spirit, she appeared to be so far beyond the savages with whom she shared the corral, that it was most wrongful to my mind to let her be enslaved. I could not save them all; I did not even see the need or the worth of sparing them all; but I wished to spare just this one. That she spoke some Portuguese and professed herself to be a Christian already marked her, in my view, as someone to be exempted from slavery: for if we countenance the enslaving of Christians, why, there would be no end to it, and soon we would all be enslaving each other, as the vile Turks and Moors do enslave captive Christian mariners to row the oars of their galleys.

I think also I should confess it that I had noticed the beauty of the girl, her sleek limbs and high breasts and bold bright eyes. Yea, give forth all the truth, Battell! But though that surely did influence me in her favor, I swear that I did not purchase her with the idea of making her my concubine. It was only that beauty in a woman makes a powerful argument of its own in any debate, just or unjust though that may be. And although in my early days in Africa I had failed to comprehend the presence of beauty in black women, and had not had any sort of sexual commerce with any of them up to that point, I had by now spent more than four years under the hot African sun, and it had worked changes in my blood, no doubt upon it. In the Book of Solomon that is called the Canticle the bride of Solomon sings, *Nigra sum, sed formosa, filiae Jerusalem*, which is to say in English, "I am black, but comely, O ye daughters of Jerusalem," and so was it with this Matamba Isabel, black but comely to my altered way of seeing. But by God's teeth I vow I did not have the use of her body in my mind at that time.

The one-eyed churlish guard returned and said, "Have you had enough conversation with this slave yet? She must return to the corral."

"Nay, she will not return to it."

"And will you prevent it, then?"

"I intend to buy her. What is her price?"

The girl knew enough Portuguese to understand that, plainly: for she threw me a look of amaze and gratitude. But the Portugal only made a shrug and said, "It is not done, selling like this. You may not have her."

"I am in need of a slave. Slaves are sold through this island. Tell me the price, and I will pay it."

"I tell you, it is not done."

Again my choler rose, and this time I seized him, bunching up his shirt in my hand so roughly that the flimsy sweat-soaked fabric tore away. I shook terror into him, making his one eye roll about in his head, and threw him from me and pulled free my sword, ready to use it if he swung that evil cutlass of his. But he did no more than to glare me his venomous glare, and slink a few steps back and attempt to restore his disarranged clothing. And at last he said, not meeting my gaze, "This is no domain of mine. Wait ye here, and I will inquire after her price."

He limped away. The girl trembled beside me, all astonished and frightened. For a long while we stood together saying nothing. Within the corral, arms did wave desperately at us and voices cried out in half a dozen African tongues; for others in there had concluded that I was taking her out of that detention, and they prayed me to do the same for them. During this time three members of my crew came along, Oliveira and Cabral and a third whose name I do not remember, and, seeing me standing with a naked blackamoor girl, they came toward us, with many a lascivious leering expression. "A sweet piece!" cried that third one. "Let us borrow her, and take her to our camp tonight!" And he did put his hands to her, stroking the curve of her buttock and squeezing her breast. At once I caught him by the shoulder and spun him around, and gave him a cuff across the cheek with the back of my hand that knocked him four or five paces, and when he was finished reeling and staggering he turned to me looking both surprised and angered, with his hand on the hilt of his sword ready to draw.

"Go you easy," I said. "I am buying this slave, and I would not have you handle her."

"I knew not that she was yours," he muttered.

"You know it now."

"Aye," said he most sullenly, still looking wrathful, but putting down the hand from the sword-hilt. He rubbed his cheek and gave me a sour look. But clearly he wanted no quarrel with me, for word had gone about the ship of my treatment of Oliveira and they knew I was dangerously strong and perhaps a trifle mad.

Oliveira said, "Are you truly buying the girl, Piloto?"

"She is Christian, and speaks Portuguese, and is unfairly taken into captivity. I would not have her suffer the fate of these savages. She will come to me to São Paulo de Loanda, and look after my domestic matters, and woe betide the sailor who fingers my property thus lewdly."

"Aye," said the man who had touched her, again. "I knew not she was yours, Piloto."

"Mark that these slave-mongers do not cheat you."

"I pray you tell me what a fair price would be."

He conferred a moment with Cabral and the other, and said to me, "At most, ten thousand reis."

Ten thousand anything would have been too great a strain on my purse, in that I was in truth a prisoner still, and had no money of my own. But I gave that no heed. When I am set on a thing, I pursue it until it is mine.

Shortly the one-eyed one returned, the ugly monoculus having with him a second Portugal of the slave-pen just as swart and unwholesome, who first told me I could not buy a slave in so irregular a way, and then, seeing me determined and backed up by three members of my crew, decided not to make a great issue of it, and with an air of extending upon me a supreme courtesy, did say, "Well, it is improper, but I can accommodate you out of regard for your master Don Jeronymo. The girl is yours for twenty thousand reis."

I laughed him to scorn. I cried out that the girl was weak in the knees and had three times coughed a cough that spoke of consumption. "Five thousand," said I. On this we went round and round a bit, he looking injured and disdainful, and at length we came to terms at ten, as both of us had known from the first. Ah, these poxy Portugals, that are but rabble, and haggle at you like a street-peddler!

"Give me your invoice," I said, "and I will have the money sent to you by morning."

This did not please him, but again there were four of us and fewer of them, and he scribbled me a bit of paper and off I went with my companions and Isabel Matamba the slave. We were all lodged in the hostelry by the harbor, and great was the outcry when I appeared with a naked black girl. The sailors crowded round as if they had never seen female flesh before. Quickly I let it be known that she was mine and not to be trifled with; and then I gave her into the custody of the slaves of the hostelry, so that she might be fed and cared for and clothed. Within an hour she was in the courtyard with a strip of red fabric around her waist, the which seemed to comfort her and give her much security: for the African women prefer to keep their private parts covered, even if it be only by a leaf or a bit of straw or a string of beads, though they care not in the slightest about hiding their breasts or their buttocks from view.

I drew Pinto Cabral aside and said, "How am I to obtain ten thousand reis, now?"

"Why, do you not have it?"

"I have not been paid so much as a single cowrie-shell in all my time in Africa."

"Why, you must borrow it, then."

"Where? How can I find me a Jew moneylender?"

He laughed and said, "You need no usurer, Piloto. I can lend you that sum, with some aid from Oliveira and a few others, and you can repay us from the profits we are to make trading at Loango on the journey south." And he went about to one and another and another, and swiftly assembled the ten thousand, which seemed to me miraculous—for ten thousand reis at that time was the equal of three English pounds, which is no trifle. But I would learn that money in these African colonies is easy to come by, when one can trade worthless beads for the equally worthless hairs out of elephanto-tails, and then trade the hairs for slaves, that can be sold for ten thousand reis each. So it was that I lightly undertook an indebtedness of the size of three pounds, that would have burdened me greatly in England, and eased myself of it in scarce any time at all.

And in that way I came to obtain a slave-girl. Truly, my life had become passing strange, flooded with novelties one after the other in such numbers that I was beginning to feel no jolts from all this strangeness, but simply took each thing as it came, accepting it as the normal flow of life.

NINE

THE PORTUGUESE governor at São Tomé returned at length from his business on the mainland and received me and endorsed my credential, and had from me the letters of Don Jeronymo asking for military aid. In a few days' time he handed me an answer, that he would supply Angola with three hundred men now and three hundred more when the equinoctial rains next arrived, in return for the license to collect slaves within the territory that was subject to Don Jeronymo. I said I thought that would be satisfactory, and took my leave of him.

We were now discharged of our duties in São Tomé, and we made our departure from that place, which none of us felt the least reluctance to do.

On our southward voyage I had a new difficulty with which to contend, that was the presence of the girl Matamba among a crew of lusty men. The pinnace was small and there were only two cabins, one of which was mine and one Oliveira's. The others slept on the open deck, to which they were accustomed. But I dared not let Matamba sleep among them, or they surely would use her most shamefully no matter what instruction I gave that she was to go unmolested: it would be only human nature for them thus to do. I could not give her over to them in that way to be their plaything. What then? Why, I had to take her into my own cabin.

My cabin was long and narrow, with my sleeping-place to the left, and an oaken chest for charts and maps opposite it, and some space between to walk. I rigged a hammock for her in that space, but she looked at it with a long face, and by pantomime told me that she feared being thrown from it by the swaying of the ship. So I got woven palm-cloth mats and laid them on the floor beside my place, which was acceptable to her.

That night I stood the early watch, and when I came in after my four hours Matamba was already asleep, curled on the floor with her knees to her bosom and her thumb thrust in her mouth, like a babe. Indeed she seemed like nothing so much as a child, peaceful there, reposing her spirit after the long horror of the slave-corral. By candlelight I looked down upon her, seeing with pleasure the smooth rich dark-hued skin of her, and the strong fleshy limbs, the firm breasts: for all the torment she had been through she was healthy and robust with the vigor of youth, like a sturdy young filly that could canter many a furlong unwinded. I smiled at her and snuffed my light and lay down in the darkness, and said a prayer or two, and dropped into swift sleep.

For two or three nights thereafter it was the same: she lay naked by my side, and I never touched her. The temptation did come to me, but I did not act upon it. By day she chastely donned her scant loin-wrap, and did simple duties aboard the ship, helping in the serving of the meals. The men favored me with their little envious knowing smiles and smirks, thinking that I was making free with her by night, to which I gave no heed.

But the natural attraction of the sexes is something that arises automatically in us, nor have I ever been notably proof against it. There came a night when I looked upon her and felt the strong pull of it. It was as I came from my watch and disrobed for sleep, and stood above her as she slept, lying on her back with her legs apart a little and not a stitch covering her, and I did think, *Why not?* She would not refuse me. I was without a woman. Dona Teresa was likely dead—how that panged me!—and Anne Katherine might as well be dwelling on the moon— that panged me, too, but not in any immediate close way, not after so many years—and I had my lusts like anyone else, and did I mean to live like a monk all the rest of my days in Africa? Here was a woman. She was handsome, after the fashion of her kind. *Nigra sum, sed formosa.* She was Christian, more or less. At least she was something more than a savage. And she was close at hand. Why not? Why not, indeed? Yet I did not. Some nicety of compunction held me from it, she being a slave and a blackamoor.

So I entered my sheets and lay awake a time, somewhat sore with need, debating these matters endlessly with myself, telling myself that I had only to reach down beside me and draw her to me, or lower myself to her and ease myself into her and that would be that. But I did not, and though sleep was slow in coming to me, it must at last have come, for I fell into troubled dreams full of teeth and claws and dark waters bubbling with hidden monstrosities.

And in the night came a spear of lightning that turned darkness to day, and a roll of thunder that was like the heavy crack of doomsday falling upon us, and such a lashing of rain as to make the sea boil and go white in its frenzy. At once I woke, and thought to go out on the deck and look to the masts and sails, although it was Oliveira's watch and I knew him to be capable in such matters. But as I sat up, blinking in the darkness and kneading my eyes, there was a sudden flutter and mutter in the cabin and Matamba did hurl herself into my bed, whispering, "I am afraid! I am afraid!"

Again the lightning. Again the thunder, more terrible.

She trembled like unto one who was on the threshold of a seizure, and did thrash and kick and leap about, so that I had to take her in my arms to protect us both from injury. And I said soothing things, and stroked her back, which was moist from the fear-sweat that had burst from her every pore. The pinnace meanwhile rocked and wallowed and slapped its sides against the great waves, and I heard men running about on deck, and knew that it was my place to be there with them. God forgive me, but I could not go. For as I gave comfort to poor frightened Matamba, gently holding and shielding her, the bareness of her body against mine became a fiery provocation to me, the twin solid masses of her breasts announced themselves irresistibly to my chest, my stroking hands did slip downward from her back to her rump, and to the hot place between her thighs. My member stood out in urgent want, pressing so hard against her belly that there was no room for it between us except if we were to insert it where nature had meant it to go. She made little panting sounds as an animal might when in heat, and scrambled about, all legs and arms, and suddenly there she was clasped tight astraddle me with my yard sunk deep in her body. It was for the mere taking of comfort, I think, a kind of primordial linking of flesh in an alliance against the great fright of dying. But, God's death! it felt good to me, that soft wet secret woman-mouth of her belly grasping and containing me and sliding back and forth over me. And she had another trick, too, that Dona Teresa also had known, that I think is general among these African women, a trick of an internal quivering of the female channel, a tightening and loosing, tightening and loosing, that gave me the most extremest pleasure.

How could I have broken away from her to go on deck, at such a time? Master of the ship I might be, but in good sooth I am a mortal man and no angel, and a male of hearty lust, and I could no more have flung Matamba from me and gone about my duties than I could have stepped outside of mine own skin. So we did the little love-wrestling on that cramped couch, lying on our sides, she half atop me, my hands clutching her buttocks and my fingers digging deep, she moving with the strange fury of one in whom terror has been transformed into desire with scarce a perceptible boundary twixt one and the other. And then from her did come a high-pitched wailing sound like the lament of some spirit of the dark misty fens, so piercing that it must have carried from one end of the ship to the other, and which affrighted me at first until I comprehended that it was only the outcry of her ecstasy, and into it I spent myself with hard hammering strokes that left me weak and whimpering. Thus drained we clung to one another in the dark, and gradually I perceived that the storm had abated, the sea had grown quiet.

She was sobbing softly.

God's bones! What does one say, when a woman sobs at you after the act of coupling? Does she weep from joy or shame or fear, or what? How can one know these things, and how can one speak without being clumsy?

Well, and sometimes it is best not to speak. I merely held her, as I had before, and she grew calm. My body slipped out of hers and she drew back a bit, but not far. I took her hand between mine to give her reassurance.

"Please," she said. "Forgive—"

"Forgive? And forgive what? There's naught to forgive."

Tears still did gleam by her cheeks. "D'ye understand my words?"

"Frightened—"

"Yea, the storm was a scary thing. It's over now."

"Frightened—now. Not storm."

"Frightened of what we did? Nay, girl! It is the kindest thing a man and a woman can do for one another! D'ye understand my words? Do you?" She made no reply, and I had no way of knowing how much she followed my speech. But then I said, "I must go on deck, and see if there is damage," and she understood that well enough, for she asked me in a whisper not to leave her. I told her it was my duty; and the leaving of her was ever so much easier now, with the magnetical pull of fleshly desire no longer holding me in its unshakeable grip. I drew on my cloak and patted her to show I meant no coldness by this withdrawal, and went without.

The sea was still high and water was sluicing over the deck, and the men were busy under Oliveira's command doing their tasks of battening and belaying. But all was well enough, the rain nothing more than a fine warm spray, the lightning having moved off to the east where we could see it marching through the dark humps of the coastal hills, and the thunder a mere distant reverberance. To me Oliveira said, "I've an hour more of my watch, Piloto! No need of you on deck now!" And he grinned his toothy grin, as if to say, Go back to thy doxy, lad, have yourself another merry roll with her. I did think of him most kindly for that carnal but well-meant grin.

Yet did I make my rounds all the same, and only when I was certain that everything was secure did I return to my cabin. Matamba had not left my bed, but now she was tranquil. I lay down beside her and would have kissed her, which I had not done in that sudden and wild conjoining of ours; but she turned her head away, saying, "Nay, the mouth is for eating."

At that I laughed. For who would find aught to object to in a sweet kiss? But I saw the great gulf that lay between us, that were two people out of different worlds.

We came close together and soon we were coupling again. And this time we did enact the rites of love no longer merely because we had been flung close together by the suddenness and violence of the storm—which I think was only the pretense we both had used, anyway—but now for sheer desirousness of it. And afterward of nights in my cabin on the homeward voyage we were unhesitating in our joinings, and did send the high wail of her pleasure and the answering rumble of my own through the ship again and yet again.

Though Matamba was scarce more than a girl she clearly had had much experience of these sexual matters. Her skills were considerable, yet in her way of going about the act she was wholly African, with practices most unfamiliar to me. I have already told you that she would not kiss, the meeting of mouths being deemed unclean in her tribe, lest there be an exchange of spittle from tongue to tongue. Nor did she care to have her private parts much caressed by my hand, nor to touch my own, except when as a particular favor to me she would rest her fingers lightly upon my member. And by no means would she countenance the putting of my mouth to her female zone, and I think she would sooner have died than do the like to me. In these things she did follow the customs of all her sort, rather than any private finicking fastidiousness, for never in African lands did I find a woman who was much fond of kissing or the other kind of mouthing: it is not their way, and they look with distaste upon Europeans who do such things.

On the other hand she was much given to tickling me, notably beneath the arms and along the thighs. The which startled and displeased me, both that it seemed frivolous in the making of love and that it was in itself not a likeable sensation to me; but when I asked her to desist, she burst into tears, thinking herself found unworthy. I learned afterward that such is the practice of her tribe, to tickle, that is as solemn to them as kissing can be among us, and is core and essence of their loveplay. Since she knew that I disliked it she attempted not to do it, but it was too deeply ingrained in her, and when the full heat of the game did come upon her she could not refrain from working her fingertips slyly into my sensitive places, the which I learned to accept from her.

So far as the manner in which coupling was achieved, there, too, she had her own strong preferences. Her favored way was to crouch above me, like one who squats by a riverside washing garments in the stream, and to lower herself until her loins were positioned above mine, and thus to impale herself. Then, too, she liked to lie alongside me and slide herself over me until I was imprisoned by her legs, as she had done that first time when the storm drove her into my bed. And often she turned and knelt with her back to me, so that I had her in the dog-fashion. What she did not care for at all was our familiar English way, the woman on her back with her legs drawn up and the man between them; this she found smothering and perilous, and somehow awkward. It was not the usage of her tribe, in fact, but I think the prime reason for her not wanting it that way was a deeper one. For during her time in slavery she was forcibly had by Portugals any number of times—they violating any handsome slave-wench without shame, whenever the fancy took them—and in such rapes they customarily flung themselves atop her, through which she came to loathe that manner of union. I may add that she loathed Portugals as well, despising everything about them, their faces and their smell and their filthiness of body. When she cried out to me from the corral that I should save her from the slave-masters, it was on account of my yellow hair and English face, for although she had no idea what an Englishman might be, she knew at first sight that I must be something quite different from a Portugal, and chose therefore to cast her lot with me. And when she discovered that I was indeed different, that my skin was not rancid with old stinks and grimes and that I would not shove my yard into her unheated slit at the first chance I got, her devotion to me manifested itself most touchingly. She followed me about the ship, as loving and tender as a puppy; and though she was courteous enough to the Portugal men, they being my comrades, she kept a cool distance between them and herself as far as such was possible in close quarters.

Thus it fell out that I did go to São Tomé a solitary man, and returned as a man of property, with my own private slave that was also the companion of my bed, and, in the best of ways between men and women, my friend.

For we were both lost souls set adrift from our native soil, two wanderers, two victims of seizure and imprisonment, and we clove to one
another. It had been my first plan to set her free in Angola and allow
her to return to her own land; but swiftly did it become evident to me,
as I guided the pinnace down the coast from port to port, that I had no
wish to dismiss her. Nor was she eager to leave me again, since in the
journey back to her native province she would surely be taken in slavery
again, if she were not devoured by Jaqqas or torn asunder by lions or
gulped by coccodrillos. As we came to these conclusions we found ourselves rapidly drawing nigh in spirit, which charmed me greatly. I began
to instruct her more fully in Portuguese, and she to teach me some
African words, so that we needed no longer to be limited to the cumbersome business of miming that was the chief means of communication
between us. She was a quick learner. I even taught her a few words of
English, telling her that this was my private language, the language of
my true nation, that was enemy to these Portugals among whom I did
find myself. It was a joy, God wot, to feel good English syllables on
my tongue again! Once in jest I had pretended with Dona Teresa a game
of talking English to stir the fires of lust; but now with Matamba I did
the like in earnest, for the hearing of mine own language in her mouth
aroused me greatly.

So we lay together and she said, "God bless Her Protestant Majesty
Queen Elizabeth," and I laughed and caressed her and would have kissed
her, if she had let me.

And she said, "Essex, Sussex, Somerset, York."

"Northumberland, Suffolk, Gloucester, Kent," said I.

And she said after me in her way, "Northumberland, Suffolk,
Gloucester, Kent."

It was a joyous time. Let the Portugals strive among themselves like
serpents and basilisks for power, I told myself: let them lie and cheat
and betray, and excommunicate each other with bell and book and
candle, and scheme feveredly for advantage. It was not my way. I had
carved out a small isle of solace for myself within their dark and tempestuous Africa. I had an occupation; I had my good health; now I had
this Matamba of mine, too. It was my purpose henceforth to continue
to live carefully and quietly until I could contrive somehow to effect my
escape and my return to England, which was the one great canker in
the sweetness of my life, that I was so far from home.

There was still the matter of the debt I had incurred in the buying
of Matamba out of slavery. But that was easily enough dealt with, in
the trading we carried out at the coastal depots. For by order of Don
João de Mendoça—an order sustained and confirmed by Don Jeron-

ymo—I stood a full partner with the Portugals of my crew in any enterprises we might conduct by way of commerce. And when we stopped once more in Loango on our southward way, those people did greet us cordially and relate that there had lately been a great hunting and slaughter of elephantos there, so that they had much merchandise to offer us, the which we were able mightily to profit upon.

The elephanto, I should say, is the most awesome of all the African beasts, the same colossus that accompanied the armies of great Hannibal that time he came to conquer Rome. It is found wandering free all over the Kongo land and Loango, and to a lesser extent in Angola, where also the dwellers are not so assiduous in the hunting of him. They are immense beasts, like unto houses that move. I have seen the imprint of their feet in the dust, in plain diameter four spans broad, and their ears are like great gray wrinkled cloaks, in which a man could hide himself. I was told in Loango that the elephantos do live one hundred and fifty years, and until the middle of their age they continue still in growing. Certainly have I seen and weighed divers of their tusks, and their weight amounted to two hundred pounds apiece, and more. These vast teeth are of course prized in civilized lands for the ivory that is cut and polished out of them.

But in Africa it is their tails that are richest valued, and from which much later I did create the fortune that for a time I assembled. They use these tails to beat away the flies that trouble them, and on their tails they have certain hairs or bristles as big as rushes or broom-sprigs, of a shining black color. The older they be, the fairer and stronger be the hairs, and they fetch a fine price, as I say, fifty hairs getting a thousand reis, that is, six of our shillings. The blacks of all these kingdoms braid the tail-hairs very finely, and wear them about their necks, and also the blackest and most glossy ones about their waists, displayed most proudly.

In the hunting of the elephantos there are several methods. They trap them by digging deep trenches in the places where they accustom to graze, which trenches are very narrow at the bottom, and broad above, so that the beast may not help himself and leap out when he is fallen into them. These trenches they cover with sods of earth, and grass, and leaves, and when the animal walks over them he falls into the hole. But another way is for light and courageous persons, that trust much to their swiftness in running, to lie in wait all smeared with elephanto dung and urine, so that the elephanto will not smell the human smell of them. Then when the beast ascends some steep and narrow place, they do come up behind them, and with a very sharp knife cut off their tails, the poor beast not being able in those straits easily to turn back to revenge himself, nor with his trunk to reach his enemy; and the hunter flees. It is a swift animal, because it makes very large strides, but in turning round it loses much time, and so the huntsman escapes in safety with his prize. And we in the marketplace of Loango did buy these things for our paltry beads and other gibcrack gewgaws that we had acquired in São Tomé, which we knew we would sell in São Paulo de Loanda far more valuably. If the Africans of this coast were seafaring folk, or had some skill at the merchant trade, it would not be so simple for the Portugals to turn such easy profits from them. But as things be, the wealth is open for the plucking, since that the native folk do not trade much with one another beyond their own borders, and leave a vacancy for enterprising Europeans to exploit them of their treasure. Well, and the race was ever to the swift; and so be it. So be it!

TEN

WHEN WE had returned to São Paulo de Loanda we did indeed hawk our cargo most beneficially, and I was able to put aside enough out of my share to repay the ten thousand reis I had borrowed of my shipmates, with some left over, the first money of my own I had possessed since leaving England. I installed Matamba at my cottage and showed her to my other slaves, who I think did resent her coming, inasmuch as she shared my bed and held other such privileges with me. They gave her evil looks and often played cruel tricks on her. But I dismissed one of them from my service, a Bakongo woman who had contempt for the tribe from which Matamba sprang; and the other two, a boy and an old woman, gave no more trouble.

The city was quiet. If there were any adherents to the former faction of Don João yet remaining, they were all now loyal to Don Jeronymo, and indeed I never heard Don João's name mentioned. Whenever I passed the palace that had been his—which still was guarded and maintained, there being an official pretense that Don João would soon be returning from Portugal—I felt the sharp pricking of sorrow over the cruel murder of that man, who had been so generous with me. And of course I lamented also and always the slaying of Dona Teresa, and prayed that the assassins, at the last, might have spared her for beauty's sake, though I did not think it very likely.

I comforted myself with Matamba, a simpler and warmer person than Dona Teresa, and good to be with, who was Teresa's equal in matters of the flesh, I think, and whose sweet and eager nature had a charm not to be found in the other woman. Yet I do confess that I preferred Dona

Teresa's beauty. Though Matamba was ripe and supple of body, she was nevertheless a pure blackamoor, and I was not then so much of an African myself that I was able to find the highest joy in her flattened nose and her full lips. And when my caressing hands passed over the rough coarse slave-brand on the softest part of her thigh, or when I stroked her face and encountered the double row of tribal markings incised as cicatrices into her skin by way of ornament, I found myself against my will yearning for the satin perfection of that woman who was lost to me.

I had yet by me the tiny wooden idol that Dona Teresa had given me long ago, the which had survived all the hardships I had undergone. This thing I regarded as most private, and displayed it not, but kept it about me in my clothes, or beneath my pillow. But with Matamba dwelling at my side, it was certain she would discover it, and one day she did. She laid back my pillow and stared at it in solemn silence, so that I heard her hard breathing. Then she crossed herself five times running and whispered, "*Mokisso! Mokisso!*"

"It is nothing, Matamba."

"Why do you have this?" she demanded.

I might have lied, and said I had found it in my wanderings, and was keeping it only as a curiosity-piece. But I saw no need to lie to a slave, and I cared not to lie to Matamba. So said I then, "It was given me by—a friend."

"Throw it away! It is witchery!"

And she trembled, as though she had found the Devil's hoofprint in the earth outside our door.

"Well, and if it is?" I said. "It has no power over me."

"Do you know that?"

"I am my own man, and suffer no witching force."

"Then throw it away," she said again.

"But I find it pleasing. It is smooth to the touch, and well carved. And the friend who gave it to me is one that is dead, or so I think, and this is all that is left to me of her."

"Of *her?*" said Matamba, and there was a very wifely something in her tone, that amused and angered me both.

"Dona Teresa da Costa was her name," said I. "A very fine and noble Christian woman of high bearing, who—"

"She is no Christian, if she gives you this. She is a witch!"

"Come, Matamba, you are too harsh!"

"I know witching. I know *mokisso*-things. This is peril!"

"A harmless little carving."

"An idol," said she.

And now my wrath did rise, for I knew that she was right and I was wrong, which always angers one when one is determined not to give way; and I would not, by my faith, part with this gift of Teresa's, if six Archbishops were to insist upon it. She tried to take it from me, I holding it in my hand, and I pushed at her and thrust her back, not gently, so that she fell to the edge of the bed. And when she looked up at me, her breasts rising and falling hard in her upset, there was a new look to her eyes, that said she was reminded I was still her master, and a man, for all that I seemed gentler than the other men she had known.

I said, "I meant you no harm. But this you must understand: the carving is mine, and it is precious to me, and I will not destroy it, and I will have you do it no harm."

"Then it will do you harm. I would not have that."

"Let me be, Matamba. I ask that you let me be."

"If you will keep it, then keep it. You are the master. But it has *mokisso* in it. It is not Christian. It can harm you."

"I will risk that," said I, and I ended the matter. And for some days I carried the carving about so she could not get rid of it; but then I saw she respected my wish, and I returned it to its place in the cottage. Whenever she saw it she crossed herself many times, but she did not raise the issue again.

Some few days after my homecoming Don Jeronymo d'Almeida sent for me, to offer me a new task. To him I did go in an ill grace, knowing him to have treacherously conspired the deaths of those two my friends, and wanting to have no warmth between me and such a Judas. But yet I had to swallow back my qualms, for he was governor and I was at his mercy; I could upbraid him all I liked over Don João and Dona Teresa, and still at the end of it he would only have me flogged, or buried away in the dungeon and forgotten, and what would that have availed me, what would it have availed Don João, Dona Teresa?

Don Jeronymo greeted me brusquely and in his usual harsh and fierce way. He was intending now, he said, to launch his expedition into the troublesome province of Kisama, that had altogether thrown off Portuguese rule. That province has its beginning on the south bank of the River Kwanza, and runs southward from there in the direction of Benguela, where there is an important stopping-place for the refreshing of Portuguese ships headed around the Cape of Bona Speranza.

It was perilous in the extreme to allow that province to remain in rebellion, and so, as soon as the São Tomé men arrived, Don Jeronymo meant to lead a large force into that land. His plan was to go by ship up the Kwanza to the former presidio of Muchima and rebuild it, and then to march overland due south to a place called Ndemba, where rich salt mines were. At Ndemba he would found another presidio, and garrison it with one hundred men: this would become his base for the reconquest of Kisama Province.

My role in all this was simply to serve as ferry-pilot. I was to take troop-ships up and down the Kwanza, delivering his soldiers to Muchima and to the larger presidio farther up the river at Masanganu.

Well, I had no great craving to go anywhere near Masanganu, where I had contracted that terrible fever that had me raving and feeble for the better part of a year, and like to have cost me my life altogether. But I reminded me of Pinto Cabral's words, that once one has survived such a fever, one does not take it again, if one has a sturdy frame. So a new voyage to Masanganu seemed to me more bothersome, on account of the awful heat, than in a real way dangerous to me. Yet I did hate the place and would gladly have been sent elsewhere, even to that salt-mine town of Ndemba. But that could not be reached by water and in Don Jeronymo's mind I was reckoned to be a pilot, not a soldier.

I was put in thought once again, also, of Don João's promise to let me go home to England after I had done him some month's service as a seaman here. Already that promise was some two years old, or nearly, and I saw no sign of its fulfillment. For it had been cast in abeyance during the strife between Don João and the d'Almeidas, and surely it was suspended entirely by Don João's death, or rather made entirely null and void: Don Jeronymo would hardly release a useful pilot in time of war. That gave me great bitterness. But I dared not bring the issue to Don Jeronymo, knowing his ferocity and the precariousness of my position. I had no choice now but to go on serving my Portuguese masters in all that they demanded of me, while awaiting God's grace in a change of my fortune.

So once again I did voyage to Masanganu, with a flat-bellied frigate that seemed to me more like the ugly boats that the Dutch call *scows*. We loaded it up with Portugals who looked most gloomy and distraught, for they felt sure they were going to their deaths, if not from native spears and arrows then from the plagues and black fluxes of Masanganu; and up the river we went, past the sluggish evil coccodrillos snoring on this shore and that, past the thick green walls of vegetation that concealed God knew what terrible mysteries and horrors, past the places where the hippopotamuses yawned and the long-legged water-birds stalked about like things of ill omen.

Into the zone of heavy foul stinking wet heat we traveled, and indeed the men began to sicken. But that was no business of mine, and I delivered them dead or alive at Masanganu or at the restored fort at Muchima, and went back for more, and did it all again. The chief thing that I remember of this onerous and dreary shuttling is my first sight of one of the gigantic serpents of this land, the which I would not have credited had I not seen it with mine own eyes.

This monster I did behold at Masanganu, when we were unloading our cargo of soldiers. The blacks of the place gave a great shout of a sudden, and waved their arms and did a kind of dance in their fright, and then we saw it coming through the low bushes along a foot-path much used by us. It was, without any hyperbole, twenty-five feet in length, I assert, and it had a head as big as a calf, and when it moved from side to side in its coilings it disturbed the bushes as much as though twenty people were advancing through them. We drew back in alarm at the sight of it, fearing that it might gobble one of us with a sudden lunge, or smite at us with its immense yellow tail; but then some among us took their muskets and fired bullets into it, which halted its advance.

It was a monstrous long time in dying, too, beating both its great head and its nether end against the ground in a slow hammering way. I think it did not know it was mortally wounded, but thought only that it had been set upon by some kind of stinging flies, or angry bees, if it thought anything at all. But at last its life left it and the natives, jumping forward most boldly now, hacked from it its head, after which it convulsed anew and continued to move for some minutes.

The meat of these serpents is eaten with great enjoyment by the blackamoors, who claim it to be a delicacy. They offered a share to us, but found no takers. Afterward I saw the bones of it, amazing delicate and beautiful, littered out over what seemed to be half an acre of the town. One Portugal who had had experience with these beasts told us a tale of a somewhat smaller one, but still immense, that was encountered near São Paulo de Loanda in the early days of its founding. A soldier did cut this one in two pieces by a lusty stroke of its scimitar, he said, but even that did not kill it, and both pieces crawled away in the thick bushes. And soon afterward, two other people happening by, the half that bore the head did crawl out again and seize upon them, devouring them almost whole. I cannot attest that I saw such a marvel with mine own eyes, only that the tale was told to me; but I am inclined to believe in its verity, knowing what I have come to know about the strength and persistence of these animals. The same Portugal told me that the Jaqqas, when they took one of these serpents alive, would urge it to gulp down one of their prisoners, and then would eat snake and man themselves, together at a single feast. This, too, I never witnessed, though I witnessed plenty else among the man-eaters.

I did my Masanganu service, finding the place plaguey hot and discomforting, as always, though I suffered not at all from its fevers. This took me all through the late months of Anno 1593 and the early seasons of '94.

Meanwhile reports came to us that Don Jeronymo, supplemented by soldiers of São Tomé, had carried out a great sweep through Kisama and had reduced nearly all of the rebellious *sobas* to submission. The work was done and I was looking toward an end to my river-shuttling, and a return to São Paulo de Loanda and the arms of my sweet Matamba. It would be a joy again to breathe the sea-breezes of the coast, I did tell myself, for even a torrid place like São Paulo de Loanda seems but a jolly holiday-place when it be compared with such an outpost of Satan's realm as Masanganu.

But then came messengers with deep disheartening news. Don Jeronymo, having completed his military work and founded his new presidio at Ndemba, had elected to go in quest of the silver mines of Kambambe in the east. Many a brave fool had been broken in the search for these mines, which for all I know are mere myth; and on his way toward them Don Jeronymo was smitten down by an ague, and had been taken back to São Paulo de Loanda gravely ill. Upon making this hasty retreat the governor had placed command of his soldiers in the hands of Balthasar d'Almeida and Pedro Alvares Rebello, two men whose judgment was not highly praised by their fellow Portugals; and those two, seeking, I suppose, to win quick fame through some independent exploit, had gone hallooing off into most bleak and inhospitable terrain in search of a certain wild native chief, Kafuche Kambara by name. That determined rebel was roving somewhere southward of Masanganu; and in the better hope of snaring him, they were summoning nearly all the garrison from that town, leaving only a small force there.

In the hasty assembly of soldiers no one healthy was spared from the service. And to my surprise and dismay I found myself compelled to take part in this rash expedition. There on the list was my name pricked out:

Andres Battell, Piloto.

Of the arts of foot-soldiery I had never known much. That is not a great English skill, we being an island race. When enemies have come to our shores we have fought valiantly but, I do admit, with little success, which is why the Romans of Caesar were able to subdue us, and the Angles and Saxons who came later, and the Normans of William. We are a brave folk—the bravest, I think, in all the world—but we have never given heed to mastering the drills and maneuvers of combat by land, that require us to march like a single animal with many heads that think alike, for that is not the English way. We are too much independent. And therefore, knowing this weakness or fault in ourselves, we have since King William's time taken good care that no enemy shall ever reach our shores again, and none ever has, and I suspect that by God's grace and the strength of our bold seamen we will be protected forever in England against further invasion.

In my own family they say there was a grandfather of my father who fought well in the wars between Lancaster and York, but other than that one we have been all of us men of the sea, as befits a family of the Essex shore. So it was a new and most unwelcome thing to me to find myself decked out in Portugee armor, with a gleaming polished casque to keep my head asweat and a great hulking breastplate and all those other foolish massive things, and then to have to go marching in one plodding step after another over an interminable wasteland. God's bones, how repellent unto me! Yet had I no choice in the matter. I could not say, "My contract with you Portugals is to be a sea-pilot for you." I had no rights whatsoever among these people. I lived by their sufferance alone. I was a prisoner of war, that could be clapped in dungeon by any commander at any time. So when I was told to march, why, I did march, and no grumble of it.

And O! the grievous dismal land we marched into! Here were no lush and leafy jungles, here were no steaming heavy vapors rising from ponds and swamps. This was a dry land in a dry season, a place where it was easy to believe that rain had fallen last in the time of King Arthur, and before that perhaps in Julius Caesar's day. The soil was a parched orange thing, cracked like old plaster where the sun had riven it, and it was all but barren. Bleached skulls and bones of animals lay scattered on the ground as omens of mortality. On that seared plain terrible crookbacked thorny trees did sprout, and other low vegetation that might have been engendered in the troubled dreams of some disordered deity. It was an empty land, except here and there where the earth was less brutal and a few native settlements clung to a sort of life: dome-shaped huts of flimsy branches and leaves, arrayed in circles of seven or nine, occupied by sad-eyed scrawny blackamoors who fouled their own territory with scatterings of bones and seeds and broken calabashes and other rubble, and hung withered chunks of smoked meat in the leafless branches of the trees.

Only once was there during that dreary miserable march any moment of beauty or joy, and that was when we entered a zone of grassy pasture that was grazed by the animal called here the zevvera, which is wondrous to behold. This beast is like a horse, but that his mane and his tail and his body is distinguished by streaks of black and white that are most highly elegant, and look as if it were done by art. These zevveras are all wild and live in great herds, and will suffer a man to come within shot of them, and let them shoot three or four times at them before they will run away. When they do run, it is in huge number, and the sight is something that not the most doltish dullard would ever forget, for they dazzle the eye with the movement of their white and black stripes, that seem to have an inner motion of their own beyond the motion of the animal itself.

We startled these zevveras and brought down a few with our muskets, and the rest fled, so as to create that miraculous effect of a river of stripes moving away from us. No man has ever tamed one of these striped horses to ride upon him, and I think no one ever will. For they do have a fierce independence of spirit, that I admire greatly.

I had one other pleasure on this journey, most unexpected, which was the companionship of my gentle friend Laurenço Barbosa, the tax-collector. Certainly he was no military man. But when I arrived of Masanganu on that last voyage in the scow I found him already there, to make some sort of enumeration or survey of Portuguese settlement in the inland region; and when generals Alvares Rebello and d'Almeida sent forth their request for an assembly of troops to conquer Kafuche Kambara, Barbosa chose to go with them instead of to remain in Masanganu. I believe he simply wished to taste a little of the excitement and fury of war, after having spent all his days traveling about the borders of the realm making lists and registers and entries in his ledger.

I did not even know until the second day out of Masanganu that he was among us. But then I saw in the column just before mine a distinguished older man with an elegant purple plume to his hat, instead of a metal helmet, and though scarce believing it could be he, I hurried ahead and found him. And we did have a cheering reunion, each being greatly surprised to find the other in such an unlikely place.

We shared wine, which he had brought with him in a hamper, and we spoke of what had befallen us in the ten months or thereabouts since last we had met. Barbosa had been all over the inland, into such provinces as Malemba and Bondo and Bangala and Matamba, where scarce any Portugal ever went, and I marveled at his diligence in making surveys of such remote places. He told me many a tale of these lands: such as the great province of Cango, fourteen days journey from the town of Loango, which is full of mountains and rocky ground, and full of woods, and has great store of copper. The elephantos in this place do excel, and there are so many that the warehouses do overflow with the teeth of them being stored to go for market in Loango. And I heard from him of certain monster apes of the inland, the great one called the pongo and the smaller one named the engeco, which are much like wild hairy men, but cannot speak and have no more understanding than a beast.

When he told me this and much else, that astonished me beyond words, I related of my voyage to São Tomé, and that I had acquired a slave-girl from Matamba who was a Christian and had become my bed-fellow, and such. Then Barbosa asked me what news I had from São Paulo de Loanda, for that he had not been in the capital of the colony in many months. In particular he craved to know whether Don João de Mendoça had returned from Portugal, and if so what had befallen between him and Don Jeronymo d'Almeida.

At this I grew most downcast, for I had not yet come round to telling him of this matter owing to the painfulness of it to me. Gravely I said, "Nay, I think Don João will never return, for Don Jeronymo has plotted to do him to death."

"What is it you say?"

"So I heard it from one of my sailors," I declared, and repeated what had been said to me by Mendes Oliveira, that two rascals had been hired to throw Don João and Dona Teresa overboard in the voyage to Europe. At that, Barbosa did cross himself several times and looked much moved, with the beginnings of tears in his eyes just showing.

He said, "Don João was the only hope of this land, to govern wisely and with effect."

"Aye. So I felt also."

"But can it truly be? He is so shrewd, surely he would have guarded himself against such an attack!"

"I do pray so," I replied. "I know only what was told me, that the scheme was so ordered by Don Jeronymo, and that when I departed last from São Paulo de Loanda there was no word of the return of Don João."

"But none of his death, either?"

"Nay, no news of that."

"Then there is still hope for him," said Barbosa. But that hope seemed scant to me.

Having this man by my side as I marched made the burden of it much more light. Within a few days more we arrived at the camp where the main body of the Portuguese army had assembled, and a fine grand force it was, filling half the plain. There must have been seven to eight hundred Portugals there, along with an army of their black allies that I could not count, it was so huge, to a number of twenty thousand or even thirty or forty thousand. All these were arrayed in a long confused mass, the Portugals in their tents with some horse grazing about, and the Negro auxiliaries to the side.

The way it is done with these auxiliaries is that the Portugals have out of Kongo a black nobleman, which is known to be a good Christian and of good behavior. He has brought out of Kongo some one hundred Negroes that are his followers. This Macikongo, as he is known, has the rank of *tandala*, or general, over the black camp, and has authority to kill, to put down lords and make lords, and has all the chief doings with the Negroes.

So now the loyal *sobas* and their armies and the black *tandala* who was their high master and the Portugal troops all were drawn up together getting ready to go in quest of that unruly and powerful *soba* Kafuche Kambara. It seemed beyond possibility to me that that chieftain could withstand the Portugals, owing to the vast size of the army that would take the field against him, with all these blackamoors and the many Portugal troops.

But God in His wisdom doth prepare many severe surprises for those who go too proudly upon the world.

The surprise that befell the Portugals on the twenty-second day of April in Anno 1594, which I did witness and which came near to taking from me my life, had the form of a sudden and most terrible ambush as the Portugals and their allies went their way through the countryside. For a great army may sometimes be so great that it is cumbered by its own size, much as those elephantos are of which I spoke, that venture into narrow places and cannot turn around, and have their tails lopped off by a cunning hunter. As we moved into a deep gorge, so long and narrow that one might scarce insert a picktooth into it, I felt a sudden sense of utter alarm over just such a likelihood, I know not why. Balthasar d'Almeida and Pedro Alvares Rebello were leading the way as if they were Alexander the Great and Hannibal, and the black *tandala* did spur his immense Negro horde along behind them, when in a trice the armies of Kafuche Kambara sprang upon us out of nowhere, the same manner as in the old Greek tale the armed men did mysteriously arise around the hero Cadmus when he sowed the earth with dragon teeth.

This was my first view of land warfare, and a wild and barbarous scene it was. In Angola and also in the Kongo they do fight more by cunning than by direct onslaught, depending much on surprise. All about us had secretly been created paths armed with thorns, and stakes tipped with the strong and hard *nsako* wood that the Portugals call ironwood, and traps consisting of ditches covered over with earth and branches. And when the enemy fell upon us there was immediate panic, with large numbers of our force behind driven into these traps at once, and either perishing straightaway or else suffering such injury that they were useless thereafter.

The native armies here do always fight on foot, this land having no horses except the wild and unmanageable zevveras. They divide their force into several groups, fitting themselves according to the situation of the field. The moves of their army are guided and directed by certain several sounds and noises, that proceed from the captain-general, who goes into the midst of the army and there signifies what is to be put into execution, that is to say, either that they shall join battle, or else retire, or put on forward, or turn to the right hand, and to the left hand, or to perform any other warlike action. For by these several sounds distinctly delivered from one another, they do all understand the commandments of their captain, as in European armies we do understand the pleasure of our general by the sundry strokes of the drum and the sounds of the trumpet.

Three principal sounds make these messages of war, and they were horrid and frightening in my ears as they burst upon us. One is uttered by great rattles hollowed out of a tree and covered with leather, which they strike with certain little handles of ivory. Another comes from a three-cornered instrument made of thin plates of iron, which are hollow and empty within. They make them ring by striking them with wooden wands; and oftentimes they do also crack them, to the end that the sound should be more harsh, horrible, and warlike. The third instrument is the *mpunga* that I met in the land of Loango, that is the fife made from the hollowed tusk of the elephanto, which yields a warlike and harmonious music. With these devices they signal and encourage one another from one part of the battlefield to the other, and some valiant and courageous soldiers go before the rest, and strike their bells and dance, and stir up the emotions of battle, and by the notes they play do signify unto them what danger they are in, and what weapons face them.

The military dress of our attackers was frightful. The high lords wore headdresses garnished with plumes made of the bright feathers of the peacock, and those of the ostrich and other birds, which made them to seem men of greater stature than they are, and terrible to look upon. From the girdle upwards they were all naked, and had hanging about them from their necks and down to their flanks certain chains of iron, with rings upon them as big as a man's little finger, which they used for a certain military pomp and bravery. From the girdle downward they had linen breeches, and wore boots in the Portuguese style. The common soldiers did not wear much, except that they were garbed about the loins. For weapons these people use bows and arrows with barbed iron tips, and clubs made of ironwood branches, and daggers, and lances that exceed the height of a man. The sword is not a weapon of battle among them, generally being carried only by kings and nobles as a mark of their office. Nor do they have the use of musket and shot, for which God be praised, though by the folly of some Portugal and Dutch traders, and some French lately, these most deadly weapons are being now sold into their hands. I do not see how the civilized races of the world will withstand the onslaught that is sure to come, once all the black and red savages do comprehend the use of firearms, that are the most terrible weapon ever loosed in the world.

But that day it was enough for Kafuche Kambara and his men to employ arrows and clubs and daggers. Like a shining black tide did they spew down upon us, making their ghastly music and shouting their war-cries, and they did cause a river of blood to flow from us. They came in waves, one group fighting until weary, then being called back by the drums and fifes and bells and fresh warriors fighting in their places.

Our black auxiliaries at once entered into panic, for all that the brave *tandala* and his *sobas* tried to form them into fighting array. It was no use, for surprise is fatal to them, and whole legions of them began to flee, trampling others and breaking down all order.

At the very midst of this the Portugals formed a stout group, back to back, shoulder to shoulder, and with their muskets tried to blow an opening in the ranks of the attackers. And sure indeed the firing did great harm. But fighting with musket is a slow business at such a wild melee, when one is loading and firing and reloading and all: in a proper formation the musket cannot be bettered, with defenders properly placed, but we were caught unprepared and we died by the dozens. They came in upon us jabbing with their lances and slashing with their daggers, and if we shot one down, two more confronted us, and all the while their deadly arrows soared above us and struck us most sorely.

This killing was a new thing for me, at least at such close range, so that I knew the face of my victim and smelled his sweat as I despatched him. It is true that when I did ship aboard the *Margaret and John* in the campaign against the Spanish Armada I took part in warfare that was no child's sport, indeed killing of the most real kind. At that time I loaded heavy shot into the guns and jumped back and watched the balls smash into the sides of Spanish ships, that promptly went up into flames and were shattered: that surely is warfare. Certainly many Spaniards died then, and I had my share of the sending of them to Hell. But there is a difference—O, a very great difference!—between toiling in a gun crew on a ship to fire balls at faceless enemies some hundreds of yards away aboard another vessel, and reaching out with your own hand to snuff the life of one single man who stands right before you. The one is a remote deed, the other a killing most intimate. So this was a baptism of slaughter for me here that day. I did not think of the death of Tristão Caldeira de Rodrigues as my killing of him, but only as his perishing by his own folly, that would not have happened but by his greed.

In the company of some two score Portugals I fought my way through the mob of howling ring-jangling blackamoor warriors to a low rise east of the main encounter. On the top of this pale sandy ridge there grew tall many-armed leafless plants whose limbs were bright green and fleshy and armed with most terrible black thorns. We squeezed ourselves between the ranks of these close-packed little trees, in the doing of which their thorns did cut me most cruelly, so that trails of blood ran down my skin in thirty places. But once we were behind them, these formidably armed vegetations formed a secure palisado that shielded us from the furious advance of the foe. We lay down or crouched, and aimed our muskets with care, and sent our shot into their hearts or into their heads by one and one and one, which created a heaping mound of fallen blacks below our ridge.

And while we did this killing, we also ventured out, a few of us at a time, to locate and bring to safety such other Portugals as passed our way. When we saw any, we slipped through that evil thicket and waved to them with our arms and cried out in the Portugal tongue until they heard us over the din of the battle, and if they were wounded we went to their side to fetch them, while our companions aimed their muskets at any enemy that periled us.

I myself went out four times in these forays, and on the fourth it was Barbosa whom I found and brought safely in. He had been skewered by a dart in the fleshy part of his arm; but he refused my attentions and called for fresh shot for his musket, and lay down beside us to fight.

So it went for perhaps the half part of an hour. We scarce had time to draw a peaceful breath, but that a new wave of the attackers came toward us. The hideous sound of their little ringing bells that dangled from their bodies did fright us terribly, and the music of their battle-orders screeched and thundered above all other sounds. Little flying insects no bigger than midges hovered over me like a buzzing cloud, settling in my sweat and most especially in the rivulets of blood, thickening and sticky, from the many gashes and gouges the green thorn-plants had inflicted upon my skin.

So long as we held safe behind our natural palisado, they could not reach us. But we had only so much powder and so much shot, and no matter how loud we called upon Jesus and the Apostles, they were not likely to supply us more.

First this Portugal and then that one exhausted his ammunition, so that our position became hopeless. The savages did crawl low and try forcing their way through the thorns, which gave them less trouble than they did us. Some worked on the outside, in the undermining of the bushes with their clubs and lances, but the doing of this they found most difficult. Yet others were able to hack entry, chopping at the limbs of the plants and cutting them apart, from which sundered places a strange milky blood did flow.

Barbosa, beside me, seized the first of them who penetrated our refuge, digging his hands into the thick wool of the man's hair and pulling him down.

"Yours!" he cried to me, and I smote the man with the butt of my empty musket, so that his head cracked and he pitched downward into the sand, blood gushing from his ears. Barbosa did seize the foeman's lance, and thrust it robustly into the next who ventured through the breach in the shrubbery, while I in turn dragged his body inward and piled it atop the first, to repair the breach. And so we fought on and on for long minutes, that seemed days to me.

In the meanwhile archers of the enemy did aim their shafts toward us in our place of sanctuary. Most of these struck the plants and were embedded therein, making more of the milky fluid gush forth—some of which, striking my lips and one eye, did sting me most fiercely, and my eyelid swelled so great that for a time I was hard put to see. For these were poison-plants, whose milk had the very fire of Satan in it, and whose deadly nature did manifest itself by the outgrowth of thorns on their skins.

A few of the arrows finding their way between the tight-laced branches worked damage among us. Shielded as we were, we suffered many injuries, and now we no longer dared venture out to recover others of our company. It seemed only a brief while before we must needs be overwhelmed. I cursed the inanity of our generals, that had led us into this impasse, and I wished a thousand times for the snugness of the dungeon at São Paulo de Loanda, where there were no ungodly plants to bathe me in their searing milk nor wild savages to threaten me with arrows. But as I thought such thoughts I also fought most strenuously, using my musket's butt until the weapon cracked in two and I tossed it aside, and then employing a lance that I took from a fallen African, opening with it the guts of more than several of our enemies. Yet were they hundreds to our dozens, and their arrows came whistling and singing in through the increasingly large openings in our palisado, and how long could we endure?

There was yet another thorny rise a fair distance behind ours. Someone among us proposed that we effect a retreat to that, and attempt thereby to lose ourselves in a parched forest that lay on the far side. If we withdrew far enough, it might be that no pursuers would detect us, and we might escape, for winning this battle was hopeless and merely surviving was our chief goal. This seemed the best of a host of unsatisfying stratagems, and we began it, some of us crawling backward while others guarded the thorny barrier before it.

But as the rearward movement commenced, three Africans did succeed in breaking open a fair gap in the thorn-plants, and a pack of them came rushing through. We struck down the first, but more were after, and we had not enough men to deal with them all. To my distress I saw Barbosa struggling with two at once, and he no hearty bravo, only an old man of gentle demeanor unused to such brawls. I made toward him.

"Nay," he cried. "Flee! Flee! I will hold them!"

That I could not countenance. So I came upon his foes, which now numbered three, and seized by the hair one great blackamoor with his cheeks painted all crimson and purple, and drew his face across a row of thorns, which wrung a hellish cry from him and sent him reeling away, blinded, and his face newly colored even further now with a mix of milky fluid of the plant and blood from his wounds. A second enemy I did catch on the tip of my lance and haul away from Barbosa, and then with a shift of my weight I spitted him through like a lamb, so thoroughly and well that I was not able to withdraw my lance, it being snagged on some interior part of him. Barbosa meanwhile had drawn his dagger and was keeping the last of his attackers at bay, chopping the air at him and defying him to come nearer. That one I did smite in the back with my fist and across the temple with the side of my other hand, a blow that I think took the life from him, for he fell like a clubbed ox.

For a moment all was tranquil in the place where we stood. My friend did turn to me with warm gratitude in his eyes, and he began to speak. But such calm on the battlefield is both deceptive and perilous, for oft it leads to worser things. All of a sudden a shower of arrows burst upon us in our clearing. One of them pierced me, taking me high in the back just where my left arm grows from my trunk. It passed through the flesh while not hitting vital parts. But so intent was I on other matters that I think I did not take the trouble to feel the fire of it; for in the same instant another arrow caught Barbosa through the throat, standing out on both sides of his neck like some new kind of ornament that I hope unto God does not become the fashion in any land where I may end my days. He said something that was only half a sound, all bubble and gurgle, and his eyes went very bright and then lost their sheen. I caught him as he fell, but there was no saving him: his wind was interrupted and he was already choking on his own phlegm and blood, or perhaps even then dead. All I could do was lower him gently to the ground.

In so doing I perceived for the first time the pain of my own wound. It burned like the stinging of a thousand thousand bees all biting in the same place. The shaft was slender but long, and jutted cumbersomely about me. But one of the Portugals, running up, employed some trick of chopping off the feathered end and driving the main part of the shaft swiftly through the wound, which knocked the breath from me but freed me of the arrow.

"Come," he said. "There is still a moment for fleeing."

I looked about. Barbosa was wholly beyond my help. The archers were aiming elsewhere at the moment, for other bands of Portugals were deployed on the far side of the crest. Most of our people had begun their flight to safety, and now I would do that also. I turned me away from that place of horrors and ran, stumbling and falling, rising again, stumbling, rolling once headlong into the warm sand, getting up, stumbling onward. I did not think I would live another ten minutes; and just then I was so weary and so sick at heart that I almost welcomed my release.

ELEVEN

I REACHED the far crest; I dropped to the ground and wriggled once more through an infernal hedge of those leafless thorny plants; I arrived to the far side, where all was quiet, and looked back and saw the battle raging in the distance. It was moving ever onward away from me, and now was only a muddle of distant shouts and bells and drums, an event seen through a haze. I crouched there and suddenly I began violently to weep—not from grief, I trow, nor from fear, but only from the complete black weariness of my body and spirit, in every bone, in every fiber. But I took some kind of healing from the tears.

When that fit was done, and it was only a brief one, I did examine my wound and I found it to be ugly and raw but not in a large way damaging: there was a numbness about the place where the arrow had ripped through the flesh, and I knew that later on I would feel a pain and an aching where now I could feel nothing, but it would not otherwise hamper me. For the moment I was in more of discomfort from the hundred fiery cuts and gouges in my skin than from that wounding.

I scouted about and found seven Portugals, all wounded in great or slight fashion, that were hiding nearby in the sands. We gathered ourselves together, a sad and battered remnant. I knew none of them, for they all were the soldiers of São Tomé; but two of them recognized me, having seen me during my visit to that island. One, that had a horrid wound to his jaw, did a sort of grin with half his face and said, "We could use that slave-girl of yours here now, English,.to bind up our injuries, eh?"

I made a shrug my sole reply. At that time I did not think I would see my Matamba ever again, and I was heartsore over the death of Barbosa, who of all the Portugals I had encountered in these years of my captivity had been the truest and gentlest of friends, and whose body I had not even been able to rescue from the vultures that already were darkening the sky.

Shortly afterward came two more Portugals to us, men of São Paulo de Loanda, who told us that Balthasar d'Almeida and his fellow general had made their escape by horse, but that nearly all the other Portugals had been slain by the remorseless warriors of Kafuche Kambara.

"The dead ones are the happy ones," said one of the São Tomé men. "Theirs was a swift going. Ours will be slow and very thirsty, I wager you."

With that he commenced an uttering of gloomy prayers.

"Wait," I said. "In five days we can be at Masanganu, can we not?"

"Do you know the way?" asked another Portugal.

"And where will we have food or drink?" said another.

"The blackamoors will hunt us down," muttered one other. We are already dead men, only we still do move about, and deceive ourselves thus that we live."

I wanted to make some inspiring speech, as I had long ago made when I was a castaway in Brazil and found myself also with men of melancholy and defeated aspect. But I could not force the words past my lips. I was too morbid of soul myself just then, too close to mine own defeat. Even though the heart of the battle now had passed us by, and we were not likely again to be molested by our enemy, we now faced a task beyond all possibility, of marching back without supplies and without knowledge of the route across this terrible desert, having no weapons to fend off beasts of prey, and bearing wounds that from day to day were sure to sap such little strength as now we had. I did not intend to give myself up to despair, for giving up is not my style and despair is not my favored tipple. But neither am I prone to embracing folly, and folly it did seem indeed to think we would come alive out of this place. And so I had little to say or think by way of good cheer.

The Portugals went at their praying. They passed around some beads that one man had, and a crucifix of another. I did not partake of the comforts of those objects.

For all their devotions, though, these men had little true faith. For one did declare, "God hath forsaken us," and the others nodded and took up the theme and embellished it, with many a somber statement that we had for our sins been cast into this valley of the shadow. And at this sort of dark talk something rose up in me that I think is wholly English within me, that does not like to rush forward and claim defeat as a bride, and, though I had not changed my own estimates of the chances of our surviving, I burst out with, "Nay, what good do such words do us? We are alive thus far, are we not? When all our comrades are dead? Rejoice in that much, that we yet live."

"Not much for rejoicing am I, Englishman, when I know I have but days to live."

"Fear not," I said. "God will provide."

"Aye," said the Portugals bitterly. "He will provide more torment, and He will provide more pain, and a lingering slow brutish death."

There was no use disputing it with them. We sat and stared and waited in silence for the day to end, for in our weakened state it seemed best to move about only in the cooler night hours. One of the Portugals, who had some skill as a surgeon, moved among us, binding wounds and offering bites of fruit from a pouch he carried. I marveled at that—that he would share his food and not save it all for himself, as I imagined a Portugal would do; but that was not right of me to think, for Portugals are not vile people, even if they have not in every way our English notion of honor. The sweetness of the fruit did refresh me, and I stood and walked about, though my head was swimming with my tiredness.

The chief center and tumult of the battle was altogether gone from us now. I saw in the distance only the bloody bodies of the fallen, and the vultures flapping about them, seeking out the most choicest titbits.

And then I saw an even more sinister thing: five naked black men that came out of another direction, the south-west, that had been quiet all the day. Three were very tall with elongated tapering limbs, and two were short and broad and exceeding powerful of frame, and all that they wore were the weapons strapped about their waists, except that one had a collar fastened around his neck, and every one had his body painted in white with certain symbols and emblems. They moved in a single file, very silent, like cats, with the tallest in the front and the second tallest at the end of the file.

I had seen such as these before, and I took no joy in seeing of them now. For I knew them to be Jaqqas, and my heart sank within me. God will provide, I had said, and God had indeed provided. But, I thought, what He has sent us are demons to hurry us to our last repose.

And yet, and yet, something within me was aroused with a fascination. As I have said before: I find myself drawn to the darkness, to the strange obscure subterranean mysteries, I know not why. The great coccodrillo that had come out of the river to me on that desert isle where I was cast away in Brazil had worked a magnetism on me, and so also had the Jaqqa prince standing by himself in the forest on the first voyage to Masanganu, and the dead one in Loango. And now I stared at these five emissaries of Satan as they marched across the horizon and I could not take my eyes away, for they exerted an irresistible pull on my soul.

They moved through the battlefield shambles, examining the dead, prodding this one and that, turning him over, feeling his flesh the way one might poke and scrutinize meat in a butcher-shop, seeing how much fat there was and how much sinew, and how firm the texture. I that had seen cannibals before, in the forests behind the town of Rio de Janeiro and after my shipwreck, knew what these men were about here, and it did chill my blood.

With great calmness and in no hurry they chose out of all the hundreds and hundreds in that field of gore three corpses, all of them blackamoors, as though white man's flesh was inferior upon their palates. These three they hoisted to the shoulders of the three Jaqqas in the midst of the file, the one that wore the collar and the two that were short and very muscular, and, looking well satisfied at their scavenging, they continued onward, crossing from south to north.

Then did they notice us.

We had not moved nor spoken all the while that they were prowling about. We huddled in our little sandy declivity, praying not to be observed; for although we were ten men and they were five, we were all of us spent and wounded, and we had no weapons other than empty muskets and broken lances, and there was not a man among us who had the least further taste for fighting that day. So shrank we down from view; but the Jaqqas paused, they sniffed the air like troubled leopards, they turned in circles to scan the terrain, and then, without a word, they put down their burden of dead men and commenced moving toward us.

"We are lost," said the Portugal surgeon. "These are the man-eaters, the Jaqqas."

I said, "And why should they trouble to slay us, when enough dead men do lie before us to feed all their nation for half a month?"

"That meat on the ground will spoil in days," the surgeon answered. "We remain fresh until we are slaughtered. We will be captives, and when their appetites require it we will be eaten."

But none of us made a move to flee. We were all so feeble and frail with strain, and they all looked to be as fleet as zevveras. And a time comes to every man when his death is upon him and he knows that there is no escaping it, and so he merely stands and waits.

I confess that of all the deaths that I had imagined for myself in the idle hours of my boyhood, when one thinks much on death and strives to understand its nature, the one death I had never envisioned was that of being roasted and devoured by my own fellow men. Which was not a pleasing notion to me; and yet how does it matter, when you are dead, whether you become food for worms or fishes or ants, or Jaqqas? You are dead; that is the essence of the thing; and it seemed to me now that I would very soon be coming to the end of my journey.

The Jaqqas neared us and stood in a ring around us, with their hands resting lightly on the hilts of their long daggers. And I saw a gesture pass from the collared one to the very tall one that seemed their leader, and it was plainly a gesture of inquiry, without accompanying words, to which the leader made quick silent reply with a single shake of his left hand. I suspected that the collared one was asking permission to kill us, and the permission was denied. In this afterward I found out that I was right, for among the Jaqqas the young men do wear a collar about their neck in token of slavery, until they bring an enemy's head slain in battle, and then they are uncollared, freed, and dignified with the title of soldiers. This one was asking if he could earn his freedom by slaying us. But clearly we were too contemptible to slay, and it would not be fair battle, and he was refused.

For a long while they studied us, and we them. They went round and round us, in strange contemplation, never once uttering a sound. Their silence was the most frightening thing of all, for it made them seem like dream-creatures, nightmare-things.

But there was much else that was frightful about them. For their eyes were bright as sizzling coals, and their bodies gleamed beneath their paint so that every muscle stood out like a statue's, and they did have two teeth above and two below knocked out, Jaqqa-fashion, which made them look like evil jack-o'-lanterns when they grinned. We remained silent, too, as they surveyed us, out of fear or perhaps out of mystification, for one does not chatter when one is in the presence of devils.

At last they reached a decision concerning us. By pantomime gesture they had us remove our battered bloodstained armor and toss it aside, leaving us only clad in the light linen surplices and such that we wore below it. Then they beckoned, indicating with a tossing of their heads that we should follow them, and led us up out of our sheltering-place toward the path they had been following before they discovered us.

They arrayed us in a line, and disposed us within their own formation, one of them followed by two of us, and again one of them and two of us, so that we all were in the single file, now three times its former size. And we began to march toward the north, they again carrying the three blackamoor corpses slung over their shoulders, we lurching along as best we could, considering our wearied condition.

"Ah, Madonna, where are they taking us?" asked one Portugal behind me.

And another replied, "To their main camp, so that they can feast on us with great celebration."

A third said, "Should we run?"

And a fourth did answer, with a laugh, "Better to take wing and fly, methinks. That way we might escape them."

I kept my peace. Night was coming on, and I was beginning to recover my strength, and I wanted to waste none of it in idle conversation. The arrow-wound in my back now was giving me extraordinary pain, that came in waves like a series of bombard-blasts that did explode within me, but I knew myself not to be badly injured for all of that. And the other exhaustions of the battle, the pounding in my chest and the soreness in my legs and the throbbing of my eyes and the cuts of my flesh, were starting now to leave me as the deep natural recuperative strength of my body asserted itself. So I thought I might wait until darkness was complete and then try to slip away from these Jaqqas, with one or two of the Portugals if they cared to come, and find my way back to Masanganu.

But it was not to be. When darkness arrived we halted at a hot dry low place where the brush was heavy and more of those abominable thorn-trees of the milky green flesh abounded. The Jaqqas drew us into a little clearing from which there was only one exit, and made us lie down, which indeed we gladly did. Two of them guarded us, standing casually before us with their arms folded, and the others went on a foray, from which they returned with a few handfuls of fruits and seeds. These they distributed to us, with a gesture that we should eat.

The fruits were bitter and the seeds were hard fare to crack and chew, yet it was good food withal, and there was a clear spring near at hand from which we were able to drink, which we had not done all the day long. The Jaqqas meanwhile busied themselves by building a fire, which they did most cleverly, by twirling one slender stick against another over a bunch of the dry straw that passed here for grass, until a spark flew forth and ignited it. Soon a goodly blaze was roaring.

We witnessed then an unholy feast, for they did take one of the three cadavers they had filched from the battlefield and most dexterously did lop its legs from it. Thereupon they carved his thigh-flesh into cubes of meat, which they affixed on skewers that they held into the tips of the flames, twisting them deftly so that the meat cooked while the skewers did not take fire. All this they did in the most absolute calmness, as if it were an extremely ordinary daily thing to butcher a dead man and make morsels out of his thighs. But in good sooth such was the case for them, it being the most daily of events, this grim anthropophagy. During their cooking they laughed and chanted, but I saw no talking between them, and as the fat dripped down and sizzled it did give them passing great delight, so that they clapped their hands like children.

They ate their fill, and then some; and when they had done with the meat, they did crack the skull, and scoop out the brains with a sort of spoon fashioned from a rib, and dine themselves with a high pleasure on that; and afterward they turned to us, who had looked on in deep horror at it all and most extremely at the serving of that final pudding, and they did make broad generous gestures to us, as though to be saying, "Join us in our banquet, comrades! There's meat enough for all!" But of course we shrank back from this kindly offer the way we would from the embrace of the Devil's dam.

The fire burned all night, and the Jaqqas sat by it, nor did they ever sleep, so far as I could tell. I was now in great discomfort from my wound and I lay sometimes awake and sometimes lost in a mazy disorder of the mind, but every time I opened my eyes I saw our five diabolical guardians sitting together, unsleeping. Now and again one of them would arise and cut for himself a piece of fresh meat and cook it to eat. All during the night the gruesome reek of charred flesh and human grease did hang over our encampment, sickening at first and then becoming merely another smell, of which one took no special notice.

Morning came. The Jaqqas prodded us awake and buried their smouldering fire in sand. We assumed our formation and moved onward.

I saw now that escape was plainly impossible. They were too shrewd in the ways of the desert, and kept us ever in check, whether on the march or in camp at night. And if I did manage to slip away it would be folly, this being an inhospitable place and I not knowing the where-abouts of the water-holes, or the plants whose fruits were safe to eat, or any such; I should be clawing at my own guts in extreme agony within two days, if I successfully fled from them into this awful wilderness. So I abandoned that plan utterly. Some of the Portugals with whom I marched made a different assessment of the situation, and on the third day of the journey two of them suddenly broke from the line and began to run, clumsily and with much staggering, across the arid waste. They had not gone ten yards before one of the Jaqqas had his bow down from his shoulder and an arrow in the ready, and I thought sure there would be a dead Portugal or two an instant later. But the tallest of the Jaqqas made one gesture and the archer put down his bow, and then he made another gesture and two of his fellows went sprinting after the fugitives I have never seen mortal man run so fast. The leopard, when he hunts, can in a short distance outpace even the fast-footed gazelle; but I think those two Jaqqas could have left even a leopard behind. In no time at all they caught the two Portugals, and seized them with an arm slipped round their necks and dropped them easily to the ground, and then lifted them, not roughly, and got them to their feet. The Portugals were shivering with fear, expecting to be slain on the spot for their temerity. But no, they were not harmed at all, they were merely sent back to their places in the line, and we continued as though nothing whatsoever had occurred.

That was the only escape attempt any of us made.

But on the fifth day north we began to perceive something amazing, that made us all rejoice we had not been more assiduous at getting away from our captors. For we took notice of certain familiar tokens on the landscape, that led to only one conclusion: the Jaqqas were not captors but rescuers, for they were guiding us in the direction of Masanganu!

"How can this be?" asked a Portugal. "Have they conquered the whole place, and is their main camp there now?"

"Nay," said another, "Masanganu is of no interest to them."

"Who knows what interests a Jaqqa?"

"Are we truly going that way?" I asked.

"Look, there, Englishman. That row of palm trees on the horizon— what else is it, but the forest at the edge of the River Kwanza? There are no rivers here, except the Lukala that comes in from above, and we are below. And there, those hills to the east—it is Kambambe, the silver-mining land!"

"But why bring us to Masanganu?" I said in wonderment.

"Why, indeed?" replied the Portugal surgeon.

And that was all the answer we ever had. You know how it is in dreams, that things take place that will not answer to the test of reason; and you know I have said again and again that these Jaqqas did seem to me to be creatures out of the misty land of sleep, like walking nightmares set loose upon our world. One does not ask questions of dream-creatures, or, if one does, one must know that one has no right to a sensible answer.

The Portugals were right that the trees had their roots in the waters of the Kwanza. Another day passed and then we were in truth within sight of the fortifications of Masanganu. Here the air did change, becoming moist and fever-laden in the horrid Masanganu way, which told us that we had come at last out of the desert where so many Portugals had left their bones. The Jaqqas did not accompany us farther. They had eaten all three of their dead men, to every last scrap of flesh, in their nightly feasts, and they had done their mysterious self-appointed task of saving our lives, and now they vanished as suddenly as they came, without a word, without a hint, and left us to find our way the last few miles into Masanganu.

A sad and sorry lot we ten were, as we struggled and tottered into the presidio. We were near naked, clad in grimy rags, and all gaunt and bulging-eyed from a diet of shabby bitter fruits and hard seed. Our wounds had begun to fester despite the best offices of our surgeon. But yet we were alive. We had neither perished on the battlefield in Kafuche Kambara's terrible ambush, nor had gone into the bellies of the Jaqqas, and that we had avoided both these fates seemed miraculous now, so that we did fling ourselves down at the outside of Masanganu and give thanks to the Lord in our own ways and languages, crying out to Him for what surely was His own compassionate intervention on our behalf.

God rest me, but I never thought I would weep with joy at entering Masanganu again. Yet this time it was as welcome to me as the shores of Paradise.

TWELVE

AT MASANGANU the Portugals did make much over us, for they had not expected any survivors of the massacre to come among them.

News of that disaster had reached them five or six days previous, when the first who got away had come into the presidio. These were the ones who had escaped by horse, mainly the ranking officers, who had galloped valiantly toward safety, leaving all their infantry to be slain behind them. Such men as Balthasar d'Almeida and his captain-major Pedro Alvares Rebello had already left Masanganu for São Paulo de Loanda, to confer with Governor d'Almeida, but others who had come safe away were still in the town, and great was their amazement when they learned that we had managed to bring ourselves alive from the place of battle.

We were taken to the hospital and given food and drink and medicines, and our wounds were treated, and an officer named Manoel Fonseca, who had the charge over the Masanganu garrison, visited us to learn how we had achieved our escape.

"Why," said our Portugal surgeon, "we were rescued by five Jaqqas, who guided us thither and provided us with food along the way."

To which Manoel Fonseca responded with loud laughter, and cried, "You are mad with fever, man!"

"No," I said, for I lay on the next bed, "it is the truth, by God's eyes! They spoke not a word, those Jaqqas, but said with gestures, Come, follow; and they kept us close by them until we saw the palm-trees that stand by the river's edge."

"I will not believe that. Jaqqas? How do you know they were Jaqqas, pray tell?"

"Because that they had teeth knocked out above and below," said I, pointing to my own front teeth. "And because that while we were with them, they did roast and eat three dead blackamoors that they hauled off from the battlefield. Is that not proof enough?"

Fonseca still could not believe it, though, and not until he had had the same tale from all the others of us did he credit it to be truthful. Which caused all the more amazement, since no one could recall the Jaqqas doing the like in all the time of the Portugals in Angola. Yet there was no denying that we were here and safe, and it had not been angels that wafted us here.

I was in Masanganu some weeks healing. That is no place to heal, with its foul air and poisonous climate, but I was too weak then to travel further, and in any case there were no ships there to make the journey to the coast. After a time I left my bed and walked about, and regained some strength. The town at that time was closed tight like a turtle in its shell, with sentinels posted night and day, for the Portugals were badly frighted and did not know what disaster might come upon them next. They had suffered the most terrible defeat in their African history at the hands of this Kafuche Kambara, having lost hundreds of men and much equipment and nearly the whole of their black auxiliary force, and they believed Kafuche might try now to finish them off, or per-adventure that the other *sobas*, emboldened, would rise and overthrow their yoke. But none of these things happened, and in July of '94 a ship finally came to Masanganu bringing reinforcements. When it returned to São Paulo de Loanda I was aboard, and did pilot it on its voyage down the river.

Vast surprises awaited me in the capital city.

There was a great huge new galleon of Portugal riding out in the harbor, a 600-ton vessel at least, and when I entered into the city proper I saw all the buildings amazingly decorated in banners and ribands and brightly colored flags, as though the Portugals had not just suffered a monstrous defeat at all, but rather were celebrating some colossal victory. Streamers in scarlet and green flew in the breeze, and the palace of the governor was especially bedecked with buntings and velvets of great gaiety.

I asked the bearers that were taking us to town, what had befallen to merit such brave decoration, and they replied, "It is in jubilee of the new governor that Portugal has sent."

"New governor? Where is Don Jeronymo?"

And they pointed most somberly toward the presidio, toward the very same grim fortress where I had been held prisoner four years before. So there had been great reversals and transformations in the colony, it did seem, during my many months of absence.

But I knew less than the half of it.

I went first to my cottage, which I found all in order and well kept. Matamba was there with my other slaves. She gave forth a little gasp as of fright and shock when she saw me, and ran to my side, tears starting from her eyes, and she dropped to her knees before me and looked up troubled, saying, "You are so changed! You are so altered!"

"Am I, now? Come, stand up, girl."

I drew her gently upward and sent the slaves away, and embraced her, and she ran her fingers over my cheeks.

"You have been ill," she said.

"Aye, and a little damaged, too. But I am the same man."

I went to my chamber, where I kept a dim old looking-glass, and peered at my image. And in truth it startled me some to see what I had become, for my face was five years older at least, with deep lines cut alongside my mouth and about my eyes, and a general shrinking of flesh, and a rising of the cheekbones. The heat of the interior and my exertions there and the wound I had suffered had all worked to boil and distill me down to the hard essence: I looked gaunt and fever-eyed, and dangerous of spirit, like some wild brawling bravo of the city taverns. Why, I trow, if I had met a man looking like me on the streets of London I would have been struck with fear of him, so mean and piratical of face had I become!

I removed my clothes, that were sweaty from voyaging, and Matamba sponged me clean. Water is always scarce and most precious in São Paulo de Loanda, since that there is no source of it in the city, but all must be brought in from the island through a trench, and that is much contaminated by the nearness of the ocean. As she bathed me Matamba did finger and inspect my new scars, both the angry one in my back that the arrow had left me, and the lesser ones, fading but not yet wholly gone, that I had taken by crawling around in those murderous thorny plants. In her thus fondling me and making much of me I had new proof of her devotion to me, and once I was refreshed I thought to take her to my bed, I having had months of abstinence in my soldiering and she looking most desirable to me, wearing a simple white shift with her breasts bare, and a blue circlet about her throat, and her eyes shining with eagerness. But then came a knock at the door and a messenger from the governor, saying that I was summoned at once to his palace, and the man handed me a writ to make it more official.

I opened the paper and read it and I like to have choked in my astonishment, for the writ was signed most boldly with the name of the new governor, and the new governor's name was Don João de Mendoça.

"But he is dead!" I cried out. "How can this be?"

The messenger, who was only a slave, looked at me as though I had gone mad, and Matamba knew nothing of governors except that the Portugals of the town had lately done much marching about in the plaza, with pompous changings of the guard and raisings and lowerings of flags, but that was all Greek to her. So, consumed with curiosity, I got me into my best clothes and bade her wait there until my return, and hurried to the palace. I could not comprehend this, for how had Don João escaped the assassins? I thought me that perhaps he had had a son of the same name, who had come from Portugal to avenge his father's murder, but I wondered much at that.

Then I was ushered into the same high-vaulted audience-chamber where I had several times met with Don Jeronymo d'Almeida, the former governor, and there, seated at the governor's great polished desk of brilliant red wood, was Don João himself, not any newly arrived son by that name, nor any ghost neither, I trow. He looked plump and hearty, and scarce a day older than when I had last seen him in the days before the Jesuit troubles, and although he did not rise from his chair of office he favored me with a warm good smile and a broad gesture of greeting, and exclaimed, "Andres! Andres, my friend, my Englishman, my Piloto!"

"Don João, it gives me joy and amaze to see you."

"And joy do I take in this meeting also. How we are all changed, eh? I am governor at last, and you—you look as if you have fought hard, and suffered no little."

"It was a difficult campaign. But by God's grace, and some help from the Jaqqas, I was spared. And you also have been spared! I thought you long dead, Don João."

He gave a little startle. "You did? Why so?"

"They told me a tale, that Don Jeronymo had plotted to have you hurled into the sea when you sailed to Portugal."

Leaning forward, he said, "Knew you of that, Andres?"

"Aye. But my knowledge came too late to help you, for I was already halfway to Loango when I learned of it, and you well out toward Portugal. But was it as I heard?"

"It was," said he in a low dark voice. "There were three men of Don Jeronymo's pay, who planned to carry it out. But I had warning, and I took care to be well guarded, and we found out the men and questioned them. And they did confess, and their scheme was blocked."

"God be thanked. I grieved much for you."

"For that I am much moved, Andres. But you see, I was prepared. I had known Don Jeronymo for what he was, and I placed no trust in his words."

"And now you are governor!"

"Yea. It was simple enough, arranging the appointments, once I spoke before His Majesty, and showed how we were in danger of losing our hold here if the rule of the d'Almeida brothers continued. It was already known that Don Francisco had fled to Brazil. Don Jeronymo's appointment had no legitimacy to it. And so I received the royal assent, and returned here with four hundred soldiers and thirty horses, and now I am putting things to right. We will go forth to punish the lawless *sobas*, and we will do a better job of it, if God wills, then Don Jeronymo did. You were at Masanganu when Kafuche Kambara made his massacre?"

"Nay. I was at the massacre itself."

"And survived? God's grace indeed!"

"And luck, and some skill. Alas, among those slain was the good Barbosa, that was like a second father to me."

"His loss is sad. I knew of that, and that hundreds of others had perished with him. Well, and well, Andres, these are the risks of empire. Were you wounded?"

"I took an arrow. It was not so bad."

"Why were you in the war at all?"

I shrugged. "Don Jeronymo had me ferrying troops to Masanganu. When he took ill, his generals ordered everyone out to fight against Kafuche, and I could not refuse."

"I meant for you only to be a pilot for us," said Don João. He looked close at me and said, "Do you think I have forgotten my promise to let you go home? Eh? I said, Serve me a little while in voyaging along the coast, and I will put you on ship to England. Eh, Andres? How long ago was that?"

"I think it was in June of '91, or the July."

"Three years. A longer service than either of us expected. The promise still stands, Andres. But I have more need of you. Will you renew your pledge a little longer?"

"I do yearn for my homeland, Don João."

"Yea. I comprehend that. But give me a little more, Andres, only a little more. Will you do that?"

He looked at me, his eyes on mine, and suddenly I saw the truth that lay behind his warm and friendly pleading words, which was that he was not pleading at all: he was commanding me. This was his method, to be kind and insinuating, as it had been Don Jeronymo's method to be fierce and domineering, and either way the result was the same, that I was compelled to remain in this land of Angola. I had mourned Don João most keenly when I had thought him to be dead, and we had taken meals and wines together many times as though we were truly friends, but at the bottom of things the reality was that I was a slave and he my absolute master, the which he softened and concealed with gentle words. But what could I say? Could I refuse service, and demand instant passage to England? I had no claim. If I did any such thing, he would, with the greatest sadness and sweet professions of friendship, commit me to his dungeon, and then I would rot there for ever.

I do not think Don João was insincere. I believe he had true regard for me, and a fondness. But he had need of me to sail his ships for him, and that need was paramount. Perhaps one day he would indeed let me go, but not now, not yet. And I could do nothing but yield.

"Aye, since you ask me, I will serve," I said. "But once the rebellion is put down, and you are secure in your power here, will you release me, Don João? Five years is a long time to be away from one's native land."

"It will be only a little," said Don João, "and then you will be on your way thither."

Which he said with such warmth and such clear profession of good will that I could not for the moment doubt him. Yet I knew that when he said, "Only a little," that little might be two months, or six, or a year and a half, or eternity, according to his changing needs of me, and that as those needs changed he would ask me again and again, with the same warmth, with the same good will, to extend my service to him. I think I would rather be compelled without deceit than cozened with such beguiling, but no matter: in Angola I would have to remain.

We talked for a time of the voyages he required of me, in sailing his pinnace along the coast in various trading missions. And when we had done with that, and as he was making ready to dismiss me, only then did I ask the question I had held back in my mind all this while, the question that I had not thought seemly to introduce in any earlier part of our meeting.

Quite casually I said, "The same who told me of the plot against you did say that Dona Teresa was to have been slain in the same manner. I trust it is not so."

Don João smiled. "Nay, she is well, and was never at jeopardy. O, she thrived in Lisbon! Her eyes were wide all the day and all the night, as she soaked up the wonders of the place. Yet the winter weather was harsh on her, and she was gladdened to return to São Paulo de Loanda. She is a married woman now, you know."

"Married?"

I did not conceal my shock; I could not, for the surprise was too great. Dona Teresa had told me, before she set sail for Europe, that she and Don João were to be wed in Lisbon, so I was not altogether taken unawares by his statement. But yet the phrasing of it was not right, for if he had married her he would have said, "Dona Teresa and I now are married," and not, *"She* is married." So I looked at him with bewilderment and I think, through showing so strong a response, I might have revealed to him that my interest in Dona Teresa went beyond mere polite curiosity.

But he gave no sign of seeing that. He said only, "Aye, she lost no time taking a husband when she came back here. Father Affonso performed the ceremony himself, and I stood up there beside her almost as a father would."

"And the husband?"

"Why, it is that man of fantastical costume, Captain Fernão da Souza. You know him, do you not? The commander of the presidio guard? I think they have long been—ah—friends, and now they are man and wife, this fortnight past. You should call on them, once you are re-established in your life here."

He rose—standing, he was so very short!—and gave me his hand, and I thanked him for all his mercies to me, and went out from there in a veritable daze of stupefaction. Dona Teresa married! And not to Don João, but to Fernão da Souza!

Well, and I had known she carried on some long intrigue with Souza. For when I had asked her how she had gained access to me so easily whilst I was imprisoned in the fortress, she had quite forthrightly explained that Souza was her friend, and that could only have meant her lover. But Souza surely had known that what went on between Dona Teresa and me in my prison cell was not merely a chaste discussion of geographical matters; and beyond any question he knew she was Don João's mistress, for all the colony was aware of that. Why, then, would he want to marry her? Had he no pride? Could he take to wife a woman who had openly been had by the governor of the colony for some years, and one whom he knew furthermore to have been had by the English prisoner Battell? I think I might not have cared to marry Anne Katherine if all of England knew she was some cast-off mistress of Sir Walter

Ralegh's, say, and if I had helped pimp her as well to a Spaniard captured in the defeat of the Armada.

But the situations were not equal, I realized, upon giving the matter some further thought. This was not England or any other civilized place, but merely a remote colony at the edge of a pagan and barbaric land. There were many men here, and few women, at least few who might be taken for Europeans, as could Dona Teresa. Those rules of chastity and propriety that might apply at home were of no substance here, I supposed. Don João, for some reason I did not fathom, had not in fact married Dona Teresa when they were in Portugal; now she did see some merit in marrying Souza, who was ambitious and of a growing importance here, and doubtless Souza saw merit in it, too, perhaps because it would bring him the enhanced favor of Don João. Perhaps. I did not know how such matters were worked. But I was shaken by the surprise of it, I who had had no small passion for Dona Teresa myself. My own embroilment with her now must certainly be ended, for as a captain's wife she could not sneak around, could she, and spread her legs secretly here and there for old lovers such as I? Or could she? Well, and I had Matamba now anyway; the cases were altered for us all.

As I moved through the town that day I found other surprises, namely, several women strolling about that seemed pure European, and protecting themselves from the sunlight by paper shades stuck to long handles. Each of these was young and handsome, and had her little following of the men of the town, who moved in close formation around her, like a cloud of gnats. I made inquiries and learned that upon Don João's return from Portugal he had brought twelve such women with him, the first pure-blood European women ever seen in Angola, to provide a gentler touch in the life of the town.

"Do you mean they are whores?" I asked.

My informant, who was a merchant of grain, laughed broadly and said, "Nay, nay, they are respectable women! They are Jewesses, but they are respectable!" And he told me that there was in Portugal a place called the Casa Pia, founded by a former queen, where unfortunate women dwelled. Some of them were criminals that had been reformed, and some were Jewesses who had been converted to Christian ways; and it was twelve of those latter, all of them now rigged out with crucifixes at their breasts and other signs of high piety, that had been introduced into this rough and harsh frontier.

And indeed they did soften and beautify the place, for each was like a little sun, giving off a bright radiance in her perambulation through the streets of São Paulo de Loanda. At another time I might have sought a closer touch of that radiance myself; but other men were ahead of me in ample number, and I had no wish to struggle through such crowds. Moreover did I have Matamba to console my nights, and that night she and I took such a reunion of the flesh as allowed me no sleep, but provided us both the most intense of delights, with many a moaning and a gasping, and making of love in this position and that, she tickling me and clipping me until I thought I would go mad of it, and then turning and crouching to present her ebony buttocks to me whilst I did thrust my stiffened wand into the hot place below them, and afterward taking me the other way around, kneeling above me in her manner, and still later even granting me the rare favor of letting me have her in the European custom with her body beneath mine, and so on and so on all through the night, in a frenzy of quivering breasts and flashing thighs and moist slippery loins and bright laughing eyes and agile thrusting hips. Which made me weep from sheer gladness of it, that I was here alive in São Paulo de Loanda in the loving arms of this good-hearted Negress, and not lying dead with vulture-picked eyesockets on the field of Kafuche Kambara.

Thirteen

It was some days before I encountered Dona Teresa, for now that she was a married woman certain constraints were upon her, and I could not merely go to visit her, nor she come to me. But I did see her in the grand plaza of the city on the arm of Captain Fernão da Souza, she all elegant in veil with cap of black velvet, and chains of gold, and a silken robe, and he thrice as splendid as ever in crimson breeches and a brilliant yellow coat. The sight of her gave me a sharp pang and thrill, to re-member how I had grieved for her rumored death. As I passed them she nodded to me and smiled through her veil, all with the greatest dignity, as if she were a lady of the court of Her Protestant Majesty Elizabeth, and Souza, too, gave me his most formal salutation. But we went on beyond one another without exchanging words.

Again the next day I saw them together, but from a greater distance, and as she went by I suddenly had a vision of myself in my prison-cell days, and Dona Teresa with me, both of us naked and she lying with her face against my thighs, and taking the tip of my yard into her mouth as she had several times done, and sliding it deep to the inner part of her throat, and moving back and forth along it until I was ready to cry out with ecstasy. That vision striking me in the public street all but smote me down. My heart began to pound and there was a dryness in my nostrils and my eyes did go bleary, and I craved her with all the craving in the world, and nothing else mattered. Then I caught my breath, and turned away, not willing to look upon her for fear of seeming a fool. The power of the moment released me and I turned again, and she was gone from my sight.

From that I learned how strongly Dona Teresa still held me in her grasp. Which I feared; for these Portugals take the chastity of their wives most serious, and I craved no quarrel with Captain Fernão da Souza, nor did I care to be drawn yet again into Dona Teresa's mischievous spells, beautiful though she was. She was too sly and perilous for me: I would remain content with Matamba, I told myself, until I could quit this place forever.

The day after that, as I was setting forth to the harbor to inspect the pinnace, Dona Teresa came by without her husband, carried by a team of bearers in a corded hammock, and she did command her bearers to halt beside me, and spoke with me from aloft, as a great lady would have done. She said she was surprised to find me still in Angola, having thought I would have obtained my release by now. To which I replied that I appeared to be of value here, in that the several governors constantly found new tasks for me, and I much doubted I would ever go home. And she said, still in that same distant way, that she had heard good report of my valor in the battle with Kafuche Kambara; and she remarked somewhat on the changes in my appearance that those hardships had worked in me. We exchanged another some few pleasantries of this kind, at the end of which she invited me to attend her at her residence that afternoon: she would send bearers to fetch me.

Her manner was altogether different when I came to her, at the handsome new dwelling that she dwelled in now with Souza. Still was she clothed in great finery; but that lofty style, that high and distant condescension, had been put aside. Now was she the woman I remembered, whose body had been coupled to mine in every several position of the act of love, and whose each inch I did know with mine eyes and fingers and lips and tongue. She glistened at me with memory of lust and desire yet unfulfilled; and I in turn responded with tremors of yearning that I controlled only barely.

Yet control it I did, as did she, for we were in the formal drawing-chamber of her house, with slaves all about us bringing us little cooked morsels and wines and the like. What passed between us, to the eyes of those onlookers, was as proper and seemly as anything that might occur between some old dowager and a decrepit monk. Only Teresa and I could detect the searing currents of powerful attraction that flowed from her eyes to mine, and mine to hers.

She proffered me a tray of sweetmeats and said, low and throbbing, "All the while I was in Europe I imagined you atop me, Andres, and I was sick to the heart from being so far from you."

"And I, lady, sick to the heart that I thought you were murdered."

"It was a near thing. Who told you of it?"

"One of my sailors, as I went toward Loango. He had heard in a tavern, rogues talking too loud of the plot. How I raged, how I pounded the staves of the ship in fury over the loss of you, Teresa! A near thing, you say?"

"We learned of the scheme only a day or two before it was to happen. Three men meant to come to us in the night and cut our throats and put us over the side, but Don João had loyal servants who scouted out the murderers, and made them admit their plan, and it was they who went into the sea instead, with their hands tied in back." She filled my goblet a second time. "It was the worst moment of the voyage for me, hearing how close I had come to dying. Nay: the second worst."

"And what was the worst, then?"

"Seeing Don João greet his wife in Lisbon."

"His *wife?* But I thought—"

"Yea, so did I. A promise of marriage made unto me. But he had never said it in so many words. He had planted the idea in my own mind, and let me think it, and embellish upon it, and imagine great things of it, but he had never said it himself. He is subtle at such twistings of the truth, is Don João. But as I sorted through my memories of our dealings on that theme, which were not many, I saw that he had not pledged me anything, but merely had allowed me to trick myself into thinking us betrothed. For how could he wed me, if he has a wife already in Portugal? The Church will allow him only one, and he cannot put her aside as easily as your English king did dispense with the queens he no longer required."

"I am sorry for your pain," I said, seeing the flaring of her nostrils in anger, and the sheen of withheld tears in her eyes.

She said, "He married her when they were very young. She is of a noble family, yea, I think of royal blood, and wealthier than he, with powerful connections in the government, and he does not dare break with her, though he has lived in Africa these many years and has had no commerce with her all the while. When we arrived in Lisbon he at once sent his messenger to her, and in the time we were in that city they did consort themselves as man and wife, with much public show of it. Although they spent their nights in separate chambers, I think."

"Then why bother to bring you to Portugal at all?"

Dona Teresa smiled a bitter smile. "Because he had truly pledged it to me, without equivocation, that if ever he returned to Portugal I should go with him. I think he never expected that pledge to be redeemed, for he planned no more to set foot in that land. But when circumstances here required him to go, why, he did not cheat me of the journey, knowing that I desired so much to see Europe. In that regard he is an honorable man. And then also it is a long voyage, and Don João is not one who cares to spend weeks and weeks without a woman in his arms. And also I think he wanted to display me at court, as his beautiful African concubine, for men take pride in such show, do they not, Andres? And even among good Christians there is no evil in taking a concubine when one has a wife already, if one is a man of high position, or so I understand it. The wife herself did not seem jealous of me. She praised me, in sooth, for my beauty, and I think gave her husband congratulation for having chosen so well."

"And is this why you married Captain da Souza?" I asked. "By way of revenging yourself?"

"That is too simple a reason."

"But Don João had done you a great injury."

"Nay, Andres, my own hopes and follies had done me the injury. I hold no grudge against Don João."

"He is most marvelously fortunate, that he can injure people and they will still love him."

"He has promised you a return to England, has he not? And not by subtlety and indirection, either, but in most straightforward outright words. Yet he has not made good the promise, and still you serve him, and still I think you love him."

"It is not the same," I said. "He has no reason nor obligation ever to release me. It is only his gift to me, which he can bestow whenever he chooses, or withhold forever, and I have nothing to say in the matter. But to allow you to think he would wed you, knowing all the while it was impossible—"

"I have told you, it was self-deception on my part. Mine eyes were blinded to the truth. I will not deny I am greatly disappointed, and that it was painful to learn how far I was from an understanding of the actual situation. But I do not hate him for it. I remain his friend."

"But you are now the wife of Souza."

"Indeed."

"Why Souza?"

"He is handsome. He is ambitious. I was eager to wed, and if I could not have Don João, why, it was time to choose another. And I chose Souza."

"And he does not object that you've been the mistress of Don João?"

"Why should he? Men do not seek virgins here. And it does him honor, to have all know that he has captured so high a prize as Dona Teresa da Costa."

"And how does Don João feel about all these matters?"

Dona Teresa said, smiling slyly, "His conscience is eased toward me, now that I am truly wed. And he has lost nothing."

I stared at her. "You intend still to—"

"He is the governor, is he not? If he still finds me attractive, is there not advantage for me in gratifying his desire? Is there not advantage for my husband, also?"

It was much like the court of England, I thought, this pandering of wives for preference, this winking at adultery. It is the same everywhere, I do suppose.

After a moment I said, "It amazes me that Souza will let himself be cuckolded before the whole community for the sake of gaining a little power. Has the man no shame?"

"Ah, it will not be so public as you seem to think. We will be circumspect. There are decencies to consider, are there not?"

"Are there?"

She laughed now. "Andres, Andres, you look so stern!"

"This kind of business is not comfortable to me, this handing off of a discarded mistress to a younger officer to be his wife, and then this sneaking around behind the new husband's back, and—"

"Ah, you are so pious! And when I thought I was betrothed to Don João, and I came secretly to you, did you find it so uncomfortable that you did refuse me, Andres?"

"That was different!" I cried.

"Was it? Not so far as I can see. I do brand you hypocrite, dear Andres, and false moralizer." She offered me the sweetmeats again, like a proper hostess, and then she leaned close to me and said in a low rich voice that went through me like a hot blade, "Nothing has changed, except that I am now called wife. I use Don João to my benefit. I use Fernão the same way. So has it been, so shall it be. What passes between them and me is a kind of business, a transaction, do you understand? It is not the same between you and me. And we remain as we are. Do you remember how it felt, when I was in your arms? Nay, you have not forgotten that. I have not forgotten, neither. And it has been a year, has it not? That is much too long. I remember your body, the size of it, the taste, the feel. I remember everything about you. I hope you will not tell me in your pious English way that I am too sacred to touch, now that I am called wife. Eh, Andres?"

Her eyes were upon me. Her skin was flushed, her lips were gleaming and parted. I think if she had asked me to take her right there, on the thick green carpet, in front of all her slaves, I would have done it. I could not have resisted. Then and there, had she bade me, would I have spread her and tupped her, without a thought of saying no. Such was her hold on me.

But of course that could not happen, and it did not happen. She leaned away from me, she let the throb and tremor go from her voice and the fire from her eye, and we did talk again like dowager and monk, all calm and innocent, until the visit had its end.

When I was outside in the full blaze of the day, though, a sweat came over me that had nothing to do with the heat of the murky air, and I was hard put to steady myself. Jezebel! Messalina! She was terrifying, that woman: she was an irresistible force, that swept down upon a man like the River Zaire.

And yet must I resist the irresistible.

Her design was perilous for me. It had been bad enough in the times gone by for me to be cuckolding Don João with her; but either Don João had not known, or he had known and had not cared, or else Don João peradventure had known and found it amusing and flattering to have his favorite concubine futtered by the valiant Englishman. For that was truly all he saw her to be, his concubine, his plaything; or he would not have acted out the cruel game of letting her travel in pomp with him to Europe and then producing upon her his proper wife.

But now that she was Souza's, it was another matter. Souza was proud; he was young; he carried a sword, and looked for the chance to employ it. I did not care to trifle with a hot-blooded young Portugal in his early manhood. Souza might choose to close his eyes if his wife did swive the governor from time to time, and would tell himself that by so doing she advanced his own position in the government: that was vile, but it gave him vantage. But I doubted much that he would accept the horns from anyone less mighty than Don João. For my part I craved no quarrels, no duels, no gangs of angry bravos setting upon me by night; I wanted only peace, safety, security, until I could get me out of this land. For the satisfaction of my desires I had the pleasant and indulgent Matamba. Dona Teresa, though I lusted for her vastly and always would, to the end of my days, could bring me only trouble, and I resolved to steer clear of so risky a shoal as she.

But easier would it have been to steer clear of the continents of the Americas, if you were making your voyage westward toward the Indies.

Twice did she send messages to me in the next few days that I should come to her at such and such a place. The message was most careful not to say why; but I knew. The first time it was an inspection of my pinnace that she desired, but I replied to her that the ship had been careened for the removing of its barnacles, and was not ready to be boarded. The second time, she begged me to convey her to the isle of Loanda in our harbor, so that she might visit the factory where the money-shells were heaped; but that island has many empty places and few Portugals on it, and it was not hard to imagine what would befall between us the moment we were alone there. Again I extended an excuse. I hoped she would take her clue from that, that I loved her no less but did not dare to embrace her. For some days I did not have word from her, which gave me heart that she had understood my meaning. To refuse a woman like Dona Teresa was not easy for me, yet I must; and I prayed she would comprehend that I was not spurning her for any reason other than that of safety, my own and even hers.

During this time a new chore descended upon me that took my mind away from these intricacies. For there appeared in our harbor a merchant-ship out of Holland, who had come to trade with the Portugals. And I was pressed into service to be the interpreter, for the Dutchmen spoke but feeble Portuguese, and the Portugals of Angola spoke no Dutch whatsoever. So Don João, greatly mystified that a Dutchman should be here at all, called me to the task, since the Dutch skipper, like most men of his kind, had a fair quantity of English, and I knew a shred or two of Dutch from my early voyaging days to Antwerp and such places.

This ship of the Dutch was of the kind they call a *fluyt*, or flyboat, and a great hulking thing it was. I would call it no more than a floating cargo hold, practically flat on her bottom, with simple rigging and no guns to speak of and the masts stepped well apart, and the length of the ship maybe five times her beam—just a big barge, really, that could carry God's own tonnage of cargo at the cheapest possible cost. I had heard that the Dutch had built many such vessels of late to fetch goods between Europe and the Americas, and were in their busy Dutch way prospering mightily by selling cloth and slaves in Brazil and buying sugar, and bringing salt from Venezuela to Europe, and such.

But it was surprising to see Dutch traders come to Angola. The Dutch they are a maritime people, and do voyage hither and yon with great success, but also are they Protestants, and enemies of King Philip of Spain, that very King Philip who also had become ruler of Portugal and thus had sway over Angola, too. Philip once had been sovereign over the Low Countries, by some trick of inheritance from his father the Emperor Charles, but the Protestant folk of Holland, so I recall, had rebelled and set up their own republic, an endeavor into which we English had given great aid. Had that republic fallen, I wondered, so that Holland was again Philip's fief? If not, what were Protestant Dutch merchants doing on a venture into Papist Africa? Had they no fear of being seized and imprisoned, as I had been seized and imprisoned by the Portugals of Brazil?

Some talk with the Dutch merchant captain, one Cornelis van Warwyck, and I had a better understanding of the complexities of the situation. The Dutch republic had not fallen; indeed in these past few years of my absence the Hollanders had expelled Spain from all their seven United Provinces. So they were as much King Philip's enemies as ever. But I had been merely privateering, going into the Brazils hoping to steal Philip's gold, the which made me forfeit to him if caught. These Dutch had come to trade, though, a thing which brings prosperity to both sides if the trading be done with skill. And so although there might be a state of war between Spain and Portugal on the one hand and the United Provinces on the other, it was a purely European war, and took second place to the necessities of profit-making out here in these distant colonies. The Portugals, moreover, had not been enemies to the Dutch before Anno 1580, when Philip came to take the Portuguese crown, and had not learned the hatred for them that the Spaniards had. Then, too, the Hollanders did bring good guilders and ducats to pay for the spices and silks and ivories and other such exotic merchandises they desired; guilders and ducats are neither Protestant nor Papist; and so these bold merchants and Don João both chose to ignore, for the sake of everyone's merry enrichment, the quarrels that divided their nations at home. Such things, I understand, were common in Africa and the Indies. Why, there were even a few Portugals who sailed in Captain van Warwyck's crew—shabby scoundrel rogues with flittering shifty eyes, that I would not have had in any crew of mine, though Warwyck did maintain that they were hard workers.

I busied myself deeply in this commerce, which involved much meeting with the Dutch skipper and with Don João, and speaking both English and Portuguese with some of my little bastard Dutch mixed in. That was hard work, but what a joy to frame good English phrases again! To hear from my own lips such words as "invoice" and "quantity" and "rate of exchange," and even such humble things as "but" and "and" and "thereunto"—what delight! Why, it was like downing a flagon of good cool brown ale, to speak forth such words!

This Warwyck was a tall round-faced man with reddened cheeks and blue eyes and white hair, who dressed in dark sober Dutch clothes, all rough and woollen in our tropic heat, and puffed away on a long clay pipe as the Dutch are so fond of doing, making heavy use of that foul weed tobacco that is the mania in his country and mine these days. He had an odd sweetness to his English, as though he did put honey on his sounds before they left his tongue, which is the Dutch accent. I liked it greatly, and, strange to tell, the more I talked with him the more the same tones did creep into my own speech. I think this was because I had scarce uttered any English aloud since Thomas Torner's disappearance years before, and I was readily swayed by his manner of speaking, English now having become almost an unfamiliar language to me.

I demanded of him news of England, he having been in London as recent as the spring of '94. For England was by this time only a sort of vague dream to me, and I needed reassurance that it yet existed.

"The Queen," I said, "how fares it with her?"

"They say that she is strong and healthy, and that her beauty it is undimmed."

"And my country, does it prosper?"

Warwyck did puff deeply on his pipe and surround himself in a great swirl of white smoke, and at length he said, "The harvests have been poor these few years past. Her Majesty has spent much on the wars in France, and in my own land. I think some Spanish treasure-carracks have been seized in the Azores, which much aided the royal funds—"

"Ah," I said, "does the Queen now take a share in such adventures?"

"Indeed. They all go partners, the Queen and her brave captains, and divide the plunder. Which she would deny if asked, but we know it to be true. Yet I think England grows poorer, despite such raids. You cannot live by piracy, my friend. Trade, yes, colonies, yes—the Englanders should settle foreign lands, and build themselves into them, as these Portugals do, and the Spaniards, and as we intend to do."

"The Dutch will colonize also? Where, I pray you?"

"In places where there are no Portugals: in the Indies, the Spice Islands, and such places. We are sailing; we are learning; we will do well, I think. Better than the Spaniards and Portugals, for they are but shallow settlers, and we will sink ourselves deeply into those lands, and export from them cloves and pepper and nutmeg and other useful things, instead of merely filching gold from the natives and giving them diseases. And we will do better than you English, too, for you seem interested only in piracy, and there is no profit in that over the long term, however glittering the rewards of snatching this ship and that one may be. Eh, friend? Do you see?"

Indeed I did see; for I had had a close view of what the Portugals did, which was more slaving than merchandising, and I knew our own maritime enterprise from within, and I was aware also of the short-sighted cruelties of the black-hearted Spaniards. And I knew that these Hollanders, if they did keep faithfully to their task, would build for themselves a great machine of perpetual money-spinning, for they are diligent people that do understand where the truest pot of gold doth lie. And I swore to myself that if ever I returned to England I would preach the gospel of colonizing and commerce, and urge my countrymen to give over piracy and slaving, as being not the best ways toward national wealth.

Warwyck and his gossiping did much enhance my longing for my own cool green country. He talked on and on! Ralegh had fallen, he said, for having got with child one of the Queen's ladies-in-waiting, and secretly marrying her, which displeased Her Majesty highly. The great man at court now was the Earl of Essex, son-in-law to old Leicester. Lord Burghley still was the Queen's most trusted adviser, but his crook-backed son Robert was rising now in esteem. There were plots on the Queen's life, which was nothing new, some Portugal living in London accused of conspiring to poison her at the behest of King Philip. And so on and so on. Food was dear, rain fell constantly, hunger was general. People died in the streets from want, but the Queen ordered grain given out to the populace from her private stores, and was widely loved for it. And so on; and so on. He told me endless things of England, that kindled in me a keen biting desire to behold thatched cottages and winding country lanes and the white line of surf licking at the fog that lies upon the coast. Only in one area did he fail me, this Dutchman Warwyck, when I did ask him of the world of plays and poetry, what new and wonderful things had been put on the stage. For the world of words has always been hot in my mind, and I had read much, as sailors go, and it seemed to me that there were in England in my time a great host of new men who would write miracles. But of all that the Dutchman knew nothing and told me nothing. So I was left all unknowing of the high deeds of our poets, though he could tell me the price of a peck of corn on the London docks. Well, and well, I could not expect everything from the man, and he had told me much. Aye, so much that it left me churning with a powerful bitter yearning to quit this torrid Angola and get myself back to the pleasant island of my birth before old age did wither me altogether to a husk. God's blood, but I had had my fill of Africa, and then some!

For day after day I did my interpreting while the Portugals and Dutch haggled over the prices of their commodities. Warwyck was not interested in slaves, but the sumptuous fabrics of Angola seemed to attract him, and he bought also goodly measure of ivory, and bales of certain medicinal herbs most sharp against the nostrils. When not occupied in these transactions I whiled away my hours happily with Matamba, or went off quietly angling, or simply strolled alone and reflective through the city. I was not living badly, that is clear; but it was not the life I wanted for myself. From time to time I did see Dona Teresa off at a distance, but there were no encounters between us. Yet I sensed there would be trouble from that quarter ere very much longer.

And so there was. I returned to my cottage one afternoon from my negotiations with the Dutch, and as I entered it I had a premonition of ill fortune, a tingling of the ballocks and a cold knot in my stomach's pit. When I looked within I saw Dona Teresa in my chamber. She had laid aside most of her garments and wore only a thin cascade of the native weaving, brightly dyed in yellow and green, a kind of damask that they do make here from the fibers of the palm. That one garment was draped so that it did reveal the supple curves of her body, with a hint of thigh and a hint of breast artfully disposed for my endazzlement.

None of my slaves were about. The house was silent; the air was stifling hot. Teresa seemed posed, as if she had struck an attitude and waited a long time so that I would find her precisely thus. Her eyes had their keenest gleam and there was an odor in the room, that musky cat-odor of her body that I knew to be the surest token of her lusts.

She said, "Since you will not come to me, Andres, I have come to you."

"Ah, you should not have done this!"

"No one has seen me. Give me an hour, and then I will slip away, and who will be the wiser?"

"For the love of God, Teresa—"

"Have I grown ugly?"

"You are more beautiful than ever. But the case is altered with us, Teresa, the case is altered! You are a wife!"

"I told you that that means nothing."

"Well, and let Don Fernão tell me that himself, and then I might feel safer," I said.

"Are you such a coward, then?"

"I will fight Jaqqas if I must," said I, "or stick lances in the bellies of Kafuche Kambara's warriors. But I have no wish to do combat with a rightfully angered husband."

"Andres—Andres—"

She gave me a look both of desire and of fury, that made me fear her very much.

Slowly she arose, and came flowingly toward me, and I did see the unconfined globes of her breasts swaying beneath her thin draping, and the darkness at her loins was apparent, too, and I felt myself losing all resolve.

"Andres," she said, "give me no more talk of angered husbands. You and I are lovers, and nothing else is significant. Come: you want me as much as I do you."

"I will not deny that."

"Then come."

I shook my head. "It is too dangerous. I tell you, we must make an end of this union."

"Nay," she said. She drew nearer, and rubbed herself against me most unsubtly amorous, with a pressing and a thrusting of her loins on me that made my yard stand out fair to split my breeches. "Do not compel me to beg you, Andres," said she.

"I beg *you*, Teresa—"

She backed off and there was rage now smouldering in her eyes.

"I cannot believe this! I crawl to you, and you refuse me? What have you done? Have you renewed your vow to that English wench of yours, and returned to your chastity?"

"She has not entered my mind often in recent times," I did declare, to my shame, for it was the truth.

"Then why do you shun me? I cannot believe this fear you claim to have of Fernão. He will not know. And if he did, he would look the other way, I swear it! Nay, it must be something else that keeps you from me." She stepped back one pace more, and the look upon her face changed, growing harder, growing colder. "They tell me that in Loango you did buy a slave-girl, a young one, and that she is your bed-toy. When I heard it I laughed at it, for I know the African women are not what you desire. You want no flat noses, you want no thick lips and heavy rumps. Or so I did think. But is it true, Andres? Do you use your little black slut, and care no more for me? Do you? Do you?"

Her words came at me like daggers. I could say nothing.

Yes, yes, I did sleep with Matamba, and yes, I took great pleasure of her, and yes, all that Dona Teresa had heard was true; but that was not the whole story of my refusal of her. It was not Matamba that had come between us, but rather the conjoining of lust with politics in this city, and my fear of letting a new embroilment with Teresa's body embroil me also in some fatal tangle of ambitions. But I had told her all that already, and she had brushed it aside, seeking a more elemental motive. I searched my brain for some new argument that might sink to the core of the matter, and prevent it from seeming a mere jealous squabble between women, but I found no reasoning worth offering her. And so I stood, silent, gaping, while within me came the insinuating devilish temptation to put all this word-spinning behind me and throw myself atop Teresa's body instantly in a willing embrace, that any other man in half his right mind would give a year of his life to enjoy.

Yet did I not do that, nor anything else, but remained as it were paralyzed. And then the worst of all possible things befell, for in that moment did Matamba enter the cottage, all unaware, and come lightly onward into my inner chamber, calling out my name in a cheery voice like a familiar lover, "Andres! Andres!"

Oh, God's bones and shoulders, what I would have given to have her choose any some other different time to appear!

In the year when I lived with my wife Rose Ullward so long ago, we did keep two cats as pets, a grizzled tabby tom and a sleek old black-and-orange female, both of them amiable and easy-tempered animals, that stood and made a purr most vociferous when I rubbed them behind the ears. They were Rose's cats, but they liked me well enough, and I them. One ghastly windy rainy winter day, when I was within the house with them and they were squatting together in the window-ledge, asleep in the warmth, some stray cat did come by outside, and perched on the sill, and peered in at them, as though yearning to join them out of the rain. I know not why, but the coming of that stray did set my two cats' fur on edge, and they rose like beasts that had seen an evil spirit, and began upon the moment to fight with one another, squealing terribly and leaping about and sending clouds of their fur flying into the air. I would not have these animals, both so dear to me, injuring each other, and so, without giving the matter any thought, I went to them and seized them to hold them apart. Which was a most grievous mistake, for with a single accord they turned on *me* as their enemy, and so clawed and bit and furrowed me that within moments was I bleeding amazingly along my arms and both my ankles, and stood in sore pain. This taught me two things: one being that the cat of your hearth, though he be old and tame and sleepy, is nevertheless a hunting animal with ferocious fangs and claws and sturdy sinews; and the other being, never set yourself as umpire between two cats in combat, for you will be the chief sufferer in that. Yet I did not learn those lessons sufficiently well, I do believe, since something of the same story now replayed itself in my cottage, and with something of the same result.

By which I mean that the moment Matamba did enter my chamber, Teresa pulled back, crouching, drawing her lips away from her teeth, shaping her hands into fearsome claws as though she meant to destroy her rival straightaway. Matamba, though wondrously startled at finding Dona Teresa here and she near naked at that, needed no time to comprehend that she was in menace.

"Ah, you are the witch-woman," said she. "You are the sorceress! I know you, idol-maker!"

"Slave! Trash!"

"Ah," said Matamba, hunching forward, extending her arms with her hands held in the same claw-fashion. "Ah, Jesu Maria, God is with me!"

And from Teresa came words in the Bakongo tongue that I had never heard her speak before, black mingo-jango words out of the souls of her grandmothers, a hard gibbering magical stuff that amazed me to hear it out of her beautiful lips. And for each word she spoke in that dark incantation, Matamba did call forth the name of a saint, though I did see the terror in her eyes, and I felt no little fright myself at this witchery magicking that poured from Dona Teresa.

For a half minute, perhaps, they circled one another, poised, taut, the one woman crying curses and sorcery, the other answering with her holy names, and I looked on stupefied, thinking I must hold them apart from one another.

But I waited an instant too long. For Dona Teresa, with a hellish shriek, suddenly leaped upon the waiting Matamba.

"Nay!" I cried. But it was like shouting commands to the wild hurricane.

They rushed together with a loud clashing of flesh and grappled one another and entered into the most unloving of hugs, tugging and pulling each to knock the other to the ground, and all the while snarling like enraged beasts. They were of about one size, Matamba being a few years younger and somewhat more sturdy of build, but Dona Teresa having a lithe leopard-like strength to her. They grasped and struck at each other while I stood by for the moment all frozen, never having seen women fighting before.

Dona Teresa's flimsy garment soon was a shred, and a reddened row of scratchings ran across her front from one shoulder over the breast to a side of her rib-cage. While at the same time she grasped Matamba's thick woolly hair and did tug at it to rip it from her head, and brought her knee up to the black girl's crotch, whereupon Matamba clawed her again, and this time flung her down, Matamba's own garment coming undone at that. Teresa rose and launched a new assault, the air being all full of shrieks and sweat.

And I, forgetting the lesson of the two quarrelsome cats, could stand no more to see these two women, near naked and so vulnerable, harming their beauty in this way. So before the gougings of eyes commenced, and the breaking of noses, and such like mutilations, I flung myself against their slippery bodies and did strive to separate them.

God's death, the foolishness of it! Ah, the silly man I was!

In the fury of the moment they turned each on me, just as had the cats, and I found myself assailed and beleaguered in a madness of bounding breasts and raking nails. They did not know nor care who it was they attacked now, but only wished to vent their rage. Aye, and vent it they did! I know not how long our triple combat lasted, but that we smashed everything in the room, as thoroughly as if we had turned a brace of bull-elephantos loose in it, and my shirt hung in rags and the hot rivulets of blood did run in channels on my arms and chest, and I was so kicked and pummeled and bruised that I feared destruction altogether, until at last I flung them into opposing corners of the room and stood panting between them, periling them with my arms lest they come at each other again or at me.

In that first moment of calmness, the three of us breathing hard and dazed from the violence, Dona Teresa did begin to cry out some new vituperation, which I silenced with a command; and Matamba muttered something dark in her own language, which also I cut off. "I will hear no more," said I. "I have had enough of this uproar!" I remained as a wall betwixt them, and beckoned to them to rise to their feet. They were both of them all but stripped bare, and sweat made their bodies shine, Teresa's dusky one and Matamba's black one, and I saw the blood all over them, but more of it on me. Yet no one was badly injured.

"Clothe yourself," I said to Dona Teresa. "And you, Matamba, stand back, let her take her leave. And not a word from either of you!"

Wearing only her outer garments, Dona Teresa went from my cottage, glaring most murderously at us both. Matamba stood rigid until she was gone, and then did begin to tremble and shake with a violence that astounded me.

"Are you hurt?" I asked.

"Blessed Virgin!" she cried. "I am bewitched! She has put the Fiend upon me, and I will wither, I will shrivel!"

"Nay, it was only words," said I, though without the fullest conviction.

I went to her and took her in my arms and comforted her, and she me, and she stood sobbing a while, and then went to fetch the sponge, so we might cleanse our bloody scratches. But the terror remained in her. I had never seen her so pale, a new color of skin altogether, the ruddiness wholly gone from her. "It is the Devil's own *mokisso* she has called down on me," said she.

"God is stronger, Matamba. God will be your shield."

"So I pray." She clutched at my arm. "I beg you, burn that idol of hers, today! Render it into ashes!"

"It is but a carved thing," said I. "It has no power."

"Destroy it! Hurl it into the sea!"

"Ah, Matamba, I would not do it."

"Even now? Even after what you have seen?"

I stroked her back, and the nape of her neck. Even now, I knew, I could not bring myself to part with that little statue, though its maker had shown herself to me in all her deep darkness of soul. And it shamed me to reveal to Matamba how fond I was of that idol, and of its maker. Yet did I say, "I have no faith in the strength of idols, and neither should you, if you be a Christian. It is but a trinket. Give it no mind. Come, let us bathe, and clothe ourselves, and put all witchery from our minds."

But she still trembled, as did I. I found myself more frighted by what had just befallen than I had been all during the attack by the warriors of Kafuche Kambara. For now Dona Teresa was my sworn enemy, and she would be no hollow braggartly foe such as the brothers Caldeira de Rodrigues had shown themselves to be. She would, I feared, cause me more grief than either of them and a whole regiment of painted savages with lances, if she did put her subtle mind to the task.

FOURTEEN

IN THE whole of my stay in Africa I had given no serious thought to escaping. That had never seemed in any way possible, there being no English ships passing within hundreds of miles of this coast, and the interior of the country being wild and unknown. Better, I had thought, to wait and serve, and have faith in Don João's pledge to free me, or in some favorable alteration of conditions between England and Portugal, that might bring me my freedom.

But this grave new breach with Dona Teresa threatened me utterly, and I felt dear need to protect myself from her; and under that necessity I did suddenly see that God's providence had given me a way to take my departure from this madhouse of a land. If I acted now, I might well be saved. If I let the moment pass, I would be at Dona Teresa's mercy: and if she persisted in her sudden hatred of me she would be an implacable foe that could do me much harm. So when I was washed and clothed and rested some, I summoned my bearers and went down to the harbor, and sought out the Dutchman Cornelis van Warwyck, that I had appointed to be the agent of my salvation.

He greeted me with warmth, a lusty clap on the back, a hearty laugh, an offer of tobacco and the good strong Dutch genever spirits that he carried in casks in his cabin. I declined the pipe but gladly took the spirits, being in severe need of its potency. We drank in the Dutch fashion, tossing the clear fiery stuff down our gullets in a quick wrist-flipping gulp, and gasping our delight and filling the glasses again.

Then Warwyck said, "You are troubled, Battell?"

"Is it so easy to see?"

"Two hours ago you looked at your ease. Now storms do rage in your face, and contrary winds rush about your head."

"Aye," I said. "You judge me shrewdly. There is trouble."

"With the Portugals?"

"With women," I said.

At which he smiled, and seemed greatly relieved, for I think he had feared some overthrow among his hosts, and his own position in this city was a delicate and easily unbalanced one.

He puffed his pipe and contemplated me in his unhurried way, and I studied him close, weighing him, for I meant to make a heavy request of him.

After a time I said, "Have you wondered at all, captain, what an Englishman is doing among these Portugals in Angola?"

He looked amused. I saw a twinkling of his eye through the vile clouds of pipe-smoke.

"It did cross my mind that you were unusual here," he said most calmly. "I thought it was not my place to ask questions. I am here to do trade, not to conduct inquiries into matters which do not concern me."

"Of course."

"Yet I did wonder. Be you some sort of renegado?"

"Nay, captain. A prisoner."

His eyebrows lifted a small part of an inch. "Are you, then?"

"Taken captive off the Brazils, while privateering. Shipped here in irons four years past."

"Ah, you English! You do love piracy so!"

"It was my first voyage in that line," I said. "And, I think, my last."

He puffed some more. "You have landed comfortably enough here, I trow. You wear no irons these days. I see you travel about on the backs of slaves when you go through the town. They tell me you have commanded their vessels in sailing along the coast and up their rivers."

"I did not go gladly into the service of the Portugals," I replied. "It was either that or stay in their dungeons. As time passed, they gave me employ and came to trust me, which is fair enough, for I am not a devious man."

"Ah. Certainly not."

There was silence between us a long while. He poured me yet another genever, and one for him, but held his glass in his hand, studying me. Nor did I drink then, either.

I said finally, "I can scarce tell you how much joy it gives me that I can speak with someone again in my own English tongue, Captain van Warwyck."

"It is a pleasing language, yes. It has much music to it. Next to Dutch I like it best."

"I would fain go, captain, to a land where English is more commonly spoken than it is in Angola."

"Ah."

"It has been a comfortable imprisonment here, for the most part. But it is imprisonment, all the same."

"Ah. Of course." Much judicious puffing of pipe.

"Captain," I said, "when do you set sail from here?"

Again the small raising of the eyebrows. "Three days hence."

"And for what port, if you will tell me?"

"We are not decided. Perhaps Sierra Leona, or Cape Verde, or the islands off that cape. Thence to the Azores to take wood and water. And to Holland."

"You will pass greatly close to England, as you make for your home port," I said.

"I take your meaning, Battell." He let his eyelids droop in a thoughtful way, and fiddled most damnably long with the embers in the bowl of his pipe, and said at long last, "There are risks in this for us."

"I comprehend that."

"And no reward, that I can perceive. You know, it has never been my custom to take risk without hope of reward."

"I have no wealth. I own a black slave-girl, but nothing else."

"Ah. Yes. I would not want your slave."

"We are both Protestants, captain. Take me from these Papists if only so that I can go properly to my church again, for it is too many years since I have heard a true blessing."

He did look indifferent to that.

"I am a Protestant, yes, but not so godly, Battell, that it matters much to me how long you have been unchurched. To snatch you from the terrible Papists is not reason enough to hazard a breaking of my courtesies here, where the Portugals have been so good as to let me trade, although I am their foe. God can spare one Protestant here and there, but can Holland spare the income of my voyaging?"

I felt some rage at being thus entered among the profits and the losses, but I throttled it back.

"Then you will not take me?" I asked.

"Did I say that, Battell? Here, we hold full glasses in our hands, and the stuff will evaporate off and be wasted in this damnable heat. Drink, man, drink!" He hoisted his genever and saluted me with it, and said, "Of course I will take you," and did gulp down his glassful as if it were water.

"You will?"

"How many thousands of men has England sent to the defense of liberty in my country, eh? How many hundreds of thousands of pounds has your Elizabeth poured into the saving of Holland from the Spaniards, as though into a sieve? And one Englishman comes to me and says, 'Cornelis, take me home, for I am sore weary of serving these Portugals,' and I shall say him nay? Do you think so? Drink your genever, Battell! Drink!"

My hand trembled so that I near spilled the stuff, which he had filled into the glass clear to the brim. But I drank most lustily, and said, "If ever I can be of some service to you or to your country—"

"I understand that. Aye." He leaned close and said, "Wednesday at sundown do you come to the harbor, and we will take you on board and hide you deep in the cargo, which is so plentiful that they will never find you, though they look all month. And at sunrise we will pull ourselves out of this place and put to sea, and that will be that. We will not discuss this thing further, eh, Battell?"

"I am most eternally grateful."

"Of course you are! I'm saving your life, man! I say we should waste no words on such talk. Shall we drink another?"

"I think we should not."

"I *know* we should not," said Warwyck. "But that was not my question. Shall we drink another, is what I asked."

And we did, and I think there was one more after that, and we may have sung a few Protestant hymns, "A Mighty Fortress Is Our God" and something else, he in Dutch and me in English, and then I think both of us in Dutch, to much laughter. And then he put me into his longboat and I was taken to shore, where my bearers waited like a team of patient mules, and thus onward to my cottage.

A great joy did sweep through my soul at the thought of returning to my true home, and an end to this close heat and this servitude and this speaking the Portugal tongue and all the rest.

In the few days remaining to me in Angola I walked about as though I were already halfway to England. I feared nothing, and no dismay entered my spirit. Even Dona Teresa and her vengeful intent meant nothing now to me; she was a mere harpy at a vast distance, who would not have time to strike. I did feel some sadness at abandoning Matamba, for plainly I could not bring her with me, and I could not come to tell her that I was leaving, because of the pain it would cause us both. And even for Dona Teresa did I suffer, the losing of her, though that had already taken place; but yet I remembered our hours of coupling, and all the great joy of that, and also the deeper union we once had had, when we spoke of our lives and our inner selves in the days of our first love in São Paulo de Loanda. All that did burn in my memory. But I comforted myself with the knowledge that I could carry her with me wheresover I went, her breasts and her thighs and the taste of her lips and the scent of her body and the feel of her rump in my hands, as vivid and as real to me as if were still together, and also the sound of her voice, that was so rich and musical and melodious. But I did not have to remain mired forever in Angola in order to enjoy such pleasures of the remembrance.

For all of Africa, now that I was going from it, I do confess I felt an odd kind of yearning. In my years here I had drunk deeply of this land, though barely a sip off the surface of that colossal goblet that Africa is, and to my surprise a part of me wished to remain and drink even deeper. I was drawn to the wild jungle that I had not really closely seen, and to the great cities of the blackamoors of which I had only heard, and even to the Jaqqas that were such devilish mysteries. I thought fondly of the coccodrillos and the zevveras and the strange and beautiful birds of many colors and the great-mouthed gaping hippopotamuses, for never would I see such things again. It is curious how, when one is at last going from a place, it can become suddenly dear to one, even though it was not so before. And I had not detested Africa, ever. I was not so much fleeing Africa as I was being drawn back to England, I think. The only deep fault I could find in Africa, other than such bothers as the heat and the insects that crawled everywhere about, was that it was not England; and for that fault, I was quitting it. But all the same I had had great adventures in this place, I had commanded a pinnace and I had fought hand to hand with savages and I had journeyed with cannibals and I had loved two women that were very little like unto the women of England, and much more, without which I would have been far the poorer in experience. And though I now was closing the African chapter of my life, yet did I feel a shadow of regret for the going forth from this place.

In my dealings with the Dutch merchants I gave no hint, by secret wink or smile, of the compact I had concluded with Captain van Warwyck, I went about my work of interpreting in a wholly businesslike way, concealing my joy and my anticipation. Yet within me I was all in ferment, madly counting the hours, telling myself that in forty-eight hours more I would be on my way out to sea, in forty, in thirty-seven, and so on, and that at such and such a time so many days hence I would be a hundred leagues off to sea, and the like.

Then it was the Wednesday, and the Dutch ship had finished its trading here, and made ready to depart. As did I. I think my heart did beat in double time all that day long. The hours crept on snail's feet, but I danced through my chores.

In late afternoon I went to my cottage, and took Matamba to me, and in my chamber did draw her clothes from her, and look for the last time on her youthful vigorous body, her high full breasts and sturdy thighs and sleek dark skin, and the tribal marks on her face and the brand of the Portugals on her thigh and the scratches of Dona Teresa here and there.

She smiled and said to me, "You are strange of mood today, are you not?"

"Nay, I am most jolly."

And O! it was not easy to hold back the truth from her.

I cupped her and caressed her and we did hold close and I begged from her a kiss, which she gave, seeing, I think, that something out of the ordinary was about to befall. And then her body opened to me and I went in unto her and we thrust and grappled and played the game of pleasure, which brought me close to weeping, for the knowledge that I was to disappear from her without favoring her with a word of explanation. Yet did I tell myself that I owed her nothing. I had bought her out of slavery and spared her from shipping to the New World, which was no small favor, and though I knew not what would happen to her in São Paulo de Loanda after I was gone, at least she was within range of her native land and might again return to it. So my account with her was balanced in my favor. And I did not want her lamentations, nor her pleas that I remain, which I was sure she would utter most piteously.

Almost did I tell her the truth, as we clothed ourselves after that lovemaking, that I was leaving that night on board the Dutch vessel. But I thought me of all the tears and sorrow, and forbore. Also I thought it was best she knew nothing, for the Portugals would surely question her about my vanishing, and they would easily see she was ignorant of it, but if she tried to conceal something they might torture it out of her: better that I planted no knowledge at all in her.

Darkness came. I summoned no bearers. I took my last look at São Paulo de Loanda and, by a roundabout route, went in the shadows through the back streets, and out the pathway to the harbor, where, in the sudden and complete blackness of night, I made out with joy the lights of the Dutch ship standing out by the roadstead. I whistled: it was the signal. There was the splashing of oars, and the longboat came for me, and soon I was on board the ship and Warwyck embraced me and himself took me through the vast cargo hold of that huge vessel, and we had one more round of genever to celebrate. And then I crouched down between the casks and bales of merchandise, all that stuff that I had helped to tally on the register-sheets in the days just past, and secreted myself in a hiding-place to wait for sunrise and the departure.

England! Home!

I bethought myself how strange a figure I would seem, with my scars and my sun-darkened skin and my gaunt hollow face well weathered by exploits, as I went sauntering through the streets of my native town. And I imagined conversations with the friends of my childhood, telling them tales of man-eaters and giant coccodrillos and the mines of King Solomon. A few hours more, and it all would have come to pass, too.

But then I did hear oars lashing the water, and a commotion on deck, with Captain van Warwyck loudly shouting in Dutch, and Portugals shouting back at him just as loudly, and no one understanding the other, but I understanding all: which was that they knew I had stowed away, and they had come here to look for me.

How was it that I had been betrayed?

I did not know. I made myself small and did crawl into the least visible place that I could see, while the dispute raged above me. And then were thumping footsteps, and torches, and the sounds of men prowling and poking nearby, and Warwyck still grumbling and protesting, and at last the lights were bright in my face and I saw six Portugals, all armed, staring down at me.

"Here he is," they cried. "The traitor, the renegado!"

They dragged me to my feet. The torches gave such a raging light as to blind me, but when I shielded mine eyes a little from the hot glare I saw that Captain Fernão da Souza himself had led the arresting party, and he was dressed now in no fancy breeches, but with armor and helmet, and his face was steely set and harsh with rage. And beside him was none other than Gaspar Caldeira de Rodrigues, who had given me no trouble worse than sour glares at a distance for a long time, but who now was puffed up with triumph and vindictive joy. For it was he—so I did learn afterward—that had discovered the secret of my escaping, by talking with some Portugals in the crew of Captain van Warwyck— those rogues, those poxy bastards!—who had overheard the preparations being made to stow me on board the vessel. And it was he who had denounced me to Captain da Souza. So it was that the hornet had had his sting into me at last, and revenge was his, for I was undone.

Souza, maddened with fury, struck me across the face with such force it nearly twisted my neck apart, and struck me again that split my lip and cost me a tooth, and he called me dog and traitor and more, and said, "Is this how you repay our kindness, with this treachery? Oh, you will be repaid yourself, for this!" And when he had done with me it was the turn of Caldeira de Rodrigues, who did punish me most severely for the death of his brother, striking me in the ribs and the gut while others held me, and in other shameful craven ways tormenting me, so that I became a mess of blood and puke everywhere on me.

Then was I taken and bound both hand and foot and pulled to the deck, and most ungently cast into the Portuguese longboat. When we reached the shore there was waiting, instead of native bearers with hammocks, a party of horses, and I was flung across the back of one as if I were nothing more than a sack of beans. They trussed me down, and into the city we rode, giving me such a jouncing and jostling as was like to break every rib. Up to the presidio we went, and into the dungeon was I conveyed, with many a kick and a slap.

It was the same filthy beshitten loathsome hole of a place where I had been when first I came to São Paulo de Loanda—I the brave pilot, I the useful interpreter, I the heroic survivor of the Kafuche Kambara massacre, I the this and I the that, now all of it wiped out, and back to the miserable starting-point for me. I lay sleepless all night, astounded by this reversal of my fortunes. And when morning came, the time of the departure of the Dutch ship, I knew it was gone although I could not see the harbor, and I felt such pain in all my vitals as could scarce have been caused my beating, or even by the thrust of a spear. For Warwyck and his Dutchmen now were standing out to sea, and I was still here, and all my hope of England was torn from my grasp just as I had been within a few hours of setting forth. That was the greatest agony, to have been so close, and to have failed.

What would become of me now?

From the severe anger of the mild and courteous Fernão da Souza I knew I was in high trouble. I wondered if my friendship with Don João, such as it was, could aid me now. For I had betrayed his trust by fleeing. I had promised to serve, and he had had need of me, and then I had slipped on board the Dutch ship after all, and that must have wounded him. And yet, and yet, he could surely understand my longing for England. He was kind of heart; he liked me; he did not need to have it explained that a homesick man would take any opportunity to depart, no matter what pledges he had given. During that long bleak night I told myself this again and again, that Don João would have me freed in the morning with no more than a reprimand, and return me to my former pleasant life among the Portugals.

But then I thought it might not be so easy. For I did remember Don João hurling the sauce into the eyes of that slave, and I remembered Don João casually deceiving Dona Teresa in the matter of their marriage contract, and I knew that I did give the man credit for being more generous of soul than he really was. So I began to fear once again. I had betrayed my trust, who had seemed trustworty to them; why then should they be soft with me?

In the morning I was brought a bowl of water and a plate of cold porridge, and nothing else, and no one came to speak with me. And so it was the next day, and the next. It was worse than my first captivity in this dungeon, for then I had the company of my shipmate Thomas Torner, and sometimes Barbosa also to visit and encourage me, and later Dona Teresa; but Torner was long since fled and Barbosa had perished and Dona Teresa had become my enemy, and who now would stand advocate for me?

I grew weak and suffered much from hunger. On the fourth day there was a clanking of gates and there came to me a priest, Father Gonçalves, one of the Jesuits. I trembled with terror when I saw him, for I knew they had years ago given up hope of converting me to their Romish way, so if they sent a priest now it must mean I was in some grave peril, perhaps even of execution. And indeed he set up his candles and began his Latin mutterings and invited me to join with him in prayer.

"How now," I said, "am I to be put to death?"

"I do not know, my son," said the priest in most gloomy tones, that brought the dark shadow of the gallows into the room.

"It cannot be, to slay a man for no more than trying to return to his homeland!"

"Your soul is endangered. Add no more sins to your score by uttering lies."

"Lies?"

"You are guilty of grave crimes," he said.

At which I cried out, "A grave crime? What? To cherish my native soil, to yearn to see my family again?"

"To force your lusts upon a married woman is no trifling offense."

"What, did I hear you aright?"

"You stand guilty of rape, or will you deny it?"

I began then to shout forth my protests, all outraged by this scurvy and unwarranted attack on my innocence. And then my head did begin to swim with dismay, for in an instant I understood which woman it was that I was accused of ravishing, and what kind of trap had been woven about me. And I feared that I was lost.

I said, when the pounding of my heart had quieted some, "Speak the truth, priest. Am I to be hanged?"

"You are a runaway and a Lutheran and a forcer of women. What hope can there be for you?"

"That I am a Protestant has been known from the beginning, and no one has greatly chided me for it in this land. That I am a runaway I do not contest, but it was a natural deed that anyone would have done, and no sin. And that I am a forcer of women is an abominable falsehood. I would wish to see my accuser take an oath before God that I have done any such crime."

"These words will not save you."

"Then the governor will! Does Don João know that I am imprisoned here?"

"It is by his express command," said the priest.

"It is a lie!"

Dourly he did hold high his crucifix and say, "Do you demand an oath from me on it?"

Then I knew all was lost. I fell to my knees, and in my own way did implore God to spare me. At this the priest brightened greatly, and dropped down beside me and offered to place the crucifix in my hands as I prayed, the which I did not accept, and he said, "If you will but embrace the true faith, I will crave pardon of the governor for you, and perhaps he shall yield."

I closed my eyes. "My life then depends upon my turning Papist?"

"Your soul, rather."

"Yea. You will fill me with Latin and then hang me anyway, and think yourselves well accomplished, for having sent another good Catholic soul to Heaven. I do see the size of it. But I will not have it. If I am to hang, I would rather hang as a Protestant, I think. For whether I go to Heaven or Hell makes little difference to me, but to die as an honest man is very much my intent."

"You speak on honesty, with such crimes on your conscience?"

Turning on him angrily I did cry, "By the God we both claim to love, I have done no crimes!"

"Peace. Peace."

And he muttered some more in Latin, with many signings of the cross over me. I think he was as sincere in his hunger for my soul as I was in my denial of guilt. So I allowed him to pray for me.

And then I said, "I will not turn Papist, for it is a matter of scruple with me. But if you are as godly as your robes proclaim you, then I beseech you do me one service: go to Don João and tell him I maintain myself to be unjustly prisoned, and ask him to grant me an audience that I may defend myself against these charges."

Father Gonçalves looked at me long and steady. At length he said, "Yes, I will speak with Don João."

He departed then. His final words did give me hope, and for a day and a half I listened intently for the sounds of my jailers coming to fetch me and take me to the governor. But when next anyone came to me, it was not the jailers, but rather a certain venerable member of the governing council, one Duarte de Vasconcellos. This stooped and parch-cheeked old lawyer, with the dust of ancient lawbooks all over him, told me that Don João had sent him to explain to me the nature of my iniquities.

Which were vast, for I was accused of plotting with the Dutchman Cornelis van Warwyck to overthrow the royal government of Angola by force and seize the city of São Paulo de Loanda for Holland, and also was I charged with going to the chamber of the lady Dona Teresa da Souza in the dark hours before my boarding of the Dutch ship, and attempting a carnal entry upon her chaste body.

"And who are my accusers?" I asked.

Dona Teresa herself was the accuser in the second offense, he told me. As for the first, it was Gaspar Caldeira de Rodrigues who cried treason against me, and swore upon his royal forebears that I had gone about town boasting that I would convey the city to the possession of the Dutch, who meant to sell it to England. Thus did he avenge his brother.

"Well," I said, "and let me be confronted with these accusers! For the deceitful Rodrigues knows that there was no plan of hostility against this city in me, but only that I sought to return to mine own homeland. And Dona Teresa, God wot, will not be capable to stand up before my eyes and swear that I had her by force, when it is well known in São Paulo de Loanda that she has many times given herself freely to—"

"Nay, say no slanders, Englishman."

"Slander? Slander? Come, old man, you know yourself that she—"

"I will not hear it." He looked at me sternly and said, "The Portugals who denounced you cannot testify, for that their ship has sailed, and they are gone with it out to sea. And I do tell you it is beyond all imagining that Dona Teresa can be put to the torment and ordeal of an appearance in court, so shaken and disrupted is she by your attack on her. But her husband Don Fernão has seen the bruises and other damage on her body, and he has entered the plea against you, by which you are found guilty and sentenced—"

"God's death, am I guilty already, and no trial?"

"—to die by hanging in the public square, at the pleasure of the Governor Don João de Mendoça."

"Those bruises on Dona Teresa's body were made by my slave-girl Matamba, when they two did fight, after Dona Teresa in jealous rage attacked the girl: she being angered that Matamba and not she herself was now my bedpartner. Examine the slave! Take her testimony, and see the wounds Dona Teresa inflicted upon her!"

"A slave's testimony is without value. And in any event the verdict has already been rendered."

"Ah," I said. "The famed Portuguese justice!"

"I am here to make formal notice to you, and to ask if you have requests we may fulfill."

"I do appeal my sentence to Don João, and demand an audience with him, to make show to him of my innocence."

"That will avail you nothing," said Vasconcellos. "But I will do as you say."

That afternoon four Portuguese warders came for me, and without one word took me from my cell. I thought joyously that I was indeed now to be brought to Don João, and it gave me heart, since that I had spent some hours resigning myself to death for these phantasmical crimes of mine. But it was a cruel disappointment, for the Portugals conveyed me only as far as the courtyard of the presidio, where they fastened me to their whipping-stake and did beat me with knotted cords, so that by the time they were done there was not a spot on all my body that was not swollen and aching, and in some places bleeding. After this punishment they did return me to my cell, and a keeper entered, and, saying he was doing this at the governor's command, did clinch to my legs great bolts of iron of thirty pounds' weight, that dragged upon me like the Devil's own grip. "This is done because that you are a known escaper," he said, and left me.

Enfeebled, shackled, sore with my whipping, I lay like one benumbed and bereft of all will. Each morning when I arose I expected to be taken out and put to death; and each night when I lay me down to sleep I tallied one more day of life, with gratitude and despair all at the same time, for what was the use of living if my remaining few days were to be so empty? I thought of Warwyck's ship, that must be halfway to Holland by now, and I wept from rage. I thought of Matamba, and wondered sorrowfully what had become of her, now that I was condemned. I thought of Dona Teresa, by whose jealousy and treachery this had befallen me, and I meditated much and deep on how love could turn to bitter enmity. And I gave my thoughts greatly to England, to my friends there and such family as I might still have, to the Queen

Her Majesty, to the soft mists and gentle rains and green fields full of sheep and all that I would never see again. In this way I passed through despair to resignation, and grew calm, telling myself that I had lived some thirty-five years, which was more than is granted to most, and had known much delight in that time along with a proper measure of grief. If I had to die now, why, I would accept that judgment, for it is true beyond quarrel that we each owe God a death, He who gave us life, and I was merely paying the debt a little earlier than was my preferred time. Furthermore there are many ways to die that are more hideous than hanging, and now I would suffer none of them.

But as it happened I was spared the gallows as well. For two months I did languish in that foul stinking prison awaiting my doom and thinking, whenever a warder approached my cell, that it was to take me to the gibbet. But then came the one that had fastened the iron hoops to my legs, and he did cut them from me; and then the lawyer Vasconcellos entered my cell and said, "I bring you happy tidings, Englishman."

"Aye, that I am to be drowned slowly in good wine of the Canary Islands, instead of being hanged, is that it?"

He looked displeased at my levity and said most soberly, "His Excellency Don João has taken mercy upon you despite your great crimes. Your sentence of death is raised."

"God be thanked!" I cried.

But my jubilation was misplaced. For Vasconcellos went on to tell me that I was not pardoned, but merely given a new sentence: which was to be banished for ever to the fort of Masanganu, and to serve for the rest of my days in that place of fevers and monstrous heat, to defend the frontiers of the colony. My first impulse upon hearing that was to call out for hanging instead, as being greatly more preferable. Which I did not say; but I did tell myself inwardly that Don João had earned little thanks from me for this show of kindness. For he had sent me into a suffering beyond all measure, to a Hell upon earth, from which death was likely to be the only release.

As I went on board the pinnace that was to take me up the river into imprisonment, I drew from my pouch the small woman-idol that Dona Teresa had given me long before, and I looked at it most long and hard. Still did it seem to embody the sinister irresistible beauty of that woman, and still did it cling to my hand as though by some secret force in the wood. I drew my breath in deep, and clamped my jaws tight closed, and with all my strength did I hurl that idol into the dark waters, and stood staring as it dropped from sight.

The which deed gave me some measure of comfort and release from constraint. I braced myself against the rail, and stood sweating and gasping in the aftermath of it, until they hurried me onward with a rude jostle onto the ship. But the discarding of that idol was the only action I was able to take against those who had brought me to this pass, and precious little good did it in truth do me. For even if I had broken free of Dona Teresa's witch-spell at last, yet still was I condemned inexorably to torment most extreme, at Masanganu the torrid, Masanganu the terrible.

BOOK
THREE:

Warrior

ONE

AT MASNGANU I lived a most miserable life for the space of six years without any hope to see the sea again.

How swiftly I am able to say that! It takes me not even two dozen words to encompass that statement of simple fact. And in so saying, so quickly and easily, I reduce to a seeming trifle what was indeed a most doleful burden. Not even two dozen words to tell of it! But the actual living of six years cannot be done in one hour less than those six years, as even a fool will attest; and I do swear to you by the Savior's own beard that to dwell at Masanganu for six years is much like living anywhere else for sixty, or perhaps six hundred.

Yet did I endure it, day by day, minute by minute, which is the only way such a thing can be done. When I think back to the years of my servitude there, the time does indeed fold and compress in upon itself, so that I can speak of six years and make it seem to have gone by as rapidly as it takes me to tell of it; and yet also I can still feel the weight of those years within me, hanging on my soul as iron gyves did once hang on my legs. A prisoner can put down his chains, when his pardon comes, but I can never put down my years at Masanganu until that last day when I do lay down all the freight that my soul does carry.

I have told you already something of this place, which lies at the meeting of the waters of the Kwanza and the Lukala, toward the inner side of the Angolan coastal plain, in a region both foggy and most stifling hot. Among the swamps and marshes of Masanganu stands the pale stone fort of the Portugals upon a little headland, in a zone where the heat is greatest, the sun hanging overhead all the day long, and, I trow, half the night as well, since it is no cooler in the hours of darkness than at noontide. This fort is well situated to guard the inner lands, for it looks toward the mountains that rise in Angola's interior, and any hostile force descending out of those jungled uplands must of necessity come within notice of Masanganu before it can hope to menace São Paulo de Loanda. So there is at Masanganu a permanent garrison to guard against any intrusion of enemies from the east or north.

Permanent, that is, in the sense that there always are men stationed at Masanganu, to a number of several hundreds; but the men themselves are far from permanent, being constantly carried off by the maladies of the place. That God chose to excuse me from those ailments is, I suppose, an example of His great mercy toward me, that He showed in many ways during my adventures in Africa; but all the while I was there, I moved among men who had been stricken horridly by this plague or that, and I learned not to form fast friendships, since there was slender chance that any such would last. There is in that place a colic that is most deadly, and a bloody flux, and a kind of headache that gives a pain beyond all understanding; and there is also the fever that smote me on my first visit, which I saw carry off any number of others, though it left me alone after the one time. And as well there is a kind of worm in Masanganu that covertly enters the body, most commonly in the fleshy parts, as the thighs, the haunches, the breasts, or even the scrotum and the yard, and I think the malady this worm causes is the most worst of all. The worm generally shows itself by the swelling of the flesh; in some it causes violent agues, with great shiverings; others it torments with intolerable pains all over the body, so that they cannot rest in any posture; others it casts into a violent fever, and continual deliriums. But those men that are afflicted in their private parts suffer beyond any others, and in their torment grow perfectly mad and outrageous, so that it is requisite to bind them very fast. The only way to cure this loathly disease is to take hold of the worm very gingerly as soon as the head has made its way out of the swelling, and make it fast to a small piece of wood, on which it is slowly and carefully drawn forth by winding the stick, sometimes for a whole month, until it emerges entire. If the worm should happen to break by being too hastily drawn out, that part which remains in the body will soon putrefy or break out at some other part, which occasions double pain and trouble. I saw men thus served, for whom no other remedy could be found to preserve their lives than cutting off a leg or an arm, or the privy parts; and if the worm is lodged in the trunk of the body, and broken, it is almost a miracle if the man does not die of the gangrene working to the vital parts. From my arrival in Masanganu in the latter part of 1594 until my departure from it early in Anno 1600 there was no single day on which I did not search my body for the intrusion of this worm, with fear and tremblings until I was sure it had not penetrated me.

Strange to say it was the Portugals at Masanganu who suffered worst from these maladies, but the blacks were rarely touched except by the worm; and there were various Moors and Gypsies there who also seemed safe against the fevers. These men had been sent to Masanganu by banishment, even as I. The Gypsies or Ciganos had been expelled from Portugal by King Philip, under pain of death if they did not quit the kingdom four months after his decree, and many of these folk had gone to seek their fortunes in Africa, which is where their kind originally did proceed from, they being Egyptians by ancestry. The ones at Masanganu were all criminals sent down from São Tomé or the Kongo, and a dangerous bunch they were, that would cheerfully slit you open just to see the color of your inner organs. As for the Moors, they were Moriscos from the land of Morocco, who did compete with the Portugals in the trading of slaves along the Guinea coast, and these had been captured and imprisoned for their pains. I never knew many of these Moorish men, who were proud and aloof and spoke a language among themselves that they would not teach to others. But I did befriend a few of the Gypsies, simply because they and I, not falling victim to the evil diseases of the place, were thrown together over a long span of time and grew accustomed to one another.

In those years the Portugals did often make war against the black nations of the interior. The mainmost of these expeditions was led by Don João himself, who had, I think, never gone before into battle. This was an entry up the River Mbengu, which lies north of São Paulo de Loanda a little way, and the purpose of it was the pacifying of the blacks along the upper reaches of Angola's boundary. In this excursion the shrewd and farsighted Don João proved himself every bit as rash as the unlamented Don Jeronymo, for against all advice he commenced it at the worst time of the year, which is March, and very quickly he lost two hundred men by fever. This I know because reinforcements were summoned from the Masanganu garrison upon these fatalities, though I was not one of those chosen. With these additional men Don João did conquer the district, and, as though to revenge himself on the natives for his own losses through diseases and ignorance of the country, he treated the defeated chieftains with unusual severity. I have it on good authority that many of the hapless *sobas* were placed in his heavy guns and blown forth by a charge of powder, to the terrible sundering of their limbs.

Well, and I suppose the Portugals may treat their fallen foes in any manner they wish, but I could not come to see Sir Francis Drake ever blowing enemies from guns, nor any other Englishman so doing. Why, I think not even our crookbacked King Richard III, that was the great enemy of our Queen's grandfather, and is said to have committed such foul crimes in our land an hundred years ago, would have stooped to such a villainy. But the souls of most of these Spaniards and Portugals, methinks, are deficient in the substance that makes other men shrink from monstrous cruelties. Perhaps it is the hot dry air of their forlorn Iberian Peninsula that bakes the mercy out of them, or possibly it is the Popish teachings by which they are reared, that cause them to hold the lives of those of other faiths to be of no account. But I doubt that latter, for the Genoese and the Venetians and the Burgundians and many others are Papists just as well, and they do not stuff their conquered adversaries into cannons.

While Don João was engaged in these pastimes, his captain-major João de Velloria, the Spaniard, was marching through the land of Lamba, which lies between the Rivers Kwanza and Mbengu, and he was doing many the same things. For these triumphs Velloria was nominated as a member in the Order of Christ, which is some holy confraternity of the Portugals, and was granted a pension of twenty thousand reis, which be six pounds a year, and was named to the office of Marcador dos Esclavos, or administrator of slaves, that brought him a fee for every slave taken in this territory. How many blacks he slaughtered in the campaign that won him these honors I cannot say. But at least none of them went to be slaves in the sugar-mills of Brazil, so to that degree he gave them a kindness: it is a quicker death to perish on the field of battle than to bleed your life away cutting cane and hauling millstones.

And I did take no part in all these heroic and pious exploits, being penned up in the hellish presidio at Masanganu. My chief duty there was to bury the dead. The colic or the flux or the fevers carried them off, and then I was summoned, along with three Gypsies and two Portugals who also were reputed to be proof against these diseases, and we did dig a grave and carry the bloated and blackened and sickening corpse to it, and give it its interment. For a time I counted the number of these dead that I saw into the earth, but then I lost the tally, when it was well above an hundred. For indeed this Masanganu was a place, as Thomas Torner had declared in fright long before, where men do die like chickens. But when a chicken dies, no one need labor to dig a great buggardly hole in the ground to put it into, under a sun that gives the heat of a thousand thousand furnaces at once.

Beyond such activities there was little. We marched patrol; we repaired the fort, which was constantly crumbling, owing to the poorness of the mortar in this clime; we made clearings in the jungle, to what end I never was told; we cleaned our guns and swept out the streets. Sometimes we hunted for coccodrillos or river-horses by way of small diversion. We had for our pleasure the native women, many of them poxed, and the soldiers did use them freely, in whatever way that suited their fancy, including one that I think would have had them burned at the stake if the Jesuits got wind of it, that is, by sodomizing them. This became the common fashion at Masanganu at a time, so that when one heard a woman screaming painfully at a distance, one could be sure that some merry Portugal had flipped her on her belly and was ramming himself between her hinder cheeks. This I never chose to do, thinking that it was folly to go poking about in the hole of foulness and excrement

when God had afforded us a much sweeter and more natural entrance
nearby. From time to time I did take me a woman by the ordinary usage,
rarely the same one twice, and never more often than the fires of lust
within me did absolutely require. A Gypsy of my acquaintance kindly
showed me a remedy for the venereal pox, that was to make a sort of
ointment of palm-oil and a new-laid egg, and to rise after carnal doings
and immediately to rub that substance all over one's yard and ballocks
and thighs. The which I unfailingly did, despite the foul sliminess of
the medicine, and I had me no poxes at Masanganu, though I cannot
say whether that was owing to the efficacy of the Gypsy medicine or
to my own good fortune.

So did the months and years pass. I felt sure I would give up all the
rest of my life in this place, and, curious to relate, I do confess that for
some span of time I did not resent that at all. What, you say? Andrew
Battell resigned to captivity, a mere passive drudge? Yea, so it was. But
I pray you remember that I had left my home in the spring of '89 and
this was six and seven and eight years after, and for most of those years
I had been a prisoner—sometimes under comfortable circumstances,
sometimes less so, but at scarce any moment my own master. That had
not broken me, but it had dulled my sharp edge of spirit. Though ever
yet I dreamed of escaping this dark and sultry land and going again to
England, that became little more than a will-o'-the-wisp to me, as remote
from reality as is the hope of heaven to a small child.

I labored. I ate. I slept. I sweated. Those were the boundaries of my
life at Masanganu. And I tell you, it let the time fly faster by, if I did
not give resistance to my captivity. In that place where there is scarce
any change of season, where even day and night are nigh the same length
all the year round, when only by alternation of wet and dry seasons can
one tell winter from summer, and the terrible heat dominates everything,
time does indeed appear to glide by in a single unbroken sheet of hours,
and I knew not whether the year was 1595 or '96 or '97. Somewhere far
away was an England where yet they had the Easter and the Christmastide and the midsummer frolic, where a Queen ruled in grace and
glory over a sparkling court of dukes and lords and knights, where maids
were wed and turned into mothers, where constant change and transformation was the rule: and here I toiled in a timeless place of the greatest
discomfort and dreariness, and each day was the twin of the last.

Only one interruption in our life of routine occurred, when King
Ngola, that was the greatest of the enemies of the Portugals in these
parts, did rise up and lay blockade against our presidio. That was in
Anno 1597, I do believe.

We had ample warning of this, for our scouts all through the province did tell us an army was massing, with drums of war beating, and a great shouting and flourishing of weapons and ringing of wooden bells by the sorcerers, that are the preliminary rituals of war among these folk. Then they came upon us, first a procession of wizards and warlocks with their bodies wrapped in the strong leaves of the *matteba*, a tree much like unto the palm, so that it seemed the forest itself did walk toward us; and then the warriors themselves, in all their wild battle-dress, their high head-dresses and iron chains and jingling bells and such, the like of which I had seen before in the attack by Kafuche Kambara. There were thousands of them, capering like grotesque phantasms and incubi before us, letting fly with their arrows and darts, and crying out in hoarse whooping tones, and doing a dance of death.

But we had builded well, and were not vulnerable behind the walls of our fort, so that they did rage and bluster for week upon week while doing us no harm. Nor could we harm them, I do add, and had the siege continued many weeks longer we should all have perished of starvation if not of the plagues of the place. We dared not come out of the presidio to our burying-ground, so whenever one of our number died of a malady we did burn his body and scatter the ashes, which may not have been pleasing unto God and Church but which spared us from the spreading of disease. And after a time the main force of the Portugals came up from São Paulo de Loanda under the command of the general Balthasar Rebello de Aragão, and drove off the blackamoors as though they were nothing more than vapors, and set us free. After which, this Rebello de Aragão did descend the Kwanza and build a new presidio near the village of Muchima, in the constructing of which I did take a part.

But then we returned to the old weary life at Masanganu, and again I lost count of the months and the years. There was a day when I learned by chance that I was now living in the November of 1598, so that it was my fortieth anniversary of my birth. That seemed a very great age for me to have attained, especially in the teeth of such many hardships. "I am forty years old," I said aloud to myself several times over, and strange it sounded in my ears. And then also it was the fortieth year of Her Protestant Majesty's glorious reign, if indeed she still held the throne. But did she? God save me, I might have been on some other star, for all the news of England I had. Did the Queen still live? And if she had gone on, who now held the throne? Was it James of Scotland, or some French prince, or the King of Spain, or someone altogether other? Nay, I could not imagine anyone else on our throne but she, that virgin and miraculous she; and I could not imagine myself being forty, which meant that my lost Anne Katherine, whose maidenhood I had had from her

when she was fifteen, must now be seven-and-twenty, long past the
bloom of her youth, almost a matron. Did she still wait for my return?
Only a fool would think so. Perhaps she grieved for me, but certain it
was she had given her love to someone else, and had by now two children
or three, and was growing plump and had a little line of golden hair
sprouting on her lip, eh? November of 1598! Forty years old, aye, and
a slave in Masanganu!

So the time journeyed, and I grew ever harder and more enduring,
and I came up out of my long resignation and bestirred myself to think
of escaping this place, before my life's time was utterly expended.

There was a certain Gypsy of Masanganu that over the years I had
come to trust, and he the same for me, because that we had labored long
side by side, suffering much and sharing much. He called himself Cristovão, though also he had a Cigano name in their own language, that
he did not offer to others. This Cristovão was a small man, very dark
of skin, with a hawk's nose and eyes of the most penetrating sort, and
the strength of his body was extraordinary, he being able to lift weights
of the heaviness of myself, though being but half my size. On one day
of amazing heat, when he and I and some few other Gypsies did labor
to rebuild a breach in the wall of the fort, suffering like Jews under
Pharaoh, an overseer named Barbosa—but surely no kin of my fallen
friend—came upon us as we paused a moment to refresh ourselves.
Cristovão had a leathern flask of palm-wine, that he drank from by
holding it high overhead and letting a stream of the sweet fluid squirt
to his open mouth; and he took a deep draught of it and handed it to
me, saying, "Here, Andres, it is time you learned how it be done."

Whereupon I imitated him, but badly, getting the stream of wine on
my cheeks and throat, and he laughed and the other Ciganos also, and
Cristovão took the flask from me to show me the trick of it. And while
he held it above him, this taskmaster Barbosa appeared and did strike
the flask from Cristovão's hands, crying, "Why are you drinking, and
not working?"

I saw the fury in Cristovão's eyes. Humbly did he stoop and pick up
his flask, the wine of which was mainly spilled, and then he cleansed
his face where the wine had stained it, and he took several deep breaths
of the hot air to constrain his temper, so that he did not strike the
taskmaster dead, as Moses did in the land of Egypt. And quietly he
murmured curses in the Cigano tongue, for he did seethe with hatred
and rage.

Then I said, taking him by the arm and leading him a little aside,
"Can you bear this any longer? For I cannot. I am minded to flee this
place, Cristovão."

"On your oath?"

"Indeed. This very night will I go, for I think it better for me to venture my life for my liberty than to live any longer in this miserable town," said I, the words rising up out of some powerful spring within my soul where they had too long been penned.

He pressed his face close to mine and grinned widely, so that I saw a fortune in yellow gold inlaid into his crooked teeth, and he said, "I will go with you, Andres, and we will take our risks together." And he clasped his arm against mine in an intricate and interwoven way that was, I think, a sign of blood-bond among the Cigano kind.

So were we resolved, and then we were swept along in our own vigor, never hesitating. Whilst we worked we planned our plan, which was to steal a canoe and slip from the fort under darkness, not just the two of us but a whole band of escapers, for we agreed there would be safety in numbers when we were abroad in the jungle. Cristovão said he would procure ten of his fellows to go with us, and so he did, seven Portugals and three more Gypsies, all of them known to me as strong and trust-worthy men.

In that tropic land the night falls swiftly once the sun goes away, and if there is no moon the darkness is absolute, owing to the thickness of the jungle vapors and the heaviness of the twined vines that tangle with one another through the tops of the trees. This was a night of no moon; and in the second hour of darkness we rose from our huts and went out from the compound surrounding the fort. We aroused no suspicion among the guards because we did go a few men at a time, and also because that they were lulled by the heat and sluggishness of the place, that in time can turn even the most vigilant of men into an imbecile and dullard.

Through the moist and fevered glades of that close-walled jungle we went one by one until we were at the little quay beside the river. There I found that Cristovão and another Gypsy had overcome the sentinel of the canoes. Simão, one of the Portugals, did take from his sleeve a blade, and make ready to thrust it into the man's belly, but quickly was he stopped by Cristovão, who seized his wrist most forcibly.

"Nay," he whispered, "be not a fool! If we slay him, and then we are retaken, what will become of us?"

I had my doubts of that, thinking it mattered little, for if we were retaken it would go hard with us whether we had this sentinel's blood upon our souls or no. Yet never have I favored slaying the innocent, and this man had done me no wrong. So I gave my agreement, and instead of killing him we did tie him with ropes of living vine pulled down from the trees, and stuffed into his mouth a thick wad of herbage to silence him.

Then we selected the best of the canoes, that was long and trim and stood like a proud lordling above the water. Aboard it we stowed our muskets and powder and shot and a little supply of the golden wheat called *masa mamputo*, which is Guinea wheat or more accurately American maize, that was the only food we were able to obtain as we departed.

"Go, Piloto," said Cristovão. "Get you to the bow, and guide us, and I will stand in the stern."

We twelve escapers then did clamber into the canoe, I taking my place fore, and each of us wielding an oar as we pushed ourselves free and set off down the black and swiftly coursing river in the dead of the night.

Two

FREE MEN!

That morning slaves, and by night we were our own masters on a voyage of departure!

In silence we did glide on the Kwanza's dark breast. Along both sides of the river the trees rose like towering palisados, and animals of the night cried out their terrible howls. With sharp dedication did we keep ourselves to the center channel, lest we crack ourselves against the shore. Sometimes in the night we saw red eyes gleaming, or yellow ones, along the margin of the river: hippopotamuses, or coccodrillos, or perchance some monster even worse. One of the Portugals, a certain Pero, began to tell a story of a journey by canoe he had had on the Mbengu in the campaign of Don João de Mendoça, saying, "It was like this, by night, and the river much narrower, and as we paddled east we were halted by an eddy in the current, and then there rose beneath us a river-horse as big as an elephanto, that overthrew our craft entirely, and scattered us in the water."

"Be quiet," said the Gypsy Duarte Lagosta, "or we will feed you to the coccodrillos. We need no such gloomy tales to dishearten us here."

"I meant only to tell you how we escaped, when—"

"Tell us after we are overthrown," said Duarte Lagosta, and the Portugal was silent.

I brooded little about meeting a river-horse in the night, but gave much more thought about fetching up into some one of the muddy isles that dot the river. For that could easily happen, and if we were beached we would be coccodrillo-meat before we could get ourselves afloat. Many times had I navigated this river, but never at night, and not in six years; yet I strained at my memories of it, contriving to recollect from the curves and swerves of it the places where the islands lay. Perhaps I did overlook a few, but yet we did not go aground. And as dawn began to creep into the sky above the treetops we found ourselves in a better part of the river, that I knew to be the territory of a little lord styled Mani Kabech, that has a territory in the province of Lamba, which is subject to Portugal.

Morning showed us a heavy sultry world of huge trees, palms and cedars and ironwood, and most especially the great bulging ollicondis, that are like houses in themselves, all spongy within, with trunks that hold rainwater, from which birds do drink. All of this was woven together like a tapestry by the festoons and drapings of the gigantic green creepers, thick as the greatest of serpents, overhead. Though it was daytime the forest was dark— O! it was dark dark dark!—and that was a good thing, for we had had more than our necessary share of sun in the Masanganu labor, and this was a kind coolness to us.

Here we went on shore with our twelve muskets, powder, and shot. We sunk our canoes, because they should not know where we had gone on shore. We made a little fire in the wood, and scorched our Guinea wheat, to relieve our hunger. Later we gathered some honey from the crotch of a great tree, where bees did fly about. And a Gypsy showed us which palm-trees were good to eat, by felling the slender young ones and biting out the pale tender succulent shoots that came from the heart of them.

All morning we rested here and ate, and talked of our plans. Since that we had had no sleep on the night of our escape, we took it now, some of us closing our eyes and some standing watch. Our vigilance was addressed more against deadly beasts of the jungle than against Portugals, for we did not think we would be pursued as far as this point.

As soon as it was dark, we took up our journey again, and marched all that night through the most difficult of thick enforestation, taking what we hoped to be a direction of north-north-west. In this everyone turned to me for counsel, I being regarded as a skilled navigator, and in every opening of the vines I did study the pattern of the stars and draw my sage advice, so it seemed, from the array of the constellations. But also I took good care to note the position of the river, that was far more useful, for it was flowing along on our left hand a short way below us and was a present guide to our way.

But then the river diverged from us, which could not be helped, for our goal was the kingdom of the Kongo in the north, and the Kwanza, if we followed it, would bring us to the sea some leagues south of São

Paulo de Loanda, a city we did not dare approach. So now I did navigate by guesswork alone, and by bluff, doing my best. It is far much easier to find one's way on the open sea betimes, for all its dearth of landmarks, than it is when one is in a jungle where every tree does look the image of his brother, and giveth one false information, which is worse than none at all.

Our second day was a grievous one, for the land grew very much more dry as we entered a great plain, and there was no water anywhere. It seemed sure that in a country so moist and lavish there would be ample springs and brooks for us, but there was not a drop, and the sun's heat did punish us cruelly, drawing the moisture up out of our bodies and making us grow dizzy.

Gonçalo Fernandes, that was a Portugal who had been shipwrecked on the other coast of Africa some time before, now told us a pretty story, saying, "I was cast upon a desert island, and in all this island we could not find any fresh water in the world, insomuch that we were driven to drink our own urine."

"And do you suggest that of us now?" asked my Gypsy friend Cristovão, making a sour face like unto an old prune that has been left in the sun a dozen year.

Gonçalo Fernandes replied, "You see me here before you not dead of thirst, and there is your answer."

"It is a very hard extreme, though," said Duarte Lagosta.

"That other time," said Gonçalo Fernandes, "we saved the urine in sherds of certain jars, which we had out of our pinnace, and set it all night to cool therein, to drink it the next morning. And I tell you by God's Mother that this sustained us. The urine we voided became exceeding red, I think because it was the same water constantly passing in and out of our bodies. But we did not die. And I tell you another thing, that when we found a way to get over to the mainland, we came upon a little river of very sweet and pleasant water, and my companion Antonio overdrank himself, being pinched before with extreme thirst, and within half an hour he died in my presence. So we must remember to be sparing when water comes to us again."

Well, and we drank no urine that day, but we suffered mightily of thirst. I think had we had any drinking-vessels with us in which to retain the stuff, we would have overcome our niceness on that score. But we did not. We pressed onward, thinking to find ollicondi trees and suck the moistness therefrom, but these trees were not native on this plain. And after a day of such travel we were dizzied and unhealthful, all but one or two of the Gypsies, who seemed of such strength that they needed neither food nor water. That night we were not able to go, and were fain to dig and scrape up roots of little trees, and suck them to maintain life, as I had done that other time of my shipwreck.

The third day we met with one of those great serpents that do inhabit these parts, this being as long as five men stretched head to toe, and as thick through as the thigh of a very stout man. The monster was sleeping and I think had lately eaten, for its middle was a bulging place that was swollen as big as a pig or a goat. We talked of killing it for its meat, but the Portugals among us were loath to eat serpent-flesh, and one of the Gypsies swore that if we angered it, the creature would breathe flame upon us and destroy us; and this argument became so impassioned that in the end, hungry as we were, we let the serpent be, and walked far around it, and continued on our way. Which led to further dispute, some saying they would rather eat serpent than starve, and others preferring starvation: and we did consume much effort in noisy parley of this kind.

But later that day we encountered an old Negro who was traveling to the town where Mani Kabech has his capital. It gave us great surprise to see any man in this forlorn place. This man was wizened and ancient, but strong, and when he saw us he at once began to run. Two of our Gypsies, being most fleet of foot, gave chase and brought him to the ground, but he struggled so keenly fierce with them that it was an amazement, he being white-haired and his skin withered by age, hanging in dry folds. When he was subdued we took from him his waist-cloth of sturdy palm fiber and bound his hands behind him, and I spoke with him, telling him in Kikongo words I had learned from Matamba that we meant no harm, if he would help us.

He looked at me most gloomily, as though I would sell him tomorrow into slavery.

"Nay," I said, "we are no slavers, and we love the Portugal government no more than you."

Mamputo is what I said for "Portugal," that being the native word for that nation, and I did pantomime my disdain by saying the word and spitting, and the like. The Portugals among us were displeased by this, but I made them hold their tongues.

With great patience I explained to the old man that we were fleeing our enemies, the *Mamputo* folk, and hoped to take refuge in the land of Kongo, and needed him to lead us to the lake of Kasanza, which we knew to be in that direction and where we could refresh ourselves. He understood my meaning and pledged himself to do that for us. One of the Portugals asked me to tell him that if he worked any treachery he would die a terrible death, but I allowed the old man enough wisdom to comprehend that without my saying it to him.

This Lake Kasanza was well known to some of those with whom I journeyed. It is eight miles across, and issues into the River Mbengu. It doth abound with fish of sundry sorts, and on its shore lives the greatest store of wild beasts that is in any place of Angola. So there we thought we might provide for ourselves as we undertook the continuance of our march into the land of Kongo.

The old man did not betray us. Traveling all that day in this extreme hot country we came to the town called Kasanza, which is near to the lake. As we neared it we crossed a small river that runs out of the lake, which was the first water that we had seen in a very long while. But the old man cried out as we ran to drink from it, saying in his tongue that the river gave bad water; and, having faith in him, I warned my companions not to take any. This was difficult for them to forego, but when we came to the edge of the water it was easier, the river being so shallow it was near dry, and the water being black and foul, with a thick scum or crust over it, and flies so numerous they were like a curtain that buzzed.

So we went onward unslaked, and a little while after came to Kasanza town. Here we were only twelve leagues east of São Paulo de Loanda. It was but another two or three miles from the town to the lake, but some of our people did not have the strength to proceed any further owing to thirst. Therefore we released our old blackamoor and went into the town to seek aid.

This town was one of those subjugated by Don João de Mendoça in his military expedition through the valley of the Mbengu, and we feared there might be a Portugal garrison here. But there was none, only a population of Negroes, that greeted us very coolly, and when we asked for water they fled into their houses and would not come out, and gave us nothing to drink.

"Let us torch the place," said that Portugal Simão who had wanted to slay the sentinel of the canoes, and who vaunted himself for bravery and resource, but to me was not much other than a common criminal.

"Aye," said Gonçalo Fernandes, who had once survived by drinking urine. "If they defy us, let us burn them like rats in a stack of hay."

"It is not the wisest way," I replied. "We can frighten them in easier style."

And I did array our party in a military fashion, and we aimed our muskets into the houses, and fired very sparingly but in a regular way, shooting into this house and that and that according to what must seem like a pattern of attack. This drove the people into the open, making gestures of surrender, and their lord the Mani Kasanza now came to us with fair speeches, inviting us to stay the night in his village, and saying we could have water.

So that night we slept under a roof again. But it was not a restful night nor a merry one, except that it is possible to see merriment in a discomfort so extreme that it takes on a character of absurdity.

This is what befell. They gave us for sleeping, one of their largest palaces, which of course was no palace but only a building of brush and straw and plastered mud, but it had many rooms. When we had eaten and had our fill to drink, we took to our chambers gladly, and quickly our joy was dissipated. My bed was against the wall, which was of fat clay ill put together, and might well be called a nest of rats; for there were so many of them and so large, that they troubled me very much, running over me and biting my toes. To prevent this I caused my bed to be laid in the middle of the room, but to no purpose, for those cursed creatures knew where to find me. The others had the same difficulty, and when an hour had passed thus plagued by the rats, Cristovão and I went to the dwelling of the Mani Kasanza, to protest the place we had been given.

He was not at all surprised at our complaint, but said he would provide us with an infallible remedy against it. This was a little monkey that would secure me against the rats by blowing on them when he spied them, and by giving off a kind of musky perfume that the rats found displeasing. We took this small agile creature to our house, and indeed it did its duty; for he was quite tame, and picked through my hair and beard for hidden creatures, which he devoured, and after doing me this service did lay down at the foot of my bed. When the rats came as they were wont, the monkey blew hard at them two or three times, and made them run away; and then he went on into the other rooms and did the same for my companions.

Thus I had perhaps two hours of sleep without interruption, which my body sorely needed after my long march across the hot land. But just as I was sinking into the true depths of my slumber, that is the most nourishing part of the night, several blacks did rush helter-skelter into the chamber, crying, "Out! Out! The ants are broke out, and there is no time to be lost!"

I was fuddled with weariness and scarce understood what they were saying, so without waiting for me to stir, they lifted me upon my straw bed and did carry bed and me together out of the building. The same was occurring to the others of my party, and we gathered outside, now thoroughly awake. The nimbleness of the blacks stood me in good stead, for the ants had already begun to run upon my legs, and get to my body, and bit in like prickling needles. A certain Portugal named Vaz Martin, much agitated by the sight of them, said, "We should give God thanks that we were delivered from these pismires, for they are most deadly." And he told me how this thing often happens in the kingdom of Angola, that men are taken in their sleep and unable to stir and are eaten up alive by them, and also cows are found devoured in the night by these ants, and nothing left of them but the bones. It is no small deliverance to escape the troublous insects, for there are some that fly, and are hard to be removed from the place where they lay hold: but God be praised that my body was not devoured by them alive.

To rid the village of the small attackers the blacks took straw, and fired it on the floor of the four rooms, where the ants were marching already above half a foot thick. But while this was being done the fire took hold of the thatch of the house, and fearing the fire might increase with the wind, we drew back to a further distance. And also the pismires broke into a neighboring cottage, where again the blacks did burn them; but the hut being all of straw, it was consumed as well as the ants, which made the blacks get out of their houses for fear the wind should carry the flame about and burn all that quarter. This may all sound amusing in the telling of it long after, but I assure you we found that comedy of rats and monkey and ants and fire to be no cheering comedy at all, but rather exceeding somber. We were without sleep that night once all this commenced, and before dawn we departed, more weary than we had come, and hied ourselves off to the shores of the lake of Kasanza.

Here at least we had some repose, and took some fish and birds for the benefit of our bellies. And at dusk the next day we proceeded onward to the north until we arrived at the river. To cross the Mbengu entailed us in great danger, for that the place is a nesting-ground of coccodrillos, in such number that they reminded us of the swarms of ants. I have told you that coccodrillos have a musky scent, but here they were so numerous that the water itself was rank with their flavor, which was distasteful in the extreme. And they are roaring beasts, that in the night do call to one another, especially toward break of day, with a sound much resembling the sound of a deep well, that might be easily heard a league away. But we found a place where we could safely ford the river between two great lairs of these monsters, and we lit torches, which they seemed not to like.

All the following day we crossed another dry hot terrain and toward night we came to the River Dande, the next one north of the Mbengu. Owing to the bleakness of the land we turned east and traveled so far that we were right against the mountains of Manibangono, which is a lord that warreth against the King of Kongo, whither we intended to go. Ahead of us we saw a village, but we were uncertain of our reception there and so we slipped most secretly into his outskirts, and hid ourselves in a field nearby.

God's death, that was folly! For we had planted ourselves right down in the great burial-ground of the village, and hardly were we established there when a procession came wending out of the town to perform some funeral rites. We could not flee, for the lay of the land was such that we would surely be seen; so we had no recourse but to huddle ourselves down behind some of the great heaped-up tumuli of the dead and hope that we went unnoticed.

So they came forth, and when they reached the edge of the cemetery they all paused while some hens were killed by their painted sorcerers, and the blood liberally scattered around. Cristovão, beside me, whispered, "D'ye know the import of that?"

"Not at all," said I.

"It is to prevent the soul of the dead person from coming to give the *zumbi* to any of the townsfolk."

"I know not this word *zumbi*."

"It means an apparition of the deceased one. They are of the opinion that to whomsoever it shall appear, that person will presently die."

"Have we then escaped the ants and coccodrillos only to deliver ourselves up to the *zumbi*?" I asked.

To this he laughed quietly, and we fell silent and watched as the ceremony of lamenting proceeded, with much singing and dancing and weeping, and the sound of drums and iron bells and ivory horns. Then the corpse, wrapped in bright clothes and blankets, was taken into its grave. They did cover it with rich goods, blankets and robes and ornaments and the like, and poured an ocean and a half of palm-wine over it, the which I would gladly have had for my own use just then, and covered the top over with straw mats. And then the sorcerers did go back and forth with a thousand superstitious interlacings and interweavings, after which the earth was heaped high. Then to the sound of a beating drum they all withdrew back into their town, and during the night we heard from afar the sounds of merriment, and I know not what idolatrous delights and abominable pleasures.

There was no sleep for us that night. Who could tell what mourners lurked about, or what sentinels, or what *zumbi*? With the first pink streaks of dawn in the sky all did seem quiet, and we stole away to the north. And we passed the river, and rested again, and proceeded by the day, crossing, as we hoped, into the kingdom of Kongo, and thinking of ourselves as much like unto the children of Israel, wandering out of the desert toward the promised land.

THREE

BEING TWO leagues north of the River Dande, we met with a party of Negroes, a dozen or more young huntsmen or warriors, well armed, but seemingly friendly. They spoke the language of the Angolan blacks and asked us whither we traveled.

"We go to Kongo," I said.

"You go the wrong way, then," said they, which much surprised me, for that I was sure I had the plan of the territory clear in my mind. But they said they would guide us, for they were Mushikongos, that is, Kongo-men, and would carry us to the land of Mbamba, where the Duke of Mbamba lay, who was one of the chief princes of the kingdom of the Kongo.

I was ill at ease at all this, and to his credit so was Cristovão and his Gypsies. But the Portugals who were with us had come to mistrust my leadership and were willing to be guided by these blackamoors, and so firmly did they argue that I yielded, thinking I might after all be mistaken about the proper direction of our travel.

So we went some three miles east, up into the land, till we became certain that we were in the wrong way. For we traveled by the sun and the sun plainly lay behind us in the afternoon as we went up into the hills. So we turned back again to the westward. At this the blacks quick took up a position before us with their bows and arrows and darts, ready to shoot at us.

I looked toward Cristovão and he to me, and I said, "We must go through them."

"Aye," said he, and we levelled our muskets at them. The blackamoors not showing fear at this, we discharged six muskets together, which killed four of them and greatly amazed the others, who fled into the woods. But they followed us four or five miles, and hurt two of our company with their arrows.

The next day we came within the borders of Mbamba, that is the south-west province of the kingdom of the Kongo, and traveled all that day. At night we heard the surge of the sea. This gave me great pleasure, I having lived all the happiest days of my life within earshot of the sea, and like any Englishman I begin to feel narrow-souled and strained when I am herded into some great dry flatland far from the surf and the ocean-breezes. But there on my ear was the rise and the fall of the waves, that is the sweetest sound our world can bestow.

My plan was this, to make my way to some civilized part of the Kongo, for that is a well-ordered land, whose people are far from backward and do obey the behests of Jesus. The Portugals have great influence there, but I did not fear falling into their hands, since they would have no knowledge of my condition in Angola, and perhaps I might pretend to be a Dutchman, shipwrecked somewhere and seeking rescue. Or else the blackamoors themselves might aid me to reach a port, and I might take ship for England. I had some other such schemes, too, in case these did not fare well. But in the final event all my planning was doomed to perish frustrate, because calamity overtook us as we made our wearisome track northward, running a few miles in from the shore of the sea.

It was in the morning and we were, I think, ten leagues or a little more above São Paulo de Loanda. To our great dismay we saw suddenly coming after us a troop of Portugals on horse, with a great store of Negroes following them. I think we had by grievous error stumbled across some outlying garrison of the army, who did patrol this region against enemies, and peradventure we were mistaken for scouts of an encroaching force.

Our company was so disheartened by this that our seven faint-hearted Portugals hid themselves in the thickets, crouching down like squirrels in a hole, where they would certainly be captured. I and the four Gypsies thought to have escaped, but the soldiers followed us so fast that we were fain to go into a little wood. As soon as the Portugal captain had overtaken us he discharged a volley of shot into the wood, which made us lose one another, for under that deadly fire we did crawl this way and that, and were separated.

I lay alone, steeped in my reeking sweat but still unwounded. All about me sounded the cries and alarums of the Negro auxiliaries, who were thrashing foolishly about in the wood, shouting halloo to one another as they sought for us. But there were so many of them that even in their folly they were like to blunder upon me, and I bethought myself that if those Negroes did take me in the wood they would kill me in some barbarous ugly way, and drag my bloodied corpse to the captain of the Portugals to claim a reward. I believed my time was up, but I preferred to die in clean warfare rather than be pounded and mangled by savages in some tangled jungly place of chaos. Therefore, thinking to make a better end for myself among the Portugals, I came presently out of the wood with my musket ready charged, intending to give a good accounting for my life.

But the captain, thinking that we had been all twelve together and I was leading my fellows from refuge, called to me and said, "Fellow soldier, I have the governor's pardon; if you will yield yourselves you shall have no hurt."

I, having my musket ready, answered the captain most truthfully that I was an Englishman, and had served six years at Masanganu, in great misery; and came in company with eleven Portugals and Gypsies, and here am left all alone; and rather than I will be hanged, I will die in the defense of my liberty.

"Nay," he said, "you will not be hanged. Are you Andres Battell the Piloto?"

"That I am."

"Deliver thy musket to one of the soldiers, Piloto Battell. And I protest, as I am a gentleman and a soldier, to save thy life for thy resolute mind."

These were right noble words, even though they came from the mouth of a Portugal. I thought it wiser to accept his pledge, for all my mistrust of such blandishments, than to reject it out of hand and die gloriously; for there is no repair of dying, glorious or otherwise. So did I surrender. And you will not be amazed to learn that I tumbled thereby into fresh misfortune.

The captain did command all his soldiers and Negroes to search the woods, and to bring us all out alive or dead, which was presently done. Then they carried us to the city of São Paulo de Loanda, which looked much enlarged and greatly more prosperous in the six years since last I had seen it, and thrust me with the three Gypsies into prison. There I lay for months with a collar of iron upon me, and great bolts upon my legs, in the very dungeon I had known before, among the rats and spiders. So I was not hanged, and the captain did keep his promise to me to that degree. But once again I was a captive in chains.

Everything becomes more skilful done with practice at it, and I had had by now such training at being a dungeon inmate that I was a fair expert at it, and carried off the task with high great virtuosity. No longer did I expend my breath in loud railings at my fate, or denunciation of mine enemies, nor did I brood long and hard upon dire revenge. Instead I quickly let myself slide into an altered condition of awareness, a kind of mystical trance, in which for hours at a time I did lift my soul from out of this dreary place and let it rove the bright realm of fancy. I think I would have gone mad in all my many captivities, had I not had that skill.

Therefore did I imagine myself in England, walking through the tangled grimy lanes of London and strolling the sweet green fields of Essex. To Plymouth I went, and Dover, that shines so fine in the sunlight, and I knelt in the great Cathedral at Canterbury, and walked on the old walls of Chester, and journeyed by cart to York, and even across into dark stormy Scotland on some errand to those dour turbulent folk. I consorted with great lords of the court and met with learned geographers, to whom I did tell my tales of Africa. I sailed again to France, and to Spain, even which I imagined now was bound by treaty of peace with England. And I pictured myself coming home to a loving wife I called Anne Katherine, though here my fancy failed me, for I could not even summon up a face to give her, nor any character of person. The Anne Katherine I had once known was only a figment, a child long outgrown, and though in pretense I could see myself married with her, she had no substance for me.

In such playing did I consume the days and the nights. I reflected often upon my own life, also, the strange twistings and turnings of it, that had me in and out of these Portugee dungeons, and back and forth up strange shadowy rivers, and moving like one ensorcelled through a realm of naked savages and man-eaters. It was as though I had fallen asleep on an April day in Anno 1589, and had entered into a long dream from which there was no awaking.

In dreams anything can happen, and nothing is cause for surprise. So now upon the failure of my bold escape from Masanganu did I resign myself to the dream-like flow of event, and let myself be carried along on its strong tide, without ever once expecting any further relief from prison and punishment, and without showing the slightest amaze when my life did undergo new transformations. By which I mean that I had lulled myself into a great calmness of spirit, from which nothing could rouse my tranquil pulse. Thus when warders came to me and smote the bolts from my legs and the iron collar from my neck, I asked no questions, and it was all the same to me, whether they were taking me next to the place of execution or to put me on board a ship to England. My blood ran quiet. My soul was accepting of anything equally.

So they took from me my rags and gave me rough but serviceable clothes of the kind a common yeoman might wear, and led me into the presidio courtyard and out into the heart of the city. And under the drumbeat blaze of noon I marched between them, a little weak in the leg from so long being cramped into a cell, but my shoulders straight, and I never asked a word, never demanded of them to know where they went with me or what fate was to be mine.

They conveyed me to a residence of the most palatial kind, with facings of white stone inset with gleaming tiles of Portuguese manufacture in blue and yellow, and sentinels with muskets patrolling outside. I thought I remembered that place from my former life in São Paulo de Loanda, but I was not sure, and the clouds did not clear from my mind until I was within. Then I realized it was the dwelling place of Fernão da Souza and Dona Teresa, but greatly rebuilt and made more splendid over the years. And setting foot in that place broke me at last from my placid trance, and put a dryness into my throat and squeezed my heart like a secret hand within my breast.

We went down a lengthy hall hung with heavy tapestries and into a drawing-chamber, where once Dona Teresa had fed me sweetmeats from a little tray. There was a woman standing there, of the greatest majesty and beauty. She wore a long black gown of Venetian silk, and a triple strand of shining pearls, deep blue in color and no two of the same shape, and in her ears were broad hoops of gold from which great emeralds depended. So opulent was her costume that the blaze of it nigh eclipsed her features, and I was slow to recognize her, even though this was, of course, Dona Teresa that I beheld.

"Leave him with me," she said.

Her voice was cool and measured, the voice of one accustomed to command. She held herself like a queen.

I thought me back six years and more to my last view of her, when she had crouched near naked in my cottage, sweat-shining and as wild as an angry animal, her clothes in tatters and red scratches across her skin, and her bare breasts heaving up and down from frenzy and wrath. And there flashed into my mind also an earlier and happier time, when I was new in Angola and scarce recovered from my Masanganu fever, and in my prison cell she did drop her shift away and show her brown nipples to me, and wrap her thighs about my body. She had been mere eighteen then, mysterious and poised but still showing the soft unformed look of youth about her. But that was ten years past, or a little more, and she had ripened into something regal, and awesome in her strength. And yet was she so beautiful still, more beautiful even than she had been, that I could have wept for anguish at the perfection of her face and form.

I should have been frighted of her, I suppose. For in our last meeting, those six years back, she had shown herself to be a true witch, a dark sorceress, a woman of the greatest malevolence: qualities which I had seen in her from the beginning, but which had risen to their peak of envenomed power that time she had contended with Matamba. She was a magnificent creature: but yet was she a kind of monster.

Strange to say, I did not fear her.

Was it that fear had been burned from my soul, under the hot sun of Masanganu? Or that I had broken her grip on me, when that I had hurled her little idol into the river-waters? Or was it only that I knew she could do me no further harm, since that I had nothing whatever left to lose? Perhaps that last was the essence of it. Whatever, I faced her most coolly, with my heart altogether still. I felt anger toward her—aye, an anger most surpassing!—but not a shred of fear.

We stood apart, with a massive burnished bronze table between us, and she studied me as though I were some rare curio from the treasure-houses of Byzantium.

Then she said, "I feared your hair would have turned white. I am much pleased to find it golden still."

"I am white-haired within, Dona Teresa."

"Indeed? How old are you now, Andres?"

"I think I will be two-and-forty this year."

"Very old, yes. Turn around. Let me see you from all sides."

I obeyed, turning as if I were displaying some new mode of cloak for her, or fashionable breeches. For I did not dare let go of my tight rein upon myself, and come into reach of my true feelings, lest I launch myself at her and throttle her to death.

She said, "You look strong and vigorous, Andres."

"Aye. Slavery agrees with me well."

"Has it been slavery for you, then?"

"Six years at Masanganu, Dona Teresa," said I most quietly. "It is not a pleasure-resort there. And then some days crossing the wilderness on foot, and afterward some months in these dungeons here, where the food is not of the finest."

"Oh, Andres, will you forgive me?" she asked, and the steel went from her voice and she seemed almost a girl again.

"Aye," said I bitterly, "for it was a light thing you did to me, to betray me on the eve of my escape, and prevent me from regaining my native land. Why should I hold a grudge for that?"

"Upon the cross, Andres, I had nothing to do with betraying your escape! It was some Portugals in the Dutchman's crew, that learned of your plan and told Caldeira de Rodrigues."

"Ah, so it was. You merely invented the tale of my raping you by force, that was all."

She lowered her eyes. "I was greatly angered with you."

"For refusing you?"

"For that, and for taking the slave-girl in my place."

"You were not my wife. Was I to sleep alone, the rest of my days, except when you chose to favor me?"

She did answer to that, "I would have favored you often. I could not bear you coupling with that animal."

"No animal, milady, but a good Christian, better than some in this city, that pretend to Christianity but deal also with the Devil. And having a warm and kind heart, where there are some here that have none whatever."

"Why did you buy her?"

"To spare her from evil, in being shipped into a fatal servitude."

"And to make her your concubine?"

"That befell afterward, which was not my prime design for her. And I had thought you were dead, do you forget? They said you had been thrown overboard on your way to Portugal."

"But that did not befall me. Why did you not put her aside, when I returned to São Paulo de Loanda?"

I drew my breath in deep, and released it slowly. "What value is there in discussing these matters, Dona Teresa? She was my servant and my companion. You had taken a husband. You and I had separate lives to live, and she was a part of mine. When I told you these things, you would not grant them, but flew at her with your claws like a wild beast, and then told a monstrous lie, that put me under sentence of death. But why poke and prod into this stuff? It was long ago."

She came alongside the table, and moved closer to me, so that I smelled the perfume of her, and I imagined there was a throbbing heat coming from her, a warmth like that of the sun, radiating out of the twin points of her breasts and from that dark hot woolly place below, that I knew so well.

She said, "It was a shameful thing that I did, accusing you falsely that way. But I was enraged, Andres, I was maddened, I was not in my right mind. Afterward I relented within myself, and felt great guilt over my sin toward you, and went to Don João and did plead for you to be pardoned from the sentence of death."

"Ah, then I owe you my life," I said, half-mockingly.

"That overstates it some, for Don João had already relented. He could not find in his heart the will to hang you, and so he delayed, leaving you in the prison. When I spoke with him, that strengthened his hand, and he decided to alter your sentence to one of banishment for life to Masanganu."

"A passing gentle place."

"Gentler than the gallows, Andres, is it not?" She stretched forth a hand to me, but did not quite touch me. "As you say: it was long ago. My fury sprang altogether out of love for you. I did repent my falsehood, and I have done private penance for it within my soul. And I beg you now to forgive me."

"What will become of me now?"

"You are again under the sentence of death, for that you have broken forth from your banishment unlawfully. But again Don João hesitates to hang you, out of an ancient fondness for you. And again I plead your case with him."

"Don João is still governor, then?"

"He is old and sick, and I think will not hold his post much longer. But for the moment he does still rule. Don Fernão argues for your death, as does Caldeira de Rodrigues. But I am opposed and Don João is unwilling, and I think we will prevail."

"Ah. Your husband still seeks vengeance for the rape that did not occur!"

"I have told him it did not occur."

"Then why hang me? Does he not believe you?"

"He believes me. He holds no grievance privately against you. But the old accusation is still remembered here. For the sake of his position, he must make a public show of enmity toward you, for having dishonored his wife."

"His position?" I asked. "And what is that?"

"He is second viceroy under Don João, and will, I think, succeed him in the governorship."

I smiled at that. "So you have almost accomplished your plan, then. Soon you shall be the governor's wife, and because he is a vain and silly man, you will in good sooth be the governor in fact, though he wear the chain of office. I applaud you, Dona Teresa! I salute you in greatest admiration!"

"Andres—"

"Why the soft word? Why the outstretched hand? Dona Teresa, you sent me into six years of terrible imprisonment."

"And saved you from hanging, and will save you again, and will pledge to do all in my power to atone for my harming of you. I ask that you give over your hatred of me. I ask that you remember our love, that burned so brightly."

I closed my eyes and looked away.

"You will not spurn me again!" she cried, and all the tenderness that had crept into her voice was gone from it again.

"Ah, do you command me to love you, then?"

"I command nothing!"

"What do you want from me, lady?"

"Nothing but what we had before."

"We are not who we were before," I said.

"I tell you, nothing has changed."

With a nod did I say, "Aye, aye, you are right. Nothing has changed, but that I have had six years of prison on your account, whilst you dressed yourself in silks and pearls and lived in splendor by the sea. You have sipped on fine wines and I have been drinking bile. You have eaten rare fowl and I have smiled the reek of coccodrillos. But nothing has changed."

"Andres—"

"O, to think I wept when I believed you dead, lady!"

"Andres," she said again, and again her voice did make the journey from steel to velvet. "Listen to me, and put aside your fury for the moment. From the first time I saw you, I loved you. You were like the sun, I thought, you with your golden hair and your blue eyes—to look upon you gave me a warmth, a strong heat, even. And ever since have I prized you above all men. If I betrayed you—and, yea, I did betray you most shamefully—it was out of excess of love, it was from a su-perfluity of passion, that does turn to rage and foul sour juices when it is thwarted. But if you will only restore yourself to me, I will make full amends, I do vow it!"

"What is it, in sharp exactness, that you want from me, Dona Teresa?"

"I thought I had said it."

"You have spoken of large vague things. Name the service you would have me do for you."

Across the gloss of her eyes there slipped a veiling cloud of new wrath.

"Andres, please—"

"Name it!"

"Nay," she said, and turned from me. "This is of no avail. Too much time has come between us."

"Time, and other things, too."

"Indeed. Go from me, Andres."

"And am I your enemy?"

"Never again," she said. "But go! Quickly!"

I could readily feel the hot waves of desire that still surged from her, and I knew that even now I had only to move toward her, to touch my fingertips to her bare shoulders, and she would be mine in a moment. I hesitated. Through my mind there blazed the image of Dona Teresa pressing some mysterious catch and causing her gown to fall away, so that she was naked before me but for her pearls and her emeralded ear-hoops, with the dark turrets rising hard out of her high round breasts, and the lust-musk perfuming her loins, and then I would kneel before her and she would stroke my thick tangled hair and draw my cheek against her smooth thighs, and I would press my face into her womanly delta, with my tongue seeking the little pink bud that was hidden within, and then—and then, and then, and then—

O! How easily I would yield myself up to her tender fleshly snare!

But I did not do it. God wot, I am no man of iron self-discipline in these matters of lust, as surely I have made quite plain by this time to you. But even so, there is a time when coupling with some certain woman becomes inappropriate, and that time had long ago arrived between Dona Teresa and me.

She was Dalila. She was Circe. She had had me in her spell, and she had used me as her plaything, and she had thrown me away when I no longer suited her needs. And in throwing me away, she had given me the strength to break from her. If I put myself back into her hands now, I might never escape again.

Ah, she was beautiful, and never more so than now, in the full ripeness of her womanhood! But I knew her so well! She was perilous, a woman-demon, a Lilith, an instrument of seduction and domination, who could pose at girlishness, or even at kittenishness, when it was to her advantage. I trembled, thinking how simple it would be to take her in my arms, and how great an error. I understood all that she was claiming, of having betrayed me simply out of wrath and jealousy. Nor were such motives unknown in the world before her time, since even Jove's queen Juno had vilely enchanted many of her rivals and ensorcelled her unfortunate lovers, and many lesser women, I trow, had done that also. But I would not be deceived again. Rather would I couple at random with some whore of the streets, than give myself into the keeping of a shedevil that I had mistaken for a true woman. I must hold my distance from Dona Teresa, for wisdom's sake, and for honor's sake, and for safety's. So I did not move toward her, as so easily I could.

I said instead, with a great distance in my voice, and a light frost, "Well, and we shall not be enemies, then. I wish you all comfort and blessing, Dona Teresa."

FOUR

THOUGH I would not submit to her, nevertheless by Dona Teresa's good offices I was once again made a free man. But it was a limited sort of freedom, nothing like that which I enjoyed in the old days when I was pilot of the governor's pinnace. There still lay over me the double charge of treason and rape, for which I had been banished to Masanganu, and there was on top of that the crime of escaping from that fort; and I was given to understand that I still would have to undergo some penalty for those offenses. Yet I would not have to bide my time longer in the dungeon here, nor was I was going to be returned to Masanganu. So my condition had improved somewhat over its former state.

I was not restored to my former cottage by the sea-breezes. Instead was I given a much humbler place, a room on the ground floor of the barracks where the common Portugal soldiers dwelled, nor did I have any servants this time. Yet I could hardly have expected anything better than that, and even the barracks was a goodly step upward from the vileness of the dungeon or the malign vapors of Masanganu. So there I resided without complaint, and took my meals with the soldiery, dining as they did on humble gruels and porridges and the stringy stewed meat of unknown beasts, and washing it down with the stale beer and flat palm-wine they were supplied.

Among these troops I formed no friendships, for they were all half my age, having come out from Portugal or its other colonies in the last few years. They looked upon me, I trow, as some sort of phantom, and found me frightening: a gaunt tall Englishman, with wild eyes, who was said to have committed terrible crimes, and who had done hard years of service in the interior of the country, a place that they dreaded. They did not understand why I was come to be in Angola at all, nor could they begin to approach me as a companion, I being so alien from their minds. There were times when I came nigh to saying, "Nay, I am only good-natured Andy Battell, who means you no harm," but I did not. For already I was beginning to see that good-natured Andy Battell, that amiable young man who had set forth from England to win a little gold with which to marry his sweetheart, was long since dead and buried within the husk of the man who now bore that same name. I had been innocent and cheerful, sweet-souled, even; and for all my sweetness God had seen fit to let me pass from captivity to captivity, from torment to torment, and it had altered me greatly, very little remaining of the original save a certain stubborn persistence and, I hope, a certain measure of honor.

Other alterations had taken place around me in this land. The most obvious was the growth of São Paulo de Loanda, which had been but a place of mud streets and thatched dwellings when Thomas Torner and I were dumped down into it in the June of 1590, and now, after ten years and some, was becoming a true city, which had fair palaces and churches and govermental halls everywhere about. That did tell me that the Portugals must be pumping heavy profits out of this place, and had made it their great headquarters along the Atlantic side of Africa, shifting themselves almost entirely from their former domain within the kingdom of the Kongo.

There had been changes among people. I have already spoken of the changing of Dona Teresa from handsome girl to formidable and awesome woman, virtually the queen of this place. A few others whom I had formerly known were yet in evidence, much enhanced. Pedro Faleiro, my shipmate in the coastal voyages, now was the high admiral here, with my other sailing-fellow Pinto Cabral as his lieutenant. Mendes Oliveira was dead; Manoel de Andrade was in the south, commanding the harbor at Benguela; Manoel Fonseca, who had had authority at Masanganu when I was brought there after the Kafuche Kambara massacre, now was the captain of the presidio at São Paulo de Loanda. His predecessor in that role, Fernão da Souza, I saw occasionally being born to and fro in a hammock by native slaves that were arrayed in the most pompous of costumes. Souza still inclined himself toward ornate dress of wondrous color, but looked softer, less gallant, for he was beginning now to slide into the sort of middle age that overcomes some of these dashing Portugals when they rise too high and are given overmuch to wine and sloth. I had no encounters with Souza and desired none. As for my other enemy of old, Gaspar Caldeira de Rodrigues, he had lately taken himself off, to my great relief, to the Portuguese lands in India.

Another whom I saw only from afar was Don João de Mendoça, and the look of him greatly saddened me. He had gone puffy and liverish, his face almost green of hue and much bloated, and his eyes, hidden within folds of unhealthful flesh, were barely to be noticed. He walked slowly and with a painful limp, and it was plain that the hand of death was closing about him in a gradual but inexorable way. I had no direct dealings with Don João. Gone were the days when he would summon me to his palace for a feast of many meats and wines, and speak with me about his dreams and hopes for this colony. I had fallen now far beneath the notice of all these great men of Angola.

Of all the transformations I observed, though, the most somber was that of one who had been closest of all to me, that is, my former slave Matamba. I found her again by accident only, and so changed was she that I nearly passed her by, unknowing.

There was now in São Paulo de Loanda a kind of whoring district, behind the main market, where soldiers who did not regularly consort with some black or mulatto woman could go, and find natives who would lie with them for a handful of cowrie-shell money. Sometimes in the early days of my return to the city I passed this place and looked in with idle curiosity, but I did no more than that, for I have never greatly favored hiring the bodies of strangers in that way, except when need is extreme. Yet from time to time the itch does become so strong in me that I fain must scratch it. It happened that an errand took me down to the harbor one day, and there I saw a few Angolan girls of thirteen or fourteen years splashing naked in the warm surf, and the sight of their firm outthrusting breasts and rounded plump buttocks, all gleaming with

sea-water and sunlight, did reawaken in me the desires of the flesh. So
I went next to the quarter where whores did consort, and looked about
to find me some reasonably clean and unpoxed black lass on whom I
could ease this sudden pressing want.

There were several young and likely ones, among whom I stood
choosing, when an old beggar-woman—as I thought—plucked at my
sleeve and said in a low downcast way, *"Por favor—"*

I would have handed her a shell without glancing at her, and continued
about my business, but some familiar note in her voice did strike a deep
level of my soul, and, not knowing why, I turned to her. I beheld a
woman in tattered and flimsy cloth of a faded orange color, with stooped
shoulders and a broken, defeated look about her: yet her eyes still retained
a glow, a spark, of some finer nature, and to my great horror I came
after a moment to understand that this was no old beggar woman but
one I knew full well; in sooth it was my Matamba, aged more than I
could easily credit in these six years. For I might just as easily have
believed this to be the mother of Matamba, as the person herself.

"Is that you?" I asked.

"I am—I forget the words—"

"You know who I am, Matamba?"

"The English—Andres—"

"Yes! But I can scarce believe this change, Matamba. Can it truly be
you?"

She seemed to tremble, and closed her eyes a moment, as if reaching
into some great depth of memory, out of which at length she fetched,
saying the words in a weak quavering voice, "Essex—Sussex—
Somerset—York—"

I was fair close upon weeping.

Instantly did I sweep her out of that whore-market and to my barracks,
where I ordered a meal for her, some palm-wine, some boiled grain and
meat. She ate hastily and in desperate greed, with both her hands, as if
she had not had food a long while, and feared it might be taken from
her before she was done. I watched her with pity and dismay. She was
then no more than two-and-twenty years of age, and looked close upon
forty, and a much-used forty at that. Her breasts, that once had stood
out before her like two firm globes, now were sagging and shrunken.
Her face was haggard, her nose showed the mark of some injury, her
rich brown skin had grown ashen-dull in its color, her woolly hair was
flecked with bits of gray. She was thin and slack-muscled, who I remembered as sturdy, a joyous athlete. There was a tremor to her hands,
not a great one but unceasing.

When she had done with her meal I took her by the chin and lifted her head, and said, "We are both much less pretty now, eh, Matamba? But at least we have both survived. Tell me your tale of these six years, and then I'll tell you mine."

"The words—too fast—"

"Forgotten your Portugee, is that it?"

"I speak—little—"

"Ah. Yes. We can talk in your Kikongo tongue, if you like. I have some words of that lingo now."

"No—Portugal—"

Aye. She wanted the language back.

So I was gentle and slow with her, and we talked a little, and she rested, and we rehearsed some words anew, and I ordered more food for her. Then she was tired, and lay down, and later I joined her in the bed; but I had forgotten all lust by this time, and merely held her in my arms until morning. Her naked body was a sorry sight, with the lines of childbearing making a map across her belly, and her thighs that had been so taut and vigorous now puckered and loose, and so on, a terrible ruination of all her beauty. Yet already, in just a day and a night, she seemed to be brightening and returning to herself. God's wounds, how she must have suffered from want and misery, before I found her among the whores!

It pained me to watch her those early days as she hobbled about my room, sighing much, pausing often to mutter a prayer and to cross herself, and always struggling to find the strength to go on. For she was a wreck, a beached hull, that had endured the worst of the elemental furies and showed all the signs of it. She did weep often, and tremble with some inner chill, or maybe the memory of an ague. But each day she was less ruined than on the day before, for the which I gave deep thanks to Him who is our preservation.

In a slow and very gradual way did she make her recovery, regaining some strength, and finding once more her command of Portuguese as her body offered sustenance to her mind. Within a week or so, months of suffering had dropped away from her, so that she was not near so frightsome to behold. But beyond doubt she never again would be that girlish black goddess I had bought in São Tomé, but at best only a shadow of her.

She told me the tale of her hardships, which chilled my blood like a wintry northern gale.

She said that after my arrest she was taken by my other servants and beaten severely, and hurled naked from my cottage and left to crawl away. Some Portugal soldiers found her and merrily had her behind a bush that very hour, one after another until she was bloodied and raw, and then they abandoned her. Later she was seized by order of Dona Teresa, and was scourged with whips—the marks still remained faint along her back and buttocks, and I think will never fade—and afterward was she given over into slavery to one of Dona Teresa's grooms.

"But this is vile!" I cried. "None of this was deserving unto you!"

"It was not the worst of it," said she very quietly.

For then was she used badly by all who came upon her, she declared: for to the men of the city it was considered a way of showing regard for Dona Teresa, to abuse the Englishman's former paramour, and Matamba was raped and maltreated more than she could tally. All this she did tell me in a soft low voice, with no fire in it, as though she were relating some events that had happened to another person in the reign of Queen Cleopatra of Egypt, far away. Yet her tales made my own blood run hot and my heart to pound for wrath, and I marched up and down the room like some caged beast as she spoke, and I wished for an hundred hands, that I might punish all those malefactors at once—as if I could do the slightest thing, I that had no privilege left to me in this land.

"The groom my master wearied of me and gave me to a fisherman," she said. "And he was as rough and scaly as any fish he ever caught, and his breath stank of fish, and his hair also, and his whole skin. He lost me by wager to an innkeeper, who hired me out as whore to his guests."

"It is not so!"

She shrugged. "In that time I bore three children. One lived two weeks, and one lived four, and one for a month and a half. My breasts were ever aching with milk. When they came to use my body, I did beg them to suckle at me, to ease the pain. And some did, and some would not."

She fell ill, too, of some colic that brought her close to death. For which release she said she prayed daily to the Madonna: her Christian faith still remained strong with her, God alone knowing why. But not even death was granted her. And upon her recovery, she said, she was subjected to whoring in the whore-market that had sprung up. Owing to the ravages of disease and childbirth and overmuch other suffering, she had grown ugly and aged too early, and only rarely did men choose her, so that she was hard pressed to pay for her food, and endured long sieges of bitter famine. And so it went for my poor Matamba, from bad to worse in year upon year, and often she thought she would simply set out into the interior one morning, hoping to be fallen upon by a lion and released from her woes. But she could not, since that self-destruction was forbidded to her by her creed.

All this, and only because I had bought her out of slavery!

I think I had done her no service by that, after all. No one can say what would have befallen her if she had gone to the New World as she had been destined to do, but perhaps it would have been no worse than this, and might even have been somewhat better, if only it had been a swift death of some killing pestilence. For I suppose there are times when death is preferable to life, if it be life of the sort Matamba had been made to swallow these years just past.

Yet was she still alive, and had hope of better things in time to come, which the dead do not have. I did what I could to atone for the cruelties she had had at the hands of others by feeding her and nursing her until some proper color returned to her skin and she began to hold her shoulders erect again and show some little semblance of vitality. Even so, she went about my room as though expecting to be whipped for any small failing, and constantly did she jump at the slightest sound like a wary cat, and cringe, and crouch; but some of that timidity passed from her, in time.

We slept each night in the same narrow bed. But I did not make any approach to her, knowing how often she had been taken by cruelty, and thinking that the act of carnal pleasure must have lost all its savor for her, being so intermixed with brutality and pain. So I would not add to her woes with yet another penetration. But one night her hand did steal shyly down my belly until it grasped my yard, and stroked it up and down to make it grow to its fullest size at once.

"Nay," said I softly. "You need not, Matamba."

"Do you not desire me, Andres?"

"You have suffered so much that I would not ask of you any such—"

"But I desire you," she said, "as in the old days. Even though I am ugly now, will you not grant me that pleasure?"

"You are not ugly."

"Yet you have no desire for me?"

"Never did I say such a thing."

"Then let us not hold back," she replied, and eased one leg across my body and did straddle me and slide me quickly into her, so that we were at last reunited in the innermost of ways, and she did tickle me in that strange African way of hers, and bite me lightly here and there and scratch me some also, and pump her loins against me with steady and increasing vigor. Then was she gasping and breathing hot against my neck, and coming to her pleasure twice or thrice or even more, peradventure the first pleasure she had known out of this act since my banishing, and in the wildest moment of her delight did she bring me to mine. And after our coupling we did both cry and laugh together, but mainly did we laugh.

Thus did I restore Matamba to herself, and to me. It gave me great keen joy to see her flourishing again, howbeit never would her early beauty be regained. One cannot pump new tautness into fallen breasts, one cannot put a cosmetic of miracles to scars and skin-gullies. I think even if she had not suffered so in those six dark years, it would have been much the same for her, since that the girlhood does go swiftly and mercilessly from these Africans: they are all black Venuses at fourteen and mere shriveled hags and crones at thirty or thirty-five, and there seems to be no help for it. I did often long for the tender and bright-eyed lass that I had bought out of slavery on São Tomé, but I knew that hope to be as idle as it would be to long for my own youthful unlined face and resilient body: folly it is to bid time return.

In that same season I discovered what punishment I was to have for my escaping from Masanganu, and for other offenses both real and alleged. The governor now proposed to send four hundred men, that had been banished out of Portugal for high crimes, up into the country of Lamba to subdue a rebellion, and from there to any other district in need of pacifying. When these criminals arrived from Lisbon I would be joined to them, and dismissed forever into these border wars, marching endlessly here and there to keep the frontier of Angola safe against Jaqqa incursion and native uprising.

I sought Don João out to appeal against this sentence, but he would not see me, I suppose out of guilt and shame at using me this crass way. So I made ready to take up my life as a soldier. It was something better than hanging, at any rate, and I think also a better fate than further duty at Masanganu, where I might die of boredom if one of the plagues did not take me first.

Yet many weeks passed before my departure from the city. I was at that time largely left to my own devices, and spent my hours with Matamba, or wandering by myself along the shore of the perplexing ocean, looking longingly off toward invisible Europe, and England shining beyond.

England! Would ever I see England again? Had such a place as England ever existed, or was it only my dream, and had I indeed been born full-grown in Africa?

Matamba said, "Speak to me in English, Andres."

"Aye, that I will! If I can remember any, lass!"

And I did speak to her, but the words were snailish slow in curling their way around my tongue, so used had I become to the Portugal way of framing speech. Yet did I persevere, and fiercely fight my way back to reclaiming my native Englishness, that has ever been so precious to me. I wondered, if I were to be dropped by angels into Essex this day, would anyone there recognize me as being of English blood, or would they run screaming, thinking me some new yellow-haired kind of Saracen, or some species of demon out of the nether? For surely I was mightily transformed, within and without, by my years in this tropic sun under such dire servitudes. But I made myself to remember my lost former life.

"These are the kings of England," I said to Matamba. "At the first there was William, who did come from Normandy to lord it over the old Saxons. And then was his son William, who was slain in the forest, and then his other son Henry, and then Stephen of Plantagenet did seize the throne, and then another Henry, and after him Richard of the Lion Heart, and John—" and so I went, telling her all the kings, the Edwards and the Henrys and the Richards, up until my Elizabeth's glorious time. And I made the black woman repeat the names after me, until she knew them as well as I, and put the second Richard in his rightful place between Edward and Henry Bolingbroke, and knew that the fourth Edward "and" the sixth Henry did change the kingship back and forth some several times during the wars of York and Lancaster, and could tell me how Henry Tudor did come out of Wales to defeat the crookback tyrant Richard, and so forth: all the names that had been dinned into me when I was a boy training for a clerkship. It did me great good to recite all that again, by way of reminding me that there once had been an England, and it existed yet. What sense it all made to Matamba, God alone can say; but often as we lay entwined at night, my yard deep in her and slowly moving, she would murmur to me, "Henry, Henry, Henry, Edward, Edward, Richard, Henry, Henry, Edward, Mary, Elizabeth," like unto a kind of litany, saying the names in a wondrous foreign way, "Ay-leesh-a-bate," with an outrush of whooshing breath, "Ainree," "Reezhard."

And I told her about our poetry, that was the great pride and wonder of our race, our special music. She asked me to chant her some verse, but when I reached into my mind all was void and dark, a dry empty well, until suddenly some scraps and shards came into view in the dusty corners of my spirit, and I did speak her some lines from Marlowe's play of Faustus, that was the newest thing upon the boards when last I was in England:

> *The stars move still, time runs, the clock will strike,*
> *The Devil will come, and Faustus must be damned.*
> *Oh, I'll leap up to my God: who pulls me down?*

> *See, see where Christ's blood streams in the*
>   *firmament.*
> *One drop would save my soul, half a drop, ah my*
>   *Christ.*

I thought I had all that speech by heart, but the rest was gone from me except the striking of the clock, and the last smallest bit:

> *My God, my God, look not so fierce on me.*
> *Adders and serpents, let me breathe a while:*
> *Ugly hell gape not, come not Lucifer,*
> *I'll burn my books. Ah, Mephistopheles!*

She listened all agape to those words, thinking them a magical music from the sound alone, as in sooth I think they are. But then she did pray to have the meaning from me, and when I translated it into her understanding, speaking part Portuguese and part Kikongo, it so terrified her that she clutched herself away from me, into a frightened quivering ball, and I had to comfort her with the laying on of my hands. Methinks she thought I was conjuring up Satan in our very chamber.

So I eased her with gentler songs:

> *Western wind, when will thou*
>   *blow,*
> *The small rain down can rain?*
> *Christ, if my love were in my arms*
> *And I in my bed again.*

And also:

> *There were three ravens sat on a tree*
> *Down a down, hay down, hay down*
> *There were three ravens sat on a tree*
> *They were as black as they might be*
>   *With a down derrie, derrie, derrie, down down.*

And then:

> *Come away, come sweet*
>   *love,*
> *The golden morning breaks:*
> *All the earth, all the air*
> *Of love and pleasure speaks.*

And all these she loved, and had me recite many times, even though on most my memory failed me, and I could but give her stray nips and fragments, and hardly ever the complete verse. Yet did the sound of them delight her, and the sense, and her eyes did gleam, and she put her hands to mine and held me while I magicked her with these incantations of my homeland. She asked me had I composed any of these, and I told her sadly nay, I was no poet but only a frequenter of poetry, and that other men with finer and more far-ranging souls had set down those words, which led her ask me how anyone could have a soul more far-ranging than mine, which had carried me so far. "There is a difference," said I. To which she shrugged, and called for more poems. Any that I said gave her pleasure, even Tom O'Bedlam's song, though when I thought close upon its meanings it made me melancholy, and I would not say it twice:

> *With an host of furious fancies,*
> *Whereof I am commander,*
> *With a burning spear, and a horse of air,*
> *To the wilderness I wander.*
> *By a knight of ghosts and shadows*
> *I summon'd am to tourney*
> *Ten leagues beyond the wide world's end*
> *Methinks it is no journey.*

And that was all of England that remained to me, a list of kings and some jingling rhyming lines, a burning spear and a horse of air, as I lay in the black woman's arms ten leagues beyond the wide world's end. Yet did I not abandon hope of home. Yet did that hope not leave me never.

FIVE

THEN IT came time for me to take up my musket and go to the wars for the Portugals, I being by then half a Portugal myself, I suppose, by the mere contagion of living among them so long. So off I went with all that rampscallery roguey army of cutpurses and rackrents and dandiprat costermongers, the dregs of Lisbon, that had been sent out by the government of old King Philip to defend Angola against the forces of darkness.

I said my farewells to Matamba, most long and lovingly and tearfully, doubting I would ever see her again, and marched off with my new companions to Sowonso, which is a town ruled by a lord that obeys the Duke of Mbamba, and from thence to Saminabansa, and then to Namba Calamba, which is under a great lord, who did resist us. But we burned his town, and then he obeyed us, and brought three thousand warlike Negroes to join our force. From thence we marched to the town of Sollancango, a little lord, that fought very desperately with us, but was forced to obey; and then to Kumbia ria Kiangu, where we remained many months. From this place we gave a large number of assaults and brought many lords to subjection. We were fifteen thousand strong, counting our blacks, and marched to the mountain known as Ngombe. But first we burned all Ngazi, which is a country along the north of the River Mbengu well eastward of São Paulo de Loanda, and then we came to the lord who ruled at Ngombe, at his chief town.

This lord of Ngombe did come upon us with more than twenty thousand archers, and spoiled many of our men. But with our shot we made a great spoil among them, whereupon he retired up into the mountain, and sent one of his captains to our general João de Velloria, signifying that the next day he would obey him. In the morning the lord of Ngombe entered our camp with great pomp, with drums and fifes and great ivory trumpets, and was royally received; and he gave great presents, and greatly enriched General de Velloria and his officers. We went into his town upon the top of the mountain, where there is a great plain, well farmed, full of palm-trees, sugar-canes, potatoes, and other roots, and great store of oranges and lemons. Here is a tree called the *ogheghe*, that beareth a fruit much like a yellow plum that is very good to eat, and has a very sweet smell, and is a remedy against bile and the wind-colic. Here, too, is a river of fresh water, that springs out of the mountains and runs all along the town.

We were here five days, and then we marched up into the country, and burned and spoiled for the space of six weeks, and then returned to Ngombe again, with great store of the cowrie-shells which are current money in that land. Here we pitched our camp a league from this pleasant mountain, and remained there for months.

In telling you of these adventures, and our burnings and sackings and conquerings, I am aware that I have told you nothing of what passed through my own mind, in those several years of marching up and down the inner provinces. That is because very little passed through my mind in those years. I had taught myself the trick of shutting off my mind, and concerning myself only with my private safety, and my three meals a day, and doing as I was told. For by now I had arrived to the central philosophy of my African life; which was, to resist nothing, to glide along uncomplainingly, obeying all my orders, serving whoever my master of the moment might be, and biding my time until I could seize some opportunity of quitting this land forever. To resist, to think for mine own self, to show independence of the spirit—I had learned that all these things led only to the dungeon, and, on the field of battle, might very well bring me a summary execution.

So I mutinied no mutinies, not even inward ones. I marched, I ate and drank, I fought. I fought well. It mattered not to me that I was fighting for Portugal. What I was in deepest truth doing was fighting to stay alive. We all every one must do our God-ordained task, whatsoever it may be, and if God in His mysterious wisdom had appointed Andrew Battell of Leigh in Essex to pass certain of his days as a soldier in the armies of Portugal, well, so be it. So be it!

Now and again I suffered a wound for my masters' sake. These were in the main not serious ones, but the trifling things one collects in battle, a slash here, a bruise there, a twisting of a leg or an ankle that has one hobbling for a week or two, and the like. But in the last of my battles in this region of Ngombe I took an arrow deep within my right thigh, that struck so heavily among the tendons and the thick muscles that I thought the leg was all to destroyed. I heard the dread whistling sound that the arrow's feathers made as it came toward me, but there was no hiding from its onrushing point, and when it went into me it made a sound like the striking of a hatchet against a tree. A cunning surgeon pried the arrow out, and bound me in such a way that my sundered tissues would quickly knit; but all the same, that put an end to me as an infantryman in that campaign, since that I would not be able to stand or walk for so many months. Along with many other wounded men I was carried to the city of São Paulo de Loanda to be cured. And most grateful was I, both that I was leaving the field of battle and that God had spared my leg, God and that Portuguese surgeon, who did not tell me his name. He had a gray beard and a squinted eye and great skill in his hands, that is all I know of him.

Now did my fortunes take a kinder turn.

As soon as I could leave my bed I was summoned to the palace of the governor to speak with Don João de Mendoça. This was the first meeting I had had with him in long years, seven or eight, since my attempt to sail home on the Dutch ship, and I knew that he was not sending for me merely to chastise me or to renew my banishment.

The sight of him was greatly shocking to me. Don João had grown immensely fat, and it was not the healthy copious flesh of an inveterate glutton, but rather something sickly and evil, a sort of spongy growth of a vegetable kind, that billowed and eddied about him like a vast flabby blanket, with the original man trapped somewhere deep within. The greenish pallor that I had noted on him earlier was now more pronounced, and did make him seem like one from the next world, who has escaped the grave and wanders among us. I could not disguise my horror at the look of him. But he seemed to take no notice of that; he sat in his great chair, slumped and old, and studied me in a most careful way, searching my face as though to read in it all that I had experienced since last we had met. He did not speak, and I dared not. I felt myself to be in the presence of Death himself.

Then Don João shook his head slowly and said, "Andres, Andres, how long has it been?"

"Very long, Don João."

"It seems forever." He stared at me interminably in silence, so that I thought he might have fallen to sleep with his eyes not closed, and after a time he did say, "You know I never would have hanged you, don't you?"

"It was my prayer that you would spare me."

"It was a bad time, you know. That time when Dona Teresa said you had abused her, and screamed most fiendish, and offered to display her injuries. And Souza was clamoring like a fury for your neck, Souza who never was more than a pimple in fancy dress, and now of a sudden was full of spirit and rage. I might have had to string you up, if Souza had pressed more sternly; but he is a weakling, and the fire went swift from him. And then Teresa admitted it was all a lie about your forcing her, a lie coined out of anger and jealousy, which much abashed her in the telling of how she had slandered you, and—well, Andres, well, it matters very little now, does it not? Nothing matters. I shall soon be dead, I think. I promised to send you home, eh? And I never did. I'm the one going home instead—in a box, d'ye follow, a long box of dark African wood, plainly joined."

"Good Don João—"

"Nay, say me no kindnesses. Can't you see the bony hand about my throat? Going home, Andres, taking with me all the elephanto meat and manatee meat and the thick wines of this place and everything else that's gone into the making of this great vile belly of mine." He grinned, showing me a gaping snagtoothed hole of a mouth. "You fought well for us, Velloria tells me. You were ever in the midst of it, no mind to the risk. You were one of his most valiant soldiers. I wonder: why did you war so hard for Portugal, eh?"

"I fought because it was my trade, Don João."

"Ah. I should have foreseen that answer. You always affect the blunt and simple way. But your trade is the sea, so I did believe."

"When I am at sea, my trade is the sea. When I am a soldier, my trade is war."

"You say it so calmly. What has happened to you, Andres? Have you no anger in you?"

"Aye. Anger enough, I trow."

"Then why this doldrum calm? Why not rage and roar, and play the lion? This land has stolen half your life away from you."

"But it is too late for raging, Don João."

"Is it? You could leap this room and choke the life from me in a minute, if you could but find my throat beneath all this swaying flesh. You could slit me like a swollen coccodrillo. The way they did in Loango when it ate those slaves, eh?"

"I would not do that," I said.

"Why not? I am at your mercy."

"Killing you will not give me back those years, but only cost me the ones I have remaining."

"Ah. Always the philosopher, Andres!"

"And I bear you no malice, Don João."

He did look genuinely surprised by that: animation for the first time came into his face, a light did glimmer in his small reddened eyes.

"No malice? No malice? But I could have sent you home, and I did not."

Sighing, I said, "I soon ceased to think you would. It makes no difference. Would you send me home now?"

"Will you do one more voyage for me, first?"

"I have heard that aforetimes," I said, with a little laugh.

"Indeed. Well, and I have no ship going to Europe this year. But later there will be one, and we'll go on it together, eh? I in my coffin, and you to guard it. And in Lisbon they'll set you free. That I pledge you, and this is a true pledge: by God, who will have the disposal of my soul soon enough, that pledge is true. The next ship to Portugal, for both of us. How do you feel about that, Andres?"

"I feel nothing, sir."

"Lost interest of going home, have you?"

"Nay, I would never lose my interest of that. But I have lost belief in pledges."

He nodded solemnly. "As well you might. But this one's sincere. One more voyage, and then home! By the cross, Andres! By all my hope of heaven, slender though that may be!"

"Just one more voyage?"

"Just one."

"And where am I to go, then?"

"Southward," he said. "Benguela, and beyond it. Will you do that?"

"How can I refuse?"

"Nay, do it gladly, Andres!"

"I will do it," I said. "Let that be sufficient, Don João."

So it befell that I did go to sea again, in a frigate to the southward with sixty soldiers, on a trading voyage, with all kind of commodities. My assent to this task did gladden Don João greatly, and he pressed my hand between his clammy fleshy ones, and I knew I would never see him alive again, which he also must have known. As for his promise to free me, why, I had heard that music before, and cared not to hum the tune again. I thought only that it was better to go to sea than once more to face the arrows of the blackamoors while wearing Portugal armor under that hot inland sun, and God would bring me to England again in His own good time.

I embraced Matamba, who said, "We are always bidding each other farewell," and I had no answer to that but to hold her close against me. "You are only newly returned to me," she said, "and now you must go again. What will I do? What will I do?"

"You are under the protection of Don João de Mendoça," I said to her, for so had I engineered it with the governor. "No one will harm you. You will not be forced back into your old sort of life."

"And when Don João dies, as you say soon will happen?"

"God will provide," I said, not knowing what else.

She and I did have a most passionate and tempestuous last night together, and by dawn I slipped away in morning mist and down to the docks, thinking the fondest thoughts of this slave-girl who had so deeply entered my soul. I thought of our talking English together, and her learning my bits of poetry, and her devout Christian way, that had her kneeling every day to her little shrine, and her skill at the venereal arts, which she performed with gusto and force and subtlety. And it seemed to me odd that the track of my life should have passed through such diverse women as Rose and Anne Katherine and Dona Teresa and Isabel Matamba, that had so little in common one with the other save their womanhood: yet had I loved them all, and they me, each in a different way.

We rode our frigate easily to the southward until we came into twelve degrees below the Line. The people of this place brought us cows and sheep, Guinea wheat and beans; but we stayed not there, but came to Bay of Vaccas: that is, the Bay of Cows, which the Portugals also call Bahia de Torre, because it hath a rock like a tower. Here we rode on the north side of the rock, in a sandy bay where any ship may ride

without danger, for it is a smooth coast. Here all ships that come out
of the East Indies refresh themselves. For the great carracks of the
Portugals heavily laden with goods now of late come along this coast,
to the town called Benguela, to water and refresh themselves.

This province is called Dombe, and it hath a ridge of high *serras*, or
mountains, that stretch from the *serras* or mountains of Kambambe,
wherein are the supposed silver mines, and lie along the coast south and
by west. Here is great store of fine copper, if the people would work
it in their mines. But these people, who are called *Ndalabondos*, have no
government among themselves, and are very simple folk, though treacherous, and do not do mining, taking no more copper than they wear for
a show of bravery. The men of this place wear skins about their middles,
and beads about their necks. They carry darts of iron, and bows and
arrows in their hands. They are beastly in their way of living, for they
have men in women's apparel, whom they keep among their wives. This
I saw, those simpering foolish queans, among the women, which did
not please me. Some of the Portugals caught one of these men-women
and did strip him of his robes, the silly creature whimpering all the
while in fear, and we saw the male parts underneath, just like any other
man's, though we had thought these disguised women might be her-
maphrodite.

Their women wear a ring of copper about their necks, which weigheth
fifteen pound at the least; about their arms little rings of copper, that
reach to their elbows: about their middle a cloth of the bark of the *nsanda*
tree, a kind of wild fig of many slender trunks; on their legs rings of
copper that reach to the calves of their legs.

From these folk we bought great store of cows, and sheep—bigger
than our English sheep—and very fine copper. Also, we bought a kind
of sweet gray wood which the Portugals esteem much for its perfume,
and great store of Guinea wheat and beans. And having laded our bark
we sent her home; but fifty of us stayed on shore, and made a little fort
with rafters of wood, because the people of this place are treacherous,
and those that trade with them must stand upon their own guard. In
seventeen days we had five hundred head of good brown cattle, which
we bought for blue glass beads of an inch long, paying fifteen beads for
one cow. The governor sent us three ships, on which we shipped these
cattle to São Paulo de Loanda, and then we departed for the town of
Benguela.

This is a small outpost that I think will grow important in later years.
It lies behind a *morro*, or great cliff, that rises straight from the sea and
is covered by the thick fleshy thorny little trees without leaves that are
sò common in these dry regions. The bay of the town has good anchoring

ground, and on the north side of it stands the fort of Benguela, built square, with palisados and trenches, and surrounded with houses shaded by banana, orange, lemon, and pomegranate trees; and behind the fort is a pond of fresh water. About it are seven villages, which pay the tenth part of all they have, in tribute to the Portugals of Benguela.

The air of Benguela is very bad, and the Portugals who live there look more like ghosts than men. In command of the small garrison was Manoel de Andrade, that had been my companion on several voyages long ago up the coast: he had aged much, and was feeble and loose-jointed. I learned from him that he had committed some grave infraction, that he would not name, and had been sent to Benguela by way of punishment. This was true also of all the other Portugals there.

There was little trading for us at Benguela, the Portugals of the place having been too indolent or too sickly lately to carry on any business. We therefore did not stay long. While we were there Andrade took us to a native town, where I saw a marketplace for dog-flesh.

"In some parts of Angola the people do love dogs' flesh better than any other meat," he said, "and for that purpose they feed and fatten them, and then kill them and sell them in an open market of meat."

In that shambles or market Andrade showed us the different sorts of meat, squeezing and handling them in an expert way, while the vendors did cry out to us in their own language, praising the qualities of their product.

To me Andrade did remark, "They breed their beasts for flavor. Last year a fine sire was sold by exchange for two-and-twenty slaves. Which is to say, at ten ducats the slave, a fortune paid for a single dog!"

"Ah, the meat must be much delectable," I replied.

Andrade, with a laugh, said, "I would not know. I am no eater of dogs. But you are a man who craves adventure, eh, Piloto? Here, will you sample this meat at your dinner this night?"

"Nay," I said, "it does not overly tempt me. I think I will live my life without the eating of dog-flesh."

And I turned away, shuddering a little. Yet dog-eaters would soon seem mild and innocent to me, by comparison with what awaited me just down the coast.

For we did move a short distance beyond Benguela and saw a mighty camp pitched on the south side of the River Kuvu. Being desirous to know what those men were, our commander, one Diogo Pinto Dourado, chose a party to go on shore with our boat, and I was among that party, owing to my skill with the native languages. When we came within close range of the beach I peered forward, and what I saw did make my blood run chilly, for these were naked men, painted here and there in white

and well armed, many of them of tall stature and powerful form: I knew
them to be Jaqqas.

Catching the wrist of our boatswain, I said, "Let us turn back, for
we are traveling to our deaths. Those are the man-eaters!"

"Are you certain of that?"

"As I am a Christian!"

This boatswain, Fernão Coelho by name, was a dark-complected man,
but he grew pale as a sheet, and at once signalled for the boat to be
swung about, we being a dozen and they on shore at least five hundred.
Yet as we rowed back to the frigate, Captain Pinto Dourado appeared
on the deck and shouted to us, demanding to know why we had not
landed, and when we told him the shore was held by Jaqqas, he said
with violent gestures that we must go to them anyway.

"Nay," said I under my breath, "they will have us boiled in a trice!"

The boatswain had some similar idea, for he continued leading us
back toward our frigate; but Pinto Dourado caused muskets to be aimed
at us, and, under point of gun, we had no choice but to head once more
toward the beach. Silent as ghosts did we take our way thither, and the
Portugals crossed themselves often. Yet I did find courage, remembering
the Jaqqas who had led me to safety when that I was lost in the desert
after the massacre of Kafuche Kambara, and I told myself that these
might be merciful. For all that, yet I was in no cheerful frame of mind,
what with muskets primed behind me and man-eaters waiting to the
fore.

We came onto the shore and a troop of hundreds of men met us at
the waterside. We were armed, but we kept our weapons down to
provoke no attack. Fernão Coelho looked to me and I said, "Aye, Jaqqas
indeed."

With a curse, Coelho said, "Then Pinto Dourado has sent us to our
doom! Be ye sure?"

"They have the Jaqqa traits. They knock out four of their teeth, as a
mark of handsomeness, and they paint their bodies here and there in
white patterns, and they carry clusters of weapons by their belts."

The Jaqqas now circled round us, saying nothing, only staring hard,
as if we were men down from the moon for a visit.

Coelho said to me, "Can you speak their language?"

"Nary a word. But I speak other languages, which perhaps they know
also. I will essay it."

I tell you that I fully expected to die that day, perhaps within the
hour. Yet was I strangely calm, as I think men often are when they are
in the presence of the certainty of death. I looked about me and found
the tallest and most awesome of the Jaqqas, and spoke to him in the

Kikongo tongue, saying we came in peace, as traders, and were emissaries from the great ship that did lie off shore.

The Jaqqa said nothing, but only looked intently upon me.

Coelho said, "Let us return to the ship, since they will not talk with us."

"Peace, boatswain. We cannot leave so soon."

"Why not? We were sent to learn who they were, and now we are certain, and therefore—"

I bade him hush. The tall Jaqqa spoke, most deep and solemnly, in words I did not understand, and then, haltingly, in Kikongo. And what he said was, "What world come you from? Are you spirits?"

"We are men," said I, "from a land far across the sea."

The Jaqqa did make a long oration to his fellows in their own tongue, and several of them broke away and ran up the beach to the main camp, as messengers. To me he said, "Are you Portugals?"

"These men my companions are Portugals. I am an Englishman!"

"And what is that?"

For answer I swung my head vigorously from side to side, so that my long golden hair did fly about and sparkle most brightly in the sun, and the Jaqqa, at that, did widen his eyes and look deeply amazed.

With my arms uplifted and my hands outstretched I cried, "An Englishman is a son of Albion, and a lord among men. And we serve Her Most Protestant Majesty Elizabeth, who is paramount among the princes of the globe."

This fine speech did cow the Jaqqa by a trifle, as it was meant to do. Coelho, who comprehended not a word, leaned close to me and said, "What is all this babbling about?"

"We are in no danger, I think," said I. "For these are Jaqqas who have never seen white men, and know of Portugals only by rumor and repute, and may believe me a god, for the color of my hair. I think they will not dare harm us."

"Let us pray you are right," said Coelho sourly.

The long-shanked Jaqqa spoke again. I did not follow his words; but it was some flowing grand announcement. Then there was a stir among the general mass of cannibals, they moving back and away from the center, and I saw that a new figure had arrived among us, led by the messengers who had gone to the camp. He strode into the middle of our group and stood regarding us with the deepest attention.

I think this man was the most frightful vision I had ever beheld, as terrifying as the fiercest of coccodrillos or the most savage of howling wolves. He was of great size, a true giant, and black as the darkest of nights. Yet for all his blackness his face looked something other than pure Negro, with a straight nose and narrow harsh lips that made him all the more cruel of visage, somewhat like a Moor, though much darker. His hair was curling and very long, embroidered richly with knots of the shells called *mbambas*, which are whelks or trumpet-shells. About his neck was a collar of other large shells of shape of twisted turrets, that I know are sold on these shores for the worth of twenty shillings a shell; and about his middle he did wear a string of beads cut from the stuff of ostrich-eggs. His loins were wrapped in a blazing bright swath of scarlet palm-cloth, fine as silk. The rest of his body was bare, but was painted with red and white ornaments of the most terrifying kind, and where he was not painted, his skin was carved and cut to raise it with sundry decorations that rose a startling height in relief, as if it were a branched damask, all covered over with pretty knots in divers forms. And he gleamed with a high gloss, so that I thought almost I could see a reflection in his skin, like unto a mirror. In his nose he wore a piece of copper two inches long, and in his ears also. In sum he was naught but the utmost image of barbarism.

And his eyes! God's death, those eyes! They were pools of night surrounded by a field of dazzling white, and they drew me and held me like the most powerful of lodestones. I felt weak of the knees when I saw those eyes.

I was minded once again of that time long ago in the isle where I had been cast away by Abraham Cocke's treachery, when a vast allagardo or coccodrillo did step from a river and smile at me and put out its tongue, and I stood transfixed, and then had gone not away from it but toward, like one who has been magicked. This Jaqqa king magicked me in the same way.

The tall cannibal who spoke Kikongo said, "You are in the presence of the great Jaqqa, Imbe Calandola."

And I felt as though I had fallen rather into the presence of the Lord of Darkness himself, the Prince of Hell, the Great Adversary, the vast Lucifer of the Abyss: Satan Mephistopheles Beelzebub, the Archfiend, the King of Evil.

Six

IN THE silence of the beach the crashing of the surf was a noise like the roll of the drums of Judgment. This Calandola did come forward and stand by me, so that I smelled the reek of his skin, which I learned afterward came from his being daily anointed with the fat of human victims, to give him that burnished gloss. Yet I dared not flinch from him as he inspected me close.

The bigness of him was overpowering. I saw now that he was not in sooth the tallest of this company, and indeed was only two inches greater in height than I, I being of no mean stature myself; but what gave him his look of great size was the enormous breadth of his shoulders and the thickness of his neck and the power of his arms and hands, which could easily seize two men by their heads and crush them at the same time like eggshells.

And those great hands did go to my own head, but not in any violent way. He scooped up my hair and let it drop again, and ran his hands through it, most lightly as if handling a fabric so fragile that it would melt at a harsh breath. He stared me deep in the eyes, as though seeking to read my soul. Rarely have I been stared so deep. He walked around me, studying me from every side, and touched my hair with the tips of his fingers, and my beard, and drew his fingers even across my eyebrows, which are thick and very golden. While so doing he muttered words to his high princes, and to himself; and when he had done with me he clapped his hands and let forth a loud diabolical laugh, as if to say, "Your strange hair gives me a great pleasure, Englishman!"

Then he swung round and marched up the beach to his camp, and Jaqqa Longshanks made a signal to me that I should follow, with my companions.

Which we did, and came before Imbe Calandola again when he was seated upon a sort of high stool in a tent. Five of his princes stood to his side, and two man-witches, and two women that might have been sisters, for both had heavy breasts, and the same face, with four of their teeth pulled out for beauty's sake and their hair piled high with *mbamba*-shells thrust into it.

A great bowl of palm-wine was brought, and Calandola drank of it, and then it was proffered to me. And when I had had some sips of it Calandola did dip his hands into it, and shake the sweet heavy wine out onto my hair, as though he were anointing me. After I was thoroughly drenched in the stuff he took my head very gently between his hands, and rubbed the wine deep into my scalp, all the while saying things in his language, with a low rumbling voice, to the man-witches beside him. To which I submitted without hesitation, for when one is in the camp of the cannibals and their king would bathe your head with wine, and they are five hundred and you are one of but a very few, one does not play the fastidious fop and refuse the honor.

When I was thus soaked, the long-legged Jaqqa who spoke the Kikongo tongue said, "Imbe Calandola would know why you have come to this place."

"To trade upon the coast," I replied. "We deal in goods of all kinds, and mean to purchase cattle and any other useful merchandise."

This he told to Calandola, who made a reply.

To me the Jaqqa said, "The Imbe-Jaqqa makes you welcome here, and instructs you to have your people come on shore with all your commodities."

I did translate this for Coelho, who showed great sign of relief, and would at once have boarded the longboat to return to the safety of our ship. But first there were certain rituals, and more passing about of the palm-wine; and then when it was plain we could go, Calandola gestured that I stay behind, with two others of the Portugals.

At this I sank into leaden despond, for my despairing imagination at once threw forth a likely sequence of event, by which Captain Pinto Dourado, fearing some trap, took his ship and crew away from these waters the instant his longboat returned, abandoning me and my two fellows here. I was an old hand at being abandoned, and ever mistrusted my position. And I doubted much that Pinto Dourado would want to march his own precious self into a den of man-eaters. Even did I take the picture a little farther, and see myself as the grand feature of the cannibal feast, at which all these Jaqqas did jostle and shove to get themselves some morsel of the flesh of the golden-haired god.

But my forebodings proved to be mere vapor. Pinto Dourado indeed hastened to come ashore with all his crew, and heaps of beads and gibcracks to trade with: if he had any much fear of Jaqqas, his love of profit altogether eclipsed that fear. We went into the Jaqqa camp, which was very orderly, entrenched with piles of wood; and we had houses provided for us that night, and many loads of palm-wine, and cows and goats and flour for our use.

There was after darkness a mighty feast, and here I expected to see human flesh upon the banquet. But no: the Jaqqas dined that night as we did, on roasted goat, and beef, and copious draughts of the palm-wine. With this was much loud harsh music of a very barbaric kind, made on drums and fifes and *mpungas* and a thing called a *tavale*, which is a board rising on two wooden sticks that they beat with their fingers. And there was dancing by the women, who wore nothing but masses of beads about their necks and arms and legs. They leaped across the fire like prancing witches, grinning widely to show their gap-toothed mouths, and laughing and screaming. And in the midst of all sat the king-demon Calandola on his stool, his oiled body glittering by firelight, his huge legs thrown far apart, his head back as he roared out his great cries of pleasure. And at all times there were three or four women about him, doing foul things to him, rubbing him and tonguing him and taking his giant yard into their straining mouths, whilst he idly stroked their woolly hair.

I felt the powerful presence of that man as a real and heavy pressure on me. Waves of force and might rolled from him like the booming of drums, like the crash of the tempest. There was no escaping him, no hiding from him.

I saw him as a giant mouth bestriding the breast of the world, and feeding, feeding, feeding.

We slept but little that night, for the festivities went on almost to dawn. And when the first early light came, and sleeping Jaqqas lay sprawled like ninepins everywhere, sleeping Portugals, too, there was a conference among Imbe Calandola and his interpreter-Jaqqa and Captain Pinto Dourado and me, and I discovered then why the king of the Jaqqas had been so glad of letting us come on shore.

Through the interpreter, whose name was Kinguri, we were told that Calandola was determined to overrun the realm of Benguela, which was on the north side of the River Kuvu. That is, he did not intend to menace the small Portugal settlement there, but he would have his way of conquest with the Benguela folk, who were ruled by a prince named Hombiangymbe (or so it sounded to me.) For this he did want our help, in bringing his men over to the other side of the river with our boat. "If you will aid us," said Kinguri, "the Imbe-Jaqqa will let you have all the captives to take as slaves, for we know you are hungry for many slaves for selling."

This astounded me, that we should go in league with man-eaters to subjugate a native tribe already giving tribute to Portugal. I did not think we would do such a thing, and was forming in my mind the words of refusal, when Pinto Dourado said unto me, with his eyes gleaming with money-lust, "Aye, it will be worth fortunes to us! We will do it!"

"Can that be so?"

"We will do it," said he sternly. "Tell him. Give him our warm pledge!"

And so it was agreed. All that day long, preparations for the war went forth briskly among the Jaqqas, and by night there was another great feast, as wild as the one before.

The women danced to the drums, and some young ones performed an obscene rite, dancing in pairs, one following behind the other and the second one aping the gestures and movements of a man pursuing a woman. At a certain moment, when the pounding of the drum came to its most envigored moment, the girl who played the man's part did grasp hold of the other and turn her around. Then they held one another by the shoulders and in a fierce and frenzied way did mime out the sexual act, with a thrusting of loins and a grinding of bellies and a rubbing together of the dark hairy zone of womanhood in high mock and counterfeit of copulation, until they fell exhausted to the ground. Then a second such couple did the like, and a third, and when everyone was suitably inflamed the chieftains of the tribe did select women from the dance and drag them aside, and spread their legs and have them in the open, all the while making hard growling sounds more suited to the coupling of savage dogs or hyaenas. But I noticed that the Jaqqas took care to pull out and spill their seed on the bellies of these girls, and not to plant it in their wombs: which I learned afterward was a feature of this rite, and not the general Jaqqa custom of coupling.

This festival ended by midnight and there was sudden silence, like a falling curtain, and everyone slept. I lay on my rough pallet a long while, listening to the soft breathing of the cannibals everywhere about, and through my mind tumbled the spectacle of the day: the naked women miming copulation, the huge Jaqqa warriors spurting their seed onto them, the Jaqqa smile with the missing teeth, the fires blazing high, and always Calandola, Calandola, Calandola, presiding over these hellish games in broad delectation, singing and shouting among his playfellows with a wondrous roar.

In the morning, before break of day, Calandola did arise and strike his *ngongo*, which is an instrument of war that has the shape of a double bell, and presently made an oration with a loud voice, that all the camp might hear. I had already in a single day learned enough of the Jaqqa tongue so that I knew something of what he was saying, which was that he would destroy the Benguelas utterly. This he cried with such vehemence as to shake the earth.

And presently they were all in arms, and marched to the river side, where they had built *jangadas* or rafts out of a light wood that grows abundantly on the swampy banks of the rivers. Owing to the strength of the current, poling these *jangadas* across the rivermouth was an awful task, that would strip the warriors of their vigor before they reached the other side; which was why they wanted the use of our boat. They swarmed about us, every one eager to have the credit of being first into the campaign, and Calandola was fain to beat them back to keep them from overflowing us. He picked his prime men and we took a load across, the bravest of the cannibals, and then another group.

On the second trip some warriors of the Benguelas appeared, and took up into a warlike position to menace the first party of the Jaqqas, who were sore outnumbered. But Pinto Dourado said, "Fire upon them," and we did shoot off our muskets, which slew many of the Benguelas and drove the others off.

By twelve of the clock all of the Jaqqas were over on the other side. Then Calandola commanded all his drums, *tavales*, *mpungas*, and other screeching and thumping instruments of warlike music to strike up, and give the onset, which began a bloody day for the Benguelas.

We took no part in the slaughter, but watched from afar, and I saw the troops of Calandola sweep down upon that helpless village the way the voracious army of ants had invaded my sleeping hut in that other village by Lake Kasanza. There was no holding back the Jaqqas, nor slowing them. With terrible wailing shrieking devil-cries did they rush upon the Benguelas, who staunchly stood fast a little while, and then, knowing the dread nature of their enemy, gave way to fright. They broke ranks and turned their backs to flee, and a very great number of them were slain, and were taken captives; man, woman, and child. These Jaqqas are mainly men of very great stature and power, and they fight with such frenzy and such energetic wielding of their swords and lances that there is no checking of them once they are fully aroused in martial fervor.

The prince of this land, Hombiangymbe, was slain, along with more than one hundred of his chief lords, and their heads were lopped off and thrown at the feet of the great Imbe-Jaqqa Calandola, who sat on his stool of state most solemnly witnessing and savoring his victory. Then the men, women, and children of the tribe were brought in captive alive, and the captive men were made to carry the bodies of the dead Benguelas that were heaped up to be eaten. For these Jaqqas are the greatest cannibals and man-eaters that be in the world, and love to feed chiefly on man's flesh, notwithstanding that they have vast herds of cattle. And I think they had made this war on the Benguelas principally because for some weeks they had been wandering in a land without settlements, and had not had the opportunity for making a dinner on their favorite sort of meat.

What happened next was frightful, though for my part I had seen something of its like among the man-eaters of Brazil long years ago, and so my soul was hardened somewhat to the sight.

The Jaqqas did build a great fire, and threw upon it much wood from the houses of the captured, and added to it certain stones and powders that their man-witches carried, to cause the flame to rise up in blue and green and violet and other stark hues. While this was being done, some older men of the tribe, using long copper blades that they wielded with great skill, worked a butchery on the dead corpses, making them ready for the meal by cutting away such parts as the Jaqqas do not prefer, and opening certain slits in the skin for better roasting. For sometimes the Jaqqas do boil their prey and sometimes they roast it, but they had not brought their great kettles with them over to this side of the river, so that it behooved them to do the roasting now. They took certain long spits and mounted them with great care, and plainly they were much practiced and expert at this task; and then they did slide the bodies of the dead upon the spits like oxen, and turn them and grill them nicely and baste them with juices as the very best cooks would do that ever served in the kitchen of a king. The meat did sizzle and crack and char quite well, and a flavor came from it that—God help me, it is the truth!—did smell most savory, so long as one kept one's back turned, and did not let one's self perceive the source of the savor.

Calandola called out to us quite jovial in his loud roaring way, and it was not hard to divine that the words he was crying were something like, "Come, Portugals, join in this our feast! We will set aside the finest cuts for you, since you are our friends!"

But of course we did not accept the hospitality of him, and in good sooth many of our men went lurching off into the woods, and I heard the sound of retching and puking coming from their direction. I myself was not so hard affected, though it did not enter in my mind to take part of this grisly feeding. As for the defeated folk of Benguela, they were made to stand in two long ranks, naked and weaponless, and to watch as the cookery proceeded. What thoughts went through their souls I cannot say, for they were very silent, except for some wounded who did groan a little, and I could not tell from their eyes whether they were deeply grieved, or else so stunned and numb that they did not comprehend the sense of what was taking place. I think if this had been Essex, and two hundred English men and women had had to stand by while their brothers and sons were roasted, we would have heard some little outcry from them, and more than a little: but these are different folk here, and their way of thinking is very foreign to me. Yet am I fair certain that they grieved, however far inward, for this terrible thing.

When the meat was ready came another great strangeness. For one of Calandola's man-witches brought him a beautifully worked wicker basket of great size, that I remembered we had carried over specially from the Jaqqa camp on the other side. And from it the witch took certain vestments and utensils of an unmistakably Christian kind, and did hand them one by one to Imbe Calandola. There was the black cassock of a priest, and the mantle called a cope, and a richly worked chasuble, which is the thing they wear when they say the Mass. All these several garments had been slitted open and reworked with rope, so that they could fit over Calandola's giant body; for the Portuguese priest to whom they had once belonged must have been a much smaller man. When Calandola had donned these things he took up a crucifix, which he held by the short end, and in his other hand he raised up a silver chalice, and with a mighty laugh he did clatter the end of the crucifix against the side of the chalice, like the ringing of a bell to summon men to dinner. And at the sound of this ringing, a great shout did go up from all the Jaqqas, and a whoop of joy, for that they knew it must be feeding-time.

It mattered little to me what blasphemy the Imbe-Jaqqa cared to work with all these Popish vestments and utensils. But I thought it would matter a good deal to my Portugal comrades. Indeed they were taken aback, and I saw their lips clamping tight and their nostrils flaring. Yet they cried out nary a word of protest. In this they took their cue from their scoundrel commander, Pinto Dourado, who stood by with his arms folded, smiling as sweetly as though this were some chorus of Christmastide revelers happening here, and not the shouting of sacrilegious cannibals. Did Pinto Dourado not mind the insult to his faith? Or was he shrewdly thinking that a protest might merely add some Portuguese meat to the banquet? Perhaps some of each; but I think also that he was keeping careful watch over his business arrangements with the Jaqqas, and would not venture any disapproval of his host's ways until the dealings were consummated.

Well, and well, the feast began.

There was Calandola waving his chalice and crucifix about, and straining his mighty shoulders against the constricting garb of some murdered priest, and there were his long-legged naked warriors turning the spits, and there were the kinfolk of the victims standing silent aside, and then the butcher-Jaqqas commenced their carving, and a great juicy haunch was brought to the king, who threw back his head and roared his vast laughter and dug his teeth into the meat.

As he ate, he pointed to his lieutenants and captains, and they one by one came to take their fill, Kinguri Longshanks first, and then each in order of precedence. Nearly all the Jaqqas are tall and straight-limbed, though some few are short, and the short ones are very brawny in the arms and legs. Since they do multiply themselves by adoption, stealing children out of other tribes and raising them as Jaqqas, there is little blood-kinship among these man-eaters; and yet they resemble each other, as if their bloody life does make them grow to look like one another. Or perhaps it is that they choose a certain shape of captive preferably to adopt into their number. But I was greatly struck by the bigness and strength of them, as I had been from the very first, long ago, when I saw a Jaqqa much the size of Kinguri standing alone and mysterious by the side of the River Kwanza.

And again Calandola beckoned us to eat, crying out what must have been the words, "You are our guests! Eat, eat, eat!"

But we did not do that.

From a distance I did watch the feast, though. And a very strange thing happened to me after a time which you may find hard to comprehend, that is, I ceased to be amazed or repelled, and looked upon what was occurring as quite an ordinary event. What, you say? How, was I become a monster like these cannibals? I think not. I think a kind of wisdom was entering me from having witnessed several previous of these cannibal banquets, going back even to my time in Brazil, and those wild Indians the Taymayas.

And what this wisdom said was, We eat cattle and we eat sheep and we eat fowl, and we think nothing amiss of that; and these folk eat man, and *they* think nothing amiss of that, and we are all God's creatures, are we not? I mean by that only that in this huge world there are differing customs, and what seems strange or loathsome to one race is quite usual to another. Are we to be angry with a Frenchman because he will speak no English, and we cannot understand his palaver? But he is French: French is his usual speech. And the flesh of humans is the usual diet of Taymayas and Jaqqas and the others of that kind. And I believe it is not fitting to condemn them out of hand for that.

Possibly, you say, I have dwelled too long among cannibals, and my soul has been tainted by their ways. Possibly; but I think otherwise. I think only that I have come to a wide understanding of the world's variety, from having lived so long on its outer edges. I dare say that somewhere on this globe is a race that not only dotes on human flesh but also would puke at the thought of eating cattle or fowl, claiming that such is unnatural and evil.

And then afterward, when all were sated, we did divide the spoils. From the captives the Jaqqas selected certain boys and girls on whom the first hair had begun to sprout in the loins, and adopted them forthwith into their tribe. These were twelve or fifteen in number, who looked to be dazed, and not knowing what was happening to them. On the boys slave-collars were placed, as is done to all Jaqqa youths until they have slain some foe in battle. The other Benguelas were given to us for slaves, as our fee for taking the Jaqqas across the river. These we loaded on our ship, knowing that we had accomplished the making of our fortune: for we had many strong and healthy souls, that we could sell in São Paulo de Loanda for twelve thousand reis the head, and they had cost us nothing, not even a handful of beads.

Then we made ready to depart. At the last, the high Jaqqas came to us, Calandola and Kinguri and some others, and they walked about on shore looking toward our ship, thinking, I suppose, that it was a miracle. And the Imbe-Jaqqa again touched my hair.

I began to have an idea now of why those Jaqqas who had found us in the desert had spared us that time, and conveyed us toward Masanganu. It was for the sake of my hair; for they had never seen its like, and thought me to be god-like in some way. For Calandola showed such fascination with it as made me feel uneasy, fearing that he would not let me set sail with my fellows, in which Pinto Dourado would most likely gladly acquiesce, or that he would let me go, but ask me to leave my hair behind, or some such thing. But the Imbe-Jaqqa was content only to touch it some few times. And then we went out toward the frigate.

And as we journeyed northward I could not cleanse the Jaqqas from my mind.

I was altogether captivated by them. Certainly they were cannibal monsters, and dreadful; and yet they seemed in a strange way not to be truly evil, any more than a storm that sweeps across the land in a rage of destruction can be said to be evil. For they had no malice in them. They were mere appetites on legs. To slay and eat one's own kind is, in sooth, a great wrong, as any child might argue. But were the Jaqqas any worse than the swarming slippery Portugals who had taken over the coast, and did press an entire race into slavery, and cheated one another and plotted all sorts of dire treacheries, all the while going piously each day to the Mass? In this land of Africa everyone was a monster of some sort or another, I did decide. And I think I preferred the ferocious Jaqqas, who made no pretense of piety, to the hypocrite folk who claimed to be civilized, but were raw savage just beneath the outer costume.

The Imbe-Jaqqa haunted me in another way. I know that there are upon this globe certain great men: Drake is one, and Ralegh, and Elizabeth must be deemed a great man, too, for a man's role is what she did adopt, and splendidly. And also Julius Caesar and Alexander and such— leaders, dominators. I have a very small bit of that thing about me myself, that they have had: for I am no king or duke, but I have observed that in any group of men, they do turn to me before long for leadership in a natural way, though I do not seek it. Had I ever sought it, or had I the kind of noble birth that confers those powers without the seeking, I might indeed have been something extraordinary and done high deeds, and I say that in no braggartly way, but in quiet simple assessment. Yet I have only a small bit of that thing. I would not have been an emperor. But this Calandola, I thought at once, had in him the stuff of majesty: like the great Genghis of the Tartars, like the Hunnish chief Attila who despoiled Europe in the long ago, like the Assyrian Sennacherib of dire repute, he could capture the souls of men, and make them follow wherever he willed. In that first encounter he had begun to capture mine, which I barely understood. For there was much that was loathsome and repellent about him, and yet he attracted. Do you comprehend? Can you? It was the pull of the coccodrillo, the pull of darkness, of the hidden chilling Satanic river that flows through the depths of the soul and sweeps all conscience and faith before it. I saw Imbe Calandola in my dreams, like a titan filling half the sky. His touch was upon me. He rang like a great gong in my skull, tolling, tolling, giving me no peace. And I did not understand what power he held over me, nor how I was meant to yield to it. But he filled half the sky; he did ring in my skull like a gong.

SEVEN

THE JAQQAS settled themselves in this country of Benguela and took the spoil of it. And we had great trade with them, five months, and gained greatly by them. First we carried our cargo of slaves to São Paulo de Loanda and sold them, the governor and other officials taking their heavy share, but still leaving profit enough so that we were all rich men. I was showered with milreis, enough money to buy me a grand farm in England, if I were in England. We stayed a little while in the city, and with my new riches I purchased good cloaks for Matamba, and other pretties. I spoke with her of the things that had befallen me, and said that I had seen Imbe Calandola. At the which she moved away from me and began to whimper, as if she feared some contagion of evil might pass from the great Jaqqa to her through me; but I calmed her and she asked me many questions, and told me that the long-legged Kinguri was brother to Calandola, and a famous man in his own right, which I had not known.

We undertook a second voyage to Benguela, bringing certain hatchets and knives and other common things that the Jaqqas needed, and brought away more slaves: for it was easy for the Jaqqas to round up the villagers to give to us at a gentle price. So I grew richer, I that had been a miserable prisoner and a banished man not too long before.

There was a counting-house in São Paulo de Loanda now, operated by a Spaniard with connections in the House of Fugger that is such great bankers across Europe, and I placed my money there, to increase it. This was a noble room of white walls and black wood panels, and a great staircase of some fine black wood rising to the upper room where the secret businesses of banking did proceed. The Spaniard was all courtesy and sleekness, and moved about like a little puppy, fawning on me, with many an eager, "*Sí, Señor Battell,*" as though I were some oiled and waxed grandee with a long Espaniardo mustachio, and gave me a receipt for my milreis on splendid vellum, inscribed most heroically in curlicues and flourishes, the way one might inscribe a passport into Paradise.

And I knew that I had crossed another unseen line in the progress of my soul into new territory, for now I was a slave-dealer and no hiding the truth of that: and what else does one call a man who buys men and women from cannibals, and sells them among the Portugals? I who rarely had more than a pound or two to my name now did hold great store of milreis at my account with Fugger of Augsburg, that is, I was a man now of substance and wealth, all of it gained by dealing in souls and trafficking with man-eaters. The which was God's small jest upon me for living an honorable life.

We did a third voyage also in those five months to the Jaqqas in the south and fetched yet more slaves. But coming the fourth time, we found them not. I knew enough of the Jaqqa way by that time to be aware that Imbe Calandola was not content to keep himself in one place for long; and he and his followers had grown weary of the Benguela country, for they had used up all their wine, and in those parts there are no palm-trees for making wine, though other foodstuffs are abundant. So they had marched toward the province of Bambala, to a great lord that is called Calicansamba, whose country is five days up into the land.

Being loath to return without trade, we determined to go up into the land after them. So we went fifty of us on shore, Captain Diogo Pinto Dourado and his boatswain among the party, and left our ship riding in the Bay of Benguela to stay for us. And marching two days up into the country, where all was green and the land was tawny and the air was filled with little glimmering midges with eyes like sapphires and beaks of fire, we entered to the domain of a great lord which is called Mofarigosat. And coming to his first town, we found it all burned to the ground and despoiled, with bloodied mangled bodies strewn here and there in a terrible way that was familiar to me from another sad slaughter long ago.

"The Jaqqas have been here and are gone," said Pinto Dourado.

He sent for a Negro slave which we had bought of the Jaqqas, and who lived with us, and ordered him to carry a message to the Lord Mofarigosat. This slave did tell Mofarigosat that we were white men allied to the Jaqqas, and seeking to meet with them our friends, and so we desired entry and free passage through his territory.

Two days went past and we thought our envoy might have been slain, which would have been a great insult and required us to make war. But then the slave returned, and with him was a dignitary of the court of Mofarigosat, a broad-bodied black with a great crimson sash of office across his breast, who bowed low before us as though we were demon-princes out of Hell, and said most humbly, "My master bids me tell you that you are welcome here."

Mofarigosat himself was less humble. This chieftain, who received us a day later in his capital village, did stand tall before us, and his eyes did flash, and there was no smile on his lips, as he bade us make our home with him. "A thousand welcomes," he said, yet his voice was cold and he did but pretend a welcome to us: I could tell, and it took little shrewdness to see it, that he was merely admitting us for fear of Imbe Calandola, with whom he wanted no disagreement.

Mofarigosat was a man of nearly sixty years, white-haired and white-bearded but with great strength and vigor. His body was lean and strong and warlike, and bore no scrap of fatty surplus upon it. He dressed only in a blue loin-cloth and in a necklace of small golden plates. The gold surprised us, that metal not being an object of much desire among these African folk. Coming before us in his council-chamber, Mofarigosat did walk from one to another of us, inspecting us close, our skins, our guns, our armor, for no white man had ever been in this part before. At last he said, in the Kikongo tongue but with a more fluid accent of the south, "Do you serve the great Imbe-Jaqqa, or is he vassal to you?"

Pinto Dourado looked to me to make reply, and after a moment, hastily constructing an answer, I said, "We are equal allies, that do trade with one another for the universal benefit of both."

"Ah," said Mofarigosat. "Equal allies."

"Go to, you should have told him the Jaqqa is our servant!" Pinto Dourado said sharply to me.

"I think it would have been a hard lie to make," I said. "They know the Jaqqa too well here."

Mofarigosat ordered feasting for us, and professed no enmity for Calandola, even that he had burned and spoiled one of his outlying villages. That small event the chieftain appeared to regard merely as the Imbe-Jaqqa's due. As he passed through this territory, it was only to be expected, a natural thing, that Calandola would pause to make his dinner somewhere, and if he dined on some of the subjects of Mofarigosat, well, then so be it. I understood now how this lord had been able to rule so long here and reach such a great age unmolested: for he, too, knew the art of bending to the breeze, lest he be snapped and swept away in storms.

Yet plainly was he no petty chief, but rather a lord most powerful, and no coward neither, but a shrewd and valiant man. Mofarigosat his town was large and well-appointed, with many dwellings and great wooden palaces covered with deep thatch, and a palisado of sharp-edged stakes set all about it, that would be difficult to breach. He had a great many warriors, strong and able, equipped with lances and large bows, that he took care to keep on display for our benefit.

I think that if Imbe Calandola had chosen to attack this lord Mofarigosat, he would have had a heavy task in the defeating of him. In the end the Jaqqa very likely would have triumphed, for I think Calandola did believe so strongly in his own invincibility that he could convince all others of that, even his foes. Yet it would have cost him sorely. So at this time Calandola had chosen not to expend his energies in a hard war with Mofarigosat, but to go on instead in a wide circle around his city and into the deeper forest, which be the true home of Jaqqas.

And seeing the size of Mofarigosat's army and the tough mettle of Mofarigosat himself, I began to feel some unease about our own safety in this place, we being but fifty men and they being many hundreds. I know that the Spaniards did conquer the entire nations of Mexico and Peru with armies hardly greater than our little band, but those folk were Indians and not Negroes, and perhaps were more readily cowed by muskets and white skins, Indians being a frailer people, and timid. I had not noticed the troops of Kafuche Kambara greatly cowed by those things that time they fell upon the Portugals in the desert. And I did not think those of Mofarigosat would greatly be, neither.

At the first it was all feasting and celebration. The palm-wine flowed like water, and Mofarigosat caused his best cattle to be led forth and butchered for our delight, and we ate and drank until we were stupored by it.

To his credit, Pinto Dourado became suspicious early of this soft treatment, thinking it might be the prelude to a massacring, when we were all thoroughly besotted. So he gave the order that at all times five out of our fifty were to take no drink at all, and that all of us were to keep our muskets close within reach during the banqueting.

The kindness of Mofarigosat toward us did not cease for some days. Each day as the orange sun fell swiftly toward the distant blue shield of the sea we gathered and we did revel with Mofarigosat and his people, and often the lord himself presided over the festivities. There was danc-

ing in which the men and women were divided into two facing rows,
and did stamp their feet in place, and rush toward one another to counterfeit the act of copulation, with thrustings of hips and the like. Yet
this dance was far less licentious than the similar one that the Jaqqa
women had performed, since those Jaqqas had rubbed their slippery
bodies together in high hot passion, and these did only mime the act in
a very chaste way, with open space between them. Still, it was not like
the dances one sees and does in England or in Portugal, and it did stir
some lusts in us.

To satisfy these, we were given women: not of Mofarigosat's own
nation, to be sure, but slave-wenches of some other tribe. All the women
of this country do sharpen their teeth for beauty's sake, but these carried
the style to its utmost, with pointed teeth like needles, that scarce hold
much beauty for me. Also were they deeply ornamented on their skins
not just with the usual carvings and cicatrices, but with colored patterns
that are pressed into the skin with sharp blades. This was done on the
forehead, the breasts, the shoulders, and the buttocks, and made the
girls look piebald and strange. I saw this skin-coloring being done to a
small girl, that was made to lie on the ground whilst the image of a
flower was carved into her belly by an artist of that kind. They say that
if the child endures these incisions without crying out, she will be good
for childbearing; but if she cannot endure them, she will never marry,
and is likely to be sold for slavery. Thus men who are looking for brides
here seek first to see if the women are perfectly ornamented on their
bellies.

Well, and in the dark one does not notice such decorations, nor is one
much offended by teeth that come to a point. So we took our pleasure
willingly with these gifts of Mofarigosat. To me it was a particular secret
sport to hold mine tight in my arms and pretend that she be Matamba,
for there was something indeed Matamba-like about the feel of her flesh
and the placing of her ornamental scars and the sweet deep odor of her
body. Yet was she not even distantly Matamba's equal in the arts of the
bedchamber, which made me long to be in São Paulo de Loanda once
again, and in Matamba's embrace.

But when we spoke with Mofarigosat about taking our leave of him,
and peradventure having from him a guide to lead us onward to the city
of Calicansamba, he only laughed and clapped us lustily on the shoulders
and cried, "Nay, stay with us! Share our meat! Why rush off so hasty?"

The which did make us even more suspicious of him. I spoke with
Pinto Dourado and told him what I believed the real reason for Mofarigosat's rich hospitality to be, that was, that he feared having us join

forces with Calandola's Jaqqas, and was delaying us here with pleasures until Calandola should be safely out of his country. In this Pinto Dourado concurred.

Then the feasting ended and we said to Mofarigosat, "Now we shall take our leave of you. Will you have the kindness to provide us with a guide to the inland?"

"In time, in time," said Mofarigosat, looking thoughtful and stroking his white beard. "But first I ask a small service of you, that will give you hardly any effort."

At that I felt dismay, for I had had a good education thus far in my life in what it meant to be asked to perform just one small service before you were free to go your own way. But we inquired of him what he would have of us, to which he replied that there was a city nearby that was enemy to him and rebelled against him, and he did crave our assistance in reducing that city to subjection.

"Surely," I said, "the armies of Mofarigosat are capable of dealing with any enemy!"

"That they are," smoothly he replied, "but it will be so much more swift, so much less bloody, if the white men and their guns show their force against these folk."

We parleyed some long while, and gradually the shape of things did become clear. Which was that Mofarigosat thought himself a mighty man having us with him, and intended to use us to terrify all his foes. He would not let us go out of his land till we had gone to the wars with him, and that was the substance of it. Of course we could refuse him and fight our way free, but beyond doubt some of us would perish in that, and quite possibly we would fail entirely. For the armies of Mofarigosat were on constant patrol around us, hundreds and hundreds of warriors, and though he respected our guns greatly, he did not fear them in any abject way, nor us. In the face of his firmness we chose the easiest course, which was to yield to him at least this once, and do him his service.

So we were forced to go with him to a town along a small fork of the River Kuvu, which was well defended but which I think Mofarigosat himself could well have conquered without our aid. He took up his position around it and called out that they must surrender, or they would be slain by white-skinned demons. To this came a volley of arrows by way of reply. Whereupon Mofarigosat turned to us and that sly old man smiled and gestured and did say to us, "Destroy them."

And we levelled our muskets at the warriors of the rebellious town and slew many of them in the first onslaught. The others fled at once, and we marched into the town and destroyed the enemies of Mofarigosat. In doing this, three of us were slightly wounded by arrows, but all the town that had opposed him was taken. We stood to one side while Mofarigosat and his troops now plundered the town and helped themselves to its wealth. I do not know the name of this place, in whose sorry downfall I took part.

When we had done this we resolved to make our leavetaking of Mofarigosat without further delay. So again the chief Portugal officers and I went to the lord, and said we would leave, I being the speaker and making my words plain and firm.

Mofarigosat replied, "I will not prevent you leaving."

"Aye," said I, "then we shall depart this hour."

"But I must have a pledge from you first."

Pinto Dourado, who had come to speak this language almost as well as I and sat listening close beside, gave me a troubled look, and I shared his distress.

I said, "What pledge do you ask?"

"That you return to my land within two months, and bring with you a hundred men to help me in my wars, and to trade with me. For we would ally ourselves with you Portugals."

"Did you understand his words?" I asked the captain.

"Aye."

"And what shall I tell him?"

"That he is an old mildewed fool," Pinto Dourado growled. Then he said, "Nay, keep that to yourself. But how can I answer him? They have nothing here that holds value to us in trade. And we have no need to fight his wars for him." With a shrug Pinto Dourado said, "Tell him we agree. We will come in two months, and give him all that he wishes."

"But—"

"Tell him, Englishman!"

So did I turn to Mofarigosat and say, as I was instructed, "It is agreed. You shall have a hundred men with weapons that shoot flame, and we will trade with you."

"Most excellent," Mofarigosat responded. "And will you give me a pawn to assure me of your good faith?"

"A pawn?" I said. "What pawn?"

"Leave one of your number with me for hostage, so that I know you will come again."

Pinto Dourado at this did spit, and scowl, and look away. I told the chieftain that we could not consent to such a thing, but he would not have it other, and in the end we withdrew to confer among ourselves.

The Portugals all seemed greatly desirous of getting away from this place as quick as possible, even if it meant leaving a man behind. "It is only two months," said Fernão Coelho. "And we will give that man a full share of all our profits in our trading!"

"If it seems so small a time to you," answered him one of our master gunners, "then you be the one who stays, boatswain!"

"Ah, nay, friend," said Coelho. "We will draw lots for it."

"Lots! Lots! Aye!" cried many of the Portugals. "It is the only fair way!"

But some of them would not agree to it, saying that even if it were only the one chance out of fifty that they be left here, they would not hazard it. And no one could make them join in the lot-drawing; and therefore the others would not draw lots, either, for only a fool would reach for a straw when half his fellows refused to share the risk. I thought Pinto Dourado would order them all to go into the lottery, to make an end of it and get us out of here before Mofarigosat devised some new labor for us. But the slippery Portugal had an easier idea.

He turned to me and said, "We will leave you as our pawn, Englishman."

I think that if I live to be eight hundred year, yet will I never grow accustomed to the casual treachery that is practiced between men on this world. For sure that Pinto Dourado's words did come upon me by surprise, and take me in the gut the way a kick by a booted foot would have done.

"Aye!" cried all the Portugals lustily, and why should they not? "Leave the Englishmen here! Leave the heretic!"

In a moment I recovered from my amaze and looked about at them, saying, "Are ye all such Judases, that you would elect me to this fate without a second thought?"

"It is only for two months," said Coelho mildly.

"Indeed. And if it befalls that you never return, what will become of me?"

"We would not be such traitors as to forget you," Pinto Dourado said, and in his oily face I saw only contempt. "But if one of us must stay, why, I tell you that it must be you, for you are a foreigner and a Lutheran, and a slave under prison sentence, but we are all free Portugals who cannot be handed off in this way. I would have much to answer for at São Paulo de Loanda, if I left any other of my men here than you. Do you understand?"

"I understand that I am betrayed," I answered him. "God's wounds, will you cast me off?"

"It must be."

"Swear, then, by your cross or something else holy, that you will return for me!"

"Ah, it would be unlawful to swear such oath," said Pinto Dourado, "you being heretical. We may not pledge upon the Lord's word to such as you."

"Never have I heard that argued before."

"You have heard it now, Englishman. Go you now to Mofarigosat, and tell him that you are our chosen pawn, and that we pledge to come back and aid him, and claim you, so he must keep you in safety. For we would not have you harmed, since that you are one of our company."

EIGHT

WITH THOSE words Diogo Pinto Dourado did dismiss me, and once again I found myself abandoned, and the victim of perfidy.

For I knew I would not be redeemed out of this place, Pinto Dourado having observed that there was nothing here that Portugals desired. Yet said to him most quietly in parting that I had done no wrong that merited me this fate, and so therefore I did hope he would not forget me, even if he had refused to swear it. And also I said, quietly and in such a way as might sink deep into his soul, that I knew the Lord God Almighty would exact a terrible revenge, upon the last day of the world, against those who broke faith with their fellow men.

Then the whoreson Portugals did hurry out of the city of Mofarigosat, not even troubling to get themselves the guide they had desired, so impatient were they of leaving. For this cunning Mofarigosat had frighted them in a way that Imbe Calandola himself had not done. To them, I think, Calandola was so hugely monstrous that they could not begin to understand him; but this lean and stringy old Mofarigosat was truly of their own kind, subtle and merciless and capable of any sort of betrayal, the only differences between him and them being that he was a pagan and his skin was a few shades darker. So they meant to flee him, before he made them all captives.

And I alone remained behind, thinking I might spend the rest of my life in Mofarigosat his town, and that that might be no very long span.

At least for the first the blacks did treat me kindly. I had a little cottage for myself, out of poles and brush, and they brought me palm-wine and meat whenever I clapped my hands, and each night when I retired there were three or four women waiting by my door, young naked hard-breasted slave-wenches with thick lips and filed teeth hiding behind those lips, from amongst whom I could take my pick. This was captivity, aye, but it was not the most woeful of durance.

By day I was free to wander about in the town, which was a place of close moist heat and of shining heavy foliage pressing close, and I could observe the customs of the tribe as I wished. And many strange things did I see among these folk.

They were idolaters, like all these blacks except the ones that live in the cities that are under the thumb of the Jesuits. For their gods the heathen Africans do choose divers snakes, and adders, and beasts, and birds, and herbs, and trees, and they make figures out of all these things graven in wood and in stone. Neither do they only content themselves with worshipping the said creatures when they are quick and alive, but also the very skins of them when they were dead, being stuffed with straw. I have heard that there are nations that carry a devotion to dragons with wings, which they nourish and feed in their own private houses, giving unto them for their food, the best and most costly viands that they had. Others keep serpents of horrible figures; some worship the greatest goats they could get; some, lions, and other most monstrous creatures: yea, the more uncouth and deformed the beasts are, the more they are honored.

I find it not easy to comprehend the holding in veneration of unclean fowls and night-birds, as bats, owls, and screech-owls, and the like, and to proclaim such things to be the incarnation of God Almighty: but yet I think I begin to understand their reasoning, which is, that God Almighty enters into all created things, even the most loathly, and to worship Him in His darker forms is nevertheless to worship Him. But this is hard for a Christian mind to encompass.

In the city of Mofarigosat, which was entirely pagan, the Gospel of Jesus never having yet come this far into the land, they did have holy houses for their *mokissos*, or idols, which the Portugals do call *feitissos* or fetishes. On their holy days, one of which befell very soon after my abandonment in that place, the people clothed themselves all in white, and were themselves smeared with white earth in token of purity. I saw them kill cocks and goats to offer to their *mokissos*, but as soon as it was killed, they tore the animal in pieces with their hands, and the owner had the smallest share of it, his friends and acquaintances falling on and every one seizing a piece. This they broiled and ate very greedily. They cleaned the guts into small bits, and, squeezing out the dung with their fingers, boiled them with other entrails, a little salt and the pepper known to the Portugals as *malagueta*, and ate it without washing off the blood, regarding it as most delicious food, and holy also.

They did solemnize their holy day in a wide open place, in the midst of which they erected a sort of table, or altar, about four feet square, supported by four pillars of clay, adorned with green boughs and leaves of reeds. This altar was set up at the foot of some tree, which is consecrated to their deities, and on it they did lay Guinea wheat, millet, and rice-ears, palm-wine, water, flesh, fish, beynonas, and other fruit, for the entertainment of their idols. I think they were persuaded that their gods do eat those things, though they daily saw them devoured by birds of prey.

A priest seated in a wooden chair before the altar made a discourse of many minutes, with some vehemence, in a secret language I did not understand. I suppose it is like the way Latin is preached by Popish priests before folk who understand only Spanish or German or such. The assembly were very attentive. The priest did sprinkle the faces of the congregation with liquor from a pot, and then they all began to sing and dance about the tree and altar, and play on their musical instruments, until the priest stood up and sprinkled the altar with the consecrated liquor. After which they all cried, *I-ou, I-ou,* which I took to mean "Amen," and they all went home.

I confess I was of two minds about these ceremonies, whether they were as evil as the worship of the golden calf against which Moses did inveigh, or whether they were only another form of honor to the true God of Heaven. For surely there is only one God, who made Papists and Protestants and pagans alike, and He does not refuse homage from any of His creatures, no matter how they choose to frame their phrases of devotion. I know this is blasphemy, for which I could be burned alive in any country of Europe, including, I am sure, my own. Yet do I say it freely here, since I am old and do not fear burning half so much as I fear hiding the truth of what I have felt and believed.

I saw the *mokisso* named Nkondi, like a man the size of a child, that protects against thieves. Mavena, a dog with slavering fangs, guards against seducers. Ntadi, a dwarfish monster with a human face, speaks in dreams to warn of danger. And there were others that brought fertility or prosperity or success in warfare or safety against sorcerers. The harvest and rainfall were in the command of Mbumba, a snake that was also a rainbow, and do not beg me to explain how a snake and a rainbow may be one.

Yet all these spirits were each a part of Nzambi Ampungu, which is the same as saying God Almighty, the supreme power. They do not worship Nzambi Ampungu directly, saying, he is too remote from human affairs, he is invisible and inaccessible, and cannot be rendered in the form of an idol to be worshipped. So they give their devotion in their hearts to Nzambi Ampungu, but say their special prayers and make their offerings to Ntadi or Nkondi or Mavena and such. Meseems that this is not immensely different from the Papist way of having one high god reigning far above, but making your prayers to Saint Mary or Saint Anthony or such, who do the real work of bringing favors to man. And perhaps that is why these pagans did take so easily to the Catholic faith that the Jesuits did bring unto them; but I think the Jesuits would not be greatly pleased, if they knew that their saints are only deemed new *mokissos* by the Africans.

I learned whatever I did about the faith of these people from a certain man-witch of Mofarigosat's tribe, whose name was Mboma. In the language of these parts *mboma* is the black python serpent, and *boma* is the word that means "fear," so this man-witch Mboma was of great power, and his name meant something like Lord of Fear. But he was not at all black: rather was he of the *ndundu* kind, what the Portugals call *albino*, with skin so fair it was fairer than an English maid's, skin more the color of paper than the color of skin, and hair of a fair kind also, though not anything like mine, being more white than golden, and eyes that were pink where a Negro's would be brown and mine are blue. This witch Mboma was a small man, very frail, who carried a sun-shade made of palm-fiber to protect himself against the scorching of the sun. And the people did seem frightened of him, and kept their distance. I recalled when I was at Loango in the beginning of my African life I did see one of these *ndundus* who seemed most fearsome, a veritable Hell-demon, and I was much disconcerted by his glares and threats; but this Mboma, for all his awesome name, did not frighten me at all. He came to me and touched me on the arm and along the beard and beckoned to me to stoop to let him touch my hair, which was beyond his reach. And he said to me, "*Mokisso, mokisso,*" which I think was his way of telling me, "You are protected by the gods," or maybe, "You are a holy man," I am not sure which.

I went about the city with this man and he did show me the shrines of the *mokissos* and let me observe their ceremonies, and told me some few things of the meaning of what I was seeing. He treated me thus out of respect for my white skin and my golden hair, which had throughout my time in Africa unfailingly brought me such special attentions.

This *ndundu*, who was a *nganga* or priest or man-witch as I say, came to me each day and tugged at my arm and took me about to some new festival. One such was the circumcision rite; for all these blackamoors do practice circumcision except the Christian ones of the coastal territories, that have forsworn it. They do this thing not for holy reasons, I think, as it is done among the Jews and Mussulmen, but to show virility:

a woman would not regard as fit for marriage any man who had his foreskin. Indeed foreskins are most strange to them, and often in my coupling with native women of the pagan tribes they would play with mine, rolling it back and forth like a toy, until I had perforce to remind them what business we were supposed to be performing with one another.

I did not take much joy in witnessing circumcisions. This was done upon boys of twelve years of age, who were smeared with white earth and did dance together a long while, looking most joyous and exalted, though I would think they should rather have looked frightened. Then they went into a dark house where they remained certain days with very hard diet; and when they came forth they were rubbed with a red earth, and animals were sacrificed, and the boys did dance about some more. The *ndundu* then spoke prayers, and the circumciser came forth, who was the blacksmith of the village, holding an iron sickle. The boys sat with their legs apart, and assistant circumcisers came up behind them and held them, and one by one the circumciser came to the novices, holding in his right hand the sickle, which was heated red-hot. With his left hand he did take each boy's yard and pull at the foreskin and quite suddenly cut it off, which made me turn my head away each time it was done. And each time I also felt a fiery impact on my own member, that made me flinch, as if by sympathy with the initiated boy.

God's wounds, what things we do to ourselves in the name of sanctity and piety!

The bleeding boys were given some potion to drink, and then older boys led them away to wash their wound, and there were other rites that I was not permitted to witness, which peradventure was no serious deprivation for me. The foreskins lastly were heaped up and taken off to the burial ground of the city and given interment with a high solemn rite. For my witch-friend did tell me that unless they were properly disposed of, they might become *zumbis*, that is, walking spirits, and return to bedevil the village.

I confess that I looked aside and did smother a laugh at those words, to think of ghosts in the form of foreskins. But later I thought it was not so foolish, to think a spirit might reconstruct itself out of a small part of a body, especially one that is removed with such a show of holy pomp. For if there are spirits at all, of which I am far from sure, why not have them emerge out of any merest scrap of humanity, and march *zumbi* thenceforth through all eternity?

The *ndundu* Mbomba did tell me something else on this subject of circumcision, that woke deep horror in me.

He said, "We cut only the boys. But I know that in the eastern lands, they do cut the girls as well."

I thought I did mishear him, and asked him to repeat, but he said it all again carefully in the same words.

To which I replied, "God's eyes, but what is there to cut on a girl?"

The white-skinned witch, by way of answer, did beckon to a girl of twelve or fourteen years who was passing by, and made her come to us, which she did in terrible palsy of terror at being summoned by such men as we. He took from her the little girdle of cloth that she wore, and bared her loins and parted her legs and the nether lips, only just mantled by the new hair, and showed me the pink hidden bud that is a woman's most secret place of pleasure.

"This is what they cut," he said.

"God's death! God's eyes! God's wounds!"

"It is not done in this land. But there are tribes that say it is unclean for women to have such things on them, or that it is the site of sorcery, or that it makes a woman unchaste if it is not cut off. They do use a kind of stinging nettle to make the organ swell so that it is large enough to be cut, except those tribes that use the cautery, where—"

"Enough," I said, and shuddered. "I will not hear more."

It was the only time, in my gathering of the lore of these foreign peoples amongst whom I was thrown, that ever I did order a halt to a narrative. I suppose I should have had the information from him, which perhaps no other man of Europe has ever heard; but I wanted it not. For all I could think of was the poor mutilated women, deprived of their pleasure-zone, and I gave thanks to my own God that He had not inflicted upon us any such custom, that seems to me far more barbarous than cannibalism itself. The life of a woman is sufficiently hard as it is, I think, without her having to give up that thing, too.

But the people of Mofarigosat were licentious by nature and did not practice such damage upon their women. For which I was grateful on those nights when I consoled myself for my fear and loneliness by taking those women to my couch. Their lovemaking was done in the style I was already familiar with, entailing much tickling and no kissing on the mouth or private parts, and in positions other than the familiar one of England. They greased their bodies with a grease not much to my joy, but it was not intolerable, and I took my will of them often enough, thinking a time might be drawing near when the vengeance of Mofarigosat might send me from this world, and wanting such comfort as I might have before then.

I learned some of the strange ways these women have of keeping from being taken with child. They believe that if they open three cuts in their thighs, and rub into them some of the blood of their monthly bleeding, they will be rendered sterile; but all they need do, to have their fertility again, is reopen the cuts and wash them in running water. Some also think that if semen be used in the place of the monthly blood, that will have the same effect. Others tie knots in a piece of string to guard against pregnancy, or put hen's eggs in their cunts after coupling, or catch a certain type of large white ant and insinuate it into the same place. As for arousing male desire, should that be necessary, they have a witchcraft of which I was told, that uses a he-goat's yard, the ballocks of a cock, and a root called *ngname*, that has the shape of the male member. Also do they make potions of salamanders and roaches, the hair of the genital zone, leaves dipped in semen, and the like things.

Another way I occupied myself during my captivity in the city of Mofarigosat was to observe their system of justice, which makes use of the trial by poison. Indeed this dreadful and deadly kind of trial is general throughout the region, but never had I seen or heard of it before, though in faith I was due for some heavy encounters with it afterward.

The way this is done is that when any man is suspected of any offense he is carried before Mofarigosat, or one of his ministers, who questions him on his guilt. And if it be upon matters that he denies, and cannot be proved but by oath, then the suspected person is given over to the *nganga*-priest whose special skill it is to administer the ordeal by poison. One of the ways this is carried out is with a root which they call *imbunda*, about the bigness of one's thumb, half a foot long, like a white carrot. This root is very strong and as bitter as gall, by my own knowledge from tasting it, and one root will serve to try one hundred.

The virtue of this root is, that if they put too much of it into water, the person that drinks it cannot void urine, and so it strikes up into the brain as though he were drunk, and he falls down, as though he were dead. Whereupon the people all cry out, "*Ndoki, ndoki,*" that is, "Sorcerer, sorcerer," and they knock him on the head and drag him away to hurl him over a cliff. But those who can make urine are found not guilty and set free.

In the like way they have another drug, *nkasa*, which comes from a certain red tree that is so noxious that the birds cannot endure even its shadow. When it is given to those who must take it, the *nganga* says, "If you are guilty of disturbing the peace or are a traitor, if you have committed such and such a crime, if you have stolen such and such a thing, if you have robbed and killed such and such a man, or if you have cast some spell or other, die from this *nkasa*. If you are innocent, vomit it forth and be free of all evil." The guilty man will discharge red urine profusely and run a few paces and fall down and die, and his body is denied holy burial. But those who are innocent puke up the drug, and their urine is unaffected, and they live.

I learned in my later life in Africa many other forms of trial by ordeal, such as the trial by hot iron and the trial by boiling water and the trial by snail-shells, or sea-shells. But I will tell of all these in their proper place.

I observed much else in my weeks in the city of Mofarigosat. One thing I witnessed was the making of the raised scars that are thought to be such a thing of beauty, by cutting the skin and inserting cinders underneath to inflame it, or by pressing certain plants into the incisions. They told me that certain scars had special meaning upon women, such as those along the thighs that are taken to say, "Squeeze me," and a circular scar on the buttock that has the meaning, "This is where a man holds me." But I learned only a little of these mysteries.

And also I saw the shame that comes upon the women when it is their bleeding time of the month, for they are thought unholy and dangerous then. Men have a deep fear of that blood and will on no account go anywhere near it, nor are the cattle of the tribe permitted to approach a woman who is in her menstruous time. They have a special house where those women go on the first two days, and there are no wells near it, nor plantations, nor pastures. Yet the blood of them is a powerful magic that they use in various rites, of which I know nothing.

Since I had naught to do but watch these things, I watched and absorbed a great deal. And I marveled much that each nation of Africa has its whole host of special customs, its myriad of tribal witchcrafts and spells and *mokissos* and philosophies, so many that it would take a thousand chroniclers a thousand lifetimes to record it all, and I think it be of high interest. Yet what will happen, if the Portugals have their way and turn all this land into Christian territory? And make everyone here wear Portugal clothes and talk the Portugal tongue and go to the Mass and forswear all their native habit? You might reply that this would be only for the good, to abolish the foul pagan way, and to some degree I would agree with that, since I see no merit in the trial by poison or the cutting of women's parts or the like. Yet when such things have disappeared wholly from the face of the earth, and everything is but the same everywhere, whether we be in London or Muscovy or Turkey or Angola, have we not lost a great deal of richness out of the world?

On all this did I ponder, while I waited for Diogo Pinto Dourado and his men to return and redeem me from my being pawned to Mofarigosat. And the days went by, which I counted by making little marks on the wood of a soft tree outside my cottage, and the tally mounted to twenty and forty and fifty and then to sixty, which was the expiration of the agreed-upon period. I was not so innocent that I expected the Portugals to return to me, but yet I was not so soured upon mankind that I would deny out of hand the possibility that they would.

And so I went on hoping and tallying and hoping and tallying. Mofarigosat, too, was keeping a tally; and as we came to the end of the second month there was a discernible change in their treatment of me, for I had no more women and no more wine and far more humble food. And the time ran out.

I will give Mofarigosat credit for this much, that he did allow four additional days of grace. But at the sixty-fourth day that was all the grace I could have, and some of the chief men of his court came to me at my cottage, and one said, "Your people have not kept their promise, and now will we cut off your head."

It seemed to me sure that I had misheard him. But I had not, for they took me straightaway to a place in the great plaza of the town where they punished their thieves and adulterers. Here there was a chopping-block, and to one side they did have the most grisly place that could be imagined, where many chopped-off hands and arms and legs were piled, and a goodly number of chopped-off heads, and old bones to be seen beneath this, and flies of a large size with gleaming green bodies buzzing around over everything. This charnel mound did speak to me of frequent and terrible punishments administered by the officers of Mofarigosat upon his people, and I understood the obedience of the citizens to him.

I looked toward that pile of human fragments and in my mind's eye I did see the golden-haired head of Andy Battell sitting high above all that sundered and withering black flesh, with the sun coming down from straight overhead and striking against my hair and beard with a wondrous radiance. And it was a vision not very much to my liking.

Yet did it seem certain I would end my life in this place within this hour. For though it was only an early time of the morning, with the mists and fogs of night still settling about the ground, a great throng did come forth and take up a place around the edges of this plaza. And the high nobility of the town had the closest place, nigh the chopping-block. I had me in mind that it must look much this way in London, at the Tower, when some great person of the realm is being parted from his head, and he stands alone by the block, and the Lord Chief Justice is there, and the Bishop of this place and that, and the Duke of this and the Earl of that, all at close range, where they can hear the sound of the axe and see the blood go flying.

And then there did come forth to me a colossal blackamoor, who must have had an elephanto for his grandsire, for he was an immensity of flesh and bone and muscle, a wall of a man; and he carried in one hand, the way you might carry a pike or a pigsticker, a sword of most ferocious size, five feet long or even greater. This blackamoor was naked except for a necklace of small bones at his collar and a chain of long lion-teeth at his waist, and his skin was oiled to a very high gloss. This was the executioner and you could see that he did relish his work, for he was smiling and singing under his breath and swinging his vast sword back and forth through the air to test the strength of his right arm.

I looked about me and said, "Ah, you would not kill me on this the holy day of my faith!"

I was minded to invent for them a fable: that this was a day of days, upon which no man was to be given to death, for his soul would be deprived of heaven if he perished that day, unless he performed certain rites that only a priest could do for him. But all this clever imagining of my fevered and frighted mind was futile, in that they paid no attention to what I said, but laid hold on me and in a trice stripped from me all my clothes, and I stood naked before that multitude.

Now, it is an awful thing to die by the headman's blade, but it is five times more awful to do it naked before hundreds of onlookers. Heigh-ho, and the onlookers themselves were just as naked, or the next thing to it; but they at least had their privities decently covered, and, besides, they were not the ones who were dying that day.

And there I stood with my yard and buttocks and everything exposed to the gaze of the curious, which robs a man of all dignity at the moment when he most needs his dignity, since he is about to lose all else. It is barbarism. King Henry, when he sent his queen Anne Boleyn to lose her head, did not also command that she be laid bare so that the gapers could behold her royal breasts and loins. Nor did he expose the equally royal belly and rump of Katherine Howard, his later queen, to the crowd when *she* went to the block. Or imagine Sir Thomas More naked on the scaffold, or Somerset, or Northumberland, or Norfolk! Nay, it is too much, to be revealed at the last before the mockers; but these savages took no account of it. I was sore afraid I would beshit myself in fear, or rouse their laughter with my urine, or, worse, have my yard stand tall at the last, as is said sometimes to happen to the dying, and there be no way to conceal any of these weaknesses of the flesh. I think I was more afraid of those shames than of dying itself.

Naked, then, and alone, and unshriven, did I march forward between two armed men to the chopping-place.

I looked about me.

"I beg you mercy," I said, "for I am a stranger in this land, and I was but left here as a pawn by my enemies, who hoped to see me brought to this pass. But I have done you no injury, as you all do know."

This brought me no response. Certain *ngangas* began an evil-sounding chanting and a making of music.

I said, having trouble finding my voice now, for my throat was dry as the sands of Egypt and my tongue was swollen with dismay, "Only give me five more days, and my companions will return, bringing you all you desire. But if you slay me, they will fall upon you and exact a terrible vengeance."

This waked only laughter in them, as well it might, since it was the direct opposite in sense from my previous plea.

And after that I said, knowing the time did grow desperate, "Let me pray, and make my peace with my Maker, before you smite me."

They indicated I might do that. But I could not find the words of prayer within my soul. I was not ready to die, and I had no summing-up yet to make to the Lord of my life and deeds, for I felt myself interrupted in mid-course. To death I had been no stranger, God wot, since coming to this land; but now that he was so close, now that I could view the very blade that would sever my neck and the very heap on which my head would be thrown, I could not speak the language of grace. So I stood still, in a praying guise, getting down on my knees, and in my head there was only a buzzing and a droning as of idle insects on the wind.

Seeing that it was useless, I rose again and stood slack, thinking that there was no delaying it further. Mofarigosat himself was arriving now, borne toward the executing-place on a high litter much ornamented with peacock feathers and the tails of leaopards. No doubt they had been waiting only for him, and would proceed with despatch to the grand event.

But then came another figure, on foot, much out of breath, making his way through the crowd with little sharp outcries that caused them all to move aside swiftly before him. This was the white-skinned red-eyed *ndundu* witch Mboma, my friend and tutor. He was flushed and wearied, as though he had run a long way, he who was so frail and feeble of body. They were already jostling me toward the chopping-block, which was a mere crude heavy log much nicked and sliced, and stained with old blood.

"Wait!" cried Mboma. "Let him be!"

The executioners paid no heed, but pushed me forward and bent me down, and the headsman grasped his weapon.

"I say wait!" cried the albino again, and added some words in the holy language, unknown to me.

Already was the great sword rising.

Mofarigosat leaned forward on his wickerwork throne. "What is this?" he said.

"Take not his life!" said Mboma.

The headsman looked toward Mofarigosat, as if to say, Let us ignore this interruption, O my lord, and continue with our morning's work. But Mofarigosat gestured, the smallest mere movement of his left hand, and in that trifling flick of his fingers did reprieve my life.

To Mboma he said again, "What is this?"

The man-witch approached his master Mofarigosat and answered, in his high reedy voice that scarce carried five yards, "He may not be slain, for his Portugals are coming, with many warriors and guns to aid us in our wars."

Mofarigosat said scowling, "Is this sure?"

"I have seen the truth of it in the rising smoke of my fire," declared the *ndundu*. "In six days will they be here."

There was muttering and grumbling among the chief lords, who had come to see me shortened that day, and would not have me set free. Mofarigosat and his witch carried on a brief colloquy that I could not hear, and then the chieftain gestured once again to the headsman, more broadly, signalling that I was saved.

I fell again to my knees. This time prayer did come to me, a flood of thanksgiving gratitude, and the dazzling light of the Almighty's mercy did shine upon my soul.

The giant headsman went slinking away disappointed, and the crowd, murmuring much, dispersed. With trembling hands I collected my clothes and covered my nakedness.

To Mboma I said, "I owe you my life."

To this he shrugged. "The message was in the images made in the smoke."

"Aye," said I. "But you could have misread it, or chosen to ignore it. And you did not." Then I laughed wildly, as one does when one is called unexpectedly back from certain doom, and said, "Friend Mboma, this is as near as I will ever come to a lordship, I think. For in my land only the high lords do lose their heads by the block, and all lesser men must die by the hanging or the burning, which is far worse, being slower. And this morning I thought sure I would die a nobleman's death. But I think I would sooner live a deckhand's life, and go on living, than perish grandly like an earl. Eh?" And I saluted him and took me back to my cottage, on legs that were so numb and shaking that it was like walking on two wooden stilts.

NINE

THE ORACLE of the man-witch's fire had spared me that morning. But I had less faith in that oracle than did these savages, and I resolved me to escape from Mofarigosat's town without further ado. Perhaps Pinto Dourado would indeed return for me six days hence, and yet I felt sure he would not: whereupon quite likely the headsman at last would have his way with me, Mboma or no Mboma.

So I spent that day in seclusion, thinking over the events of the morning and gradually casting aside my fright, which for some hours after my reprieve had still reverberated in my bones. It is no small thing to walk to the place of the chopping-block and stare at the edge of the blade, and the dread it inspires is not shrugged off in a moment. Moreover still I did think it might all be suddenly reversed, the blacks coming for me an hour hence, saying Mboma now claimed to be mistaken in his reading of the smoke message, and they would smite off my head. From time to time did I wriggle my neck to make certain it was still whole; and I imagined that blade descending and felt a peculiar choking in my Adam's apple, and it was some days before I was able to put that preoccupation behind me.

When night came and the fullest depth of darkness arrived, no moon being in the sky, I did arise and leaving my cottage I made my way quietly toward the edge of the town. I had with me my musket and shot and powder that Pinto Dourado had provided me with, for the blacks had not thought to take it from me, and a leathern flask of palm-wine, but nothing else.

The town was quiet. But as I went by one group of houses a dog sprang up and nipped and yipped at my heels, which aroused a watchman, a tall black warrior who came forward as if to block my way. I dared not take the time to parley, so I commended his soul to God and put my knife into his throat, and kept going.

Only one other man did I see as I left the town. But this was Mofarigosat, who was walking the boundaries on some dark inquiry of his soul. He did not spy me. He went head downward and hands locked behind his back, deep in thought, and I prayed that he would not glance my way, for then I should have to take his life also, and I did not greatly wish to do that. With all the stealth at my command did I glide behind a tree and wait there, peeping out from moment to moment as that chieftain proceeded to pace up and down, murmuring to himself. Once

I thought he was coming in my way, but then he turned, still deep in contemplation. What a noble figure he was, that rigorous old man, spending his sleepless hours in communion with his pagan gods! If God had cast his soul into a Christian body he would have been some prince for sure, or an archbishop.

Like a ghost he floated away from me, his black body becoming invisible in the night and only his white hair in view; then he was gone and I darted into the jungle.

Once more was I free.

But I was the only white man within fifty leagues, doubtless, and I had no slightest hope of finding my way alone through these wastelands and wildernesses to São Paulo de Loanda. Nor did I have much yearning to return to that place, except that there I would find the sweetness of my Matamba once again. But otherwise I had no hunger to see those Portugals: for a traitorous lot they all were, and I was done with their kind.

I intended now to go to the camp of the Jaqqas. Aye: the Jaqqas.

How far was I traveled, now, from that innocent young man who first had set to sea! That boy had held all kinds of fanciful notions of honor, and proper behavior, and rights and wrongs; and he had parted one by one from all those holdings, in his long education under the African stars. Now was he setting forth toward the most dreaded cannibal tribe of this land to give himself over freely to their service, and raising no questions of honor over it. For I did hope in God that in their diabolical marauding the Jaqqas would travel so far to the westward that we should see the sea again; and so I might escape to England by some ship, and holy grace. Only that thing mattered: quitting this accursed land, and homeward sailing. I would pillage, I would kill, I would if need be forswear myself thrice over, all for the sake of getting myself shipped out of this hellish Africa, where I had never desired to go, and where I had been detained against my will for close upon a dozen years now.

All that night I marched through the terrible darkness. I heard sounds I could not name and smelled smells of animals I could not see. Sometimes there was a loathsome snuffling sound, as of a great snout pressed close against the ground, and sometimes there was a craven sickly whining, followed by a growl and then a scream of pain from some other creature. I knew that skull-faced Death did pad along beside me on silent paws, and that he could have me at any instant did he choose. But he did not choose. I put great distance between myself and Mofarigosat before I would allow myself repose; then did I sink down on a moist mossy hummock and take some sleep, which came over me as if I had been drugged.

Two things at once awakened me. One was the coming of morning, sunlight very pale penetrating the green canopy of vines over my head; and the second was the creeping across my body of certain small round insects, bright red with black speckles, that did bite me most abundantly in every exposed place. Each bite was like the prick of a hot needle. I looked at them in amaze and saw the small creatures thrusting their sharp tubes into me, and sucking forth my substance; and with a howl I swept them away, but the tubes often remained in me most painful, and I had to pick them out with great diligence. Within moments each bite grew inflamed, and red swellings rose all over me, so that I looked like one who had taken a pox. But that was the worst that befell me from those vermin; and afterward an African told me that I might have died of it if they had stung me more copiously, for among the blacks the juice of these insects causes a dissolution of the flesh and bones, so that a man becomes a mere bag of vile liquid within his own skin some hours after being bitten. I do not know if this is so: it did not happen to me.

I breakfasted upon some glossy yellow fruits that looked to be safe, and proved sweet and tender. Then I found the River Kuvu, which was here shallow and brackish, with a few sickly-looking coccodrillos dozing on its bank, and I made my journey inland by following its course. The jungle was so deep overhead that I was hard put to see the direction of the sun, but in an opening I spied the mountains of the eastern land ahead of me, and thereafter I kept close by the river, knowing it would take me in the direction that the Jaqqas had gone.

By afternoon I met two Negroes, not of Mofarigosat's nation, that gaped in wonder at me, for in this place there was never any white man seen before me. These two were sore affrighted and stood like statues in their tracks, but I put them at ease and asked if they had seen the Jaqqas, and they said, "Yes, they are in the town of the lord Cashil," and showed me the way. Then they gave me some meat they were eating, which was a roasted monkey, and I gave them five beads that I found in my pocket, and we went our separate ways.

The meat did afford me strength, and I pressed onward through very close heat that made my body stream with sweat, until I came to footpaths that were well trampled, and I knew the town of Cashil must not be far beyond. Outside it I found a tree with a great hollow, where bees were flying, and boys came and drove the bees off with smoking torches, and helped themselves to the honey. And they gave me some without asking me what I was or from whence I came, but their hands were shaking, and I am sure they thought me to be a *mokisso* visiting out of the spirit-world. The honey was passing sweet, far finer than any of England.

Then did I enter Cashil's town, where all the people, great and small, came to marvel at my whiteness of skin and at my hair, the like of which was a great mystery to them. Here among the Negroes of the place were some of the Imbe-Jaqqa's lieutenants, who were abiding peacefully in Cashil, for the Jaqqas do not always destroy the lands they enter. I was right glad to see them.

This town of the lord Cashil was very great, and is so overgrown with ollicondi trees, cedars, and palms, that the streets were darkened with them. The streets of this town were paled with palm-canes, very orderly. Their houses were round like a hive, and, within, hanged with fine mats curiously wrought. In the middle of the town there was an image, which was somewhat in the shape of a man, but strange, with tusks and great staring eyes, and stood twelve feet high; and at the foot of the image there was a circle of elephanto teeth, pitched into the ground. Fastened to these teeth were great store of dead men's skulls, which were killed in the wars, and offered to this image. I saw them pour palm oil at his feet for an offering, and pour their blood at his feet also. This image is called Quesango, and the people have great belief in him, and swear by him; and do believe when they are sick that Quesango is offended with them. In many places of the town were little *mokisso* images, and over them great store of elephanto teeth piled. On the southeast end of the town was a most fanciful *mokisso* in scarlet and gold paint that had more than three tons of elephanto teeth piled over him, that would be worth a princely ransom if taken to be carved into ivory pieces.

In this dark and cool place the Jaqqa lieutenants came to me, for they knew me as the golden-haired man from that other time by the shore. They spoke with me, using both their own language and the Kikongo tongue, so that I learned deeper into the Jaqqa sort of speech. When they asked of me why I was here, I said that I had been left by my own people and had been captive of Mofarigosat, and now was faring into the dark wilderness to find the Imbe-Jaqqa and give myself into his care. To which they replied that the Imbe-Jaqqa was in the town of Calicansamba, which lay two days' journey further into the country.

"And will you take me to him?" I asked.

"That we will," said the Jaqqas, and grinned their gappy grins at me, and slapped my shoulders as though I were some old comrade of theirs, that they were greatly joyed in seeing again.

But first there was feasting at Cashil and much drinking of the palm-wine: for the lord of the place, seeing me favored by the Jaqqas, was most earnest to show his favor to me, too. That is, they stand in such fear of the man-eaters that they will spoil themselves of half their goods, to make a brave show of hospitality for them, and oftimes afterward the Jaqqas will despoil them of the other half anyway.

I saw here what I had never seen before, how the palm-wine is procured. These palm-trees in which it is harbored are six or seven fathoms high, and have no leaves but in the top. There is a way the natives have of climbing the trees swift as monkeys, by wrapping a cloth about the stem and pulling on it with their hands while pushing against the wood with their bare feet, and when they get to the top of the tree they do cut a hole, and press a bottle into the place that is cut, and draw the wine into the bottle. This is a fluid of a somewhat milky look, that they set aside a few days for greater richness, and then it becomes sweet and powerful, so that it makes the head spin from the drinking of it. This wine they drink cold, and it moves one to urine very much: so that in those countries where it is favored, there is not a man that is troubled with gravel or stone in the bladder. Thus are they spared one of the most evil of torments. The wine will make them drunk, that drink too much of it; but indeed it is of a very good nutriment. After a time it turns sour, and becomes very vinegar, fit to serve for salads.

The Jaqqas love the palm-wine more than any other beverage, and drink a great muchness of it. But their way of producing it is altogether different from that of the village folk. For the Jaqqas, being a tribe of wanderers, keep no long-time plantations of the wine-palm trees. Instead do they go into a land where groves of palms abound, and cut the palm-trees down by the root. The tree must lie ten days before it will give wine. And then the Jaqqas do make a square hole in the top and heart of the tree, and take out of the hole every morning a quart, and at night a quart. So that every felled tree giveth two quarts of wine a day for the space of six and twenty days, and then it drieth up. When they settle themselves in any country, they cut down as many palms as will serve them wine for a month: and then as many more, so that in a little time they spoil the country.

I saw this done in the town of the lord Cashil. The Jaqqas went into the plantation, which was already well destroyed, and cut themselves down five of the finest trees for their future delectation. Some of the men of Cashil stood by as this was being done, and they looked sorely sad to see this, but they dared not speak out, lest they provoke the Jaqqas and bring about the general destruction of their town.

The Jaqqas stay no longer in a place than it will afford them maintenance. And then in harvest-time they arise, and settle themselves in the fruitfullest place they can find; and do reap their enemy's corn, and take their cattle. For they will not sow, nor plant, nor bring up any cattle, other than they take by making of war.

So I remained in this town some days. Which I did not like, for it is a place close by the country of Mofarigosat, and I feared he might be sending messengers in search of me, since that I had killed one of his watchmen and escaped his custody. But I could not hurry the Jaqqas to take me to Imbe Calandola. It is plain that only a fool will hurry a Jaqqa. For even a friendly one, and the ones in the town of the lord Cashil were friendly in the extreme, will turn savage and snarling if he is offended, and he will growl and strike out with his hand or his knife. I have seen this. They are a fearsome folk, and will kill for a trifle. So I abided in the town of Cashil and showed no impatience. And sure enough, five men of the country of Mofarigosat did come to the place, and ask if any white-skinned demon with golden hair had come this way.

"Nay," said the men of Cashil, "we saw no such," while all the while I did remain out of sight.

"We know he is here, and we want him, for he has given offense to our master."

"He is not here," said the men of Cashil. But there was less firmness in their voices, and in my place of hiding I felt the sweat rolling down my skin.

The men of Mofarigosat did say, "He has slain a prince of our city, and he has broken his pledge to our master. We have put to death a false *ndundu* who lied so that the white man's life would be spared. And now we must slay the white man also, so that the *zumbi* of our *ndundu* does not come to us and harm us."

At this talk of *zumbis* and *ndundus* the men of Cashil showed great fear, and conferred among themselves, and I think were making themselves ready to sell me to Mofarigosat. But the Jaqqas of the town, hearing what was taking place, did go to the emissaries and say loudly, "Begone, fools, or we will slit off your skins and tie them around pigs, and send you back to your master in the guise of the beasts that you are."

"We demand—" said one of the men of Mofarigosat, and then he said no more, for the Jaqqas slew him that instant, and the others turned and fled. I was summoned from my hiding place so that the Jaqqas might tell me all that had befallen. Very cool and easy did they seem about the murder they had done.

"And will not Mofarigosat make war upon us now?" I asked.

"Nay," replied the Jaqqas, "for he fears the Imbe-Jaqqa, and does not want you that much. But we will leave this place tomorrow, and take you to the Imbe-Jaqqa."

That night the Jaqqas boiled the man of Mofarigosat in a great metal tub that they had with them, and threw in spices and savories of many kinds, to make a soup in which morsels of flesh did float. The people of Cashil watched this festival from afar, looking most gloomy over it, for man-eating was not to their liking, and this was going on in the center of their own town. When the meat was ready the Jaqqas did carouse with great gulpings of the palm-wine, and called to me, saying, "Ho, white one, dine with us, it is tender flesh!"

I said a nay to that, claiming an illness of the stomach that would not let me eat meat just then. The which gave them no offense, and they took their bellies' fill of their awful delicacy without me. And afterward they lay about the plaza very satisfied, sleeping that light Jaqqa sleep which is almost no sleep at all.

In the morning they brought me onward to the camp of Imbe Calandola at the town of Calicansamba.

This way passed through a grove of giant ollicondi trees, the biggest I had yet seen, that darkened the air with the spread of their leaves. This tree is one of the marvels of Angola, very tall and exceeding great, some of them as big around as twelve men can fathom, all bloated and distended of trunk, and of limb. Some of them are hollow, and from the liberal skies receive such plenty of water at the time of the rainy season, that they are hospitable entertainers of thousands in the hard thirsty months that follow. I have seen whole villages of three or four thousand souls remain at one of these trees for four and twenty hours, receiving watery provision from it, and yet not empty it. I think some one tree can hold forty tuns of water. Also do they have in them great store of honey, for this is the favored tree of the bees here, and as I have said the blacks do drive the bees off by smoke, rewarding the laborious creatures with robbery, exile, death, and stealing their produce. To get the honey the Negroes climb up with pegs of hardwood, which the softer wood of the ollicondi easily receives.

When we passed through this forest of mysterious tree-monsters, which are like unto whales that have taken root in the ground—albeit whales with gnarled arms and myriad little leaves—we entered into the town of Calicansamba.

The great Jaqqa had made his camp here for some months, and all the place was greatly despoiled by his triumphing, drinking, dancing, and banqueting. The native folk of Calicansamba did stand about like sad ghosts, helpless to resist the Jaqqas and forced to give them all that they desired: the Jaqqas being like a plague of locusts that had come this way to help themselves to cattle, corn, wine, and oil, not to mention the flesh of human beings. The town was full of them. I think there were more Jaqqas here than villagers, the difference between them being readily apparent, for the Jaqqas had their skins ornamented differently, and did practice the knocking out of front teeth, and wore scarce any clothing, but mainly just beads and shells. And also the Jaqqas did comport themselves with terrible pride, like grand swaggering masters, even the humblest of them who still wore the slave-collar of boyhood about his neck. Whereas the Calicansamba people had been utterly defeated without striking a blow, and their manhood was altogether humbled, and they went with drooping shoulders and dim eyes, the look of conquered folk.

The town of Calicansamba was very like the one of Cashil, except that nearly all its palm-wine trees were cut down, save only one grove at the eastern end of the place. It too had a great idol in the center of the town and many elephanto tusks thrust into the earth in front of it. And here also was an altar of human skulls, very grisly indeed, and making me think how close I had come to leaving my own skull for Mofarigosat's pleasure.

But also in the great square of Calicansamba were certain things that I had not seen in Cashil, for they were things of the Jaqqas. Lined up all in a row were three gigantic metal tubs, which I knew to be their cooking-pots. To one side of these was a great vat made of woven fiber very tightly drawn, and smeared on the inner side with a sort of dark wax. It contained some several hogsheads' full of a thick purple fluid, and when I asked what that was, the Jaqqas who were my guides did dip their hands merrily in it and anoint themselves with streaming runlets of it, and laugh, and say, "It is blood, that we save for our feasts."

I did not ask, nor did I need to be told, what sort of blood that blood might be.

And on the other side of the three tubs was another such wickerwork basket, the contents of which were even more repelling, for it was a kind of soft pale blubbery stuff that did make my stomach heave and churn to behold it, a great store of fat that had been carved from thighs and breasts and bellies and buttocks, and I turned away, gagging, holding my gut in distress.

"It is the Imbe-Jaqqa's own supply," they told me, "but we have so much in this town that he shares it freely."

Aye! Such was his generosity, this grand Calandola, that he did let others of his nation besmear himself with the fat of fallen foes that made his own skin so glossy, and they deemed it a rare privilege.

And these were my hosts. And these were the beings to whom I had fled for safety, because I had found my own Christian kind to be too traitorous toward me. Aye, in such a way do we choose our friends and allies, in this bleak and sorrowful world, as we make our path through the pitfalls and turmoil of life toward the joyous reward that lieth at the end.

TEN

NEVER HAD most of these Jaqqas seen a white man before, and the amazement that I caused among them was tenfold greater than I had ever previously created. They circled round and round me with their eyes wide and their mouths agape, and they pointed, and muttered, and jostled each other and said things, and came close, and rubbed my skin and my hair, and made strange soft cries deep in their throats, like the sound of no other man nor beast on this earth. So many of them came to view me upon my arrival in Calicansamba, that I thought I might be crushed in the frenzy. They snuffled and snorted and pressed in, murmuring, "Skin is white, hair is gold.... Skin is *white*, hair is *gold*.... Skin is WHITE, hair is GOLD.... O Calandola! O Sumba-Jaqqa! O Kalunga! Skin is *white!* Hair is *gold!*" And many more such outcries, and a howling like that of tormented spirits, and a dancing on the round part of their heels, with their arms thrust upward stiffly as though they were joined on wires to the sky.

This frightened me greatly. But I stood my ground, smiling at them and nodding and bowing slightly, and accepting their curiosity for all the world like the Pope of Rome accepting the homage of a tremendous multitude of Papists, or like a king greeting subjects crazed with awe. But my hand was close upon my musket, and I resolved to fire off some loud shots into the air if the crowding of them seemed to grow more perilous to me.

They were all of them oiled with loathsome greases, whether the fat of animals or of men I could not tell, and they were painted and bejewelled, and their mouths, that did gape so wide at me, were missing all of them two top teeth and the two bottom, that is such a mark of beauty among them. I felt myself at the center of a great whirlpool of strangeness, that might be sweeping me downward and downward to the far circles of Hell. It was as if in all my time in Africa I had been pulled through jungles and deserts and swamps and rivers toward this place and this time and these people, the wild man-eaters whose prince the Imbe-Jaqqa was surely of the substance and being of the Lord of Darkness. And now here I was, my weird destiny fulfilled.

As this dance proceeded there came a sudden sharp outcry from the rim of the circle, and it widened and fell apart entirely, admitting a

Jaqqa of great height and poise. I recognized him after a moment to be Kinguri, the brother to Calandola. He embraced me as though I had been his brother also, and bade me be welcome at their camp. When he spoke everyone else fell silent, so that there was a great hush, against which we could make out every sound of the forest that lay close beside the town.

Kinguri said, "What is your purpose, white one?"

"To live among you."

"Ah, and will you be a Jaqqa?"

"I will no longer be a Portugal," said I. "For they have given me only pain, and loaded many treasons upon me, and now I make them my enemy."

"Then our enemy is your enemy also, which makes us kin," Kinguri said. "For we do purpose to bring deep grief upon the Portugals your enemy, and we will place you beside ourselves when we undertake that thing. How are you called?"

"Andrew Battell is my name."

"Andubatil," said Kinguri.

I thought to correct him. But then I smiled, and told myself nay, for that I was beginning a new chapter of my life in this sultry forest, or indeed a new life altogether, and I could readily take on a new name here in the same bargain.

"Aye," I did answer most ringingly. "Andubatil am I!"

"Come to the Imbe-Jaqqa," he said.

Thereupon was I conveyed to the dwelling-place of the Jaqqas in a far part of the town. For they had built a habitation of their own alongside the settled place of Calicansamba, opening into it, so that they could go freely from the Jaqqa town to the village-folks' town. It is the custom of the Jaqqas, wheresoever they pitch their camp, although they stay but one night in a place, to build a strong fort around their resting-place, with such wood or trees as the place yieldeth. So when they arrive at a place, the one part of them cuts down trees and boughs, and the other part carries them, and builds a round circle with twelve gates. Each of these gates is in the charge of one of the captains of the Jaqqas, being twelve in number, and all of them pledged forever to loyalty to their prince and general Imbe Calandola. In the middle of the fort they place Calandola's house, which is severely entrenched about, and fortified by a triple hedge of thorns.

So was it done here. I think it would have been a valiant army indeed that could have thrust itself to the inner sanctuary of the Imbe-Jaqqa.

At the lone entrance to Calandola's place there were warriors in double rows, well armed and very frightful of size and strength. Though these were eager to look upon me and touch me, they held their positions as I went past them. To the innermost place I came, where great sharpened stakes were thrust into the ground, that had points at both ends, and embedded in the tops of each stake were lopped-off arms and legs, withering and shriveling and parching in the heat, with whitened bones showing upon their nether sides. And each of these was of an enemy, and displayed here like a banner of triumph. And beyond this stark palisado was Imbe Calandola, in the midst of all his household people, his lieutenants and his man-witches and his wives, to the number of twenty or thirty, for I do think all those women were his wives.

Even though this was the second time I had laid eyes on him, I felt the same shivering surprise and astound that I had felt the first, so overwhelming was his presence.

He was dressed as before, in a strip of palm-cloth about the middle, though this was bright yellow now, and not scarlet; and he had the shells knotted in his hair and the copper pieces thrust through his ears and nose and the beads about his waist, and the painted ornaments on his shining skin. He sat in a kind of saddle half as high as a man, that rose on three legs of some very fine jet-black wood that looked almost like stone. In his hand he held a cup brimming with palm-wine, the which cup had been fashioned most artfully from the top part of a human skull.

When I entered, the Imbe-Jaqqa nodded very calmly to me and plunged his face into the bowl, taking so deep a draught of the wine that I thought he would drain it all at a gulp. When he lifted his head he was dripping with it, and it ran down his cheeks and jowls, like the slaver that runneth down the face of a wolf when it has bitten deep.

Kinguri said, "This is Andubatil."

"Andubatil, welcome." The voice of Calandola was like the growling of a bear. "Drink, Andubatil!"

To me he handed the cup, which still held some half its wine. I took it as he had, with the weight of it against both my hands and the smoothness of bone to feel, and I put my lips to it. The beverage was even more sweet than other palm-wine I had tasted, as if honey had been put into it. But it was not honey, as I understood after a moment. For the wine had a red tinge of hue, and I realized what substance it was that had been mixed in it to give that color. And I did shiver, though I strived hard to hide it. Aye! The muzzle of a wolf, lifted bloodied to bay the moon!

Kinguri said, "Does the wine please you?"

"That it does."

"It is the royal wine, that only the Imbe-Jaqqa may drink. You have a great honor upon you."

"I am grateful," said I to Kinguri, who repeated my words to Calandola. At that time I knew just a scattering of Jaqqa words and Calandola did not deign to speak Kikongo, nor did he comprehend Portuguese.

Calandola smiled his frightful smile, all coccodrillo-teeth of a great sharpness and evil length, except where the four were missing and made holes black as jet. He stared me as he had stared me before, deep as a blade into my soul.

"Drink, Andubatil," said he again.

I did not hesitate.

Let them mix blood with my wine, I would drink all the same, and drink me deep, and feel flattered by the great honor. Ah, I thought, I have done the Papists one better! For they drink wine and pretend it is blood, while I drink blood encumbered in my wine and pretend it is mere wine! Yet something in my gut did recoil at it, or perhaps it was in my mind and not my gut, and on the second draught I felt myself on the verge of retching, which would have been a deadly insult. God be thanked, I did find means to control that movement, and put the nausea wholly away from me, and smiled, and drank again, lightly but with great show of willingness and pleasure, and handed the wine-skull back to Calandola.

He clapped one great hand against the heavy muscle of his arm, which was his way of showing approval.

Then he said, "What is your nation, Andubatil?"

"English, O Lord Imbe-Jaqqa."

"Angleez?"

"Aye, Imbe-Jaqqa."

Kinguri said, "What nation is that?"

"Of an island," I replied, "far away in the western sea." I waited to see if the Imbe-Jaqqa's brother had understood that, which seemed to be the case, and I went on, "Where the people are as fair-haired as I am, and do stand tall and square, and go to sea and travel far, with the finest of courage. And where our ruler is a great prince who is also a woman, and a virgin, and the finest master that Heaven ever did send our people."

It was a long speech and in my joy at talking of England I let it all come rolling out at once, and I thought for sure Kinguri had become lost in it. But he had not, Kinguri being a man of extraordinary sharpness of sense. He repeated all that I had said to Imbe Calandola, who leaned forward, listening with great intentness, and twice taking great noisy draughts of his wine. I could follow most of Kinguri's words, and I saw that when he arrived at the part about our prince being a woman, the

Imbe-Jaqqa did sit up straight with his eyes bright and wide, and when Kinguri said that she was a virgin, Calandola did slap his leg with amaze, and made a loud snorting sound like that of a river-hippopotamus.

There followed a lengthy colloquy between Calandola and his brother, scarce a word of which I could comprehend, so fast did the Imbe-Jaqqa tumble forth his words. But he did also a pantomiming with his hands, thrusting one finger back and forth between two of the other hand in the unmistakable manner of a male member being thrust into a woman's hole, and I knew they must be discussing the virginity of Her Majesty.

Then Kinguri turned to me and said, "My brother asks, is this Queen of yours a woman?"

"Aye, that is what all queens are."

"And she rules by proper right in your land?"

"That she does, for her father was Great Harry our king, the eighth of that name. And she is Queen and her sister was Queen before her, and also her brother, who did die a young man."

"And your Queen-woman, she has never known what it is to lie with a man?"

I smiled. "That is the report that is widely given out, and we call her the Virgin Queen, and it would be a blasphemy to argue against its truth. Besides, I think it is so."

Kinguri, shaking his head, did say, "And the people of your land easily accept her, and she has always reigned in peace with her subjects?"

"Aye."

"And if a man came to her, and said, Queen, I would fain lie with you, open yourself to me, what then?"

"Why, she would strike his insolent head from him, if he spoke with her like that!" I then added, "There are those who assert that in her youth the Lord High Admiral Seymour did trifle lewdly with her, and that later she was had by the Earl of Leicester, and still later by Sir Walter Ralegh also. But I do believe these are but scandals and slanders, and that she is a true maiden to this day, and I would wager my head on it."

"A virgin queen," said Kinguri in wonderment, and Imbe Calandola did say the same words, wondering also. But neither of them would give me the lie, for I suppose they thought that a land where men had white skins and long golden hair could well also have women for its princes, and virgin ones at that.

Calandola said, "I will send you to England, Andubatil, and you will tell your Queen to come here to me. Will you do that? You tell her, Imbe Calandola offers her *this*."

And he did move his yellow garment aside, to reveal a black yard

that was as thick as the trunk of an elephanto, though not quite so
lengthy, and two great heavy ballocks like dark round apples. At the
sight of this formidable virile equipment several of his wives did clap
their hands and laugh in delight or approval, and Calandola seized those
women amiably by the flesh of their hinder parts, and hugged them
against himself, and looked vastly amused by this jape.

I said, when his roaring laughter had subsided some, "By all that is
holy, Lord Jaqqa, you have but to send me to England, and I will deliver
her your message, that I vow!"

"And will she come?" asked Calandola, when that Kinguri had explained the meaning of my words to him.

"That I cannot say, for she is a prince, and I cannot command her,
nor can any man. But I will ask her: that I do pledge."

"Good. Good. How far does England be from here?"

"Many days' journey, Lord Jaqqa."

"Farther than the land of Kongo?"

"Ten times as far," I said. "Twenty times, perhaps."

Calandola said to several of his man-witches, "We will go to England
some day, and drink of its wines. Eh? Eh? And spurt our fiery seed into
the belly of its Queen." And he did laugh and slap his arm, and called
for more wine, his cup being empty. One of his wives supplied him,
and he took his fill, putting back his head and letting the bloody sweet
stuff roll down his chin. His last draught he did hold in his mouth for
a time, and then spew it forth upon the earth around him in a wide
spitting spray. Which seemed merely vile, but was, I learned later, a
holy deed, a consecration of the soil by the Jaqqa way.

When he was done with that he signalled to me in a sweeping fashion,
waving his hand back and forth, but I did not catch his meaning.

Kinguri said, "Take your clothes off from your body."

"Shall I?"

"The Imbe-Jaqqa wonders if you be white all over."

"Aye, that I am," I said, making no move to disrobe.

"He would see it," said Kinguri.

"And would he?"

"Come, no more delay. He would see it!"

There was no refusing, I saw, and so I removed my clothes, which
were half in tatters anyway, and stood naked before this crowd of Jaqqa
warriors and witches and princes and the Imbe-Jaqqa and his many
wives. Well, and my body is a good and a healthy one, and I have no
shame of it; and to be naked here was less distressing than the other
time in Mofarigosat's town, where I was expecting the headsman's mortal
blow and did not welcome being shamed besides. All the same, it is no

trifle to be revealed in front of strangers, even savages, and it was with discomfort that I exposed my private places. It was all the worse for me that Calandola had so lately laid bare his giant member and swollen ballocks: for compared by those I would seem most insufficiently male, though no woman has ever found me so.

Calandola rose and came to me and did put his finger to my flesh here and there, pressing into it at belly and thigh to watch the way the color of it changed at his pressure. That seemed a marvel to him, and he did press at his own flesh in the same places to observe it. Then he tugged at the hair on my chest, he being perfectly smooth and sleek there, and he turned me about, I suppose to see if I were white on the other side, too, and he turned me back again. He had me open my mouth, where I had all the teeth God meant me to own, and he did touch those four front teeth that Jaqqas do knock from their heads. When he gripped my teeth I feared he meant to pull those teeth from me right there, with a twist of his mighty fingers, and the thought gave me a sickly tremor from my gut to my ballocks. But I showed no outer sign of my apprehensions. And great was my relief when at last he took his hands from my mouth.

Then the Imbe-Jaqqa moved his close inspection of me downward a distance, and did take my yard in his hand, as coolly as though he were lifting a cup or a piece of fruit, and remarked on it to his brother. I knew not what he said. But being so idly handled of the *membrum virile* and so intimately discussed brought a blaze of hot color to my face: and that bright reddening so amazed Calandola that he let go my member and touched my cheek, to see, I suppose, how I had managed that trick of changing colors.

Kinguri said, "The Imbe-Jaqqa wonders if all the men of England have yards like yours, Andubatil."

A little angrily I replied, "I think that they do, though in sooth I do not spend much time examining them. I venture that some are larger and some are smaller, but mine is quite the usual kind."

"We do not mean the size," said Kinguri, "but the shape."

I did not at first comprehend the sense of his words. So he gestured, and the men of the court did push aside their loin-cloths and blithely bare their members, and lo! every man of them was circumcised.

"Aye," I said. "I understand now. We are not like you in that way, nor are any white men, except only the Jews. We have a few Jews living in our land, though they are supposed to be banned. But the rest of us do not cut our foreskins off."

"Why is that?" asked Calandola, when he had heard my answer.

"Why," I said, "it is not our way to do so. Under the Christian law that we obey, we leave that part untouched."

"But then you are not men!" said Calandola.

"It does not seem that way to us."

"A man must have that part removed. For it is a female part, and all that is female in him must be cut away, when he enters into a man's estate."

I did not propose to dispute this point with the Imbe-Jaqqa, it being a new philosophy to me, and difficult.

"The Bakongo people of the coast," I said, "leave themselves uncircumcised, now that they are Christian."

"And their men are mere women," said Calandola. "Is it not obvious?" Deeply did he frown. "Your prince is a woman who will not admit a man to lie between her legs, and your men will not remove the female piece from their members. So there can be no children born among you."

"I assure you that that is not the case."

"But if your Queen—" He broke off, mystified.

"She is the only chaste woman of our realm," I said, which was not precisely the proper meaning I meant, but it sufficed. "And as for the men, we are quite able to perform our deeds of manhood as we are, which is as we came into the world, which is as God our Maker did intend."

I thought the Imbe-Jaqqa was angered at that. Perhaps he took God to be his direct rival, and cared not to hear His name. But his anger, if such it was, quickly passed, and he pointed again at my uncircumcised yard and said, "In this land you should be as we are. We will make you now as we are."

Which struck me deep with a fear that softened my bones. For I mistook the import of his words, being still mostly unfamiliar with the subtleties of the Jaqqa tongue, and thought that he was commanding me to undergo a circumcision on the spot. Whereas he was merely making a friendly offer, or perhaps it was a jest: I am not sure. He did beckon to one of his witches, who drew from a sheath a lengthy knife of commendable sharpness. I shrank back from him and put my hands over my private parts, which had shriveled to the size of a child's in my terror. Covering myself in that way brought a hearty laugh from the women.

I said miserably, "By your leave, great Lord Jaqqa—"

"Come, Andubatil, we will not cut it all off! Only that one part!" he said, laughing.

"I may not, O Imbe-Jaqqa."

"And why is that?"

"It is forbidden among my nation to undergo such a surgery, for that would make me a Jew, which was a slayer of our God."

"Your god is dead?" asked Kinguri quickly, with show of deep interest and surprise.

"Aye, He was killed, but then He rose again—"

"How say you?"

Glad of the diversion of the talk away from the condition of my foreskin, I responded, half babbling my words, "When He came down to earth in human guise to save us, He was taken by enemies and nailed upon a cross, and a spear thrust deep into His side also, and so He perished, who was the Son of God and the Redeemer, but then as was prophesied He arose from the dead—"

"The son of god? But you said it was the god that died!"

"The Son is equal unto God," I answered, "for He is one Person of the Holy Trinity, which be God the Father, God the Son, and God the Holy Spirit." Kinguri's eyes showed me his mystification, and upon my soul I could not have given him much true enlightenment of these matters had he pressed me concerning them. But I hurried on, saying, "On the third day afterward of His crucifixion He did arise from the dead, and go to sit on the right hand of the Father—"

"And who was his mother?" Kinguri demanded.

"He was born of a virgin, Mary by name—"

"The Queen of your land, then, is the mother of your god?"

"A different virgin," said I, "a long time ago, and not in the same country from which I come."

"But a virgin also, was she? What color was her skin?"

"Why, like mine."

"No darker?"

"We do not hold it to be the case that she was dark."

"And the god, he is white also?"

"We do not think of Him as having a color, or a size, or any of the attributes of mortal flesh."

"But he can die? Is that not an attribute of mortal flesh?"

"It was His son that died," said I, beginning to think it might have been easier to submit to circumcision than to have to explain these complex and cloudy matters to the cannibal prince.

"Ah," said Kinguri. "And why did he let himself be killed, if he was a god and the son of a god?"

"To redeem us from the sin that came upon us in the original paradise, when our first father and our first mother did wantonly eat of the Tree of Knowledge, and thereby brought wickedness and death into the world, that had been created free of it."

Looking most pensive and perplexed, Kinguri held up a hand to shut off my flow of doctrine. "Let me understand these things. Your god, who was his own son by a virgin mother, did come to the world to save you from death, which had come upon you when—"

At that Calandola did break roughly in, demanding, "What are all these words?"

Kinguri turned to him, and again the two engaged in lengthy talk, this time on the mysteries of the Christian faith as I had begun to expound them. How much sense they could make of it all, I know not; but the essence of the thing is that they grew so interested in these fine holy niceties that the question of my circumcision slipped away from the Imbe-Jaqqa's mind for a time, and the man-witch did put away his blade, and when Calandola returned his attention to me he had lost interest in my foreskin. Which is just as well for me, I having little need of that part of my body but yet no wish at all to see it severed from me by a pagan savage, and I being somewhat past the age when any such surgery is agreeable.

The Imbe-Jaqqa now proceeded to question me on how I had come to this part of the country, he having last seen me on the coast with the Portugals. I explained how I had been pawned to Mofarigosat and falsely abandoned there by Pinto Dourado, and told of my narrow escape from the block, and of my flight into the forest. This interested Calandola greatly.

During this conversing I grew much wearied of standing with my privities exposed, so I begged permission to put on my clothes once again; but Calandola, saying, "Those are no fit garments," ordered Jaqqa raiment to be brought for me. Several women came forth, and drew from a wooden chest a handsome piece of green palm-cloth that they wrapped about my loins, and then Kinguri took from his own waist a string of bright beads, and one of the witches gave me a collar of shells polished very smooth. I felt at first in this stuff that I was costumed for the masquerado, playing the part of a wild jungle-man, but it was with amazing ease that within the hour I came to feel comfort in such garb, as though I had worn it all my life. My worn and frayed old clothes they took from me and I never saw those things again.

"A feast!" Calandola now did cry. "Make ready a feast, for the English Andubatil!"

These words, which I understood full clear, did strike me with horror deeper than any other. For they brought me face to face with something I had attempted not to consider, since first I had resolved to give myself over to these man-eaters, and that was their choice of favored meat. Oft do we put out of our minds that which we have no stomach to contemplate; and in this case was it most literally the truth that I had no stomach for it. But the moment was coming when needs I must deal with it. I had taken refuge among the Jaqqas; they had clothed me as one of their own; they were mounting a grand feast in my honor.

Could I then refuse their hospitality?

Politely had I declined circumcision, by the claim that it was a matter of religious belief not to give myself over to it. Well, and I had kept my foreskin, though at the time I still was not sure I would be excused from the surgery altogether. But how, at a feast, could I turn away the meat they would proffer me? More religious qualms? Would they accept that answer, or would Calandola's lively spirit, that had been so amused by my whiteness of skin and the virginity of my Queen, suddenly turn against me, so that in wrath he condemned me to the stew-pot? Perilous indeed it was to throw myself upon the mercies of these cannibals: for they were devils, in good sooth, and I was minded of that old saw, that he who sups with the Devil must have a long spoon.

"A feast!" they all cried. "A feast!"

Whereupon the Jaqqas rushed as though caught by a whirlwind out of the house of the Imbe-Jaqqa, though each, as he took his leave, did spin about and make a sign of respect to their terrible master. Calandola and Kinguri and the wives and witches were the last to leave, and they took me with them. Across all the town of the Jaqqas did we walk, and into the town of Calicansamba, and to the open square where the three gigantic metal tubs were seated. Now was the feast prepared before our eyes, to the accompaniment of much beating on drums, and hellish playing of trumpets and fifes, and awful screeching on other instruments the like of which I had not seen before, that were something like the viols of Europe, but with only a single string.

Fires were lit, and the kettle-water was heated. And into the kettles went these things:

The flesh of a cow, that was butchered before us with a single stroke of a sword against its neck, and then fast work done with a flaying knife.

The flesh of a goat, slain the same way.

The flesh of a yellow dog, that howled most piteously until the knife took its throat.

A cock. A pigeon.

And into each pot, also, the body of a prisoner that they summoned out from a pen and slew before my eyes. These were three heavy-muscled warriors of some interior tribe, that spoke out curses in a language I did not know, and raged, and pounded his fists together. As much avail them to rail at the Angel of Death! Each of these three was killed with a wound that preserved the blood within his body, and fell away from life with a long sighing gurgle of despair, and then the blood was carefully drained off by artisans whose science this was, and shunted into the storage vessel where that fluid was kept. Jaqqa carvers next did work upon these new corpses to make them ready for the cooking, and when they were well carved to fit the vessels, in they went, alongside the other meats.

To the bubbling cook-pots also were added fruits and vegetables of the region, heaps and mounds of them, the bean called *nkasa* and the hot pepper and the onions, and cucurbits, and I know not what else: for I must tell you that my brain was so numbed by seeing those protesting men slain and chopped and put to boil that I failed to observe some of the latter details of the cooking.

And all the while did the drums resound, the trumpets shriek.

And what did I think, what did I feel?

Why, I tell you on my oath, I felt nothing. Nothing did I feel. For there comes a time, I tell you, when the mind is so overladen by strangeness and shock that it merely sees without reflecting and that was what I did now, standing beside the lord of the cannibals and his brothers and the priests of the tribe. And I said nothing, I thought nothing, I only watched. This was what the voyage of my life had brought me to, that I had drifted as though by sea-wrack to this place at this time, among these harsh folk, and they were readying their evening meal. And God in His wisdom had caused me to be here, wherefore I was not to ask questions of Him.

I did pray, though, that when it came to the serving out of the meat, they would give me to partake of the cow, or of the goat, or even of the dog, and of no other kind of flesh.

Now the palm-wine did flow freely, the Imbe-Jaqqa drinking in his gluttonous way from his special skull-cup, and having his wine mixed with blood the half to the half, and all the others of us taking our fill from a seemingly limitless supply that came in vessels of wood. My head did sway and my face came to be flushed and moist. There was dancing, most lewd and lascivious in its nature, by the younger men and some of the women, and the drums grew even louder, so that they pounded against the temples of my skull like hammers.

Calandola now rose and stepped from his garment. Several of his wives reached into the vat where the human fat was stored, and gathered the same and rubbed it on his naked body to renew his gloss, covering every inch of him, his belly and his thighs and his huge privities and all else. After which, new ornaments were drawn upon him with colored stones, and he clothed himself once more in his beads and shells and fine waist-cloth. Some of the wives did also swab themselves with the glistening fat, but no others. There was loud singing, and forty or fifty women did come and stand about the Imbe-Jaqqa, holding in each hand the tail of that wild horse called the zevvera, which they switched back and forth. The handles of these switches, so it was said, contain a potent medicine, that protected the Imbe-Jaqqa from all harm.

And after a long while of these barbarous festivities, the cry went up that the meat was cooked, and the eating could thereupon commence.

Kinguri said to me, "It is first-feast for you, and so we make great holiday tonight, Andubatil!"

"I am grateful for this high honor."

"It is the law that the Imbe-Jaqqa must eat before all others. But you are to be second."

For this, too, I did give most courteous thanks.

Then did a man-witch of the royal court, covered from head to toe with chalked markings that made him look himself like a capering zevvera, go to the centermost of the three cauldrons, and take from it with his bare hands out of the boiling water a joint of meat, and hold it high, and show it to the Jaqqas. Who set up at once the most hideous howling and wailing, as is their way of showing approval, though it sounds like the shrieks of Pandemonium itself.

And there was no mistaking this haunch, that it was neither cow nor goat nor dog, and I knew whereof that meat had come.

The witch did carry the steaming meat forth to Calandola, and held it out to the Imbe-Jaqqa to be inspected. Calandola made a sound of assent, and took a deep slavering draught of his bloodied palm-wine, and seized the haunch after that with both his hands, and put his jaws to it and ripped away a great piece.

"Ayayya! Ayayya! Ayayya!" cried the Jaqqas, capering ever more wildly.

And then did the Imbe-Jaqqa turn to me, with the great slab of meat in his hands.

O! The world did spin about me, so that I was the very center and vortex of it, and thought I would be whirled apart! O! And there was a storm in my brain, and a throbbing of my soul, and I felt my breast would burst!

O! and I prayed that the earth might open and swallow me, that I should not have to partake of this that was offered me!

Yet was I not engulfed, nor did I fall down faint, nor was there any hiding place. And I grew calm and told myself, as I had told myself often enough before, that all this was meant for some high purpose beyond my understanding.

"Take and eat," said Calandola.

"Lord," I said, saying it aloud and in English, "I am Andrew Battell Thy servant, and I have fallen into a strange fate, which no doubt Thou had good reason for sending upon me. I will do Thy bidding in all things and I look to Thee to preserve me and to keep my body from peril and my soul from corruption. Amen." This was mine own prayer, that I had invented myself long ago among the Portugals of São Paulo de Loanda. That prayer had stood me in such good stead thus far, and in uttering it now I felt a great ease of the soul. I took the meat from Calandola, who smiled upon me as benignly as though this were my baptism.

I stared at the thing I held in my hand, that warm and most tender piece of meat, as though never had I seen meat before, of any sort whatsoever.

I will eat of it, I told myself. And if I gag and retch and puke it forth, and give offense to the Imbe-Jaqqa, why, let him slay me and cast me next into the pot, and it will not matter to me, it will not matter to me, it will not matter.

I put my teeth to the forbidden flesh and took a hesitating bite, and closed mine eyes a moment, and swallowed it down.

I did not gag, I did not retch. That was the greatest amazement I have ever known. The meat was succulent and well seasoned, and had a flavor of it not unlike a fine degree of pork, from a pig well nourished. I felt it pass my tongue and make the juices of my mouth flow forth, and I swallowed it down, and all of this was strangely easy for me. It is only meat, I thought. And meat of a passing good taste, which the Lord hath created and put upon the earth.

"Andubatil!" cried Imbe Calandola in loud delight and approval. "Eat, Andubatil!"

I had accepted of their hospitality, and now I knew I was free to hand back the haunch, and ask for some other meat more closely kin to my usual choice. And yet, and yet, and yet: I had not eaten meat of any kind but for those pitiful few scraps of monkey, and so easy was the first bite, and so surprising to my palate, that I thought to myself, If I am to go to Hell for this, the one mouthful will have damned me, so there is no reason not to have another.

God grant me forgiveness, said I within, and took for myself a second serving of the meat.

"Andubatil!" cried Calandola again. "Andubatil Jaqqa!"

And the cry went up on all sides, and became general, as they beheld me eating of their feast, that no other stranger had ever shared with them, and that made me now one of their number: "Andubatil Jaqqa! Andubatil Jaqqa!"

BOOK
FOUR:

~~~~~~

Jaqqa

ONE

AND SO that night was I entered into the man-eater tribe, and became one among them: the first white Jaqqa that has ever walked this earth, and, God grant it, also the last.

I had shared their monstrous meal. Within my body now lay shreds of meat that a few hours before had been the flesh of a child of God, a son of Adam. So be it. I made no orations upon that in the inwardness of my soul: for if I had learned anything in this my African sojourn, it was to take each thing as it comes, and ask not to live in English ways in a place that was so alien to all that was English. And thus I might hope to survive until the next morn.

All that raucous evening the Jaqqas feasted and drank and danced, and I among them did the same. They asked me to dance an English dance for them, but I was hesitant at that, it being so long since I had been in England that I had forgot most of their amusements. Then I recalled the dance that is called the hornpipe, that is done by our sailors aboard the ships, and that I had learned of my brothers Henry and John so long ago in Essex by the water.

"Dance!" cried Imbe Calandola.

"Ah, I must fain have music, if I am to dance."

He waved to his musicians, telling me to take my choice of them, whichever met my need.

I went down the ranks of all those painted and gleaming gargoyles and cacodaemons, and lit upon one that took my fancy, a fife-player, that did play the *mpunga*, which is fashioned from elephanto-tusk.

"You," said I. "Give unto me your instrument, so that I can show you the melody I require."

He laughed and handed me his instrument, and put my hands into the fingering. I found it not hard to bring a sound from this barbarous fife, though what I made at first was doubly barbarous, harsh and awkward, that drew great gawfing bellows of amusement from the man-eaters. But then did I find the tune, and played it most lively, with a nodding of my head and a prancing of my feet, and gave back the fife to its owner so he could essay the same.

And lo! he caught the music by its heart, and delivered it so well in a moment that he displayed himself five times as skilled as any English-man that fifed. The hornpipe that he did play was of course a strange

373

and most discordant one, the Devil's own hornpipe tune, but yet it had a wild delightful strength in it. And as the sound of it rose high above the Jaqqa camp all of them fell solemn still, and I did my dance.

Ah, such a dance it was! In the dread frozen silence of these man-eaters I did jig up and down, kicking high my legs, and putting now this hand afore my belly and now that, in the hornpipe manner. The Jaqqas had never beheld its like, and they were thrown into stupor by it, statue-still, amazed, as the long-legged white-skinned man in beads and shells and a palm-cloth loin-clout hopped about amongst them, up one row and down the next, to the wailing melody of that eerie fife.

"Andubatil Jaqqa!" they began to cry, when the surprise had lifted some from them. "Andubatil! Andubatil!"

And they rose, and danced behind me, a band of frightful black apparitions with great long spectral legs and arms. They flung out their limbs, they threw back their heads, they shouted, they cried, they stamped their feet. *"Ooom-day!"* they called. *"Oom-da ooom-day ooom da! Ooom-Jaqqa Ooom-Jaqqa ooom ooom ooom! Andubatil! Andubatil! Ooom!"*

When they had had their full share of that, and the fife-man was compelled to stop from soreness of the lips and an excess of laughter, for this was a passing riotous dance, and a most rollicking sight withal, these Jaqqas doing the hornpipe, Kinguri did turn to me and say, "Do you know another dance, Andubatil?"

"Aye, that I do," said I.

And I bethought me of the dance of our village known as the longways dance, and called forth eight Jaqqas to take part, and tried to instruct them in the movements, while telling certain musicians how best to imitate the rhythm of our tabor and the squirling of the pipes and the shrill sounds of the fiddle. All this brought great merriment, and the huge black men did leap and fling like Bedlam lunatics, in a dance, God wot, nothing at all like anything the village greens of Essex had ever seen. But they danced until they were sore weary, and would have had more. And I saw myself becoming their dancing-master, and teaching them square dances and round dances and maybe even the morris-dance, too, with tuned bells fastened to their legs and a Robin Hood and a Friar Tuck and a Little John, and one of the Imbe-Jaqqa's heavy-breasted scar-faced wives to dance the Maid Marian. And then in all this high jollity there came a sudden halt. For Calandola had risen from his throne-stool and was handling my musket, that all this time had lain to one side, unheeded.

He fingered it most close, the lock and the stock and the barrel, admiring its workmanship, sniffing it at both ends, hefting it to have the weight of it. I thought then he would put it to his shoulder and mimic the firing of it, but he did not seem to comprehend the holding of it.

Then he looked to me and said, "Show us how."

I took the gun from him and put the powder to it, and rammed a ball down the barrel, and saw to my match, and looked about for a place to shoot. A night-owl stood perched on a dark-leaved tree high above the camp, and it croaked its ill-omened sound, and I turned my gun to it. It is no small feat to strike an owl from its perch by night with a musket, but in my time as a soldier of the Portugals I had learned some little skill with that weapon. And so I took my aim and pulled my trigger, and the Jaqqas did gasp aloud at the sight of the flash of the powder in the pan, and I struck the owl fair in his breast and knocked him aflutter to the ground.

Again the cry went up, "Andubatil! Andubatil Jaqqa!"

And the Jaqqas did turn outward their hands, and slap against their temples, and cut the air with their elbows, which all are their ways of showing amaze.

This display of killing sank deep in the soul of Imbe Calandola. He stood a long time brooding, looking toward me and then to the shattered fallen owl, and to the musket, and to me again. For he had never seen our weapons in action, and certainly not the musket: for the Portugals are more given to the older instruments, such as the arquebus and the caliver, and muskets are uncommon among them. And a way of striking death from a distance, with so loud a roar and so bright a flash—yea, that caught the Imbe-Jaqqa's interest, and held it firm!

Then Calandola did make a little grunt and a gesture, and out of the crowd of women about him came one of his wives, a woman of perhaps thirty years, who bore a maze of tribal scars on her body, and whose teeth were few and whose breasts were long and low-hanging. The Imbe-Jaqqa ordered her to take up a stance at some hundred paces from me, or a little less, and there she stood, unmoving, and seeming as uncaring as a tree.

"Do it to her," said Imbe Calandola.

That command struck me as would a knee in the gut. Cold-blooded slaughter of an innocent woman? God's eyes, that was worse than cannibalism!

"Nay," I said. "I cannot."

"Cannot?" Calandola repeated, turning the word around in his mouth as though it were some rare delicacy. "Cannot? Who says this to the Imbe-Jaqqa?"

Kinguri, closer by me, murmured, "The Imbe-Jaqqa fain would see how your weapon works on such a target."

"I understand," said I, "but it is not in me to slay her."

"She has no life except at the Imbe-Jaqqa's pleasure," returned Kinguri. "That has now been withdrawn from her."

"I am tired, and the weapon is heavy, and I have had so much wine tonight that I fear my aim will be untrue."

"Your aim was true enough when you shot the owl."

"God guided my eye then," said I, "but He will do that but once a night, and before I may shoot again I must make special prayers to Him, that will be quite lengthy."

In thus speaking of God and long prayer I hoped to divert them, until they forgot this evil enterprise, as my circumcision had been forgotten. It did not thus befall. Kinguri spat and said something to Calandola; and the Imbe-Jaqqa, growing impatient, folded his arms and grunted, and his eyes blazed and a ghastly raging scowl came across his features.

Kinguri said, "Andubatil, why do you wait?"

"This is not easy for me."

"The Imbe-Jaqqa would see the display."

"I beg you—"

And all this while the woman stood unmoving, waiting the fatal shot. Whether she was aware of the essence of our talk or no, I cannot say: but I have seen dumb animals in the field look with greater sense upon the huntsman that in a moment will blow out their lives.

Then Calandola, angered to madness now by my slowness, cried out something to me in the Jaqqa tongue, his voice so thick with roarings and snortings that I could not identify the words. He did stamp his foot and spit and pound his fists, and his black face grew blacker still with rage. He appeared at that moment a pure madman, capable of any deed.

While that he raged, I did begin to reload my musket, which is a painful slow business. I was thinking that if he should launch some attack upon me, and in his anger condemn me to the cauldron, or worse, I would at least turn my musket on him, and take his life before he could have mine.

Yet that idea went from my mind the instant I conceived it, for it was the greatest folly: among these cannibals the Imbe-Jaqqa was near to being a god, and if I were to harm him even slightly, I knew, the death that his followers would give me would be the most foul this world doth hold, a slow boiling, perhaps, or something far more terrible even than that. So I banished the plan, and searched for some other way to mollify him, but there was none, save to do his bidding. His rage yet mounted and I feared to defy him, and to my disgrace I could no longer find the will to say him nay in this terrible thing.

Kinguri said, "It will go hard for us all if you do not obey."

"Shoot!" howled the Imbe-Jaqqa.

"Lord give Thy unhappy servant mercy, and forgive me," I whispered, and I touched my finger to the trigger and discharged my shot.

Mine arms were trembling and mine eyes were half blinded with tears of shame. Yet did the musket-ball fly true to his target and take the woman between her breasts, and knock her back five or ten paces and drop her sprawling to the ground.

Some Jaqqas ran to her, and danced about her, and held her up bleeding, and lifted her like a trophy. And they did set up a wild howling of glee.

Thus did I for the only time in my life slay a purely innocent person, that had done no harm to me, and promised none, and made me no obstacle. And for that I think I will do penance long years before I am let see Paradise. But yet in the moment of doing it I felt I had no other way, but to gratify the dark demand of the Imbe-Jaqqa.

Who now was entirely at his ease, and smiling, and applauding me for my marksmanship. That crazed wrath of his of only a moment before was altogether gone from him, as though it had never been. He came to my side and wrapped his great arm about me and hugged me joyfully, and gave me warm praise in coarse Jaqqa words I scarce understood, and caressed the hot barrel of my musket, and called for his cup-bearer to bring me a draught of the royal wine that was mixed with blood. And lifted the cup high, and pronounced a long pronouncement, and gave me the cup to drain.

Kinguri and the other Jaqqa lords did circle close about, and I saw their eyes glittering like shining stars, and their faces set in deep expressions, and some of them not amused, nor friendly in the least.

"What is it he says?" I asked Kinguri.

"Ah, Andubatil, he names you to be the chief of all his warriors."

"Do you tell me so?"

"And makes you the lieutenant of the battlefield, and says all honors will be yours."

"But I am white! I am Christian!"

"You are Andubatil Jaqqa. He calls you also Kimana Kyeer, that is, Lord of the Thunder."

And with the saying of that new name the other Jaqqas about us did shout, "Kimana Kyeer! Kimana Kyeer!" But some were joyous and some were scowling, as well they might, if this white stranger had been raised in rank above them in the twinkling of an eye only because he carried a thunder-stick.

Calandola gestured in his impatient way, and made the sounds that I knew now to mean, "Drink! Drink!"

Therefore did I drink. And they blackslapped me and handled me, so that the drink did run down my chin and chest, and the wine dripped all the way to my loins, where I felt it sliding over my privities, that wine that was mixed with blood.

"Kimana Kyeer!" they all did cry.

And I all the while could think only of that poor dumb woman that I had blown to Hell with my musket at his cruel inhuman command, the which I had not had the strength to resist.

Kinguri to me did say, "You are fortunate. He will make you great among us, and give you great gladness, for that you have the power to slay from afar."

I looked to the other lordlings and saw them discussing among themselves, and some nodding and some spitting, and I knew that it was perilous delicate to be elevated to lieutenant and duke among these folk. Yet had I been a prisoner and a pawn overlong, and if my musket did win me acclaim, well, be I then Kimana Kyeer in gladness, said I to myself, and Devil have the hindmost.

But then, to my horror, Calandola did make a signal most imperious, and a second of his wives was thrust forth out of the crowd of them.

What, and was I meant to massacre the Imbe-Jaqqa's entire harem, one by one? God's death, I would not! Lieutenant or no, Kimana Kyeer or no, chief of all the warriors or no, I would not! On that I meant to stand firm, and not be swept away again by Calandola's bluster or by his strange resistless power to command. I looked about in appeal to Kinguri, who even then I understood to be more reasonable a man than his great brother, and I began to frame some words of protest. But Kinguri was smiling; and so, too, was the woman who had come forth out of the group of wives.

"The Imbe-Jaqqa is well pleased with you, Andubatil," said Kinguri, "and he gives you this favorite among his women, to be a wife to you."

God's wounds!

I a cannibal, and a cannibal's husband! Well, and what was I to say? I looked at her close.

She was of that early womanhood that Matamba had had when first I bought her out of slavery: sixteen years, or perhaps even younger, it not being easy to tell. Her flesh was ripe, with high heavy breasts and great round buttocks, and solid smooth thighs like ebon columns, and everything about her was youthful and firm, with her skin drawn tight over the abundant vigorous flesh beneath. Her eyes were mild and her smile was gentle, but her face was not beautiful to me: for even though her features were sharp and well sculpted, and indeed were graceful and far from coarse, she was so heavy adorned with the cicatrices of their barbarous fashion that she scarce seemed like a human being, but rather some sort of fabulous monster. Ornament in the shape of lightning-bolts and triangles and serpents had been laid upon her cheeks and forehead, and between her breasts, and down the outside of one thigh and the inside of the other; and each of her buttocks, which were bared where her tight loin-cloth passed between them, had a design of circular rings, one within the other, raised amazing high. Then also she was oiled with the grease of the fat of men, which gave her a high shine but made her reek most strangely, and her hair, which was long, did hang in heavy plaits waxed with oil and red-colored clay, and sprinkled with the scent of something much like lavender, but more sour. And this woman, and not Anne Katherine, whom I had all but forgot, was to be my wife, I who had been unmarried since Rose Ullward's time. God's bones, such a strange dream has my life been, such a walking sleep of phantasms!

The cannibal woman came to me, all demure, eyes downcast, and knelt, wife-like.

"Raise her, Andubatil," said Kinguri.

I drew her to her feet.

"How are you called?" I asked.

"Kulachinga," she said, in a low murmur barely within the range of my hearing.

"She is full of juice, Andubatil!" Calandola cried. "She is soft and tender! A fine wife for the Kimana Kyeer!"

I looked at him and saw that he had brought forth his Romish gear, his cassock and his chalice and his crucifix. He had donned the cassock, and now did bang the crucifix against the chalice most gleefully, to signal a new start to the festival, which now had become my wedding feast. No meat remained, but they brought forth fruits and great store of wine, and there was more dancing—first the wild capering of the old Jaqqa manner, and then a renewal of the hornpipe I had taught them, and the longways dance—and all the while bridegroom and bride stood in the midst, hand in hand, as flowers were showered upon us.

This went on for some hour and more. And then to us came Calandola, and laughed and put one hand to the small of my back and one to hers, and pressed us together so that her breasts did flatten into me, and pushed us back and forth, by way of miming that it had arrived time now for the consummation of our nuptial.

God's cod, was I to perform it in front of them all?

Surely such a thing would be impossible, I being full of wine, and half dead with weariness, and shaken by all the frenzy and clamor of the evening, so that it would have been hard to couple under any circumstance, but trebly so with a whole tribe of leering cannibals looking on. And also this Kulachinga being so remote from my ideal of beauty, with her oiled skin and mud-thickened hair and the cicatrized scars all over her. And her with her memories of Imbe Calandola's massive yard in her, so that how could I begin to equal him?

Well, and yet I told myself I would essay it, come what will.

The Jaqqas were already building a bower for us under a vast ollicondi tree, piling high the torn-off limbs of some flowering shrub, most sweet and fragrant both of wood and leaf, arranging them in a roundel, with an open place for us to lie at the center. And they clapped and danced and sang, and pantomimed us into the bower, and pantomimed also the joining of man and woman with the finger-mime. And grinned their jack-o'-lantern Jaqqa grins at me. I was gamesome for anything, I the man-eater, I the bead-wearer, I the woman-killer, I the Kimana Kyeer, I the English Jaqqa, Andubatil.

I took my fair young bride by the hand and I did draw her down upon the soft tender young grass.

Then we made away with our loin-wraps and our shells and our beaded bangles, of which Kulachinga wore great store about her neck and arms and legs. And when we were naked as Eve and Adam we faced each other, and she made a little whistling sound through the places of the missing teeth, and said, "Andubatil."

"Kulachinga," said I.

Her skin was bright by the flaring torchlight. I touched her skin and drew my fingers along the greased tracks, over the ridges and hillocks and bumps of her ornaments. I held her breasts in my hand and let the weight of them arouse me, for they had a great merry exuberousness. I cupped the buttocks of her, and touched her hot thighs, with their markings high and strange. And she with great sly skill did caress my arms and my back, and then went lower, to my rump, even sliding her fingertips between my buttocks and into the hole a little way, which felt passing strange to me but excited me. And from there she traveled to my yard, which had not hardened yet except a little, but she took it deftly with the fingers of one hand, and drew upon it, as one draws on the udder of a cow, a gentle firm tug, and with the other, most skilfully, this woman Kulachinga Jaqqa did seize my ballocks, stretching her fingers about to contain them both. And to my amaze I did respond despite all of the challenge of the public moment, and grew stiff and huge to her touch, and she laughed just as a little girl will laugh when presented with a pretty frock, a playful laugh of pleasure in her own attributes, and she drew me down on her and widened her thighs to me and with one good thrust I speared her, while from all about me the jungle resounded with the crying of my name by the Jaqqas, "Andubatil, Andubatil, Andubatil!" In and out, in and out, moving easily and surely, and Kulachinga lay back, her head lolling, her lips slack, her eyes open but the dark of them rolled up far into her head, and I reached down and with the tip of my finger did burrow in the thick hair of her, and found her hard little bud, and touched it only twice and she gasped and moaned and had her fulfilling. Which we did three or four times the more, until at last she drew her knees up toward her breasts and outward, and clamped her heels against my back, and with sudden violent movements of her hips did push me onward to the venting of my seed. After which a heavy sweat came upon me like unto that caused by the greatest heat of the jungle, and rivers of hot fluid did burst from my every pore, so that I was slippery as a fish, and I sank forward onto her breasts and she held me and I dropped into a sleep that was none very different from death itself, I trow, for I did not dream and I did not know I slept, but lay like a stone until morning. And so did I pass the first night of my life among the Jaqqas, and so also did I accomplish myself on the night of my wedding to my African bride Kulachinga.

TWO

FOR ANOTHER two months did the Jaqqas remain at the town of Calicansamba, until they had utterly laid waste to everything that had belonged to those people, and most of the villagers had fled to Cashil and Mofarigosat and other lords, and the town had become an empty thing where those mean beasts the jackall and the hyaena did roam, snuffling for scraps. Then the word came down from Imbe Calandola and his viceroy Kinguri that the tribe was to take up its wanderings again, and they did gather their cattle and their gourds laden with palm-wine and their weapons and make ready to go on the march, inland toward the mountains of Cashindcabar.

These mountains be mighty high, and have great copper mines, which the blackamoors do work, going in and taking the ore and melting it some, and hammering it to use for ornaments and weapons. The Jaqqas do none of this themselves, but only prey on the metal-working tribes. Kinguri explained this to me as a matter more of religion than sloth, saying, "It is forbidden by our custom to draw metal from the earth, this being a shameful handling of our mother. But we must have tools; and so we do allow lesser nations to engage in the commerce of metals on our behalf."

As we passed toward Cashindcabar, the Jaqqas took the spoil all the way as they went. The towns of the makers of copper bells and chains and bracelets did unresistingly surrender their hoards, out of fear of Imbe Calandola. Also did he take from them their goats and their cattle, and destroyed many of their palm-wine trees, in that manner most wasteful that the Jaqqas practice. And now and then when the hunger for human meat came upon the tribe, they did choose a few townsfolk whose flesh they coveted, and killed and ate them in their great feasts, which were ever a heavy spectacle to behold.

This devouring of men was done not only for the flavor of it, though that was very dear to the Jaqqas, but also because it did strike terror into the nations of this land, being so unnatural and monstrous. Thus it invested the Jaqqas with a mantle of strange grandeur and frightfulness: ofttimes a town would surrender without a struggle, so fearful of the Jaqqas were they.

Onward did we proceed, looting and eating, eating and looting. I took each day as it came, and lived easily my life among them, doing as they did by quick nature, the way one breathes without thinking on it. Yet also did I hold myself back in at least one part, that was the observer, the scholar of their doings and the doings of the nations that were about them. For I did know that no man before me had had the opportunity to witness such things, and that if God's grace ever brought me to a place where I might set down my experiences, I would have such a tale to tell as few wanderers and journeyers before me had had, except peradventure for the great Marco himself, of Cathay.

In the mining country of Cashindcabar I saw how the working of metals is carried out among the Bakongo peoples, who used molds of wax to shape their bangles, the wax melting away and leaving the bracelet or armlet behind, full formed. In the working of iron they are very skilful also, and even amazing. For the blacksmiths do light a fire on the ground and, sitting nearby, practice their art in a most tranquil way, using neither hammer nor anvil. In the place of the hammer they employ a piece of iron large enough to fill the hand, and whose shape resembles a nail. The anvil is a piece of iron to the weight of some ten pounds, that they place on the ground like a log. On this they do their forging. The bellows is made of hollow logs over which a hide has been stretched. They raise and lower this hide by hand, and in this way blow air on the fire; this serves them very well and without difficulty. With these three simple instruments they do fashion all their iron goods, even the most elaborate.

I asked a blacksmith what art of magic he used in accomplishing this, and he replied most blandly, "It is in the arm, the directing of it, the weight of the thrust. Which we learn as boys, and it must be of the soul, of the inner spirit: I mean there is a *mokisso* in it, or the work is worthless." And perhaps that is true of whatsoever labor any one does, in any land, that if there is no *mokisso* in it, and the spirit is not just right to aim the thrust and shape the weight of the task, then it matters not what fine tools you do employ.

These blacksmiths have other special skills. If someone is troubled by a disease, he goes to the blacksmith, makes some payment to him, and has his face blown on three times by the bellows. When you ask them why they do this, they reply that the air that comes out of the bellows drives the evil from the body and preserves their health for a long time. At one of the mining towns under Cashindcabar all the lordlings of the Jaqqas did form a long line, that stretched far out into the country, and one by one all the day long they came forward to have the blacksmith of that place blow air thus into their faces.

Gold is of little interest to all these peoples. At Cashindcabar I picked up a Jaqqa hatchet to admire it and found some gold inlaid into its handle, along with other workings of copper. This I showed to Kinguri.

"Where is this metal to be found?" I asked.

"You mean this copper?" said he.

"Nay, not the copper, but this other bright stuff, which is gold." I said the name of that word to him both in English and also in Portuguese, which is *ouro*, for I had never heard any African name for it, they having so little respect for it.

"Gold?" said Kinguri. "Why, this other metal is copper also, but of another color."

"Aye," I said, not wishing to dispute it, "and from whence does this other copper come?"

"Out of a river that is to the southward of the Bay of Vaccas," he said, "that has great store of it. In the time of rain the fresh water drives grains of this metal out on the sand, and we gather it then, for it is not forbidden to us to take metal that we find lying on the surface of our mother's breast. It has a good shine, but it is soft and useless stuff."

I pressed him to tell me more precisely where this river lay, but he could only say, southward of the Bay of Vaccas, that is, the bay about Benguela. Certainly I had heard nothing from the Portugals about finding gold there when we made our voyages thither; it was slaves that they sought, only slaves and slaves and slaves. But I may hope that one day Englishmen will scoop up this easy gold of the river-sands, if ever we do displace the Portugals from that part of the globe. And so I set the information down now that it not be forgotten.

Kinguri became my close companion in these first months of my wandering with the Jaqqas. Though he was a frightful man-eater and monster and all of that, yet also was he a person of thought and wisdom, with a far-seeing mind, that would have carried him to a high place in whatever country he was born: it was only the jest of fate that gave him off to spend his life in so barbarous a fashion. In this tribe he was a counsellor and companion to his elder brother the Imbe-Jaqqa, but in no way was he a partner in the government, for Calandola held that absolute unto himself. There was not room in that great tyrant's soul for a sharing of power, though I know it to be true that he did love Kinguri and hold him in high esteem—while at the same time he was jealous of him, and most watchful that Kinguri should not usurp so much as one shred of the Imbe-Jaqqa's authority and privilege.

Since in time I came to be close friend, if "friend" is the true and proper word, both to Calandola and Kinguri, I felt the pull of conflict sometimes between these two, and was much torn in my loyalties and strained by their brotherly rivalry. But the extent of that was not apparent to me at first, though of course any man of even slight wisdom knows that there are risks in getting too close to princes, or of seeming to favor the brother of a prince over the prince himself. The prince does love his brother, but also does he fear him, and for good reason, generally: so then does he fear the brother's friend.

But there was more than mere court intrigue to all this, for the brothers did have a feeling for me that went beyond such simple intrigue. Each wanted for himself the *mokisso* that was within my white skin; each coveted me, each desired me, almost as rival lovers do, for each thought I had in me that which would illuminate and exalt his spirit.

I had some hint to this early, when the man-witch Kakula-banga, a high sorcerer of the tribe, came to me to paint me with magic signs to warn off the threat of *zumbi*. Those spirits were much in fear just then. This witch was a small wrinkled man with one eye and a scar that made much of his face seem that it had been melted in flame; but that one eye saw with keen sight. And he said, as he drew his zickzacks upon my skin, "Calandola is fire, and Kinguri is snow, and so Calandola does rule, for fire rules over snow. But yet snow can kill, and it is a passing cold death."

"What is the meaning of this witch-talk, old man?" said I.

"That you lie between the flame and the ice, and both can burn you, O Andubatil Jaqqa. But you cannot endure both burnings. You will have to choose, some day, between Kinguri and Calandola, as will we all. Give it thought, O Andubatil Jaqqa! Give it thought!"

But these dark forebodings had no substance for me, except in the most broad way, that I knew one must be careful in the proximity of great men. In every realm, and not only that of the man-eaters, does greatness glut itself on the blood and flesh of those who are not so great, and who hope to rise, and die in the rising. Beyond such wisdom I knew nothing here, and resolved to watch and wait, and tread carefully.

From Kinguri I learned something of the history of these dread Jaqqas. They had come, he told me, out of the land known as the Sierra Leona, that is high above and inward somewhere in Africa. But long ago did they leave that place, giving up all settled habitation and wandering in an unsettled course. Thus they dispersed themselves as a scourge, one might say as a pestilence, throughout much of this continent, invading this land and that, and over time drifting southward through the kingdom of the Kongo and onward to the eastward of the great city of Angola, which is called Dongo. Thus they came to infest both these territories that the Portugals have colonized, and to threaten constantly against the little Portugal outposts and the Christian blackamoor nations that the Portugals have made subject to themselves.

As they marched, the Jaqqas in time transformed themselves into the likeness of the tribes they conquered. For they allow the bearing of no children of their own, but adopt into their nation the strongest and best of their foes' children, as I have already told. Thus in all their camp there were but twelve natural Jaqqas of the true blood, that were their captains, and fourteen or fifteen women. For it is more than fifty years since they came from Sierra Leona, that was their native country. But their camp is sixteen thousand strong, and sometimes more, and all of them know themselves only as Jaqqas, being without any knowledge of the tribes from which they were taken, or concealing it if they do.

This matter of bearing no children is one of the strangest of their ways. Of course they do engender babes, and carry them to full term, and the women are very fruitful, since the Jaqqas are a lewd nation and constantly perform the act of coition. But their women enjoy none of their children: for as soon as the woman is delivered of her child, it is presently taken from her, and placed in a hole in the earth, and in that dark prison of death the newborn creature, not yet made happy with the light of life, is allowed to perish.

Their reason for this cruelty is that they will not in their travels be troubled with such cumbersome burdens as babes, nor do they wish to undertake the education of infants. This is most monstrous. I witnessed it myself many times, the digging of the hole, the placing of the babe, all this done with the greatest ease and calm, as if it were the drowning of kittens. I did tax Kinguri with the manifest evil of this, and he said, "But it lets us grow stronger, for we choose only the best for our number, and discard all others."

"But since you are so valiant, are not your own children apt to be stronger than those of other tribes, and best suited to become as you are?"

"That may be, Andubatil, but it may also not happen that way. Great kings do engender feeble princes. Did you not tell me yourself that your King Henry brought forth only sickly sons, that all died in youth, so that your kingdom had to be given over to women?"

"It can happen so, aye, but it is not the rule. Have you not had sons yourself, of your wives?"

He looked indifferent. "I have not come to know them. They are of no concern to me."

"They are of your get, of your blood, of your valor!"

"They are only half mine, and who knows what corruption the other half brings? I tell you, Andubatil, these babes are mere insects, that buzz and drone for a day, and are gone."

"Nay, nay, nay," said I, pressing him close. "Strong men with strapping wives do bring forth fine and lusty children, so I believe. And in the murder of your babes you and your fellows have forfeited great strength in your armies, and—"

"Have care, Andubatil!"

"Do I transgress?"

"You transgress in the extreme."

"I speak from my heart, though."

"I was told by my brother Calandola that your heart was Jaqqa."

That did give me a moment's pause. Jaqqa-hearted, was I, in their eyes? Well, and I had thrown myself most lustily into their festivals, and did ape Jaqqa ways, and now did bear a Jaqqa sort of name: but was my heart truly Jaqqa? In faith, that brought me some amaze, and then some second thought, and I recalled to me the harsh croakings of that white-skinned witch, that demon-eyed madman of a *ndundu*, that in the city of Loango long ago had moaned and gestured at me and called me "white Jaqqa." Was his prophecy now fulfilled? Well, and so be it, though this was passing strange to me.

"And is my heart not Jaqqa then?" I asked Kinguri.

"So it seemed to my brother, and so it seems also to me: which is why I took you near, and showed my love to you. But am I mistook? Is your heart still white?"

"I think it is both white and Jaqqa at once," I said. "I find myself making the voyage between the one life and the other, and taking on new ways, and casting off old ones. But in some things I do find my heart as white as ever. In the matter of the murder of babes—"

"It is not murder!"

"I understand the killing of innocents to be murder."

"You understand nothing!" cried he most furiously.

"I think I have some little wisdom."

"None! None!"

There was a blaze in his eye and a froth to his lips. My own brain was heated, and to my tongue there came a crowd of arguments, why it was not right to do as the Jaqqas did with their young. But I caught my breath, and held myself still. For from the fury that was rising upon him, I knew it was the moment to cease plaguing him on this, lest I lose his love entirely, and inflame him into enmity. We had reached our boundary in this discourse, and any crossing of it would be a breach irreparable.

"I will not press you," said I.

"Nay, best that you do not."

He still was enraged. And I was yet fevered with the heat of my convictions; but I gave over, I held myself still, and after a time we did grow calm, and restore our amity.

Never did I open that subject again, even for the sake of hearing what mysterious profundity he could bring forth to justify the slaughter of babes. To see into his mind was like a powerful potion to me, so strange and other were his thoughts, but here I kept the boundary. Peradventure there was no profundity to be found there on this matter anyway, but only bloodlust: for I reminded myself that it might be an error to regard this man as wholly a philosopher with whom I could hold unrestricted discourse of the mind, when in fact I dared not forget that what he was was a savage and a cannibal and a killer who gave no quarter, even though his mind be deep and discerning.

Kinguri told me that the first of the Jaqqa kings was a chief of his own name, Kinguri, that when he came south did marry a wife named Kulachinga out of one of the local nations. After him came Imbe-Jaqqas that had the names of Kasanje and Kalunga and Ngonga, all of the same original Jaqqa family of the first Kinguri. These presided over this mixture of many tribes that was the Jaqqa nation. Some of the Jaqqa monarchs fell into friendly relations with the Portugals of Kongo and Angola, and did ally themselves with them in certain battles in return for the privilege of crossing territories unhindered. But these alliances came and went like the shadowy events of a dream, and the Portugals never knew whether the Jaqqas were their friend or their mortal enemy, which was how the Jaqqas preferred it to be.

The Imbe-Jaqqa just before Calandola's reign was called Elembe, and it was he who conducted the spoiling of the Kongo that led to the great massacres of the last generation, in which so many Portugals and Kongo folk lost their lives. Calandola was a page unto this Elembe, and may also have been his son, for I think the Imbe-Jaqqas do spare some of their own offspring from the general rule of destruction. I believe Calandola did overthrow Elembe at some time, much as the god Jove did overthrow his father in a mighty revolution upon Mount Olympus. But this again was a matter that was perilous to explore, and I did not probe deeply in my talks with Kinguri on this, when I felt him withdrawing and sealing himself off. Certain it is that in recent years Calandola was the utter master of the Jaqqas, and the sole architect of their exploits.

They have no *feitissos*, or idols. That they leave to the other tribes. They do have gods—is there a nation on earth that does not?—but images are not kept by them.

Their gods are two, so far as I know, but I cannot tell you their names, if names they have. One they refer to as "the mother," by which they mean the earth itself, our sphere of habitation: they do hold her sacred, and abhor any kind of profaning of her wholeness, such as mining or even farming.

Thus it is that they will not plough the earth, and without ploughing it is difficult indeed to raise crops, even in this most fertile honeyed land of Africa. (I think also the Jaqqas abjure ploughing because that they regard farming as fit only for humble peasant folk and serfs, and they look upon themselves as a race of kings; that is, it is more pride than piety that leads them to seize the produce of others and raise none of their own.) The sole violation of the mother earth that they will countenance is the digging of holes for burial, either of children at birth, or the dead of the tribe. But this they see, not as a profaning of the mother, but merely as a returning of her children to her.

Their other god is a dark *mokisso* or spirit that is the force of destruction, the whirlwind of warfare and killing. But also is he the god of creation, the quickener of life in the world.

This union of destruction and creation was explained me by the witch Kakula-banga, who had appointed himself my ghostly father in this tribe. "In the beginning," he said, "there was only the mother, and she was empty and shining, like an uncarved piece of stone, pure, void, whole. But although she was perfect, she did not feel complete: so she did stir in her sleep, and roll about, and flail from side to side, until she awakened a mighty wind, which had *mokisso* in it. And this wind did come roaring down across the face of the land, and cut great gouges in it, which were the valleys and lake-beds, and threw up great ramparts, which were the mountains. And round and round the mother did the *mokisso*-wind blow, ever more fiercely and deeply. Until at last the wind did set seed inside her, and make her fertile, and quicken the first life. Out from her caverns in time came the first man, and the first woman, and the other creatures each in their turn, and so the world was peopled by the union of the whirlwind and the mother. And when the time comes, it will be destroyed in the same way."

"When will that wind rise?" I asked.

And Kakula-banga said, "It has already risen, O Andubatil Jaqqa Kimana Kyeer. For the Imbe-Calandola has the summoning of that wind in his hands, and he has summoned it!"

I do believe that this god of storm is in fact the Devil, though the Jaqqas do not know our idea of the Devil as the adversary of God, but rather worship him as a spirit who is a god himself, and worthy of the highest admiration. Yet as always in Jaqqa thought creation and destruction are entwined, and killing is a form of giving life, and I suppose a god can be a devil, too, and quicken the seed of the great mother at the same time that he does great injury to her perfection.

Whenever the great Jaqqa Calandola did undertake any large enterprise against the inhabitants of any country, he first invariably made a sacrifice to his stormy god the Devil, in the morning, before the sun arose. He would sit upon a stool, having upon each side of him a man-witch: then he had forty or fifty women which stood round him, holding in each hand a zevvera-tail, wherewith they did flourish and sing. Behind them were great store of drums and *mpungas* and other instruments loudly playing. In the midst of everything was a great fire; upon the fire an earthen pot of white powders, wherewith the men-witches did paint him on the forehead, temples, athwart the breast and belly, and on one cheek and the other, with long ceremonies and spells and enchantments. This would continue until the sun was down: thus did they conjure all the day long.

Then at night the witches brought to the Imbe-Jaqqa his *cassengula*, which is a weapon like a hatchet of great size of shining black metal with fair gleaming crystal set into its handle. This they put into his hands, and bade him be strong against his enemies: for his *mokisso* is with him, and victory shall be his. And presently there was a man-child brought, which forthwith he would kill with a blow of the *cassengula*, a weapon too heavy for most men to lift. Then usually were four men brought before him, slaves or prisoners: two whereof he would presently strike and kill in the same way, and the other two to be taken outside the Jaqqa camp and slain there by the man-witches.

Here I was in the first weeks of my stay among the Jaqqas always ordered to go away by the witches, for I believe they did not want a Christian to see a ceremony at which the Devil did appear. Then certain most holy rites took place. And presently after, Calandola did command five cows to be killed within the fort, and five without the fort, and likewise as many goats, and as many dogs, and the blood of them was sprinkled in the fire, and their bodies were eaten with great feasting and triumph. And also too they did eat the bodies of the men and the man-child that they had sacrificed.

Later, when the wind was in my sails and it had carried me much deeper on my voyage into the Jaqqa commonwealth, they decided I was no longer a Christian, and could be indoctrinated into their most secret rites. And so it was done, as I will tell in its rightful place. But never once, though I witnessed all the holiest of their holies, did ever I see the Devil himself, unless that I saw him and did not know him by his face. But I do doubt that he was truly there.

Kinguri did tell me, as we sat in their camp on the moist black earth beneath the great spreading arms of an ollicondi tree, of the many wonders that he had seen through his marchings across these lands. He spoke of a beast called the empalanga, which is in bigness and shape like oxen, save that they hold their neck and head aloft, and have their horns broad and crooked, three hand-breadths long, divided into knots, and sharp at the end, whereof they might make very fair cornets to sound withal. I saw none of these creatures, but I think they are harder to find than the Devil, since he is everywhere around and they are shy and rare.

Then also he told me of the great water-adder called the naumri, a serpent that goes forth of the water and gets itself up upon the boughs and branches of trees, and there watches the cattle that feed thereabouts. Which when they are come near unto it, presently it falls upon them, and winds itself in many twines about them, and claps his tail on their hinder parts: and so it straineth them, and bites so many holes in them, that at last it killeth them. And then it draws them into some solitary place where it devours them at pleasure, skin, horns, hoofs, and all.

Upon hearing this tale I did tell Kinguri of the coccodrillo at Loango that had eaten the whole *alibamba* of eight slaves, at which he laughed and said, "Nay, it is impossible for one coccodrillo to hold so many!" When I swore I had seen the monster cut open myself, he at first grew angry, and gave me the lie, and I thought would strike at me with the flat of his sword. But then he relented, and later I heard him telling the tale to Imbe Calandola, except that when it was told this time it was eleven slaves that the coccodrillo had devoured, not a mere eight.

From Kinguri I learned of the great bird called the estridge, taller than a man, and with feet that can kill a man with a single kick. It does not fly, because of its immense size. And he told me of certain other strange creatures, which being as big as rams, have wings like dragons, with long tails, and divers rows of teeth, and feed upon raw flesh. Their color is blue and green, their skins bepainted like scales; and two legs they have, but no more. I had heard of these dragons in Mofarigosat's town, that some were worshipped by the blacks and kept for a wonder in special cages. No dragons did I ever see, neither. But Kinguri promised he would show them to me when we were near some, a promise that he did not keep.

I could tell you many more tales I had from Kinguri, and very likely I shall. For he was a man much traveled and very shrewd; and as we talked often, he came to master the Portugal tongue, and I the Jaqqa tongue, and also we both spoke the Bakongo language, so that we had rich store of words between us and could communicate most easily and well.

Kinguri asked me much about life in Europe, that was of keen interest to him: our kings and our churches, and our way of dress, and our beliefs about the size and shape of the world, and much much else. In this I was often hard pressed to make reply to him, for though I am an educated man in my way, I had not held a book in my hand since leaving England, and much that I had been taught was forgotten to me now over so many years. Nor were his questions easy ones, since that he probed right to the heart of our mysteries, asking such as, Why did we use gold for our money and not iron, when iron was the more sturdy and useful metal? And, Why did we build great stone houses in which to worship our god, when God is everywhere? And, Why had our god created the first man and the first woman pure and innocent, and then let the Devil tempt them with sin, and then punish Eve and Adam with shame and death, when it would have been easier and more just to create them resistant to such temptation, while He was taking the trouble to bring them into existence? All this did I answer, more or less, but inasmuch as these were problems with which I found some difficulty myself, I think I did not give the Imbe-Jaqqa's brother great satisfaction by the firmness of my reasoning.

I had one question for Kinguri of a similarly deep sort, that was, To what purpose did the Jaqqas travel up and down this land of Africa, consuming all that lay in their path? What fury drove them, what hunger for destruction? To this, Kinguri made no reply for a great long while, so that I feared I had angered him by impertinence; his eyes seemed to turn inward, and he brooded in a chill and far distant way. Then at last he did reply, "I will not answer this. You must ask it of the Imbe-Jaqqa, who is our guide and master in these matters."

In those days I did not readily approach Calandola for such conversation. He held himself apart from the camp except at feasting-time, and his presence in it was like that of some smouldering volcano, a huge terrible Vesuvio that might erupt at any instant, hurling fiery rivers of lava over those nearby. So I let that question go by, thinking that perhaps it was a fool's question, inasmuch that the Jaqqas might merely do their killing and destruction out of the sheer joyous love for harm, and nothing underlying. Yet I suspected otherwise. In my study of the world it has seemed to me that there are very few nations that practice mere harm for harm's sake, but rather always do have some reason for their deeds, that to themselves seems to be the purest light of righteousness sublime.

And so it was with the Jaqqas. But I did not learn that until some while afterward.

We were done now with the spoiling of Cashindcabar, and moved onward toward the north and the east. The Imbe-Jaqqa's plan now took him across a river called Longa, and toward the town of Kalungu, that lies on the edge of the province of Tondo. Here we stood as it were between two worlds. For Kalungu is a place most fertile, and always tilled and full of grain, and is all a fine plain very level and rich, with great store of honey. But beyond it is that evil desert in which the Portugals underwent their massacre at the hands of Kafuche Kambara, who was also a great enemy of the Jaqqas. We did camp outside Kalungu for some time, while Calandola strived to decide whether to go inward upon that pleasant city, or to strike upward upon Kafuche Kambara. In this time of indecision he did hold many ceremonies in honor of the Devil, and feast greatly, and seek the Devil's counsel.

Then one time in the night we were all summoned from our sleep. I looked to the north and saw in the air many strange fires and flames rising in manner as high as the moon. And in the element were heard the sound of pipes, trumpets, and drums, most spectral.

I had been told long ago by older mariners of such strange noises, which may perhaps be caused by the vehement and sundry motions of such fiery exhalations in the sky as are wrought by wind and heat: for those fiery exhalations, ascending into the powerful cold of the middle region of the air, are suddenly stricken back with great force, and make a noise not unlike the noise that fire makes in the air, such as the whizzing of a burning torch. But to Calandola it was a great omen. He stood looking out over the plain and said to me, "See, Andubatil, there is heat coming from the beams of the moon! That means we must march and destroy Kalungu."

In faith the moon's beams felt as cool as ever, to me. But I would not gainsay Calandola.

He rested his heavy hand on my shoulder and waved the other toward the sleeping town that lay before us. "See, see, Andubatil, the farms, the ploughed earth! Those people have enslaved our mother, and we must set her free."

"Indeed, enslaved?"

"Yea. All across the land, there are men who would make themselves the mother's masters. And they scourge her dark warm skin with their ploughs, and they cover her with their houses and their roads. It is not right. Those men spread like a plague of insects across the land."

I would have said, rather, that it was the Jaqqas that were the plague. But that I held to myself.

Calandola went on, "Do you understand me? Very few understand. We Jaqqas know the truth, which is not given to other men, that this enslaving of the earth through farming and commerce is a great evil. It was not meant for mankind to do thus." He spoke most gently and softly, like a thoughtful king rather than as a madman. "It is our mission," he said, "to undo that evil. And so we sweep from land to land, and we rage, and we slay, and we devour; and behind us everything is made more simple, more clean, more holy. We will restore the earth, Andubatil. We will make it what it was in the first days: green, pure, noble." And with a laugh he said, "Your Portugals, they build in stone, do they not? Well, and we will drive them into the sea, and give their stone houses over to the jungle, and the vines and creepers will pull the heavy blocks apart. And then will we rejoice, when the motherland is wholly cleansed. Do you understand, Andubatil? So few understand. We are the forces of the purifying. We take into our own bodies those who are the enemies of truth, and we absorb them, and we make their strength our own and we cast forth their weakness. And thus we conquer and prevail. And we will go on in this way from land to land, from shore to shore, to the farthest rim of the sky. Tomorrow it will be Kalungu; and then later it will be Dongo, and Mbanza Kongo, and those other great cities; and in time it will be São Paulo de Loando, too, and when that city is gone, all will be whole again. After that we will see what work remains to be done in farther realms. Do you see? We have the semblance of ones who smash and destroy, Andubatil: but actually what we do, in truth, is make things whole again."

And we stood side by side all that night, looking toward the desert and watching the witch-fires dancing in the air. And that witchery did enter my brain and inflame my blood, for the words of the Imbe-Jaqqa seemed crystal-clear and reasonable to me, and I made no quarrel with them. I saw the world as swarming with ugliness and treachery and corruption, and the good green breast of the earth encumbered with the ill-made works of man; and it seemed to me most peaceful and beautiful to sweep all that away, and return to the silence of the first Garden.

And when morning came, Imbe Calandola did mount a high scaffold and utter a warlike oration to his troops, inspiring them with the frenzy of battle. Whereupon they did sweep down upon the town of Kalungu and take it, and put its people to the sword and its high slender palm-trees to the axe, and devour many of its folk boiled and roasted, and take its children by impressment into the tribe of Jaqqas. And in that way was yet more of this land returned into its ancestral purity. And in doing this, I truly believe, the Jaqqas were aware of no hypocrisy, but were altogether sincere, in fullest knowledge that this was their divine mission, to smash and destroy until they had made all things whole. Aye, and God spare us from such terrible virtue!

THREE

I MAKE my full confession. In the warfare that the Jaqqas had launched against all the civilized world, I confess I did play my full part, with much heartiness and vigor.

For Calandola had not spoken in jest, or in idle vaporing, when that he had named me on my wedding night to be his lieutenant, and the chief of all his warriors, and dubbed me Kimana Kyeer, the Lord of the Thunder. For love of my musket or for love of my golden hair had he in a single stroke lifted me to a lordship among these people, I who had been a prisoner and a slave and a pawn for so long with the Portugals. Now that we went into battle he looked to me indeed to act my role, as the right hand of the Imbe-Jaqqa, and act it I did, with all the fervor of my soul.

In giving me this high place he did of course displace others, that might have reason to resent me. There were, I have said, twelve high captains of the Jaqqa nation. Firstmost was Calandola, and then, a long distance behind, Kinguri, by right of blood. I will tell you the names of the other ten, which were Ntotela, Zimbo, Kulambo, Ngonga, Kilombo, Kasanje, Kaimba, Bangala, Ti-Bangala, Machimba-lombo: all of great stature and awesome presence, though in the beginning I could scarce tell one from another. I knew them only as long-legged figures that stalked like spectres through the Jaqqa camp with followings of their own, and stood close beside Calandola and Kinguri at the festivals, and had privileges in the feasting. But of course with time came familiarity, and I learned to know each in his way, and saw that some were mine enemy, and some were friendly in their hearts toward me. But that knowledge came later.

When we went down into the valley of Kalungu to take it, I was with them, with Kinguri on my left hand and Kulambo, who had the longest arms I ever have seen on a man, to my right. Calandola was not with us, for he had had himself borne ahead of us on a great scarlet palanquin in which he sometimes rode, and was directing things from the fore. But the others seemed to be looking to me to see what I would do.

When we came to a high position outside the besieged town, where the ground did rise up into strange little tawny hillocks more than three times the height of a man, and very narrow and twisted, I said, "Here will I take my stand, and show them what a musket is used for!"

And I did climb one hillock that gave me a view into the town, and was within musket range. And with my musket I did set up an uproar of fatal power, that terrified the blackamoors that had come forth from Kalungu to defend themselves, and sent them fleeing in an instant.

"Kimana Kyeer!" came the cry, as I fired me my first shot. I think ten men fell, though in good sooth I could not have hit more than one, and the others dead of fright.

I aimed and I shot again. And again came the cry, "Kimana Kyeer!" from the Jaqqas, but also now it came, not so jubilantly, from the throats of the Kalungu men.

With those two shots did I put the town into rout. Imbe Calandola came from his palanquin, and watched what was befalling; and he grinned a great grin, and hauled forth from his robes his mighty yard, and made water in the direction of the town, with a great yellow stream that was like the outpouring of a giant spigot. For that was his token of conquest, to piddle on the threshold of an enemy that was giving over the fight.

That was the first of my battles on behalf of the Jaqqas; but it was far from the last.

I became so highly esteemed with the great Imbe-Jaqqa, because I killed those many Negroes with my musket, and frightened an hundred for every one I slew, that I could have anything I desired of him: the best wine, the choicest meat, captured maidens, little pretty ivory trinkets. I needed but to name it and it was mine. I confess I took some glee in this. I do not conceal it. After so long not my own master, I was Lord of the Thunder, and I was like some vast force let loose from leash. There was a joy in it, that had me looking keenly forward from battle to battle. And when I fought I was like a king, or like a god. All the same I used my shot with caution and parsimony, not knowing where I would replenish my powder when it was gone, but being skillful in my aiming I made full advantage of my weapon's force, and slew great numbers, and those who were not slain were rendered helpless out of terror of my weapon.

Terror was a key to the Jaqqas' success. Their foes were half dead with fear before battle ever was joined. Calandola had seen at once that

I was a new kind of terror-wielder, and so it was that he did put me again and again in the fore of his troop, and I would fire, and the battle-cry would go up, "Andubatil Jaqqa! Kimana Kyeer!" And mighty was the weapon of Andubatil, and easy was the conquest of the town that never had beheld a musket before, or a white man. And to protect me, when we went out to the wars, Calandola did give charge to his most valiant men over me, even his high captains. By this means I was often carried away from hard battle in their arms, by giant Ti-Bangala or broad-backed Ngonga, and my life thereby saved: for there was ever a phalanx of puissant Jaqqa swordsmen to shield me and rescue me.

The way of fighting of the Jaqqas was most shrewd. When they came into any country that was strong, which they could not the first day conquer, then Calandola would order them to build their sturdy fort, and they would remain sometimes a month or two quiet. For Calandola said to me, "It is as great a war to the inhabitants to see me settled in their country, as though I fought with them every day." The houses of the Jaqqa town were built very close together, and outside each the men kept their bows, arrows, and darts; and when the alarm was given, they all would rush suddenly out of the fort and seize their weapons and be ready to do battle, no matter the hour. Every company kept very good watch at the gates in the night, playing upon their drums and the wooden instruments called *tavales*, and there was never any relaxing of vigilance.

Sometimes some of the most rash of the beleaguered townspeople might come out and assault the Jaqqas at their fort; but when this happened, the Jaqqas did defend themselves most staunchly for two or three days. And when Calandola was minded to give the onset, he would, in the night, put out some one thousand men: which did bed themselves down in an ambuscade about a mile from the fort. Then in the morning the great Jaqqa would go with all his strength out of the fort, as though he would capture the town. The inhabitants coming near the fort to defend their country, the Jaqqas gave the watchword with their drums, and then the men hidden in ambuscade did rise, and fall upon them from the other side, so that very few did escape. And that day Calandola would overrun the country, which in fright and panic yielded itself up without further struggle. I saw this tactic worked many times, and always in success.

Of the courage of the Jaqqas there seemed to be no limit. But there is good reason for this, since like the Spartans of old they are trained from boyhood toward valor. First there is the custom of putting the slave-collar to the newly adopted Jaqqas, that they must wear until they have killed a foe in battle. For a boy to wear this collar is accounted no disgrace, at least when he is thirteen or fourteen. But if he go a year or two beyond that, and still is collared, the men do mock him and the girls will not lie with him, and he will rush forward in battle to slay or be slain, lest he be accounted worthless.

You may readily see from this that only the warlike Jaqqas live to manhood, and the weak ones are culled from the tribe early. But if by some accident of fortune a weakling endures, he will not endure long into his mature years: for those soldiers that are faint-hearted, and are seen turning their backs to the enemy, are presently condemned and killed for cowards, and their bodies eaten. I have seen this.

I asked Kinguri once why they would make the flesh of a coward part of their own flesh, and he looked upon me frowning as if I had asked of him in Greek or Hebrew, and said at last, "The cowardice of them is boiled away in the pot, and what remains is their inborn vigor, which we consume."

They had many other ways of increasing themselves in courage. One I saw during the time after the conquest of Kalungu, where we remained five or six months, making use of the substance of those farming folk. It happened that some Jaqqa huntsmen did capture a lion of great fierceness, which they took in a very strong trap, using a kid as bait. This lion, which was a she-lion—and they are very much more fierce than the male—they chained down to the trunk of a great red-barked tree in the midst of a spacious plain outside their fort. Nearby, in the top of another tree, the Jaqqas did erect a sort of scaffold, capable of holding the Imbe-Jaqqa and the chiefest of his lords, among whom I was now reckoned.

When Calandola and all his court had mounted this scaffold, the other Jaqqas who had assembled in a great circle began to set up a huge noise, which joined with the untunable discord of a great number of odd musical instruments to compose a hellish concert. Then a sudden sign was given for all to be hush and silent; and then the lion was immediately loosed, though with the loss of her tail, which was at the same time whipped off to make her the more furious.

At her first looking the lion stared about, comprehending that she was again at liberty, but not altogether free, by reason of the multitude of Jaqqas that surrounded her. At once she set up a hideous roar, and then, greedy of revenge, she launched herself into the company of onlookers. Who did not flee, but rather ran toward the lion. She did fall upon them, rending one, and tearing another, and making a fearful havoc among them: all this, while the people ran round her unarmed, being resolved either to kill her with their bare hands, or to perish. I had never seen the like of this bloody event even in my strangest dreams, and I thought for an instant I was at the Circus in old Rome, seeing Christians tossed to the wild beasts. But these were no Christians, and they had gone joyously and willingly toward that ravening she-lion.

In utter amaze I watched as the bleeding beast raked this Jaqqa and that one with her claws, or griped at them with her fangs. She slew more than a few of her assailants, spilling their entrails in the dust with great sweeping onslaughts of her limbs. And all this time the Jaqqas closed their ring, moving inward, and fighting and jostling with one another for the privilege of being of the innermost ring, that confronted the she-lion most closely.

It seemed like madness to me. And yet I was stirred by it: my heart did race, my blood did grow heated, my sweat to flow. I hunched myself forward to the edge of the scaffold, and clenched my fists so that my nails did nigh pierce my palms, and shouted out to the ones below, "Beware! Turn! Jump! Guard yourself!" as the lion worked her rampage.

The other lordly Jaqqas likewise were well gripped by the carnal spectacle. Calandola did growl and roar to himself, eyes half-closed as though he were lost in a dream of gory welter. Ferocious Kulambo, who was a great huntsman, shouted encouragement to those in jeopardy, and clapped his hands and cried out at their bravery. The dark-souled and brooding Machimba-lombo made low sounds in the depths of his throat, and strained in his seat, plainly yearning to be down there with the crowd. Even the austere philosopher Kinguri, who trafficked in such high questions of faith and money and government, showed himself now as bestial as the others, as deep in the sanguinary passion of the moment. Yet were we all but onlookers, constrained to remain in our scaffolding. That was made clear when Machimba-lombo at last could stand no more, and rose, and cried, "I will go to them!"

"You may not," said the Imbe-Jaqqa, cold and sharp.

"I beg it, Lord Calandola! I cannot sit longer!"

"The lion-circle is no longer for you," replied his master. "You are of the captains now, and here will you stay."

There was palpable strain in the air between them: I saw the throbbing in the proud Machimba-lombo's throat and forehead, like that of a Titan enchained. He moved most slowly, as if through a tangible fog, toward the ladder, and he was trembling with the effort of it. Calandola hissed at him: Machimba-lombo halted. He fought within himself. Kinguri touched his wrist lightly and said in a soft way, "Come, take your ease, and watch the sport. For it is not fitting to go below, at your rank, good friend." It was like the letting out of air from some swollen bladder. Machimba-lombo, moved by Kinguri's gentle words where Calandola's rage had not swayed him, subsided and resumed his place, and the moment passed.

Below, there was scarce any room at last for the beast to make her attack, so tight was the pressing crowd of Jaqqas about her: and they rushed in, with a terrible cry, and seized the beast and forced her down, and by sheer weight and force did crush her and choke the life from her. Each of the Jaqqa warriors strived to outdo the others in the taking of risk and leaping on the lion. And after a time a vast outroar went up from them all, saying, "The beast is dead!" They all did withdraw to the outer edge of the circle, leaving in the midst the dead lion, now looking merely to be a great tabby-cat that was asleep, and about her some members of their own tribe that she had slain.

Whereupon the kettles were heated and they did all greedily devour the dead bodies of the fallen. The choicest parts were handed up the scaffold to Calandola and his nobles, and we did pounce upon the meat like vultures, since that there is much virtue in consuming the flesh of those who have died bravely in this sport. I held back a while, letting them have their fill, for they were so eager.

But when I went for mine, I came in the way of Machimba-lombo, whose lips and jowls were besmeared with grease and whose eyes were wild with hunger and something else, a sort of frenzy. I thought he would strike me as I reached past him for my slice: but again he controlled himself, holding taut, and I heard him rumbling in his throat. For this man was mine enemy, and I was coming now to learn it. Yet I could not let him threaten me before the others. So courteously I said, "I pray you, good cousin, let me have my due share."

His eyes were wolf-eyes upon me. But what could he do? I had spoken sweet words, yet not in any sweet tone. And he gave ground, and let me eat.

The music now began again, and singing and dancing, and crying, "Long live our Lord Imbe-Jaqqa! Long live our Lord Imbe-Jaqqa." And some of the strongest of the warriors below commenced a kind of wrestling, that was most graceful and beautiful, like unto a kind of dance, for all its fierceness. This was the first time that ever I beheld Jaqqa wrestling. They twined their long arms, they matched each other's movements like men in a mirror, they bent forward and backward, and leaped about, and pounced, and cast each other down with the greatest of elegance.

As for the lion, her flesh was not eaten, but her skin and head was taken, and used for ornaments in the Imbe-Jaqqa's household. And all the week that followed I saw Jaqqas in the camp that were scratched and torn from the rage of the lion; and in this manner did these man-eaters train themselves to greater bravery; as though more of that commodity were needed amongst them.

The other thing they did for valor's sake was hunting of elephantos to take their tails. This was not done, as among the settled Bakongo folk, to make ornaments out of the dark and glossy tail-hairs. Nay, it was the entire tail of the giant beast that the Jaqqas prized. For when any one of their captains or chief lords came to die, they commonly did preserve one of these tails in memory of him, and to which they paid a sort of adoration, out of an opinion they had of its great strength. They would say, holding up the shrine in which a certain tail was kept, "This is the tail of the elephanto of the Jaqqa Ntotela," or, "This is the tail of the elephanto of the Jaqqa Zimbo," or whichever. So to increase the number of these tails they did pursue the elephantos into narrow places, as I have told earlier. But the amputation had to be performed at one blow, and from a living elephanto, or their superstition would allow it no value.

I did not see this elephanto-hunting myself, for it was a most sacred thing that was done privately by Jaqqas to enhance their ghostly stature, and not the sort of quest on which one would invite a companion. But three separate times I saw a Jaqqa come running into camp holding a fresh-cut elephanto tail aloft, and each one of them was shining in the face, and altogether transfigured with radiant joy, as though the bloody thing he carried was none other than the Holy Grail of the Lord.

We saw elephantos often, wandering hither and thither across the land. And frightsome things they were to behold, at close distance, though they are in the main gentle and tractable creatures. As is well for all other creatures, when one considers their great size. For if there were an animal with the bulk of an elephanto and the spirit of a wolf or a she-lion, it should have conquered all the world.

When elephantos came near us, even the Jaqqas gave them a wide way, since, when angered, they are beyond being killed by any weapon, and do great destruction. They have great hanging ears and long lips, and a tongue that is very little, and so far in their mouth that it cannot be seen; but the snout or trunk is so long and in such form that it is to him in the stead of a hand, for he neither eats nor drinks but by bringing his trunk to his mouth. Also can he overthrow trees with it, to eat the tender shoots high up. Once I saw an elephanto take a boy around the middle with his trunk, that had done something idle to annoy him, and hurl that foolish boy far away, flying through the air with arms and legs wildly waving, so that he landed all shattered against a remote rock.

The male elephanto lives two hundred years or at the least one hundred and twenty, the female almost as long. They love rivers and will often go into them up to the snout, wherewith they blow and snuff, and play in the water; but swim they cannot, for the weight of their bodies. I know from reading the Greek and Roman writers that the elephanto can be trained, and made to bear burdens and be a beast of war, but the Africans do no such thing that I ever heard. The eye of the elephanto is very small, and high up along its head, yet it shows great wisdom and even a kind of sadness, and always when I looked at the eye of an elephanto I did feel a little shiver go down my back, for I told myself, This is a deep and thoughtful creature, that lives long and understandeth much, and has something holy in its aspect.

We saw another ponderous famous beast in our wanderings through this district of Kalungu that I had heard much of, but had not previously encountered in Africa. These were rhinocerotes, which are a sort of elephanto, but not so tall, and without the snout or the great ears, but having horns upon their noses. Like elephantos, the rhinocerotes are massive and armor-skinned, and gray or white in color, with heavy flat feet, and they can make the ground shake when they run. I saw two first, that my Jaqqa wife Kulachinga pointed out to me, saying, "They are mother and daughter," and soon after came the husband, such a monster as I could hardly believe, gigantic, like unto a fortress on four thick heavy legs. They went past without anyone doing them harm, and I stared after them as if I had seen three phantoms out of nightmare.

Kulachinga said, "Do you not have such animals in England, Andubatil?"

"Nay," said I, "not rhinocerotes, nor elephantos, nor coccodrillos, nor zevveras, neither."

"You have no animals, then?"

"Ah, we have cattle," I said, "and sheep, and goats, and pigs, and dogs, and cats, and the like. And in the forests are great stags, and perchance a unicorn or two, though I think it is many years since one of those was seen upon our shores. But of rhinocerotes not a one."

"What a strange land," said Kulachinga.

And I thought to myself, Yea, how very strange, with its green fields like tended carpets, and its little hills, and its cool rainy air, and its oak trees and elms and such that did drop their withered leaves when the first chill blasts of autumn came by. I had by now lived half as long in Africa as ever I did in England, or close upon that, and I was growing used to ollicondi trees and palms and thorny things, and elephantos and coccodrillos. And in time even rhinocerotes would seem as comfortable to me as a roebuck on a hillside, I could readily believe.

I was in these days living in most congenial harmony with this Jaqqa wife of mine, and that of itself was strange. For surely we were not designed to companion one another. At the first we could scarce speak to one another, I having only the bare smattering of the Jaqqa tongue and she no knowledge of my languages. In my usual way I did come to be fluent quickly in Jaqqa-speech, but even that did not by itself augur any true marriage, since there are in England many millions of men and women who speak each other's language as though they be native to it, and yet would make most woeful consorts to one another. And here was Kulachinga with her scarred and ridged skin, and her body all greased and oiled with strange substances of alien odor, and her hair done up with red clay and yet more grease, and she should have been as unsuited for me, and I for her, as a coccodrillo for a rhinocerote. But yet we did pleasantly together.

This was in part, I think, because she was a lusty wench, and I had always taken such keen joy in the pleasures of the flesh. When there is hot passion between a man and a woman, many other points of great difference can be overlooked, for lust is a bridge that links the most remote of islands. And we did frequently play the game of tangled bodies, and play it well, she in her Jaqqa style and me in my English way. She would not kiss, and often she liked to give herself to me dog-fashion, with her strong rump upturned, but no matter: I thrust, we joined, back and forth I slid in the deep but narrow channel of her, that was so frothing with the sweet natural juices of her, and into her, night after night, I shot my hot tallow and she responded with cries of delight.

It was the case that I had by gradual ways come to be enrolled in the very life of Africa by women who, stage by stage, were ever darker, ever more barbarous. My first instructress was Dona Teresa, who gave the outer appearance of a Portuguese woman, and one of serene beauty that any European would recognize; yet mingled within her somewhere was the seed of her African mothers, that showed only in the hue of her nipples and in the mysteries of her soul. After her had come Matamba, that was pure black, a creature of the jungled interior of the land: still she was Christian, and spoke the tongue of Portugals, and stood midway between savage and white in spirit, if not in appearance. And then had come various tribal women, whose names I could not tell you, that had satisfied my lusts in Masanganu and other places along my pilgrimage, leading me step by step toward the depth of this black world: so that by the time I was given Kulachinga to be my Jaqqa bride, I was ready to embrace without reluctance that woman of the cannibal race, and sleep placidly beside her night after night, and only now and then reflect with amaze upon the journey I had taken to bring me over the arch of the years from Rose Ullward and Anne Katherine Sawyer, so sweet and English, to this my Jaqqa wife.

Kulachinga had no wish to learn Portuguese, and did not even know English existed. Only rarely did she show curiosity about that other world out of which I had fallen. Indeed she was not of a searching and probing mind at all, which set her apart from Dona Teresa and from Matamba, both of whom I remembered fondly as being lively in their wit and perceptions and eagerness for learning. Kulachinga did not know what nation she was native to, though it could have been no more than a few years since she had been adopted into the Jaqqas. Nor would she speak to me at all concerning her marriage to Imbe Calandola, except to say, "He was a good husband to me," and not a word of what the carnal ways of that dark lord might be, or what it was like to have been one of so many wives. Soon I saw that I would learn little from her, and learning has ever been one of my passions. Yet was I content simply to dwell with her, and let her comfort me after I had been a troublesome day on the field of battle, and to take from her the bowl of palm-wine and the meat she had roasted for me at nightfall. And often did I reach for her in the night, and take her breasts into my hands, and slide my stiffened yard into her ready entryway. So when I was with her I was a happy man.

FOUR

WHEN WE had done with the sacking and consuming of the town of Kalunga, which we did entirely ruin, we arose and entered into the province of Tondo, which was a deep way to the north and east. To be sure, this was the direction opposite to that in which I most wanted to go, which was toward the coast. But I could no more then influence the Imbe-Jaqqa in the movements of his army than I could control the surge of the tides. And also I was finding life among the man-eaters uncommon pleasing, which was the last thing I would have expected. To run free with them in pagan revelry was like the throwing off of tight garments and constricting boots, and going naked and easy of spirit. Among the Portugals, whom I had found to be generally a people of deceit and petty treacheries and little mean betrayals, I had been a captive and a slave; but among the Jaqqas, who were monsters but yet bore themselves with a certain lofty nobility, I was a prince. So I was in little hurry to depart them. I abided my time in the forest without distress, becoming more Jaqqa in my ways each day, and thinking, I had already waited a dozen year and some to see England again, I could wait a little more.

We came to the River Kwanza, that I had sailed many times in going between the coast and the presidio of Masanganu. Both those places now were far to my back, we being a long way inland, beyond even the supposed silver-mining place called Kambambe. Following along the south side of the river and continuing ever eastward, we entered the domain of a lord that was called Makellacolonge, near to the great city of Dongo.

Here we passed over mighty high mountains, and found it very cold, we being near naked in the manner of jungle folk. In these steep passes the air was very blue and sharp, and there was frost on the ground at morn, like a little white crust; though by midday in the full blast of the sun we were greatly hot, and remained that way until twilight, when all the heat fled from the world. The things that grew on the high country were different from those of the lowland, there being no palms or vines or creepers, but instead certain things without stems, with fleshy thick leaves that bore pale stripes and spots, sprouting on the earth, and out of the heart of them came high spikes trimmed with a myriad little red flowers, that was most beautiful and strange.

On the other side of these passes the Imbe-Jaqqa did camp his forces for some days, making no attack on Makellacolonge. We sent out our scouts and our outriders, to get the lay of the land, but we did not move forward, nor did we give our enemy any hint that we were in their territory. Calandola often consulted his man-witches, and most particularly the *nganga* Kakula-banga, that was oldest and holiest of that kind. The Imbe-Jaqqa looked solemn and distant much of the time, but did not share with us his captains the nature of his fears.

Yet he had it in his mind to attack Makellacolonge when the omens were right. For we did gather a score of times to plan our strategy, Calandola and Kinguri and the ten other high captains and I. And the Imbe-Jaqqa did shape and reshape his plan, so that it shifted like a running stream in a shallow bed; but one thing was always constant, that I was to be the center of the thrust. "You will take up your post with your musket," said he, "and when the trumpet sounds, you will give your fire, five times into the town, and then—then—then—"

It was the *and then* that was always changing. I had never seen Calandola to be so indecisive. For his mind was altogether scattered and would not come into clarity.

It was at this time that often he took me aside, and walked with me, saying little, but I think carrying on some sort of colloquy with me in his mind, a long discourse that he did not deign to share with me, but which satisfied him. Plainly I was the favorite, now. I saw his brow knitting and his jaw working, yet he gave me little hint of what occupied his soul. I came to feel close to him, withal, and there were moments when he appeared to be not some kind of titan and monster, but only a man, albeit of great size and strangeness, with a man's cares on his spirit.

And finally he told me in one of these long walks together, "I think they are planning my overthrow. Do you think that also, Andubatil?"

"Who could overthrow you, O Imbe-Jaqqa!"

He glared at me most fierce and said, "Give me no courtier talk now! I have enemies in this nation."

"They are unknown to me."

"And unknown to me also," said he darkly. "Yet I feel them crowding about me in the shadows. There are men here hungry for my place. There are men who would cast me down."

I knew not what to say; I said nothing.

He leaned toward me, his eyes near to mine, and muttered, "It would be a great wrong. They cannot achieve my tasks. They lack the strength within their souls. Do you know what I say, Andubatil? There is strength of body—" and he snatched up a stout log, that lay before us, and snapped it in half as though it were a straw—"and there is strength in *here*, which is a different strength." He pounded upon his vault of a chest. "I have that strength, and they do not, and so I am the one Imbe-Jaqqa! And so I must remain!" His eyes grew wilder, his face became slick with sweat. He was moving from a solemn brooding humor to one of mad intensity and rancor, and I felt the huge force of him gathering like a great rock rolling down the side of a mountain, to crush all below. "Look, there is the world, Andubatil! Fouled! Stained! Corrupted! And it is given to me to cleanse it! Not to them is it given, but to Calandola, to go forth into that rotten and debased and unsound world, and make it clean and holy. They do not understand that. They think of power, not of purity; they think of ruling, not of cleansing. And I will not allow them to displace me. An' I know them, I will break them, as I break these." Whereupon he dropped to his knees, and seized on all sides the fallen wood of the forest, and bundled it into thick faggots, and broke those faggots with no effort, and scattered the pieces aside. "I will break them!" he cried.

You will say, from my account of his words, that he was mad. And yea, there was madness in him. But also was there a terrible strength, and a force, and a burning heat of conviction, that you could only have known, had you stood close beside him as I stood close beside him.

"Who is it that opposes you, O Lord Imbe-Jaqqa?" I asked.

"I do not know," said he. "But if you hear things, come to me with what you hear. For it would be a wickedness and a criminal deed, if I am overthrown before my time, and before my work is accomplished.

Will you? Will you come to me with the names of the traitors, Andu-batil?"

I pledged him that I would, for how could I say him nay? But I knew no traitors, not then.

The planning of the new war proceeded, and went on endlessly, as if the enemy that Calandola faced was Portugal itself, and not just some little lord of the inland. I think he was held immobile by his own doubts, he who all his life had been a stranger to doubt and hesitance. So still he embellished and enhanced his plans, which always exalted the part of the Kimana Kyeer and his peerless musket, and made the white Jaqqa ever more central to the conquest that was seemingly never to be begun.

I noticed that after these goings off with Calandola for such private discourse, I began to see less of my first friend Kinguri, who now hung back, and sought my company rarely. I remembered the warning of Kakula-banga, that I would have one day to choose between Calandola and Kinguri, between fire and ice, and I bethought me that perhaps I was being maneuvered now toward making that choice. But I could do nothing in that regard except watch, and wait.

Also did I watch, at Calandola's behest, the ten captains of the nation. But although I now knew them one from the other, and had some idea of each man's soul, I saw little enmity in them toward Calandola. In the wranglings of the high council, I did perceive that certain of the lords always disposed themselves at once toward any measure that Calandola proposed, and some frequently took issue, and gave their support of times to counter-measures suggested by Kinguri. The ones most solidly with the Imbe-Jaqqa were Kasanje and Kaimba and Bangala, and the adherents to Kinguri they were Kulambo and Ngonga and Kilombo. But that of itself said nothing: for frequently a king's most loyal and loving advisers are those men who dare to offer him independent judg-ment, and the traitors are those that feign total submission. Of the other lords, Zimbo and Ntotela were men both old and wise, who did not seem to have the stuff of treason in them, and Ti-Bangala was a mighty and lion-hearted hero, and Machimba-lombo, though full of pride and often trembling like an overtuned harpstring from some hidden rage within him, had so many times on the field of battle risked his own life in the defense of the Imbe-Jaqqa that I could not imagine him false. So it seemed to me that Calandola, like many a Caesar before him, was inventing conspirators and enemies out of moonbeams and cobwebs, for his rule here did seem absolute to me, and maybe only a torment of his soul did require him to contrive such fears. Yet I remembered that the first Caesar had had conspirators indeed about him, and not mere moon-beams; therefore did I keep my eyes open.

But perhaps not open wide enough, or I would have been more on guard myself.

We were in the third week of our hesitation before Makellacolonge, and a kind of tautness did grip all the Jaqqa camp, like the tight silence before a great storm, or before a quaking of the earth. We Jaqqa lords had feasted well, and Calandola had shown great favor to me, giving me the choicest cut of the meat, and pouring blooded wine for me with his own hand. Afterward I went to my sleeping-place and took my will most joyously and noisily of my wife Kulachinga, and then I toppled into sleep like a stone statue overturned by a tempest.

And woke some time in the darkness to hear a little whimpering sound, like the cry of a cat in pain, and felt Kulachinga's hand, or someone's, against my shoulder, shoving me most vehemently to the far side of the mat. And looked upward, and by cold clear shafts of moonlight saw a figure great as a mountain looming over me, and a weapon raised high and descending; and I rolled aside just as it fell and cleft deep through the mat.

Though I had been strong gripped by sleep, and almost drugged, I might say, by overmuch wine and the venting of lust, yet there is nothing quite like the crashing of a vast sword into one's pillow to clarify one's mind and bring it awake. I came to my knees, and saw my assailant striving to pull his weapon free of the ground into which it had cut; and when I put my hand to his wrist to stay him, he flung me aside like a bundle of rags. Now I saw his face. It was the captain Jaqqa Machimba-lombo.

"Aye, and will you kill me?" I said. I grasped about, and found a spear, and my sword; and Kulachinga, unbidden, knelt to fan the fire, so that I could have clearer sight. Machimba-lombo left his sword where it lay, and went for his dagger, which he raked against my right arm, lightly cutting it. I thrust my spear between his legs and twisted, putting him off his balance, but the stratagem was a faulty one, for he fell forward atop me instead of, as I had hoped, broadside into the wall. We went down, losing all our weapons in the turmoil, and rolled over and over, fighting not in the graceful dance-like manner of Jaqqa wrestling, but in the bloodiest of coarse brawling, intending to do a lethal injury upon one another.

I heard Kulachinga shouting, and running for aid.

Now Machimba-lombo held the upper hand, and now I. He was a heavier man, and some years younger; but I was quick and no weakling, and the knowledge that I was fighting for my life gave me an added power. His hands were at my throat, but I forced them back, and got my thumbs against the sides of his neck: this hold he broke by swinging

his shoulders clear of the ground, and then he brought his knee up to
my loins, which stunned me and made me choke with pain. But that
very action liberated a torrent of puke that sprang from my injured belly
and spewed out upon him. He grunted and, in his disgust, gave over
for an instant, turning from me just long enough for me to drive my
elbow crashing into his gut, and then the side of my other hand across
the back of his neck as he rolled away. It was done with such force that
I felt it through my whole shoulder, and I dare say he felt it worse, for
he writhed as if I had smashed his every bone with that one blow. I
took his shoulders in my grip and forced his face hard into the ground
and cried, "Will you yield?"

"You must not live!"

"Come, Machimba-lombo, give over. Give over!"

"Filth-Jaqqa! Thief-Jaqqa! Offal-Jaqqa!"

"These names have no force," said I.

But there was force left in him: that I soon learned, for he pried
himself upward, and gave me a great buffet of his rising shoulder against
my chin, that left me with my head spinning. Then he reached past me
for the dagger he had dropped. I caught his arm just in time, chopping
at it with the edge of my hand so that it was numbed, and mine fair
numbed also. I took him arm in arm and rolled him over, so that he
went through the fire of our hearth and was singed of the face, and
howled. But on the far side of the hearth he landed against his sword,
that was still stuck in the ground, and this time, such was the direction
of his movement, it came free when he pulled at it. He sprang up like
a demon and brandished it and swung it in a wide circle through the
air, making it hiss and sing.

I saw my spear and snatched it up, and waited for him. For all his
dire attack on me, I did not wish the slaying of him; but now I knew I
must do it, or perish myself. It was a great loathly sharp sword he had,
but a sword is not a good lunging weapon, nor a throwing weapon, and
I could stick him from afar, and I would.

I readied myself for the cast. But then suddenly there were torches
everywhere, and the place was full of warriors, that swarmed on us and
seized us both, and took from us our weapons; and Imbe Calandola
himself came to the scene an instant afterward, demanding to know the
cause of the uproar.

"I awoke to find him over me with his sword poised," I said. "And
we fought; and we were stopped from fighting. I beg you, Lord Calandola, let me finish this thing."

And I glowered at Machimba-lombo, all grizzled on one side of his
head from the flame in his hair, and battered, and enraged. The full

anger was upon me, too, now, and my chest was full of it so I could scarce breathe, for that this man would have done me cowardly to death as I slept, butchering me like a calf. I felt fifty pains from our wrestling, that I had not noticed two moments before. There was across my eyes a mask of hot red rage.

He too was enfuried. He spat toward me, and cried, "Slave-Jaqqa! Pig-Jaqqa!"

"Night-creeper!"

Machimba-lombo did struggle to break free. As did I, and nearly I succeeded, but I was restrained.

Calandola said, "What is this treason, Machimba-lombo? This is the Kimana Kyeer you do menace! Explain your attack."

But now Machimba-lombo said nothing.

Kinguri and Ntotela and Ti-Bangala and one or two of the other lords entered. They conferred in whispers; Imbe Calandola summoned them to him; after a moment Machimba-lombo was bound with thick plaited withes, and taken off, still cursing and muttering. Only then did the warriors who held my arms pinned behind my back release me. I rubbed at the bruised places I felt all over me, and Kulachinga most timidly came to me, and stroked me to soothe me.

I said, "I know not why he did this ambuscade upon me, for I have done him no injury never, unless my rising so fast in your esteem did enrage him."

"It was nothing else than that," said the Imbe-Jaqqa. And he looked dour and thoughtful, that by his ennobling me as Kimana Kyeer he had driven this valued prince of his to despair, and to treason. "He could not abide your triumphs."

"And would he kill, out of envy alone? Ah, that is it! I should have seen!"

Kinguri said, "He has been greatly angered by your high repute among us, Andubatil. Before you came, he was the most valiant of our warriors, but your musket has darkened his light. We have seen him change in recent weeks. But I had not thought him changed so much, that he would come to slay in the dark."

Though he would have killed me most foully, I felt a sadness for this lord Machimba-lombo. My anger was passing. I am a man of even temper, as you know. Yet what pain there must have been upon Machimba-lombo, to see me climb so swift in his people! For I knew these Jaqqa lords to have a nobility, that would not permit them so shameful a murder, were they in their proper minds.

To Calandola I said, "What will be done with him now?"

"He will be tried and slain."

"And is there no sparing him?" I asked.

The Imbe-Jaqqa looked perplexed. "What, you would spare him?"

"It is the Christian way," said Kinguri quietly to him. "They do love their enemies, by command of their great *mokisso*."

"Ah," said Calandola to me, "you love him, then?"

"By God's feet, I love him not, O Imbe-Jaqqa!" I cried. "When he was in my hands on the floor, I would have had the life from him if I could, for his treachery on me. But now I am more calm. I think it would be a grievous waste to slay him, for his strength is great, and his valor huge."

"He is worthless now," said old Ntotela. "He is an animal now, a wild beast."

"He will recover his wits," I said. "Look ye, it was only that he was jealous of my honors among you, as the Imbe-Jaqqa has said, because I am newly come and already risen high. But he can be led out of his wrath."

"Nay," said Calandola. "This is foolishness. Defend him not to me, Andubatil. He will never leave off his enmity to you now. There is only one way to end this enmity, and that is to put an end to the one who dares attempt murder upon the Kimana Kyeer. Come."

It was dawn now. A great red blaze of light, that looked like a giant bonfire, was rising over the eastern mountains. The air was soft and heavy, with the hint of a later rain. All the Jaqqas were up, and all appeared to know of Machimba-lombo's invasion of my sleeping-place, for they were agitated and vehement.

Kinguri, falling in alongside me, said, "This is never done, the striking of one Jaqqa captain by another. It was noble of you to speak in his favor, but you ought not to persist. He is doomed."

I shrugged. "It is nothing to me, if he die," I said. For my outburst of mercy had gone from me as swiftly as my earlier red rage had. I felt now all the pains that Machimba-lombo had inflicted upon me in our struggle, and also I felt the strange belated dismay that comes over one when one has had a near thing with death, and has had no time to comprehend it for the first while. But for Kulachinga's warning I would be cleft halves painting the earth-mother's breast with my good blood now.

They had Machimba-lombo in the midst of a circle, like the lion-circle of before, and Zimbo and some of the older men were speaking with him. His bonds had been undone, and indeed he seemed quieter now, almost reflective, even saddened. But it was only his failure to slay me that made him downcast. The sunrise fell upon him so that his deeply black skin did shine with a bronzy brightness, and I saw my marks upon his flesh. When he beheld me he glared with new fervor, and I think if he had been freed he would have leapt me all over again.

Imbe Calandola said, approaching him, "Speak, Machimba-lombo, tell us what was in your mind."

"It was in my mind. O Imbe-Jaqqa, that this man is not one of us, and does not deserve his rank."

"And so you would slay him?"

"If not I, then who? For I knew you would not remove him. And he should not be what he is among us, for he is not of our kind, I think."

"Then you are wrong. He is truly of our kind, Machimba-lombo."

I found it passing strange, to hear the man-eater king say this of me. But I kept my silence, and chewed inward a little upon those words.

"How, of our kind?" cried Machimba-lombo. "His skin is white! His hair is gold! He is Christian!"

"He is taken in with us, and adopted into our number."

"Aye, and made a captain, even! But he is not of the blood, O Imbe-Jaqqa!"

"I say that he is blooded with us by his soul," replied Calandola. Then impatiently he said, "I will not dispute this with you. You know that it is treason to raise your hand against a high Jaqqa."

"He is no Jaqqa," stubbornly said Machimba-lombo.

"Yet I say he is. And you have done treason; and therefore you are put down from all your high place, and we grant you only this one mercy, that you will have an elephanto-tail dedicated for you as though you had died in honor. For you were a man of honor before this." To the captain Ti-Bangala he gestured, and said, "Bring to us the tail of the elephanto of the Jaqqa Machimba-lombo."

At this, the face of Machimba-lombo turned stony and ashen, for he knew that his death was upon him. And I think he heard his *mokisso* singing to him out of the ground, which soon would draw him down to Hell.

I felt some sorrow for him, though he would have felt none for me. But I kept it locked within my breast, and only glared at him like an enemy. For I was Kimana Kyeer, and he had done treason against me and all my adopted nation.

Ti-Bangala returned. A great heavy hairy elephanto-tail was in his grasp. Calandola took it, and draped it like a whip about his shoulders. Then to Machimba-lombo he said, "We grant you the death of honor, Machimba-lombo Jaqqa."

What next befell filled me with stupefaction and amaze. They did not put Machimba-lombo to death with weapons, as I had expected, nor any poison. Merely did Calandola lay the coiled elephanto-tail at the condemned man's feet. And Machimba-lombo nodded, and looked downward most somber at it a moment; and then he swayed and went sinking down upon the earth like a puppet-doll whose strings had been let loose. For he simply did release his life, and let it from him upon a wish, and that was an end to him. It is a trick these Africans have, that I do not understand, that when they grieve extremely, or are dishonored and must die, they can do it by willing it alone, and saying to themselves, "Depart this world," and they do depart.

Six of the high captains bore Machimba-lombo's body away, and there was a ceremony that I did not attend, and they laid him to rest. And afterward another Jaqqa that was named Paivaga was named to be captain in his place, being slender and swift, with the thin lips and narrow nose of a Moor, though his skin was jet. For some days Calandola did keep to himself, thereafter, brooding on the death of Machimba-lombo, for he had been a great warrior. But his life had been forfeit, since it is forbidden for one high Jaqqa to harm another. And in the eyes of all in this nation, now, was I recognized to be a high Jaqqa: I Andubatil, I Kimana Kyeer.

FIVE

FOUR DAYS after the death of Machimba-lombo, Kinguri the Imbe-Jaqqa's brother did summon me quietly, and say, "Tell no one, but make ready for a journey, and take nothing with you but a knife and a sword."

"Not my musket?"

"Nay, it will be only a hindrance."

Though I knew not what he had in mind, I did as he said, and at his orders I arose in the night and said to Kulachinga that I would return, but I knew not when. I went to the edge of the camp by dawny mists, and there I met Kinguri.

He and I left camp stealthily together, only us two, and made our way eastward across a broad open plain. By the sunrise hour we halted, and he said, "You told me once of the city of Rome, that is the Pope's house, and sits on seven hills beside a river. Is it a splendid city?"

"So I have heard, though I have never seen it."

"Is it as splendid, do you think, as *that?*"

And he led me a little way around a low grassy hill, and I looked beyond it and saw a city perched atop a stony mountain some seven leagues in compass, that had been hidden from my view by the winding of our path. Between that city and us lay rich green pastures, fields, and meadows, that surely did yield God's own bounty of provision for everyone who dwelled therein.

Kinguri said, "It is the city of Dongo, that is the residence of King Ngola. Tell me, Andubatil, do you know anything so splendid in all of Christendom?"

What could I say? That Dongo is a mere squalid town of thatched cottages, and Rome is the capital of the world? Nay, I would not hurt him so. Besides, in its way this Dongo was a fair wondrous place, perched so high, like the habitation of the former gods upon Olympus, and in the early light it did shine with a pale beauty quite unearthly.

"Is it the Imbe-Jaqqa's thought to assault that city now, instead of Makellacolonge?"

Kinguri smiled and shook his head. "Not yet, Andubatil, not yet! You see there: there is but a single passage into the mountain, and that is well fortified, so that in the forcing of it we would suffer great loss of life. The Imbe-Jaqqa is not ready for that forcing. First we must grow our numbers, threefold beyond what we are now; and then we will camp below Dongo, and cut its road to the fields, and starve it a little. And when it is enough starved we will burst into it, and take it, and remove it from the world. And that will be the end of King Ngola and his nation, whom we have hated a long while."

This he said most calmly, seeming without blood-lust. It was much like Calandola's talk of a divine mission to purge the world of its cities and farms: this did Kinguri also share, and in a dispassionate way he longed to turn everything back to the fashion of the beginning, to render Africa a new Eden of simple naked shepherds.

Well, and I suppose that is no worse a reason to go to war than any other, and better than some. For what profits it to march into a land simply to force Papistry upon its people, or to take Papistry from them, or to make a change of government that puts one lecherous greedy prince in place of another? And the war that the Spaniards did carry against the people of the Indies, stealing their gold from them and giving them poxes and plagues in return: was that any more noble than the Jaqqas' dream of cleansing the world of everything that mankind had builded upon it? I was still under Imbe Calandola's spell, and his monstrous ambition, though I did not truly share it, had substance in my eyes. I saw in it a kind of strange poetry, and a stark simplicity, that seemed to me to be in its way most deeply felt. Aye, clear them off, those who profaned the earth! Pull down the cities, push the perfidious Portugals into the sea! Why not? It had a merit. Dongo tomorrow, and São Paulo de Loanda the day after that: aye, why not, why not? And then the land would be at peace, and sheep might safely graze.

Kinguri now drew me onward toward the city of Dongo. I wondered if he meant to enter it, which would be sure death for us, I being as conspicuous in this land as a three-headed calf, and he with his Jaqqa stature and ornaments being scarce less visible.

But that was not his plan. When we neared the place where the path to Dongo turned upward into the mountain, he gestured to the left and said, "In that meadow live the sacred peacocks of King Ngola, that he prizes above all else. To take a single feather from one is to forfeit your life, if you are seen. Let us enter that meadow, Andubatil, and gather us some feathers."

"And if we are caught?"

"Then we will die. But we will do it bravely."

I could not see the sense of this effort. I had had one touch of death's wings already this week, and the soreness of my struggle with Machimba-lombo was still upon my limbs. But it seemed most urgent to Kinguri to enter here, and having come so far with him I would not turn away now.

So we did steal into the meadow, which was moist and bordered by thick-columned plants of a bluish hue in stem and leaf. Before us lay the royal birds, flying up and down the trees, and spreading their tremendous tails and making wild shrieking sounds. The place seemed to be unguarded, which was strange to me, these birds being so precious to the king. But Kinguri said there were guards hidden about, and charged me to stand watch for them.

From his pouch he drew a strip of leather with two round stones attached to its ends. Most warily he walked toward the peacocks, meaning to cast this thing at them and entangle the legs of one. On his first two casts he failed, the birds being faster-moving than they appeared; but on the third he did snare one, that set up a vast squawking and rioting as the leather wrapped itself by the deftness of Kinguri's throw about its body. "Come!" he cried, and we rushed forward, and with our knives we cut the beautiful bird's throat, that gleamed with many colors.

Then he caught me by the upper arm, and did make a deep but narrow slit in my flesh, very swiftly, before I could pull back, and the same to himself. And took the throat of the peacock and let its blood run over his wound, and put his arm against mine, rubbing it so that our three bloods did mix, his and mine and the bird's, and as he did this he glared into my eyes with wild savage glee, behind which I saw his subtle intelligence burning brightly.

"We are brothers now, you and I, Andubatil Jaqqa!" he said in a hoarse thick voice.

"Brothers of the blood, is it?"

"Yea. And if we had done this earlier, Machimba-lombo would have feared to touch you, knowing your *mokisso* and mine were joined. But this will guard you now against other such enemies, for I think you do have some yet, Andubatil."

"And who do those be?" I asked, staring in wonder at the bleeding place on my arm.

"Ah, we can talk of that another time. Come, now."

In haste we did gather tail-feathers of the peacock, and thrust them into the bands of beads we wore, and cast aside the carcass of the bird and made ready to go. Just then the sentry of the place, making his early rounds, came upon us, and stood in surprise, his mouth opening and closing like that of a fish on land, at the sight of a white man and a Jaqqa looting together one of the holy peacocks. He was a short blackamoor, past middle years, in a brocaded green robe and a high turreted hat, and he pointed at us and made a little choking sound without voice to it, so great was his amaze. At once Kinguri sprang toward him, knife in hand.

The guard took a heavy breath, as though at last preparing himself to utter a great outcry: and the Jaqqa slipped his blade very easily into the man's throat, so that all he let forth was a tiny bubbling sound, and went to his knees, gushing blood like a fountain. And had he walked first to the other side of the meadow that morning, he would on this day yet be alive, I think.

"We must hurry, brother," said Kinguri.

Through the dawn mists we fled that place, clutching our brave peacock feathers in both our hands, and my arm did throb and tingle where the alien bloods had entered it.

On the return journey to the Jaqqa camp Kinguri was most animated and alive. He walked with such bounds that I could scarce keep pace with his long-legged stride, and he overflowed with new questions for me, asking, What is the color of the sky over England, and, How big is the Queen's palace at London, and, Does God ever visit the kings of Europe, and more like that. And he demanded also to know who it was that decided how much grain a piece of gold would buy, and why it was that God had let His only Son be slain by men, and was it true that English were born black and turned white upon exposure to the cold air of our land, and such. I could hardly finish the answer to one question when he was upon me with the next, or two or three others, like a man in fever of knowledge: and this the man who had grown furious when I made objection to the killing of babies, and told me I was a fool for not seeing the obvious wisdom of the custom, this who now interrogated me like a hungry scholar. Only as we reached the camp did he grow more quiet; and at the end he turned to me and looked me close in the eye and said, "This is no small thing, what you and I have done. A Jaqqa takes a brother but once or twice in his life, and not without much considering of it first. And almost always it happens on the field of battle."

"Why did you choose me, then, Kinguri?"

"Your blood has wisdom in it, Andubatil. And now we are sealed to one another, and the wisdom of the whites streams in my flesh. I tell you, I could not abide not having it within me!"

And therefore the ferocity of the Jaqqas now streamed in my own flesh, I thought, but did not say. I took their food in my gut and their blood in my veins, and step by step was my life flowing in the river of their life, and mingling indistinguishable.

I grinned at him and said, "I hope I am worthy of the choice, brother!"

"So will you prove to be," said he. "Of that I am sure."

We entered the camp together, bearing our dazzling feathers held high; and some boys of the Imbe-Jaqqa's court saw us, each with our bloody slices on our arms. Within an hour every Jaqqa knew what had passed between Kinguri and me in the meadow under the city of Dongo. All that day long was there whispering, and furtive glances at me. Kulachinga herself, although my wife and a former wife of the Imbe-Jaqqa, looked upon me from afar, as if I had attained some sublime new ennoblement beyond what I already had, that made me awesome to her.

For this was one of the highest customs among the Jaqqas, that two men who respected and loved one another should go off in the night on some long journey that had an aspect of peril to it, and perform some unusual deed such as the stealing of King Ngola's peacock, and celebrate the rite by a mixing of blood. And thenceforth were those two sealed to one another in a way that transcended the ordinary kind of kinship, since that in a tribe that got its members by stealing them, kinship of the ordinary kind meant very little, there being no descent from known mothers or sharing of a common father. I was bonded now to the second man of the realm, who was natural brother to Imbe Calandola himself, which made me in a way a member of the royal family.

Like all such honors this carried a heavy price; for it plunged me even deeper into the rivalries of the court, which already I knew to be strong and severe.

These Jaqqas, like the Turks or Tartars or anyone else, like even us English with our wars of York and Lancaster, are jealous of high rank, and do intrigue and maneuver mightily among themselves to surpass one another. That I perceived only slowly, for at first they were all alike to me, and all seemed united in a war against mankind that joined them into a single being. That was but an illusion, which the falling of Machimba-lombo's sword upon my sleeping-mat had dispelled in me forever. United they might be, yet they had rivalries among themselves, and factions, like any other nation.

So my elevation to blood-brotherhood with Kinguri won me the safety of his own greatness, that extended over me like a glow, but it ran me the risk of gaining other foes such as my late enemy had been. When I pressed Kinguri to name those I must be wary of, he slipped away from the theme like quicksilver, and said there was no one special. But yet he urged me to keep my eyes sharp for signs of resentment. I watched; and I saw that among the high Jaqqas, the three who were most loyal to Kinguri, that is, Kulambo and Ngonga and Kilombo, seemed to hold the same love for me. And those three who ever basked in the close favor of the Imbe-Jaqqa, that were Kasanje and Kaimba and Bangala, now gave me glances, and scowls, and sidewise glares, that made me uneasy. But though I thought often of it, I did not again ever awaken to find an assassin raising his sword above me.

I wondered, having mind of the witch Kakula-banga's warnings, what Calandola's feeling toward me would be, since my joining of blood with Kinguri. I did not think Kinguri would have dared do such a thing without the Imbe-Jaqqa's consent, but I did not know. And because the essence of his nature was so unlike that of other men, never was I sure how he responded to what we had done. On the day of my bonding to Kinguri, the Imbe-Jaqqa did embrace me in that crushing way of his, causing my new-healed wound to open, and he cried most roaringly, "The brother of my brother is my brother!" And called for blooded wine, and had me share it with him. Yet afterward I saw his face most somber and thoughtful, as though he brooded upon this matter, and did not like the new union between Kinguri and me.

In the days that followed, Calandola often had me by his side hours on end, and would not let me go from him. Sometimes he did not speak a word, only stared and drank; and I was silent alongside him, feeling the powerful emanations of his presence, that worked secretly and silently upon my spirit. Other times was he most garrulous, and boasted endlessly of past conquests, saying he had ruined this city and that, and roasted this chief and that, and laid waste this province and that. And still other times did he speak in a more reflective way, almost as deep as the wise Kinguri, on the purpose of his wrath, and on the hope he had of ending wickedness on earth—by which he meant settled civilization, that is—and on the differences between Africa as he perceived it and Europe as I described it. I think he had no real understanding of such places as England and France and Spain, and thought of them just as somewhat more busy places much like Angola and the Kongo. For he could not easily grasp my talk of roads and highways, of great harbors, of cathedrals and palaces, and all such things unknown to this land. He imagined he saw them when I spoke of them, but his own vision of them, as I understood it from his words, was very much smaller than the reality. Or did I misjudge him? Never truly do we see what is in another's mind, but we must stumble about, doing our best to make our thoughts known, and always failing, until we come to Heaven, where all is transparent.

Often now did I go hunting with certain princes of the tribe, most usually Kinguri, but also sometimes his comrades Kulambo and Ngonga. These men were valiant and fierce, and said little, but moved with the strong and lethal speed of huge deadly cats. We would go apart from the tribe, taking with us lances or bows or swords, and for our pleasure fall upon the beasts of the field, the gazelles and zevveras and antelopes, and now and again a leopard prowling the treetops by night, or a young lion. Never did I use my musket in these exploits, the powder and shot being too difficult of replacement. But there was one time when I did regret its absence, when I hunted alone with great wide-shouldered Ngonga.

We had gone into the thickets to the east, pursuing the track of some swift creature, and getting ever closer to it, for its scent grew greater. But then suddenly we made our way into an opening between two thick vines that twined like angry serpents, and there was our beast fallen, and five men of some inland tribe gathered round it, pulling from it their spears.

Upon the sight of us they pointed and shouted in unknown jabber. I think they came from so far away that they knew not what a Jaqqa was, for they showed no fright of Ngonga for all his size and majesty and his Jaqqa emblems and his Jaqqa teeth. But any forest folk who knew they were with a Jaqqa would have fled at once. As for me, they were more perturbed, I suppose thinking me a spirit from the next world; but they displayed no fear of me, neither, so either they were most mightily valiant or else more than passing silly.

Still crying out their garboiled noises, thick-tonguedly, *"Yagh ghagh ghagh yagh,"* or the like, they rushed toward us with their weapons drawn. But their valor was not matched by their skill. I parried a thrust with my spear, and pushed the man away to Ngonga, who sliced him lustily upon his shoulder with the edge of his sword and cut him downward in two. And in the same moment Ngonga did jostle an attacker toward me, within range of my own blade, and swiftly I took the man's head from his shoulders. The three remaining would not flee, but stubbornly renewed the onslaught: to their great cost, for that we cut them to pieces. All was done in a moment. The clearing was a charnel shambles, with heads here and legs there and blood bubbling everywhere, and Ngonga's body and mine soaked and crimsoned with it, though we had neither of us been injured.

We looked toward one another, breathing hard, but joyous in the fine heat that comes from fighting well accomplished.

"Who are these foolish folk?" I asked him.

He shrugged. "They are meat," he said. "That is all they are, and nothing more than that."

"Do you think there are more of them nearby?"

"Most certainly I do," said he. "They hide behind every tree. Come, let us show them what we are!"

And to my amaze he did slash open the belly of one of the dead men, and forage most expertly into that tangle of glistening various-colored gewgaws that we all of us carry in our middles. From amongst those things he plucked forth the man's liver, and held it high, so that any concealed onlooker might have a good look. And then most coolly this Ngonga did sever the raw red liver into some smaller pieces and hand me mine, and he began to devour the fresh meat, which I did also. Slippery was it on my tongue, and hot and strange, but I bolted it down as though it were breast of partridge, or something even finer.

I think we were a most terrible sight to the unseen watchers. For in a quick while we heard rustlings out there, and saw a swaying of some treetops, and then all was silent: they were fleeing those eaters of human gore that had fallen so fiercely upon their fellows. It would not astonish me to hear that they were fleeing even unto this day, not daring to look back behind them lest we be following in our monstrous hunger.

In such ways did I pass the time as we camped outside the land of Makellacolonge. We did not attack, neither did we depart, and the air was troubled among my Jaqqa brothers, who grew tense and suspicious. They did not understand why we waited so long. Nor did Calandola give any clue: he was guided by his witches, and by the stars and the things he saw upon the horizon, and he kept his own counsel in these matters. So we diverted ourselves in whatever ways we could. But the death of Machimba-lombo overhung our minds, and created much unrest.

In this uncertain time there was revived in the Jaqqa camp a practice of which I had heard much, but had not yet witnessed here, which was, the trial by ordeal. I had seen such things among the people of Mofarigosat, where trial by poison was the customary measure. But that was only one of the many devilish forms of this manner of justice that the Jaqqas favored.

Moreover, they did not hold their trials merely when some issue at law had to be decided. Nay, they did them as general signs of innocence, as a grand show of bravery, to prove their loyalty to Imbe Calandola.

Perhaps ten days after my brothering with Kinguri came the first of these events, when all the Jaqqa lords marched before Calandola as he sat upon his high throne. The Imbe-Jaqqa did demand of them a renewing of homage, by means of the ordeal called *chilumbo*, which was done with fire. In this, a red-hot iron was passed over the thigh of each man, the reasoning being that any who are faithful to the Imbe-Jaqqa will be unharmed, but those who harbor secret discontents will be blistered and injured, and thereby their treachery exposed.

Thereupon the old wizard Kakula-banga, wearing his finest feathers and paints, and a coat of shining grease over his whole skin, did take a kind of holy hatchet which he had, and laid it in the fire. Then one by one every great man of the tribe did step forward, while musicians did make a horrid drumming to excite everyone the further.

The first of these was Kinguri, who cried out, "By my *mokisso*, I do vow I love the Imbe-Jaqqa Calandola before all else in the world!" And the wizard did take the hot iron from the fire, and pass it across Kinguri's leg, not touching the skin but coming close upon it. During this, Kinguri held high his head, and his arms outstretched, and he smiled broadly without the least show of fear or pain. And lo! when the wizard stepped back, there was not the merest blister upon Kinguri's skin.

The trial of *chilumbo* proceeded now to examine the Jaqqa generals Kasanje and Kaimba, who came forth from it unscathed, which I could not comprehend, the fire being so hot and the head of the hatchet glowing full ruby red. After them came Kulambo, who was so dear to Kinguri, and he, too, was unharmed, smiling throughout his ordeal. The wizard now plunged his hatchet back into the flame to renew its heat, and I looked about to see who would be next, and was much surprised and amazed to see that Kinguri was beckoning to me that I should join the line.

I stood frozen a moment, not knowing what to do.

"Go, Andubatil!" Kinguri did command.

I had thought me exempt from these sports, being a foreigner and no native of the tribe. But that was folly: I was Andubatil Jaqqa, blood-brother to the great Kinguri, and the Imbe-Jaqqa had named me Kimana Kyeer, and had proclaimed me to be a true Jaqqa when he condemned Machimba-lombo. I could not have the high privilege of my rank without accepting its perils.

I would lie if I told you that great fear did not pass through my guts, at Kinguri's command. For I knew not by what magic this ordeal was conducted. Nor did I think myself fully loyal to Calandola, as these men were: I still stood with one foot in Christendom and the other in the Jaqqa nation. When the hot metal came near to my skin, would it reveal the secret Englishness that I still held within, the part of me that was not yet wholly given up to revelry of the cannibal sort? And if I blistered, what then would befall me?

Yet had I no choice. If I failed to come forth, I would proclaim myself traitor and coward, and this was a nation that knew not mercy.

So I put the best face on things, and marched me forward, and cried out to the Imbe-Jaqqa, proclaiming my loyalty to him, and trusted to God to bring me through this ordeal as He had carried me through so many others. And the witch Kakula-banga did lift the glowing hatchet, and bring it close, pressing his scarred and wrinkled face upon me and staring into mine eyes with his one blazing brilliant eye. I could not tell if he were mocking me or giving me assurance that all was well, so strange and intense was the look of that eye.

He passed the hatchet-head near enough to me so that I felt its heat on my naked thigh, and did smell the burnt smell of the fine hairs that sprout on my skin. Throughout which, I did compel myself to smile securely and stretch out my arms, as though for all the world I was being given some great new honor, some Jaqqa dukedom.

Then the hatchet passed from me, and still I stood for an instant, not realizing the ordeal was over for me and I was unharmed: and I at length eased my stiff pose and joined those who had succeeded in the test, to drink some palm-wine with them.

"Ah, I had no doubts of you, brother," said Kinguri, laughing.

Thus it went, man after man, and no one of them being touched by the heat. Which left me thinking that the ordeal was a mere hollow mummery, done to amuse the Imbe-Jaqqa. But then a certain Nbande, a deep-chested warrior of the second rank, with a dry and sullen manner about him, had his turn in the line; and when the hatchet came to him he howled and clutched his leg, which was singed and well-nigh cooked in a great red patch. This man Nbande then did fall to his knees and implore Calandola, claiming that this singeing was some mistake and that he stood higher than any man for love of the Imbe-Jaqqa, but it was no use, for justice was swift, and five or six of the Jaqqa lords did stick him with their lances, and cut the life from him.

"It is no surprise," said Kinguri beside me. "He was ever untrustworthy, that one."

That night the Jaqqas did feast on the flesh of the traitor Nbande, with many lewd remarks about the dead man's wickedness; and the wives of Nbande, five of them, were brought forth weeping, and were offered as concubines to several of the Jaqqa high ones. Bangala had him one, and Paivaga chose a woman also, and old Zimbo took two; but I declined when they offered me the last, and she was taken by Ngonga. Afterward there was a wrestling, between Paivaga, the newest of the high lords, and Kaimba. This was done most gracefully, with many a fall made to look like a simple feint, and even when they did much harm to one another, they did it without crying out by the injured man, but only delicate incatchings of the breath. Paivaga was proclaimed the victor, and he threw his arm most warmly over Kaimba. This Jaqqa wrestling, I thought, was one of the most beautiful things about these people. When the match was done, they called for others to come forth, and some looked toward me.

But I was still sore from my blooding with Kinguri, and the injuries done me by Machimba-lombo had not altogether healed, either. Nor were my spirits so high that I welcomed this exuberance, for the ordeal trial had darkened my soul some, and the slaying of the man Nbande. I declined the wrestling-match, saying I was not ready for it, and sat back, somber somewhat. I thanked God for my narrow escape, thinking, This might be my flesh that is being eaten in banquet this evening, had the heat raised my skin. And it might be my wife Kulachinga who was offered about for the pleasure of others. And I saw, that among these man-eaters one lived always on the edge of the sword.

Six

THERE WERE trials of other sorts on the days that followed. These were not large spectacles for the sake of demonstrating loyalty to Calandola, but rather the settling of disputes between one Jaqqa and another. For they were in sooth a quarrelsome and contentious lot. A way they had of dealing with such disputes, that seemed most strange to me, was the trial by sea-shells, which occurred between the Jaqqas Mbula and Matadi, when they quarreled over the ownership of a fine sword. Kinguri did summon both to appear before him, and when they were come he fixed to each of their foreheads a grand yellow and purple sea-shell, and at the same time commanded them to bow down their heads. The shell did stick to the forehead of Mbula, but fell from that of Matadi, and he was taken for the liar.

Another was the trial by boiling water, the which I saw upon a dispute concerning possession of a woman, that two men both claimed as his own captive wench. Here each of them took an oath, the oath *nole fianzumdu* it was called, and then a wizard did heat an iron red hot, and quench it in a gourd of water. This boiling water was immediately given to the two who took the oath. One swallowed it without labor, the other could not easily get it down: and the woman was awarded to the first.

Also did I see the trial by poison again, that was here practiced with the fruit of a certain palm called *embá*, which yields much oil. Here, one Jaqqa had accused another of a treachery toward Calandola, that is, even planning the Imbe-Jaqqa's murder. "This I greatly deny," the accused man cried, and such a clamor burst out between them that they were taken up for the ordeal. Then were all the great Jaqqas called together, and a bowl of the *embá* fruit was brought to Calandola, who held it on high. The Imbe-Jaqqa then did have one of his man-witches select a fruit from the bowl, and bite of it himself, to show that it was harmless and innocent. After which, three other fruits were chosen, and into one of them a poison was injected by means of a long thorn. Then the poisoned one was mixed with the other two, and the bowl was offered, after certain prayers by the wizard, to the two Jaqqas.

The accuser chose first, and he did bite a fruit and find it harmless. That one was thrown away, and a new fruit from the bowl was added, so that the second man might have the same risk of one out of three. He took his bite, and instantly began to swell at his throat, and to choke and make horrid gurgling sounds. And within three moments he had fallen down dead.

"Thus die all traitors," said Imbe Calandola, and the body was carried away.

All this I found most sinister and disagreeable, for I could not see how justice was discovered with hot irons and poisoned fruits and the like. I reminded me that even in England we had known the trial by ordeal, such as the carrying of red-hot irons, or the ordeal by combat. But all of that had been abolished long ago, in the reign of Henry III or even before him, as something not worthy of a civilized people: except only the trial of witches by ducking them in a pond, for it is known that a witch cannot sink in water, which will always cast her up. But that applies only to witches, who are a special case, and not to ordinary matters at law.

After these trials, there was some quiet among the Jaqqas for a time. We did gather our strength once again to make our long-postponed onslaught against Makellacolonge, but at the last instant Imbe Calandola decided once more against it, saying the omens were not right. What fear he had of attacking that lord, I never knew, and peradventure neither did he. But we closed our camp, having never made battle from it, and marched to the westward again.

Coming along the River Kwanza once more, we reached the city of a lord that is called Shillambansa, uncle to the King of Angola. We burnt his chief town, which was after their fashion very sumptuously builded. This place was very pleasant and fruitful. Here we found great store of wild peacocks, that were everywhere about. Also was there great store of tame ones. In the middle of the town was the grave of the old lord Shillambansa, father to the present one, and there were an hundred tame peacocks on his grave-site, that he had provided for an offering to his *mokisso*. These birds were called *Njilo mokisso*, that is, the Devil's or Idol's Birds, and were accounted as holy things. He had great store of copper, cloth, and many other things laid upon his grave, which is the order of that country.

By command of Imbe Calandola we touched none of the *Njilo mokisso* birds, nor did we injure the goods on the old king's grave. In this I had me in mind of a certain other time when a Portugal had not hesitated to plunder the dead: but a Jaqqa had more respect for the departed, or more fear of his *mokisso*, one or other.

The town itself we did destroy utterly, and of the wild peacocks we captured many, the tail-feathers of which we plucked as ornaments.

In the festival to celebrate the sacking of Shillambansa the palm-wine did flow most freely, and we danced and ate and greatly rejoiced ourselves. It seemed as though the time of the trials by ordeal was well behind us. To Kinguri, as we sat passing the cup one to the other, I said, "Now there is peace among the Jaqqas. It seemed a good war was all that was needed, is that not so?"

"Ah," he said, "war is always a delight to us. But there will be more trouble, I think."

"And more trials?"

"More trials. Always more trials."

"They are so strange to me, so different from our English way."

"And what way is that?" Kinguri asked.

"Why, that the accused is put forth before a judge and a jury, that are picked from among the citizenry at large, and they hear the evidence, and decide the rights and wrongs by vote."

This did startle him. "Why, then, is anyone at all allowed to serve on these juries?"

"Anyone worthy. That is, he must be a man, and neither low nor base. But we are most of us called out to serve, and listen and weigh the tale, and make our decision."

"But how then can the king be certain of the result?"

I did not understand. "He is not," I said. "First the rights and the wrongs must be discerned, by examination of what has befallen, and testimony of witnesses, and the like."

Kinguri shook his head. Plainly he was astonished. "That is no way," he said. "It is madness. There is no government, where justice is left to chance."

"Not to chance, but to investigation."

"It is the same thing," said he. "For the king has no voice in the outcome, and he is not king if he cannot rule his people."

Though I was well gone in my cups, I tried some several times more to explain how justice derives from the facts of the case, and not from the king's wishes. But this seemed stranger and stranger to Kinguri the more ways I expressed it. And finally, being deep in his cups himself, he did impart to me certain truths about the workings of the Jaqqa system of trial, that did make very much clear to me that had been obscure before. For I had been fool enough to think there was some witchcraft involved upon it—if ever there was a place where witchcraft could thrive, and magics of all kinds, it was among these Jaqqas—but, as I had in part already guessed, there was a much more ordinary scaffolding to these ordeals.

It was not justice that the trials served, he said, so much as it was the overarching will of Calandola, that shaped all the destiny of the Jaqqa nation. In the general trials of loyalty, those suspected of being unloyal were chosen aforehand by Calandola; and the wizards, Kinguri declared to me, were put on notice to deal with those men. And then it was done by sleight of hand that the hatchet is put closer to the skin of the victim than of any others, and held there longer, so that he alone is burned, though it is made to seem that all are having equal treatment. So justice becomes an instrument of policy by the Imbe-Jaqqa, who pretends that it is divine will speaking, but it is merely his own plotting. To Kinguri this seemed a most wise way of maintaining order.

"And the trial by shells," I said, "is there some special trickery to that as well?"

"Trickery? Who speaks of trickery? I speak of assuring that a proper verdict is reached."

"It is all the same," said I wearily.

"In the case you witnessed, I knew whose sword that was, and who was the false claimant. We all of us did know. But we must make the outcome seem a holy decree. Look you, Andubatil: there is a special way of fixing these shells to the forehead, with a little twist of the hand, so that it will stick there a moment, while the other man's falls off. This did I do, giving that twist to one, stinting it to the other that was the liar."

"So I wondered," said I.

I did not ask him about the trial by boiling water, for I thought I understood that one through my own reasoning: since that it sometimes happens that by apprehension alone a man is unable to swallow, it can be that guilt will close the throat of one petitioner but not the other, who is the innocent one. And I saw no way that that could be arranged aforetimes by the judge, so perhaps in this instance Jaqqa justice provided true justice.

"And the poisoned palm-fruit?" I said. "How is that done?"

Kinguri laughed. "Why, it is simplicity itself. In the saying of the prayers over the bowl, the *nganga* does conceal palm-fruits in his fingers, and move them about very quickly and cunningly. So that when he offers the bowl to the accuser, all three of the fruits are free of poison, for the *nganga* has taken the poisoned one away. Then when he gives the bowl to the accused one, he drops back in the poisoned one, and secretly puts two more poisoned ones in the place of the harmless ones. Thus all three are deadly, and there is no unsureness of the outcome."

"Ah," I said. "Simplicity itself, as you say."

"Indeed. Is it not?"

"But why does anyone submit to these trials, knowing that the result is foredoomed, and not flee at once?"

Kinguri, looking troubled, replied in a dark voice, "But they do not know what I have told you."

"Ah."

"You understand, these are high secrets of the Imbe-Jaqqa, that I have told you because you are my brother." He seized my wrist. "They must not be revealed, brother."

"I understand—brother."

"They *must not* be revealed," said he, tightening his hand on my arm so that I could feel the bones moving about within, though I made no motion to withdraw from his painful grasp. "Must not, brother."

"Brother, they shall not be," said I.

Nor have they been, until this moment, when any pledge I might have made to Kinguri Jaqqa is long since cancelled and voided by the passage of time and the turning of events.

Having been made privy to such great secrets, though, I began to fear anew for my life, thinking that Kinguri might regret what he had confided in me even more, when the wine had burned from his brain. So when I went to my sleeping-mat, I slept that night with one eye open, and both my ears. But no dark figure came upon me in the night, and in the days that succeeded Kinguri showed me only cordiality, and gave no hint that he was uneasy with me.

It was the warm and rainy season, and several of the Jaqqas fell ill of fevers. For these sick ones, wickerwork houses were built at the far side of the camp, and they were made to dwell there, untended except for the bringing of a little food. No treatment were they given, though the man-witches of the tribe went to them and chanted prayers from a distance. The Jaqqas are generally very kind to one another in their health; but in their sickness they do abhor one another, and will shun their company.

Some of the sick recovered, and some did not. Of these there were burials. To bury the dead they made a vault in the ground, and a seat for him to sit. The dead one had his head newly embroidered with beads and bangles, his body washed, and anointed with sweet powders. All his best robes were put on, and he was brought between two men to his grave, and set in seat as though he were alive. Then two of his wives were set with him, looking most solemn and in terror, as well they might be: for they were to be buried alive. The arms of these wives were broken, I suppose so they might not dig their way out of the grave. And when they were seated, the vault was covered over on the top. After this, comrades of the dead man mourned and sang doleful songs at his grave for the space of three days, and killed many goats, and poured their blood upon his grave, and palm-wine also.

In the fullest of the season of the rain, when it came like greasy warm bullets out of the gray sky and turned the land to a quagmire and a mud-sea about us, this outbreak of fevers did become something like unto a great plague in the Jaqqa camp. Fifty, one hundred, two hundred fell ill, and perhaps more, with new victims every day. On the rim of the camp were whole villages of sick-houses, and the sound of moaning and retching was a hideous counterpointing of harsh symphonies under the drumming of the rain.

The two great men of the Jaqqas took exceeding different outlooks upon this calamity. I saw Kinguri going each hour through the encampment with his shoulders hunched in despair and his black face even blacker with grief. With desperate energy did he strive to halt the spreading of the malady. He conferred often with the witches, and set them to work beating on drums to drive off the spirits, and when the rain permitted it he caused great fires to be lit, with powders hurled into them to send blazes of violent crimson and yellow hues into the air. Every death seemed perceptibly to diminish him. "These are valiant warriors perishing," said he to me. "This is a curse upon us, and I cannot abide it!"

"It will pass with the rain," said I by way of consoling him, though I had no more idea of the truth of that than I did of the sort of birds that do live on the moon.

"It is a curse," said Kinguri again most gloomfully.

He brooded and paced and boiled within as the outbreak became wholly epidemic amongst us. With ever more intent purpose he sought for some remedy. But meanwhile his brother Calandola held himself aloof, like a great mountain looming high above the mists and fogs, that dwelled in utter serenity in the midst of the chaos and the dying. From time to time I saw him moving through the camp among his special followers, observing in a most cool dispassioned way the downfall and wracking of his own armies. But at other times was he encloistered most placidly within his own dwelling, holding court amid wives and witches as if nothing untoward did progress. It was as though his view of the world, that was something that needed purging and cleansing and much destruction, did extend even unto his own nation: that he regarded this plague as a cooking away of needless impureness and dross from the hard gleaming core of the Jaqqa force. But that is only my own speculating; I could not tell you truly what enfolded in Imbe Calandola's mind during this dark time.

One thing I greatly feared, as the dying proceeded, was that there would be some in the Jaqqa camp that would lay the plague to my door, saying, "He is a stranger, he is not one of us, he is white-faced, he has brought a pestilence upon us." And that they would insist on the placating of their *mokissos* by my death. If such an outcry went up, would Calandola yield me up in sacrifice? I lived in daily caution of this.

So I did tremble when a day came on which Calandola summoned me to his inner sanctuary, sending me the word by Kasanje and Kilombo. And I thought, Ah, they have resolved at last that I am the cause, and I am to be slain.

I found the Imbe-Jaqqa sprawled on his great throne, toying with bangles of bone, and only some four or five of his wives about him. His face was somber but yet calm, and out of that dark glistening mask his terrible eyes did shine like beacon-fires as he looked down upon me and said, "I must have a service from you."

"Ask it, O Imbe-Jaqqa."

"I would have you end this sickness that is among us."

"Ah, I am no surgeon, Lord Calandola."

"You are more surgeon than you think," replied the man-eater king. "And it is you must cut the heart from this plague lest it devour us all. For I have given it its free run, and let it to blaze like a healthy fire, but now a finish must swiftly be brought to it."

"And I am to be the finisher?"

"Only you can do what is required, my Andubatil, my Kimana Kyeer."

He did explain to me that in his prayers and meditation he had identified the causing of the disease. Which was, that certain members of the tribe who lay ill but neither regained their health nor died were the centers of the infection. From their wicker-house shelters they did pump the taint of their souls into the tribe, said he, and corrupted new victims every day. Therefore must these plague-bearers be eradicated. And that task he did assign to me, because the *ngangas* had decreed that the slayer must be one whose heart is Jaqqa but whose body is not, and that man could only be me.

"How am I to know which those persons are?" I asked.

"You will be shown," said he.

He heaved his vast body from his throne, and descended, and walked out into the rainy deluge. I followed him, and a throng of witches and courtiers behind me. Kinguri too came to him, and a great witch of the tribe with his hair painted scarlet red, who carried upon a heavy palm-frond a long shining sword polished most brilliantly.

"This is your instrument of surgery," Calandola declared.

Then did we march across the whole width of the encampment to the place of the sick-houses; and the hangers-on fell back, leaving only Calandola and Kinguri and me. Those two and I did enter a certain sick-house where the chieftain Ti-Bangala lay suffering. I had not come to know this man well, who was a great hunter and wielder of the bow, but I respected him greatly. Though he was of formidable stature and majesty, now he was huddled and shivering, and half drowning in his own pouring sweat. Upon our entry he looked up and said in a small tired voice that was scarce his own, "Imbe-Jaqqa? Lord Kinguri? Ah, I suffer, I suffer: when does this end?"

"It ends now, Ti-Bangala," said the Imbe-Jaqqa.

Then the two brothers moved to the side, revealing me standing there like the angel of death, with the great bright weapon in my hand. Ti-Bangala did not show fear of my sword, only a kind of mild surprise, and he feebly smiled to me, saying, "Ah, Andubatil, will we ever hunt together again?"

"Nay, I fear not," said I.

"Are you the death-*mokisso*, then?"

"That is what I am, Ti-Bangala."

And at a signal from Calandola I thrust him through, and he made a soft outrush of air and gave up his ghost.

From there we went to the sick-house of the Jaqqa Paivaga, who looked to me near death unaided, but I despatched him with the blade all the same; and from that to the chamber of Nzinga-bandi, a master of music, who took my thrust in silence; and then onward to another, and one more, and some eleven beyond that. All of whom did I send from the world without giving a second thought to it. Most were so ill, with a glassy look to their eyes and the gleam of shining sweat to their skins, that they scarce perceived what was upon them until my sword descended. But one, Mbanda-kanini, that was a man near as massive and huge as Calandola, looked upon the weapon and drew himself up to his knees, and cried out, "Smite me not, Andubatil! What is this, that you would do me to death?" And with his eyes he did both implore me to let him live, and glare his defiance at me. But I ran him through all the same, and it was no easy task, for there was such a wall of muscle about his belly that it was like pushing the blade through a band of stone. Yet did I do it well, with a sharp fatal twist to my arm at the end, and he fell back and expired with a great rush of dark discolored blood from the wound.

I think I would have gone on serenely all day, striking down these certain Jaqqas that were fancied to be the causes of the plague: for my arm grew hot and supple from this use, and I made an art of seeking the vital places, so that I needed not to thrust a second time with any of them. I did not question the need for this work. It was simply my office, this surgery, this eradication. I did it well. I was in the service of the Imbe-Jaqqa.

At last Calandola said, "It is enough. We have slain them all."

Then he and Kinguri and I did go down to the river and strip forth our clothes, there in the rain, and march into the muddy swollen coccodrillo-infested stream and bathe ourselves, as if to sweep away any pestilence that might have attached itself to us upon these deadly errands. After which, we repaired to the lodgings of the Imbe-Jaqqa, where his servants did restore our body-paints, that we had washed away; and I yielded up the sword, which was a holy one, to its witch-keeper.

That night the rain came to its termination. By the morning sun, when steaming banks of yellow fog did rise from the baking earth, a grand ceremony of burial was begun. And from that day the pestilence began to leave us, and life returned to its usual state among the Jaqqa nation.

SEVEN

WHEN THE dead were buried and the sick were recovered and the elephanto-tails dedicated to the fallen lords had been placed into their shrines, we marched westward, along the south side of the River Kwanza. This brought us right against the mountains of Kambambe, which the Portugals call the Serras da Prata, or Mountains of Silver. Now were

we not far east of Masanganu, so I was coming back at last to the region
that was frequented by Portugals. And I prayed me that I would not
encounter any. For they were become odious to me, those men of jerkins
and doublets and breeches and cuffs, of stone houses and noisy taverns,
of garlic and saffron and sugar. They had the reek of perfidious civilization about them: I wanted no whiff of it. The forest life was cleansing
me of all that grime and stench of Christendom.

I had not been to Kambambe before, though I had been within some
leagues of it, years earlier. Here there was a great fall of water on the
river, that falls right down a vast distance, and makes a mighty sound
that is heard thirty miles, a noise that swallows all other noises like a
great greedy mouth. We visited this plunge, Kinguri and I. The place
is sacred to the Jaqqas, I think because the torrent of falling water
dropping vehemently into that great chasm does put into their minds
some image of their mother the earth. When we departed from it, its
deafening roar remained in my head for some hours, and I felt as though
swathed in thick wool over my face and ears.

Kinguri asked me why Portugals came to this place so often, wondering if it might be holy also to them. "Nay," I said, "not holy in any
way you would understand, for the god they would worship there is
called Mammon, and you know him not. At Kambambe they do seek
a white metal that is said to be found there."

"There are no white metals," said Kinguri.

"There is one, that we call silver, very precious to the Portugals and
other Christians. And it lives in the ground here."

He shrugged, and said again that there were no white metals, and
certainly none at Kambambe. But that led us into talk with some other
Jaqqas, and none of them knew aught of silver-mines here. However,
the lord Kilombo, who had fought many campaigns in the province of
Matamba, told us that a white metal was plentiful there, and was fashioned into bracelets.

This talk of the province of Matamba did touch me at the heart, for
it put me in mind of a cherished person that had been far from my mind
and soul.

"I knew a woman of Matamba when I lived among the Portugals," I
said. "She never spoke of such a metal. But if ever I see her again, I
will ask her."

"Where is this woman?" asked Kinguri.

"In São Paulo de Loanda, if she still lives."

"Then I think you will see her soon, Andubatil."

"What?"

He smiled, and stretched himself back, preening himself on his lordliness among these folk. "I have spoken this day with the Imbe-Jaqqa, and he has disclosed his plan to me. We are shortly to aim our war against the Portugals."

This news did make my heart pound fiercely in my breast, and my skin to turn chill.

I said, "What, will you attack São Paulo de Loanda, when you did hesitate to invade the city of Dongo?"

"It is not the same. Dongo is sealed tight, and is not simple of approach; and King Ngola knows our ways, and how to defend himself from them. We will deal with Dongo, aye, but at some farther time. The Portugals will not be so difficult. Imbe Calandola has come to believe we must destroy them now, before they have done more grievous harm to our mother, and before they are so numerous that we will be hard put to defeat them. They are the true enemy: and so we have believed for these ten years past. And their time now draws nigh."

These words gave me some deep pause. Yea, and I detested the Portugals for what they were and all they had done to me; and there had been moments of late when I wished their utter destruction as fervently as Calandola himself, a sweeping clean of all of them from the African land. But yet, would I let myself truly be part of this war against São Paulo de Loanda, or no? Was I become that much a Jaqqa? To partake of butchering and eating those folk, and putting their city to the torch?

The Christian within me cried, "Nay, it is monstrous, you may not do it!" But the Englishman in me did shout most lustily, "Aye, take your full revenge upon the oily bastardos, Andy-boy!" And then also the Jaqqa that was in me, coursing dark and hot in my veins, whispered hard and tempting, "Strike, strike deep, for the mother must be cleansed of such vermin!"

Kinguri said, "You look sore troubled, Andubatil."

"A passing griping of the gut," said I, with a shrug. "Those small yellow fruits we plucked yesterday were not ripe, I think."

"Ah. I wish you a proper heaving of the belly, then, brother." He laughed. "There is a leaf I could give you, that would make you puke out all your torment in an hour."

"Would that there be such a thing," said I.

"Let me show you, good my brother!"

But I waved his help aside, and said, "It will pass, Kinguri. The weight will lift. I feel it already clearing."

Which was untrue. But I was able then to put the matter somewhat from my mind, for it emerged that Calandola's scheme of war was no more ripe than the imagined fruits upon which I had blamed my malaise.

The Imbe-Jaqqa, said Kinguri, did not propose to attack the Portugals until he first had dealt with the army of Kafuche Kambara. That great blackamoor chieftain, whose fury I myself knew well, was a mighty rival to Calandola, being just as fierce, and just as shrewd in battle, though no man-eater. The Imbe-Jaqqa intended now to slay Kafuche Kambara and then to press his strong army into his own, and with joined forces to march upon São Paulo de Loanda for the destruction of the Portugals.

So entered we into the province of Kisama, which I remembered well but not fondly from long ago, and in that drab wasteland we presented ourselves to one of its greatest lords, which was called Langere. This black prince wanted no war with Calandola, but came out from his town most hastily and paid homage to the Imbe-Jaqqa, bowing low and making offerings of meat and drink. Kinguri stood to one side of Calandola and I to the other, holding my musket as a kind of staff of office, and Langere did grovel and pray for the love of Calandola, until the Imbe-Jaqqa did say, a little disgusted, "Rise, Langere, we would not eat you."

The chieftain rose trembling, and asked what was the Imbe-Jaqqa's bidding, and Calandola said that he wanted Langere's warriors, to employ in a war he proposed to make against Kafuche Kambara. At this Langere looked pale. If one can speak of a blackamoor going pale, then pale is what he looked, or more yellowish, from dismay. For Kafuche Kambara was not only a mighty warrior, he was also the high prince of the province, and Langere's own master. Caught between one doom and the other, Langere chose the more remote one: the Jaqqas were already at his town, and would punish him cruelly if he did not yield to their will. So then Langere obeyed, and gave his army over to the Imbe-Jaqqa, and we all marched onward to the city of Kafuche Kambara.

Before we were there, Imbe Calandola drew me aside, and smiled most fondly upon me, and said, "This will be the largest battle you have fought since you came to us."

"Aye. That I know, for I have seen the troops of Kafuche Kambara at work, and they show no quarter."

"We must destroy their prince, but not the warriors, for them shall we need in our campaign against the Portugals. Take you your musket, Andubatil, and aim it for the high ones of the city, and if it goes well for us they will surrender when their chiefs are all fallen."

"I will aim my sharpest," said I.

"You are a great treasure to me," Calandola said. He was fully greased with the grease of human fat, and his body gleamed like some terrible idol, and he was a giant even sitting down, so that I felt the waves of power emanating from him, beating steady upon my soul like the heavy surf. And he said, "You are a true Jaqqa, in all but your skin, and we can do nothing about that. But before this battle we must admit you to our deepest mysteries, so that you will fight with the highest loyalty."

"My loyalty could not be higher."

"Ah, that I know. For are you not blood-brother to the wise Kinguri? But still—still, Andubatil—there is one rite, there is a further close-ness—"

I knew not what he meant.

He did frighten me somewhat by this talk, for he was speaking most quietly, and by this time I was aware that when Imbe Calandola roared and stamped his feet and pounded his fists together, it was mostly for show, to cow and humble the foolish; but when he spoke quietly, it was because he had some dark and devious plan, most subtle and perilous. And his talking of my being blood-brother to Kinguri—why, I knew that was a sore thing with him, and did fester within the murky fevered caverns of his devilish soul, in that it was a source of jealousy and private pain to him. He never spoke outwardly of it, and now he had, and so very calmly at that.

What, then, was his scheme? To make me his blood-brother as well, and equal Kinguri in making a bond with me? Well, and if he did, I could give him that, for what would it cost me? A bit of pain, but there was room on my skin for one more scar, even now. Yet that was not his plan. What the Imbe-Jaqqa had in mind by way of bond was something far more intimate, a full initiation into the core and heart of the Jaqqa nation.

To me he said, "These rites are such as no Christian has ever beheld. We guard them even from slaves of other tribes. But I have spoken with my witches, and they are in agreement that you are fit to share our secrets."

Imbe Calandola had his head close to mine and his eyes staring into my eyes, that had ever overwhelmed me, and his voice was low and deep and persuasive, and he said, "Come, then, will you be one of us, Andubatil?"

"Aye," I said, "that I will, and gladly."

And so I did, and monstrous things did I undertake, and I think you will condemn me for them. Nevertheless will I tell all. I say to you only that you were not there, and I was; that you had not traveled the long journey I had traveled; that you are you, turning these pages safe in safe England, and I was who I was, the sum and essence of all my perilous and toilsome adventures. And so I was willing at that moment to partake of whatsoever the Imbe-Jaqqa chose to offer me.

I will tell all.

Once it was openly agreed that I would have the rite, the news was published generally in the Jaqqa camp, and from that instant on I was regarded in a special way, as one who had taken on a high radiance. Certain slaves that the Jaqqas did keep at once commenced the building of a ceremonial house apart from the main camp, by the riverbank, hidden from view by a tight-woven wall of palm-fibers. I watched them building it, until I saw that they were looking upon me with fear, and could not work well. In my own place, Kulachinga took a sleeping-mat apart from me, and said she could not embrace me until I was initiate: which I regretted, but I abided by the rule. In fact no one touched my skin in all those days, as if I would burn them with some god-like fire from within: those who passed me by took pains to walk far around me, and I was not let play in Jaqqa games or dances.

On the day appointed for the rite, I was summoned and taken to the house of ceremony by Imbe Calandola himself, and led within, and the wall of palm-fibers was woven closed behind me.

Some dozen Jaqqas were already in the house, sitting crosslegged awaiting me. The Jaqqa Ntotela was among them, and Zimbo, and Kasanje, and Bangala, and also the witch Kakula-banga; the others I did not know except distantly. Kinguri was not there: I had not expected him to be.

Calandola took his place at the head of the solemn group. A music began, from outside the house: a low thick beat of drums, and then a winding high sour outcry of the ivory fife, a sound that reminded me of the weaving of the serpent from side to side as it readies itself to strike.

There was a great bowl of palm-wine, mixed in the royal fashion, that is, stiffened with human blood. We all did drink of this, as the first step of the rite, and we drank freely of it throughout.

Also was there the wicker vat that contained human grease. I removed my ornaments and my loin-cloth, and Calandola nodded to two of his man-witches, who begreased me thoroughly with this stuff, leaving no inch of my nakedness unoiled. All the others in the group also submitted themselves to this greasing. At the first I found the reek of it loathsome, and the slipperiness disagreeable, but after some short time I ceased to notice it.

Now the Imbe-Jaqqa turned to me and said, "Swear to me, by wind and sky and the bones of the great mother, that what occurs here will remain forever secret. And if you violate this oath, your body will crumble and you will be eaten upon forever by ants, but you will remain eternally alive while they do eat. Swear upon this!"

And he did put into my hand a talisman, that was carved from some ebon-black wood of great weight, and was in the form of a yard and a pair of ballocks. This I gripped by the middle of the yard, and he said, "Do you swear?"

"I so swear," I replied. "By wind and sky and the bones of the great mother, that I will divulge to no man what occurs in this house today."

So did I swear. Yet am I telling all, in setting down these words. And if I am to be eaten forever by ants, so be it, but I have sworn unto myself a higher oath, to be true in all that I relate of my adventurings. I think that oath does take precedence above my oath to Imbe Calandola. And I shall tell you all.

Having sworn, I was given to drink a cup that contained some bitter fluid, a potion made from certain dried roots and leaves, I know not which. Swallowing this stuff was not easy. Before long I grew flushed and mine eyes refused to serve me properly, but showed me everything in double or triple. And I felt a great strange uprushing with my brain, as though I had become a copious waterfall that rose heavenward, and poured and poured into the sky. And my hearing grew more sensitive, so that the drums and fifes outside grew swollen and immense, and I could detect also the little harsh chittering sounds of insects, and—so I thought—the whispering noise made by the growing of the grass. And flaming colors streamed in the air, a wild blazing torrent of red and green and purple banners that had no substance, but only hue.

As I sat muddled and dazzled by these things, all the others began to dance most threateningly about me and about Imbe Calandola, who sat by my side. They waved their arms and shook their fists and lifted their feet as though to kick me, but they never once touched me, and only kept churning round and round me. This part lasted some long time.

Then I drank again, a cooling draught out of a new cup of high burnish, that had the figure of a male member rising from it on the one handle, and the shape of the female parts on the other, with long lips extended. When I had had my drink of it, Calandola took it from me, and drank also. This beverage we had had, he told me, was a kind of strong wine into which the dried powder of the sex parts of a dead witch had been sprinkled. What, you recoil? Aye, so do I, now. But I tell you I did not find it strange just then, or in any way displeasing.

Now everyone danced once more, and I with them, hard put to keep my legs from tangling; but they gripped me by my wrists and drew me along as we pranced around the circle, faster and faster, to louder and louder music. They sang all the while, in a language I did not know, which I took to be some holy kind of Latin that these people spoke in their rites.

At the end of the dance we fell down exhausted to the ground. The man-witches lit a fire, and threw powders on it to make colors rise like ghostly phantoms in the air, and for a long while there was a chanting in a low mumbled way. Their voices never left the same one or two tones, as they said again *Yumbe yumbe nimbe hongon,* or words much like that. By the ten thousandth repeating of it I was saying it along with them, *Yumbe yumbe nimbe hongon,* and they did smile and encourage me to do that by gestures of their hands. And then they stood, still doing the *Yumbe,* and lifted me to my feet, and rocked me back and forth a bit, and led me into an inner room of the same house.

It was entered through a broad arch that was draped with red and raw entrails, that I thought quite calmly were probably human ones. But they were only the intestines of a sheep. Beyond, decorated with the shining bluish leaves of a sacred bush, were the sexual organs of that sheep, which was female, and other parts of the sheep attached. And kneeling beside the sheep were two of the wives of Calandola, naked except for the abundance of beads they wore. I thought I could see even beyond the sheep, and it was an open shadowy place, a great blue space stretching far to the horizon and over the sea; but perhaps I dreamed that.

I was by now very uncertain on my feet. Calandola came behind me, supporting me by his arms under mine, and holding me up as easily as though I were a babe. He walked me to the center of the room and put me down kneeling before the sheep, and stayed crouched just behind me.

I smelled many smells. There was the odor of a dry hillside overgrown with rare herbs, and the charred musky perfume of seared flesh, and the sweet heavy scent of oils of Araby. There was a wine-smell; there was a meat-smell; there was a woman-smell. All these fragrances went to the roots of my soul, and tugged at them, and hauled me loose of my moorings.

The two women held bowls, one of blood and one of milk. With these they proceeded to lave me, first my arms and my legs, and then most lovingly my private parts, doing it so cunningly with their wetted fingers that most swiftly my yard did rise. The potions I had drunk were at their height in me now, so that I scarce knew whether I waked or dreamed, and did not care.

"Forward, and enter the gate," murmured Calandola, and tipped me toward the mounted parts of the sheep, so that my member did penetrate the swollen hole of the dead beast. I rocked back and forth in it, while the Imbe-Jaqqa sang a low song that was much like a long groan, into my ear. But also he whispered, "Be of great care not to spill your seed just yet," and so I strived to withhold it, though I was in great excitement from all the wine and potions and throbbing music and the hands of the women upon me. As I coupled with that dead sheep's cunt, other Jaqqas did place rings of sheepskin about my wrists and ankles, and about those of Calandola.

I thought for sure the Devil would appear in that room, out of the smoke and haze. I thought also that he would have my soul from me, and I was lost forever, damned by my willing entry into these diabolical rites. Yet did I take those fears most lightly. If I was become a slave of the Devil, so be it. If I was now enrolled in the company of witches, so be it. Prudence had fled from me. I was a Jaqqa of the Jaqqas in all truth, at that moment. I do confess before God and His Son that I felt no shame in what I did, though I suppose it was because I was so mazy with their strong potions. But peradventure it was not that, but only that I had lived so long in the Devil's jungles, far from the realm of the good Jesus. In such places even a saint could turn by easy passages into a witch, and I had never been a saint.

There was more. I have sworn to tell all.

They withdrew me gently from the sheep before I had spilled my seed, and a ram was brought into the room and slain with a great sword. The blood of this animal then they poured over me and over Imbe Calandola. The male member of the ram was cut loose, and it was thrust some several times into the hole of the female sheep, and taken from it, and roasted upon a sharp stick; and the meat was divided into morsels, and each of us did eat a morsel of it. And the blood of the ram and the ewe were mixed together, and pounded fruits and grains were put into it, and of this porridge we all ate, except for the two women. When we had done with it, the remainder was poured into the laps of the women, and Calandola and I came forward and knelt, and licked it all from their thighs and bellies and from their private parts. And then the women were sent from the room. I had supposed that we would couple with them, but I was wrong in that.

Night had come, I do think. Certainly I perceived the world to have grown dark, but by this stage of the ceremony I could not have told the sun from the moon. My memories of it now become confused. One of the women did return, I believe, bearing an ivory box that held two shriveled worms, and I was told to take one of those worms and thrust it into her arse with my finger, and Calandola did put the other into her cunt; but perhaps it was I that gave her the front worm and he the rear, I can no longer remember. And I think there were other such rites, using objects of witchcraft such as dried leaves and amulets, but I am not sure. It may be the case that my mind has expunged from itself the most horrid and dreadful of these witcheries, by way of protecting me against mine own doings: but I am concealing nothing, God wot, of what I can recall. I gave myself fully up to all of this, the way one surrenders oneself fully to the experiences that come in a dream.

Though I have forgotten some of these latter events, there is one I cannot forget. Nor do I dare shrink from imparting it here, though it be the worst of all. It was far into the night, and I had had other drugs to drink, and more of the blood-wine, and fires were lit all about the room, and low chanting went forward, when suddenly I did feel a hand upon my yard. The touch was light and supple, and in my bemusement I thought it must be one of Calandola's wives returned to caress me, and I moved in slow thrusts against its grip, deriving great pleasure of it.

"Mine," said a thick heavy voice. "Do the like to mine."

The voice was Imbe Calandola's, and the hand on my yard was Calandola's also, sliding up and down the shaft of it with great skill. And he sat alongside me, his huge body pressed close upon mine, and as I sharpened my eyes in the dim smoky haze I came to see that his member did stand upright like a giant black scepter, frightsomely thick and high.

I did not draw back from that which he offered.

I put my hand to his yard as he had to mine. I opened my fingers wide to span that immensity, which seemed to me as thick as an arm, and I wondered fleetingly how any woman ever could take him into her without being split by him. And I stroked him up and down, having no more sense of sin about it than if I had been stroking mine own yard, or the railing of a stair. This was the deepest point of my voyage toward that Lord of Darkness, the Imbe-Jaqqa Calandola: for I was wholly his creature, totally in submission to his will, entirely unknowing of the existence of myself as an independent being. My hand was to him, and his was to me, and nothing else did I perceive. And the last shred of that innocent English boy who had set to sea on the seventh day of May of Anno 1589 was lost now in the beating of the drums and the rising of the many-colored smoke and the wild swirling of the drug in my veins. I had become altogether a thing of the jungle. I was swallowed up in this mystery. I was truly Andubatil Jaqqa, that never had had a former life as anyone other.

Ah! The spurting of my seed did come, with a power and an intensity I had not known since I was a rammish boy. It wrung from me a great shout, that must have sounded none too different from a cry of pain, though it sprang from the supremest of pleasure. I felt myself covered with my hot outpouring from belly to mid-thigh.

And still my hand moved in its unchanging motion, grasping that mighty black rod; and soon from Calandola came a deep rumbling sound, something like the sound that I imagine a volcano-mountain to make as it prepares to loose its molten rock. And then I felt the heavy quiver and shake of his flesh, and the spurt, and his outcries split the air most thunderously.

He cried my name, and I cried his, and we let go of one another and fell backward against the warm moist earth, and lay there unmoving. I think that was the end of it. At any rate, I remember no more.

I was as one stunned. The fires died down, the music trailed away into silence, and all was still.

Whatever happened in the late hours of the night, if there was anything, it was without my knowledge, for I lay in the deepest of slumber. I have told all that I know of that night. So did I vow; so have I done. I have told all.

EIGHT

IT WAS midday before I awoke, and found myself still in the house of the ceremony. Two Jaqqa warriors sat beside me as a kind of guard of honor, but Calandola was not there. I looked at them the way a man looks when he has been half drowned, and comes to himself. They said nothing, neither Kasanje nor old Ntotela. I rose, feeling like the merest burnt husk of myself, and with an uncertain stride I made my way out of that place, and down to the river's edge, and washed myself free of all the greases and stains of the night's revelries, and washed and washed, scrubbing myself most thoroughly in that fast-rushing stream.

At the first I had no clear memory of what I had done, but then gradually at first, and then in a torrent, it all came back to me from the first to the last. And I did feel a kind of numb frosty amaze, that I had done such things, and especially that I had done the last thing. But I gave myself no shame over them. It was too late for shame. Some while back, so I knew, I had passed a certain boundary within my soul, and I lived now, in the inner sense, in a land other than my native one.

Only one thing that troubled me, and that was that I might henceforth be expected to be Imbe Calandola's constant paramour. I was not yet so wholly transformed that I was ready to reckon myself a willing catamite, gladly given over to sodomy. I am well aware of the evils of the sins of Sodom and Gomorrah, and I have never known any inclination toward the same within my soul. Many times aboard ship during long voyages I have been covertly approached by men of that sort, who did risk their lives to offer me invitations, saying they would give me pleasure

with their hands, or their mouths, or their bums, any part I liked, and
would I peradventure care to play some buggery with them as well? It
was easy enough to say them nay, for that was not my game: it is the
soft moist hole of women that draws me, and for the rest, why, it is all
so much dead meat, that interests me not at all. I would not burn the
buggers upon the stake, or skewer them from the rear as is often done,
or hurl them into the sea, for that also is not my way. And I know many
great men have had that vice and still been great, aye, some even being
King of England. But it is not my pleasure. I did not wish to indulge
it again. But there my fears proved needless, since the Imbe-Jaqqa was
no more dedicated to buggery than I: what had passed between us was
a ritual deed, of some high spiritual meaning, and it portended no change
in our relations. He went back to his many wives, and I went back to
my one.

But other things had changed.

Kinguri came to me that morning, and said, looking remote and much
cast down, "Well, and so he has taken you for his own, brother."

"It was for the making of me into a deeper Jaqqa."

"Aye, so it was. And are you the deeper Jaqqa now?"

"I have seen new things, brother," said I. "But look you: nothing has
altered between us, and I am still your brother, and your nearest friend,
and we will spend long hours still speaking of the laws of England and
how they differ from the laws of France, and such matters."

"We are brothers still, but you are now *his*."

"He is the Imbe-Jaqqa. I had no refusal."

"That is so," said Kinguri. "You had no refusal. And you are one
with him now."

"We are all one with him," said I, finding this conversation most
awkward and discomforting, like the conversation a man might have
with his wife after he has left her for a new lover. "Come, Kinguri,
reproach me not! I had no refusal."

"So I am given to understand."

"Have you had the same rite with him?"

"It could not be. I am his mother-brother."

"But you have had the rite?"

"I have," said he.

"And with whom?"

"With Ngonga, once. And with a man who is dead."

"But yet they did not become your brothers?"

"Nay," said he, "I have only Calandola for my brother, and you."

"Then the brother-rite is a closer one than this other, so why do you
reproach me? I am dearer with you than I be with him, even afterward."

"Ah, so you are," said he. "But what you had with Calandola, no one else has had with him ever."

And therefore was he sulky and wounded, and felt betrayed and cast off. It is like all lovers, and in a way that was not of the flesh we were surely that: he had shared me with another that was more powerful, and felt now that something had been spilled that could not be put back in the bowl. All the same he could not have been greatly surprised that it had happened, knowing that Calandola did hold him to be a rival, and thus that he coveted all that Kinguri did have; and from the first I had to Calandola been something most precious, a giver of light and brightness in the dark of the jungle, as I had seen from his handling of my fair hair. So there was no repairing it: I was the plaything of these two powerful brothers, and I had to take care for myself, that they did not tear me asunder in their struggle for me.

So thereafter Kinguri was polite with me, and I with him, but we were cool, and did pretend that nothing had changed while both aware that a great change had come. And no longer did he invite me to go hunting with him, or come to my cottage to draw me into deep discourse, which I lamented. But we sat side by side at the feasts, and smiled, and gave outward show of warm brotherhood, even so.

With the other Jaqqas was I altered also, in another way. Owing to my golden hair and white skin they all had taken me to be some kind of *ndundu*-creature, an albino of a new sort, with warlock powers. That had been greatly heightened by my becoming blood-brother to Kinguri, and now was elevated even more by my having shared this deep rite with the Imbe-Jaqqa. So I walked among them now like a man eleven feet tall, whose feet did not touch the ordinary ground. They made a hand-gesture to me of obeisance, and cast down their eyes, these swaggering devilish cannibal lords and princes. And at their feasts I had the finest morsels and all the wine I chose to drink, and I am certain I could have taken any woman, too, though I was content with Kulachinga.

In a day or two after my initiation with Calandola, we resumed our march toward the city of Kafuche Kambara. Shortly we drew up our position on high ground to the northeast of it. I saw it far below, dry and dusty, the color of a lion in the hot sunlight, and crouching like a lion at the base of low dark hills. The city was a great one, but it seemed a swarm of ants and nothing more, from here.

I cleaned my musket thoroughly and made ready my remaining shot and powder. And on a day of great heat and some little rain the Imbe-Jaqqa did mount his lofty scaffold, and utter a long and most ferocious oration, and we did sound our battle-drums and *mpungas* and other musics of war, and with a great rush we swept down on Kafuche Kambara.

It was Calandola's stratagem to terrify Kafuche, and break his spirit on that first day by a sudden onslaught. But it did not happen that way. This lord did stoutly withstand the Jaqqas, and we had that day a mighty battle, but neither side had the victory. In this warfare I was placed upon a wooden engine that the Jaqqas had constructed, so that I could shoot my musket downward upon the enemy, and perhaps slay the opposing general. Three bold Jaqqas stood before me with great shields of elephanto-hide, to form a phalanx in my protection, and again and again they parted at a signal, and I did thrust my weapon through the opening, and discharge it with a terrible roar.

But Kafuche Kambara did not fall. At sunset we withdrew with many of our men dead on the field, and made ourselves a palisado of trees in the Jaqqa fashion behind which we might encamp. And the next day it was the same, and the next, a battle without outcome.

We remained close on four months in the wars with them, to great cost. Some days we had the better hand, some days they did; but it mightily perplexed Calandola that he could not shatter the forces of Kafuche Kambara no matter what tactic he employed. Never had a blackamoor lord withstood him before in this way. We held a long council to discuss it, at which I was present along with Kinguri and Kulambo and Kasanje and the other great Jaqqa princes, and I could see the wrath of Imbe Calandola smouldering within him. And he did look toward me from time to time, as though I might offer some plan to break the stalemate. But the only plan I had was one I thought he would deeply mislike, so I did not voice it.

And at length it was Kinguri, after we had talked for hours, that put forth the same idea that had come to me. "Since it seems we cannot defeat them, let us make alliance with them against the Portugals."

At this, Imbe Calandola's eyes blazed with fury, and he snarled like a jungle beast and clenched his fists tight. Peradventure only Kinguri could have made that proposal without giving mortal offense. For alliance with an enemy was not Calandola's way; and he was not eager to admit he had failed against Kafuche Kambara.

Yet around the council-house the other princes did nod and give assent to Kinguri, first old Zimbo, and then others, in a cautious manner, for they knew how perilous it was to support that which the Imbe-Jaqqa opposed.

Calandola turned then to me, and said, "What say you, Andubatil, shall we parley with Kafuche Kambara?"

His eyes did gleam most craftily. Clearly it was a test, to see whether my love lay more with him or with his brother. So I chose my words with some care, and said, "What is our greater goal, O Imbe-Jaqqa? To destroy Kafuche Kambara, or to wipe from our soil the Portugals of the coast?"

"That question does not answer to my question."

"Aye, but it does! If Kafuche is the higher foe, why, then we must stay here until we break him. But if our greater thrust is destined to be against the Portugals, Lord Calandola, then it behooves us not to slaughter many more of Kafuche's warriors. For we will need them in the attack on São Paulo de Loanda."

I saw a keen smile quickly cross Kinguri's face, and knew that I had spoken myself rightly.

Calandola, too, showed pleasure. "Yea, that is so. Each day do we kill great number of his men."

"And also do they kill great number of ours," said Kasanje, but not so loud that the Imbe-Jaqqa might hear.

Kulambo, that was a wise and bold commander, now said, "The Andubatil Jaqqa speaks sooth. Let us spare Kafuche Kambara's army, and put it to our own uses. And when the Portugals are destroyed, why, then we may turn again against Kafuche, and deal with him as he deserves."

Calandola did ponder this a long while in silence, and I saw his face change from moment to moment as he weighed this argument and that. And then he did brighten, as though he had weighed it all, and saw the truth.

"So be it, as Kulambo proposes," he said at last.

And so it was that on the next day a negotiation commenced, under a flag of truce, between the Jaqqas and their foes. I say "a flag of truce," that being the way we do understand such things, but in fact the way it was done was quite other: for a pig was slaughtered, and turned so that its entrails were on the outside, and this was carried into the open ground by six of the Jaqqa women, with two dozen Jaqqa warriors behind them as a guard. By this display was signified a willingness to parley, which Kafuche Kambara did comprehend, and he did send forth by way of agreement a slaughtered calf, similarly opened, so that there was blood and entrails all about. These meats were cooked and shared by the ambassadors of both sides, and after that it would have been unholy to make war, so that truce was struck.

I was not present at this parleying, though all the other Jaqqa high lords did attend. As I was making ready to set forth with them Calandola said, "Nay, not you, Andubatil."

"And why is that?"

"Because of our skin that is dark, and yours that is white."

"This I do not understand," said I. "Am I not a Jaqqa?"

"You are Jaqqa within, by right of initiation, and blood-brothering, and marriage. But yet are you still a white man to the outer semblance, and I fear you will give dismay to Kafuche Kambara on that score."

"Do you, then? Even though I wear Jaqqa emblems?"

"Even though," said he, and I knew there was no appeal from that. So I withdrew my pleading, much as I did resent to be excluded from the meeting. And in this I think Calandola was not wrong. This Kafuche was a man of quick suspicions, who was known to have no liking for whites, and I would be far too strange an article for him to accept with ease. Therefore did I yield, although feeling shamed by my having to remain behind.

I did have one glimpse of the formidable Kafuche, as he came out from his city to meet with the Jaqqa lords. He was a splendid figure indeed, being very tall and strong, though old, with whitened hair, and when he came forth it was in such state as befitted a king. For he did ride upon an elephanto in great pomp and majesty, and on either side of the elephanto he had six lordly warriors, and there were slaves who carried a high golden canopy as it were a cloth of state above his head, and some five hundred archers as his guard came before him.

More than that I did not see, for Calandola had another task for me, that took me into new and grievous adventure. This was that we were to prepare the way for the invasion of the Portuguese territories, and so I was sent to explore the lands that lay between this place and Masanganu, and be a spy against the number of Portugals who defended the presidio there.

To accomplish this the Imbe-Jaqqa gave me for my protection some ninety fine warriors, of whom one, a tall and slender man that was called Golambolo, came to me with a great laugh and said, "Do you not know me, Andubatil?"

"Aye, you are the warrior Golambolo," said I.

"So I am. But does nothing else concerning me come to your mind, now that we are about to cross this dry wasteland together?"

"I do not take your meaning," I said.

"Have you no remembering of five Jaqqas that found you wandering in this same desert, after the Portugals had been smashed by the army of Kafuche Kambara?"

"That escorted me safe over the dry lands to Masanganu?"

"Indeed," said Golambolo.

I looked close at him, and feigned that I recognized him; but in truth I did not, since that in those early days one Jaqqa had looked much like another to me.

"My gratitude is great," said I. "To you I owe my life."

"The life of Andubatil is precious to us all."

"But I was not then Andubatil. Why did you save me, then?"

He smiled and pointed to my hair, and said he had thought me to be some powerful *mokisso*, or at the very least an important witch belonging to the Portugals, and he had not wanted to risk the enmity of the spirit world by letting me come to harm. Which was the confirming of what I had long suspected. I took from my neck the beads I was wearing, white with inlays of jet, and placed them about his throat, and he took both my elbows in his hands, which is a Jaqqa embrace of loyalty and affection, and we smiled upon one another for the sake of that other time.

With Golambolo and my ninety warriors did I now set forth to the direction of the River Kwanza, across Kisama province by way of a place called Agokayongo, where a lord subject to Kafuche Kambara did reign. At this town we were greeted with a hospitality of an uneasy sort—for none of these villagers relished the sight of Jaqqas ever, be they one Jaqqa or ninety-one—but they fed us and gave us to drink, and then they told us that a party of Portugals had passed just that way, traveling from the presidio of Ndemba to the west, and heading for Masanganu, where they proposed to take ship back to the coast.

This news gave me some alarm. "How many were there?" I asked.

"Not many," replied the lord of Agokayongo. "Less than the fingers of two hands."

"And said they anything about events in the Kisama province? Of a Jaqqa army, or of warfare in the south?"

"I heard from them not a thing of such matters," answered that lord.

But the Portugals, had they known Calandola was moving through the province, might not have deemed it important to share that news with the lord of Agokayongo. Nor, even if he did know it, was he necessarily telling me the truth. And if there were Portuguese travelers moving through these regions, who knew of Imbe Calandola's movements, it would go hard for us if they conveyed word of this to the forces of Masanganu. So I did summon Golambolo and my other lieutenants and say, "We must overtake these Portugals and make them prisoners, and keep them from bearing tales of us to their countrymen."

At once did we set forth in their pursuit. Which did not seem to me to be any easy matter, for there is no fixed road in this part, and the terrain is much broken. But when we were only a league beyond Agokayongo we came upon the first sign of them: a dead horse by the base of a cliff, most pitiful to behold, for it was shrunken and withered and lying flat with sprawled limbs, like some cast-off doll out of which all the straw has fallen.

"They travel by horse?" Golambolo said. "Ah, then they are undone!"

I felt the same. For it is a risky thing to travel by horse in this torrid country; there is sparse forage for the poor beasts, and the air itself does suck the life from their lungs. Better by far is it to go afoot, and be light of burden, for there are some places, and this is one, where a man can go and a horse is only a drain and a disadvantage.

Indeed that had been the case amongst these Portugals. For we proceeded onward, and surmounted a steep rise in the valley, and looked down a short way to the west into a deep cleft between two sharp hills, and there they were. They sat gathered by the shade of a broad-spreading tree that was rooted in a small brackish pond. There were six of them, and four horses, and one of the horses looked to Golambolo's keen eyes as being near unto death, and the other three not much more vigorous. Plainly the Portugals had made camp to allow their steeds to regain strength: and a somber error it had been for them, since that it had delivered them up into our hands.

"I will take them," Golambolo said.

"Aye. Choose nine men, and ride down there and seize them, and return them to Lord Calandola for safekeeping. Tell him that upon my coming back from Masanganu, I will question them and get from them valuable information about the dealings of the Portugals in this province. And when you have done that, proceed onward and meet me by the town of Ndala Chosa."

"So shall I do," answered Golambolo.

With his nine men he moved out and down into the valley where the six Portugals lay. I knew I could trust him to accomplish the task with ease; therefore I did not wait, but continued on northward with the remainder of my force. We saw nothing of note in the bleak country ahead, until that we came to the place called Ndala Chosa, which lieth on the south side of the River Kwanza a few leagues upstream from Masanganu. For a day or two I rested in this village, for I had had the misfortune of twisting my foot and injuring it most sorely, so that I could not walk. While I lay in this fashion I sent forth scouts, who came back to me swiftly with news of the district that runs from Ndala Chosa to the great waterfall. There was a Portugal army ahead, they said: not just the usual complement of Masanganu, but some hundreds of troops camped outside that place, as though they were contemplating a war.

"Take me thence immediately," said I.

It is not in the Jaqqa nature to carry men in a litter, after the servile manner of the Bakongo folk, but there was no choice in that now. So they did cobble together something by which to bear me, and took me forth toward Masanganu, until I came to a sloping low hill that gave a prospect of the hot tableland ahead. And indeed the Portugals were drawn up encamped there, with much weaponry and a great force.

"What is this?" I asked. "Are they patrolling, or do they plan some conquest of Kisama?"

To this no one could make answer. And as I looked down upon them I felt within me a pounding of the heart, and a swaying of the soul, and a great overwhelming urge to reach out with the tip of my finger and brush those Portugals aside, or grind them into the earth like offensive insects. Aye, that was the Jaqqa rising in me! By what right did they camp there, I asked myself, with all their gear and their tents and their refuse and trash? Let us wipe them aside, I thought! And all like them, even to São Paulo de Loanda! Let there be war between Jaqqa and Portugal, and let us drive them into the sea!

Even as those savage war-like feelings did course within me, and loose the blood-thrill in my soul, so also did I calculate in a more civil way the practical merits of such a campaign of extermination and expungement. For when Portugals were gone from this land, the English might enter. Through my dazzled mind floated a vision of myself taking ship to England aboard some Dutch trader, and organizing a company of adventurers, and returning to Africa to lead a venture that would wholly supplant the Portugals here. Aye! Strike up a treaty with Calandola my brother, and pledge him never to offend against our mother the earth as the Portugals had done, and then drive the slavers from São Tomé, and build a new England in this hot West African country!

You can see in my words the conflict, the contradicting. For how could I think both of destroying and of building, and each equally holy? But there were two souls in my breast just then, one English and one Jaqqa; and the wonder of it was that I encompassed them both and did not go altogether mad. I stood there a long while dreaming of Portugals abolished and English established here, with the blessing of the Imbe-Jaqqa my lord and kinsman. Madness? Aye, madness! But within the madness, I tell you, lay a core of the soundest reason; and within that core, another core yet, of the dark madness that Africa does kindle in the soul.

"Come," said I finally to my men, "we must bring news of this army hastily to the Imbe-Jaqqa."

So turned we back southward. On our return journey we did spread ourselves out in a wide company over several valleys, so that we would have a better chance of meeting with Golambolo, as he came northward to rejoin us. But we saw him not, though we gave every attention to noticing him. I continued onward into the south, as far as Agokayongo. Approaching that place, I looked down into the cleft where those six

Portugals had been camped, and saw their horses lying dead beneath that wide-crowned tree. But of the Portugals themselves, or of Golambolo and his nine Jaqqas, I saw nothing. That perplexed me, for I did not care to have part of my force wandering in search of me in this land, but I saw no help for it other than to go on into Agokayongo.

And as we came in view of the town, I beheld a vast and unexpected sight: not the little Jaqqa party of Golambolo, but uncountable thousands of men, the entire force of Imbe Calandola, and the troops of Kafuche Kambara as well, laid out upon the plain in immense array, with banners flying most jubilantly. I sent one of my fleet Jaqqas forward, to discover what event was unfolding, and he came back soon with the word, "Alliance has been made between the Imbe-Jaqqa and Kafuche Kambara, and they have begun the march northward upon Masanganu."

Well, and there must have been some swift and cunning bargaining in my absence, that the two enemies were so cozily merged so soon! I regretted me not having been there to take part. But that mattered only lightly now. I was the bearer of significant news; it behooved me to bring my tale before Calandola forthwith.

My injured foot by this time was largely healed. So at the head of my men I walked swiftly into the heart of the Jaqqa encampment at the sunset hour, when the sky was richly stained as though by spreading blood the whole length of the horizon. And I discovered that a festival was being begun, with much beating of drums and chanting and dancing. This wild noise gave me pause, for I recognized it as the cannibal-feast music. There would be dining on human flesh tonight: but what foes were these, that would be the Jaqqa dinner?

The great kettles were in their position, and the raging fire was already lit. And the drummers were pounding, and the dancers were dancing, and the *nganga*-witches were crying out their screeching blessings, with old Kakula-banga hopping about to the forefront, and the water was just coming to its first boil. Under the gathering darkness all the high lords of the Jaqqas were assembled for their grim festivity: there was Imbe Calandola proud upon his great tall stool in all his shining ornament, and there was my solemn-faced blood-brother Kinguri beside him, and Ntotela and Kaimba and Kasanje and Ngonga and Zimbo and Kulambo and Bangala, which were the totality of the great ones yet living, since none had been named in the place of Ti-Bangala and Paivaga, that had died by my sword during the pestilence.

At the sight of me they all did give salutes and cheers, and Calandola raised his hand toward me and cried out, "What, Andubatil, back among us just in time for dinner?"

"Aye, and what feast is this?"

"Why, we shall dine well tonight, on plump white meat! Come, take your place with us, and swiftly!"

He laughed and gestured, and I looked toward the other side of the clearing. On the ground behind the kettles lay the dead bodies of three white men, naked and bloodied, with their torn clothes in heaps about them. And three more, in Jaqqa manacles, did huddle together in terror and fright against a thick tree. Because the air was dark with smoke and the encroachment of night, I could not see those three clearly from the distance at which I stood, but it was plain from their garb that they were Portugals, and surely they were the ones Golambolo had caught, and brought back to be prisoner here. Prisoner: not dinner.

To Calandola I said, bluntly and forgetting all diplomacy, "This is a great wrong, O Lord Imbe-Jaqqa."

"What do you say?" he answered, in a growl and a snarl.

"There is a new army of Portugals camped beyond Ndala Chosa, and I know not why. I have come all this way from Ndala Chosa to speak with these Portugals, and interrogate them on the movements of that army, which is why I plucked them from the desert and had them borne here. And I find you cooking them, O Imbe-Jaqqa, as though they were mere beasts!"

"Ah, is that the reason you are so angered? Not that you mislike the boiling of Portugals?"

I shrugged. "Boil them, roast them, do as you like. But not before I have spoken with them!"

Calandola's great booming laughter floated downward to me like the white water that tumbles down some mighty waterfall-cascade, and he said, "Ah, we have saved a few for you to give questions to, Andubatil! Feast with us tonight, and you can speak with them tomorrow, and then another night we will feast on them as well, Eh? Does that suit you, Jaqqa prince?"

The butcher-Jaqqas were already at work readying the dead men for the kettle. Well, and that was beyond any remedy: whatever information I might get from them was perished, and would not rise to the kettle's skimmings when they were cooked. My anger at Calandola was extreme, and another time I might have suffered for reproaching him this way before his people, but it seemed that tonight he was in high good humor. Yet I had best master my fury, since that even in good humor Calandola would accept only so much reproach, even from me, and then he would grow ugly.

I said, "I will join you in a moment, Lord Calandola. I ask leave to speak with the captives first."

He nodded and turned from me, to take a bowl of wine from one of his wives. I walked to the far side of the kettles to inspect the prisoners, whether I knew any of them from my days amongst the Portugals.

And when I went to them I had a mighty surprise, that shook me to the foundation and base of my soul: for two of the Portugals were men, but the third, that I did not expect, was a woman. It was unmistakable, even though she had her hair bound tight in back, so that it looked no longer than a man's. Her garments were in shreds and tatters, and by the coppery gleam of the firelight I was able to see her bare breasts rising steeply, full and round and most beautiful, and dark tipped. Aye! and those were breasts I knew most excellently well, by my faith. I knew the feel of them in my cupped hands, and the taste of them to my lips. For this woman was that dark-souled witchy creature Dona Teresa, that I had loved and been loved by when I was Andrew Battell the English seaman of Leigh in Essex, and by whom, also, I had been most shamefully betrayed, what seemed like half a lifetime ago. I could not have been more dumbstruck nor appalled to find her here, than had that woman chained to the tree been my mother.

In the dimness of the heavy twilight she did stare at me, and her reddened eyes grew bright, and she made a gesture of amaze. And in a voice choking with astonishment did she say, "Andres? Andres, is it possible? Is that who you are? Andres, in those savage beads?"

"Aye," I said. "I am Andres."

Her lips trembled. "You are much changed, Andres!"

"Aye," said I. The Portugal words came hard and uncouth to my mouth, after these long months of speaking the Jaqqa tongue. "I am much changed, indeed. I am scarce Andres any longer."

"If you are not Andres, then what are you?"

"I am Andubatil Jaqqa," I answered her.

"Mother of God," she said softly. "I am lost, then!"

NINE

I CAME close to her, this woman who had done me so much wrong, and who before that had given me such pleasure, and I let her have a good look upon me by the light of the leaping blazing fire.

And I saw the wild panic fear in her eyes, that was as revealing to me as the most costly of polished mirrors. How frightening the man that she beheld must have been! For what stood before her was a kind of man-monster, near naked, with paint on his body and barbarous beads and bangles and a host of battle-scars, I must have looked like something out of the wild dawn of time. She stared at the certain tribal marks that I had let the Jaqqa witches carve into my skin with most excruciating pain, and a new brightness of horror shined on her face. My hair hung well past my shoulders and was a tangle of great snarls; my beard was as rough and shaggy as a goat's; my hands and feet were unkempt; and though I had not had any mirroring of my own face for more months than I had counted, I knew I must now have a savage countenance, with fierce hard eyes and sparse flesh and all the corners hard and sun-baked by that merciless tropic orb, so that my Englishness was fair roasted from me. Dona Teresa shivered and made to cover her breasts with the one arm of hers that was unfettered. Such a gesture of shame never had I seen before from the haughty and imperious and lustful Dona Teresa.

And I, what did I feel, looking upon her?

Hatred, first and primary, and the craving for revenge. For I might have been at sea to England, but for her, who had plucked me from the Dutcher's ship on that false libel of a rape, and sent me off for six years of soul-breaking torment at the presidio of Masanganu. And all for jealousy, a petty spitefulness over my living with Matamba: for that she had stolen my life from me, as much so as Cocke that had abandoned me to the Portugals, and all those perfidious whoreson Portugal governors that had made me their servant in my long years of Angola. I am, Got wot, a man of even keel: but yet I have feelings, I am no stone statue, and I do hate those who give me over to injustice, and I did rejoice just then to see this Dona Teresa in peril of her life, with the kettles already heating for her companions and her boiling soon to come.

But that was the first moment only, that hatred: for her beauty melted my heart, withal how long I had yearned to be revenged on her. That seemed so long ago, her crime against me. I could not, try as I might, hold my vengefulness in my grasp that long. It did slip from me, like some writhing eel, even as I glowered at her and tried to take pleasure in her downfall.

How, and am I so light of resolve? I think not: but it was her beauty undid me. I tell you, her beauty melted my heart, for all that she was soiled and disheveled and tear-streaked, and for all that she had given me into that terrible six-year servitude out of petty spite, and that there was the brimstone reek of witchcraft somehow about her.

She was magnificent in my eyes.

That time when first she came to me in my prison cell in São Paulo de Loanda, she had even then been queenly in her poise. But in the thirteen or fourteen years that intervened she had grown superb, a woman of imperial splendor, and not even her present sad state could disguise it.

Standing before her, peering eye to eye, I found myself trembling and unmanned with the surprise of resurgent love. Yet had she no inkling of this, seeing as she did only the strange Jaqqa-monster that I had become. And another thing began to happen, which was that the wondrous beauty of her began to wash from me not only my long-cherished anger toward her, but also the strangeness that I had put on, the Jaqqa self within which I had cloaked myself: I had come before her as Andubatil, but I heard the voice of Andrew Battell within my skull, speaking with her in English most playfully, such words as "scavenger" and "stonemason" and "turnip-greens," in our games of love. Which brought a confusion over me, a slipping and a sliding of my soul, so that I felt like one who is battered and pummeled by heavy surf, and knocked to his knees whenever he tries to rise, and loses his strength in the struggle and begins to drown. What was I, Jaqqa or Englishman? And did I hate her or love her? I was drowning in the contraries and antitheticals of mine own bewildered soul. But as one who feels himself drowning may begin at the last to swim upward to salvation, so, too, did I out of that maelstream of fuddlement commence the ascent toward some measure of understanding. For I knew that I was more English than Jaqqa, for all my journey into the man-eater's ways, and that I held more love than loathing for this woman. And I swore then a mighty vow within myself, by God the Redeemer and by every *mokisso* of this somber jungle, that I would see her spared from the cannibal kettle, or go into that kettle myself. Nor was this any witchcraft at work upon me this time, but mine own free decision.

Yet was I slow to reveal that to her. Merely did I circle her from side to side, like leopard contemplating trapped prey, and study her in all regards. She hovered on the borderland between fear and boldness, mastering with wondrous strength the terror that she must feel.

"Well," she said at last, "have done with it, drag me to the pot and hurl me in, Andres!"

"Do you think I will do that?"

"You are so rigged and geared for savagery that it would amaze me if you did not."

"Ah, you are fierce, fierce, Teresa!"

"Am I, then? But not fierce enough to gnaw through these bonds, I fear."

"How has this befallen you? To be in captivity here?"

"Don Fernão and I were journeying through the interior," said she. "From Ndemba to Masanganu to Kambambe, to inspect the presidios, at the behest of the governor."

"Don João de Mendoça still?"

"Nay," said she. "He is long dead, poor sweet man, and there is a new one come from Portugal, Don João Coutinho by name, that is very bountiful and well loved. He is to build new castles in this land, and conquer it supremely, by order of the King of Portugal. And so are there armies marching now through all parts of the province."

Ah, I thought. That explained the troop I had seen beyond the city of Ndala Chosa.

She went on, "And so this governor sent us outward here—but our horses perished, and the Jaqqas came upon us in the road—" Her lips trembled, and her strength broke a moment, and she began to snuffle and weep, which was strange to behold in that regal woman. But only a moment, and then she had her strength again. "Don Fernão is slain, and we are to be eaten," said she bitterly. "And are you to feed upon us as well, Andres? Are you transformed into a man-eater? For that is what I believe you now must be."

"Which is Don Fernão?" I asked.

She indicated, with a gesture of her head, one of the dead Portugals, that even as we spoke were being quartered and thrust into the bubbling kettles. And as she looked that way, such a revulsion and terror came upon her that her gorge did rise, and she writhed in nausea and turned her head from me to choke back the tide of vomitus that was surging upward in her. I felt nigh the same way, to think of that finely garbed vain foppish man Souza, that had had little real harm in him, cut to pieces by my Jaqqa brothers and put up to boil like so much mutton; for though he had been weak and trifling, he had been Dona Teresa's husband these many year, and for that long companionship she doubtless felt a deep pang to see him perish so before her eye.

Then once more she regained herself and said, "How much longer am I to live? And can you bring me a swift death, so I need not endure this limb of Hell in which I am?"

Most gently I did say, "I mean to preserve you from doom."

"You? The capering painted jigging naked man-eater?"

"I am indeed much changed, as you see, Dona Teresa. But something in me remains, of the man you knew."

"This is no moment to mock me, Andres."

"I do not mock. I will save you from this feast."

Her eyes went wide. "Jesu Cristo, and can you do it?"

"I have much power among these people, for I am become close kin to the Jaqqa king, and to his brother as well." I put my hand to her arm, and gripped it most fondly; from which touch she shrank away at first, but then yielded and softened against it. Aye, how could I let her be slaughtered? That were too heavy vengeance for the wrong she had done me: and she had done me much benefit, ere that one betrayal. I would right then have pulled free her bonds and taken her against my bosom to comfort her, in the midst of all that cannibal nightmare. But first I needs must beg her liberty from the Imbe-Jaqqa.

Softly I said, "I cannot save your comrades. But your life I will at once make venture for. Fear no more: you shall be spared from the kettle."

On the far side where the lords of the Jaqqas did sit, all was wild and merry. They swilled their blooded wine and laughed most uproariously and showed much joy over their feast. I approached the Imbe-Jaqqa. He looked upon me with a little display of anger or at least displeasure, and said, "I told you, Andubatil, you might interrogate the prisoners tomorrow. Come, now, join us, and share our wine!"

"By your pardon, my Lord Calandola, but I was not interrogating the prisoners."

"Only the woman, eh! I saw you at it." He slapped his great thighs and merrily rubbed his hands over his greased body and said, "She is fair and juicy, that Portugal! I will have her breasts, and Kinguri her rump, and the thighs, Andubatil, will you take the thighs?"

His callous words did strike me to the quick.

"Nay!" I cried in sudden heat. "Nay, Lord Calandola!"

"Not the thighs, then?"

I shook my head most vehemently. "No part of her! She shall not be eaten!"

"What is this you say?" he asked, in his curious way, for it always amazed him much to have his will gainsaid, and he would stare at the gainsayer the way he might at a flea the size of an elephanto, or at an elephanto the size of a flea. "Not eaten, Andubatil, by your command?"

"Good my lord," I said, with more humility, "I crave a great boon. I ask you not to slay this woman."

"So that you may have her, is that it?"

"O Imbe-Jaqqa, that Portugal woman was my wife, when I did live in São Paulo de Loanda."

"Ah, your wife," said he, the way he might have said, *Your boots, your cap, your drinking-mug.* "Well, what of that? You have another wife now. You can have three or four more, or seven, if it please you."

"Nay," said I, sweating freely and struggling to conceal my unease. "I loved her dear, and I preferred all other women before her. I beg you speak not so hungrily of her."

"Your wife, Andubatil?" said he, musing on the idea.

"Aye, we were joined in the highest way before our God," I lied most fervently, "and greatly did it amaze me just now to see her among your captives. For we have been parted these some years past, since my betrayal into the hands of Mofarigosat. But all this time have I yearned keenly for her, and now she is reunited to me."

Kinguri, leaning close, said in a dark voice, "You should know, Andubatil, that she clung very near and familiar to one of those Portugals, that now is dead and being readied for the feast."

"Her brother," said I hastily.

"Ah."

"Aye. Don Fernão da Souza: I knew him in my old life, a man of much fantastical taste in garments. They were very dear, the brother to the sister, the sister to the brother. Lord Imbe-Jaqqa, let me go to her now, and cut her free of her bonds."

Kinguri did say to his brother, but I was able to hear it, "The woman is dangerous. I saw her with the other Portugals, and they did look to her as though she was their queen. There is great strength in her. I feel it, I see it clear. If we let her live, she will bring us harm."

"She is the wife of Andubatil," Calandola did rejoin.

"He has another wife now."

I saw that this was becoming a dispute between the royal brothers, that had questions of power at the root of it, and perhaps also some question of my turning away from love of them toward the woman I said was my wife.

Stretching forth my arms to Kinguri, I did cry, "Brother! How can you speak so callously before me?"

With a frosty smile Kinguri did make reply, "I would not imperil all our nation to save one woman, even if she be your woman."

"And one woman, naked and frightened, imperils all the grand nation of Jaqqas? Fie, Kinguri, I thought you to be a man of wisdom!"

"That I am, Andubatil Jaqqa, my wisdom and yours that mingles in my blood, and that shared wisdom tells me to fear this Portugal woman. I say, smite her while she can do no mischief."

I turned from him.

"I appeal to you, Lord Calandola—"

"You do cherish her?" the great Jaqqa asked me, still most curious, as if this sort of passion were a vast mystery to him.

"That I do. I cherish her close upon life itself. I could not abide seeing her slain for this feast."

"My brother Kinguri dislikes her, and he is rarely wrong in such judgments."

"I tell you she will work no evil, Lord Imbe-Jaqqa."

Calandola shrugged. This was becoming tiresome to him, I saw. He lowered his face into his wine-cup, and took a deep draught, and when he emerged his cheeks and mouth were slavered with the purplish bloody fluid, that made him look ten times the monster he was. Yet was there now a benevolence to his smile, and he nodded amiably to his brother, saying, "Andubatil has served me well, and I would not deny him, brother. He craves the Portugal woman. I see the heat of him for her, and I would not deny him."

"I am uneasy, brother," muttered Kinguri.

Stretching my hand to that devilish shrewd Jaqqa I did say, "I pledge myself as surety, brother. She will do no harm to our nation. I would have my wife restored to me, and I ask you withdraw your opposing it."

"So be it," said Calandola, with an imperious wave. "Take her, then."

"A thousand thanks, mighty Imbe-Jaqqa," I said, making a low bow. When I looked up I saw the cold enmity on Kinguri's face, for plainly he did not want me to have her, and even more did not want my pleading to triumph over his words to the Imbe-Jaqqa.

Calandola said, "As for the other two Portugals, they will be tomorrow's feast. Mark that you speak with them before then, and learn what you may from them."

"That I will do," said I.

I went then to Dona Teresa and ordered the Jaqqa who guarded her to strike her fetters from her. He made a move to do it, out of respect for me, but then a doubt did smite him, and he glanced across toward the Imbe-Jaqqa. Calandola nodded, and the guard set her free.

Dona Teresa, gathering her rags about her to hide her breasts, gave me thanks with a squeeze of the hand, and said, "How was this thing accomplished?"

"I swore to them you were my wife, and they have given you back to me."

"Ah. There is no penalty for perjuring here, then?"

I leaned close to her and said, "Your case was desperate. Shall I cling to niceties of truth, and let you be stewed?"

"So I am to be your wife in this place?"

"Either that, or offer yourself to the fetters again," said I.

"Ah. Ah, I see." There was mischief in her eyes, and a little anger, and also much amusement, I think. "Well, and I suppose I can play at being your wife, then, Andres."

"You will do more than play," said I.

"You are very blunt, now that you are a man-eater."

"Lady, I have won you your life back. But I have pledged mine own as security, that you will work no trouble in this camp. So therefore you will bear yourself less imperiously, and carry me along in this pretense of our marriage, or I will in this instant revoke what I have done. Is that understood?"

"Ah, Andres, Andres, I mean no difficulties! I but jest a little."

"Jest at another time," said I. For I was much angered, and newly cold toward her, for this pride of hers. It had cost me something with Kinguri to have saved her: but I need not explain that to her, only be assured of her consenting in the falsehood that had saved her life.

After a moment she said, "And these two?"

"I have no grasp on their lives. They will be slain."

"Ah," she said. "Well, and then I suppose we must pray for their souls." She did not look deeply grieved. "You are kin to these man-eaters, you say, Andres?"

At this I hesitated some. "They have taken me as close companion," said I finally. "It is for my hair and skin, that I think they revere for its color. And my musket, which I have put to strong use in their service."

"You do battles on their behalf?"

"Aye," I answered. "I am one of their great warriors."

She stepped back a bit, and stared at me as though I had sprouted a Satan-tail, and breathed fire. Behind us, the sound of the drums and other musics grew more fierce. It was altogether night now, and a heavy heat was descending, with droplets of moistness hanging in it, and creatures cried most raucously beyond the zone of our fires.

She said, hushed and strange-voiced, "You speak to me in good Portuguese words, and I think you are the man I knew in São Paulo de Loanda, that was so straightforward and upright. And then I look at you, and see these marks of paganism on your body, and I hear you say you fight in Jaqqa wars and do them great service, and I know you to be a changeling, Andres."

"A changeling. Aye," said I. "I think that is what I am, that has had some other soul slipped in behind my face. And the face is much altered, too, is it not?"

"I barely knew you when you first came close," she said. There was a trembling in her arms now, and perhaps elsewhere, and her eyes were fixed and harsh with fright. "I said, What is this creature, that has the skin of a white man, but the bearing of a Jaqqa? And I was sore affrighted. And I am sore affrighted now."

"Are you, then?"

"Listen. Listen! The fifes, the drums, the singing. They are devils, Andres, all about us!"

"Aye."

"And you: you are half devil now."

"More than half, perhaps. But why would that trouble you? You are of that kind yourself."

"Nay," she said, making the sign of the cross. "Nay, you do not understand me."

"You, with your idols, and your witchy incantations?"

"I am a Christian, Andres. I but use the other older things, when I feel the need. But I am no witch!"

"Ah," I said. "It must be so, if you do say it."

"Mock me not. I am not the witch you think me, and I am sore affrighted. I think this is Hell we are in. But where are the fires? Where are the imps?"

"See the fires, there?"

"Those?" she said, shivering. "Will they leap higher, as the night goes on? Are they true Hell-fires, Andres? And are these demons about me, or only men and savages? O Andres, how have they conjured you so?"

I thought she would weep again, from her quivering and pallor, but she did not. But she plainly was smitten to the core of her soul by all she beheld about her, and even by what she could read in my face.

"Come," I said, "let me take you to the Jaqqa lords."

"What, and shall we dine grandly with them, as though we are all lords and ladies here?"

"We dine with them," I said, "or they dine upon you. Which is your preference?"

"And we will eat the flesh of—"

She could not say it. She was yellow-faced with loathing.

"You are not compelled to do it. But they are the masters of this place. We must make a show of friendship."

"Yes. Yes. I understand. It is for the sake of staying alive."

"Exactly."

"And for the sake of staying alive, have you on such occasions also eaten—"

"Come," said I. "Ask fewer questions, and take my arm, and be you my true wife, if you would save yourself from the pot."

Yet did she shrink back from me. I offered arm to her anew, and she shook a little, but then recovered herself once more, standing tall, making her shoulders squared. Averting her eyes from the kettle and its bubbling contents, those floating disjointed limbs that surged now and again to the surface, she walked with me like a veritable consort to the other side of the fire. All about us were hordes of frenzied Jaqqas, flinging their knees high in the capers of their dance, who paused in their wild leaping to salute me, which did not fail to have its measure upon her.

We went up to the banqueting-place of the high ones. Quite as if I were presenting her at the court of Her Majesty, I did show Dona Teresa to Calandola, and felt the taut grip of her hand on my arm as he turned his blazing and chillsome eyes upon her, penetrating her to the veriest mysteries of her soul: she breathed in bursts, her breasts rose and fell most vehemently, so keen was her terror. And yet I think if I had put my hand to her loins, in the moment of her meeting Calandola's diabolic gaze, I would have found her hot and wet, in the lustful way of one who finds the monstrous most arousing.

I offered her next toward Kinguri, who smiled most frigidly upon me and scarce more warmly to her, and then to the other lords; and we were seated, and given wine; and they placed before us vegetables and porridges, which we both did toy at much uninterestedly, neither of us having great appetite under these pressures; and the witches did their dance, and lit fires of strange colors, and sang their screaming hymns in praise of the Imbe-Jaqqa.

And Dona Teresa looked out upon all this quite as if she had been transported to the nether Pit, and was witness to the terrible celebrations and rites of Belial and Beelzebub and Moloch and Lucifer. Yet did she remain outwardly calm, though tautly held and trembling like the tuned string of a harp.

She said at length, "How many months have you dwelled among these creatures?"

"I think close upon two years. It is not easy to retain account of the passing of the time."

She held her wine-bowl, and looked into it as though into a wizard's sphere, and swirled it about.

"Why have they not slain you, Andres? They do slay everything in their path."

"It is not so," said I. "They are philosophers—"

"Ha! Are you drunken, or only mad?"

"Philosophers," I said again, "and follow a great mission, to bend the world to their way."

"That much I know, but it is not philosophy."

"I tell you it is!" I cried.

"You are mad, then."

"Listen to me: they mean to reshape the world into something that is holy by their way of seeing. They slay as need and appetite demand; but they do not slay indiscriminately. They serve a higher cause than mere destruction."

She looked about her, at the riotous roaring Calandola, at cool scheming Kinguri, at the dancers, at the witches.

"Then they are greater devils," she said, "than even I had thought."

"I think you are right in that, Teresa."

"And yet you serve them."

"I serve them, yes."

"What use have they for you? Strong though you are, you are nothing next to a demon Jaqqa."

"Ah, I have a musket," I said.

"That is it. I had overlooked it. They desire you for your musket, Andres."

"Aye, my musket, and me for myself, also. I am the white *mokisso* with golden hair, and they think I have divine force within me."

She looked me inward long and steady. A server came by with wine, and offered us; and she took, making him fill her bowl to the brim, and drank of it deep, and asked for more. It was not the blooded wine. I think I would not have told her, had it been that stuff. But here only Calandola was drinking it.

After a time she said, "I am much astounded by all this, Andres."

"For a time, so was I. But I am alive: that is the justification for everything."

"Sometimes it may be preferable to accept death."

"Sometimes," said I. "But I have not met that sometimes yet."

"How came you to them?" she asked.

I laughed a sour laugh, and replied, "By the usual treacheries of your brothers the Portugals, who left me as pawn to a blackamoor king, and did not redeem me. Then the blackamoors would have slain me, and I slipped away, and gave myself up to the man-eaters, who seem the most honest of the peoples of this land, since they alone pretend to no virtue they do not possess."

"Ah. And so you enrolled in their number."

"I was welcomed gladly there. They gave me a place, and a rank, and one of the king's own wives for my own—"

"A wife?" cried she in amaze. "But now I am your wife!"

"Then I have two."

"Ah," she said. "I understand. You are heathen through and through, deeper ever all the time."

"I could have had more wives. I took only one. I would still have only one, Teresa, but that I saw a way to save your life. If you prefer, you need not be wife to me. As you said only a moment before, sometimes it can be preferable to accept death. And death is waiting for you in those kettles. Eh?"

"I am your wife," said she sullenly.

"Then cry me no shame, for having two of them here."

"Where is this first wife of yours? Why is she not at your side, then?"

"She is dancing, there, with the other women. See, the young one, with the reddened hair?"

Dona Teresa followed my pointing finger, and squinted some in the smoky dark, until she spied Kulachinga, who did prance and leap most grandly, her breasts swaying, her body shining with sweat and oils. To me did Kulachinga seem quite fine; but an instant later I saw her through Dona Teresa's eyes, with her cicatrice-scars, her thick lips, her heavy rump all crying forth her jungle birth.

"That one is your wife?" said Dona Teresa. "You lie with her, Andres?"

"Aye, that I do."

"When first you came to this African land, you held yourself proudly apart, and thought even me to be too foreign for you. Yea, and now you couple joyously with greasy cannibal wenches that put red clay in their hair."

"I came to this land many years ago, Teresa."

"How you are transformed!" And in a lower voice, husky, quavering, she said, "I cannot put aside my fright of you. And I cannot abide feeling fear of you."

"Am I so frightening still, then?"

She turned to me, and her nostrils were aflare, and her eyes hard and bright, and I knew that she feared me, and that she hated herself for fearing her old dear Andres that could be so easily led about once by the nose. "I am part African, you know," she said after a moment, "although I pretend that I am not, and hide that side of my blood even from myself, and put on the airs of a Portugal lady. But you! You, who are pure fair-skinned English: you have become three-quarters savage, and most devilish savage at that. I knew you when you had a boy's way about you, a kind of schoolboy honor that was most charming in you, if a bit foolish. It is a metamorphosis most terrifying."

"Is it? I did not ask it. I could have been living quietly in England years ago, and doing none of this."

"Is there anything left of England in you now, Andres?"

"It is deep below."

"Do you think so?"

"It is my hope," said I, not sure at all. To her most intently I said, "I adapt to my surroundings, Teresa. It is my way of surviving, and surviving is a high goal for me, as I think it is for you. We are more alike than different, I think, and that is why we were drawn once so close, and that is why you struck at me that time, when you thought you had lost me."

"Speak not of that time, Andres. You said we would not be enemies over that."

"Ah. So I did. And we are not enemies, eh? Are we? Now you are my wife, are you not?"

"Truly?"

"Truly," said I.

"I and also the cannibal woman, your wives."

"Two wives, aye. The king has some forty. I can have two."

"In England, do they take their wives two at once?"

"This is not England."

"I think you speak sooth," said she. And she smiled, and seemed to ease a little, withal. "You are so strange, Andres, as you are now. But I think I grow used to it. I will be your wife here, though you frighten me some. I will lie on the one side of you, and the man-eater woman— what is her name?"

"Kulachinga."

"Kitchlooka. She will lie on the other. And we will press you close between us, and smother you amongst our flesh. Is there any better way to perish?"

"I think your spirits are returning, Teresa."

"It is this wine," she said. And smiled again, but it was a dark and sharp-angled smile, for dead Portugals did boil in the kettle, and live ones were chained to the far tree, and man-eaters roared and pranced all about us. And those were realities that could not lightly be thrust aside by jest.

The meat now was served, to the Imbe-Jaqqa first, and then to Kinguri, and then to me. Teresa hissed a little when the platter was brought to us, and looked away, and much of her fragile newly-won ease went from her.

"I will have none," said I to the servitor. For I would not let Teresa see me partaking of such stuff; and in truth, though I had grown casual to Jaqqa fare in my long time among them, I could no more have made a meal of the flesh of Don Fernão da Souza, which is what most likely was being served us, than could I have taken my own right arm to my mouth, and bite off a gobbet of myself to gnaw. So the joint was passed, and we drank our wine and ate our porridge. It was an ordinary evening's amusement among the Jaqqas, that I had known many times before, but tonight I saw it as Dona Teresa did see it, and I think it brought me to my senses somewhat to perceive these festivities with her eyes.

She stayed contained, and held back her tears and her fright. The feast became too mad and noisy for the exchanging of words, and we sat side by side saying little. At our high table there was much pounding and laughing, and great abundance of wine being consumed.

Yet also were there some frictions apparent between the Imbe-Jaqqa and his brother: I saw them whispering, and glaring hotly, and once the witch Kakula-banga came to them, and seemed to play the role of a mediator in a hard dispute. I think, from the words I could catch, that they quarreled over the sparing of Dona Teresa, which Kinguri still thought to be an error. Cunning Kinguri, to see in her the force that lay coiled there! To know, almost by second sight, that she was a woman of power and purpose, which it was wisest to slay out of hand while yet she was fettered! I admired the keenness of him, and I feared the consequences of having thwarted him; and in a way I knew that by wheedling the life of Dona Teresa from Imbe Calandola against the strong counsel of Kinguri, I had widened the wedge that was opening between the two brothers, and had increased the difficulties of my own position in the Jaqqa camp.

At length the brothers put the matter aside, and Calandola diverted himself by commanding a wrestling match. My man Golambolo came forth in the first, and one named Tikonje-nzinga, and they faced one another and reached forth their long arms and began the slow and stately dance that was the praeludium and introduction to their combat.

Such wrestling had I seen many times at these man-eating feasts, and always was there a fierce beauty to it. The essence of the sport was in the display of agility and suppleness it afforded, not in the winning or losing: little heed seemed to be paid to victory, but only to excellence of performance, and one who displayed grace in the manner of his defeat often was hailed as warmly as his conqueror. So now did Golambolo and Tikonje-nzinga go artfully through their pavanes and allemandes of combat, until in the press of the struggle Tikonje-nzinga was thrown, and fell most serenely, which won him acclaim.

The next pair to wrestle was Kaimba and Ngonga—for high lords of the Jaqqas did eagerly take their turns in the arena—and after them, the venerable Ntotela, with a man nearly his age, much muscled and brawned, by name Kulurimba. And they all were elegant and splendid in their movements, and I did envy and admire them, thinking, Lord, give me the grace and skill to wrestle as they do! And I wondered what would befall me if I were to go into the arena, which never yet had I done.

I looked to Dona Teresa, and in faith she was moved as I was moved by the beauties of this sport. Her eyes did gleam and her face was held fixed and her breathing came slow, and her lips were a little apart, and as one man or the other gained briefly the supremacy, she did clench and unclench her hands in silent concern. And at last turned to me, when Ntotela knelt upon his opponent's chest, and said in a thick whispering voice, "Ah, they are like angels, when they wrestle! How can that be, that devils may be like angels?"

"It is the great art amongst them, this combat."

"And have you learned it?"

"I? I have watched, but I have never fought."

"But would you, Andres, if you were called out?"

"That I would, and most gladly," said I. "And God guard me well, for I fear the callowest of these Jaqqas would be my master at it, but yet would I joy to engage with one."

"Why, see, then, the high lord devil is looking about for the next wrestlers, this moment. Go you, Andres!"

"Ah, not this night," said I, and would not meet Calandola's questing eye.

For indeed I had a different sort of wrestle in mind. Now I had me two wives, and my mind did dwell uncomfortingly on what would occur when I brought Teresa together with Kulachinga. We are not trained in England, after all, in the keeping of harems.

"Will you not fight, then?" Teresa asked, and I saw her blood stirred by the battles that had been enacted.

"I tell you, not this night. Come: the festivity is entering its late hours, and I would have you meet my Kulachinga."

I took her by the arm, and led her down into the midst of the Jaqqas. And lo! there was no chill between them. My Jaqqa wife only smiled without rancor, for it was the custom for these people to take wives by the score, and perhaps she had thought me overdue. And Dona Teresa, who once had given me grief enough over her rival Matamba, now greeted Kulachinga most graciously. Though neither spoke a word of the other's language, they seemed instantly to enter into a communication.

Together we went to the habitation the Jaqqas had set aside for me in this new camp of theirs outside Agokayongo. It was a fine fair wicker-work cottage, with straw strewn over the ground, and some brocaded scarlet-and-purple draperies on the wall that I had carried with me since being given them by Kinguri in the town of Shillambansa that we sacked. I was weary with long travel and much excitement of the evening and the heavy wine, and upon entering the place I sank down upon my knees to the ground. My two women did come to me then and ease me with caresses, which was passing strange to me, to be with two at once. For there they were, the handsome Portuguese woman in her torn finery, and the strong-bodied black woman with her skin all greased and her hair thick with clay. One could scarce conceive a stranger tripling of souls than we.

There was a difficult moment at the outset, when I did feel the closeness of Dona Teresa by me. For there had been a great gulf of years and feeling between us since our fiery early love, and such gulfs are not readily bridged. So many seasons had swept through time's great brazen gate, since last our flesh had met in this sort of embrace, that I felt sore estranged from her, and uneasy at resuming our lovemaking.

But old skills well learned do swift return. I put my hands to her breasts, and my lips to her lips, which drew a giggling burst of laughter from Kulachinga, to whom kissing was strange. And then Dona Teresa and I were pressed body to body from thighs to chest, and her fingers did dig deep into my flesh, and mine into hers, as though with one great seizure of one another we could atone for all the years apart.

Yet was there also Kulachinga, and I would not spurn her. So I did ease my grip on Teresa after a bit, and turn to the Jaqqa woman, and we embraced also in our different manner. During this, Dona Teresa did stroke her oiled skin most familiarly, most lovingly, with no show of shame at the handling of another woman's body.

The two of them then drew me down together with them.

Ah, I was hard put to know what to do, I having but one member and they each a hole! But the wine and the weariness made my head swim, so that I gave no heed to difficulties, but merely allowed myself to float on the flow of the instant, going whithersoever I found myself journeying, just as a mariner cast into the sea gives himself over to the bosom of the water, if he be wise, and makes no attempt to direct his passage.

God's blood! It was a wondrous time! Their hands were upon me, here and there and everywhere. Their bodies, so various of shape and sensation and odor, encompassed me close. I had one hand between these thighs, and one hand between those; my fingers moved busily; there was warmth and wetness upon them; I heard sounds; I closed my eyes; fingers traveled the length of my yard, and back again; someone bestrode me and impaled herself upon me; someone else put hard-tipped breasts to my lips; I fondled one woman and futtered the other; and withdrew, or was withdrawn from; and futtered one and fondled the other; and my senses were engulfed, and my mind dissolved, and my soul was swept away, and all the universe became but a sea of action, of gasping and thrusting and laughing and writhing, with streams of hot sweat making slippery our skins; and a moment came when I discharged my lusts with a ferocious explosion, into the one or the other woman and I could not, for all the gold in Peru, tell you which; and I dropped into sleep as though I were a man drugged, and when I awoke, on account of the whimpering, or so I thought, of some jungle animal prowling near by me, I beheld by dawn's thin light the two of them in one another's arms, breasts against breasts rubbing, and legs intertwined like those of wrestlers. But they were not wrestling. And I smiled, and watched Teresa and Kulachinga at play for a while, and shook my head in wonder, and turned from them and closed my eyes, and fell into a heavy sleep from which, God wot, the arms of Venus herself could not have pulled me.

TEN

ON THE morrow I found me Golambolo, and asked him if he had heeded me, in telling Imbe Calandola that the Portugal prisoners he had brought were to be held for questioning. Most aggrieved that I should suspect him of a default, he swore by the mother-*mokisso* that he had done so, and begged me to slay him if I found it was not so.

"Why then were some killed?" I demanded.

"Ah, it is the hunger of Calandola, that brooks no check," said he, and I knew that to be the case, so I dismissed him with my pardon.

Then went I to the surviving pair of Portugals. They were not men I knew: one was named Benevides, and the other Negreiros, and they had only lately come to São Paulo de Loanda, in the retinue of this new governor Coutinho. From what they had witnessed the night before they were well-nigh dumbstricken with fright, and the sight of me in my Jaqqa ornaments gave them no great ease. I knelt down beside them and offered them some comfort, telling them I would see to their freedom if they could tell me of the army that was gathered near Ndala Chosa, how many men it contained and for what purpose it had assembled. But they knew no more of it than that it was there, though they strived most piteously to invent a few scraps of news that would be of value to me. They wept, and begged for their lives, and implored me to spare them from the stew-pot. But I could only offer them the hope of God's mercy, and a swift release from suffering. And they saw there would be no salvation for them forthcoming of me, and turned away, and said no more, and they were silent still until the last. At the next feast did they perish for the fulfillment of Jaqqa appetites.

I lived in those days in strange double matrimony, and there were no discordancies out of it, miraculous to relate. Why it was that Teresa and

Kulachinga should have found so easy affinity, I cannot say, except perhaps that there is some innate lubriciousness of womanhood, that came to them at the time our first mother did accept the apple from the serpent in Eden, by which they glide easily and without reluctance into such amorous interknottings. Or else it was only a happy combining of traits, Kulachinga being a natural child of the jungle, and Teresa being wanton and insatiable in passion, and thus the two of them did conjoin out of wholly separate motives, one from sheer innocence and the other from deep craft. Whatever it was, they seemed to enjoy one another as powerfully as either of them did me, or I either of them.

In the early days of reunion Dona Teresa and I did strive to span the gap of event that had opened between us over the years. Of my own adventures it was swiftly told, for she knew of my voyages south to Benguela by order of Don João de Mendoça, and after that I had naught to tell but my captivity under Mofarigosat and my going to dwell among the Jaqqas. What she had to tell moved me deeply, for it was the death of Don João, that had already been ill when last I was in São Paulo de Loanda. "He came upon a bloating disease," she said, "that turned him into a swollen ball, and we could not recognize his features. Toward the last he did lose his mind, and hold long conversations with his fathers, and with King Philip and many others, and with you."

"With me, forsooth?"

"Aye, he spoke in his ravings with you about England, and said he would send you there by the next ship, as his ambassador, for he would be King of Africa. The poor man! And then he died, in the dry season of 1602, and it took a coffin fit for an elephanto to hold him, and ten strong men to carry it."

"The dry season of 1602," I said, in a wondering way, for I had given the numbers of the years little thought in my Jaqqa time. "And what year does this be?"

"It is the mid-part of the year 1603."

"Ah," said I, revolving that in my mind, and striving to make some sense of it. "It was fourteen years this season that I left England, though it seems fourteen hundred, betimes, to me. The boy-babes who were born that day have beards now, and the girl-babes are sprouting breasts! And Queen Elizabeth is an old woman, if still she hold the throne. And if she do not, who has come to take her place?"

"I know nothing of that," said Dona Teresa. "But King Philip is dead in Spain."

"What, that old monk? I thought he would live forever. How long since?"

"Five years," said she. "It was in 1598."

"But why did I not hear, then? No one spoke of it in São Paulo de Loanda, and I was there at that time."

She shrugged and replied, "The news was slow in coming. And then another Philip his son came to take the crown, and for a time we thought it was the same Philip as before."

I laughed at that, seeing now Angola as a place at the end of the world, where the mightiest king in Christendom might die and his own far-off subjects not get the true report for years. Well, and I had no illusion that we were at the heart of things here. In sooth I scarce cared about these matters: they were white man's business, Europe-man's business. Some other Philip was on the Spanish throne, and he was said to be a weak and silly man when he was prince, and might be a weak and silly king as well, which would allow England to make an end of the war with Spain that was such a waste of English substance. I gave that some moment of thought. But it was like a filmy thing blowing in the gale, a mere inconsequential tissue, all this talk of kings and nations. I could find no fullness of texture in them now. My world was bounded by cauldrons and drums and ollicondi trees.

"Tell me of events in São Paulo de Loanda," I asked, to be cordial.

"The city is much enlarged. There is a grand new church, and the governor has made his palace greater."

"This governor is your Don João Coutinho, you say?"

"That is the one. When Don João fell ill, the new King Philip sent him to us, with authority to conquer the mines or mountains of Kambambe. To perform that service, the King of Spain has given him seven years' custom of all the slaves and goods that are carried from Angola to the West Indies, Brazil, or whithersoever, with condition that he should build three castles—one in Ndemba, where the salt mines are, another in Kambambe, and the other in the south, at Bahia das Vaccas."

"And will he come to Kambambe, while these Jaqqas lurk so close?"

"He knows nothing of the Jaqqas. It was Don Fernão's commission to investigate these provinces, and report to him. Well, and I see there is large report to make." She leaned near, and plucked at my arm. "What is this army the Jaqqas have formed, in league with Kafuche Kambara?"

"It is as you see: an army."

"To what end?"

"The usual end," said I. "War."

"But who is left for Calandola to conquer, if he has made peace with Kafuche? Will he march against King Ngola in Dongo?"

"I think not," said I.

She was silent a time. Then she said, "But there is only São Paulo de Loanda otherwise."

I made no reply.

"Is that the scheme? Will they march westward, and attack the city, as in my father's time they attacked São Salvador of the Kongo?"

I could not lie to her. "I think they will," I said after some troubled hesitance. "It has been discussed."

"More than discussed! It is determined, is it not?"

"That it has," I said.

"How soon?" said she fiercely. "When will they march?"

"I cannot tell you this, Teresa."

"Come, come, hide nothing from me! How do you say, you cannot tell me?"

"Because I do not know," I did reply. "We will march when the auspices are proper, by Calandola's lights, and no man knows that but Calandola. I do swear it, Teresa. I conceal nothing in this. There will be a war: but the time of it is not yet chosen."

"Ah," she said, and looked most solemn. After a moment she said, "You know that these are the Jaqqas that slew my mother, and put her in their kettles. And they have slain my husband now also."

"Your husband, yes. But these are not the same Jaqqas as long ago slew your mother."

"That matters little. Jaqqas they be, all the same. I dread these folk, Andres. I would banish them to the dankest caverns of Hell, and be rid of them."

"They are much maligned, I think."

Her eyes went wide and she laughed most scornfully. "What? You defend the man-eaters? Are you altogether mad, Andres, from your jungle wanderings? They are monsters!"

"Aye," said I.

"How can you speak aught that is good of them?"

Softly and sternly I said, "This land is a den of monsters, both white and black, that do steal each other's land, and take each other's lives. The more I saw of Portugals, Teresa, the less I did loathe Jaqqas."

"And so you are become one of them, then? And will you fight beside them against my people, when they march on São Paulo de Loanda?"

To that I gave her no answer.

"Will you? What will you do, in that war? What have you become, Andres? *What have you become?*"

As we exchanged these words, we did move along the perimeter of the Jaqqa camp, that did spread like floodwaters over the dry plain outside the town of Agokayongo. And on all sides preparations for war were going forth, the fashioning of blades and the stringing of bows, which Dona Teresa did not fail to note. Beyond us lay the second army, that of Kafuche Kambara that was joined with us in alliance, nearly as strong as ours. This, too, Dona Teresa did observe, and I knew that in the eye of her mind she was seeing this barbarian horde pouring in a torrent into São Paulo de Loanda, to the number of ten savages or more to each Portugal, and unleashing there a hecatomb and holocaust of terrible slaughter and rapine. I noted the somberness on her face, and comprehended the fears in her heart: yet did I proffer her no comfort then.

Not far away from us I spied a towering figure moving slowly through the camp. It was the Imbe-Jaqqa, taking some survey of his men, alone but for a bodyguard that lingered some paces behind him.

"Andubatil!" he called, upon the sight of me, and beckoned.

"It is your king summoning you," said Dona Teresa in a bitter way. "Go to him!"

"Let us both go."

"I will not," said she, and drew back, and lingered near a tree of great coiling roots like swollen serpents on the ground.

I found Calandola to be in a reflective and somewhat tranquil frame of mind, with none of his great roaring manner about him; yet even so did he give forth that manifest sign of grandeur, of barely controlled power wound and ready to spring forth, that I think was the most terrifying thing about him. He rested his hand upon my shoulder and stared deep into my eyes with his cold glistening diabolical stare, and said, deep-voiced, awesome, "Well, Andubatil, and are you pleased to have your wife with you once more?"

"That I am, and greatly, Lord Imbe-Jaqqa."

"It has cost me much fury out of my brother Kinguri, who dislikes her with a heavy disliking."

"This I know," said I. "I would see Kinguri, and ease his fears of her, but he avoids me."

"You and he were deep friends, so I thought."

"So thought I as well, Lord Calandola."

"He is very wise, is he not?"

"His mind is a searching one," I said.

Calandola smiled, and looked away, putting his hand to his vast bull neck and squeezing it, and after a moment he declared, "Kinguri is also a great fool."

To this I replied nothing.

"A fool," said Calandola, "because his mind is thick with thoughts of Portugal, and England, and Europe, and other places that are of no importance. And he wants to know of your God, and your Devil, and the other Christian *mokissos*. Why do such things matter? They are unreal.

They are trifles." All this still calm, though I sensed, as ever, the smouldering furnace within this man, or demon, or whatever he might be. He continued, just as calm, "All these things I will sweep from the world. And then will come a time of happiness and simplicity. There will be only one nation. There will be only one tongue. There will be only one king. It will be better that way."

I met his terrible gaze, and I nodded when he spoke, and gave him no gainsaying. And he did go on, expounding his vision of the purity and virtue of the Jaqqa realm when extended to every nation of the world, that I had heard before, but he said it much grander this time, with the zeal not of a demon but of an archdemon. I was engulfed in it. You may laugh, to think of the cities of Christendom blotted from being and replaced with wild forests full of dancing painted cannibals, and you may say it can never be; yet I tell you that as Calandola spoke, painting for me once again that vision of all our vices abolished, all our crooked streets and soiled lanes ploughed under, all our encrustations upon the skin of the earth purged away, saying all this in the most level of tones in that deep and magical voice, it seemed to me almost as if it would be mankind's great gain to surrender all that we had built since Caesar's day, and yield ourselves up to the whirlwinds of pure nature. It was madness. I felt the philosophy of Imbe Calandola running anew like quicksilver in my veins, and it burned me like fire, for that it was foreign to my nature but yet had impinged itself deeply into me. I knew it to be folly. I knew he could never extend his sway beyond the forests of this wild land. Yet out of the dusty plains of deep Asia had come the Khan Genghis of the Tartars with much the same dream, riding down upon the settled nations of the world like a whirlwind of scimitars, and had he not made all of Europe tremble in his day? And who could rightly say but that it would not all happen again, under this Calandola? For the moment, if only for the moment, I saw the Imbe-Jaqqa marching in triumph at the head of his black legions through the streets of London, and on to Canterbury for wild bacchanal amid the tumbled paving-blocks of the cathedral, and I did feel the hard chill of that dread fantasy, and the frosty beauty of it.

Then he said, "Would you have another woman, Andubatil, or do two serve you sufficiently?"

"Quite sufficiently, Lord Calandola!"

"Good. Good. I would not have you suffer for the lack. You are most valuable to me, Andubatil, you are cherished deeply by me. When we march on São Paulo de Loanda, you will lead the column beside me, and I would see your hair gleaming like a beacon in the hot sunlight. Is your musket in good repair?"

"Aye, that it is."

"And with powder, with shot? I gave orders that the weapons of those Portugals were to be given unto you."

"That has been done," I said. "I have enough powder now for all my uses, and great store of ammunition."

"Good."

"And when, Lord Calandola, does the march begin?"

"In four days' time, I think. Or five. I must consult with Kakula-banga, whether it be four days or five, and have him read the omens."

He turned, and took my hand in his, and squeezed it in that ferocious way of his, that conveyed his love; and once more the Imbe-Jaqqa's eyes met mine and had my measure; and then he strode away.

I stood looking toward him, wondering. What power was it he had, that was so compelling over me? Not just his size, for there are many big men that are but oafs, and not just his voice, and not his visage alone, nor the vision that possessed him, of world dominion and destruction; but it was all of those at once, I suppose, that drew into one thick cable that could bind entire nations. Certainly he did bind me, though I have never otherwise felt myself to be a man easily led; this Calandola did ever impress his will into me in a way most mysterious, and reduce me to something far less than my true self, so that I moved often not of my own accord but in the general frenzy and thrust of a larger and irresistible mass. And so I give my thanks to God Almighty that He made Calandola an African, and kept him far from our shores. But one day, I do fear, a man of that sort will arise closer to home, and take all the civilized world in his grip and do the Devil's own work with it, and it will go hard for us. May God preserve us from the coming of that man's day.

When Calandola was gone from me, Dona Teresa returned.

"That is Satan himself," she said.

"Perhaps. Or Satan's own son."

"Why do you not slay him while he stands so comradely beside you, and spare the world from this monster?"

"I would not live an hour, an' I do any such thing," said I. "And I think he is less monstrous than he chooses to appear."

"You have become a fool, Andres."

"Have I, then?"

"You defend him ever, him that is indefensible. Which marks you as a fool, and a gull."

I shook my head. "Beyond doubt he has a sway on me, yes. But I think I see him more exactly than most. It is easy to say, He is a monster, He is a monster, and in some ways indeed he makes himself monstrous.

It takes a keener perception to find the philosophy beneath the frightsome surface."

"Philosophy!" cried she most scornfully. "Aye, I know his philosophy. Kill and eat, kill and eat, carve and gorge, carve and gorge! It is a wondrous thoughtful philosophy! Have you come to like the flavor of man-meat, Andres?"

"You are wife indeed, if you beshrew me this way."

"I seek only to know your soul. Are you yet a Christian? Or do you give yourself over fully to these cannibal revels?"

"Let me be, Teresa," I said wearily.

"You have eaten of the forbidden flesh, have you not?"

"By whom forbidden?" I asked.

"By the mouth of God and the laws of man," said she. "But you have dined of it. That I know. And you will again, and the love of its savor does possess you, and make you mad."

"Nay, Teresa, I am no madman at all, but only a poor lost sailor, who longs for his home."

"You delude yourself."

"It is so. I ship myself under whatever flag I must, until the day I am free of Africa."

"So you have been saying. But I think a deeper sea-change has come upon you, and your talk of homegoing is now mere talk, that you repeat because you have long repeated it, which has lost its urgency for you some years back."

"That is not so," said I, but I did not say it with conviction.

With much fire she said, "That man is no man, but a devil, is he not? And you are ensorcelled by him, I think, and transformed into something accursed. And you do not see it, but believe you are only pretending to serve him, while biding your time. Or else you lie to yourself as well as to me." She glared into my eyes, and I compelled myself not to flinch. "Of what were you and he talking, I ask you, pray?"

I said, "Of his brother Kinguri: for I have caused a rift between them. And we talked also of the war that Calandola would make against all the world, and his hopes for conducting it. He dreams of invading Europe."

"Which is madness."

"So I would not deny. He will never achieve that. But soon will he march against São Paulo de Loanda, at any rate."

She grasped my arm. "How soon?"

"I cannot say."

"So you told me before. But that was because you did not know. Now you know. How soon, Andres?"

I drew deep my breath. "Four days. Or maybe five. The time depends on the horoscopes his witches cast."

"We must send warning!"

"We will do nothing of the sort," said I bluntly.

"It is monstrous, that he would burst into the city. Fie, Andres, let us escape this place, and carry the word to the governor, before everyone is slaughtered!"

"There is no escape from here. They would have after us, and we would be in the kettles by nightfall of the day we are caught."

"But we cannot stand idly by, and let the city be destroyed," she said.

"We will."

"This war must not be!"

"I am not convinced of that," said I. "I think it might be well, if São Paulo de Loanda perished."

"What, Andres? Now comes forth the truth! You are wholly of them!"

"I have my reasons for what I say."

"Reasons of madness!"

"I have no cause to love the Portugals. What love did they ever show me, except Barbosa, that is dead? And Don João, who spoke sweet of one side of his mouth, and traitored me with the other? And you, Dona Teresa, who did the same?"

"I have had forgiveness for that."

"Aye, so you have. But the others? Those who chained me, those who beat me, those who mocked me, those who kept me from my home for all these years? Am I Jesus, that I should embrace them, and ask God to spare them?"

"You need not destroy them, though."

"Ah, but perhaps I welcome such a vengeance."

She stared long at me. "You are not a man in whom such hatred is natural. Of that am I certain."

"Perhaps I have changed, Teresa."

"Then it is a mighty change indeed, I think. Come, Andres, forget this wrath, and join with me to save the city. We must do something! I will devise a way."

"I remind you, Dona Teresa, that I have pledged myself for your good behavior. Whatever you do, it will bring down catastrophe upon me. Will you betray me a second time?"

"The city, Andres, think of the city!"

"Aye," said I. "I do think of the city."

She scowled at me, and tossed her head, and strode away in the direction of our cottage. I did not follow her thence, but paced like an anxious lion, throughout the Jaqqa camp, and my mind did swim and flutter with the chaos that was in it. I scarce saw where I was going; but as I wandered freely I came to a place where the musicians of war dwelled, and they were tuning of their instruments, or whatever it is they do with them. These men grinned at me most amiably and offered me their fifes and viols to play, but I shook my head, and walked on, and from behind me in ten discordant tunes at once came the wild and jangling sounds of Jaqqa harmonies.

ELEVEN

FOR SOME several days the preparations for war went on at an increasing fervor. Weapons were gathered and made ready; war-chiefs met in council to construct their web of stratagem; Kakula-banga the high witch did busy himself in the casting of omens and the lighting of foul-smelling witch-fires on the borders of our camp. In this time I had my role to play as lieutenant to Calandola, and spent much time with him, sketching for him maps of the city of São Paulo de Loanda, showing the approach routes, the location of the citadel, the quarters where the soldiers dwelled. I saw little of Dona Teresa except at night; but she was more calm now, with that wrath and anxiety gone from her, and a new serenity over her countenance.

Then on a night a few days thereafter was I awakened suddenly in mid-sleep, and pulled roughly to my feet, and caught from behind by both my arms. Greatly did I struggle, but it was useless: I was held fast, a prisoner, still half befogged by slumber.

"What is this?" I cried. "Help! Assassins!"

Our cottage was full of Jaqqas. By their torches I saw their scarred and gap-toothed faces, and they were men I knew, Golambolo and some others who had served me in the wars. But now they seemed forbidding and hostile, and as much like demons as were the first Jaqqas I had ever seen, long ago, when I had known nothing of these folk but their fearsome repute. They gripped me so I could not break free, and gripped Dona Teresa, too, whose face in the torchlight was a stark mask of fear. Kulachinga lay untouched, at my feet, on the straw couch that the three of us had so cozily shared together until just moments before.

They swept me off, and Dona Teresa as well, through the camp to the inner fortification behind which the Imbe-Jaqqa dwelled. And there I saw all the high ones of the man-eater tribe already assembled, with their visages seeming most grim and somber. Imbe Calandola sat upon his high throne, garbed in a necklace of whitened bones and holding in his hand a scepter that was of bone also, a shin perhaps, and beside him was Kinguri equally solemn, and other lords. And on the ground before them, trussed and bound so that his body was arched most painfully in the manner of a bow, was a blackamoor I did not know, one of the Bakongo slaves that the Jaqqas did keep about them in their camp. At the sight of this man, there came from Dona Teresa a little hissing sound, and then a deep groan of pain or of sorrow. The which served to provide me with the unraveling of this mystery that encumbered us and with a melting feeling in my legs I came to understand what must have occurred. In shock and anger did I look toward Dona Teresa, but she did not meet my gaze. Then those who held us did lead us to separate sides of the council-hearth, far opposite one another. My heart beat with frightsome force and I glared across the way at her, knowing she had betrayed me yet again and not being willing to believe that of her; but she would not look at me.

Kinguri said, "There has been treason here."

Ah, then it was so! Yet was I determined to separate myself from the deed, for I had had no part of it.

"Good brother, what has happened?" I asked. "And why am I restrained this way? I have done no wrong."

"That shall we discover," said Kinguri. He gestured toward the Bakongo slave. "Is this man your creature, Andubatil?"

"Never have I seen his face."

"Aye. But perhaps you have spoken with him through some intermediary, to give him a commission on your behalf."

"I do not take your meaning," I said. I looked toward Calandola, who sat above this assemblage as remote as Zeus, and seemingly as uncaring, his eyes far away, and I said, "Mighty Lord Imbe-Jaqqa, I ask you what this proceeding may be."

"Address yourself to me," coldly said Kinguri, Calandola making no response to my words.

"Then I ask you again—"

"You have not hired this man to undertake some task for you?"

"I have not."

"Nor your Portuguese woman?"

In sore rage I looked across to Dona Teresa, who met my gaze for an instant, and her eyes were hard and bright with terror.

"I do not know what dealings she has had with this man, if she has had any," I said. "I have, as you know, been preoccupied of late with the planning of the war."

"Ah," said Kinguri. "Of course: how could I have overlooked that? But there has been treason here, Andubatil."

He made gesture to a hulking Jaqqa, who stepped forward and tightened the bonds on the Bakongo slave, the which did draw a yelp of distress from the tormented man. Then Kinguri said, in the slave's own tongue, "Tell us once again what you were hired to do, and by whom."

"To go—to São Paulo de Loanda—" the man said softly, for he was so bent and strained that he could scarce get out the words, this being the Jaqqa approximation of the rack upon which more civilized folk do stretch their inquisitions.

"For what purpose?" demanded Kinguri.

"To warn—Portugals—Jaqqas coming—"

"Ah. To give warning! Do you hear, O Imbe-Jaqqa? Do you understand the man's words?"

Calandola scowled most darkly.

Kinguri leaned close by the slave, and signalled for another twisting of the trusses, and said to him, "And by which persons were you charged with this message?"

"Woman—Portugal woman—"

"The one you see there?"

"That one."

"And by which other person?"

"Woman—the woman—"

"The woman, yes, but who else?"

Naught but moans and whimpers came from the slave.

"Ease him a little," said Kinguri, and this was done. Then, as severe as any Cardinal of the Holy Office, the longshanked Jaqqa did hover above the sweat-drenched man and say again, "What accomplice did the Portugal woman have?"

"Spoke—only with—woman—"

"Name the other!"

"Don't—know—"

"Tighter again," said Kinguri, and the cords were pulled, and the slave did cry out.

"Enough," said Imbe Calandola.

"He has not yet confessed fully," Kinguri did protest.

Calandola waved impatiently. "It is enough. He knows no more. Destroy him."

"My Lord Imbe-Jaqqa!" cried Kinguri.

But there was no halting the order of Calandola. A Jaqqa that was one of the headsmen of the tribe stepped forth, and with a stroke of his immense blade, that whistled as it fell, he cut the hapless slave in twain.

There was a sharp sound of metal against bone, and a dull sound of metal against earth afterward, and the severed parts of the dead man, released so instantly from the taut strings that held him, did fly apart most horridly, with a scarlet spraying going most wondrous far, even to the feet of Calandola's throne. Kinguri, at this, did whirl around and throw up his arms in expostulation, for he was maddened by this hasty slaughter of his source of confession.

Calandola looked downward toward Dona Teresa and said, "You are named by this slave as treasonous toward us. What statement do you make?"

"None," said Dona Teresa, when the words were explained to her in the Kikongo tongue; but she said it with throat so dry that no sound emerged, only the silent mouthings of her lips, and perforce she had to say the word again.

"You will not deny the charge?" asked the Imbe-Jaqqa.

"Why waste the breath?"

Even now I could not let her so doom herself by acquiescing thus in the indictment. Even now I felt constrained to defend her, though she had put my life in jeopardy.

"Lord Imbe-Jaqqa!" I burst out. "I pray you, forgive this foolish woman! Whatever she may have done, it was done rashly and without thought, and was only an idle thing, for she has no understanding—"

"Silence, Andubatil. This nonsense ill becomes you." To Teresa he said again, "You stand accused of treachery, by the words of this dead bondsman here, that we all did hear several times over since we captured him by the edge of our camp. He said you promised him many shells, to carry your message to the Portguals. Is this so?"

"I say nothing," she replied, with a flash of wrath in her eyes, and an imperious look, for her courage seemed to be returning even though to me it was plain that all was lost.

The Imbe-Jaqqa now turned toward me. "And you, Andubatil, you are charged with conspiring also with her in this treason."

"I know not a thing of it, O Lord Imbe-Jaqqa."

"He lies," said Kinguri.

"Do I, now? And did the slave name me? Did he speak of me before I came, yet in my presence did not know me?"

"Your guilt is known to us," said Kinguri.

"Not so, brother, not so!"

"You are no brother of mine."

"By this scar I bear, and yours also, Kinguri! What, will you reject me now, that you fondly once spoke with so late into the night, about the kingdoms and laws of Christendom, and so much else?"

"I am no brother to a liar and traitor," said he, all ice and contempt. To Calandola he did cry, "You who are my brother of the flesh, do you not see the guilt of Andubatil?"

"I see it not," said Calandola.

"They had conspired together, the woman and the man! They both must die, O lord!"

"Andubatil has done no treason," the Imbe-Jaqqa said.

"Nor has my woman!" I said, perhaps too rashly. "There is no proof! The slave was paid to perjure upon her!"

"The woman," said Calandola, "surely has hatred for us. You take grave risk by defending her, except if you do it out of love. We think her guilt is certain, and we will put her to the trial to demonstrate it."

"I beg you, good my lord, by all that passed between us on that night you remember, spare her!"

This I said in a low voice, to him alone. But he did not look pleased at being conjured by the force of that rite we had shared. Glowering most saturninely at me, he did continue, "She is a traitor. You stand accused by my brother of the same offense, the which you deny. It is a heavy charge, that may not be ignored. This must we examine with care, and there will be consultation of the witches. You will be prisoned until we arrive at our proper path."

He lifted his hand, and Teresa and I were dragged away from that place, I to a wickerwork enclosure not far from the place of the great kettles, which was not a cheering sight unto me, and she elsewhere, beyond my vision. There I was left to ruminate in solitude upon these latest turns of fate.

It enraged me that she had forsworn me so, and, after I had given pledge she would do no harm, had tried to send word to her people of our attack on São Paulo de Loanda. For such a thing could only work my downfall along with hers, if it miscarried, and it had miscarried.

Of her guilt I had no doubt. Plainly she had hired that man to bear the warning to the Portugals; and plainly she would die for it. She stood incriminated and had no defense, nor would she attempt to devise one, whether out of overarching pride or a submission to inevitable destiny. She was in the hands of Jaqqas, and no claim of innocence would save her. She would die. And for all the pain she had given me, I found myself sore stricken with grief over that. How could she perish? She was so vital, so deep with life, so magnificent of beauty: if she was not a witch, then she was some sort of goddess. And yet she would die, nor was I at all sure I would survive this attainder of treason myself, with Kinguri now become my implacable foe. Surely he saw me as rival for Calandola's affections, and enemy to his own ambitions; and with so potent an enemy at the court of the Imbe-Jaqqa, I would be hard put to come forth of this with my life.

For a day, and half a day more, I did remain in my cage, guarded all the while by silent Jaqqas and giving myself over to the most melancholy of thoughts, and to occasional moments of prayer. Then was I summoned once again to the council-hearth, where the same great Jaqqas as before were in their positions of state. And thither also was Dona Teresa brought, with her arms bound behind her, though I was unchained.

She looked to me, and in her eyes I saw no fear, but only strength, resignation, courage.

Imbe Calandola said, "My brother Kinguri has spoken with the *nganga*-men. They are of the verdict that treason is likely here, and must be searched out by the trial of ordeal."

"Ah, then I am a dead man!" I cried.

"If there has been treason, then that is so," replied Calandola most serenely.

"And which of us is to have the ordeal first, the woman or I?"

"There is only you to be tried," said the Imbe-Jaqqa, "for the woman's guilt is certain, and her doom is fixed."

At this, Dona Teresa did utter the smallest of sounds of despair, a mere issuing-forth of air, quickly cut off; and then she did resume her staunch demeanor.

And I, seeing myself standing at the veritable brink of extinction, with the earth crumbling before me and bidding fair to pitch me into the abyss, what then did I feel? Why, once again I felt nothing at all, no fear, no dismay, I who had been at the same fatal brink so many times before: I was cold in my heart, numb like one who has clasped himself to the great ice-floes of the north, but I was wholly still at the center of my soul, and calm. For one can face death only so many times, and then the fear of it is gone from the spirit, and one becomes void and wholly at ease, like one who is so fatigated by constant warfare that he takes no notice of the deadly arrows singing past his cheeks. They would give me the ordeal by poison, which I knew from the testimony of Kinguri, when his lips were unsealed by wine, to be concocted aforehand by the will of the king. So the only question to be answered was whether the fraudulence of the ordeal would be the fraudulence of Kinguri, who wished me dead, or that of Calandola, who I believed did not associate me with Teresa's treason, and meant to preserve me. Calandola was mightier; Kinguri was craftier; I had no notion which of them would prevail. But though I had not lost the love of life that has imbued me deeply since my first years, though I longed as passionately as ever to go on and on, and see what lay beyond the next headland and the next, yet was I untroubled by distress over the outcome of this test: whatever would befall would take its own course the same way, whether I fretted and worried over it or no. And so I was wholly tranquil.

"Bring now the fruit of the *embá*," said Calandola.

So it was to be the poisoned fruit, and not the snailshells to my forehead, nor the boiling water that I must drink, nor the singeing of my flesh with the red-hot iron.

A *nganga* in heavy paint and glistening grease did step forward, carrying with him the bowl of the fruits of these palm-trees, which were about the size and shape of a small peach-fruit, but smooth and shining of skin, with a golden hue and faint red streaks in it. As I had seen that time before, the witch-man did draw from the bowl one of these fruits and eat it himself for show, and spit out the hard kernel of it, and stand before us unpoisoned and hale, and smiling. Then did a second of these witches advance to him with a flask made of highly polished dark wood, that was meant to contain the poison, and he did dip a great lengthy black thorn into the flask, bringing it out dripping with a fluid, and this he thrust deep within one of the *embá*-fruits, and a second, and a third.

Imbe Calandola did extend his scepter of bone to me from his high throne to say, "You are accused, Andubatil, of treasonably betraying our intent to the Portugals of São Paulo de Loando. What say you to this charge?"

"This I wholly deny."

"Make an oath upon this rod."

I did touch his scepter, just at the tip. Which made me faintly shudder to think that next week someone might be swearing by some bone of mine. I said most loudly, "Be it known by this that I have done no treason ever against the Jaqqa nation, nor against Imbe Calandola its master, nor Kinguri his brother and mine."

And so saying, I looked deep at Imbe Calandola and then at Kinguri, who looked back at me with eyes that were like fiery coals, all blazing and hateful.

Calandola gestured. The witch who held the bowl did say to me, "We have mixed within this bowl three fruits that bear a killing poison. Seek, and take, and eat, and if you have done no crime your *mokisso* will guard you from harm."

And now my strange tranquility fell from me like a discarded cloak, and I felt great fear from crown to toes, I that had thought I had outlived the sensation of mortal dread; for I did remember that time I had seen this oath administered to Jaqqas, and how the man designated for death had made terrible noises, and had swollen in his throat and died choking, which is a horrible way to die. But I did present myself boldly as I advanced to select the fruit. The *nganga*-man held the bowl high, to give me no clue by way of mark or puncture on the fruit, and I reached in, and again I grew calm and easy, saying to myself that I had been ready many times to pay God the death that is owing by me, and if this were the moment, so be it, since that if it were not now, it would merely be later. And took a fruit and put it to my mouth, and found it passing sweet and comforting to the taste, with no hint of venom in it, and ate it down and spat forth the kernel, and grinned most widely and said, "There, it is shown now that I had no complicity."

"Draw another," said the witch-man.

"I have drawn!"

"The trial calls for three," said Kinguri.

"It was not so the other time, when three fruits were presented," said, I, "and only one was poisoned, and the accused did take the jeopardy but once—"

"This is a trial of another sort," said Kinguri, and when I looked in appeal to Imbe Calandola, he met my gaze without response, and waited like a stone statue for my next taking of fruit.

The *nganga* did proffer me the bowl. And I did choose again.

I was sure now that they would do me to death this day, that Kinguri would have me go on choosing until I hit one of the venomed ones; and to make a haste for the outcome I bit and spat kernel and swallowed, and stood, and wondered, and felt no murder in my veins.

"Again my innocence is proven, Imbe Calandola!"

"Draw one more," said the witch most inexorably.

Ah, then, so the sleight of hand would be practiced on me now, and they had saved the poison for the last, to heighten the game for themselves! The bowl was on high. I reached to it and made my choice.

"Jesu guard me," I said. "The Lord bring mercy upon me. The angels defend me."

And took the third fruit into my mouth.

This time did I have the pure certainty that I had come to my final moment, and would soon be gathered to my last repose, and walk in Heaven with my father and my dead brothers. And I knew no tremor of fear, but only the greatest assurance that the Savior is the Resurrection and the Life, and that my Redeemer liveth, and that although now I did walk in the valley of the shadow of death, I need fear no evil, for He was with me, and His rod and His staff did comfort me. I consumed the fruit and spat forth the kernel, and looked toward Kinguri, my dark brother that was now become mine enemy, and saw the fire of his eyes, and the sternness of his gaze that did run like a cable taut between his soul and mine. And a moment passed, and I did not fall, and I did not choke and swell, and I did not perish; and there was a snapping of that cable between Kinguri and me, for he sat slumping backward in the greatest of disappointment and the deepest of dejection, snarling a little to see that I lived. From Calandola came a thundering laugh, and the Imbe-Jaqqa did stand and clap his hands, and cry out, "It is done, Andubatil! Thy *mokisso* is with thee, and proclaims thy innocence!" And taking the bowl of palm-fruit from his witch, he hurled the remainder into the bushes, and reached out his arm toward me in jubilance of fellowship.

TWELVE

THUS WAS I returned back into the good graces of the Imbe-Jaqqa, and lay no longer at risk of my life. I was set free, and carried up beside Imbe Calandola to share his wine, and all men of the Jaqqa nation hailed me once again as one of their lords. All save Kinguri, who drew apart, sulking, as had Achilles in his tent; for Kinguri's former love for me now was turned entirely to enmity, and he could not bear that I was a favorite of his brother.

There was still the matter of Dona Teresa to be played out: for she was under mortal sentence, and that could not be appealed. Nor did I have enough credit with Calandola to win her free, since that she had committed indisputable treachery, and would have worked the ruin of his scheme of war, had her slave managed to bring the warning to the Portugals. So she would perish, without further trial, but not until the *nganga*-men said that it was an auspicious moment for the execution.

Calandola's plan of marching upon São Paulo de Loanda had been entirely put into abeyance and suspension by these recent events, and now was further suspended, for the moon had passed into an improper phase. No heavy action now might be taken until the sorcerers gave their consent. The moon does have great import to these Jaqqas, who think it has forcible operation in the body of man, and is the planet most prejudicial to his health, and to be shunned. On nights when the moon is fullest they do utter special prayers to their *mokissos*, and postpone any major deeds. Indeed, Kinguri once did tell me that he had forgotten his prayer of a certain time, and the moon shining upon his shoulder left him with such an extraordinary pain, and furious burning in it, that he was like to run mad, but in the end, with force of medicines and cures, after long torment was he eased. The slaying of Dona Teresa required a grand feast, and the feast could not just then be held owing to the moon, and the war could not begin until the feast, and therefore all stood still, held unmoving upon the brink.

God's blood, but I would not have her slain!

She was huge in my mind, and for all that she had done against me, I could not forget how she had cared for me in that ancient illness of mine, and our early love, and the closeness we once had had; nor was I unmindful of her beauty and the fire that it kindled in me; and I think that even though I had hurled her carven image into the river, yet even now it still held a power over me, reaching forth across many leagues to impinge upon my soul. How could I let her perish? I had vowed to protect her; that vow still bound me; and if I stood idly by and let her die the death, I should be no man. Yet she was doomed, and she was well guarded, and it would be worth both our lives for me to make any sort of rash attempt at freeing her. Nor could I win her pardon from the Imbe-Jaqqu. So I did brood a day and a second day, without reaching a resolution, and time was running short for Dona Teresa. Soon I should have to act, or know that I had failed her. He that is in the dance must needs dance on, though he do but hop.

At this time Golambolo did come to me, who had command of the scouts that occupied the outlying districts. He made his obeisance and said, "News, O Andubatil, of the Portuguese army!"

"And what is that, Golambolo?"

"That it has left Ndala Chosa, and begun to move through the countryside."

"In which direction?" said I, much excited.

"They seem not to know themselves. First they go toward the great waterfall, and then they turn westward again, and south as if they would march upon Langere. I think they have no plan except to move across the land and hope to encounter enemies."

"Ah. We must keep close watch on them." I closed mine eyes, and summoned up the image of the region, and the place of each town alongside the River Kwanza, and of our own position well south of it. And said to Golambolo, "Send forth double the number of scouts, and check their movements every hour. And when there is a change in their march, send your men running in relays, that is, one runner bearing the news to another who is fresh, and him to the next along the route, so that the tale comes to me swift as the wind. I must know at once."

He saluted and hastened to obey. And in the next day and the next the reports that he brought me were frequent, that the Portugals were moving swiftly though still without evident purpose, a large force of them marching in the territory that formed a triangle on the points of Ndala Chosa, Langere, and Agokayongo. There was no indication from this that they were aware of the force we had gathered at Agokayongo, nor had Golambolo's men seen sign that the Portugals were scouting in this direction. Yet something was brewing, for now they were only a day's march from us, or perhaps just a little more than that. Again I doubled the number of scouts under Golambolo's command, so that we might have exact knowledge.

Calandola at this time was preoccupied by meeting with Kafuche Kambara, at a midway point outside Agokayongo between his army and that of the other lord. I was not privy to these meetings, nor were any of the other Jaqqa generals: it was just the two high masters, coming together to discuss their tactic for sacking São Paulo de Loanda. But I think there was some dispute of policy between them, and rising tempers that grew hotter with the continuing negotiation; for rumor did journey in the Jaqqa camp that the other force was going to sever its alliance with us, or even to renew an onslaught against us, and that Imbe Calandola was hard pressed to hold Kafuche to his treaty. Certainly the Imbe-Jaqqa was morose and distant when he returned to us, and closeted himself with some several of his wives, and we saw nothing of him.

Thus I did not report to him the movements of the Portuguese force. I took it purely as my province of authority, to keep watch over that force by means of Golambolo's men, and to reserve all decision concerning it until its movements were clear. It was but a few hundred men, and we were many thousands: if they blundered within our neighborhood, we would easily be able to overwhelm them.

Then—the moon being still inauspicious—Calandola suddenly did summon me and declare, "Load your musket, Andubatil, for we will go to the wars tomorrow."

"Lord Calandola, is this not hasty?"

He swung about on me like an enfuried coccodrillo, and gaped and bared his teeth. "What, do you tell me my own mind?"

"We have relaxed our fine edge of readiness," I replied. "Surely we cannot regain it so swiftly!"

"We must," said he. "I feel necessity rolling down upon us. If we make not the war against São Paulo de Loanda this day next, we will lose our moment entirely. Tonight we feast; tomorrow we break camp. I am making the order generally known."

"The moon—"

"The moon will turn in our favor," said he.

I dared not dispute with him further.

This was the time to tell him that a Portuguese army was not far away, and that we must enter it into our planning. But something held me from giving forth that news at just that instant, and in the next he drove it utterly from my mind by saying most offhandedly, "And also, we will deal with the Portugal woman tonight. I give you leave to pay your farewell to her, if you so desire."

That struck me most heavily, for in recent days it had seemed to me that under the press of circumstance Calandola had forgotten Dona Teresa entirely, or else was no longer set on having her life. The force of his words must have had its conspicuous effect in my features, for he noted my look and said more gently, "She must die, Andubatil. There is no other way about it. Have you not resolved yourself to it?"

"That woman is most dear to me."

"Aye, but she is a traitor, self-confessed. I cannot let her live, or it would be the end of all government among my nation. Kinguri cries for her blood."

"And who is lord here, Kinguri or Calandola?"

"Calandola is lord!" he howled. "Calandola will have her slain! And take care, Andubatil, lest he take your life, too, for insolence if not for treason!"

"I meant no offense, my lord. You see how strong I regret her slaying, that I would speak that way?"

"She must die," said he more calmly, though I knew I had wounded him deep and would not be soon forgiven. "Speak no folly, Andubatil. Go to her, bid her be resigned, comfort her, take what comfort you can yourself; for it is sealed."

"There is no sparing her?"

"None."

"I will go to her, then," I said.

And as we parted he called after me, "Andubatil? Attempt no desperate treason, when you are with her. I pray you, do not do any foolish thing. It would grieve me to see you slaughtered beside her at the festival."

"I shall not be rash, O Imbe-Jaqqa," I did reply, though he had read my heart.

I went at once to the place where Dona Teresa was kept; and her guards, knowing that it was Calandola's will, admitted me freely to her cage. Thus was it that our first meeting was reversed, she now being the prisoner and I the visitor, whereas in the presidio of São Paulo de Loanda upon my coming to this land it had been the other way.

Her captivity had gone severely with her. They had not starved her, for I saw food and drink within her cage; but she must have eaten little of it, and she was most haggard and diminished, as though the flame within her did burn low. Her garments, that had been in rents and tatters before, now were loose and soiled and she made no show of fastening them, so that her breasts and belly were all but bare, and her skin seemed slack to me, her bearing feeble, her nobility and beauty in retreat. When I entered I found her bent over, crouched over some small thing of twigs and straw, and muttering words to it, and she looked up, alarmed, and hid it behind her back.

"What is that, Teresa?" I asked.

"It is nothing, Andres."

"Show it me."

"It is nothing."

"Show it."

She shook her head; and when I reached for it, she hissed like an angry cat, and backed away from me to the corner of the cage.

"It is some idol, is it not?" I asked. "Some *mokisso*-thing that you have fashioned, and that you are praying to?"

"It does not concern you," said she.

"This is no time for idols and witchcraft. This is a time for true prayer, Teresa."

She looked toward me with dull and somber eyes and said, "They are to slay me tonight, Andres, are they not?"

"So the Imbe-Jaqqa declares."

"And will they eat me afterward?"

"Speak not of such things, Teresa, I pray you."

"They will eat me. It was as my mother died. I will go into their pot, and they will carve me, and this one will eat my breasts, and this one my thighs, and—well, and what does it matter, when I am dead?" She stared me cold in the eyes and said, "And will you eat your share of my flesh?"

"It is a sickening thing you have said."

"Andres—O! I would not die, Andres, not so soon! Is it to be tonight?"

Softly I said, "That is their intent."

"And will you not save me? Is there no way? You are brother to these Jaqqa lords: go to them, plead for me, ask a pardon, tell them they can banish me instead, that I will go to the Kongo, to Benguela, to any place they choose, an' only they let me live, Andres!"

"I have pleaded for you strongly. It has not availed."

"But you have power with them!"

"I count myself lucky not to have been drawn down into your guilt, as Kinguri would have had it befall me. For I did stake my honor you would not do a treason. They would be within their rights to punish me for your deed."

"What could I do, then? Allow the city to be sacked, and send no warning?"

"It was folly. They were on their guard against some such thing from you."

"Well, and what does it matter now? I am to die," she said, wholly dejected and defeated. "You cannot save me? You will not?"

"I cannot. Though I have tried, and will try again, at the very last. I will speak again with the Jaqqa king, when he has had some wine, when he is easy among his women, and perhaps then at last he will give you pardon."

"You do not sound hopeful of it."

"I will attempt to save you. I can give you no promise I will succeed. I will attempt: I will ask again, Teresa."

She said, "Let them not eat me, at least."

"If I cannot have your life spared, I will beg the Imbe-Jaqqa to allow you a Christian burial, if it come to that. But I hope it will not come to that."

"O Andres, I am not ready for this! I loved my life. I was a great woman in Angola, do you know? I was like a queen in that city. Look at me now! I am ten years older in a single week. My beauty is destroyed. I am afraid, Andres. I was never afraid of anything, and now I am a column of fear, and naught but fear, the whole length of my body. Will I go to Hell, Andres?"

"You should not fear it, if you die a Christian."

"I have sinned. I have done sins of the flesh—"

"They were acts of love, which are not sins."

"And other sins, of pride, of avarice, I have been treacherous to you whom I loved, Andres, I have told lies of great evil nature to work harm on you—I did love you, is that known to you?"

"Aye, Teresa. And I had love for you. Mingled with a certain fear, I think, for you were so strong, so frightening in your strength."

"My strength is all gone from me now. I will beshit myself with fright when I walk out to be slain."

"I think not. I think if it must come to that, you will do it well. Like a queen."

"Like an English Queen? What did your King Harry's Queens say and do, when they came forth to lose their heads?"

"Why, I was not born then," said I, "but the tale is that they were most courageous, and faced their doom without the least quiver. As also did Mary the Scottish Queen, that was done to death just in the years before I left England. And you will be bold and strong like all of them, for you are queenly too. If it must come to pass that way."

"Hold me, Andres."

I took her into my arms. She was trembling, and folded herself against me like a frightened child.

In a voice I scarce could hear, she said, "When first I saw you in São Paulo de Loanda so long ago, I said within myself, He is beautiful, he shines like the sun, I want him. You were a pretty plaything. And then I came to you in the fortress, and I nursed you when you were sick and gone from your rightful mind, and as you slept I looked upon you and loved you. And when you healed, and I bathed you with the sponge, and your manhood rose, I wanted you as I have wanted no other man, and so we became lovers, and would have been lovers all the years since, but for circumstance. I dreamed of you. When I was in bed with Don Fernão I pretended he was you. When you got yourself that blackamoor wench as your slave and concubine, I thought of killing her—or you—or myself, so strong was my love. Well, and so I felt, and I could not help myself for it. And did you love me, Andres?"

"That I did, most deeply, Teresa. For I think you have been the great love of my life."

With a little laugh she said, "And the wonderful Anne Katherine of whom you spoke so much?"

"Long ago. A ghost that flits in my mind. I knew her only a little, when I was a boy. You have been at the center of my heart these fourteen years."

"Andres—"

"Aye, Teresa. It is true."

"I am afraid of dying now."

"We will pray together."

"I am afraid of praying, also," said she, with a glance behind her, where she had dropped her little magic-thing of straw and twigs. "I have fallen away from the true God, Andres."

"He welcomes always the strayed sheep," I said. I reached past her and took the little pagan thing in my hand, and said, "You must not damn yourself, so near the end. Put this witchcraft aside from you, and spurn it, and give yourself over to the loving Son of God."

"Will you pray with me, now?"

"That I will."

She shredded her idol, and strewed its fragments on the ground.

"Pray in English. Pray what prayers you would pray for your English wife," she said.

"If I remember the words, I will do that," said I.

And the words were slow to come, but come at last they did, and I knelt beside her and I did say, "The Lord is my light, and my salvation; whom then shall I fear: the Lord is the strength of my life; of whom then shall I be afraid?" And I said the words then in Portuguese also, and she said them with me. And also I said, "I will lift up mine eyes unto the hills: from whence cometh my help. My help cometh even from the Lord: who hath made heaven and earth." And she said this after me. And I said, "Lighten our darkness, we beseech thee, O Lord; and by thy great mercy defend us from all perils and dangers of this night." Which she the like did say.

Then Dona Teresa on her knees alongside me did begin to speak to me as though I were her confessor, and to tell me her sins, which I had no right to hear, I being no priest and scarce even of the same faith as she. But I listened, since that she had a need of telling, and I would not ask of her that she go unshriven to her death, if this night were indeed to be her last. And the sins that she told me were some of them trifles, and some of them not such trifles, and some that gave me great amaze. But though I have spoken in such fullness of all that befell me in Africa, I will not speak of Dona Teresa's sins here, since they were hers alone, and if I was her confessor then I must respect the sanctity of the confessional, and let God be the only witness to my knowledge of her heart. So I heard her out, and when she was done she spoke the Credo to me, "I believe in God the Father Almighty, Maker of Heaven and Earth," saying it in Latin while I spoke in English with her, and at the last I did say to her, this one last thing, "Good Lord, deliver us, in all time of our tribulation; in all time of our wealth; in the hour of death, and in the day of judgment, Good Lord, deliver us," which she did pray most fervently.

Then we rose and we embraced, and through my mind there rolled as though upon an endless scroll all the images of my life with this woman, from first unto last, our great carnality and high joyous lusts, our sorrows and disturbances, our partings and our reunions, and I felt tears within the threshold of mine eyes, and I withheld them lest I induce grief in her. But at last I could withhold them no more, and we wept together. And I kissed her tenderly and she said, "Go now. I am ready for what must come, Andres."

"We will have faith, and you shall be spared."

"I do not think so, Andres."

"We do not abandon hope, lady, until hope is rendered hopeless."

As I turned to go, she reached for my hand, and pressed something into it, and folded my fingers over it, as once she had done long ago with that carven love-idol of hers. I opened my hand and saw that she had given me a little golden crucifix, that often I had seen between her breasts.

"Take it," she said. "To remember me."

"You should keep this upon you."

"I will have no need of it soon. Take it, Andres."

I could not tell her that to me this piece of gold was as much an idol as that other one; indeed, at that moment, strange to tell, I did not entirely feel that way, but recognized in it a kind of power, which I suppose meant that Africa had seeped into my soul a little, and had made of me not a Papist but an idol-worshipper to some degree. But I think mainly it was because it came from Dona Teresa that I felt the power in it. So I took it and placed it safe about me, and thanked her.

And I went from her, and the cage was closed behind me, and I walked me a long while around the Jaqqa camp, listening to the strange and barbarous sounds of it, the chanting and the singing and the playing of instruments, and the sharpening of knives, and when I came to the place of the kettles a fire was already lit, and the water was aboil. And at the sight of that, a vast rage rose in me, so that I pondered seizing Calandola and holding him as hostage for Teresa's life, and breaking forth from this camp with her beside me and the Imbe-Jaqqa at my sword's point; but I knew that to be folly.

Yet was I beginning to draw away from my immersement in the Jaqqa way, and commence my voyage back toward civilization. For I did boggle at this purposing of theirs to slay Dona Teresa, and all the rest of their intent did now begin to take on the taint of blood, and I pulled myself back from it, and stood hesitating, drifting between the side of God and the side of Satan. For I did see that God is the spirit that cries *Yea*, and Satan is he that cries *Nay*, and I in my African captivity had become as great a crier of *Nay* as the Fiend himself, willing to tear down anything to ease mine own pain. For a time I had been mad, I think, or adream. And in that time had I given myself unto Calandola, for whom the act of destruction was the act of creation: I had for a time seen the poetry within that strange pairing of ideas. But no longer. And now I wandered, desperate, lost, between one world and another.

In that moment Golambolo came to me, running, breathing hard, as though he had run a great distance. He lurched to me on his long legs and gasped before he could speak, and finally the words tumbled from him.

"The Portugals! They are advancing, O Andubatil! They are coming toward us!"

"Is it an attack, then?"

He shook his head. "I think not. I think it is but by chance that they move in our direction. But when morning comes they will surely stumble upon our outlying forces."

"How far are they now from us?"

"An hour's march, perhaps, or two or three. They have camped for the night."

"Ah. And where are they?"

"In the direction of Langere, between the two gray hills."

"The Imbe-Jaqqa must be told," said I. "I will go to him at once." Then did I take Golambolo by the wrist and look him close in the eye and say, "Speak nothing to anyone else of what your scouts have told you, not to Kinguri, not to Ntotela, not to anyone, until I have been to the Imbe-Jaqqa: for I would not have the news going running wild through our camp, until the high council has met to resolve on a plan."

"I understand. I will obey, O Andubatil."

"You do well, Golambolo," I told him, and sent him on his way.

Now all fate was in my hands; and I stood poised on the knife's-edge, between this way and that; and I did make my choice.

To Kulachinga my Jaqqa wife did I go, she who was so sturdy and reliable, and strong of leg and wind.

"I have urgent need of you," I said. "Go now, run eastward, toward Langere way, to a place of two gray hills, that we have seen in recent days. There will be an army there. Take this, and give it to the high commander." I put into her hand the golden crucifix that Dona Teresa had bestowed upon me. "And tell him these words, that you must repeat to me until you have them by heart." And I told her the Portuguese words that meant, *"Come at once, strike tonight!"* These she said after me, and on the fifth time she had them perfect, though she had no idea of their meaning. "Show them by signs where our camp is located, and lead them to us: for it is the Imbe-Jaqqa's plan to deceive them, and fall upon them when they least do expect it. Go now!"

"I will go," said she, and turned from me, and sank herself into the forest like a stone into the depths of the sea, and was lost to my sight.

So it was done. I had made me my choice.

And night descended; and the Jaqqas did gather for their grand festival of death.

THIRTEEN

THE PRINCES of the man-eater nation bedecked themselves in their finest finery, their paints and beads and ornaments of bone; and I who was a Jaqqa prince did do the same, it being incumbent upon me to play my part. So certain servants to my naked body applied white circles of paint, and stripes of red and blue, and on my face where certain tribal scars had been incised I did color myself with the special Jaqqa powders, and I wrapped palm-cloth over my loins and put on my jingling necklaces of honor, and donned my sword on the one hip and my dagger on the other. All this while Kulachinga was running through the darkness, with Dona Teresa's little golden crucifix clutched in her hand and the words, *"Come at once, strike tonight!"* going over and over in her mind. And would they come? And would they come in time? And what price would I pay for my treason, when they came? Those questions I could not answer. In my grand insignia of office, then, I went me down to the festival to sit beside Imbe Calandola and my brother Kinguri.

When it was full dark they brought forth Dona Teresa.

Her rags were stripped away and they had bathed her body and painted it somewhat, too, and given her nothing more than a ringlet of some animal's teeth about her loins to wear, that hid nothing, so that she came forth as I once had come to a place of execution with all her privities laid bare, the high round breasts and the dark curling mat of lower hair put on exhibit.

Yet was she tall and proud and queenly as she strode, for all her nakedness, this Christian woman whose most secret places were displayed to ten thousand savages. I think I might rather have seen her feeble and frightened; for the sight of her so regal awoke on me sharp memories of the woman of São Paulo de Loanda that I had loved, that soon would be lost to me forever unless some miracle came, and time was growing monstrous late for miracles. And I did feel a powerful sense of onrushing disaster impending over this place, and not for Dona Teresa alone. And I bethought me of those words of Master Marlowe's play of Faustus, when the clock is striking eleven, and Mephistophilis approaches to claim the soul of the damned man:

> *Stand still, you ever-moving spheres of heaven,*
> *That time may cease, and midnight never come;*

> *Fair Nature's eye, rise, rise again, and make*
> *Perpetual day; or let this hour be but*
> *A year, a month, a week, a natural day....*

Now the musicians did play, now the *nganga*-men did dance and shout and invoke their *mokisso* the Devil. And the slaves of the Jaqqas brought forth great leathern sacks of palm-wine, enough of the stuff, God wot, to set afloat the entire Spanish Armada, and they passed among the Jaqqas, filling their cups again and yet again. And all this while did Dona Teresa stand naked in the midst of this barbarous multitude, awaiting her death most calmly with her hands together behind her back.

Let it be a lengthy ceremony, I prayed. Let them dance and prance for hours and hours, so that the rescuers, if they are to come, will have time to come. I put great faith in that rescue. I was confident of God's own providence that would spare Dona Teresa from her death.

But yet—what was that speech of Faustus?

> *The stars move still, time runs, the clock will strike,*
> *The Devil will come, and Faustus must be damn'd.*

They will not understand Kulachinga's message, I thought; or they will not believe it, thinking it to be a deceit; or they will ignore it. Why did I not go myself? Why did I not send to the Portugals earlier? I belabored myself with a thousand such *whys*, every one of them futile.

My brooding was broken by the touch of the Jaqqa Kasanje against my arm, and he said, "Calandola would speak with you, O Andubatil."

Terror! O mountains and hills, come, come and fall on me, and hide me from him! For I was sure he knew of my betrayal: that Kulachinga was taken, that she had confessed all, that I would be reproached for my treason and sent down below to die beside the Portugal woman.

I did make my face firm and unrevealing, and went me down the high table to the Imbe-Jaqqa. Who greeted me in somber fashion, most stark and grim; and when his eyes met mine it was needful that I call into play all my strength of will, so that I did not go down to kneel before him and babble forth my contrition.

To me he said, "When this festivity is at an end, Andubatil, I must speak most urgently with you."

Ah, then, he knew my treachery!

But no: it was another matter entirely. For he said, as I so stonily faced him, "I have learned much that is important to me, this day. The conspiracy against me that I feared, and of which I have spoken to you: it is real, it is ripe. Its leader is known to me. He is planning shortly to strike. But I will strike first, Andubatil, and you will be at my side in the slaying of my foes."

Then he knew nothing at all of my betrayal, for which I felt vast relief.

"Ah, then, who is the enemy?" said I.

"Afterward will we talk, in private." He clasped my hand between his great paws. "You alone can I trust. You alone are my brother."

Which filled me with shame, that he should have such love for me and I having done such treason against him. And also it made clear to me who the enemy must be, from Calandola's words, *"You alone are my brother."* So this night would be a night of many reckonings.

But one above them all was primary. Thinking that out of need of me, or out of love, he might yet grant me that one great boon, I said in a low voice to him, "May I ask you now one more time, O Imbe-Jaqqa, to relent toward the Portugal woman, and—"

"Nay!" he roared, like an angered lion.

"I beg—"

"Nay," he said again, more quietly, shaking his great head to and fro. "It may not be, Andubatil. I ask you, plague me not on this score. She is doomed. Nothing can save her. Nothing! She has done treason against us; she must die, or my power will be wholly without credit here."

"Ah."

"Forget her. She is lost to you. Go, now: to your place. But afterward, come to me, and keep ready your sword, for tonight I think you will need it."

There was no hope. He was fixed upon her death.

And what now, how did I halt time? Of Portugals there was no sign. There was no one to whom I could turn but Calandola, and he had refused me, and short of some madman's deed that beyond doubt would cost me mine own life, I could do naught but stand and watch, and pray, and wait. *Ugly hell, gape not! Come not, Lucifer!* Yet could I not turn back the striking of the final hour, which was all but upon us now.

The wine-bibbing had reached a high moment, and the Jaqqas did mill about, spilling the stuff down their chests and bellies in their wild surfeit. Imbe Calandola arose, and gave his signal, and the giant black headsman of the tribe stepped forward with his titanic blade, and the drums went still and the fifes ceased an instant, long enough for me to hear Dona Teresa say most sorrowfully, *"Sancta Maria ora pro nobis,"* and some other like phrases.

Now, Portugals! Now erupt, and fall upon this heathen band!

But they did not come. And, I came to see, they would not come, and the clock could not be halted, and the last moment was at hand. And I was helpless.

I looked toward Dona Teresa and had my final sight of her bare supple body, still so beautiful and full of life, and I thought me of Anne Boleyn the Queen's mother, and of Katherine Howard, and of many another whose death had early been inflicted in this fashion, for truly this is a vale of tears: and there was a sudden frightened cry, *"Andres!"* and she bent forward.

And the huge Jaqqa did strike from her her head. I did avert mine eyes for the pain of it in my soul, but I heard the terrible sound of it; I cannot ever forget that sound. And when I looked again I would have rejected the awful evidence of my vision, but I could not.

So it was done, the which I was witness to, and yet even after I saw it carried out I did not fully believe it, so sharp was my memory of her in my arms, so warm was the impress of her upon my soul. I could not associate the sundered thing lying bloody in the clearing with the slender girl who had come to me in my prison, or with the noble woman who had gone striding so queenly through the avenues of São Paulo de Loanda, or with the companion of my arms of only a few days past. It was done.

"Give me wine!" I cried, and pulled a cup toward me, and gulped it down to ease my pain.

"So it will be," said Calandola, "with all the Portugals of that city. You will see it, Andubatil: we will take them prisoner while they slumber, and we will cut from them their heads, and we will swallow them back into us and they will be gone from the land. You alone will wear the white skin on these shores, Andubatil. We will have no others here."

And he did call for wine, and pound his cup until he had it. And when he had it he poured for me, and then for him, and for Kinguri; and I saw Kinguri smiling with special joy for the pain he had brought upon me by the death of my beloved.

"We will wrestle, you and I," said Kinguri, "after we have eaten. Eh? Will you face me in the match, Andubatil?"

"With the Imbe-Jaqqa's leave, that I will," said I.

He turned to Calandola. "What do you say, brother? Am I to wrestle the Christian tonight!"

Calandola stared at him a long while, and finally he said, "Yea, you will wrestle with him, Kinguri. So be it, you and Andubatil."

Kinguri's eyes gleamed. "I have waited long for this, Andubatil."

"As have I, brother," I said to him.

"Ah," said he. "You will call me brother no longer, after tonight!"

I shrugged and turned away. My soul was still stunned by the death of Teresa, and I wanted no bickering with Kinguri to intrude on my grief, not now: there would be time later to wrestle him, and, if God gave me the strength, to break him in pieces, and pull his long limbs from his trunk, and cast him like offal into the bone-pit. But that would be later.

Because that there was a cold place now beneath my breastbone like a lump of ancient ice, I drank heavily to warm it, a stoup of wine perhaps and then another, a bucket of it, a hogshead, a barrel. Yet it barely moved me and did not stir my soul; the coldness within burned it all away.

Some Jaqqa servants meanwhile gathered up Dona Teresa's body and took it to the kettle, and her head they did remove from the scene, to give it interment and prevent the *mokisso* of her from molesting their souls, I suppose, or to keep her *zumbi* from haunting their sleep. To all this I paid little heed. For I was sunk deep in gloom of her death, that cut me so deep. And I thought me of her ambitions to greatness, her dreams of glory and lust for high place, and all those other aspects of her, reduced to nothing now, for that she was mere dead meat, and that gave me great sadness, at the injustice of her death and the injustice indeed of all death.

Yet as the wine entered at last upon me and lulled my sorrow, I came to be more accepting. Truly what did it matter that Dona Teresa had died now instead of then, since that it was foreordained that one day she must die? I remembered me the words of one of the wisest men that ever was, the Emperor Marcus Aurelius, whose book of meditations I had pored over as a boy, and his words now floated through my soul, that were, "Do not act as if thou would live ten thousand years. Death hangs over thee."

Aye! And where today is Marcus? And where are all those who stood beside Henry Tudor at Bosworth Field an hundred year ago, so proud as they were then at the winning of the commonwealth from King Richard Crookback! So why feel torment for the death of a woman now, or fear indeed for mine own death to come, when our lives are like unto that of a butterfly? Everything is only for a day.

These thoughts did ease me some, and also the wine. But I did sit morosely while those about me were in wild frenzy. There were Jaqqas making festivity as far as my gaze could encompass, all of them heavy gone in drink, and rolling about with their women, and coupling on the warm bare earth. Slaves went among them, bringing slabs of meat from the slaughtered cattle, and all manner of fruits, and other dainties.

And then came the monstrous moment when the banquet was at its fullest and the flesh of Dona Teresa was deemed to be ready, and they did bring this most awful food to the high bench for the delectation of the Jaqqa lords.

Kinguri rose, and smiled a cold savage smile upon me, and addressed his royal brother, saying loudly, "O Imbe-Jaqqa, since that this woman was Andubatil's wife, it is fitting that you surrender unto him the choice of all the meat of her, though it be your right to take the first selection."

Calandola did at that look startled, for he had not expected it, and I suppose was not sure whether Kinguri meant some mischief toward him from it. But then he considered, and I think it did seem proper to him. Turning to me he declared, "Aye, that is the fitting thing. I grant you the Imbe-Jaqqa's portion, O Andubatil!"

I gaped at him in amaze. "You would not have me do that, my lord!"

"It is honor most great."

"Nay," I said, deep in my throat. "I will not eat of it!"

But this enraged the Imbe-Jaqqa, for he was not accustomed to refusal, nor was he practiced at being told by Kinguri how he should comport himself, and all this had put him in a whirl. His eyes grew furious and veins stood out upon the great thickness of his neck, and he cried, "Take her and make her into you."

"I beg you, Lord Imbe-Jaqqa—"

"I command you, Andubatil!"

To which Kinguri said, "Would you dispute the command of the Imbe-Jaqqa?"

"Give over, brother," I answered him. "I want no part of this festivity."

"Ah, we should have slain you at the first," said he. "Instead of cherishing you, and nurturing you, and feigning that you were of our own kind. A white Jaqqa! What madness! You are the cause and root of all our woe! Take and eat!"

And Kinguri did seize and shove into my face the broad green leaf of a jungle tree, wide as a platter, upon which lay steaming a cut of meat, a section that—nay, I will not write it, my mind rebels, even now my gorge rises—

But this dreadful meat the Imbe-Jaqqa's brother did most insistently offer to me, exclaiming all the while in stentorian voice that high acclaim was being done to me by this, and urging me to have it for the good of mine own spirit. I was steadfast in my refusal, and he in his insistence, and he pressed the steaming meat upon me, and I did force it back. Both of us were shouting most furiously. I did not fear Kinguri's wrath. I did not at that moment fear even death: but I would not die with the shame of this bestial meal upon my soul.

Calandola, too, was in outrage that I had refused the meat.

"You will not say nay!" he cried. "Eat! Take, eat!"

And he held me and shook me, and I fought back at him, which made me indeed feel like a butterfly in his mighty grip; but the wine and my grief and rage did arm me, and with a strength I did not expect I pushed myself back from him a bit. Yet did he seize me again.

"Eat! Eat!"

And from behind him came Kinguri, cackling with delight at the strife he had let loose, crying, "Eat, Andubatil! Eat!"

Calandola's strength was diabolical and could not be resisted. He held me and forced me backward, and that loathly fillet of once-beloved flesh he did most terribly bring into approach of my mouth, though I resolved I would not open for it, no matter how frightsome the torment he applied. His face hovered an inch from mine; his sweat fell upon my skin and scalded me; his eyes were great beacons that burned into my skull; truly he was the incarnation of the Dark One, truly the authentic Diabolus, and in that nightmare noise of shouting and battling and musicking my spirit began to reach the limit of its tether, all but overcome by the dread force of this cannibal chieftain.

I know not what would have happened then, save the Imbe-Jaqqa would have had the flesh of Teresa into me to satisfy his crazed need to overmaster me; but at the moment of it, as the meat neared my lips, Calandola did utter a sudden great cry of surprise and pain, and released me. I beheld Kinguri standing behind him with a war-hatchet raised, having struck at his brother and cut him deeply.

So the insurrection had begun, and the enemy had had his first blow. I saw that all this was a ruse on Kinguri's part, a diversion, this business of the meat, to enrage Calandola and cause him to put aside his prudence so that he could be slain. Now blood poured down the Imbe-Jaqqa's back and he looked dazed and stunned by his wound, and Kinguri was making ready to strike a second and fatal time.

At the sight of this, the Jaqqas below and around us began to shout also, and caper, and strike one another; the dissension at the high table seemed to act very like a kindling, that struck into the dry tinder of the camp, they being so far gone, all of them, in wine, and so wrought-up from the long delay before marching into battle. And the striking of Calandola by Kinguri was, I perceived, the signal for a general affray, a war between two Jaqqa factions, one faithful to the monarch and one loyal to his brother.

The Imbe-Jaqqa's bodyguard, stupored somewhat by wine but not yet altogether incapable, rushed toward Kinguri and pulled him some dozen feet away before he could strike the second blow. All was engulfed now in madness. Thousands of drunken Jaqqas roared and thrashed about like ape-creatures, scarce human, more like hairy baboomas or wild pongos and engecos, smashing whatever lay in their way, tipping over the kettles of scalding water, hacking at trees and at cattle and at one another. I looked to escape, but no escape was possible, for that a turbulence of berserk men surged on all sides, a stew of flailing crazed humanity, and it was like the great maelstrom or whirlpool of the northern waters, that becomes so irresistible a vortex as to swallow everything, and there is no fleeing from it. So was I buffeted about, and swept here and there. There was killing everywhere; and I saw the bloody Calandola roaring and bellowing and fighting a dozen men at once.

Then in the general upheave I found myself nose to nose with Kinguri. Blood did flow along his scalp and forehead in torrents, and his eyes were a wild man's.

"You!" he cried. "The peril, the curse among us!"

"Let me past you, brother," said I.

He struck at me with the butt end of his hatchet, and laid bare my cheek almost to the bone, cutting athwart the older scars of my tribal ornamentation. I felt the streaming of my blood, but there was no pain, not then, not yet. He came to me with a second blow, but there was good frenzy upon me also, the kind that in battle does arm a man to surpass his own power. And as his hatchet descended did I catch his wrist and hold it high over me, so that neither of us could move.

We stood there maybe five hundred year, or maybe five thousand, frozen, wholly stilled, with all the drunkard Jaqqas circling about us and none daring to come near. Kinguri could not bring his great long arm down upon me to do injury, and I could not push that arm above me back to shake the weapon from it, so well matched were we, and so thoroughly equal in force. But if hatred alone had heat, I would have fried to a sizzle beneath his gaze.

To me he said, as we stood in that way, "You will die now, and you will join your Portugal witch in our banquet."

"Ah, nay brother, nay, not so! I will have my vengeance upon you for her death!"

And with a surging of strength, such as comes upon a man perhaps once or twice in his life when he is at his greatest need, I took his arm and drew it down, and twisted it so that it snapped: for we were wrestling at last, but it was not the graceful dance of the Jaqqa sport-wrestling, but rather a wrestle for life or death, and the contest was to me. I heard the bone yield in his arm; his lips drew back in a horrid scream; the hatchet fell, and I snatched it up, and made ready to have his life from him.

Then there came above us a great spreading darkness, like unto some vast bird that had opened his wings over us to blot out the glitter of the stars. I did not understand. But after a moment I perceived it was vast Calandola that loomed over both us twain as an avenging-demon.

"He is mine," said Calandola to me, and from my hand he plucked Kinguri's hatchet, the very hatchet that had wounded him, taking it as lightly as it were a straw; and Kinguri, hissing, crouched down to shield himself with his hands.

"Slave!" the Imbe-Jaqqa cried. "Go! Go from me! Go from the world!"

And with a fearsome blow of the hatchet he did maim his crouching brother, lopping off an arm, and then struck again, the blow the second time being dire and the blood of Kinguri leaping forth to spew us both.

"Nugga-Jaqqa!" Calandola exclaimed. "Shegga-Jaqqa!" And spat upon his brother's corpse, and trampled him into the reddened earth.

Then did he turn, and confront me once again, and a more hellish sight I hope never to see. His own blood and Kinguri's painted his body utterly, that also did shine with the grease of slaughtered men, and his eyes were lunatic eyes, for that he had seen his kingdom dissolving about him in this war of brothers that had sprung up so suddenly.

"Come, we must kill them all!" he cried.

"Kill them yourself," said I. "I want no part of your warfare."

"What say you?"

"I am no longer of your kingdom, Calandola!"

"Ah, and is that so?" Advancing upon me, he did say in thick half-strangled tones, "You will fight when I tell you to fight, Andubatil, and you will eat what I give you to eat, and you will obey me in all things. You are my creature, you are my toy!" And then he did cry out in a language I did not know, perhaps no language at all save the language of madness, or the language of Hell, some belching coarse mazy gib-berish, the language of coccodrillos, the language of dream-warlocks. And leaped high and brought down the hatchet, but I lurched aside, and went unharmed, and he leaped again, and swung, and came near to trimming my beard, and cried out in his coccodrillo-crazy jargon anew. I was sure I would die at his hand, so berserk was he, but I meant to make him work at it. Thus he pursued me about in the narrow space we had to move, chopping at me and cursing me and weeping and moaning, while blood poured over him, and all his followers did battle drunkenly amongst themselves. I longed for a pistol, that I could thrust it into his face and explode him to Hell; but of pistols I had none, and my musket was in my cottage, that would have been useless here anyway in such close quarters. A sword I did have, and was able finally to hoist it out, and for an instant we faced one another as equals. But only for an instant, since that as I lunged at him with my blade he struck downward upon it with his hatchet in such force that my arm was made numb, and I dropped the weapon, not knowing whether I still had an arm or not.

"Jesu receive me," I cried.

"*Inga negga bagga khagga!*" cried Calandola, or some such wild garboil.

And he readied himself to come upon me and make an end of me. But in that instant came a thunderclap and a burst of flame in our midst, and a second such uproar, and a third. In mid-stride the Imbe-Jaqqa halted, and looked about.

Cannon!

Aye, Christian weapons erupting from all sides! For we were surrounded, the army of Portugals having come at last, and setting themselves up in surround of this place while the maddened Jaqqas did blind themselves with wine. Too late for Dona Teresa, alas, but in time, in time for my salvation, the forces of the Masanganu garrison had appeared, and were making deadly war into the Jaqqa multitude.

Imbe Calandola did look at me most melancholy at this onslaught, much as Caesar must have looked upon Brutus: for I think he guessed that it had been I who brought this army onto him. "Ah, traitor, traitor," said he in a low sad voice, and reached out to grip my shoulder, and held it tight a long moment, as brother might hold brother in a dark time, so that I felt the full flow of his powerful soul rushing from him to me. And having done that, I thought he would slay me, but merely did he scowl, and he spat upon me and turned on his heel without one more word to me. Then did he cry for his lieutenants by name, "Kasanje! Kaimba! Bangala!" Fully sobered was he by this invasion of the Portugals. I think he would fain have had Kinguri by his side now, and Andubatil as well; but Kinguri was tatters in the dust, and Andubatil was Andubatil no longer, having repudiated altogether his Jaqqa allegiance and taken on once more the name of Andrew Battell of Leigh in Essex.

Calandola, like a thwarted Lucifer, went running off one way, and I went the other, thinking to tunnel down into darkness in the bush, to strip from myself the beads and bangles of the man-eater nation; better to be naked now than a Jaqqa. As he vanished I saw old Ntotela and Zimbo come toward me, both of them wounded and looking more than half dazed. They hailed me and cried out, "Andubatil! Imbe-Jaqqa Andubatil!"

"Ah, nay, I will not be your king," I said, for that was their purpose, to offer me the Jaqqa crown, I think, with all else fallen into turmoil.

"Imbe-Jaqqa!" said they again, sadly, in bewilderment, but I shook my head and ran past them.

Fires were blazing, clouds of dusty smoke were rising. From their fortifications around us the Portugals fired again and again, exploding a sunrise on the darkness, and the Jaqqas did stampede most wildly, all their brave courage peeled away by the confusion of their leadership and the surprise of the assault. They went this way and that, a headless mob. Some rushed into the adjoining camp of Kafuche Kambara, where I think they were slaughtered; some stood their ground, and made war against one another while the Portugals in regular formation sent them to Hell; some went into madness, and screamed and raged into the trees; and I know not what the others did, save that the camp of many thousands was dissipated, and reduced within an hour or two to nothing.

There came at last the dawn. I stood alone in a field of dreadful carnage. Black bodies lay everywhere, and a very few white ones in armor. The great kettles of the man-eaters were overturned; their banners were down; their shrines were all trampled. Mists drifted over the ground, and streams of blood ran like wine, and streams of wine alongside the blood, so that they mixed in hard mockery of the Imbe-Jaqqa's own favored tipple. Of Calandola I saw nothing. He had slipped away; he had surely not been slain. I do not believe he could have been slain, nor that he will ever die. He is too dark a force, too deep in league with Satan his master, whose incarnation I do think him to be. Search I did for that great body, and I did not discover it. It would have surprised me much had it been otherwise.

And at sunrise the Portugals found me. I was naked but for shreds; I was bloodied and injured; and I sobbed, not out of grief nor fear but of simple relief and ease, that this eternal night was over, and the demons were fled, and I still alive.

Three soldiers that were little more than boys came upon me and pointed their muskets at me, and I threw up my hands to show I meant no harm.

"What is this?" they asked. "Is it Jaqqa, or demon, or what?"

"English," said I in their own Portuguese tongue. "I am Andres the Piloto, of São Paulo de Loanda, captive among the Jaqqas these past years, and you have freed me."

"Go you to the governor," said one Portugal to another, who rushed off at once. And to me he said, looking wide-eyed upon me, "I have heard tales of you, but I thought that they were all but fable. What has befallen you, man? Are you hurt?"

I replied, "I have been in the Devil's own paw, and he has squeezed me some. But I am whole, I think, and will go on breathing some while longer. Jesu Cristo, it has been a dream, and not a cheerful one, but now I am awake. Now I am awake!"

And I did fall to my knees, and give thanks for my deliverance to Him who guardeth me.

Through the forest now came more Portugals, and at their head was the Angolan governor, João Coutinho, of whom Dona Teresa had spoken. This man looked at me long, without belief, as if I had a second head beside mine own, or wings and a tail. At last he said, "It was you, then, that summoned us."

"Aye. But I had given up all hope of your coming."

"We came as swift as we could. There were tales of a massing of the Jaqqas, so that we were poised for the attack, and needed only to know the place. What is your name, Englishman? Andres, is it?"

"Andrew, in good sooth. Andrew Battell."

He gave me his hand, and drew me to my feet, and ordered up a cloak to be thrown over me, and sent for his surgeon to examine my wounds. This João Coutinho was a man of perhaps four-and-thirty, very sleek and handsome of face, with a warm and kindly way about him; I saw by the mirrors of his soul that were his eyes, that he would use me well, and that he felt great compassion for me in my long travail, so that perhaps my betrayals were at their end.

He said, "And the Portugals who were prisoner with you?"

"Dead. All."

"Dona Teresa? Don Fernão?"

"Dead," said I. "Dead and eaten."

He looked away, choking with a deep revulsion.

"They are monsters," said he after a moment. "We will hunt them down, and they shall all perish. Did they torment you greatly?"

"Nay," I answered. "They treated me like one of themselves. I think it was for my golden hair, that made me seem as some kind of spirit to them."

"Golden hair?" said Don João Coutinho in wonder. "Is it golden, then?"

"Is it not?"

He put his hand to it, and ran his fingers gently through it, and said, "It is white, Senhor Andrew, it is most altogether and entirely white."

BOOK
FIVE:

Ulysses

ONE

So ENDED my sojourn among the Jaqqas. But there is much more to tell. For I was not yet done with Africa, not by a great long while, and much else went into the tempering and annealing of my soul before that land would let me free. Nor am I fully free yet. Nor have I escaped wholly from the malign sway of the Imbe-Jaqqa Calandola, to this hour.

Don João Coutinho would not have me walk with his army, but gave orders that I be carried by bearer as we left the place of the battle, and returned to Masanganu. There was no war now to be pursued, the Jaqqas having scattered in all directions, and that other army of Kafuche Kambara having decamped very swiftly and taken itself to its home territory some way south and east of this place. Which was just as well, since that the only advantage that this Portugal force had had was that of surprise, that now had been expended; for they were only some four hundred men, though they had in that night routed many thousands.

In Masanganu, that had been so hateful to me before but which now seemed like a veritable Jerusalem, did I quickly regain my strength. I was very well used by this new governor, who regarded me as some kind of holy sufferer, a pilgrim, even, that had undergone a great ordeal and must now be recompensed with the kindest of treatment. Thus as I lay at Masanganu he gave orders that I was to have the best of wine and drink; and his surgeons did what they could to close my wounds, and heal them without further mutilation of my skin. And the natural strength and resilience of my body did manifest itself, so that after some time I felt myself beginning to grow strong again, and recovering somewhat of my weariness. But all the same I knew I had been transformed, in a way from which there was no recovering. My body bore scars, both those of a tribal nature and those of warfare and rough usage. And now I had the visage of an old man, which was the outer mark of my experiences, the sign and symbol of the horrors I had witnessed and those that I had committed.

Dona Teresa visited me often in dreams those first nights, and said to me, "Weep not, Andres, I am with the saints in heaven." Which was but mocking comfort to me. My philosophical quietude over her death had fled me. I bethought me often of the sage Marcus Aurelius, but his teachings just now seemed of no worth: for she was dead that I had held most dear and lost and unexpectedly regained, and I would not regain her again no matter how close I explored this sultry jungled land. And that great loss did burn more hotly in me the more fully my weary body renewed its health.

Then I went to Don João Coutinho in his place at the presidio of Masanganu and he greeted me most warmly, with an embrace and good wine, and asked what service he could do me.

To which I replied, "Only one, that you put me aboard a pinnace bound for São Paulo de Loanda, and you give an order that I am to be set free, and shipped to England, since that I am old now, and would die among my own people."

"Why are you here at all?" he asked.

I told him everything of it, the great tangled tale of my setting to sea with Abraham Cocke and being taken in Brazil and made prisoner and then being a pilot and then imprisoned again, and so on and on and on down all the winding years of it, in which he was much interested. Only of the Jaqqa part of my life was I chary, telling him merely that I was kept by them.

When I was done he embraced me and said, "You shall have your freedom, Senhor Andrew. But no ship will be departing this land for some months."

"So that I am aboard the next one, I can wait a little time more," said I. "For in truth I am not fully ready to see England again."

"Ah, is that so?"

It was indeed, though I could not tell him why. Which was, forsooth, that there was still too much Jaqqa in me; that my mind and soul were corrupted by the dark rites of that jungle people, in which I had partaken; that I needed some time yet to cleanse myself of all that, and to have a full purge, before I could enter myself into the clean quiet life of England, from which I had been absent so long that I scarce felt I belonged there.

The governor gave me his pledge that I was to go home. And in good sooth it was a pledge I had heard often before, as you know. But I think this Coutinho was sincere. I might go home whenever I pleased, said he, and in the mean time, could I do a little service for him?

Ah, I thought, it is the old song sung anew; it is the wheel to which I am ever yoked. If I am not to be a pilot for them, I am to be a soldier of the army, or some like thing, I who want only to retreat from the fray and meditate upon my travail. But yet was I beholden to him for my rescue. So what was the little thing he desired of me? Why, that he was going to march down into Kisama province, and bring all the rebels to heel and make an end to the Jaqqas if he could find them, and destroy for all time the power of the chief Kafuche Kambara. And since I knew these peoples so well, and spoke their languages as though I had been born to them, would I join with them in that endeavor?

Well, and what could I say, but yes? I was beholden. So then I journeyed again to the wars. The governor made me a sergeant of a Portugal company, with an hundred men at my command. We marched into Muchima first, the place where first I had seen the bloody fury of the Jaqqas expended long ago, and at the presidio there we gathered further soldiers; from thence it was south-easterly to a place called Cava, and then to Malombe, that was the city of a great lord subject to Kafuche Kambara. Here we were four days, and many lords came and obeyed us, so that our armies were swelled mightily with our black auxiliaries.

From thence we marched upon Agokayongo, where lately I had experienced such terrible events. The chief of this town was a Christian, and we settled ourselves here for eight days, finding it a very pleasant place, and full of cattle and victuals. But here a further misfortune came upon me, for the bountiful Don João Coutinho fell ill of the fever that is so widespread at Masanganu, and that he had carried secret in his body from that place. He sickened quickly and did roam wildly in his mind for a few days, and then he died, which was a great loss to us all, and most especially to me.

To serve as governor now the army did choose its captain-major, whose name was Manoel Cerveira Pereira. I did not find him greatly to my liking. This Cerveira Pereira was small of stature and very hard-fleshed and dark, as some Portugals are, as though the sun has baked all mercy and charity from their bodies. He was of somber mien and very deeply religious, constantly fingering his beads and crucifixes and the like such holy apparatus. The Jesuits of Angola did hold him in the highest esteem, and he gave them much advantage in the colony, which earned him the enmity of many of the powerful men. To me he made outward show of courtesy, and confirmed me in the sergeancy that Don João Coutinho had bestowed upon me. But because he was so devout a Papist and I a mere Protestant heretic, Cerveira Pereira privately did not regard me as one to whom he needs must be faithful of his oath, and he did sadly play me false in many ways.

Yet this will I say for him, he was a most excellent warrior. As soon as he had seen the late governor given proper funeral, he addressed his army and made ready to march. We were eight hundred Portugals, or more, and I know not how many thousand blacks: a very great army indeed, and well armed. Eastward we did press. The Jaqqas were wholly dispersed, having melted into the land like the phantoms they be, but the army of Kafuche Kambara was not far beyond Agokayongo, with more than sixty thousand men, whom we did fall upon mightily. We had the victory, and made a great slaughter among them, and took captives all the women and children of Kafuche Kambara. This took place upon the tenth day of August, Anno 1603, and in the very place where Kafuche had slain so many Portugals years before, so that that terrible defeat was wholly avenged.

After we had been two months in the country about Agokayongo, we marched towards Kambambe, which was but three days' journey, and came right against the Serras da Prata, and passed the River Kwanza. At the great waterfall that was the holy place of the Jaqqas we did see signs that the man-eaters had been there of late: some remnants of their feasting, and certain painted marks on the rocks. But of the Jaqqas themselves we yet saw nothing, they being as elusive as ghosts. This was finely suitable to me, I having seen enough of those folk for one lifetime and being in little urgency to encounter them again. At night Imbe Calandola came to me in dreams very greatly often, floating through the seas of my mind like a malign monster of the depths, and laughing and stirring up turbulent maelstroms, and crying out, "Andubatil Jaqqa! Return unto me, Andubatil Jaqqa, and let us devour the world!" For which meal I had small appetite remaining.

Presently we overran the country at Kambambe, and built a fort hard by the riverside.

No chance presented itself to me for my return to the coast, nor to seek ship for England. Governor Cerveira Pereira, when I reminded him of the promise of Don João Coutinho to release me after a time, only shrugged and said, "I find nothing in his journals of such a promise, Don Andres."

Aye, and what could I say?

So I bided my time, a skill in which I had developed no trifling aptitude. I lived a private life apart from the Portugals now, friendly with them but not close, nor had they much wish to befriend me. I think they knew not what to make of me, and, God wot, I hardly knew what to make of me myself, for I was so changed by time and monstrous event. I had seen a quantity of gore and horror sufficient to leave its impress on me in the deepest ways. Often when I closed mine eyes I saw the headsman's blade falling upon Dona Teresa; or I imagined myself in Kulachinga's greasy embrace, her body slippery against mine own; or I sat between Calandola and Kinguri at some dread festival, and awoke with the savor of human meat in my nostrils and on my tongue. I had made a voyage that was passing strange, into the darkest of the realms of this world; and though I smiled upon others, with a cheery greeting, a *"Bom dia"* for all and a friendly *"adeus"* upon parting, yet was I a man alone within their midst, one who has looked upon things that put him beyond the pale of common society. I felt almost like a wanderer out of some other world: which I was, in good sooth, in some five or six various ways.

We marched about upon the tribes outside Kambambe, and mastered many nations there. Among our conquered was Shillambansa, uncle to the King of Angola, that I had helped to sack utterly when I was with the Jaqqas. He had rebuilt his city to something of its old sumptuousness; when this chief did see me again in the triumphant army of Portugals, he looked upon me as a demon who particularly oppressed his destinies, and hissed *"mokisso"* at me, and "white Jaqqa," and turned away in dread. Well, and I suppose he had no cause to love me for working two utter devastations upon him, and my appearance now was frightening to behold, with my scars and my long tangled white hair and my golden beard and my blue eyes to manifest me as a devil to him.

Cerveira Pereira founded a presidio at Kambambe, and once again the Portugals set about the search for the silver mines, but I think they got small share of silver, or perhaps none at all. This new upstart governor, who held no royal commission from his king, was very cruel to his soldiers, so that in time all his voluntary men left him; and by this means he could go no further. So we remained at Kambambe month upon month, I now being past forty-five years of age, but still, thank God, strong and healthy.

Then there did come to us a pair of Jesuits, that had traveled up the Kwanza to bring certain news to the governor, and not finding him at Masanganu had continued on to this place. These two were closeted with Cerveira Pereira a long while, and two days afterward messengers came to me, saying, Cerveira Pereira did wish to speak with me.

I went to him and he declared, without any pleasantries of conversation, "Your Queen Elizabeth is dead."

"Nay, it is not so!" I cried, taking the news like a hard blow upon the back of my neck.

"It is brought me by the Jesuit fathers, who say she is long dead, of the April of 1603."

"Then who is King in my land?"

"James of Scotland, that was the Scottish Queen's son."

"Aye, I suppose it would have been he," said I. "For she died a maid, did Elizabeth, and the Scottish King is of the royal blood." And I did fall to thinking inwardly, *King James, King James*, trying to get the sound of it to ring honestly in my head, for at the moment it was entirely false. *King James*. Never had there been a James King of England before, but only Henry, William, Edward, Richard, in the main, and your stray lone John and Stephen, so James was a strange noise upon the throne.

And furthermore there had been no King of England at all in my lifetime, but only the Queen, that was Elizabeth, and before her Queen Mary Tudor, the bloody one, so that the rule of women had been customary to my mind. King James? Aye, then, King James, King James, King James: I would try to learn the music of it by heart, discordant though it now might seem. *King James.* Of that man I knew little or none, save that he was a Scot, and said to be not fair to look upon, and a Protestant, though his mother had not been one. A Protestant for good and aye, surely, else Elizabeth would not have bestowed upon him the crown.

"There is more news, Don Andres," Cerveira Pereira said. "The war is ended between Spain and England, by command of King James and King Philip, and so there is peace between Portugal and England as well, this having been proclaimed in August last."

"God be praised, then, I am no man's enemy in this land!"

"That is the case," said he.

"I do make petition to you, Don Manoel, to grant me license to go into mine own country, since that I am no longer a prisoner of the realm, but only a sojourner here."

He studied me a long while out of those harsh and beady dark eyes of his, and I felt me to be a fish upon a hook, dangling in air while the angler decides if he is to be thrown back into the freedom of the water.

I said, into his silence, "You could consult the archives in Sao Páulo de Loanda of Governor Serrão's time, that would record how I was brought here out of Brazil, upon my capture from a freebooter's expedition, and—"

"This I know," he replied. "And most bravely have you served us, Don Andres."

"Surely that service is at its end now."

"I think so," said he.

"Then may I go?"

"Aye," he said. "Make to me a petition by writing, and I will grant you license, and you may go home."

Such simple and easy words! Such a trifle, falling from his lips! England to be mine again! I for King James' land, by Governor Cerveira Pereira's freely given license!

Aye, but not so lightly, for nothing is light or swift when one is dealing with Portugals. I did make my application that afternoon by writ to Don Manoel Cerveira Pereira, and then I went off apart to give thanks unto God for my deliverance, and to pray for the repose of Her Protestant Majesty Elizabeth of beloved memory, and to offer also the hope of God's benevolence upon my new King and master James I, who unknown to me had been my monarch some two years already. But still was I in Kambambe, many leagues from the coast. Nor did Cerveira Pereira favor me with a written reply to my petition, though I had the promise in words from him.

Shortly it was time for the governor to return himself to his capital; and I departed with him and his train to São Paulo de Loanda. Scarce was I able to recognize that city, so great had it grown, with majestic new buildings now rising on the hill and in the flat places, and the old palaces and cathedral dwarfed in their midst. Slavery had become the main sustenance of the city, and it looked not much unlike the depot of São Tomé, with great pens everywhere in which the sad human merchandise of this commerce was penned.

Strange was it to be back in civilization, to sleep in a true bed, to eat Portuguese food and drink claret and wear fresh clothes. I still felt the Jaqqa pull, the lodestone force of the jungle. I was in part yet one of that nation, even after some years away from them; I think I will always be, for Jaqqa blood does throb ineradicably in my veins. And also was there in me a void and chilly place where Dona Teresa had occupied mine affections, that left me hollow and bereft.

In merely the few years that I had been gone from São Paulo de Loanda I had become a total stranger, without links to this place. I looked about most diligently, and all was unfamiliar. Those men known to me of old had died or gone elsewhere, even the streets I had known being engulfed into the new ones. I could not find Matamba, nor any who knew of her. The very names of Don João de Mendoça and Fernão da Souza and his wife Dona Teresa seemed lost to oblivion in this greater and noisier place. And as for Andrew Battell, why, he was forgotten also. I had no attention of any special kind, not even on account of my coloring, since my hair was no longer golden, nor was golden hair a scarcity here, the city being full of Dutchmen partaking in the slave trade, and some Frenchmen also.

Aye, and did I board the first ship bound for Europe, now that I had license to go? Surely that is what I did, you say. But I did not do that. For they would not ship me home by courtesy of the crown: I had to buy my passage, and at most dear a price. And among those who had forgotten me were those bankers to whom I had entrusted my store of wealth. I had placed at deposit in the counting-house in São Paulo de Loanda all the proceeds of my trading voyages to Benguela, before my abandonment into the hands of Mofarigosat, and a heavy sum it was, too. But when I came calling for it, thinking it had compounded into a pretty pile, they left me standing in their velveted outer chamber a long span, and when they returned to me they feigned not knowing why I had come, and left me standing there another long while, and so on, before coming at last to deny any knowledge of my credit with them. Had I any certificate of that funding? What could I say, that I had been roaming naked in the wilderness, wearing beads and paint, and had had no purse to keep my documents in? "You will see," I said, "I am Andrew Battell, or it may be that you have me down as Andres, who served as pilot under Don João de Mendoça—"

But they knew not Don João, and they knew not me, and they had not my money, nor any record thereof.

I went to the governor to make complaint, but he would not admit me, and his secretary told me bluntly that the counting-house was known to be honorable. I had no further recourse. These Spaniards who kept the bank were sly dogs, and I was English, having no rights in this land. And they had cozened me of all my wealth and that was the end upon it. When I returned to England, so one official opined, I might bring an action in court against the counting-house. But without that money I was unable to return to England!

So, then, how to pay for my passage? Pawn my scars? I had no friends in this place, and of moneylenders there were none who would deal with me, and in fine I was as helpless a beggar here as I had been on the day Thomas Torner and I were led in chains into our prison.

But at that pass a good Portugal came to my aid. This was a certain merchant, by name Nicolau Cabral, that was the younger brother of Pinto Cabral that had sailed with me on my voyages when I was a pilot here. This younger Cabral, knowing of me from his brother's stories, sought me out and said, "I intend making a journey of trade into the kingdom of Kongo, where I think there is much profit to be had. And my brother says you are a man of valor, and of skill in languages, and with great knowledge of the peoples of the land: so I would have you as my partner in this venture."

I embraced this Cabral most warmly, and told him he was my salvation, for that I was penniless and seeking earnings for my homeward passage and the comfort of mine old age when I should reach England. And so it was agreed, that I would guide him and shield him from harm, and I was to have a portion of the profits of the venture to mine own, even though I put up no capital for it. Moreover, he said, even if we did not return a profit on our commodities, he undertook to pledge me enough money to pay for my passage. The which offer gave me great joy, although I said, "It will not be necessary to exact those terms from you, I think, since we will return well loaded with treasure."

Two

In this way I found myself yet again a wanderer in the forests and wastelands of Africa, who had thought by this time to be long since on his voyage home.

Yet was it not a burdensome ordeal. When one has been gone from home beyond fifteen year, as was now the case with me, what matters it to have a little more delay? I could not let myself go home a pauper. I confess to you also that I was fearful of returning to England, though it had been my dream so long, for it frightened me that I might be altogether bewildered in that land from its many changes. And the other thing that led me away from my great homeward goal was the knowledge still that there was too much African in me, that I was out of consort with the spirit of my native land and must yet strive to put Calandola behind me; for the taste of forbidden meat still sometimes rose to my tongue.

We set forth, Nicolau Cabral and I, into the province of Mbamba, that lieth northward of Angola, through cities that were named Musulu and Lembo and Nkondo. These were Christian places, having long been under the influence of the Portugals. Yet it was a strange kind of Christianity they did practice here, that I found strongly repellent.

This was, I suppose, in the town called Musulu. One evening an hour after sunset, I heard abundance of people singing, but in such a doleful tone as caused horror. I inquired of my servants what that meant, and they answered, it was the people of the town that came to discipline themselves in church, because it was a Friday in March. I went to the church to see it for myself, and found a Romish priest there, who lit two candles and rang the bell. The blackamoors in the meanwhile remained outside the church on their knees, singing the *Salve Regina* in their language, with a very doleful harmony; then being come into the church, the priest gave them all holy water. He offered some of it to me, but I did not take my place at the stoup. The worshippers were about two hundred men carrying great logs of wood of a vast weight, for the greater penance. The priest spoke a few words to them, saying, "If we do not undergo penance in this world, we shall be forced to endure it in the next," and again he looked toward me, thinking me a good Paptist and expecting me to kneel down. I did not, but I stayed to watch, telling myself that although I could never do penance enough for my sins, yet I was not about to do it under the auspices of Rome.

The blackamoors were all on their knees, and they disciplined themselves a whole hour, I suppose, with leather thongs and cords made of the bark of trees. Several times did the priest with gestures invite me to participate. But of what value would flagellating my body be to the purging of my soul? It was prayer that I needed, and the descent of divine grace, not whips. So the ceremony soon grew wearying to me, and I went out, to find Nicolau Cabral in search of me.

"What," he said, "are you a Roman now, Andres?"

"Not quite yet," said I. "But I have been witnessing a most joyless rite." And I took him within, and showed him the blackamoors still flogging themselves in Jesu's name. And the priest still exhorted them, saying that they had committed sins against the majesty of God, who is merciless to the penitent but most harsh to those who are not. Cabral drew me by the arm and took me out of there, saying it saddened him to watch it; for though he was of the Roman faith he held no sympathy for this flogging, and I think he inwardly believed it had been better to leave these folk in their paganism than to give them so bitter a taste of the love of our gentle Savior.

But before we left that place we found the true reason for this extreme penitence, which was that the people of the town had learned that the Jaqqas were menacing the frontier, and by punishing themselves did somehow hope to win God's favor against the man-eaters. At the sound of the name "Jaqqa" I caught in my breath, and bit down hard on my lip, for I was much appalled.

I said, "And are they far from here?"

"No one knows that," replied my informant, a Bakongo man named Nsaku that had been traveling inland. "They flit like ghosts from place to place, as always."

"Is Imbe Calandola yet their king?" I asked.

"Their king is said to be a dread monster, that eats children for his noon-meal," said Nsaku, "but I know not his name. I know only that we must implore God's mercy against these creatures, or they will destroy us."

Cabral to me said, "It is reported that you lived among them a time, Andres."

"Aye," said I. "That I did, before they were defeated under Don João Coutinho."

"And was it a terrible torment to be their captive?"

"Aye. I would not speak of it, so painful was it."

"I quite understand, my friend. The marks of the suffering are inscribed on your face." And he smiled kindly upon me, and we gave Nsaku some shell-money for his information, and we made ready to move on from that place. As we went forth into the dark forest I felt heavy fear descending upon me, like a tangible weight, that we might meet with a troop of Jaqqas in this deep wilderness. It is not that I dreaded dying at their hands; I think I had long since passed beyond such fear of death as I might once have had. Nay, what I truly feared was that I would see them encamped in some clearing, with their kettles and their music and all, and I would throw off my Portugal clothes and run to them, and fling myself before Imbe Calandola and beg his forgiveness, and give myself into their nation once again.

Does that sound like madness to you? Aye, so it does to me. But it was a most plausible madness; for Calandola was real to me and England only a phantasm, now, and much of the time my mind lay in a hazy borderland between the real and the unreal. I had at first embraced the Jaqqa way only so that they might bring me closer to the coast, and hope of home; but in some fashion along my travels with them the infection of them had entered my flesh, and I was still raging with it in a distant corner of my being. I thought I had broken with the Jaqqas when I did send Kulachinga to Don João Coutinho to betray Calandola; I thought then that it marked my adherence forever to civilized Christian things; and yet here was I in the Kongo forest all atremble, lest I should find them in yonder ollicondi grove and be swept willy-nilly into new allegiance to their dark lord and master.

But we encountered no Jaqqas, God be thanked, and came unhindered into the capital zone of the kingdom of the Kongo.

Now this was the place where the Portugals first had taken root on this side of Africa, insinuating themselves into a kingdom that already was rich and well advanced to civility. There were black kings here long ago, some of them great ones. When the Portugals came, an hundred year and some ago, they gulled these folk into accepting the Papist faith, and into becoming allies of Portugal, which meant, in time, that Portugal swallowed them up. Christians did they become, with Christian ways and dress and names, and strutted about telling themselves they were much enlarged by these new customs, while quietly the Portugals did suck the wealth from their land through flattery and deceit. It is the old story, that will be repeated wherever the guile of Europe meets the innocence of Paradise, I fear.

The capital city of this kingdom was named Mbanza, which in their tongue only means "the city" or "the royal court," and when the Portugals settled here they named it São Salvador de Mbanza, which is how it is called now. Though it was somewhat fallen from its greatest days, owing to the Jaqqa invasion of thirty years ago and other calamities, yet was it still a grand sight as we came upon it, traveling as we had through thick forest, past marsh and swamp, over ravines and rivers, to the highland on which it is seated, about one hundred fifty miles from the sea.

It is upon a great and high mountain that the Portugals call Outeiro, being almost all of rock, but yet having a vein of iron in it, whereof they have very great use in their housing. This mountain has in the top of it a great plain, very fertile and furnished with houses and villages, containing in circuit about ten miles, where there do dwell and live the number of one hundred thousand persons. The soil is fruitful, and the air fresh, wholesome, and pure: there are great store of springs of good water, and of all sorts of cattle great abundance.

This town of São Salvador has neither enclosure nor wall, except a little on the south side, which the first king built and afterwards gave to the Portugals to inhabit. Also enclosed are the royal palace and the houses of the nobility. In the midst between the Portuguese district and the royal compound is a great space, where the principal church is set, with a fair marketplace beyond it. The walls of the Portuguese town and the king's are very thick, but the gates are not shut in the night time, neither is there any watch or ward kept therein. The buildings of the great men are of chalk and stone, but all the rest are of straw, very neatly wrought: the lodgings, dining-rooms, galleries, and other apartments, are hung after the European manner, with mats of an exquisite curiosity. Within the innermost courts are gardens, pleasantly stored with variety of herbs, and planted with several sorts of trees. There are ten or eleven churches, in honor of various saints, and a Jesuit college, and schools where youths are brought up and taught the Latin and Portuguese tongues.

We called first at the court of the king. This monarch's name was Don Alvaro II, though his private name was Nempanzu a Mini, but it was an offense to call him that, it not being Christian. He had already been king more than thirty years and was said to be a zealous Christian, but not fond of the Portugals. Cabral told me that he had given favor lately to Dutch merchants, of whom many now abounded in the Kongo; and I knew already that this king had leagued himself several times with the King of Angola and other enemies of the Portugals during the wars.

Yet did he receive us graciously enough, and in high pomp. When we came upon him, amid a great noise of trumpets, fifes, drums, and cornets, we found him clad with a scarlet cloak and gold buttons, and white buskins upon carnation silk stockings. Cabral remarked that he has new clothes every day, which I could hardly believe in a country where fine stuffs and good tailors are scarce. Before him went twenty-four young blacks, all sons of dukes or marquises of this kingdom, who wore about their middles a handkerchief of palm-cloth dyed black, and a cloak of blue European cloth hanging down to the ground, but all of them bareheaded and barefooted.

Near to his majesty was an official who carried his sun-shade of silk, of a fire-color laced with gold, and another who carried a chair of carnation velvet, with gold nails, and the wood all gilt. Two others clad in red coats carried his red hammock, but I know not whether it was silk, or dyed cotton. We bowed and saluted His Majesty, who spoke with us in passing good Portuguese, and asked me if I was a Dutchman.

I said I was English, and he found that worth noting, saying, "There has never been an Englishman to this court. Come closer, and let me see you near."

Which I did, whereupon he spied the Jaqqa markings on my face, and said, "What are these, and how did you come by them?"

"They were placed on me by the man-eaters, when I was captive among them."

At that he made the sign of the cross, and told me how when he was a child the Jaqqas had come into this city, and slaughtered thousands and driven his father to take refuge on the Hippopotamus Island in the Zaire River. All this I already knew, but I listened most attentively. Then he asked me if I had seen with mine own eyes, in my sojourn with those folk, the great Jaqqa Imbe Calandola.

"That I did," said I, "and a most frightsome being he is."

"Then he is real, and not just a tale told to frighten boys?"

"He is as real as is Your Majesty, by my faith!"

"And he is a monster?"

"He is most frightsome," I did say again, and nothing more, not wishing to speak of the feasts and other secret things that I had shared with the Lord Imbe-Jaqqa.

King Alvaro closed his eyes, and seemed to brood inward; and then after a time he said, "It is fated that the Jaqqas will eat the world, and bring us all unto judgment, but that Christ will rise upon the last and overthrow them. I hope that warfare is long yet in the coming."

"As do I, most fervently, Your Majesty," I responded, thinking that this was a most strange kind of Christianity that had the gentle Savior doing battle with the terrible Imbe-Jaqqa at the end of the world. But I did not say it. I think these people are very fine Christians indeed, that obey their priests and go to Mass and all the rest, but I do quietly suspect that mixed into their catechism is a very great store of encrusted pagan belief, that would give high surprise to the men of the Vatican if they did but know. Yet that is no business of mine, if these good black Romans have stirred a few *mokissos* into their creed, and have made an

Antichrist out of Calandola. For all faiths are true faiths, and if the Imbe-Jaqqa be not an Archfiend he is something very close upon it.

When we had paid our respects, and met other members of the court and certain sons of the king, both true ones and bastards (for so were they introduced to us) we were free to go about our trading. Cabral had brought to this land all manner of useful commodities, such things as chamber pots and shaving bowls and iron kettles and blankets of Flanders and Portugal and French linen and dyed caps and much else, which we took into the marketplace. Here we found fine brassware and pottery, and splendid woven mats, and elephanto teeth, and the skins of leopards and other handsome beasts, and carved staffs of a most beautiful design, and other such produce of the land, which we were able to buy at a most advantageous exchange, so eager were the Kongo folk for our foreign goods. Let it only be made in Europe and they will rush to own it, however humble an object it may be.

Also did I acquire two young Negro boys to be my servants, they being offered at a good price and I feeling the need of their aid with my baggage.

Now had we turned enough of a profit to see me safe aboard a ship to Spain, but I was not ready to halt in my trading, nor was Nicolau Cabral. We went on deeper into Kongo to Ngongo and to Bata, where they had great heathen images set up. Then, having sold most of our commodities, we brought ourselves back to the coast at the mouth of the Zaire. Here a pinnace was waiting for Cabral, to bring our goods south, but here also was another ship of the Dutch bound northward, and I proposed to sail with them a little way, leaving our merchandise with Cabral. This shows you how much faith I had in that man, that he would not cheat me of my share; and that faith for once was not misplaced. We parted most warmly and I journeyed up the coast a few days with the Dutchmen.

I tarried briefly in the province of Mayombe, which is all woods and groves, so overgrown that a man may travel twenty days in the shadow, without any sun or heat. Here they have great store of elephanto flesh, which they greatly esteem, and many kinds of wild beasts; and great store of fish. The woods are covered with baboomas, monkeys, apes, and parrots, that it will fear any man to travel in them alone. But the Jaqqas are not feared in this land, indeed are scarce known among them except as some sort of distant menace.

Here dwell two other kinds of monsters of which I had once heard from my dear friend Barbosa of blessed memory, that are apes, the pongo and the engeco. This pongo is in all proportions like a man, but that he is more like a giant in stature than a man; for he is very tall, and has a man's face, hollow-eyed, with long hair upon his brows. His face and ears are without hair, and his hands also. His body is full of hair, but not very thick, and it is of a dunnish color. He differs not from a man but in his legs, for they have no calf. He goes always upon his legs, and carries his hands clasped upon the nape of his neck when he goes upon the ground. They sleep in the trees, and build shelters from the rain. They feed upon fruit they find in the woods and upon nuts, for they eat no kind of flesh. They cannot speak, and have no more understanding than a beast. I saw these creatures now and again, but always from a great distance, they being very shy.

The people of the country, when they travel in the woods, make fires when they sleep in the night. And in the morning, when they are gone, the pongos will come and sit about the fire till it goes out, for they have no understanding to lay the wood together. They go many together, and kill many Negroes that travel in the woods. Many times they fall upon the elephantos, which come to feed where they be, and so beat them with their clubbed fists and pieces of wood that they will run roaring away from them.

Those pongos are never taken alive, because they are so strong that ten men cannot hold one of them, but yet they take many of their young ones with poisoned arrows. The young pongo hangeth on to his mother's belly, with his hands clasped fast about her, so that when the country people kill any of the females, they take the young one which hangeth fast to her. I did much desire to purchase a young pongo, that I might take it back to England with me as a curiosity to present it to King James, but I could not obtain one. This being a great pity, for I am sure no such monstrous ape has ever been seen in that land.

The engeco is much different, being smaller, to the height of a boy of twelve years, and covered with coarse dark hair. It walks upon its legs, that are bandy and have bright pink feet, and its face is most comic, like unto that of a mummer's or buffoon's. They also eat no flesh, or very little, and are said to be much quicker of wit than the pongo. Here also did I attempt to obtain this creature for England, and in the city of Mani Mayombe one was brought for me that was no more than a babe, and most piteous, being like a little very hairy human person, with sad eyes and a great ugly yawning mouth. I think the King would have made me a knight had I given him that creature, but I did not have the purchase of it, for it died of yearning for its mother soon after.

There is another lord to the eastward of the town of Mani Mayombe, which is called Mani Kesock, and he is eight days' journey from Mayombe. Here I was with my two Negro boys to buy elephanto hairs and tails. And in a month I bought twenty thousand, which I later sold to the Portugals for thirty slaves, so that I was again a wealthy man. From this place I sent one of my Negro boys to the prince Mani Sette with a looking-glass. He did esteem it much, and sent me four elephanto teeth of great size by his own men, which did further increase my wealth.

To the northeast of Mani Kesock are a kind of little people called Matimbas, which are no bigger than boys of twelve years old, but are very sturdy, and live only upon flesh, which they kill in the woods with their bows and darts. They pay tribute to Mani Kesock, and bring all their elephanto teeth and tails to him. The women carry bows and arrows, as well as the men, and one of these will walk in the woods alone, and kill the pongos with their poisoned arrows.

Here ends my recitation of the wonders of this province, for I had now acquired such riches, by God's grace, that I needed no more, and I did return to the coast, where in good time the Dutch traders did call for me and carry me back to São Paulo de Loanda. It had now become Anno 1607 and I was well ready to begin my passage at last back to England: as ready as I could be, though still I feared somewhat the entry into that placid sweet land out of this realm of nightmare. For I had not shaken free, in the inwardness of myself, of the grasp of this land. I dreamed sometimes still of Imbe Calandola, shouting and raging and marching to and fro with blood dripping from his jowls, and into my mind at untoward moments came images out of the death of Dona Teresa, and other such horrors, and now and again some loathly coccodrillo would drag its scaly huge form through my slumber's repose. Yet I told me that if I waited for such matters to escape themselves from my mind before I set forth for home, I would dwell in this land to the end of my days. If one goes among devils, one must expect certain dregs of deviltry to crust the borders of one's soul forever, said I to myself. And so I resolved to take me to England now that I had the funds for it, and complete my healing there. But as usual I was too hopeful of a happy outcome.

THREE

NICOLAU CABRAL indeed did not betray me, for he had turned the value of our trading mission into gold, and my share was waiting for me. That and the sale of my thirty slaves gave me such wealth as any man could desire, so the voyage that I had begun eighteen years previous had resulted, after many a turn and twisting, in the fortune I sought.

And now for England!

I purposed to have shipped myself for Spain, and thence homewards, there now being peace between Spain and England. But for that I needed the writ of Governor Cerveira Pereira, and I went before him, saying, "You gave me license to go, and now it is my time to depart, and I would have the paper from you."

This little man, who was so dark and gaunt, with a black beard that came to a point, did shuffle and shove the documents before him for long moments, making me no answer. Then at length he looked up to me where I stood uneasy, and said, "It may not be."

"What, and you deny your word?"

This angered him. High color came into his face, and he rose, he being half my height, and cried out loudly at me, "I will let you go when I will let you go! But at this time you may not go, for you are needed."

"God's eyes, am I to hear that again? For close on twenty years you Portugals have needed me! Why am I so everlasting useful for you? Aye, and must I be a pilot again, or what? Shall I cut paths in the forest for you? Shall I caulk decks, and sweep away dust? In Jesu name, how can you ask more of me?" And I cried this forth, you may imagine, in no smooth flattering way, for I was bubbling with surprise and wrath and a fury that was close to a killing one.

"It is the Jaqqas that are once more upon Kambambe, almost," said he, "and they must be driven back, and we know you are the match for them. So we are to begin the conquest, and you must aid us. I command you to go up to the wars, two days hence."

God's death, but I came close to striking him down!

Two days, and then I was to resume the wars? And they would take me out to do battle with the Jaqqas? Nay, nay, I would not, it was beyond all conceiving! In my long travail I had learned much philosophy of the Stoic kind, to be strong and all-withstanding, and bide my time and quietly pursue my purposes; but this was far too much, this went beyond the bounds, and there was no philosophy honeyed enough to help me swallow so prickly a lump.

At the least I was philosopher enough to take my leave of Governor Pereira without making any mayhem upon him. But it was close, aye, it was parlous close, and were I not a man of temperance I would have left him disjointed on the floor, fit for a Jaqqa stew and nothing more.

But I choked back my fury and got me out of there, though a red mist was in my eyes. Two days, to go off to the conquest! It would not be. Here was I determined not to yield.

But what now, what now?

There were Dutchmen in the harbor, that would give little heed to the writs and decrees of that coxcomb Portugal. I could go to one, as I had long before to Cornelis van Warwyck, and beg him to give me secret passage, and reward him freely with my gold. But what if the scheme miscarried? I bethought me how my dealings with Warwyck had ended, bringing me near to a sentence of death, and I knew it was not the part of wisdom to try the like again under Cerveira Pereira. He would not have the mercy on me that Don João de Mendoça had had.

But a much more easy solution offered itself that night, as I sat most morose in a tavern of the town, and heard some Portugals saying that a new governor had been sent out from Portugal, and would arrive in two or three days, or at most six. For I knew that Cerveira Pereira had no royal commission, but only served by vote of the soldiers, and he had had three years and more of that. Now was a rightful man, whose name was Manoel Pereira Forjaz, to arrive.

So my way was clear. I determined to absent myself for ten or twenty days, till the other governor came, and then to come to the city again. For every governor that comes does make proclamation for all men that be absent, to come with free pardon. And I felt certain this Pereira Forjaz would give me the writ to go home, I being of no use or significance to him.

The same day, at night, I departed frokm São Paulo de Loanda with my two Negro boys that I had, which carried my musket and six pounds of powder, and a hundred bullets, and what little provision of victuals that I could make. In the morning I was some twenty miles from the city, up along the river Mbengu, and there I stayed certain days, and then passed Mbengu and came to the River Dande, which is northward.

Here I was near the highway of Kongo, that I had taken the year before on my venture with Nicolau Cabral, and merchants passed it every day. I sent forth one of my Negroes to inquire of those that went by, what news was in the city.

The boy returned soon, saying, "There is no news."

"What of the new governor?"

"He is not come. The old one still rules, and it is certain that the new governor comes not this year."

At this dreary report, my heart did sink deep.

Now I was put to my shifts, whether I would go to the city again and be hanged, or to stay and live in the woods. For I had run away before, and they had never treated it lightly; and this time I had done a great crime, Cerveira Pereira having ordered me out to the wars, and I having fled instead. What could I do? Walk into the city and say to him, "I have given half my life to you Portugals, and that is enough. I will no longer do your service, so let me go to my home?" He would laugh in his foul way and reply that I was a fugitive from the conquest of the Jaqqas, and must die. God's blood, it was enough to drive me to the side of the Jaqqas once again, and aid them in their war against all humankind!

But I kept my peace, and did none of that.

So I was forced to live in the woods a month, betwixt the rivers of Dande and Mbengu. Then I went to Mbengu again, and passed over the river near a place called Mani Kaswea, and went to the lake of Kasanza, where I had taken refuge once before. That was upon the time of my escape from Masanganu prison with the gypsy Cristovão, what seemed like eight hundred year before.

This lake of Kasanza was an easy place to make my habitation, for that such a great store of wild beasts did abound there. About this lake I stayed six months, and hunted the animals with my musket, such creatures as buffaloes, deer, mokokes, impolancas, and roebucks, and other sorts. The mokoke he is a very large gray animal, most graceful and swift, and the impolanca another of these running beasts somewhat similar, of a sort somewhat like a deer. These animals when I had killed them I dried the flesh, as the savages do, upon an hurdle, three feet from the ground, making underneath it a great fire, and laying upon the flesh green boughs, which keep the smoke and the heat of the fire down, and dry it. I made my fire with two little sticks, as the savages do. I had sometimes also Guinea wheat to eat, which one of my Negro boys would get for me of the inhabitants of the town of Kasanza nearby, by exchange for pieces of dried flesh.

This lake of Kasanza does abound with fish of sundry sorts, that gave me variety of my eating. I took once a fish that had skipped out of the water on shore, four feet long, which the heathen call *nsombo*. This fish is long and serpent-like, and does give off a sort of emanation, or power, that if you should be so rash as to touch it will feel much like a lightning-bolt. But when the life is gone from the *nsombo*, so also is its Jove-like force, and its flesh is passing fair to the taste.

The greatest danger of this lake is not the *nsombo*-fish but the river-horse, or hippopotamus, that wanders along the shore, especially by night. These creatures feed always on the land, and live only by grass, and they be very perilous in the water, because that their temper is most sharp. I think it is that they suffer from the bigness of their heads, that are heavy in the extreme, and this makes them churlish; for they will snap and snarl and bite at anything, though you would think them otherwise to be as placid as pigs. They are the biggest creature in this country, except the elephanto. The claws of their left forefoot are thought to have great virtue, and the Portugals make rings of them, and they are a present remedy for the flux. I saw many of these beasts and gave them a very wide passage, for I feared them more than coccodrillos, that also are not unknown here.

After I had lived six months with the dried flesh and fish, sharing my abode with hippopotamus and coccodrillo, and seeing no end to my misery, I wrought means to get away. For though I was dwelling quietly and in peace here, with a strange tranquility of my soul that I think arose from a deep and utter weariness of adventure, yet did I hope for a change of habitance, and perhaps to resume my long-interrupted voyage home. For, like wandering Ulysses, though I might dwell this season among the Lotus-eaters and that season on the isle of Calypso, and in this place and that, yet always did I dream fondly of mine own bed and mine own hearth in the land of my birth, even if that land had become as strange to me as any place in the world.

So did I make a departure. In the lake of Kasanza are many little islands that are full of trees called *bimba*, which are as light as cork and as soft. Of these trees I built a *jangada* or raft with a knife of the savages that I had with me, in the fashion of a box nailed with wooden pegs, and railed round about, so that the sea should not wash me out; and with a blanket that I had, I made a sail, and prepared three oars to row withal.

This lake of Kasanza is eight miles over, and issueth into the River Mbengu. So I entered into my *jangada* and my two Negro boys with me, and rowed into the River Mbengu, and so came down with the current twelve leagues to the bar that crosses the rivermouth. Here I was in great danger, because the sea was great, and my boys, seeing the upheaval of the waves, did cry out that their last hour was come.

"Have no fear," I told them cheeringly, "for I am Andrew Battell that comes of a great line of mariners, who are pilots of the Trinity House."

I will confess long after the event that I, too, knew fear just then; but I could not believe that God my Provider, having sustained me so long and through so much, had it of His plan to drown me in this surf. And I carried my raft safely over the bar and rode into the sea, and then sailed afore the wind along the coast, which I knew well, minding to go to the kingdom of Loango, which is toward the north.

And why did I not go to São Paulo de Loanda? Ah, but I knew naught of what befell there, except that in all likelihood Manoel Cerveira Pereira was yet governor, and he was mine enemy. It seemed me much wiser to chance the voyage in this little raft of my devising, and be blown along the upper coast, than to put my head back into the jaws of the lion in that city. And if I spent the rest of my days in Loango, never seeing England again, well, so be it, but at the least I would cheat the Portugals of my death.

So northward aye I went, and the boys with me, all that day and the night. The next day I saw a pinnace come before the wind, which journeyed from the city of São Paulo de Loanda, and she came near to me. There was no escaping from this ship, so I stood by, waiting for her to fall upon me, and ready to sell my life at a very fine price, and it come to that. But when the Portugals drew nigh and hailed me, great was my amaze and joy, for the master of this ship was my great friend Pinto Cabral of old days, elder brother to Nicolau. Who looked at me high and low and said, "Andres? Is this Andres the Piloto, that I shipped with in years gone by, and had the saving of my life when I was drowning upon that devil-shoal?"

"The same," said I. "Much changed without and within, and yet somewhat unaltered in essence, I do hope."

We embraced, and he gave me wine, in which I greatly joyed, and some beef and biscuit, and fed my boys also. I asked him of the city's news, which was very little. Cerveira Pereira was yet governor, said he. Pereira Forjaz was said to be sailing soon from Lisbon, but they had been saying that for a year. "I know not this little Cerveira Pereira well," declared Cabral, "for I have been to the north, in São Tomé, these two years. But he is much hated, and I think will not be lamented when he goes."

"Most especially by me," I said, "for that he did deny me my passage home, after pledging it."

Pinto Cabral laughed, and said, "It is ever thus with you, Andres, is it not? But your time will come, and your breeze will waft you homeward at last."

"May God grant it, friend," said I.

I asked him of his brother Nicolau, my partner. But here the news was grievous: for that faithful man was dead, slain by brawlers in the streets of the city. This left me downcast, both for that I had loved that man in the little time I knew him, and that I had entrusted the major part of my gold to his keeping, which surely was all vanished now. Of my treasure there remained only the pouch at my waist, in which I had prudently taken some pieces of gold when I slipped away from São Paulo de Loanda. And Pinto Cabral, in recognition of my misfortunes, did give me some other gold also.

He was bound for São Tomé to do business in slaves. But because that we had been shipmates together, he took me for pity's sake to Loango, and set me on shore in that port, where I had gone with him in ancient days when I was the pilot of the governor's pinnace; and there he left me.

Well did I remember this place, where I had seen the coocodrillo that ate the eight slaves, and the dead Jaqqa that so frighted everyone, and the burial-ground of the kings, and other wonders that struck me so strange when I was new in this land. Now I walked the three miles from the waterside to the town, calm as a tree, and when I saw the people of the place I saluted them and bade them good morrow in their own tongue most fluently, and entered into the city like a townsman coming home. I remembered, as if I had seen it but yesterday, the great house of the Maloango or king, and the wide street to the market, and all the rest. And at audience-time I did go to the Maloango and sit before the king, which was the same king from my past visit, much older and white of hair, and I cried "*Nzambi! Ampungu!*" in salutation, that is, *O Most High God*.

To which he replied with that greeting once so mysterioius to me, "*Byani ampembe mpolo, muneya ka zinga,*" that means, *My companion, the white face, has risen from underground and will not live long,* which was so strange a thing to hear, though it was but a ritual phrase.

"Are you come in trade?" said he then.

"Nay, I am come to take sanctuary here from the fury of the Portugals, who have barred me from my native land. And I have been here before, when my hair was golden."

This king the Maloango Njimbe remembered me then, and spoke of the time when I had gone diving in the sea in the hope of recovering the *mokisso*-idol that they had dropped there. And then came forth another who remembered me, which was his white-skinned *ndundu* wizzard of the red eyes, that had seen me long ago and at that time did send a coldness into my soul. This creature was now of great age, and withered and hideous, and came shuffling forward to inspect me.

At length he said, "You are the white Jaqqa."

"Aye, so you called me once, and I did not understand it."

"But now understanding has come into you?"

"That it has, and burned me deep."

"You are a Jaqqa still," the albino creature said, "and yet there is no danger about you. For you have made your voyage, and you have come to rest, and all is well within you. You are a Jaqqa-*ndundu* now."

Now that is a hard thing to comprehend, a Jaqqa-*ndundu*, nor did I ask him to spell me the meanings of it. Yet so far as I can fathom, what he was saying was, I was a white man who had turned black inside, and now was white again, but my color now was the whiteness of the albino, the changeling, and not the whiteness of the white man. Well, and I do not pretend to be a penetrating scholar, but I think I have the drift of it. The one thing is certain, that on my first visit here this sorcerer had looked on me with dread and loathing, a monster to be shunned, but now he bade the Maloango make me welcome in this land, as something holy that had been cast up on their shores.

So it befell me. I remained in Loango three years, and was well beloved of the king, because I killed him deer and fowls with my musket.

Another thing that I did was go down again in the recovery of that sunken idol, which in all these years they had hoped to bring to the surface. This time I caused to be made a suit of leather all greased and pitched, that no water could enter into it, and I caused a great head to be made all pitched, with a great nose, and at the nose were three bladders, and at the mouth two. Putting on this suit of leather, I had them cast me into the sea in eighteen fathom deep, with a mighty great stone tied about me. The weight of the stone carried me downward, but yet I was able to breathe somewhat, although the air quick became hot and foul. In the depths did I grope about, and lo! there was the leg of the *mokisso* coming forth from the muck and silt that had enveloped it. I was in much pain by then, for the stone pulled me downward and the air in the head pulled me upward, so that I thought the cord I was tied withal would have cut me in pieces. When I felt myself so tormented, I took a knife that was tied in my hand, and cut the cord, and held fast to the idol. Upward was I carried, and as soon as I came above water, I tore the bladders from my face, and cut my suit before, for I was almost stifled. After this I was greatly dizzied and walked in circles close upon an hour, and did not feel a healthy man for some days or peradventure a week. But I had found them their idol after all so many years, and they hailed me as a great hero for this, and bestowed many rich gifts upon me.

I think I would have passed all the remainder of my days in Loango. For, as the *ndundu* said, I had made my voyage, and I had come to rest. Striving was no longer my way. I lived peaceably among them and ate of their foods and went to their festivals, and was not shunned by them. When I passed the house of Kikoko the great *mokisso* I did clap my hands for good luck, as they did. The king gave me a wife, who was the last of my African wives, whose name was Inizanda, and gentle and tender she was, though she spoke little, and I think regarded herself as my slave rather than my wife. Yet when we lay together she stroked me soothingly and gave me good pleasure, such times as I required it. Which was not so often as in other times, I now being fifty years of age, and a little more. That is a fine full age, and the fires burn a little low when one comes to it, if one has lived as arduously as I have lived. But when I turned to my Inizanda and placed my hand upon her thigh, her legs did open to me and she did take my head against her breasts, and my yard into her warm nest, and that was a great comfort upon me.

So was I lulled by life in Loango, and one year glided into another. And I thought me of all my struggle and avowal to reach my homeland, and how far from my soul that aim was now; and I smiled over that, to think I now no longer cared. England? What was that, and where? I was in the Lotus-eater land! Be the English nation under the rule of King James, or King Peter, or King Calandola, it meant nothing whatsoever to me. Did Englishmen now dress in Scots garb? Were shilling coins struck these days of clay? Had London slipped into the sea? Why, it was all one to me: foreign, dreamy. I was content. I had made my voyage, and I had come to my rest.

Then one day a band of Portugals did march into the city of Loango, and at the head of them was Pinto Cabral, who was returning to São Paulo de Loanda from yet another voyage to São Tomé, and who had come to inquire after me.

I was summoned. I came forth in my palm-cloth skirt and my necklace of shells, which took him somewhat athwart. But he laughed and embraced me and said, "At last we find you! We stopped here coming north, but you were away on a hunt. I carry good news for you, Andres."

"And what might that be?"

"Why, that you are sought, and urged for England, by Governor Pereira Forjaz! Your tale is known to him, and he has sent word along the coast, that your pardon is fully granted."

"Nay, it is a jest," said I. "They will take me, and send me off to make war on King Ngola, or some such service. Or make me pilot on their voyage to the Pole Antarctic. It cannot be that I am pardoned."

"You are too much hardened by adversity," Cabral replied. "This is God's own truth."

I laughed at that.

"Why do you laugh, Andres?"

"I laugh because I no longer care," I replied. "It is ever thus, that we are granted our deepest wishes when they have come to have no weight. I am happy here. My life is quiet. It is a good harbor for me, this place. And now you come, saying, I am pardoned, I am free, the ship is waiting to bear me home. Home? Where is my home? I think sometimes Loango is my home."

Pinto Cabral at this grew most solemn, and stared me close, and took my hand.

"Is this so? Shall I leave you here, old friend?"

I did not at once answer. I was not sure of my way.

He said, "It is all the same to me, stay or come, if only you be happy. I would not tear you from this place."

"Nay," I answered, after a long quietness. "Nay, I am old and foolish, and I know not what I say. But it is England that I want. Take me from hence! Of course, take me, friend Cabral, take me and send me toward England, for that is what I want, and nothing other!"

"Be you sure?"

"I am sure," said I.

And I was, after that moment of hesitance; for Andrew Battell had awakened in me, that was slumbering, and did say unto me, You are an Englishman, you are no man of this black world, no Jaqqa, no *ndundu*, you are Andrew Battell of Leigh in Essex, so put off your beads and your palm-cloth, and get you down to the city, and take you home to England where the cold rain does fall all the year long, and sit by the fire and tell your tales to the fairhaired children that crouch wide-eyed at your knees. And I did hear that voice within me say those things, and my strength returned, and my resolve sharpened, and also there came back to me my sense of who I was and where God had designed me to dwell.

And I gave over my habitation in Loango and went with Pinto Cabral down into São Paulo de Loanda.

FOUR

THIS TIME there were no deceptions practiced upon me. This time they meant to deal most honorably with me.

Governor Cerveira Pereira had gone home to Lisbon to face certain very serious accusations concerning his rule in Angola, and the governor now was Pereira Forjaz. Cabral said that this man was no better admired than his predecessors, for he was laying heavy taxes on the tribal chiefs and draining this money into his purse and those of his favorites. But such things were mere vapors to me; and to me this Pereira Forjaz was a veritable saint and a Solomon of wisdom. For he said to me, "I have looked into your record, and a great injustice has been done upon you these many years. So you are to go home."

"And may I have a writ to that effect?"

"That you may," said he, and gave me a document in writing, and a purse of gold as well. It was not much money, and little enough recompense for the fortunes I had twice lost in this land, but I would at any rate have some coins to jingle when I set foot in England. There was but a short time to wait, until the next ship departed from Europe for Spain. I was sure that in that short time they would find some means of retracting this gift of my liberty, but it was not so.

Whilst I was in São Paulo de Loanda waiting, a Dutchman named Janszoon that was trading there said to me that there was another Englishman in the city, old and ill, living in an inn by the waterfront. The news that a countryman was here did buoy my spirits greatly, for that I had not seen anyone of mine own race in twenty years, since Thomas Torner had made his escape from Angola. Indeed, I did have some wild notion that this old Englishman might even be Torner, who perhaps had been wandering all this while on paths similar to mine, and in the end had been beached upon the same place. So I went me to the inn, and said to the Portugal that was the keeper, "Do you have an English lying here?"

"That I do, but he is a foul wretch, and most surly."

"I would see him, even so."

"You will only catch a plague of him."

"And if I do, then I will die aiding a countryman, which is not a scurvy thing to do."

The innkeeper shrugged, as if to say it was on my own head whatever happened, and took me to an upstairs room, dark and stale, and called inside, saying, "You have a guest, fellow!"

Out of the darkness came a bitter grumbling muttering noise, and no more.

I went in. So sure was I that this was Torner that my mind was filling already with the tales to tell him, of all my travels and pains and wives and the like, one story tumbling over another in a wild hasty scramble in my head, and which was I to tell him first?

But the man in the room was not Thomas Torner.

He was a small pasty-faced shrunken withered man, with a round bald head and a stringy thin beard, who sat palsied and feeble by the window. When I entered, he looked up at me but did not see me, for his eyes were pale and sightless, and he sniffed at the air as though he would find me out by smell alone.

I said, and it was not easy to frame English phrases after so long a sojourn here, "They say you are an Englishman."

"Aye."

"So am I also, that has been twenty years on this shore."

To this he said nothing.

I said, "Are you unwell? Can I give you any aid?"

"I would die, but I cannot. My life is over, yet I live on."

"Never say you would welcome death, until the moment when death is upon you. Come, brother, let us walk about, and seek the fresh air of the shore."

"Let me be."

"The breeze will set your blood coursing again, and restore you to life," said I.

"Let me be. I have no wish to be restored to life."

"I beg you, brother—"

"Damn you, let me be!" cried he in a screech-owl cry, that had more pain than anger in it. Spittle flecked his face, and he rose part way from his seat, making claws at me, but he could not rise, and trembling he fell back, huddled, shaking. In a very low voice he said, "D'ye see, I am too weak to stand! And yet I am unable to die. Yet death spurns me."

"I see that," said I. And my heart went out for him, for that he was a sorrowful mortal man in dire distress, and it was my Christian duty to comfort him. I pulled over a second chair, and sat beside him, and said, "Let me help you in what way I can, for if one Englishman does not help another here, who will do it for us?"

He looked at me less darkly, and some ease came over him.

"Tell me how you came to this place, friend," said I.

"By the Portugals," he replied, "who had me a slave in their galleys five years, and whipped me once until I could no longer walk aright, and then afterward my sight went from me; and they had me in São Tomé, but did not want me there, and dumped me down to die."

"You have suffered much."

"I am altogether destroyed at their account. But they had reason to injure me, for I once was a privateer captain, and roved King Philip's seas and took heavy plunder from his ships, until I was taken in my turn."

"Ah," I said, "and I was a privateer once also, though precious little plunder fell to my share. What is your home place?"

"Essex," said he. "I am of the town of Leigh, that is close by the sea. Do you know it, perchance?"

"Aye," I said.

And a great shiver did run down my spine at what I had heard from him, and I was half stricken by amaze, and my breath came in sudden ragged bursts out of my pounding bosom; for I did peer close, seeking to discern the outlines of his face beneath the changes the years had worked on him, this being a man not so much older than I, from my very town, and I saw that I did know him, though it was almost outside the scope of belief that this man could be—this man—

"My name," said he, and though he said it in a scratchy whisper it exploded in my ears like the bombard of an hundred cannon, "My name is Abraham Cocke."

"Ah, so I thought!"

And for an instant I thought me to strike him dead, as many times I had fancied I would do, if ever I met with that man again. But how strike this feeble ancient villain, that was so ruined by time and adversity already?

"You know of me?" he said.

"You are that great captain," said I, "that sailed out of the Thames in the April of 1589 with two pinnaces bound for the River de la Plata, that were called the *May-Morning* and the *Dolphin*."

He half rose again, and opened his blind eyes wide, though it availed him naught to do it, for he could see me not.

"You know those ships? You recall that voyage? Who are you? In Jesu's name, who are you, man?"

"I am Andrew Battell."

"Andrew Battell?" He said the name quietly, curiously, as someone would who had never heard it before. "Battell? That is a name of Leigh, is it not?"

"Thomas James Battell was my father, and my brothers were the mariners Thomas and Henry and John."

"Ah. I know those names."

"And the name of Andrew Battell is unknown to you?"

"It rings in my mind, but I do not place it properly."

"Nay," said I, "it is so many years, you surely have forgotten. But we fought together against the Armada, on the *Margaret and John*."

"Aye. I remember that ship well."

"And afterward, you were going with the *May-Morning* and the *Dolphin* privateering—"

"Aye."

"And I was of your crew."

"It is so long ago, good Andrew."

"Aye, twenty-one years, this April. And we sailed in African waters first, to São Tomé, even, and then westward, a hard voyage, and much loss. D'ye recall, Captain Cocke?"

"Aye, a hard voyage."

I shivered with the rage I felt, remembering. "And there was an isle called São Sebastião, beneath the Tropic of Capricorn, where we were sore hungry. And you did choose a party of men to go ashore for gathering food and water."

"It was so long ago. I cannot recall. There were so many voyages, so many islands."

"You did choose a band of sailors, and send them to the isle, and then a party of Indians fell upon them. And slew some of us, and some escaped. But we were lost there on that isle, for that our captain had sailed away without making search for us, and I was among those men, Captain Cocke."

"Ah," said he, in a voice from the tomb. "Ah, I do think I recall it slightly, now."

I put my face near to his and most sternly said, "I recall it more than slightly, for it stole all my life from me, to be marooned there. For I came into the hands of the Portugals, and by June of '90 they had me in Angola as a prisoner, and I have been here ever since."

"Ah. And you are Andrew Battell, of Leigh?"

"The very man."

"I thought those mariners were dead, that went to the isle for food and water."

"And never came near to look for us?"

"But if you were dead, why then should we have risked the lives of the others?"

"And if we were not dead? And if we still lived, Captain Cocke, and were to go on into a life of slavery, because that you would not turn about to seek us?"

His face was gray, his head was bowed. His body shook as if with tears, but his cheeks were dry.

I said, "I vowed that if ever I found you I would tear you arm from leg, Cocke, for destroying my life."

"Aye. Then slay me," said he bleakly.

"You had my life from me. You sent me into monstrous perils and torments."

"Slay me, then," said he again. "It was not my intent, leaving you there. I felt sure you were all of you dead. But it was a sin, a most grievous sin, not to have looked. Slay me."

He was not afraid. He was pleading for my vengeance.

Ah, then! Strike him now?

"I will not," said I.

"What is that you tell me?"

Darkly I said, "We are old men, and my life has gone its course, and I think the sands are nearly run out for you. What pleasure is it in killing you now? What revenge? Will it give me back my twenty years, Cocke?"

"For Jesu sake, do it!"

"That I will not." And I said, "Why are you so eager to die?"

To which he said, "Do you not see me. Blind and broken and feeble as a trampled spider? Why should I live? Ah, you hate me so much that you will punish me by letting me live, is that it, Battell? Aye. Aye, I understand that. I took your life from you, and you punish me by giving me mine. But that is cruel of you, most monstrous cruel."

"I hate you no longer," said I. "I loathe the deed you did me, but you were only the first of many betrayers, and how can I have room in my heart to hate them all? Nay, Cocke, I feel nothing toward you now, nothing!"

"I am in pain. For Christian mercy's sake, put me away, and end my suffering."

"That I will not do," said I. "Sit here and reflect upon your life, and tremble, and grow old in this room, for aught I care. I sail soon for England. Shall I convey your greetings to friends in Leigh?"

"I know no one . . . no one. . . ."

He commenced the weeping movement again, and this time tears in faith did come, most copious, a river down his withered cheeks. I rose and departed without taking my leave of him.

"Battell, in Jesu name!" he called after me. "Come back! Give me my despatching!"

I walked swiftly through the dockside streets, my head all in a whirl at seeing him here, and him brought so low, and begging for death. I thought of the words that had passed between us, and my telling him that I hated him no longer. But did I? Nay, my anger had not subsided; but the Cocke I detested was the one of the isle of São Sebastião, and not this wretched old man. I would gladly have struck dead that other; for this one I felt only sorrow and compassion, that he was a sufferer on the earth like us all, and a sinner, who was in his punishment and would have punishment more, and who showed at least the outer signs of repentance. Methought me that the finest revenge I could have taken upon him was the one I had taken, that is, to leave him alive in his misery and his pain, and not to destroy him, which I think I could have done with the back of my hand, as one destroys a buzzing fly. Now there sat he in his room, knowing that the deliverance of his death had been within ten inches of him and had not been granted him. That must be bitter indeed to him.

And so did I leave him, for another two days. Then did my heart soften to him: even unto Abraham Cocke of the *May-Morning* and the *Dolphin*. And I resolved that I would meet evil with good, as the Lord hath enjoined upon us. So I did send one of my Negro boys to the marketplace to obtain a certain poison that the blackamoors do use in the hunting of fishes, by which they cause the stunned creatures to rise to the surface of a pond to be netted. And I told the boy to take the phial of this stuff to the inn, and give it to Cocke, and say to him, "This is of Andrew Battell, for charity's sake, to speed you on your way."

I know not if he did use it, but I think he did. For the next day my wanderings took me toward that inn, and I saw a coffin being carried from it, and I asked of the innkeeper, who said, "It is the churlish Englishman, who died in the night most suddenly."

And so his soul now undergoes purgation for his many misdeeds, even the grievous one that by negligence or malevolence he did upon me; and that account is now closed, between Abraham Cocke and me. I have sometimes said a prayer or two for his repose: even for the repose of that man Cocke.

In my last days at São Paulo de Loanda I did also meet a second person out of prior years, that was also mightily transformed and gave me much surprise. This was as I passed outside the great church of the town, when its bell was tolling, and a dozen black nuns did come forth, all clad in their zevvera-striped habits, and their heads downcast. These holy women went in a file past me and toward their nunnery, all but one, who dropped from the rank and stood hesitating, looking back to me. And I looked to her, but only in a casual way, for I knew no nuns. Yet did she stand, and look, and search my face, and at last she moved closer to me, and said in a soft and gentle voice, "You are Andres, are you not?"

"That I am."

"And am I a stranger to you?"

I smiled and said, "I know you not, good sister."

"Ah, I think you know me very well," said she.

I peered close, and still it was a mystery, she being a woman of middle years with a round hearty face, and bright warm eyes, and a skin that was more of a reddish-brown hue than black. And as I stared upon her, the veil of the years did drop away, and I saw in my mind not a nun, but a girl of perhaps fourteen, bold and naked, with high outrising breasts and strong plump buttocks, and a mark of slavery inside her thigh over against her loins; and I felt shame at that, for it is no noble thing to hold so intimate a vision of a nun. But also I did see that saucy naked girl entwined about my body, and in my memory I heard her gasping sounds of delight, and hot waves of astoundment did surge through my soul.

"Matamba?" I said, with a stammering.

She nodded. "But that is not my name now. It was not ever my name, though I did not mislike it that you called me that, Andres. I am Sister Isabel now, and as Sister Isabel will I die."

"Ah, this does my heart good, to see you once more!" I cried. "For I searched some long time for you upon my return to this city. But no one knew of you."

"Nay," she said, "the Matamba that was your slave is dead, and the Matamba that was used so commonly in the whore-market is dead, and only Sister Isabel lives within this body. Oh, Andres, Andres, how I joy that the Lord has preserved you! Come, take my hand, let us renew our friendship!"

And she did seize both my hands in hers, and squeeze them most firmly, which caused me new shame.

"Is this permitted?" I asked. "You a nun, and all?"

"There is no harm in our touching," said she. "For we are old friends, and we have no secrets between us. Will you follow me within?"

"Aye."

I went with her into the church, Roman though it was, for it was cool and dark and empty in there, and we could sit, I no longer being eager to stand about under the hot sun. We took to ourselves a bench and sat facing one another, this nun and I, and her eyes did gleam with pleasure, and her smile was like the clear dawn light.

"I thought you had perished among the Jaqqas," said she. "For so was the story given about, that you had been taken by them, and slain long ago."

"It was not so. I gave myself unto them, freely, preferring their company to that of Portugals."

"Aye, and did you? You dwelled with the Jaqqas, then?"

"And dined beside their king, and mixed my blood with the king's brother, and did many another strangeness of which I do not care to speak. For these things I know some little guilt."

She studied my face with care, and said after a time, "God will pardon you for all."

"So do I entreat Him constantly. And you? This nunning—what led you there?"

"Why, what other harbor was there for me? When you were gone, they would have made me a whore again, and indeed some of the Portugals did treat me so; but I took me to the Fathers, and offered myself into their service, and they gave me my vows four years past. And I am greatly happy. I am escaped of all torments now."

"Aye," said I. "Your voyage is made, and you are at rest."

"So it is. I comfort the ill; I console the dying; I make my prayers and do my offices. It is for this that I was put into the world, Andres, though I was a long time finding it. And to you I owe my life."

"To me, forsooth?"

"Aye," said she, and took my hand again, warmly, more like a lover than like a nun. "For that you bought me out of slavery, and took me to dwell with you, and showed me how it is that decent Christian men do live their lives. That was my salvation, since otherwise I would have been a slave in America, and very likely long ago worked to death. And then you saved me a second time, when I had been thrown to the whore-market; and you nursed me, and recovered me into my health. I give thanks ever, that you were bestowed upon me by God."

"And I have given thanks many times for you, Matamba."

"Sister Isabel, am I now."

"Pardon. Sister Isabel. But I have been mindful of our love, and the sweetness of it. Is it a blasphemy to think of such things now? Now that you are—"

"Nay," she said. "It was true, and real. It need not be denied. I gloried in your embrace, Andres."

"And I in yours."

"And we had our time, and a fine time it was, and now we have moved on into other worlds, and so be it. What will you do now?"

"Return to England at long last."

"Ah. When is that?"

"A few days, no more."

"The Lord go with you, and speed your journey, and give you a happy return."

"So pray I also, Sister Isabel."

"You go alone?"

"I have two boys, slaves. I will ask them to accompany me, for I know not what will become of them here, and they are fond of me, and I of them."

"There was a Portugal woman once—"

"Dona Teresa, yes. The Jaqqas slew her." And I looked away of a sudden, for that terrible scene awoke in my mind, and I heard sounds and saw sights that I fain would not have had recalled to me.

In my anguish Sister Isabel did draw close beside me and say, "You loved her greatly, I know."

"I will not deny that."

"It does not matter. I know that you loved me, and you loved also her, and there was room in your heart for us both." With a laugh that was almost girlish she said, "Do you remember, when she and I did fight like wild beasts, and claw and scratch each other naked for jealousy?"

"And how could I forget that?"

"Nor I. She was like a demon. But I gave her as good as I received.

I think that woman was a witch, Andres, and I think she is suffering for that."

"She prayed God for forgiveness, at the end, and she prayed sincerely. I was with her."

"So long ago, Andres, so very long ago."

"There were good times, then, when we were together."

"There were. Without shame I tell you, I had great joy of your body."

"And I of yours," I told her. "Dare I say such things, with a holy sister?"

"In that time, it was rightful that we did what we did, and our joy was the measure of its rightfulness. I am so pleased, at seeing you this last time, and looking back upon all of those things with you." There was a deep glow in her eyes, of remembrance of things past, that was altogether radiant. Then she stood to her feet. "Come. I have my duties, and I must not shirk them."

"But a minute more with you," said I.

"Of course."

I looked toward her. A fantastic scheme then did blaze into being in my mind, that she should come back to England with me, and we live together—chastely, that is, she and I—in the renewal of the love we bore one another. For we were the only survivors of the past time, and it was pity that we should part, having found one another again at this latter day.

But that scheme, which for an instant did seem so valuable to me, decayed into absurdity the moment after, as I considered the madness of it, that I should set up housekeeping in England—chastely or no— with a black Catholic nun in that Protestant land. It could not be done. Nor was she likely, even for love of me, to follow me away from her devotions and her native continent. So I did swallow back the words even as they were rising in me, and said nothing, and only pressed my hand to hers in all of love.

Then said I at last, "Farewell, Matamba Sister Isabel."

"Farewell, Andres. God's love go with you. You know that mine own does."

And she made with her lips the little shape of a kiss, that never was part of her lovemaking craft when we were lovers; and then she was gone from me, most serenely gliding toward the door of the church and into the bright blaze of sunlight without.

FIVE

SOON AFTER, a messenger from the governor came to me at my lodging, and said that the ship was ready, and that I should prepare myself to go. Which I could scarce believe, after having dreamed of this day so long. For when we dream too long upon a thing, the coming of it becomes indistinguishable from the dream, and loses the power to sustain. I thought I would weep for joy when the day came when they told me I could go; but the day had come, and I did not weep. Joy indeed I felt, but of a subdued sort; one does not weep for joy when one has rehearsed in one's mind that very weeping. It must take one unawares, I do believe.

I gathered my few things, and my bit of gold, and walked one last time about the city of São Paulo de Loanda under the hot African sun. That sun was descending, and in the west a stain like blood lay upon the horizon, of terrible fine beauty. I felt a strange sorrow rising in me that I should be leaving this place, that I had so unwillingly entered. It had become my home, in these twenty years.

But England is ever the greater and truer home, no matter how wide we stray. And the ship was waiting, and I had no farewells to pay, having taken already my leave of Matamba, and Pinto Cabral being abroad on a slaving journey, and most everyone else of my African life being now in the next world: Dona Teresa, Don João, Serrão, Barbosa, Nicolau Cabral, Kinguri, and all those many others, save only, I think, the Imbe-Jaqqa Calandola, who would not die. And of him there was no leavetaking never: he rides forever in my soul, like a black fog that rises unbidden out of the depths by night.

The ship was a merchant-carrack of six hundred tons, the *Santa Catalina*, that was richly laden with a cargo of elephanto teeth and other such African treasure, with a mixed crew of Portugals and Spaniards. She was bound for Cadiz and then Lisbon, where I was assured of obtaining a passage to England. Her captain was a Pedro Teixeira, of great courtesy and kindness to me, who offered me a good cabin that gave me comfort. "You are old," he said, "and they tell me you have given great service to Portugal, and I would have you sleep well of these nights." Which was a statement that struck me deeply in two ways: for I did not inwardly comprehend that I had become old, nor would I say of myself that I had given great service to Portugal, that was my country's enemy so long. Yet those two things were altogether true, whether I like it or like it not.

I took me only one of my blackamoor boys to accompany me, that was twelve years old; for he was greatly desirous of seeing England, but the other would not go at all, and begged to be sold in Angola, which I granted him. This boy that I took with me had no name whatever, he having forgotten it in his captivities, and I now gave him one, which was Francis, in honor of the great Drake.

On a March day of superb brilliance of the sun in Anno 1610 did we hoist our sails and make our way past the isle of Loanda and into the open sea. And I did turn, and look back at the baked earth and thick trees of Angola, and at the fortress of the city atop its hill, where I had lain prisoner. And it was as though all my life in Africa did pass in review before mine eyes at once, my warfares and my servitudes and my injuries, and my dealings with the Portugals and with the Jaqqas, and my wives and beloved women, and all of that, in one great flash that dizzied me and made me grasp at a spar to hold me upright. And a Spaniard sailor did leap toward me and say, "Lean on me, old man, and I will bear you safe."

"I am not so old," said I, pained to hear that word twice in the same hour, *velho* from the captain's lips and *viejo* from the other, but the meaning being identical, and cutting identically deep. To which the boy smiled, for he was no more than three-and-twenty, and I old enough to be his father with some years to spare. In my own mind I was yet the golden-haired lad that had come out of England, but to his eyes, I fear, I seemed much parched by time, and whitened and shrunken. Well, and he smiled at me, but he did not laugh. And I said, "It was the rush of memory that unsteadied me, for I leave a land that I have dwelled in for a very great long while."

"And are you loath to leave, father?"

"Nay," said I, "I go home joyously."

But yet I knew there was a mixture in my feelings on that score, all the same.

I stood a time longer, looking backward at the hills. And a cloud came and darkened the land, and I thought I saw the face of Imbe Calandola in the curvings and twistings of the great hill, and that he was calling out to me in his great deep voice, "Andubatil! Andubatil!" So I did turn my back on him, and all of Africa, and looked to the vast sun-sparkled blue-green breast of the ocean sea.

Our ship was heavy and slow, and the winds were wayward as winds always are; but yet we beat our way up the coast in steady order. I looked landward again, thinking as a pilot does, that this cape I know, and that, and over there must be Zaire mouth, and there Cabo de Palmar in the land of Loango, and there Kabinda, and so on and on. These names I did speak to the sailors, who had done little African service and were unfamiliar with those marks; and they, too, smiled at me, doubtless thinking me a foolish gaffer, but a good-hearted one.

But some did come to me and ask me my tales of Angola, and I told them a few, and shared with them some of my piloting knowledge that still was sharp in my mind. These were good sailors, men of valor and sufficiency, from youth bred up in business of the sea. I was uneasy at first being among so many Spaniards, they having been the enemies of my nation since I was a boy. But that war was ended, and these bore me no enmity. And why should they? Most had been only babes at the time of the Armada. They said that England and Spain were not only at peace but did do much trade with one another, and there was talk that the King of England's son Charles might be married to a Spanish princess, which I found most marvelous to consider.

"What?" I said. "And do Drake and Ralegh swallow all this, and pay civil calls at the court of King Philip?"

But the names of Drake and Ralegh meant nothing to these lads; and it was from Captain Teixeira that I had the truth, which was that Drake was long dead, having died in '96 with John Hawkins on the Spanish Main of fevers, in some miscarried voyage; and Ralegh had fared little better, having been clapped into the Tower by this our King James in Anno 1603 on charges of treason, and being still prisoner there these seven years later. So I knew me that I was entering an England greatly altered, where old heroes were branded traitor and the Spanish lingo was heard in the chambers of our King. And that taught me much about the changes carved by the tooth of time.

We journeyed under a burning swollen sun into the high tropic lands, and to Guinea, and off the headland of Sierra Leona, and into the latitude of Cape Verde; and a few days thereafter we were directly under the Tropic of Cancer. On the next day we had sight of a ship to the windward of us, which proved to be a Frenchman privateer of ninety tons, who came with us as stoutly and as desperately as might be, and coming near us, perceived that we were a merchantship, and judged us to be weak and easily taken. The Frenchman then thought to have laid us aboard, and there stepped up some of his men in armor and commanded us to strike sail; whereupon, we sent them some of our stuff, crossbars and chainshot and arrows, so thick that it made the upper work of their ship fly about their ears, and we spoiled him with all his men, and tore his ship miserably with our great ordnance.

And then he began to fall astern of us, and to pack on his sails, and get away; and we, seeing that, gave him four or five good pieces more for his farewell; and thus we were rid of this Frenchman. Such are the hazards of the sea. In this hot action I took no part, being a mere passenger, and not needed. But it put me in mind of my young days, this being the most vigorous passage at sea I had witnessed since the Armada. Which I did remark to the sailors, and the young ones looked as empty-eyed at mention of the Armada as though I had been speaking of the Crusades! Well, and they will be fifty years of age one day also, those that are granted such good fortune. For no man be immune and exempt from the passage of time, however much he may think so when he be young.

Then sped we onward, and in an amazing short time we hove into the road of Cadiz. Here we unladed much of our cargo, and I went ashore, to say I had put foot in Spanish soil. There was some rain then, and the air was cold, and I did huddle close into myself, this temperate air being most intemperate to me, that had become thin-skinned from long African life. And afterward shipped we for Lisbon, where I lay two weeks in kinder weather, until I could board the English vessel *Mary Christopher*, that took me home.

This was a journey finally that went by so swiftly it seemed a dream; for one day I entered the ship, and—thus did I fancy it—the next was I in mine own land. But in sooth it did not quite occur that way, except that I took a fever and was raving for some few days; but I was restored fully to health. The captain's name was Nicholas Kenning, and his pilot John Loxmith, and they looked upon me, as did their men, as though I were something most rare and fragile, for they knew I had long been abroad in African captivity. We took a merry wind for England and by the good blessing and providence of God brought ourselves by the twenty-seventh day of June in Anno 1610 to the sight of the Lizard, where we bore in under heavy wind, and the next day about nine of the clock in the morning we arrived safely in Plymouth, and praised God for our good landfall. Kenning and Loxmith were beside me as I came on deck, and the captain did say, "Well, and you are in England again."

"I thought I would weep for joy at this sight, but look! Mine eyes are dry, for I can scarce believe I am here."

"Be most assured, this is England."

And as so he spoke, the sky that had been gray did release some rain upon us, by way of my welcome; and at that trick of fortune I laughed very heartily, which all of a sudden turned to tears, most copious ones. For indeed this was England and I was in it once again, and as I have said, tears come in unexpected ways: I who had looked dry-eyed into the harbor of Plymouth was surprised by joy in this rainfall.

I came forth onto the land and would not do anything for show, such as kneel down and kiss the earth, or the like. But I felt a quiet gladness that was deep and pure in every fiber of my being. For I was an Englishman in England again, after ever so trifling a side-journey of only one-and-twenty years.

Plymouth always is full of sailors fresh in from strange corners of the world, and so no celebrity was made upon me, for the which I was right grateful. I desired only to slip back into this land in quiet, and adapt me to its ways, that had become more strange to me now than those of Calicansamba and Mofarigosat. But it was not so easy. From a money-changer I got me English money, and found the silver pieces showing King James' face to be most very curious, though he did look kingly enough, with his sweeping mustachio and beard and heavy brow. I stepped into a tavern, and took a lodging for the night for me and the black boy Francis, that was all eyes, wild agog with wonder at this country. That night I dined on meat pie that to me had no savor at all, and was mere bland stuff without spice after the foods of Africa, and I drank some tankards of foamy beer, but I missed the heavy sweet taste of palm-wine. And in the chill of the night I thought I would perish, though I hid deep below my blankets, on my soft bed that seemed altogether oversoft.

And so on and so on: it was my first day, and I knew not England any more, but I was as Moses had said of himself, a stranger in a strange land.

There was another odd thing about my first impression of this new England. It seemed I had entered a smaller and a quieter time than was the one I left. In Elizabeth's day all was bubbling and excitement, a great upheaving turmoil of life and vigor and earthy outspanning growth: and now, under James, I sensed right at the first that men trod more cautious, and looked often over their shoulders out of timidity, and spoke in less robust voices. Was it an illusion? I think not; for that first impression was confirmed by my succeeding days and weeks. A certain great moment of time has gone by, for England, and is but memory now. It is as though once the world was all fire and crystal, and now it is mere wool and smoke, and dull red sparks in the ashes. And I do regret that I was not here for some of that time of fire and crystal; but, by Jesu, at least I saw its borning and its early ripeness!

As ever, I swiftly accustomed me to my surroundings; and in a day or two, Plymouth seemed quite ordinary to me again, not much altered from my memories of it, and its houses and lanes and carts and such all having the semblance of a proper town, though not very like the towns in which I had spent the last twenty years. I found me the captain of a fishing-skiff out of Essex who was going homeward, and hired him to take me as far as my village of Leigh, and in that afternoon we put to sea, under a brisk and loving wind. That captain did carry me to my native place without ever once asking me where I had been, nor how long absent: some English lack these curiosities, I suppose.

At last, then, did I step forward into those familiar streets of Leigh, that I had never abandoned hope of seeing again.

My wanderings were over. Even as wily Ulysses was I come home again; but there was a difference, for no faithful Penelope waited me here, nor good son Telemachus, nor trusty dog and herdsmen and the rest. In these lanes and byways of Leigh I was as lonesome as if I were trudging the avenues of ruddy Mars: though I knew this house and that one, and this grassy spot, and that stable, yet was there reflected from those places a sheer chill unknowingness, as if the whole town did say, *What man are thou, old stranger, and why have you come upon us?*

Yet were there quick amazements for me. My feet did take me along one lane and another, until, like one who drifts in dream, I found me standing before the house of my father, where I was born. There was an old woman, much bowed and shrunken, sweeping out the steps most vigorously with a broom, and when I paused there she looked up, with beady suspecting eyes, at me with my scarred and sun-blackened face, and at the Negro lad gape-mouthed beside me, as though we were both of us apparitions.

I said, "Be this the dwelling of Thomas James Battell?"

"It was, but he is dead these many years, and all his sons as well."

"That good Thomas is dead, I know right truly," said I. "But not all of his sons have perished."

"Nay, and is it so?"

"So it is. For I am Andrew, that went forth from this place in '89."

"Nay! It cannot be!"

"In good sooth, grandmother, so it is, and I am back from the wars in Africa where the Portugals took me, with this blackamoor child as my companion, and a bit of gold in my purse."

She did squint and scry me this way and that, twisting her head and peering at every angle. And with a shake of her head she declared, "But Andrew was a fine strapping great lad, and you are bowed and bent!"

"Ah," said I. "He was a man of thirty year when he went from here, which is no lad. And I am one-and-fifty, and time has used me hard. But I am Andrew Battell."

"Aye, I think you are," said she a little grudgingly.

"I swear it by my father's beard!"

"Ah, then, you swear most strongly. Andrew Battell, come home again! So I do perceive, that you be he. But how is it that you are

Andrew Battell, as you say, and you know me not?"

"Good my lady," said I, thinking her to be some domestic of the house that once had been my father's, "it has been so many years—"

"Indeed. And I did not know you at first, true. Yet you should have known me, since I am less changed by time than you."

I gave her close scrutiny. Her cheeks were like the map of the world, all lines and notations. I thought of all the old women of Leigh that I could recall, and she was none of them; and then I thought of the younger women, those that might well be seventy or thereabouts now, the mothers of my friends; and then the truth broke through to me, and I was overcome with shame for my folly, that I had searched all about the barn, and had not gone straightaway to the essence of her identity.

"God's blood! Mother Cecily!"

"Aye, child." And she laughed and dropped her broom, and gathered me close, and we did embrace. For who was this, if not my father's wife, that had raised me from a babe, and taught me my first reading, and walked with me by the Thames mouth to give me my early taste of the salt air? Without thinking had I taken it as granted that she was dead, since that so many years had passed; but she had been much my father's younger, and must now be no more than six-and-sixty, or even less. Why then should she still not live, and in the same house?

When at last I released her, we stood back and looked at each other anew, and she said, "Once I held you at my breast. And now we are two old people together, more like brother and sister than mother and son. Oh, Andrew, Andrew, where have you been, what has befallen you?"

"It would take me twenty year more to tell it all," said I.

We went within the house. It was all much the smaller with time than I remembered, and darker; yet was it familiar, and beloved. I had me a long look in silence, and stood before the portraits of my father Thomas and my mother Mary Martha, and bowed my head to them as a greeting, the father I had revered and the mother I had never known, and said, "I am come back, and I have done much, and I tell you, the blood of yours in my veins is good substantial blood, for which I am grateful."

And then I remembered that I had the blood of the Jaqqa Kinguri in my veins as well, by solemn transfusing, and I turned away, confounded and shamed.

To Mother Cecily I poured out questions so fast she could scarce answer them, of this person and that, playfellows and schoolmasters and all, and some were dead and some were gone to London and some, she said, were still to be found in Leigh. Lastly I asked her the question that should have been first, save that I did not have the strength to confront it without long postponement:

"And tell me also, mother, about my betrothed of years ago, Anne Katherine. What became of her, and how did her life unfold, and did she ever speak of me? Where is she now?"

And I waited atremble in the long silence that was my stepmother's reply to me.

Then at last she said, "Wait here, and have yourself a little ale, and I will return anon."

So did I sit there in the kitchen of that ancient house, and my heart was racing and my lips were dry, and I did not dare to think, but sat as stiff as a carven statue. Long minutes went by, and the boy Francis wandered off, touching walls and floors in wonder, and putting his lips to the windows, and the like. Then did I hear footsteps on the stairs, and my stepmother came back into the house. And with her was such a miracle that I received it as a thunderbolt.

For she had brought Anne Katherine. And I mean not the wrinkled aged Anne Katherine I might expect to see in this Anno 1610, but the fair and golden maid of long ago, of no more than sixteen or seventeen year, or even younger, with hair like shining silk and bright blue eyes, and about her neck, resting on the sweet plump cushion of her breasts, was the pearl that looked like a blue tear, dangling from a beaded chain, that I had had of my brother Henry an age ago and had given as a gift to her, by way of betokening our betrothal.

I trembled and shrank back and threw up my hands, and cried out, "God's death, woman, are you a sorcerer now?"

"Andrew—" cried my stepmother, afraid. "Andrew, what ails you?"

The girl, in fright at my wild outburst or perhaps at my rough looks, did back away most timidly, she who had been smiling a moment before.

"How can this be?" said I in a thick and fearful voice. "She is unchanged, in one-and-twenty years! What *nganga*-work is this, what wizardry?"

My stepmother, understanding now, came to me and said in a sharp short voice, "The sun has addled your wits, boy! D'ye take her for your Anne Katherine?"

"She is the very image."

"That she is. But it's folly to take the image for the reality. Girl, tell him your name."

"Kate Elizabeth," answered she in a tiny voice, but sweet.

"And your parentage?"

"The daughter of Richard Hooker and Anne Katherine Hooker, that was Anne Katherine Sawyer before."

"Ah," said I. "Her daughter! Now is it made clear! But you are just like her, Kate Elizabeth!"

"So it is often said. Only they tell me she was beautiful, and I think I am not so beautiful as she was."

"*Was?*"

"Aye," said the girl, "my mother is long dead."

"Ah," said I. I came a little closer to her, and looked, and said, "I thought you were her image, but it is not so. For you are even more fair than your mother, girl."

Color blossomed in her cheeks, and she looked away. But she was smiling. And excited, for her breasts did rise and fall most swiftly beneath her frock, as I could not help but see.

"And when did your mother die?" I asked.

"It was seven years Michaelmas."

"I will visit her grave. You know, that she and I were once betrothed?"

"I heard tell, there was that sailor she loved, that went to America apirating."

"I was that sailor."

"Yes," she said. "That I know." Her shyness and her fear of me were melting swiftly. She touched the pearl and said, "My mother often spoke of you, when I was a child. She said you gave her this, and promised to come back from the Spanish Main with caskets of doubloons, but that you were lost at sea, and perished in some raid against the Brazils."

"Ah. So it was reported, eh?"

"She would not believe it, when they said you were dead. She waited long for you, looking toward the sea, hoping you would come in from Plymouth some afternoon."

"This is true, Andrew," said my stepmother Cecily. "Every day did she go down to the water, and look, and pray. And she was urged to marry, but she said she would not. Until at last it was certain you must be dead, and then she did at last bestow herself to Richard Hooker, the lawyer's son."

"I think I recall him. A dark-haired man, very brawny, with a gleaming good smile?"

"Aye, that was he!" cried the girl.

"I trust he cherished her well, then."

"Aye, he was a most loving husband. And he gave her two sons and a daughter, and then she died, and he was sore bereft. Which I think led to his too early death as well."

"Then he is also gone. I see."

"These three years past."

"How old are you, girl?"

"Fifteen, sir."

"Fifteen. Aye. And you keep the household yourself, as the eldest?"

"That I do," said she.

Fifteen. Well, and then Anne Katherine must have waited three or four years in hope of me, and then had yielded to Hooker's suit in '92 or '93, if this girl had been born by '95. So I did calculate. Well, and that was as good a display of love as anyone need make, to wait those many years. And I was not grieved that she had married at last, for had I not done the like, with my Kulachinga and my Inizanda, and also my Matamba and my Dona Teresa, that never were my wives, but might just as well have been?

I said, "This gives me great pleasure, to see that my Anne Katherine is reborn in you, with all her grace and beauty unaltered, or perhaps enhanced."

"You are very kind, sir."

My stepmother said, "Kate, have the goodness to go outside a moment, will you, girl?"

She curtseyed and departed; and when she was gone, Mother Cecily did say, "It is almost like sorcery, is it not, Andrew? She is Anne Katherine come again, indeed. I comprehend now why you looked so amazed when I fetched her."

"Aye. The same age, even, as when first I fell in love with her mother."

"She is fatherless, and bears the toll of keeping her house."

"So she just has said, aye."

"And you are far from young, and newly returned from great adventures, and I think would settle down and spend your years quietly."

"So I would, Mother Cecily."

"Well, then—"

I looked to her in utter amaze. "What are you saying?"

"Is it not plain?"

"That I am to take her as wife?"

"Ah, you are slow, Andrew, but you do find the answer in time."

I scarce believed mine ears. She was altogether serious. I blinked and gaped, and imagined myself in the marriage bed with that girl, the old leathery hide of me rubbing against her tender bare skin, and my hand that had groped so many strange places probing her maiden fleece, and my yard that had warmed itself by Jaqqa loins and so many others gliding into her tender harbor—aye, it was tempting, but it was also monstrous, was it not, such a mating of April and November! I played the idea in my mind as I had played the bringing of the nun Sister Isabel to England, and found it just as impossible. And shook my head, and turned to my stepmother, and said softly, "She is not Anne Katherine. And I am not the Andy Battell of five-and-twenty years ago, that gave Anne Katherine that pearl. I do love this child, but not as my wife, Mother Cecily. I could not ask that of her."

"I told her you might ask it, when I went to fetch her."

"You did?"

"She is of an age, almost. You would be husband and father to her at once. I thought it was a good match."

"And did she?"

"So I believe. Though you dismayed her a little, with your wild hair and beard, and that cry you made, when she came in. But you were taken then by surprise; and the hair can be trimmed."

"Nay," I said. "It is beyond thinking."

"She would do it."

"So I know. But I could not. It would not fit my sense of the rightness of things. But I have a different idea. Summon her back, Mother Cecily."

Which she did, and the girl came into the room, and I saw the fear still in her eyes; for I knew she would marry me if I asked, since she needed a man's protection, but that she did not greatly crave so old and worn and rough a seafarer as I.

I said, "Kate, I have come home to live, and I am weary by my adventures, and I would not live alone. Will you dwell with me, and be my daughter?"

"Your—daughter?"

"Aye. The child I might have had by Anne Katherine, had fate treated us another way. For I have no one else, save old Mother Cecily and this black boy my servant. And this world of England now is greatly strange to me. So we can aid one another, you and I, in facing the mysteries ahead, for that I have some hard-won wisdom, and you have youth and vigor. If you share my house we can share our efforts and our strengths. Shall we?"

"Your daughter," she said in wonder.

"Stepdaughter, let us say. I will adopt you as mine own. Will it be thus, Kate Elizabeth?"

"Aye," she said. "Aye, let us do that, for I like it very much!"

And her eyes did glow with happiness, as much, I trow, of relief as of joy.

SIX

THUS HAVE we lived, these three years past, in the old house of the Battells: Kate Elizabeth in her bedroom and I in mine, and Mother Cecily in her own, until death came for her last Easter quietly in her sleep. Kate Elizabth cares for me, and I for her, and we both for her two young brothers and my blackamoor Francis, who serves us well. And to the world we are father and daughter, and so shall we be until some swain comes and takes her from me. Which I suppose will be any month now, so much courting does she do.

I wonder often whether I should have wed her when I could. For she is warm and beautiful and loving, and would have gladdened my bed greatly; and I am not yet entirely without lust, for once I did see Kate Elizabeth by chance at her bath, and the sight of her breasts and thighs and golden loins did awaken in me a desire so fierce as to wring tears from me; but it was quickly enough quelled. She knows nothing of that, nor will she ever.

I have occupied myself in these years by setting down this my memoir of all that befell me. It is a great long tale, I know, but for that I make no apology, since much befell me, and I would record it complete. Not that I am anything unusual in myself, only a simple and fortunate man, honorable enough to win God's grace, and sturdy enough to have endured mine adversities. But where I have been and what I have seen are not unimportant, and I would make record of it, just as other travelers of the past have made their records, from Marco Polo of Venice onward.

For I do have a vision of a new world of England overseas, and I hope to advocate it with my words in a way that will leave an imprint. This is a very small island, and it has little wealth of its own, only some sheep and some grass and some trees, and the like. But we are English, which means we have an inner strength that has not been given to most other folk, and I believe that we should go forth upon the world, and shape it to our pattern, and put it to our increase and the general good.

It is not a new idea. When that I was a little lad I heard Francis Willoughby saying to my father that the time had come for us English to be scattered upon the earth like seeds: or thrown like coins, he also said, bright glittering coins. That is a prettier image, but I like his one of seeds better, for seeds do in time have great growth into mighty oaks. Well, and many of us have been truly scattered upon the earth: but it is time to think what the deeper purpose of that scattering is to be.

The present way of England, in pirating and such, is futile. We cannot grow great by stealing the wealth of others. Nor can we merely go into tropic lands and and take from the people there the treasures they have. We must settle, and plant ourselves, and build; and we must create an empire that sinks deep roots everywhere, like the most lofty of trees. For in that way will we achieve the greatness that is marked and destined in our blood.

The Portugals have done a fine thing by opening Africa, by the efforts of their valorous explorers of more than an hundred years ago. But they have opened only its edge, with their ports widely spaced, and have made no successful ventures to the inland.

I think the Portugals could be displaced with ease—or, better, peacefully contained and overmastered—if we were to move from the Cape of Bona Speranza upward, and through the interior. Then the wealth of Africa would be ours: not its slaves, nor its elephanto teeth, but the truer richness of its farmland and its pasture. We could build a second England in that wondrous fertility, an England fifty times as grand as ours.

And if we went among the blacks not as tyrants and overlords but as elder brothers, giving them our wisdom and forcing nothing upon them, I think we might incorporate them into our commonwealth as partners, rather than slaves. This is a most bold and strange idea: but I do know those people, more closely than anyone else of England, and I tell you it could be done, if only we grasp the nettle now, and seize our moment. For in another fifty years it will be too late; the Portugals and Dutch and French will have sliced Africa amongst themselves, and they will destroy it, as in the New World so much has been destroyed already by the coming of greedy men of Europe.

So that is my vision. Of course, there is another vision as well, which I may not forget, and that is the vision of the Imbe-Jaqqa Lord Calandola.

That dark being comes to me yet, in my sleep or sometimes even as I sit by the fire, drowsing over my ale. He visited himself upon me just a week before, turning solid out of a pillar of smoke, in the way of magic, and filling my sight, that enormous hulking mass of power, black as night, shining with the evil grease on which he dotes.

"Andubatil?" he said, in that voice deep as the deepest viol.

"Aye, Lord Imbe-Jaqqa!"

"Are you comfortable, there in England? Look, the white snow falls outside. Do you not freeze?"

"I am inside, Lord Calandola."

"Come back. Come and join me, and bring a hundred English of your quality, and many muskets. For we will soon march. The world cries out for destroying."

"I have no taste for destroying, Lord Calandola."

"Ah, Andubatil, Andubati! I thought you were one of us! I thought you had adopted my wisdom. Look ye, you dream of building great empires as you sit there dozing: that I know. But it is altogether wrong, Andubatil! Tear down! Build nothing! Make pure the earth! The great mother is stained and defaced by all this building. Can you not hear her weeping? By my *mokisso*, it is loud as thunder in my hearing! I still see my task, and I yearn to complete it."

"I think you will not succeed, O mighty Imbe-Jaqqa!"

He laughed then his diabolic laugh, and said, "I sometimes fear you may be right, Andubatil. There is not time, there is not strength enough. I have had defeats, and they have wasted years for me. But I will persevere at it. It would have been easier, had you been loyal, and not betrayed me. But I do forgive you. Did not your Lord Jesus know betrayal, and forgive his Judas?"

"You are not content with being Satan, you must be Jesus as well, O Imbe-Jaqqa?"

"I am the world and all it contains," said the Lord of Darkness unto me. "I grant you forgiveness, and I call you back to my side, and we will be brothers, you and I, the white Jaqqa and the black."

"Nay, Calandola. That is all over for me."

"Is it, then? But there is Jaqqa in you. There is Jaqqa in every man, Andubatil, that I know: but especially is there Jaqqa in you. It is a part of you and you can never escape it."

"But I can resist it, Lord Calandola. That is my pride: that I do resist the Jaqqa within my soul, and put him down, and triumph over him. Go, Lord Calandola, let me be: I am old, I have no wish left to wage war, and I have defeated you within my heart."

"Ah, and is it so?"

"It is so."

"Very well," said he. "I will go on alone. And if I have not time enough for my task, why, there will be other Imbe-Jaqqas after me. I know not who they are, and peradventure they will be Jaqqas with white skins, born in your Europe, or in lands yet unknown. But they will rise, and come forth, these kings of the sword, and they will complete my work, and sweep away that thing which is known as civilization, and then will the earth be happy again. That I do foretell, O Andubatil. That I see quite clear. And now farewell: but I think I will return to you again."

And he did turn once more to black fog, and was gone, and I sat alone with my tankard.

I pray he be wrong in his vision.

Yet with a part of my soul, that is perverse and mysterious to mine understanding, I do almost welcome such a sweeping away. It would be like unto the flood of Noah, ridding the world of evil. You see, do you not, how intricate I am, that talks in one breath of building empires, and in another of purging them? But you know from the tale of this my long adventure that I am a man of opposites, and great inner differences. I would not have the world despoiled; and yet I see the strange beauty of the Imbe-Jaqqa's dream. And if the end is to come, and he is to have his way, why, perhaps it will be for the best, since that it would give us a new beginning, if only the best of us survive and endure and prevail, to build again. For so the eternal cycle goes, from building to destroying to building again.

But it will all happen without me. I sit here and write, and dream on far lands, and grow old, and the world moves about me. They say Walter Ralegh will lose his head, for having given offense to Spain by going to search for the land of El Dorado. God's death, but his fate rings strange in mine ears! And I can hear what Queen Bess would say, if she knew that her Ralegh would be chopped for being overly unkind to Spain. But this is a new time, and it is not much like her time, nor Ralegh's, nor mine. I do write my book, only, and think, and sometimes shake my head.

My sweet Kate Elizabeth has brought a man to see me, a little dreary pedantic man named Samuel Purchas, who is the vicar in Eastwood, that is two miles from Leigh. This Purchas is a dry and pious fellow, forty or fifty years of age, that has his degree in divinity out of Campbridge, and pretends to scholarship. He has inherited the papers of Master Richard Hakluyt, that compiled so great a volume of the travels of the famed voyagers, and this Purchas means to put together a new work, even larger.

Now, I have read the Hakluyt books, and a great epic they are, the work of a supreme compiler; and I do not think this Purchas can fashion their equal, for though he is industrious he also seems haphazard and hasty of ambition. He talks of "abridging the tedious" from his narratives, by which I think he means to take out all the details of routes and pilotage, and leave only the wonders and marvels. Master Hakluyt was wiser. But Master Hakluyt is dead, and Purchas is our only hope for bringing our tales to print. I have talked several times with him, he pumping me thoroughly about my adventure, and taking copious notes. He will write about me, and tell the world where I have been and what I have done. God grant he get it true.

And he will take my big book and slice it down, to put it in his collection of voyages, and I think he will mangle my words into some silly garboil, and put everything out of order, for that seems to be his way; but I pray that he will not. I know these scholars, that take a man's book and change it all around, so it bears no more resemblance to what he has written than a discarded greatcoat does to the earl who wore it. But we shall see. I will not see, for I think I will not much longer be here; but perhaps my words will outlast me. And if not, why, it may not matter, if the Imbe-Jaqqa Calandola has its way, and all this our world is swept to oblivion under the tide of destruction.

That my time is close gives me no dismay. I have fared far, and seen much, and done my best. I went forth, as England and Her Majesty required of the men of my day, and I was sown upon the earth like good English seed: and, God willing, I shall have left some crop behind me, and some increase of the realm. I am reminded now of some words of Marcus Aurelius, that are much like other words that I heard in Africa near the end, from the old *ndundu*-wizard that said I had made my voyage and come to rest, and all was well within me. For what Marcus wrote is near the same: "Thou hast embarked, thou hast made the voyage, thou art come to shore; get thee out."

So I will do, when I am called.

Almighty God, I thank Thee for my deliverance from the dark land of Africa. Yet am I grateful for all that Thou hast shown me in that land, even for the pain Thou hast inflicted upon me for my deeper instruction. And I thank Thee also for sparing me from the wrath of the Portugals who enslaved me, and from the other foes, black of skin and blacker of soul, with whom I contended. And I give thanks, too, that Thou let me taste the delight of strange loves in a strange place, so that in these my latter years I may look back with pleasure upon pleasures few Englishmen have known. But most of all I thank Thee for showing me the face of evil and bringing me away whole, and joyous, and unshaken in my love of Thee. This is the book of Andrew Battell of Leigh in Essex, that went voyaging on the Spanish Main in Anno 1589 and was carried to many another place before he found safe harbor. It is offered to Thee, to whom be all glory, and praise everlastingly, world without end: Amen.

AFTERWORD

ANDREW BATTELL and many of the other characters of this novel actually existed. But all we know of Battell is that he went to sea with one Abraham Cocke in 1589, was captured in Brazil and shipped to Angola, and had twenty years of adventures there; and that when he returned to England in 1610 he dictated a memoir to the geographer Samuel Purchas. An abridged and apparently garbled version of that memoir was published in Purchas' vast compendium, *Purchas His Pilgrimes* (1625), and a modern edition of it appeared in 1901: *The Strange Adventure of Andrew Battell*, edited by E. G. Ravenstein (London, The Hakluyt Society.)

I have used that brief narrative of Battell's as the foundation for *Lord of Darkness;* but I think it is best to regard this book not as a volume of history, but rather as a historical fantasy. For I have taken the liberty of reinventing Andrew Battell, since he left only the scantiest of information about himself, and no one has been able to learn even the dates of his birth and death, or what the outlines of his life were like before and after Africa. I have imagined a family background for him, and some wives, and several lovers, and a philosophy, and a great deal more, much of which he might find scandalous or even libelous if he were to read this book. I have followed the broad outlines of his tale of adventure, making only minor changes in the order of events for the sake of dramatic force; but I have filled in those broad (and often vague) outlines with a world of imagined detail. For that, I hope the real Andrew Battell will forgive me. The man in the book is my own creature, whose life story overlaps in some aspects that of the other Andrew Battell who sailed the seas in the reign of Elizabeth. My purpose was to show *what it might have been like* for an English seaman to have spent twenty years in the jungles of West Africa in the late sixteenth century; Andrew Battell's true but sketchy story was useful for illustrating my theme; and since Purchas did not deign to give us more than the outline of what Battell told him, I have invented the rest.

—Robert Silverberg
California, October 1982